HOT SIN IN YOUR AREA

Book fairies

Camp Wiggaws, Truro, Cornwall.

HOT SINGLES IN YOUR AREA

JORDAN SHIVELEY

unbound

First published in 2024

Unbound
c/o TC Group, 6th Floor King's House, 9–10 Haymarket,
London SW1Y 4BP
www.unbound.com

Text design by Jouve (UK), Milton Keynes

A CIP record for this book is available from the British Library

ISBN 978-1-80018-341-4 (paperback)
ISBN 978-1-80018-342-1 (ebook)

Printed and bound in Great Britain by Clays Ltd, Elcograf S.p.A.

1 3 5 7 9 8 6 4 2

FSC www.fsc.org MIX Paper | Supporting responsible forestry FSC® C018072

For all the cold flames who ever sought to keep their hearts dark and true and their teeth sharp and many

Please imagine that we could afford to print a very insightful quote from that one indie darling band that functions both to signal something about the soul of this book/what is to come and also to make you think: 'Huh, he knows about _____ I bet his writing is good if that is what he consumes.' Yeah, imagine *that* here.

Noah

Burnt toast.

Rancid butter.

Dried blood.

Good morning, world; time to limply fumble at your throat before collapsing into muttered apologies and backpedaling.

Burnt toast was better than no toast at all.[1] You put enough butter on anything and you could eat it. Noah Bezden actually looked forward to his burnt toast and butter sandwiches. After all, sometimes there was no butter and then it was just burnt white bread from the food bank, so glass half full, right? He looked again at the job advertisement as he waited for the bus to arrive, toast protruding from his mouth.

It wasn't often that a job ad led with 'No experience preferred' so that was a good sign.

---

[1] Debatable. As was seen at the last conference of Grilled Grains and Olfactory Devices that was held in Copenhagen in 1987. Professor Burnhaegen was booed from the stage when he proposed dark rye untoasted as the premier form of Neu-Toast.

Probably.

He definitely wanted a job that hopefully involved less blood and piss than his current one. Or at least a job that wouldn't give him the same recurring nightmares. Even now he could feel the phantom rasp of the dream. The pull of thousands of small teeth held together in a constellation of prickling points, a blanket of something wet and red that he could never shrug off.

At least those were the parts he could remember.

Janitorial work was usually his shit: work nights, listen to podcasts, get your work done way faster than your shift and all the rest was gravy. But this janitorial job at the bus station on the way out of town . . . was less than ideal. He had had to mop up a pool of blood and teeth once, blood and fucking teeth. Human teeth, probably. Just in a pool with no one around to explain why they were there. Although thinking about it, that was probably the best-case scenario. That was the night he stole a newspaper out of the supply room on the way home and started looking for jobs. Ad Sales and Customer Management[2] had to be better than teeth and blood . . . it had to.

The offices of Printed Matter weren't down a set of dingy stairs lined with trash and time. Nor were they in a basement you could only access through an alleyway solely lit by the sodium flare of a single guttering streetlight. Instead Printed Matter occupied the corner spot of the Langdon Silencio Heights strip mall between the China Moon restaurant and an obviously failing Play It Again Sports. Noah straightened the always-twisting-itself knit tie whose square end, no

---

[2] His actual job title was Opener of Doors Thought Lost and Hound of the Crimson Court but it would be a long time before he found this out, if in fact he ever did.

matter how much he tried to fold it back in on itself, always curled up. He had put it on with his good blue Oxford shirt and now looked at himself critically in the reflection of the sporting goods store window, a row of faceless mannequins ghosting behind his features. He didn't hate how he looked most days. His nose was long and sharp, yeah, but he thought it made him 'interesting', and messy dark hair with just the beginning of silver threads in the temples was cool, right? Like whatshisname, Dr Stranger? He probably should have shaved before he came to this interview but it was only a few days' worth so fuck it. No experience preferred, right? He had one of those builds people liked to call stocky and they were always surprised when he told them that technically, according to medical professionals, he was actually six foot one. But that was what it was and fuck 'em if they couldn't take God's joke. Noah ran a hand through his hair and let out a long breath.

Calm the fuck down, dude, he thought to himself. *You're interviewing for a job that* wants *no experience. As long as it's still there you got this in the bag. Fucking chill, my baby.*

My baby? What the fuck, Noah? Alright, let's do this.

The glass front door to Printed Matter swung open not unlike the dying warble of a wounded mechanical bird heard from deep within a well.

Printed Matter was nothing special.[3] From the less-than-standard job advertisement Noah had expected either a super yuppie sort of business with glass-partitioned 'work zones' and someone in the back gesturing to a whiteboard with the word 'SYNCHRONICITY' circled on it, or a hipster Pinterest-ready

---

[3] One cannot help but laugh here. Or weep. Is there really a difference in the human animal?

hand-printed sort of business with enamel trays and felt pads artfully holding business cards with antiqued brass paperclips. But Printed Matter was neither of those.

It was, if anything, aggressively . . . intimidatingly . . . average. The floor was grey almost astroturf carpeting that was worn to a sheen in the places where foot traffic passed on a regular basis. Despite being a customer-facing storefront, it only showed wear going from the front door to the door marked STAFF ONLY. The counter was beige Formica with a neat stack of brochures and a 'take one, it's free' stand[4] of the Printed Matter newspaper insert. Apparently, the company did not print the entire newspaper as he had assumed but just the personal/ads section that went in the back.

Noah craned his neck looking for anyone who might seem like they were in charge but the room was surprisingly empty; not even a desk clerk or anyone to ask about the job application. The morning sun was streaming in through the plate-glass storefront behind him and the room was filled with specks of floating dust that reflected like amber ants in the light.

He sidled over to the stack of inserts and picked up one to look over. *Never hurts to have a little inside knowledge going into an interview, right?*

---

[4] Never take one of these. I physically cannot type out the explanation of why but trust me on this one. Or don't and I'll see you soon.

Hand Hewn | 0 ¢

Printed ● Matter

Ad Saver

Fresh Harvested — People News

28 CLASSIFIED ADS—PHONE 4-4141

EMPLOYMENT

Help Wanted 20

HOT SINGLES IN YOUR AREA, LOOKING AT YOU WITH VOID DARK EYES, EYES LINED WITH ROWS OF TEETH EVER SPIRALING INWARD, EYES YOU COULD GET LOST IN

[redacted] dolor [redacted] or [redacted]

Want Situations 26

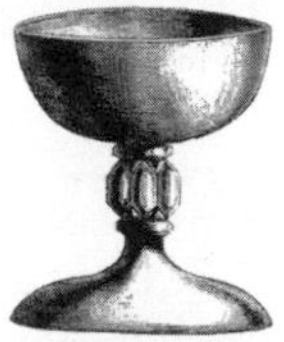

SOMETHING TO FILL

Ring if you know what we need 349-2198

TEETH teeth teeth
TEETH TEETH your-
teethteethteethteeth
TEETH teeth teeth
teeth TEETH your-
teethteethteethteeth
TEETH teeth teeth
teeth TEETH your-
teethteethteethteeth
TEETH teeth teeth
teeth TEETH your-
teethteethteethteeth
TEETH teeth teeth
teeth TEETH your-
teethteethteethteeth

teeth.

SALESMEN—Experienced shoe men

EMPLOYMENT

Help Wanted 21

AGING COUPLE SEEKS YOUNG COMPANION

Must provide evidence of strong teeth and warm but not too warm blood. Must be deep sleeper. Preferrably no living relatives. A large supply of crimson robes is a bonus. No need to call. We will call you...

TOOTH DIVINERS

No jaw too small

No tooth too hidden

No questions

12 Redber Lane

HOW MUCH MEAT CAN YOUR BODY HOLD?

Call for the surprising answer

209-918267356

HOT SINGLES IN YOUR AREA, JOGGING PAST YOUR HOUSE, AGAIN AND AGAIN, SMILING, WAVING, EACH TIME LOOKING MORE LIKE YOU, EXCEPT FOR THOSE TEETH

EMPLOYMENT

Help Wanted 21

Who wrote this?
Was it you?
Are you sure?

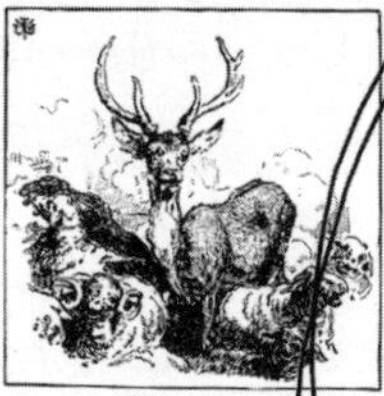

fig. 11 Wake up...wake up...wake up...

THE EARLY BIRD GETS THE EARLY GRAVE

BUTLER WANTED

Discreet. Blood not provided. Accomodations on site. Late nights. Mornings off.

Help Wanted 22

HOT SINGLES IN YOUR AREA, DIGGING TIRELESSLY THROUGH THE NIGHT, PACKING EACH OTHER'S MOUTHS WITH DEEP COLD EARTH, UNCEASINGLY WHISPERING DOWN INTO THE WET LOAM, PROMISING THAT WHICH LIES WAITING THAT SOON SOON THEY WILL BE REUNITED, THIS COULD BE EVERYONE AND THEY ARE NOT PLAYING

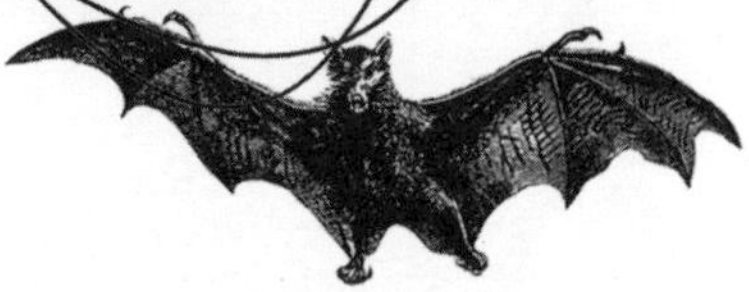

fig. 9 a dream forgotten

LIVESTOCK

and Supplies

Whatever is beneath your floorboards. We want it.

HOT SINGLES IN YOUR AREA, STANDING EVER SO STILL, LISTENING SO SO CLOSELY, HEARING THE SOUND OF THE DEVOURER THAT HIDES JUST AT THE EDGES OF YOUR SIGHT, A SLOW HUNGRY BREATHING, IT WILL NEVER LOG OFF THEY CROON

FOR SALE

Miscellaneous

A dream you thought you had forgotten

A dream you wish you had
87-594-32

[redacted]

What was written here is lost

Hand Hewn

Printed Matter

Ad Saver

Fresh Harvested

People News

CLASSIFIED ADS—PHONE 4-4141

EMPLOYMENT

Help Wanted 20

HOT SINGLES IN YOUR AREA, HARVESTING THE CORNERS OF THE NIGHT, WEAVING THEIR ROBES UPON THE LOOM OF EXULTANT SORROWS, DROPPING CROONING PRAYERS INTO THE WELL OF CARRION DELIGHTS, VOID SIGILS OF POSSESSION BLOOMING ON EVERY CHEEK, MONDAYS AMIRITE

THERE ARE MORE BONES NOW THAN THERE WERE BEFORE. You hear this as you stand looking at your reflection in the mirror. THERE ARE MORE BONES AWAKENING, SOON THEY WILL BE HERE. What the fuck? You swear you just saw your lips move in the mirror but that's not possible.

...SMEN—Experienced shoe men

EMPLOYMENT

Help Wanted 21

Wait. What is that figure behind your reflection? It is unclear, like a smeared oil painting, like smog swirling against glass to billow in on itself. CAN YOU FEEL THE BONES. THERE ARE SO MANY OF THEM.

HAVE YOU SEEN me? Reward offered for seeing me. Have you? I have seen you. Yes, YOU. Such tears and wailing. You would think you had caught at least a glimpse of me. HAVE YOU?

HOT SINGLES IN YOUR AREA, HANDS COLD AND HUNGRY, GRASPING THE GIFTS LEFT BY THE THING THAT KNOWS EVERY WORD, MOUTHS DISTENDING, JAWS UNLOCKING AS THEY SWALLOW THE WRITHING GIFTS, HOWLING IN UNHOLY FERVOR AS THEY BEGIN TO CHANGE, SOMETHING DARK AND ANCIENT GROWING DEEP WITHIN

EMPLOYMENT

Help Wanted 21

HOT SINGLES IN YOUR AREA, HOLDING DARK OFFERINGS BENEATH UNQUIET WATERS, LETTING THEIR CANTS DRIFT DOWN TO WHAT SLEEPS IN THE DEPTHS, RAISING THEIR DARKLY SHINING EYES TO THE RISING HUNTRESS MOTHER IN ANTICIPATION OF WHAT IS RISING UP TO MEET THEM. XOXOX

Help Wanted

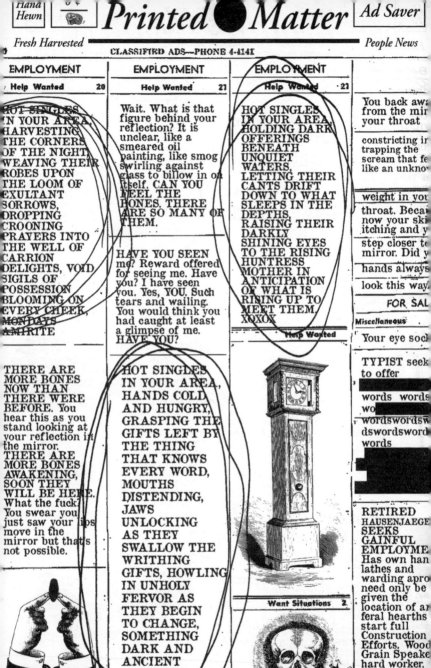

Want Situations 2

You back awa... from the mir... your throat

constricting i... trapping the scream that fe... like an unkno...

weight in you... throat. Becau... now your ski... itching and y... step closer to... mirror. Did y... hands always... look this way.

FOR SAL...

Miscellaneous

Your eye sock...

TYPIST seek... to offer [redacted] words words wo[redacted] wordswordsw... dswordsword... words [redacted]

RETIRED HAUSENJAEGE... SEEKS GAINFUL EMPLOYME... Has own han... lathes and warding apro... need only be given the location of a... feral hearths start full Construction Efforts. Wood Grain Speake... hard worker.

Did you [redacted]

If I am different in this world maybe you

Hand Hewn | 0 ¢ | **Printed ● Matter** | Ad Saver

Fresh Harvested — *People News*

CLASSIFIED ADS—PHONE 4-4141

EMPLOYMENT

Help Wanted 20

HOT SINGLES IN YOUR AREA, SKIN WILTING BENEATH A NEWLY RENT SKY, TONGUES SNAKING OUT TO HISS AT THE NEW CRIMSON MOON OF THE HUNTRESS MOTHER'S FAVOR THAT RISES ABOVE THEM, TALONS TEARING AT THE EARTH THAT WILL SOON FORGET THEM, LIKE TOTES GRODY WE KNOW, WHATEVER, GAWD

Want Situations 26

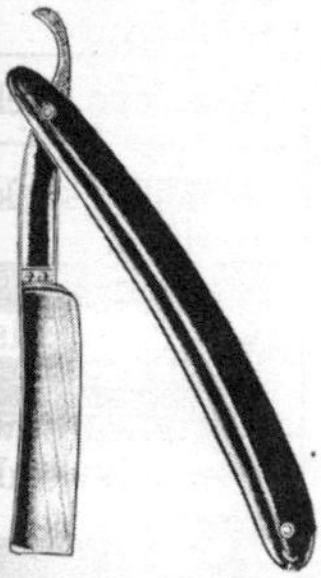

CALLING CARDS PRINTED CHEAP

teeth.

[redacted]

[redacted]

SMEN—Experienced ... men

EMPLOYMENT

Help Wanted 21

AGING COUPLE SEEKS TRAVEL COMPANION

Must be of good upstanding moral fiber. Well read in most binding rituals. Knowledge of flensing not required but a plus. Willing to be a self firestarter on occassion

TOOTH ASSAYERS

No tooth too small

No jaw too large

No provenance too murky

13 Redber Lane

HOT SINGLES IN YOUR AREA, UNNATURALLY LONG LIMBS UNFOLDING FROM THE DARKEST CORNERS, LIMBS CRACKING AND REFORMING, COLD FINGERS TWISTING AND SNAPPING, BACKS ARCHING AS UNHOLY HYMNS STRETCH BULGING THROATS, 'This is the day, this is the day, this is the day our lord has UNMADE'

EMPLOYMENT

Help Wanted 21

APPRENTICE BUTCHER

Pays in OPPORTUNITIES

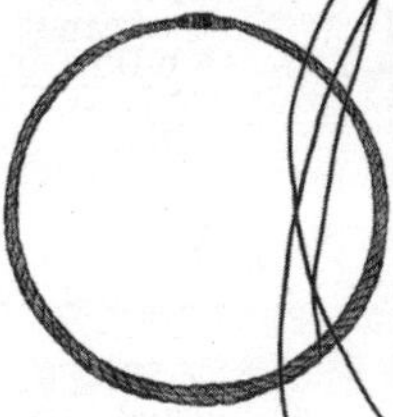

LEAVE THEM AT THE BOTTOM OF THE GRAVE THEY DUG FOR YOU

Help Wanted 22

HOT SINGLES IN YOUR AREA, WALKING THROUGH ABANDONED DEPTHS, DESCENDING ECHOING STAIRWELLS THAT ONCE USED TO BREATH AS IF ALIVE, TALONS CLICKING ALONG WALLS THAT NO LONGER HUM WITH BURIED HUNGER, 'I GUESS WE JUST GREW APART' THEY WHISPER DOWN INTO THE CARRION WELL THAT'S ALL

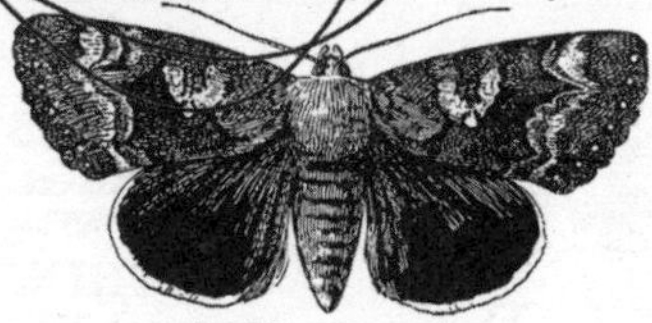

fig. 12 quit running

lost meat.

YOUR WALLS ARE ~~NOT EMPTY~~

HOT SINGLES IN YOUR AREA, KNEELING BEFORE THE THREE CRIMSON MOTHERS OF THE CARRION HOST, LIPS WET FROM THEIR BLOOD OATHS, MURMURED PRAYERS FILLING THE FETID AIR 'one taught me love, one taught me patience, one taught me pain...'

FOR SALE

Miscellaneo [redacted]

ARE YOU INTERESTED IN THE SCIENTIFIC ARTS?

Please report this treason immediately

208-7654

Why here why did the powers flee to this specific world and to printed Matter

Hand Hewn | 0 ¢ | **Printed ● Matter** | Ad Saver

Fresh Harvested — CLASSIFIED ADS—PHONE 4-4141 — People News

EMPLOYMENT

Help Wanted 20

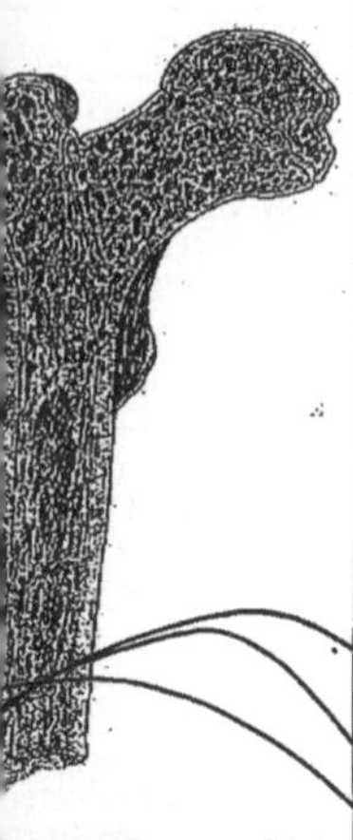

OT SINGLES
YOUR AREA,
ASSING IN A
RITHING
OUND OF
NNATURALLY
ONG LIMBS
ND LUMINOUS
LESH,
ANDIBLES
OCKING IN
NHOLY
OMMUNION,
EENING THE
ORGOTTEN
ANT BACK
ND FORTH, IT
E IT ME IT
E IT ME IT
E IT ME IT
E IT ME IT
E IT ME

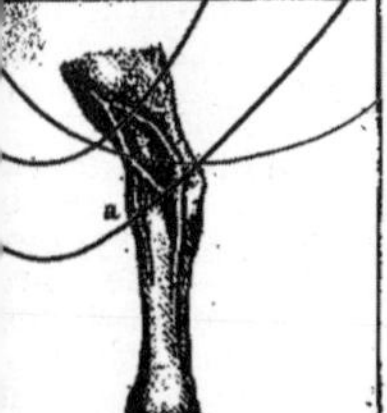

EN—Experienced shoe men

EMPLOYMENT

Help Wanted 21

You go to open the fridge but what is inside is not what you remember. Later you go back to open the fridge again. Something stops you,

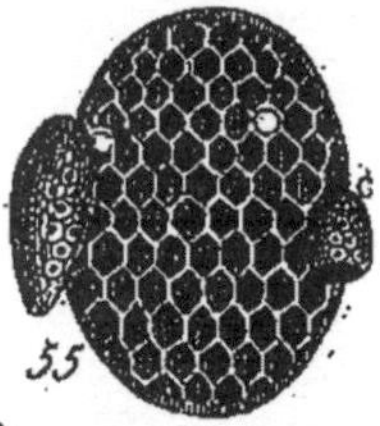

55

a scrambling in the animal part of the brain, a pounding at the sealed basement door of your memory. You go to open the fridge.

You go to open the fridge. You don't remember the door being so dirty. Rust dried smears flaking in patches the same color as your your hands. Your hands, your hands shake as you grasp the fridge handle, the veins in your forearm bulging. What is inside is not what you remember.

You go to open the fridge. You lean your forehead against the humming door of the freezer. Your skin feels flushed and the door is deliciously cool. Your teeth ache and when you run your tongue over them they wiggle loosely and your mouth fills with the familiar taste of iron.

EMPLOYMENT

Help Wanted 21

You go to open the fridge. With your hand on the door you look back over your shoulder and the hallway swims in and out of focus, a lens smeared with vaseline, a pulsing liminal canal. The fridge hums waiting. You think you know what is inside ...you're wrong.

You go to open the fridge

Help Wanted

HOT SINGLES IN YOUR AREA, MOUTHS ENGULFING A SWELLING TIDE OF SHADOWS, LONG FINGERS SEEKING THE SEAMS OF CREATION, REPLACING WHAT THEY FIND INSIDE WITH SOMETHING OH SO HUNGRY, UPVOTING THE CHARNEL HOST

Want Situations

You go to open the fridge You go to open the fridgeyougottoopen thefridgethefridget hefridgeyougoto open You go to open the fridge You go to open the fridge

LIVESTOCK

and Supplies

HOT SINGLES IN YOUR AREA HANDS UNEARTHLY BENEATH THE HUNTRESS MOON, PEERING INTO ECHOING VOID, COLD MOUTHS WHISPERING, NEW PHONE WHO DIS?

FOR SALE

You go to open t
fridgeyougotoope
ougotoopenopen
[redacted]
fridge You go to
pen the fridge Yo
go to open the
fridge You go to
open the
fridgeyougottoop [redacted]
hefr [redacted]
fridgeyougoto op
You go to open th
fridge You go to
[redacted]
ougotoopenopen
nIT IS OPEN ope
[redacted]
fridge

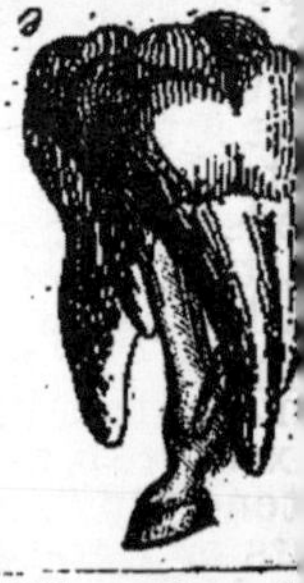

Did you know?

look into the red moon noah keeps babb

sh Harvested

People News

| PLOYMENT | EMPLOYMENT | EMPLOYMENT | LIVESTOCK |

| lp Wanted 20 | Help Wanted 21 | Help Wanted ·21 | and Supplies |

Column 1 (Help Wanted 20):

T SINGLES IN
R AREA
KING UP NEW
BBIES, MAYBE
N DARTS
OKING INTO
ASSES TO
DIT AT THE U
ALOGUING
R EVERY
K AND SIGH
KNITTING,
A NITTING
E AY
NDS PLUNGED
O YOUR
TRAILS

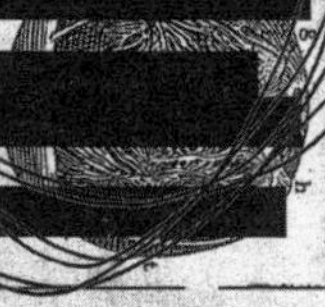

They couldn't tell
you when they did it
for the first time. It
wasn't something
you could really just
bring up in polite
conversation.

ger seeking band. Must be
und beneath the Gloaming of
hispering Knives. Those bound
neath the Writhing of Carrion
lights need not apply. DRAMA
EE environment. Singer has
cess to all-bi...ircles and
uals needed...for practice
ds. I don't know how
g I...to be in control
...
swe...
most impor...
the...h the
pect o...
e Crone o...ll
low w...
n't answer this...the...ing
at "...the door only
eds or...husk...it can
rt the...ly
ally don't want...tual to
ppen. The ban...mostly heretic
th with a bit of blood wave
xed in so anyone who has
tened to bands like the Mangy
ts or Dead and Disorderly
uld fit right in.

Column 2 (Help Wanted 21):

78(F) seeking
compatible (F)
preferably with long
legs, legs that glisten
beneath the gaze of
our Huntress Mother,
legs (many) that
clack and bend in
impossible ways,
their serrations
dripping with
heart's poison and
ready for the Hunt.

Column 3 (Help Wanted 21):

'Hiya Marge, when
was the first time you
tremblingly tore a
page from a book and
pressed it to your
fevered sweating
flesh because you
couldn't bear to be
apart from the words
you had just read?'
See doesn't exactly
make for small talk
does it? But still it
was the truth. As
long as they could
remember they had a
hunger for the words
on paper.

| Help Wanted |

HOT SINGLES IN
YOUR AREA,
STANDING
BEFORE THE
CRONE MIND,
R ING THE
HORRIBLE
SPLENDOUR OF
THEIR HEXSELF,
LIFTING COLD
BLADES UP TO
THE HUNTRESS
MOTHER'S GAZE

| Want Situations 2 |

And not just to
read them but to
have them close by
to feel them, the ink
and paper fibers
pressing into their
skin. They could tell
you the paper
weight and tooth of
almost any page in
their collection
much more readily
than the eye color
or hairstyle of any
of their coworkers
they saw on a daily
basis. The only
problem was that
after awhile where
did you keep the

Column 4 (Livestock and Supplies):

It hadn't been a
problem for a lon
time because ver
few pages were
SPECIAL most
them were filled
with dead lifeless
words but the
special ones...we
year after year
they did start to
add up.

At first they trie
to carry around
satchel, but that
was only a
solution for a yea
or two. Then they
started keeping
the best ones
pressed to their
skin, underneath
their shirt...then
their pants. Word
and phrases beg
to peek past thei
collar and shirt
cuffs.

Finally one day
they put a page
tentatively to the
lips, hesitant as
that first kiss
from a new lover
that soon swings
to the intimate
familiarity of
things created fo
each other. This
was what they ha
been looking for
all along. This is
what the words
had wanted.

Their jaws now
moved tirelessly,
worshipfully. The
lips soon took on
the dark stain of
ink and paper
dust. Now no one
would ever be ab
to separate them
from all the word
that called to the
and when they
moved it was wi
the dry rustle of
distant library.

N-Experienced shoe men

Mansions of silence there is more there than

EMPLOYMENT	EMPLOYMENT	EMPLOYMENT
Help Wanted 20	**Help Wanted**	**Wanted**

For rent. Teeth and jaws, various.
Available weekends and for parties

HOT SINGLES
IN YOUR AREA,
SLITHERING
THROUGH
IMPOSSIBLE
CRACKS, RISING
PALE
LUMINESCENT
AGAINST DEAD
NIGHT SKY,
UNKNOWN
STARS FIDGET
SPINNING

As you walk towards the triangular door of the Sealed Library you murmur a benediction of Lesser Motives and Winding Humors. As the words sigh out from the cage of your teeth like a soft wind from a tomb's mouth you can see the lines of power the Confessor had been holding in place begin to unravel and blow away on an unfelt wind.

The door to the library begins to open retracting like an iris in three pieces, the dust and calcification of the centuries

HOT SINGLES IN YOUR AREA, RISING HALF-FORMED FROM THE WRITHING MIRE, PALE EYES BULGING, DISTORTED MAWS TURNED TO AN ILL-OMENED MOON FOR WHAT

follow up at Mansions of Silence
unsure if this is the real deal

Speed Dating Weekends.
Inquire Within if Seen.

falling in great sheets from its face. It is obvious that it has been quite a while since a Librarian came down here to take Accounting.

Finally the doors finish their groaning retreat with an echoing thud that travels past you bringing with it a damp fetid breeze not unlike the exhalation of some great slumbering beast. Gathering your robes

falling in great sheets from its face. It is obviou that it has been quite a while si a Librarian cam down here to ta Accounting.

Finally the door finish their groaning retrea with an echoing thud that travels past you bringin with it a damp fetid breeze not unlike the exhalation of some great slumbering bea Gathering your robes you walk

HOT SINGLES IN YOUR AREA RISING FROM SUNKEN WRITHING NESTS, FILING THEIR TEETH DOWN TO POIN SHEDDING PAPERY HUSKS STREAMING T RISING DARK

SALESMEN—Experienced, shoe men

Hand Hewn | 0 ¢

Printed Matter

Ad Saver

Fresh Harvested — People News

CLASSIFIED ADS—PHONE

EMPLOYMENT

Help Wanted

1
6
3
4
2
5
6
7

WHOLESALE PRICES

know for certain
hat my bedroom
nd the kitchen
xist.
am not so sure
bout the hallway
onnecting them.
But the bedroom is
ixed in my mind.

The fevered blur of
he air as I try and
link sleep away,
nly to slip back
inder.
The bedside table
hat always has a
glass of water
vith only enough
eft in it to remind
ne what water
tastes like.
The sheets are
lways wrapped
round my limbs
so I'm swimming in
damp river of my
wn sweat.
The yellow light that
lants across my
body from the blinds
striping everything
n bars of amber
and dark.

I am sure of these things.

The kitchen is more muted than the waking room. Like a reminder to myself that has been erased and rewritten too many times. I'm sure it's there . . . when I'm in it . . . but I am in the bedroom now and the kitchen is sketched on the wet bar napkin of my memory, the lines bleeding and blurring together.

comehomecomehOmEcOMeH
OmecomehomeCOME HOME

I know that there is a sink full of clean dishes beneath a dripping faucet. I can hear the drone of an unseen refrigerator. The linoleum is faded yellow with a brown stain growing across it like a spreading bruise. The kitchen and the bedroom; I know they exist because they bounce off of me like echoes down a forgotten well. Sometimes I sit in the corner of the bedroom, the rough edges where the carpet staples are coming loose sharp against my bare skin.

I bring my knees
up close to my
chest like I am
trying to pull
them into myself
become smaller,
less of a receivin
vessel for the
building.

I remind myself
what I am by
running my hand
over my face.
Feeling their cold
wet clamminess
meet the feverish
glow of my cheek
the dull but not
unpleasurable pa
of pressing hard
against my close
eyes. I set them
into my memory
each time. I find
my hair in long
matted clumps o
the pillow.

ALESMEN—Experienced ... men

...en was the last time the Crimson Mother
...ose a bound this is not good

Hand Hewn | 0 ¢ | **Printed Matter** | Ad Saver

Fresh Harvested — People News

CLASSIFIED ADS—PHONE

those Without are stirring

EMPLOYMENT

Help Wanted

HOT SINGLES IN YOUR AREA, SEATED ON NINE THRONES OF HISSING BONES,CARRION CROWNS FIXED TO SHADOWY BROWS, DESECRATE ALL THAT IS HOLY AND CHILL

It is brown . . . or blonde . . . the light makes it hard to tell.

I like my hands. I spend long hours running them over my lips, touching each knuckle to the slick cage of my teeth. Biting down gently till I know their contours like sounding depths on a chart of their two oceans. Anything really to not think about the Taste.

But the Taste is inevitable, it is always in my mouth when I wake. Morning or night it is there filling the crevices under my tongue with the hot tang of sour saliva. My jaws are always aching like I have been clenching or chewing all night long.

Once I think about the Taste it is all I can do. I don't know what it is from but it sits there like an aftertaste that only appears on your tongue when you inhale. But no matter how many mouthfuls of air I swallow I can't place what it is. I run my tongue up and down the inside of my teeth hoping that there is something there that will shake loose, something more physical than this phantom that disappears the first time I swallow. I wander to the kitchen but no matter what I eat it's not the same. Nothing matches. I begin to think about the other rooms that must be in the building?

Maybe the taste is there.

Maybe I just need to find it.

blink if you can see this

Unlost Child: Have You Dreamed Me?

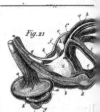

Fig.21

Call for Weekly Quote: Fresh Da

HOT SINGLES IN YOUR AREA HANDS UNEARTHLY BENEATH THE HUNTRESS MOON, PEERIN INTO ECHOING VOID, COLD MOUTHS WHISPERING, NEW PHONE WHO DIS?

HOT SINGLES IN YOUR AREA SILENTLY TRODDING INTO THE CARRION OAK'S DOMAIN, VEINS WRITHI TO ITS CALL, SKIN STRETCHING, SPLENDID AN RIPE

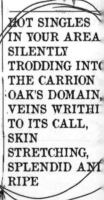

SALESMEN—Experienced shoe men

Hand Hewn | 0 ¢

Printed Matter

Ad Saver

Fresh Harvested — *People News*

CLASSIFIED ADS—PHONE

EMPLOYMENT

Help Wanted

eing scared of
evators is silly.

know this.

live in the Verdvis
uilding. Yes, that
ne. All concrete
nd arrow slit
indows. And I'm
ot complaining
bout that, I love
nat part of it. It's
hat happened a
w weeks after I
oved in. Well, I
ink it probably
appened the very
rst day I moved in,
ut as you will come
see it is a gradual
ing that has
tarted to creep up
n me, like boiling
ater to a frog, the
low tightening hand
round the throat of
sleeping child.

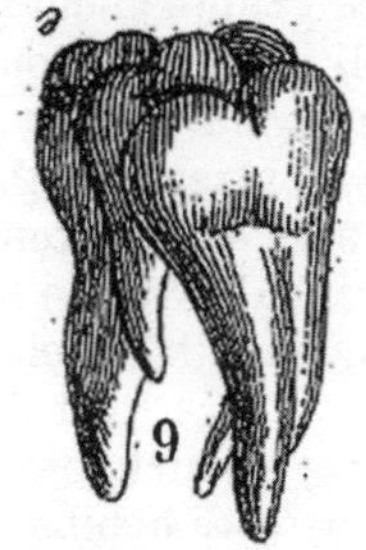

So I can only describe when I first noticed it happening.

I live on the twelfth floor. Twenty flights of stairs, two per floor, so I was thrilled to see that there was a large, almost-to-the-point-of-being designated 'freight' two-sided elevator directly in the middle of the main lobby. Three weeks after moving in, I was on my way up, adjusting my other hand around four plastic grocery bags that were trying to cut off my circulation. The elevator dinged and I started to step forward, my eyes still on my phone, but something made me look up. Something about the weight of the air, the way it too damply pressed against the nape of my neck, like a long-held and now exhaled breath.

Maybe there was a distant ringing of phantom tinnitus too? When I try and lock down the particulars I feel nauseous and the twinges of a migraine begin. But something made me look up and stop my forward motion just as I was about to step past the threshold of the elevator.

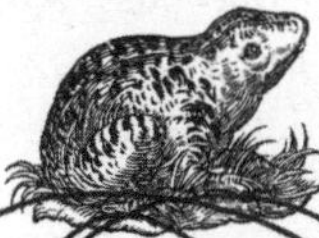

HOT SINGLES IN YOUR AREA FINGERS TRACING THE SEAMS OF THE NIGHT,FINGER TEARING OPEN THE CORNERS OF THE EVENING, GESTURING FOR YOU TO ENTER

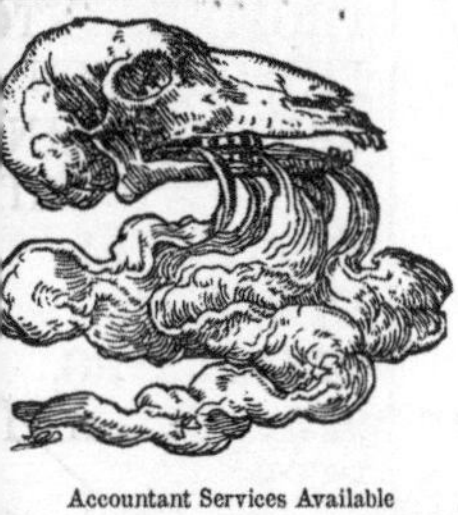

Accountant Services Available

LESMEN—Experienced . shoe men

Hand Hewn | 0 ¢ | **Printed ● Matter** | Ad Saver

Fresh Harvested — *People News*

CLASSIFIED ADS—PHONE

EMPLOYMENT

Help Wanted

[redacted]

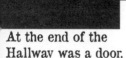

At the end of the Hallway was a door.

There is no door at the end of my hallway.

And while the doors of my hallway were flat featureless panel doors painted with a now dingey taupe-adjacent color, this was a four-panel wooden door painted red. The paint was bubbled and peeling all around the edges of the frame. The Hallway itself was also Wrong. Instead of apartment doors lining the sides of the hallway, the walls were covered with carpet. An orange-brown shag that bulged out in places, like the walls were swelling with water damage - or something behind them was pressing to escape.

The air in the hallway was hazy with dust, and the wells of light that shone from the row of sickly yellow fluorescents running down the Hallway were alive, amber motes swirling back and forth in an invisible rhythmic draft.

All of this entered into my brain in the second it took me to pull up short, letting my grocery bags fall from my now nerveless fingers. By the time they hit the floor and I had inhaled one full breath of consternation, the hallway was back to normal. The empty pizza boxes stacked in front of tenants' doorways had never looked so welcoming. Even as I stood there, heart pounding in my chest and tongue drying out behind my teeth, I found I could barely remember what the other hall had looked like. What other hall? Maybe I had even dozed off in the time it took me to ascend from the lobby to the twelfth floor. That had to be it. A momentary plunge into a dream.

Yes, I was sure this is what happened. And I didn't think any more of it.

Until it happened again.

I have been in this Hallway

A week later I was leaning lazily against th back door of the elevator, secure in the knowledg that they would stay shut since I had only used th buttons on the opposite panel. Except they didn't. As soon as the elevator arrived at the twelfth floor, th two doors behin me slid open without a sound and I felt mysel spill backward onto the floor.

lewn | Printed Matter | Ad Saver

resh Harvested | People News

CLASSIFIED ADS—PHONE

MPLOYMENT

lelp Wanted

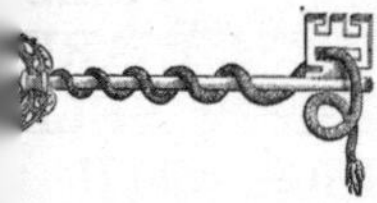

ried clumsily to
o at the sliding
rs to stop
elf, but this
den violent
ion only made
gs worse, and I
ed up cracking
head when I
led half in, half
of the elevator.
vision blurred
a moment and
en it cleared I
the other
llway. The red
r was there
in. It was hard
ell with my
ion swimming,
the Hallway
med shorter than
ore. The red door
s now open just
barest fraction.
e floor was damp
l warm against
cheek, and I
ık more than the
ingeness of the
llway, this is what
de me scramble
my feet.

I immediately had the image of it stretching down the passage from the red door like a misshapen tongue from an eager mouth flash through my brain. Since then it's happened five more times. And not just when I use the elevator. Now, any door in this building has the potential to momentarily show me this humid, undulating Hallway and the red door at Its end. Even when I take the stairs. Each time I see it, the Hallway stays for a few seconds longer. Like something seen vaguely on the horizon that comes closer every time you look back up. A radio station tuning itself into clarity.

I don't know what to do. I can't afford to break my lease. And what would I even say to anyone?

What will happen if one day when the elevator dings and the doors slide open and the Hallway stays?

What will I do when everything is Hallway?

this has to have something to do with the Mansions

HOT SINGLES IN YOUR AREA JAWS GNAWING THE CORNERS OF THE NIGHT, FINGERS SLITHERING THROUGH THE ENTRAILS OF YOUR DREAMS, SWIPING LEFT

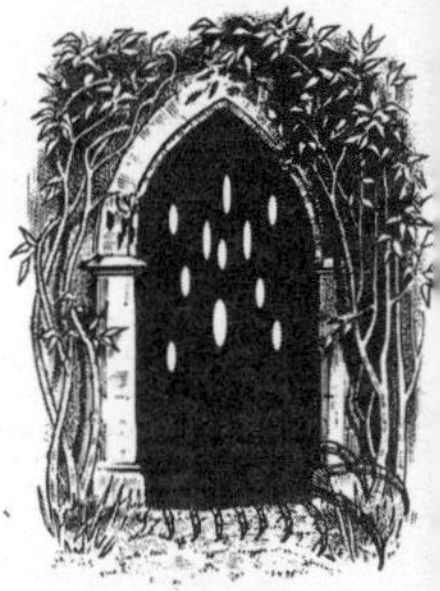

okay fine fuck it

HOT SINGLES IN YOUR AREA JAWS GNAWING THE CORNERS OF THE NIGHT, FINGERS SLITHERING THROUGH THE ENTRAILS OF YOUR DREAMS, SWIPING LEFT

MEN—Experienced . shoe men

WHAT. THE. ACTUAL. FUCK.

So this was why there was no experience preferred. The benefits had better be great if he was going to have to try and sell ads in a . . . what was that? A fictional newspaper advertising section? If this was just someone's glorified zine, Noah swore to . . . Well, actually, what did he care if the ads were fake or real or written in elvish for fuck's sake? As long as they paid him on time and the benefits were good he would be golden.

Still . . . kinda weird . . . Who would even buy something like this?[5] Nerds? Yep, probably had something to do with nerds.

Noah rang the counter bell that he had not seen hiding behind the stack of *Printed Matter* and scratched at the scruff on his cheek as he nervously waited for someone to answer. His mirror-window pep-talk high was slowly fading back to the normal toe-tapping, key-jiggling anxiety of pre-job-interview jitters.

'How can I help you, young man?'

The voice at his elbow twanged with the ever-present but unable-to-pinpoint Midwestern accent that seemed to be so prevalent in this city. Noah startled at the proximity and almost stumbled sidewise away from it out of reflex before he got a hold of himself and turned to see who was talking to him.

They were short, compared to his six-foot-one frame; a femme-presenting person dressed in a beige cardigan and blazer that distressingly matched the Formica counters and sensible tweed slacks with loafers. They had their sandy-blonde hair cut into a severe bob and red, plastic-framed glasses pushed up

---

[5] The majority of the subscribers to *Printed Matter* did not so much buy the newspaper as it was assigned to each of them upon their migration. Many of them would go to great lengths to . . . unsubscribe.

high on the bridge of their not unsizeable nose. So basically every 'Karen' he had ever worked for through temp agencies.

Where the fuck had they come from? Noah had been looking directly at the . . . yep, still closed Staff Only door at the back of the store. But here they were, standing definitely too close for comfort.

'Ummm . . .' Noah took a step sideways to orient himself and turned to face them. 'Yeah, I'm here about the job position for Ad Sales and Customer Management?' he replied in what he hoped was a *hire me I'm super dependable and will probably only miss work slightly more than the average employee* tone of voice.

They extended a hand in greeting. 'Well, then I am the exact person you're looking for! My name is Linda and I handle the HR and most other things around here in the day-to-day.' They smiled widely, revealing almost too perfect teeth except for one chipped front incisor which gave their grin a slightly conspiratorial slant. 'So happy to have you on board, and if you come with me we can start setting ya up with all the boring paperwork and other new hire stuff.' Linda positively beamed at Noah and then continued without pausing for breath. 'I know, who likes paperwork, amirite? Well, except me, but I've always had what my mothers called a "voracious appetite of unending means and scope" for the stuff . . . MOTHERS . . . can't live with them, can't betray them to the Council of Nine.[6] Amirite?'

Mothers? Council of Nine?[7] What the actual . . . Noah was not used to this much stimuli after working janitorial nights and sleeping days for the last who knew how long.

---

[6] There is no Council of Nine. Mind your business.
[7] Ibid.

'Hold up . . . please,' he managed to squeak out. 'Are you hiring me, just like that? I, uh, have a resumé. Don't I need to do like an interview or somethi—'

Goddamit, shut up, you idiot, they are apparently just giving you the job; don't look a gift-Linda in the mouth.

Linda just smiled even wider than Noah would have thought humanly possible and he couldn't help but look directly into their mouth with its perfect rows of teeth[8] and pale pink tongue peeking up from behind them like a moist, hungry slug tasting the air. Noah blinked; for a moment he'd thought there had been more than one set of teeth in Linda's mouth, another set clicking into place, an ivory horizon line looming up from the wet, pink sea of their mouth, but then it was gone and Linda was saying something he hadn't caught the beginning of.

'. . . so that explains the majority of your duties and we can move on to paperwork and inducting if that is all fine and dandy.'

Fuck, how long was I spaced out staring at their mouth like some sort of weirdo? Noah thought in a blind panic while nodding and putting on what he hoped was his best *oh yes, this is all old hat for me and there is no way I have no idea what you're talking about and I'm going to make you regret hiring me* smile and posture. What was with their mouth? He wasn't even into mouth stuff . . . or was he? *Wait, did I zone out again while yelling at myself about zoning out to begin with? Get it the fuck together, Noah!*

'. . . and that might seem like a strange employee clause and all but lots of jobs are doing blood tests these days, you know, just as a precaution, so if that won't be a problem, then

---

[8] You know the drill. Teeth, teeth . . . teeth?

just sign here one final time and we can move to the back office to watch the new hire tutorial video.'

Now Linda was gesturing to the counter in front of Noah, where there was suddenly a large stack of yellowing paper. The text on it was tiny and crammed, having been typed on what would seem to be an old typewriter in desperate need of a new ribbon. The place at the bottom of the document where Linda was gesturing had several previous signatures crossed out and several more peeked rebelliously from under the edges of chalky white-out.

'Ummmmmm . . .'

Noah briefly thumbed through the rest of the pages and there was his signature on all of them. The cramped typed letters swam before his eyes and some of the pages just had diagrams and schematics except the lines were disturbingly organic.

'Oh, you don't have to go back over those, you already signed them. Just worry about that final page while I set these up,' Linda chirped as they put out several large empty medical vials. 'If you can take these to the conference room in the back there, we can get started and have you out on the road by lunch.'

Linda turned on their heel after gathering up several sheaves of papers from the counter between them that Noah had no memory of reading or in fact signing and started back towards the room they had gestured to with the placid walk of someone who expects beyond a shadow of a doubt that they will be followed.

Did he have the job already? On the road by lunch? How good were these training videos?

Before he could either vocalise his confusion or just follow them blindly, the bell over the door jangled and a man

entered. He was dressed in a well-worn but obviously recently washed and pressed repairman's uniform; it was a faded blue material and the white patch with black border stitching over his breast pocket read RFGRTR RPR in block letters and then Svenn in cursive stitching. Svenn's face, with its middle-aged care-lines and a mustache that would have been the envy of Tom Selleck, and the salt-and-pepper hair sticking out over his ears from beneath his cap moved him firmly into a mental folder labelled *Daddies?*. At least Noah hoped he was Svenn, and not someone who had murdered Svenn, taken his outfit, laundered all the blood out of it – he really should ask him how he got blood out of it if that was the case – and then worn Svenn's uniform for the beginning of a refrigerator-repair revenge-slasher murder spree. Maybe he'd had his t-shirts shrunk one too many times (this was based on the murders being related to ALL appliance repairs and not just fridges); maybe the lint trap had caught fire and burned his family alive when he was a child; maybe he'd had to do all the refrigerator repair work at a summer camp and the campers had locked him inside one and he'd frozen to death and now whenever he came back for his revenge, the victims would say something like, 'Oh, do you feel cold all of a sudden?' and he would burst in with a meat hook and say, 'I hope you don't catch a CHILL!' before beginning the slaughter . . .

Noah hoped none of that was the case and that Svenn was just . . . Svenn . . . the repair person.

Linda stopped, and turning on their heel they eyed the repairman with their back rigid, for all the world like a cat who has just seen a dog wander into its alley and is deciding not if they are going to give it hell, but how much.

Without taking their eyes off Svenn, Linda held the stack of paperwork out towards Noah. 'Noah, sweety, take this

paperwork back to the conference room and get started on your new hire orientation. You won't be able to miss it.'

Noah didn't know what was more disconcerting: this odd stare-down or the fact that his new boss had just called him 'sweety'. Either way the vibe had gotten fucking weird and he was glad to have an official reason to go hide from it in another room. So he took the stack of papers and tried to walk and not run back to the rear of the office where Linda had gestured.

As he walked away he heard Svenn say in a calm, not-quite-southern-drawl-not-quite-northern twang, 'Why, Linda, were you expecting me? You must have been. I would hate to think you were making new hires without sending the request up the ladder first?'

To which Linda replied in their cheery but clipped office-manager tone, 'Of course, Svenn, it's all in the mail. Maybe the *couriers* are just late as usual.'

Their emphasis on the word couriers was full of the same sort of workplace venom that you usually associated with the phrase, 'Someone *accidentally* ate my lunch from the employee fridge.' Noah quickened his step and slipped into the conference room just as Svenn was saying, 'I wasn't actually coming here about your new hire, Linda, but we might as well discuss that now . . .'

What the heck kind of repair person is Svenn? Noah thought as he looked around the room.

The room might have well come from a catalogue for Conference Rooms to Impress Until Success from the seventies. Everything was brown and orange and beige. A neat, short-nap, orange carpet covered the floor, and the walls had twin brown stripes that zigzagged across them in an ascending path that reminded him of a stock market price chart or a temperature-rising graphic from the news. In the centre of

the room was a beige, plastic conference table that looked like it was left over from some lost Bauhaus furniture museum. At the far end of the room was a black AV cart with a blocky television and a VCR set on the shelf below it.

Noah could vaguely hear Svenn and Linda talking. *What the fuck kind of job have I gotten myself into?* he thought dazedly as he firmly pushed the door closed behind him to block them out. There was a solitary swivel-style office chair, a desk mat and a yellow manila envelope waiting for him. The lights overhead hummed in a drone that undulated in pitch over a few seconds or so to give the illusion of there being some swarm of glowing insects that were travelling down the fluorescent bulbs instead of mercury vapors. Now that he was in the quiet of the room Noah felt suddenly bone-tired. He hadn't planned on *starting* a new job today but really anything was better than going back to mopping up that bus station every night. Right? Right.

He walked over to the manila envelope, which he could only imagine contained the new hire materials Linda had mentioned he needed to go through, and picked it up. The flap was creased and had a dirty outline where it had been taped and opened repeatedly. Something at one time had been stamped over the envelope's closure in red ink like a seal but it was faded and worn away in places and all Noah could make out now was something that looked like a tooth? A tower? A . . . a . . . printing press? He had no idea. The envelope was light but whatever was in it pressed outwards in a square, blocky shape. Opening it, he shook the contents out onto the mat and unsurprisingly it was a VHS cassette. Turning it over in his hand, he smiled to himself. There was something about obsolete technology like the VHS that always pleased him. Like just by it still existing and

stubbornly refusing to be replaced by more modern and convenient means of informational dissemination, it was a
confederate in his own similar life of anachronistic goals.
Well, not goals . . . achievements? He had given up on the big
life goals after the first year or so of trying to keep current
with student loans and now . . . just paying rent was his big
life achievement. Eating three meals a day, hot water . . .

Anyhoo, he liked VHS tapes and had a collection back at
his apartment, liberated from the dumpsters of chain book-
stores and libraries when they updated their collections. The
label on the tape just said:

EMP. MNL. SRC. 4 of 9

Illuminating.

Noah walked over to the AV cart that was already pow-
ered on, a mass of cords snaking out from the back of it and
into the ceiling via a missing drop ceiling tile. It seemed like
entirely too many cords and wires for just a television and
VCR but he was here to be an ad salesman, not IT, so he slid
the tape into the machine, which accepted it hungrily, and
flipped the lid of its mouth closed with a click. The screen
flickered for a moment, a static storm exploding across it
that wavered, and he saw a silent image of someone standing
in front of a gigantic tree that looked like it was growing . . .
inside . . . an office building. Then the static consumed it
and the screen flicked to glowing blue with a time stamp in
the bottom right corner. In the centre of the screen in a
glowing yellow sans serif was the title, 'EMP. MNL. SRC.
4 of 9', just like the label of the tape. Noah sighed and sat
down in the office chair, spinning it around to face the television just as it began to emit that countdown beeping
sound that so many of these corporations didn't bother to
edit out of their training tapes. The blue screen flashed green

with tiny clusters of static artifacts before blinking to a scene.

There was an AV cart, in a room with orange carpet and brown striped walls and . . . a table where a young man with disheveled hair that looked to have been hastily plastered down sat, wearing a blue button-down short-sleeved Oxford with one front tail untucked, khaki dickie work pants and large horn-rimmed glasses. The man leaned forward towards the television as if he could not believe what he was seeing; it was his own face staring at him. He looked over his shoulder at where the camera for the scene would have had to be. There was nothing in that corner of the room except an almost imperceptible yellow water stain creeping into the drop ceiling tile that bordered it.

Turning around, Noah swore softly but urgently. What the actual fuck? Was this one of those mental acuity tests? Were they wanting to find out how he performed under stress? But what kind of job would have . . . a television doppelgänger . . . as a scenario? Was this the beginning of a snuff film? Was this how snuff films started? Noah couldn't remember ever seeing one; he hadn't even watched that *Faces of Death* tape that had gone around in college, mostly because the dudes who'd always tried to get him to watch it with them had all been waaayyy too eager to get someone else into it. But also life was short, man, and his brain, as he had proven time and time again in college and later jobs, was a finite quantity and could only store so much before things began to fall out. What if *Faces of Death* had bumped out the memory of riding his first bike or the way Mitchell Simmons' mouth had tasted beneath the bleachers in eleventh grade? No, thank you. Also just gross?

He was about to stand up and walk out of Printed Matter

as calmly as he could before breaking into a panicked run that he wouldn't have stopped until he was home with the door slammed shut, triple locked, and he was hyperventilating in the bathroom – but just then the screen switched perspective and now it showed a waist-height stone wall in front of a spread of white birch trees; three of the trees stood apart from the others, the other trees growing away from them as if attempting to escape their orbit. In the sky just above them hung a red orb.[9] Noah tried to form the idea that it was a moon or the sun but he couldn't; the thing resisted those names. It was now in the middle of the trees, looming larger, the red circle thrumming and the CRT screen of the television crackling with waves of light that passed across it in time to the thrumming like tidal swells across an ocean of light and static. Noah could feel tears leaking out of the sides of his eyes and knew that his mouth was gaping open but he couldn't do anything about it; all he could do was lean closer and closer as the red circle grew until it swallowed everything.

---

[9] '. . . the depth and breadth of those whose minds have tried to comprehend the call of the Huntress Mother have never been fully catalogued before. It runs the gamut of forgotten mystics, everyday labourers and often celebrated artists whose visions were often attributed to a febrile mind instead of a conduit to something greater. For instance, the artist René Magritte over the span of his lifetime obsessively painted and chronicled something he referred to as the Banquet . . .' *Notes Upon the Crimson Mother and Those that Hunt*, Racliffe Press, New York, 1967.

2

Malachia

Malachia was sure there had once been a reason that she got up every morning to go and shuffle the hallowed bones of the past saints into new niches and altar lecterns. But if there had been, she had trouble remembering what it was besides the need for it. The mandibles with their long, yellowed teeth and black, almost translucent pincers were hard for a single novitiate to move from altar to altar but Malachia still schlepped them up and down between the musty chapels of the Congregation of the Hallowed Unspoken.[10] Sometimes after she was done with the first of her curatorial duties she would climb the rickety service ladders that crisscrossed the back of the church and led across the cacophony of pale stone-shingled roofs to then climb the arching stone steps that led to the very top of the main chapel's central dome.

Here, there was a chair, better described as a throne of yellowed bone that grew out of the centre of the dome to a height of twelve feet or more. It faced away from the Mansions of Silence and their tenements and palaces of echoing

---

[10] It has been remarked upon by many that for a sect with 'Unspoken' in their name it is remarkably hard to get some of these undead proselytisers to ever shut up.

dust and feral silence to look out at the grey of the Expanse. The Congregation of the Hallowed Unspoken was built upon the very edge of the cliff where the white clouds that filled the streets during the daytime poured up from.

Malachia could not remember anything about it other than it was the Expanse and even that she didn't truly remember. It was as if it was just her mind giving it a functional term or something nominative . . . and there was no one left that she could ask about it.

She only knew the names of the other members of her order because of the large membership ledger she had found while exploring the empty rooms and the chore board down in the kitchens. But much like the rules of necromancy and osseomancy,[11] which she apparently had no trouble remembering in painstaking, mind-numbingly boring detail, there was an exception to this when it came to the name Bene. The first day she had awoken and found the church empty, that name had been on her lips, almost as if she had been repeating it in her sleep to keep it from slipping away like all the others. She had also found an incredibly ornate wimple beneath her bed that had that name stitched into the lining, the mundanity of which, in contrast to the complicated black on black embroidery that covered the headpiece, had made her laugh aloud, the sound breaking the heavy silence that had been hanging over her since waking. She had surprised herself by pressing the

---

[11] On the matter of osseomancy, instead of boring the reader to tears with the entire catalogue of each bone, their saints and the canticle derivations thereof, I will merely refer you to the work of Annabelle Dimitrov, specifically her book *On the Morrow of Our Sunken Hopes: A Monograph Concerning the Phalangeal Tabernacle and the Heresies That Resulted*, Racliffe Press, New York, 1876.

cloth to her face and inhaling deeply; the odour of bone dust and old paper and the warmth that bloomed in her breast at this both comforted and confused her in equal measures.

From the detailed log tallies on the hallway chalkboards that lined four entire corridors, it seemed like she had been doing far fewer chores than the rest of them and spending most of her time in warding walks. And because her brain seemed to be filled to bursting with the history and practices of the Congregation of the Hallowed Unspoken – not that any of this academic knowledge was helping her with the mystery of everything *outside* the walls of the Congregation – she knew that these walks were an important part of the Congregation's responsibility of keeping the Sainted Sleepers . . . well . . . sleeping.

Also, maybe she would find whoever had carried the name and scent of Bene.

This walking seemed like something that was still a manageable task so she set herself to it. Out through the crumbling gate of the Congregation's expansive if austere grounds, a narrow cobblestone road that hardly deserved the distinction from 'path' wound down a narrow hillside and was bordered on each side by graceful if bleak walls that leaned into each other like mourners in a funeral procession made of stone and mortar and dusty whitewash.

Malachia began these walks by taking a hymnal from the stacks that were mouldering in baskets by the doorway of the nave and putting a handful of the yellowing warding finger-bones that were in the stone font[12] next to the books. She

---

[12] I find the fact that such powerful relics were left in a bowl like forgotten car keys on a mantle to be staggering. Their historical value alone . . . not to mention the power within them.

knew to do this because it was what the murals all over the chapel depicted. And if nine murals that showed her swathed in grey funerary robes walking over a miniaturised city scattering fingerbones along her path were not enough to say what she should be doing, it was also stated in the first appendix of *Ordinances of Regret and Lacrimae of the Novitiate Ascendent*, a well-worn copy of which had been in her room when she'd woken to find herself alone.

So with a handful of bones in one of her robe's pockets and a rolled-up hymnal in the other, she walked down the winding path to the city that sat like a breath held, waiting to exhale . . . or swallow.

Malachia listened to the echoing slap of her sandals on the dusty white cobblestones and watched each footstep as it puffed the fine powdery dust out in a cloud. In some of the buildings that she walked past she could remember the inhabitants easily, static images firmly anchored in the palace of her memory. Here was the salon where the spider-limbed and many-veiled Night Sisters of Carrion Whispers would hold long, quiet vigils where interested parties could come to forget their dearest held beliefs. If you were one of the fanatics of Oblivion, that is. Malachia had never gotten the allure of the Forgotten or the orgiastic rush they seemed to get from losing something dear and welcoming the gash it left behind, but to each their own.

Here and there were shops she remembered frequenting. The baker Almondov, with his chalky loaves of bitter ash and long, thin flatbreads dusted with bone shavings and time that all the restaurants in town came to buy for their breakfast customers. She had come just in time to get one warm from the overnight ovens on the morning she'd had to hold vigil out on the furthest reach of the Mansions of Silence district,

and remembered the way he'd smiled so the fine parchment paper of his skin stretched tight and translucent over the yellowed bones of his jaws and teeth.

Almondov was no longer there and the great ash kilns were now silent.

Next to the bakery was a room of mirrors, and sometimes she stopped to walk amidst them to remind herself of her face. But not all the reflections could be trusted to tell the truth. The mirrors sometimes frowned when she smiled or showed far more teeth than she knew to be in her mouth or eyes in places she was sure she had none. One mirror particularly disturbed her with its unwavering image of a red orb hovering above a low stone wall backed by white-barked trees. She couldn't remember why but she knew that she should not spend too much time staring into that mirror. All that she *remembered*, but the inhabitants were an empty, echoing void in her memory. And so it was the rest of the walk down to the Quarter of Dust Fountains.

The Quarter of Dust Fountains was at the base of the Congregation's hill and Malachia loved the graceful, translucent bone archways that led into the main square. The fountains that ringed the entrances to the square were all dry as the bones they were made of, as was the towering central fountain. In the middle of the dried bowl of the central fountain's pool was a large, soaring monolith that was darkly stained down its flat sides. The stain had faded with time but Malachia still had the memory that it used to run a deep, brackish obsidian on high holy days, though she could not remember the last time one had been celebrated.

She usually stopped here to hold out the first of the handful of fingerbones that she brought on these walks and pick a Precept from the hymnal at random to keen to the flat grey

sky above. Today, however, as the last lines of the Canticle of
Perceived Losses Ascendent left her lips – '. . . the shadow
that brushes across the doorway, the shadow that whispers
beneath the Lie of Earth, the shadow whose whispers we
deny nightly, so say we the Congregation, so hope we the
Unspoken . . .' – there was a frisson of energy that caused her
teeth to vibrate and for a brief moment the dust around her
feet to spiral up before suddenly falling back down to lie as
inert as always.

Across the square, there was a figure with its back to her.
A figure that had most emphatically not been there when
she had arrived. It was seated all alone at a small table that
normally was not present in this square; an incongruous
battered brown wood affair surrounded by drifts of sheets of
paper, some large, some small, that fell from it like a whispering waterfall. Malachia stared. This was the first time
since everyone had disappeared that she had come across
something substantial like this. Sure, certain alleys had lin-
gering shades or the echoes that would boil up from beneath
the stones if you got too close, but this was something . . .
someone solid.

Malachia clenched the fingerbone, in this case the *Fourth
Metacarpal of Binding Weight*,[13] in her fist and moved towards
the figure, her footsteps echoing across the square in dying

---

[13] This is impossible. The *Fourth Metacarpal of Binding Weight* was lost
in 1726 during the pogroms of the Night Wardens, whose despicable
influence upon Silence was finally excised when the Carrion Oak along
with the other current Foundational Entities rose reluctantly to the positions they currently hold. Malachia is either incorrect or . . . or the
Congregation for some reason lied about it being destroyed and have
had it hidden all these years.

ghosts of cautious movement. As she got nearer she saw the figure was a tall lanky man wearing a short-sleeved blue button-down Oxford shirt whose collar was unfolded in the back and subsequently lost amidst a tangle of unruly dark hair. He had large horn-rimmed glasses perched low on a not insignificant nose. The figure's knees, clad in some sort of khaki work pants, were uncomfortably jammed under the table and they moved as if working on something that Malachia could not see from the angle she was at. Several sheets of paper blew towards her and stopped, plastered against the base of her robe. Malachia gathered them up and looked at them one after another.

Hand Hewn | 0 ¢

Printed Matter

Ad Saver

Fresh Harvested — People News

CLASSIFIED ADS—PHONE

EMPLOYMENT

Help Wanted

OT SINGLES
N YOUR AREA,
ONES WRITHING
NSIDE PALE
USKS, EYES
ONG SINCE
ALLEN TO ASH,
JUST WISH
FELT MORE
ERTAIN
HEY HISS

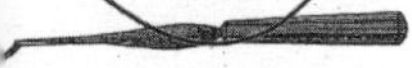

what do you see here?
wrong answers only

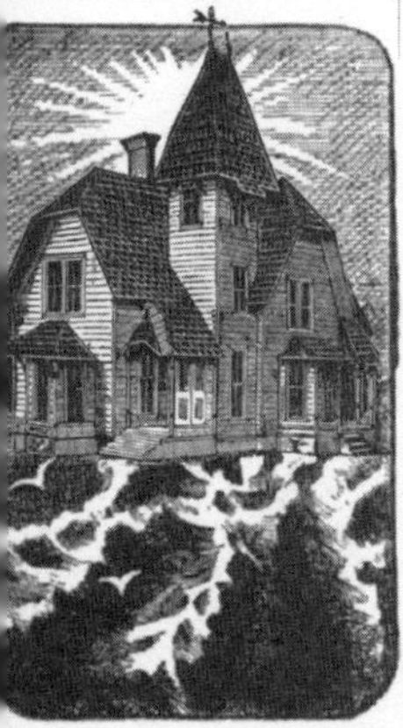

ontinued from last
eek our lifestyle
nd living
orrespondent
ADNIL brings us
heir experience
vith the new viral
Would You Live
Here challenge:

Day 1: Everything is going so great! The boat ride out here was so beautiful! The water was like a smooth dark mirror that didn't even reflect the sky! Finland is glorious! I can't wait to really disconnect and recharge.

When I first submitted my video application for this competition I was thinking about how great it would be content-wise for you my #eachdayablessingarmy but now . . . now I think this might be a chance for some real self-awareness checklists.

I'll leave a link below to my video about how to be perfectly self-aware and what notebooks you need to buy! Oh lookit, so many sea crows!

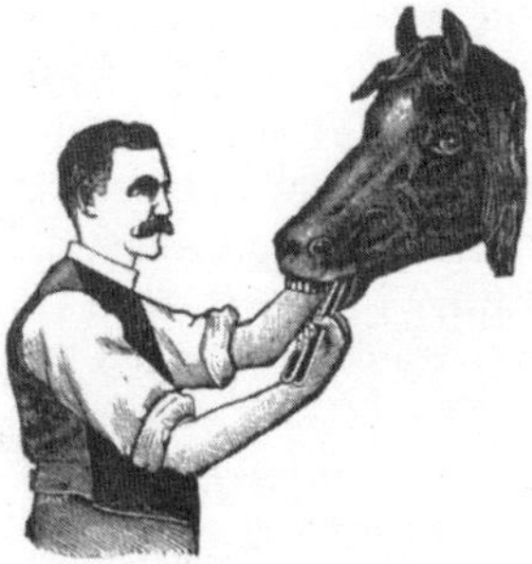

do you have your tithing ready?
can you hear their hoofs in your dreams? call us for help with dental budgeting!

if you see one of these report it to your local pomme authorities

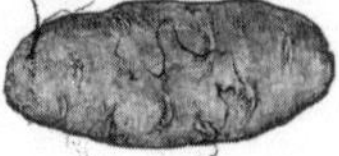

do not trust it

Day 2: Just finished unpacking. It wa sort of weird how the boat captain threw m stuff onto the shore and then sped away, his boat weaving erratically as he cast a last glanc back over his shoulder. It must be something special about th water here but the surface didn' even ripple with the ship's passage. I bet it' like the salt content or something. Let me know what you think about it in the comments!

Also, let's not forget YOGA SUNSETS amirite!

ESMEN—Experienced shoe men

EMPLOYMENT

Help Wanted

Day 3: So this island is so much smaller than it looked in the picture. I mean it seems smaller than when I first arrived . . . but that isn't possible, right? Right. Glad I brought so many books! This is going to be just what I needed. I'm also going to start working on the lesson plans for that Mindfulness Through Selfies seminar I've been promising all of you! Oh, look the sun is setting already.

That's odd.

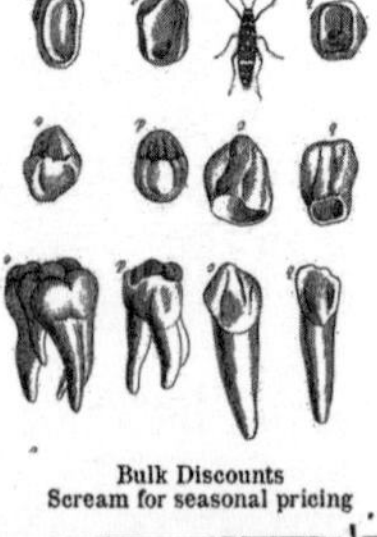

Bulk Discounts
Scream for seasonal pricing

something is changing the script

Day 4: Didn't sleep very well last night. You never really realize how physical the dark is until you are in the middle of it. Woke up and the candle I had left burning was out. For a moment it seemed like the dark was a wet velvety thing pressing down on my face, pushing into my mouth. But then I saw a light spark on one of the neighboring islands. It went out as soon as it appeared but I felt better for it. I'm starting to like this Muesli stuff.

this is new i dont like it

Day 5: Oh man I must have just been in a funk yesterday this place is the best. The rocks are covered with this soft green downy moss. Like Pinterest perfect . . . except my phone is dead. Oh well, the mind is the best camera, right? The moss is growing on the house steps as well. Didn't notice that when I first arrived. It is positively luminescent in the setting sun. Must be a seasonal thing? I haven't even finished one book yet. I need to get my act together. Ooh, maybe I'll start a bullet journal! I bet I can make some videos doing dramatic readings of it with some inspographs in the background.

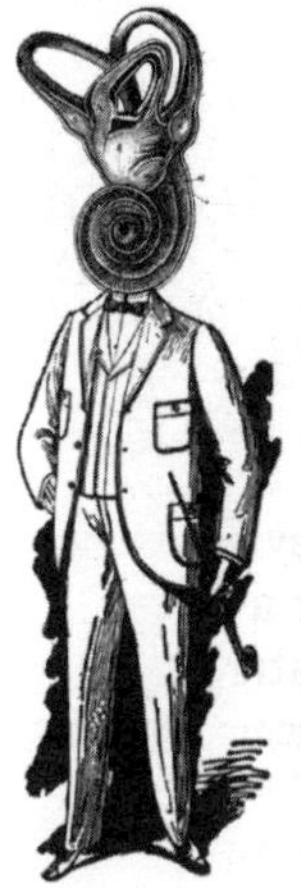

this is not your father
do not believe them
this is not your father
yet yet yet yet yet yet

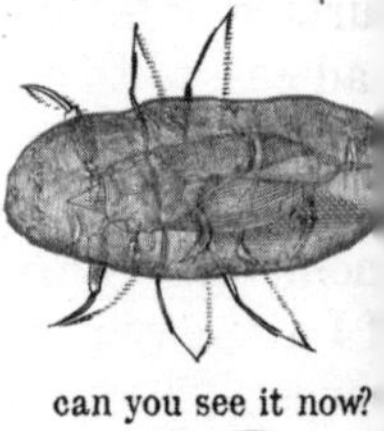

can you see it now?

HOT SINGLES IN YOUR AREA BRINGING OUT THE HARNESS OF WRITHING TORMENTS, THE NETS OF RAVENOUS SHADOWS, GOTTA CATCH EM' ALL THEY CROON EAGERLY

LESMEN—Experienced shoe men

Hand Hewn | 0 ¢ | Printed ● Matter | Ad Saver
Fresh Harvested | People News
CLASSIFIED ADS—PHONE

EMPLOYMENT

Help Wanted

You can avoid the annual teeth tithing with this One Simple Trick! More on page 2-7

)ay 6: Decide to go)r a swim today. The 'ater was...bracing. Actually, it was so old I couldn't feel ny limbs after a few ninutes. It felt like ny body below the till ridiculously calm urface of the lake ad ceased to exist.

'here in that noment, I wondered f I dipped my head eneath the surface f I would also lisappear into its larkly dreaming lepths. Ha! No phone or six days and look t me waxing poetic. should do like a 'edTalk when I get ack. I was about to vrite let me know vhat you think in the omments, but there ren't any right now re there? Weird.

LESMEN—Experienced shoe men

Day 7: I must have fallen asleep outside looking at the lake. I mean I woke up outside on the shore so that is what happened right? I had some of that green moss in my hair too, that stuff is amazing! I bet they could run a great terrarium supply business with how fast it grows.

Day 8: Okay there are some drawbacks to no electricity. I'm not complaining. This trip is an amazing opportunity. It's just...how long are the nights here? They seem REALLY long.

Like the darkness is comfortable here, like it has sunk its roots deep and every morning recedes ever more begrudgingly. Also, I didn't bring a watch that wasn't my phone, which is dead. Epic fail. But the water is still gorgeous. I find myself just staring out into it, for hours.

nope

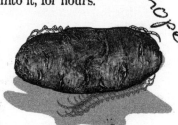

what must you see to believe?

can you hear them?
do you want to?

HOT SINGLES IN YOUR AREA, PALE FINGERS CRACKING THROUGH RIBS,HISSING IN DELIGHT AT YOUR WHIMPERS, TAKE A DEEP BREATH THIS MIGHT STING A LITTLE

friday at 9 pm

Hand Hewn | 0 ¢

Printed ● Matter

Ad Saver

Fresh Harvested — People News

CLASSIFIED ADS—PHONE

EMPLOYMENT

Help Wanted

HOT SINGLES IN YOUR AREA, PERCHING ALONG ROOFTOPS, TALONS CLICKING, SMILES STRETCHING UNNATURALLY WIDE, EIGHT OUT OF TEN DENTISTS AGREE

Day 9: I think the moss has started growing under my fingernails? Maybe it's from swimming in the lake? But how else am I supposed to bathe? There is no electricity or hot water heater. Maybe I just touched some in the dark and didn't notice?
I HAVE started finding some growing inside of the house, pushing its way up between the floorboards in long green rows like blood welling from a scratch.

This is way more stressful than I thought it would be, the having no light at night part. But I have been finding standing in the lake up to my ankles to be calming. I've been doing that most afternoons now

RIP Geneviève Elverum (Geneviève Castrée). The world is darker without you in it.

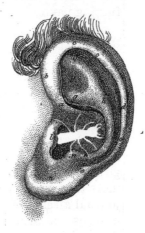

listen to MOTHER

which one though

Day 10: I must have dozed off while standing in the lake or maybe I've started sleepwalking because of my erratic sleep cycle here. Either way, I woke up today, tonight, up to my chest in the dark glassy water of the lake.

Tonight, however; it didn't feel cold, it was so warm it was almost uncomfortable. The lights on the neighboring island were back as well . . . I must have been staring at them. I should try rock stacking tomorrow!

Day 11: I stack all the rocks o this island. There weren't that many. Or least I think I did? I don't remember doi it but there the are all stacked in a row of thr rock high piles leading straigh into the lake. I wonder how many likes tha would have got me on insta? I' going to sketch the rocks then take a picture that when my phone is recharged. Tho likes aren't getting off that easily!

[redacted]

SALESMEN—Experienced shoe men

Hand Hewn | 0¢

Printed Matter

Ad Saver

Fresh Harvested | *People News*

CLASSIFIED ADS—PHONE

EMPLOYMENT

Help Wanted

Day 12: This morning I woke up and had planned to have a new attitude. To REALLY take advantage of this culture detox! I was going to take a book and sit out on the moss-covered dock until I read the whole damn thing! However, every book I brought with me was sodden and oozing.

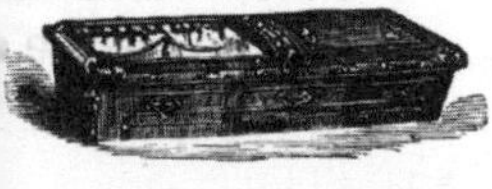

rental properties available

HOT SINGLES IN YOUR AREA, GOING DOOR TO DOOR,HAIR COIFFED, COLLARS PRESSED,SMILES WIDE FULL OF BRIGHT TEETH, TEETH THAT USED TO BELONG TO YOU

SALESMEN—Experienced . shoe men.

The pages are beginning to weld themselves together with green veins of moss. The ink just a grey blur, pages falling apart like . . . well like wet fucking paper.

Okay, deep breath, I mean twelve days seems fast for something like that to happen but this is an adventure, right? This journal seems fine. You know what, eighteen more days to just write and doodle. That in itself is a gift. Right? I've already filled more than half of this journal already. Just sketches of ferns and moss covered things. I had no idea I'd drawn so much. Is sleepsketching a thing?

Day 13: I've started to become curious about what the moss tastes like. Eating the same canned soup and crackers is fine, I'm not a food snob, but this stuff is SO GREEN. Like power ultra cleanse herbal matcha GREEN.

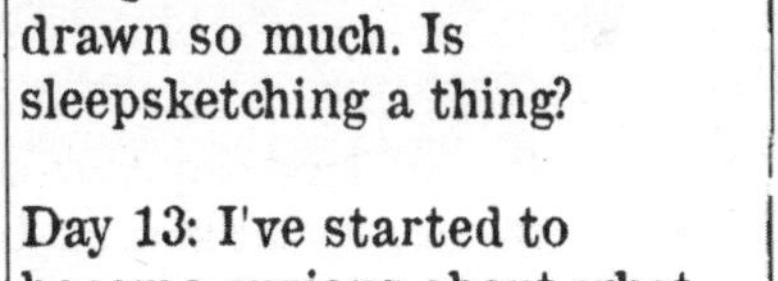

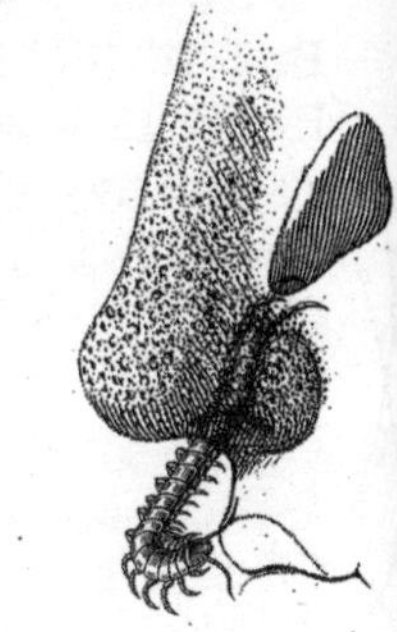

rental properties availabl

And it's EVERYWHERE now. When I grab a can of soup I have to tear it fre from the moss that has begun to grow up the sides of the cans inside the cabinets. It's definitely growing under my fingernails now. But that'll go awa once the month is up right? One good manicure and I'll be back to doing nail tutoials in no time. Ooh I wonder if I can get decals made that look like this moss hashtag meta hashtag goals!

EMPLOYMENT

Help Wanted

·AY 14: Okay. Okay, ıe island is ·EFINITELY smaller ıan it used to be. The ·ater comes up to the ·ft side of the house ·nd that semicircle of ·ocks that used to be ıst off the shore are ·ow completely gone. ·he water is right up · the very top of the ·ocks as well.

·hey look like floating ·reen-carpeted ·allways surrounded ·y black glass. This ·ıust be a tidal thing, ·ght? I'm sure I'm ·ıfe though, I mean ·ıe house has been ·ere a long time right? ·ny way it's scary and ·don't like it. But I'm ·ot giving up. If worse ·omes to worse I can ·ıst swim to that ·land where I saw the ·ghts.

fine! but dont say we didn't warn you, hmpf

Day 15: I ate some of the moss. It's all I want to eat now. It has this amazing mouth feel like even as I chew it is pushing back against the inside of my mouth. Oh I know it's just like the seaweed salad you get at a sushi restaurant but so much more . . . al dente? Good thing there is so much of it. I don't know why I was so upset about my books before? This moss is so much more interesting than any book. I think I'm finally getting the hang of this island thing.

DAY 16: I've stopped sleeping in the house. Why would I want to? The moss and the lake are out here. I lie out on the mossy carpet of the dock, which now seamlessly connects to the obsidian surface of the lakes.

The water stretches out around me and I can't tell where it stops and the dome of the night sky starts. The nights stretches so long now. I'm sure there was a time when it wasn't the velvet dark of the night pressing down gently on my face, pushing me deep into the whispering bed of moss . . . but I can't remember it . . .

nothing to see he

HOT SINGLES IN YOUR ARE ROBES CAKE WITH THE DARK SANDS FROM BEYON TIME, EYES RIMMED WIT THE FROST O BETWEEN WORLDS, BES HAIR DAY EVER

mind your business

EMPLOYMENT

Help Wanted

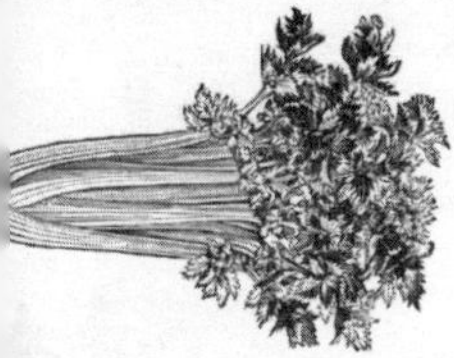

not the enemy

)T SINGLES
YOUR AREA,
SSING AT THE
RIGHTENING
Y, TALONS
ARESSING TAUT
)RROWED FLESH,
AGERLY PUTTING
)UR FRESH FACE
)RWARD

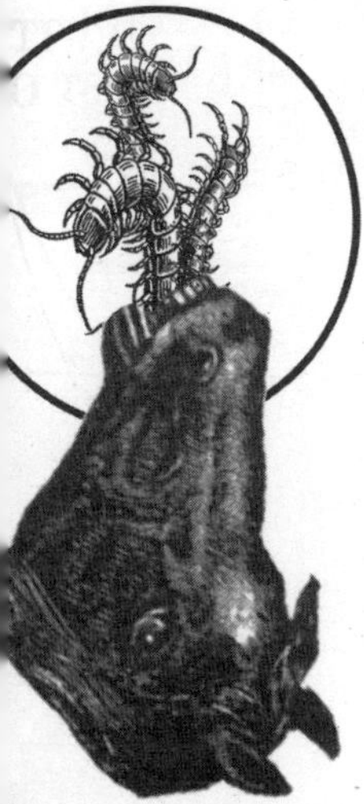

story continued on page 9-9-9

The water silently meets the shore of moss-covered rocks.

The moss breathes softly, an undulating pelt of green that covers everything.

A bird flies overhead calling out to its mate. It is not reflected below in the dark water.

The moss undulates. The water is still silent.

A bird lands on the moss-covered mound at the end of the dock.

Something lunges up from below the water shedding the mound like a sloughed off skin. It is green and glistening as it thrashes for a moment towards the house. There is a wet gurgling sound, a mewling of a wounded animal as it calls out once, twice . . .

The water ripples and then is still.

The moss grows thicker . . . greener . . . unfettered.

A crab scuttles across the mossy rocks, something pale and glistening clutched in one claw.

HOT SINGLES
IN YOUR AREA,
ANCIENT
STEEL AND
GLISTENING
ENTRAILS
BENEATH A
HUNGRY MOON,
CLICK, CLACK,
THIS KNITTING
MEETUP IS
REALLY
TAKING OFF

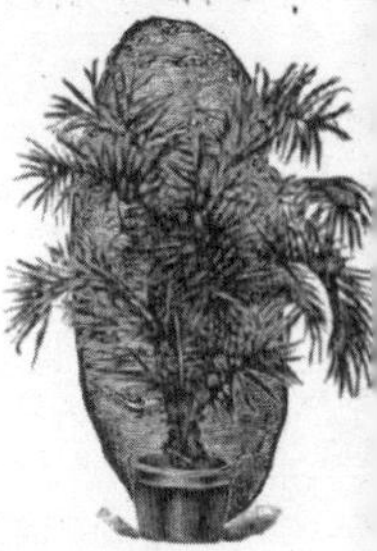

HOT SINGLES
IN YOUR AREA
MOUTHS
ENGULFING A
SWELLING
TIDE OF
SHADOWS,
LONG FINGERS
SEEKING THE
SEAMS OF
CREATION,
UPVOTING THE
CHARNEL
HOST

ESMEN—Experienced . shoe men

Hand Hewn | 0 ¢

Printed Matter

Ad Saver

Fresh Harvested — People News

CLASSIFIED ADS—PHONE

EMPLOYMENT

Help Wanted

HOT SINGLES IN YOUR AREA, FOOTSTEPS HOLLOW AMONGST MANSIONS OF SILENCE,EYES MILKILY REFLECTING UNDULATING PIT MOTHERS,A CRIMSON DOOR BECKONS

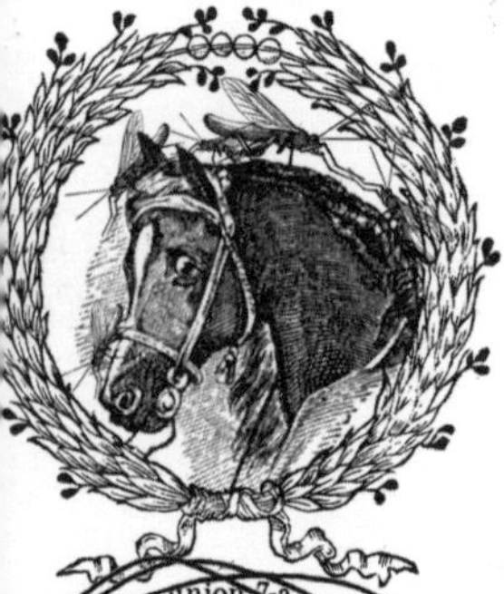

union 7-a

HOT SINGLES IN YOUR AREA, TEETH FILED INTO HUNGRY POINTS, DONNING WRITHING VESTMENTS OF WHISPERING DARK, PRE-ORDERING THE FRESH NEW APOCALYPSE

SALESMEN—Experienced . shoe men

The water recedes but is still smooth as a sheet of darkened glass.

A few darkly glistening rocks show from amongst the moss like smaller jagged islands in a sea of green.

A constant slow wind blows across the island. Bits of green moss float gently into the air.

Rain sleets across the island. Moss sluices through the rocks into the water of the lake, verdigris swirling into black, but still not a ripple breaking the surface.

The house creaks as it continues to settle. The lake is an unending black only broken by the green of the islands.

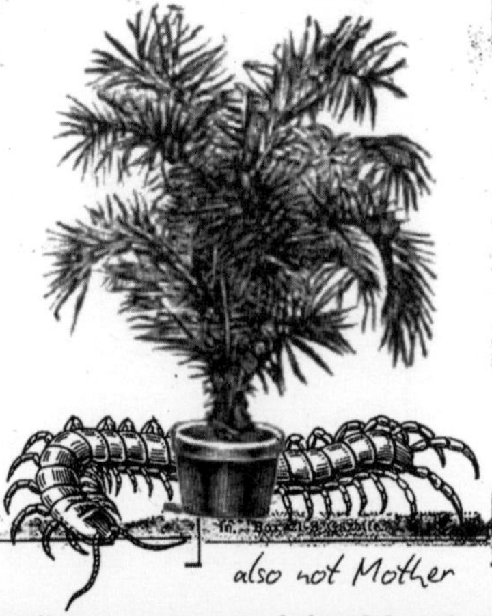

also not Mother

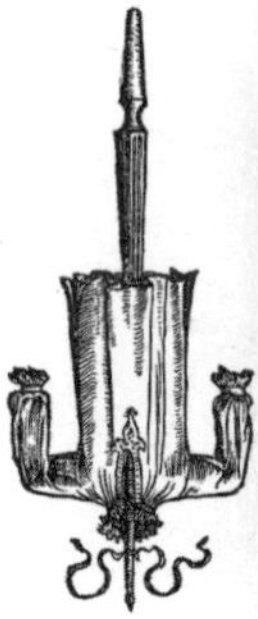

HOT SINGLES IN YOUR AREA, OPENING DOORS THAT WERE NOT THERE MOMENTS BEFORE, DESCENDING BREATHING STAIRWAYS, SINGING TO WHAT WAITS BENEATH

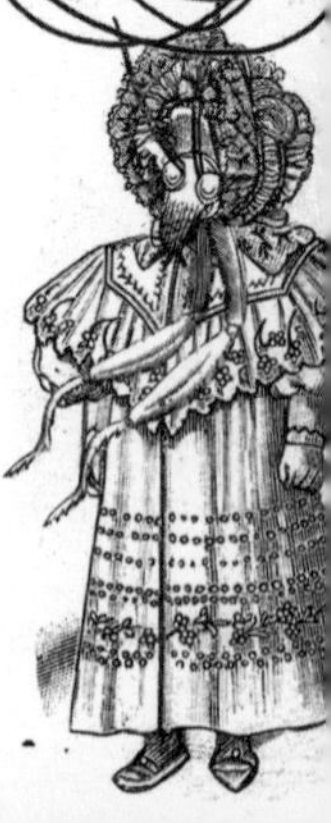

Hand Hewn | 0 ¢

Printed Matter

Ad Saver

Fresh Harvested | People News

CLASSIFIED ADS—PHONE

EMPLOYMENT

Help Wanted

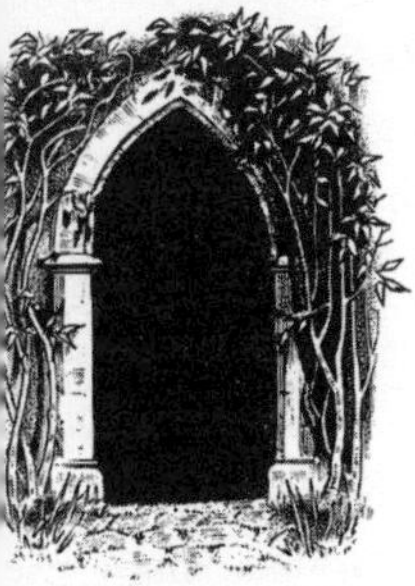

no

)T SINGLES
 YOUR AREA,
ANDS CLASPED
EHIND BACKS,
ANDS THAT
CHE FOR THEIR
RUE PURPOSE,
ANDS THAT
EMEMBER
RIMSON
RIPPING
RUTHS

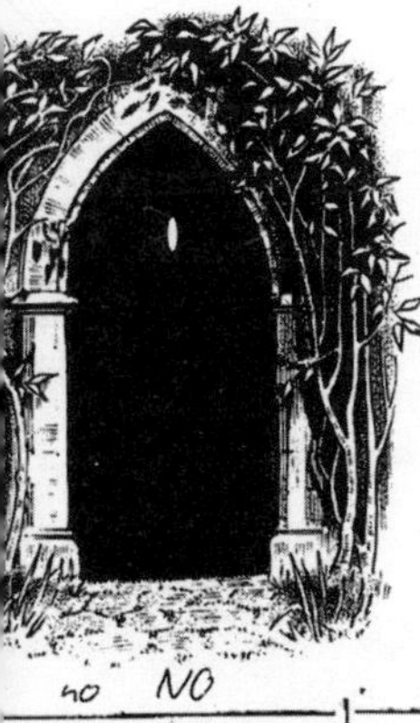

no NO

SMEN—Experienced . shoe men

DAY 30 This has been such a great experience. I feel so . . . so full of life, so relaxed. Like the gentle green quiet of these moss-covered rocks has slipped under my skin and filled me with its curling quiet depths. I think I am becoming spiritual? I bet I can do an entire video playlist on Things I Learned From The Moss or something like that. Maybe a whole separate channel for moss? I could be the Moss Queen! Lulz.

I was going to take some moss back with me but overnight its all been washed away. The island is still pretty in a rocky palette of greys and blacks sort of way but I miss the moss. Is that a weird thing to say?

The boat should be here soon and I will be returning to civilization. I hope I manage to bring back some piece of this island with me when I return despite there being no moss left. Something from my nights here that will settle into the fertile ground of my daily life, spread its roots . . . and begin to grow . . .

HOT SINGLES
IN YOUR
AREA,
CALCULATING
THE DEPTH OF
THE CARRION
RIFT, CARVING
THAT NUMBER
INTO THE
SPINE OF THE
SLUMBERING
PIT FIEND,
8675309

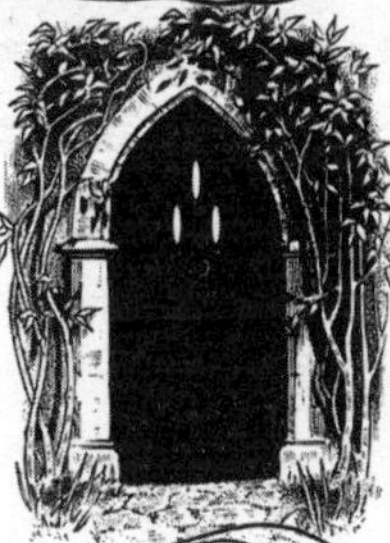

no no noNo No

HOT SINGLES
IN YOUR AREA
TALONS
SLEEPING
INSIDE MILKY
FLESH, BEAKS
SILENT
BEHIND
SULLEN MASKS
NOT SO GOOD
THINGS COMING
TO THOSE WHO
WAIT

Interesting.

Malachia carefully folded the paper and continued closer to the figure. She stopped and cleared her throat.

'Hello. Are you a shade?'

The figure did not acknowledge her. She walked cautiously around him, keeping a reasonable distance; after all, there were many things in the city that it would not be wise to startle. She saw that he was writing on a typewriter. It was much more plain than the intricate ones she saw the Writers using when they were paraded around for the Feast of Words,[14] their long pale fingers intertwining over the bone keys that swayed up to receive the blessing of their touch, but still a typewriter all the same.

This man was obviously not a Writer because . . . well, the lack of visible mandibles was a good place to start. Also, he was human like her, not a glistening being of chiton and dreams. Being a human was not something she thought about, ever. Even in a city as odd as Silence, with its plethora of dimensional gaps, both natural and via the transit authority, it was rare to see another human like herself. So she should have cared about it, logically. Maybe it was the changes that were beginning to happen in her body due to her service to the Congregation or just a general disinterest but she had never felt any sort of kinship with other humans. Some of the

---

[14] Ah, the Feast of Words! It has been so long since I have lost myself amidst the drift of revellers, a particularly savoury stanza or hauntingly sweet definition melting on my tongue. The last time I was in Silence was, I think, two hundred and seventy years since I left my larval crèche, so around 1981 to you, the reader of this account. Youth truly does not comprehend the gift of their home until they have left it. I miss that city.

younger, more unruly novitiates would gossip about the rumor that part of taking your vows to the Congregation erased your past, severing the ties like the cut string of a lost kite. But Malachia had always dismissed that because if it *was* true, how would you even know that you had lost something after it was gone? There was no point in idle speculation besides the shirking of chores and prayers. Today was different, though. Something about seeing another human in the middle of the silent echoing corpse of the city, something about this person in particular, gave her a rush of relief and made her wonder *why* she had never thought much about it before.

Malachia cleared her throat again, this time with a touch of annoyance.

'Excuse me. You are obviously not a shade and it is usually held to be polite to answer when spoken to.'

Malachia took a step closer, moving into what she guessed would be the person's line of sight, and indeed as she neared the figure did notice her. He jerked upright or at least tried to . . . Malachia could now see that his fingers were somehow enmeshed with the keys of the typewriter, his nails peeling back to let the metal shunts of the key levers slide into the meat. In fact, the papers on the table were stained with a dark oily substance that leaked from the base of the typewriter in a disturbingly organic rhythm.

The man looked at her, eyes wide and shining, the whites flashing like an animal caught in a trap that senses the hunter coming to collect their quarry.

Malachia approached the table which she now saw was a battered wooden writing desk that had once been painted black but was now mostly scuffed wood with just small speck

islands of black paint remaining. On one end was a hand-cranked pencil sharpener which jutted out of the sea of papers that covered the desk, a solitary outward sentinel from the mainland of the typewriter.

The man now sat still except for his fingers, which continued to move across the keys of the typewriter as he watched her.

'Can you hear me? Can you understand what I am saying?' she tried again, stopping directly in front of the desk this time. The man looked down at her; even hunched over the desk, he towered a good foot above her. His eyes locked with hers and held them for a long moment before darting back to the paper currently in the typewriter and then back to her and back again.

Malachia stood there weighing the choice before her, and in the end it was easy. If she walked away, all that she had was more grey, mist-filled days of sainted knuckle-bones and keened hymns as she roamed the empty, echoing streets of this necropolis that was only populated in her memory. But here was something new, something *possibly* breathing or at least not a memory. So taking a breath and muttering the first line of the Lament of Tangled Bones[15] to steady her nerves, she walked around the desk to see what he was writing.

---

[15] '. . . between you and I the sea of loss, between you and I a forest of doubt, between you and I a bridge of bone and faith, between you and I this theft of clarity held close . . .' – a particularly poetic canticle from the 43rd Edition of the *Primer of Petal and Bone*, the first mention of which dates back to even before the founding of the Congregation of the Hallowed Unspoken and is credited to a sect of heretical osseocantors whose name has been purged even from my records by the fourth Convention of Wurm.

3

Noah

While it did not really live up to the Mansions part of its name, the Mansions of Silence apartment complex definitely seemed silent alright. Noah sat in the company car that Linda had assigned him as they'd shooed him out the back loading dock of the Printed Matter office, handing him a set of keys on a bright orange floatation fob like you got when you rented a paddle boat and an address scrawled in surprisingly messy handwriting on a sheet of Printed Matter memo stationery. At least that's what his memory told him had happened, but it had the feeling of something he was reading off a note card as he remembered. A certain wet warbling warpedness like sound heard underwater or light shining through smeared glass. Ever since he had left Printed Matter he had a line running through his head like a pop hit earworm – '. . . between you and I a bridge of bone and faith . . .' – and for the life of him he couldn't remember if it was a song he had heard or a gothspirational meme or what have you. Most likely it was an ABBA[16] lyric; when in doubt, always just

---

[16] Normally I would frown on putting the name of such powerful practitioners down in ink and paper like this, thus drawing their Gaze, but any attempt to limit their power over reality became a lost cause with the

assume it is ABBA. It was driving him to distraction and he had to make a conscious effort not to whisper the line to himself under his breath as he sat there in the car. He probably wasn't getting enough sleep. Yeah, that had to be it.

He shrugged off the feeling as he looked around the interior of the company vehicle. The car was an El Camino and Noah didn't know what surprised him more: the fact that this job came with a company car at all or that the car sported burnt orange pinstriping and faux wood panelling down its sides with the Printed Matter placard attached to the doors with magnets. The catalytic converter ticked loudly in the sudden hush of the engine being shut off and Noah just sat there looking at what in name was an apartment complex but looked for all the world like the sort of Overnight Motor Inn[17] you stashed government witnesses in while waiting to testify against the mob.

The sign was one of those large swooping ones in the shape of a painter's palette or a weird stretched-out blob, sort of like the logo for *The Jetsons*. It must have at one time lit up but even in the daylight Noah could see that the previously white translucent plastic was now the dull yellow of nicotine-stained teeth, and all along the bottom edge it was singed black from some long-past short circuit or fire. Then the complex entered into the shape of a long L. The bottom bar was a short, squat area

---

release of 'Tiger' in 1976. The vast scope of the amount of life lost that year by occultists and varied and sundried sects not wishing to bow to the power behind the infernal syncopation of the *Arrival* album is still being discovered even to this day.

[17] I sincerely doubt Noah had any idea about the actual Overnight Motor Inn (*Über dunkle Nacht Motor Gasthof*) and its many feral appetites. And we can only hope it never gains any ideas of him either.

where the manager's office/lobby was housed, and then through an archway that was flaking an old coat of faint blue paint you could see the long part of the L stretching in a three-storeyed row of rooms with balconied hallways running down their fronts. To the right and just out of his full eyeline was something with a short, half-brick wall that was topped with a sagging chain-link fence. There were some signs attached to it but Noah couldn't read them from where he sat in his car. On a whim, Noah popped open the glove box, and inside, besides the normal registration and title in a blue plastic sleeve, was a canister of vinyl wipes, a mileage logbook and a half-full box of Printed Matter business cards. Noah pulled the wipes out and out of habit began wiping down all the plastic and metal of the dashboard, steering wheel and cup holders before he could stop himself. *Once a janitor* . . . he thought but still finished the task, which had a calming effect on his general sense of anxiety. As he did this he noticed the tips of all his fingers and stopped in confusion. Each had scar tissue like decades-long calluses had grown there overnight or he had burned them against hot metal. Repeatedly. He had no memory of this happening. He would remember if his fingers had been like that before, right? Or was this one of those betrayals of your body like nearsightedness or bad knees that crept up on you as quietly as a thrill killer hiding behind the louvered slatted doors of your washroom? *Can't wait for middle age,* he thought ruefully. *That's gonna be fuuuuuuun if I'm already falling apart now.*

Shaking his head, he returned the wipes canister and grabbed a handful of business cards that he slipped into his breast pocket; after a quick and mostly fruitless attempt at grooming in the rearview mirror, he got out of the car with a bone-popping stretch and tucked his shirt in. In the glove box there had also been a brown knit tie with a squared-off tip

and a cheap gold-plated tie pin clipped to it that had the logo of Printed Matter on it, so he took a moment to put that on as best he could, taking off the very similar tie he was already wearing and leaning over the car to see his reflection in the window. He left the top button of his shirt undone but was generally satisfied with the job he had done with the knot. Putting on a tie always felt like donning a bit of armor or weaving a mental shield. Now he was Noah Bezden, salesperson and employee of the month four years in a row.[18] (How were these people going to know he wasn't?)

So it was with a fairly confident step that Noah cut through the yellowing grass and bedraggled poinsettias that bordered the sun-baked overhang over the entrance to the lobby. The door didn't give off a chime when he entered but it did make a horrible screeching noise where the corner of the door dug into the tiled floor. Everyone in the lobby, all two of them, looked up at him as he stood frozen for a moment. Noah found himself wishing absurdly that they had given him a name tag that he could just point to, but they hadn't so he just awkwardly forced the door shut behind him with a juddering, shuddering screech back into place and then smiled gamely at them with a small, quickly aborted attempt at a nonchalant wave.

The lobby's occupants did not look very impressed by Noah's entrance. The person behind the counter had a square jaw that looked like it had been carved from unmarred ivory

---

[18] It is lucky that Noah had no idea at the time the severe and usually spectacularly fatal consequences of becoming an 'employee of the month' at Printed Matter or any of its sister corporations or he would never have been able to get out of that car for the abject terror that would have transformed him into a pile of quivering, mewling jelly.

and possibly the fullest lips that Noah had ever seen. He immediately thought of caricatures he had seen of Steven Tyler or Mick Jagger, but where those were exaggerated and leering, this person – for they completely evaded any attempt at gender classification – was perfect in every way, and even though he knew it was just a trick of the light, had to be a trick of the light, they looked so velvety soft that he imagined if he reached out to touch them he would leave trace runnels like you got from stroking a carpet or velour material. Their eyes looked at Noah not so much with suspicion but with the annoyed fore-knowledge of some new wrinkle having been added to their workday; they were the lightest golden amber he had ever seen and took up the majority of the space on either side of a per-fect if very dominant aquiline nose. Their hair was cropped short but still long enough to have a tight circlet of ringlets that had been dyed an intense, silvery lavender. The overall effect was that of looking at a perfect Roman bust like the ones they made of emperors, albeit with proportions more akin to the work of Margaret Keane or something else in the velvet painting subgenre. They were clad in a bleach-stained maroon polo that had 'Mansions of Silence' stitched in gold thread over the right breast with the weird blob shape from the sign outside behind it in outlined relief.

The other individual in the lobby could not have been more different. Well, Noah assumed that they were different but, in honesty, he really couldn't get a very clear view of them because they appeared to have draped every magazine and newspaper over themselves where they lay on the couch. If he hadn't been able to hear the sound of them coughing at regu-lar intervals, he would have wondered if they were alive at all, but just as he had that thought the pile of magazines shifted and a brown hand with several gold rings and long nails that

had been painted jet black and manicured into the approximation of bird talons slipped out from underneath them and hung down the side of the couch they were lying on. The nails had splatters of gold sparkles on them, and now that he was paying closer attention he could also see a pair of red running shoes with yellow stripes on the side also peeking from the magazine mound.

Noah had no idea how to react to this, so he didn't. Turning on his heel as smoothly as he could, as if any small squeak on the tile would wake the Rip Van Couch Winkle, he headed to the counter where the small clerk/possible fallen angel was still staring at him askance. He waited for a beat, expecting them to say something along the lines of 'And how may I help you today?' or 'Whatchya want?' or 'Hail and Well Met, Fair Traveller, for Unto You This Fair Couch Gremlin Child Is Born' but all the desk clerk did was raise an eyebrow at him and turn the page in the book they had been reading on the counter without looking down at it.

'Um, I uh, I'm here to see, um, let me see, I have it here . . .'

Noah began fumbling in his shirt pocket for the slip of memo paper with the information Linda had written down for him. The clerk cleared their throat and with exaggerated deliberateness closed their book; folding their hands on top of it, they turned the full attention of their large golden eyes on him with the *you've made me stop what I'm doing so you better not waste my time* air that only veteran customer service representatives can truly muster. Flattening the piece of paper on the counter, Noah realised with a sinking sensation that Linda had only written the address and the name of the establishment on the paper and nothing about who he was supposed to be visiting. He stared at the paper, trying to will more writing to appear or for the ghost of the conversation he *must*

have had with Linda to reappear in his mind like the dregs of a dream that you could feel the aftereffects of in the morning but never the particulars.[19]

'I uh, I was sent here from . . . I'm supposed to . . .'

He could feel his mouth drying of all moisture and the sides of his lips sticking to his suddenly dry teeth. This was too soon; just yesterday he had been mopping bus stations. He should have had some sort of training or at least a dossier or manual or client list, right? All he'd had was that video. The video with the red[20] orb. Just remembering made his heartbeat begin to slow. The video hadn't been that long, had it? No matter how hard he tried to remember how it had ended and what had happened between that time and Linda handing him the keys, all he could think of, all he could see, was the red orb, the red . . . moon.

THE CRIMSON MOTHER, he heard in his head, a sibilant wave of static. The red orb filled the screen and he leaned closer and closer and the RED

red

RED

---

[19] Noah often had a dream where he was certain beyond a shadow of a doubt that in it he had written word for word the next great American novel but when he would wake all he could recall was that it was 'kinda yellow' or 'really shaggy and had a muzzle'.

[20] Every time you see the word 'red' you must imagine it is printed in red. We had the printer make it red #EF3340 but within minutes the colour would fade and migrate to, well actually we cannot legally tell you what it migrated to but just trust us. Anyhoo, imagine the colour here and in every instance of the word in the future, both in this book and any other that you have the misfortune to read.

'. . . like I told you, Mrs Galloway usually informs me of any guests she or hers will be entertaining well in advance. So I'm not sure I should tell you what room she is in, you know, for privacy and safety reasons? But I do owe Linda from the last time I had to have one of their clients evicted. They did pull my ass out of the proverbial and literal spectral fire so . . .'

Noah heard all this like he was coming up off the mat from a near knockout in a boxing match, or at least what he imagined it was like; he had just seen a few of the *Rocky* films on local cable so that was all he had to go on as far as boxing experiences. But this had that warbly, slowed down and suddenly speeding up to snap back into normal speed and intonation like Balboa had had when he'd blearily hugged his bloody mess of a face against Apollo Creed's gorgeous sweaty chest. The last thing he remembered was RED and then this conversation which was obviously in response to something he had said but could not for the life of him remember what it was. And that was why he was just letting a phrase like 'spectral fire' slip past without the normal query that would have elicited. The way this day was going he wasn't sure he even cared what they meant by it . . . or if he could be sure he had heard them right in the first place.

The clerk continued, 'You Printed Matter employees are always nothing but trouble but I know what side my bread is buttered and the last thing I need is Svenn poking his big nose around my business. You'll tell him I was helpful if you see him, right? Mrs Galloway is on the second floor, third door after you exit the stairs, Room 206.'

Noah swallowed the sour saliva that had started collecting under his parched tongue and managed to croak, 'Sure thing . . . ummm . . .'

He paused for a second, realising he had never gotten their

name and they didn't have a name tag on. They must have seen Noah glance at their shirt because, with an aggrieved sigh, they reached behind the counter and retrieved a bronze-coloured metallic badge and carefully attached it to their shirt, then stared at him with an expression that wasn't blank but definitely didn't invite any camaraderie or further conversation.

The tag said 'SAM' and had a set of googly eyes stuck to the bottom of it with one of the eyes having ripped open and the googly missing from it.

'. . . Sam,' Noah finished awkwardly. 'Sure thing, Sam.'

4

Malachia

Malachia strained to see what was written on the paper that was beginning to spool from the typewriter in one long continuous sheath. The letters or characters or . . . symbols – because at this speed who knew – were swimming together and began to form a kaleidoscope image like something seen through the spinning blades of a fan, a stuttering and stumbling picture that slowly swelled to stability and jerkily moved across the now hissing stream of paper that was beginning to pile around the desk in a crinkling nest.

AN OAK TREE.

The flickering mirage of ink spread its branches, growing out past the edges of the paper. Malachia felt tears she had been unaware of squeeze themselves from her lashes to gather in the corners of her eyes. Her teeth suddenly vibrated so violently that she was worried they were going to fall out of their sockets, and without even a conscious thought she brought her hands, clenched in fists, up in front of her face with her forearms together, forming a barrier in front of her. She was already humming the Intonation of Banished Hungers, an automatic reaction instilled in every novitiate who had undergone the painful but glorious etching of the thirty-two foundational marks upon the back side of their teeth. The tone she was

humming rose in pitch and her teeth began to quiet in her jaw as she consciously worked her way through the pitch and weave of the intonation to its prescribed ending. She had no idea what was happening on the other side of her forearms but she trusted her tutelage and didn't lower them till the last lonesome vibrating tone had died out in the air. In front of her, where the man had been typing with blood-soaked hands and bone on the typewriter, there was now a small five-foot-high facsimile of an oak tree growing out of the desk, and the man . . . thing was nowhere to be seen.

'Well, that's par for the course,' she muttered to the now once again empty square as she squatted down to peer at the tree.

It was made of twisted skeins of the paper that had poured from the machine, and in places it seeped a dark crimson treacly sap from gaps in its trunk. Malachia was sure that she saw the sodden paper trunk swell in and out like a papier-mâché lung for a moment and thought if she got close enough she would be able to hear a deep shuddering breath coming from inside. As she watched, dark roots slithered out from beneath the tree and began to cover the desk and the typewriter, their tendril ends groping blindly for the ground below.

Now Malachia knew where she needed to go next and that someone . . . some*thing* was, if not alive, still present in the city.

The Carrion Oak.

She needed to go see the Carrion Oak.

Malachia left the square and the throbbing tree behind. She stepped onto the Way of Cold Flames, one of the nine streets that radiated out from the square. The buildings that represented the entrance to the Ministry of the Carrion Oak were in the southern ward of the city. She would have to go

through the glistening bone mounds of the financial district to get there. Malachia sighed and with a tightening of the braided rope that bound her initiate robes around her, set off down the paving-stoned street.

Malachia arrived in the Ward of Hunger and Sighs much quicker than she had expected, owing to the abandoned nature the city of Silence found itself currently enshrouded in. The bone mounds, while still towering in glistening bleached certainty, had been bereft of the usual traffic of diaphanous worms that flowed from one gaping mound entrance to the next. Their occupants were visible through their partially transparent ghost flesh as they commuted from one meeting to the next in the normally ever-busy district. She had not had to wait for any unbinding rituals at the crosswalks either. The worms occasionally broke free from their paths and would start to casually devour, well, anything in their path, not to mention begin to digest their passengers. If it had been a normal day, Malachia would have avoided passing through that way altogether but it was far from a normal day so the commute had been eerily easy.

However, now that she stood facing the three interlocking towers that made up the front-facing entrance to the Ministry of the Carrion Oak, she almost wished she had had the time traffic would have afforded her to compose her thoughts. Malachia had never been to the offices of the Carrion Oak before, and until today had counted that a good thing. Those summoned before the ancient being were either bound for sainthood or the Gristlemaw,[21] and she had never aspired to

---

[21] The Gristlemaw gets a bad rap. I spent a very formative decade being partially digested (due to a clerical misunderstanding that I completely own up to. I did indeed forget to register for a visa to the Withered Spiral,

either. But here she was and there they were and fucked if they weren't the only game going in Silence currently.

The entryway to the MoCO was tiled in large, bone-white squares that instead of yellowing with age continued to give off a ghostly luminescence; Malachia couldn't tell if it was just a trick of the light or some necrocraft inherent in their making. Desiccated leaves and yellowing rubbish crunched around her feet as she walked through the drifts that covered the steps. Their existence just deepened the oddness of the mystery of where everyone in the city had fucked off to. Yeah, she needed to get answers and soon. The echoing emptiness of the city was starting to grow on her. She could feel it seeping into the corridors of her mind and she didn't want to wait to see what would happen if she let it begin to rise.

The large glass doors to the ministry were open and yawning as she walked through them. The moment she crossed the threshold the piped-in music for the lobby started as if a switch had been thrown. One moment she had been walking up to an imposing building maybe made of living bone, maybe not, and the next she was in a somewhat dingy lobby with several islands of low-slung beige couches and a reception desk that had a small half-wall backdrop behind it with a mosaic of an oak set into warm copper against dark . . . oak? She couldn't remember if that would be a heretical use or if the Carrion Oak liked its employees to use its own separated flesh for decorations. You never knew with these Powers.

'I am the Question that the Quiet asks. I am becoming the Answer the Quiet abhors,' she whispered to herself, taking a

---

not to mention I lacked any of the required paperwork needed to import ▮▮▮▮ especially in their ▮▮▮▮ molting state) through its bowels and look at me now. Kids will be kids, amirite?

small moment of solace in the practice of the psalm-saying. Then with a practised motion she smoothed the front of her acolyte robes and reached up to push stray hairs into the bone-strewn net of her rosarius head covering. She would be damned if she let the Carrion Oak or its representatives ding her for propriety and dress.

Walking behind the reception table she flipped through the assorted binders and stacks of paper until she found a laminated chart of the building's office layouts. The Nave of Carrion Praise, the Well of Their Many Branched Sorrow, the Dwelling of the Charnel Blessed and Copy Room were on floor 49.5, almost exactly halfway up the tower and what unsurprisingly enough would be the very heart of the building.

The ride up the elevator was uneventful. It had the same blood sigil puzzle powering the buttons that most of the large buildings in the city had switched to a few years back so Malachia had not wasted any time with the trap buttons, instead drawing the figures in the opposite order than the instructions seemed to indicate and shrieking the floor number into the small speaker that was in the recess that slid open. She didn't know why they kept these sorts of artifacts of how management had run things before the two previous Silences had been absorbed into the current Silence. Probably for the same stuffy ornamental reasons the Weepers had still gone door to door every Saturday collecting unused tears and cast-off sorrows even though everyone knew they had long been subsidised by the local taxes and zoning arrangements.

But all thoughts about the bureaucracy of dead cities had to wait because the elevator doors had slid silently open at the 49.5th floor.

The sanctum . . . grove? The office of the Carrion Oak was one massive echoing room that looked to take up the entire

49.5th floor except for a small door immediately to the left of the elevator that was marked 'Copy Room. Please use employee code when making copies' and a smaller note taped below that one: 'This means you, Xalanth'. The ceiling for the majority of the floor soared much higher than it should have been able to based on the layout of the building but logic and the laws of physics very rarely shook hands in the city of Silence, and Malachia had long stopped questioning such things. If she squinted she could make out that the ceiling was tiled with the same sort of polystyrene squares that the other city services offices had but the squares arched up into a dome somehow, their lines bending and merging in a way that made your eyes blur if you tried to follow them too closely.

In the centre of the room . . . was the Carrion Oak.

Malachia caught herself holding her breath as she looked up at the tree and forced herself to release it little by little and breathe normally. She was sure the Carrion Oak could sense everything about her down to the hole in her worn grey wool socks, but she wasn't going to give it an easy sign of her nervousness if she could help it. The tree's roots spread across the tiled floor like canyons through the ground. The tiles lay shattered and pushed up into ceramic hillocks where the roots passed through, emerging and then submerging into the floor, a barked serpent winding its way between cubicles and upended furniture.

The roots climbed the walls in places and wrapped themselves around the few desks and chairs that were spread throughout the room. A path wound through them from the elevator, apparent only for its lack of roots or furniture, and terminated at a small raised ambolic lectern that sat directly in front of the towering Carrion Oak.

Malachia made her way down the path, slowly taking in

the same dried and yellowing stacks of paperwork and general dust-rimmed status of the room that she had seen most everywhere across the city. As she got closer to the raised lectern she could see that the ground around the tree was littered with faded memo sheets and spools of dot-matrix printer paper. The paper crunched beneath her feet in an unnatural parody of walking through a leaf-strewn forest floor. Then she stopped in her tracks and bit back an involuntary hiss of surprise. What she had at a distance thought were just tangles of vines or drooping branches were in fact bodies.

Quietly twisting in the air, desiccated bodies.

All throughout the Carrion Oak, mummified bodies hung by their ankles, bound in thick red cords that disappeared up into the tree's impenetrable maze of branches. Their limbs were held close to their bodies by drifting strands of what at some point might have been burlap sacks or some other type of monastic garb but now they were woven into the dried flesh of the corpses by time. Their heads were all thrust free from the lines that bound their limbs, and the flesh was withered tightly against their skulls; the eye sockets were empty gaping holes except for an occasional small green branch of the oak tree pressing outwards. Their mouths yawned open and downwards and a sound, not unlike distant hollow wind chimes, drifted from them as they all swayed in an unfelt breeze.

This sort of thing was nothing new for an acolyte of the Congregation but Malachia still felt a sort of cautious reverence filling her as she mounted the lectern steps. The Carrion Oak was still one of the nine Powers that had run this city since . . . well, since ever? That alone helped to quell the unease she felt at seeing bodies displayed in this way and not safely mouldering away in a catacomb where they would be daily blessed by eager novitiates and nuns alike.

At the top of the lectern was a small curved semi-circle railing and a built-in table with a rusted and darkly stained drain in the centre. Malachia leaned against the railing that came up to the middle of her chest and took a long moment to just look at the Carrion Oak.

Nothing happened.

It was just a tree.

Suddenly she was so, so tired. From the moment she had woken to an empty city, she had not allowed herself to stop. Now leaning on the railing, every part of her felt like it was ready to achingly slide off her bones into a sleeping pile of failure and never wake up. She was just a fucking acolyte. Her whole job was to memorise cants and walk the Congregation's ward lines. That was it! She was basically a spiritual janitor and here she was trying to what? Talk to the Carrion Oak? Find out . . . why . . . everyone had left her? It was too much. There wasn't a canticle or hymn she could recite for this situation. Unless maybe she made a very situational interpretation of the Hymn of the Mouth That Laughs in the Dark Beneath but that would have to be a *very* liberal, bordering on heretical interpretation, and starting a new gnostic sect of one member based around a hymnal from the Third Silence Movement seemed just a tad bit one try-hard bridge too far for Malachia right now.

She slumped to the floor of the lectern and, with her back to the railing, closed her eyes.

She would just take a short nap here. Or a long one, who the fuck was going to stop her? If they didn't want her to nap, they could very well come back from wherever they had all fucked off to and tell her. She was just going to settle in here and not give a . . .

Something tapped her on the shoulder.

This was the sort of moment where someone else might have frozen, body shaking and eyes dilating as their hairs turned grey one by one, but Malachia didn't even have the emotional juice to gibber or flail around in panic. Instead she hoisted herself back to her feet and, rather than whirl around, she rotated in place like a tired door on rusty hinges. Any words she might have been about to say dried up on her tongue.

The tree was very much not just a tree.

The Carrion Oak was definitely bigger than it was before. The trunk undulated softly in and out like a breathing body. *Or*, Malachia thought suddenly, *a bark-clad appendage that has emerged from the earth, wormlike and searching.* The mummified corpses moved in a way that belied the laws of physics and were more like the arms of an anemone than rigid branches. One of them was in the act of retreating from the edge of the lectern and she realised that its open rictus of a mouth must have been what had touched her.

She felt a rush of relief so intense her knees almost buckled beneath her. She wasn't alone amongst the dust and ghosts. Gripping the handrail, she leaned forward to say something. She had no idea what was going to come out of her mouth but the need to talk to someone . . . some*thing* else was suddenly overwhelming.

The Carrion Oak beat her to the punch.

'DAUGHTER OF BONE. DAUGHTER OF DUST.'

The words didn't come from the central trunk of the tree but instead issued from the multitude of mouths in the corpses that hung from the tree, the words slithering around each other in dry, reedy sibilance. The corpses swayed outwards with each syllable like a garden of desiccated larynxes.

'DAUGHTER OF TIME AND ROT. ARE YOU HERE BECAUSE THE HARVEST IS LONG PAST DUE AND A GARDENER IS NEEDED?'

What do you fucking say to that?

What she wanted to say to the Carrion Oak was, *Hey, Mr Fuckface Carrion Oak, maybe you could just drop the shit and tell me why everyone . . . left me?*

But you couldn't just say that to a foundational Entity . . . could you?

'Proud One of the Root and Mother's Shadow . . .' She began using the honorifics for one of the Nine that every acolyte learned since the crèche. But the corpses swayed again and the Carrion Oak interrupted her.

'DAUGHTER OF . . .'

Something snapped inside Malachia. Whether it was the fact that this Entity that could apparently speak through corpses' mouths had let her wander the city for days without contacting her, or the way she could almost taste the entitlement and capital letters of its words, she didn't know. But enough was enough, fuck these corporate titles and even the Congregation's deference.

'I'm not your fucking daughter . . . *tree.*'

The silence that followed began to deepen but Malachia wasn't having it. If the tree – she wasn't going to call it Carrion Oak until it did more than talk over her – wanted to say something useful, it was going to have to wait its turn.

'And if you think I came here to be another ornament in your branches, you have another think coming. Where is everyone? Why is the Congregation silent? Who is keeping the hymnlines sung? Why are there those revenants? Aberrations? Intruders? Ghosts? Why are they popping up in the

city? Where are the people who are supposed to be here? What are the Nine doing about it?'

Her words tumbled out in a shattered glass spray of emotions, and when she ran out of them she stood there breathing heavily, almost hyperventilating.

The tree just stood there, not even swaying in the unfelt breeze anymore. It stood there and Malachia felt like if she listened hard enough, she could hear it growing, becoming more solid. In its quiet insistence on being there, it felt like the only thing that was real. And that pissed her off.

'You know what?' she said with a savage, wolfish grin. 'You know fucking what, you *weed*? Fuck you. Fuck this bureaucratic shit. I don't know why I even came here for help. I'm going to go and find out where everyone is, and who Bene is because I know she was pretty fucking important to me, and why the Congregation is gone and . . . I'm going to find everything . . . ugh, FUCK YOU!'

The urge to weep crept back in around the corners of her eyes, tightening the muscles of her neck. She turned away from the tree and took one step back from the handrail.

'NOTHING BELONGS HERE . . . DAU . . . MALACHIA ACOLYTE OF THE CONGREGATION OF THE HALLOWED UNSPOKEN. NOTHING.'

She stopped with one foot out over the first step, swallowed, and turned around. Her skin felt hot and tight over the bones of her face like a robe washed and dried too many times in the sun.

'What?'

'YOU ASKED WHERE THE THINGS THAT BELONGED HERE HAD GONE. WE ARE SIMPLY STATING FACT. NOTHING BELONGS HERE. THE CITY OF SILENCE IS, AS ITS NAME

IMPLIES, MORE OF AN ABSENCE, A VOID, AN . . . ABYSS . . . IN ITS NATURAL STATE. YOU, THE CONGREGATION, EVEN WE THE NINE FOUNDATIONAL ENTITIES, ARE ALL VOICES EMERGING INTO THAT SILENCE, ECHOES THAT BY OUR VERY NATURE DEFORM THE VOID AND LEAVE THE TRACES THAT WE CALL A CITY. THE REASON THEY ARE ALL GONE IS BECAUSE THE THINGS THAT HOUSED THOSE VOICES HAVE . . . MIGRATED.'

Malachia blinked once . . . and then again, as if that was going to make the Carrion Oak's words suddenly make sense. Nope. Still gibberish.

'What. The. Actual. Fuck?'

She hissed through her ground teeth like dark rainwater surging through a sluice gate.

'What do you mean the city isn't real? We are standing in a fucking high-rise with a fucking talking tree in the middle of it. I know Silence is full of weird shit but it's weird shit that's real. I fucking live here. I have a cell and a cot and a stack of catechism books. I have this fucking itchy robe.'

The tree seemed to shrink, if that was possible, like it had used up all of its official One of the Nine Who Stand As Pillars Before the Deep bureaucratic persona and now was just as tired as she felt. The corpses swayed.

'THOSE THINGS. THEY ARE HERE BECAUSE OF YOU. WHEN YOU LEAVE THEY WILL FADE. AND WHEN YOU RETURN, IF YOU RETURN, THEY MIGHT GROW SOLID AGAIN DEPEND-ING ON HOW MUCH YOU WILL HAVE CHANGED. AND I SEE YOU OPENING YOUR LITTLE MEAT-AND-BONE MOUTH TO ASK

MORE QUESTIONS AND ARGUE BUT JUST
LISTEN. YOU NEED TO LEAVE HERE. YOU
MUST LEAVE HERE. THIS MIGRATION IS NOT
THE FIRST OF ITS KIND. ALWAYS ONE OF THE
NINE STAYS BEHIND TO WATCH THE CITY
FADE. LAST TIME IT WAS THE HUNTRESS
MOTHER WHO LAY IN HER TALL GRASSES
AND RED-SPLASHED BONES. THIS TIME IT IS I
AND THE DEAD AMONGST THE ROOTS THAT
KEEP VIGIL. ALL THE OTHERS LEAVE SO THAT
THE CITY OF SILENCE CAN BE REFRESHED.
THEN THEY RETURN AND ALL IS REWRITTEN
ANEW. IF WE STAY TOO LONG THE CITY
BECOMES FRAYED. IT SINKS ITSELF INTO
THE VOID. EVERY GHAUNTPRIEST AND
SCRIBE WHO GOES ABOUT THEIR DAILY LIFE
HERE. EVERY FUNERARY PARLOR AND NEON
MAUSOLEUM WRITES ITSELF INTO THE
FABRIC OF THE ABYSS, BUT LIKE A SENTENCE
REWRITTEN AND ERASED AGAIN DAILY THE
VOID CAN BEGIN TO WEAR THIN IN THOSE
PLACES. SO THE MIGRATION RESETS IT EVERY
SO OFTEN. BUT ... MALACHIA, THEY HAVE
NOT RETURNED WHEN THEY SHOULD.'

Malachia swallowed and after a moment nodded. It made
sense. Horrible, stupid, beyond the bounds of reality and
anything that she had wanted to have the Carrion Oak say to
her sense. But really she was the acolyte to a church committed to the concept of dead, who never uttered words in a city
full of haunts and twisted, many-legged Entities. She was
standing in front of someone called the *Carrion Oak*, for
fuck's sake. Was it really any stretch of the imagination to

then believe that the city she lived in was formed anew every morning by the intent of those living in it? Wasn't the fact that she was a human and very obviously not a natural denizen of this place just more evidence that *no one* was from Silence, that everyone who called it home came and went from other places like so many limbed and mouthed tides receding and returning even if they were not all aware of it?

'Sooooo . . . what am I supposed to do with any of this?' she asked, even though in her heart, swaddled in its canopic reliquary deep in the dusty bowels of the Black Chapel, she knew with a sinking feeling that the answer was going to be travelling to wherever it was humans came from. Because that had to be the reason she'd been left behind, right? There were more powerful members of the Congregation, if that had been the metric for deciding. But the fact that she was human *and* had just seen another, albeit very weird, human this very day . . . well, the maths added up.

The Carrion Oak stared at her and waited, or more accurately the array of mummified corpses all twisted on the red cords they hung from until the empty sockets in their heads pointed in her direction. Their mouths yawned open in unison.

'WHAT YOU ARE SUPPOSED TO DO IS GO AND SEE WHY THEY HAVE NOT RETURNED LIKE THEY WERE MEANT TO. I CANNOT HOLD THE FORM OF THE CITY IN MY MIND INDEFINITELY. EVENTUALLY, I WILL SLEEP AND ALL THIS WILL BE GONE. NOT THAT IT WOULD BE A TRAGEDY. MAYBE SILENCE HAS JUST RUN ITS COURSE AND THE OTHERS HAVE GONE ON TO BECOME DIFFERENT THINGS, AND PLACES. BUT I AM FOND OF WHAT WE HAVE MADE HERE AND I WOULD IF POSSIBLE LIKE

TO SEE IT RETURN FOR ANOTHER CYCLE.
AND IF THAT IS NOT ENOUGH OF A REASON,
THEN LOOK AT IT IN A PURELY SELF-SERVING
LIGHT. IF THEY DO NOT RETURN, WHERE WILL
YOU, MALACHIA, EXIST WHEN THE CONGRE-
GATION AND ITS BONE-LINED HALLS FADE
INTO THE STATIC OF THE VOID? IF NOT FOR
THE WORRIES OF YOUR GODS AND ONE VERY
OLD TREE, YOU SHOULD AT LEAST BE WOR-
RIED   ABOUT   YOUR   OWN   CONTINUED
EXISTENCE. I DO NOT THINK YOU WOULD
ENJOY WHAT THIS PLACE WOULD BECOME
WITHOUT US.'

Malachia let out a long sigh that segued halfway into a groan. Her head was starting to throb with the beginnings of a migraine and even more than saving the universe, or the part of the *not* universe that the city of Silence sat in, even more than finding whoever the name Bene belonged to and why her breath quickened just at the mention of it, and definitely even more than avoiding whatever ominous fate the Carrion Oak had alluded to if she decided to just wait it out in Silence doing her little chores and staring at her hands, more than all that she really wanted this conversation to just be over.

'Just fucking tell me where to go and what to do, tree. I fucking swear you talk like a catechism hymnal.'

A few days ago she would never have even imagined talking like this to one of the Nine, but she wasn't exactly the same woman she had been then, or even who she had been when she'd walked into this room for that matter. So she just jutted her chin out and looked up into the boughs of the Carrion Oak.

And then the tree told her what she had to do . . .

Noah

The hallway from the lobby to the outside stairwell was unimpressive. White faux-wood wall panels, light tan and brown speckled linoleum tiles and dingy drop-ceiling panelling reminded him of the back halls of his high school, where the art and music rooms had been stuck and used mostly for storage, and making out and smoking. He had given and received his first handjob from Gary Williamson in the ninth grade back there under the pretense of doing the detention labour of stacking all the chairs from the pep rally in neat if dangerously leaning towers. Even now he could remember the taste of dust sifting down from the supply closet he had been leaning in, head back, mouth open to receive that baptismal dusting.

He exited the hallway through what at some point must have been a security door but now was just the remains of a glass-panelled door where the top half had been repaired with a piece of plywood. On a folding chair next to the door was a toolbox and an unopened box that proclaimed itself 'Sertonic No. 1 Card Reading Lock VAULT-TITE™', but from the stack of old newspapers on top of it he could guess the level of priority that little modernisation had with the staff.

He was under the overhang of the first floor with door 12 at

his immediate left; he could only assume that the numbering of them started at the far end of the row instead of at this end, which was odd. To his immediate right, Noah could now see over the brick wall with the chain-link fence he had seen earlier, and there was a smattering of upside-down rotting plastic lounge chairs, two shattered tables, one with the desiccated corpse of a sun umbrella still sticking out of it, and the far lip of an empty pool. He could also read the sign that he hadn't been able to earlier. It was written in bold sans serif and red paint on a piece of plywood that had been painted white at some point but now was a faded dingy grey and divided into two quadrants by a red line down the middle. On one side was what he had expected: a list of pool rules and etiquette. No running. No food in the pool. No urination in the pool. No alcohol. But on the other side, mixed in with instructions for how to reserve the barbecue pit (which was nowhere to be seen), were . . . other lines. NO LEAVING ESCAPED FOOD OUT OVER- NIGHT. NO CULTIVATING OF TALL GRASS FOR STALKING. NO FILLING OF POOL WITH ANY- THING OTHER THAN WATER (under which someone had appended with a thinner line of black paint letters: YES, THIS MEANS BLOOD OR ANY SORT OF ICHOR AS WELL, QUIT ASKING).

Well, that's just about as fucking weird as everything else so far. Pool of Blood would be a great band name though, Noah thought to himself, and took a moment to let it sink in how quickly he was starting to just take this sort of shit in stride. Then out of idle curiosity and some small amount of nostal- gia for a youth where an abandoned empty pool would have been a goldmine for skateboarding (which was really just an excuse to break into a place at night and drink beer in the echoing bottom of a pool), he walked over to the chain-link

to get a better view. The fence dipped away from him with a sway that spoke of disrepair and abandon.

Now Noah could see that the bottom of the pool was filled with the usual trash of broken beer bottles, yellowing plastic water containers and dead leaves . . . but also down in the deep end, where the shadows let about an inch of water and sludgy decomposing leaves remain safe from the sun's evaporation, stood a well-worn but entirely intact writing desk. It was one of those metal ones with the linoleum tops you saw facing each other in old cop movies or documentaries about the Space Race in the seventies. For a moment it was an odd enough thing that Noah was tempted to go see if there was anything interesting in its drawers but then he straightened. He could do that after he got his sales call done. As weird as this fucking day had been and as bizarre as Linda and Svenn and Sam and the whole Printed Matter job application had been . . . he did need this job. Rent was due in three weeks and a little weirdness with a company car . . . and apparent if not wholly remembered blood drawing . . . and creepy training videos that gave him a migraine if he even tried to remember what they were about, any and all of that was better than mopping up puke and shit with no company car any day of the week . . . and benefits. Jesus fucking Christ he couldn't even remember the last time he had gone to a dentist. Yes, he would do this job, how hard could it be? Sit down with Mrs Whatshername and talk about ad space in a newspaper, maybe help her write a personal ad, one of those HOT SINGLES IN YOUR AREA ones you always saw in the back of the paper next to ads for Bulk Dirt and Restaurant Foreclosure Sale All Units Must Go. Although she might want something more along the lines of 'Gentle Gazelle Seeks Ferocious Hyena to Prowl Water of Life Hole Must Have Own

Car and Be Good With Kids'. Who knew? Perhaps she just had an ad for her floral-arrangement or cement-laying business. The scrap of paper Linda had given him with her details hadn't even had her fucking name on it so this sales visit could be about anything. They would play it by ear.

Turning away from the pool, Noah headed up the zigzag concrete and steel stairwell to the second-storey landing. It was a long balcony walkway with a handrail and wrought-iron cage wall on the right, a row of doors set in water-stained and weather-baked stucco on the left. At some point, there had been an attempt to give the motel-cum-apartments some sort of pizazz because beside each door was a nameplate that had a mid-century spray of rays around it like the arms of a sea urchin but in the centre of it was just the room number on a black plastic shingle that had been attached to the top of the nameplate with a zip tie.

Based on the number of rooms on the first floor, there should not have been a 206 on this floor unless they were doing that weird numbering convention where each floor started in the hundreds even when there were only twelve rooms. But the first room downstairs had been 12 not 112 so that didn't make any sense, and indeed as he went down the walkway he saw that none of these rooms adhered to any sort of numbering logic he could make sense of. There was Room 45, there was Room 98, here was Room 9, there was Room . . . a polaroid of a cat wearing a birthday hat instead of a number shingle, here was Room hole-in-the-wall-with-decidedly-not-up-to-code-wires-dangling-from-it and then in the middle of the building, finally, Room 206. Wait, now it read Room 9. Noah blinked and it once again read as Room 206. He suddenly had the horrible thought that if he looked to his right or his left all he would see would be smooth endless walls on each

side without a single door to be seen. And if he then blinked it would be nothing but an impossible, unending kaleidoscope of door on top of door filling every inch of the walls. So he didn't look. This was the only door he had the energy to perceive anyway.

Room 206 had a red, metal-looking door with the paint flaking off but around the doorknob it was festooned with the sort of generic cartoon character stickers you got from a box of cereal as prizes. Close to actual known cartoon characters but just off enough to be eerie: a lanky grey rabbit holding a butternut squash instead of a carrot; a cupped hand holding several fingerbones; a leopard with sunglasses and a bag of pretzels; a large tree with several ropes dangling from its branches that had at one time had something attached to them but someone had scratched that part of the sticker away; a mouse wearing red shorts with big yellow buttons and one white glove that he was removing with the other hand to reveal something that his facial expression showed he was clearly horrified by.

He remembered Sam the Lavender-Curled had said something about 'Mrs Galloway *and hers*' so he assumed she must have children. Small pets? Hostages? Maybe Mrs Galloway was an installation artist and the detritus of breakfast-cereal gimmicks were her subjects. It could be a grand statement about the permanence of cultural icons and the housing market bubble, both bursting like the ephemeral nature of the cereal's crunchiness before an onslaught of milk and trickle-down economics. Or it could just be some fucking stickers.

Noah straightened himself, smoothed his tie, straightened his collar and knocked.

6

Malachia

Malachia exited the Ministry of the Carrion Oak not by the way she'd come through the bone-tiled front entrance but instead through a service entrance the Carrion Oak had opened for her at the rear of its office. That was why she was picking ritual viscera out from between her teeth and brushing excess bone dust from the sleeves of her habit; a little bone dust was natural, desired even, but too much would draw the eye of ████████████████; even if they were not still around that would be both a venial sin in the eyes of the Congregation and the premature end of the job the tree had given her. She didn't allow herself even in her mind to say words like 'mission' or, Forgotten Whispers of the Host preserve her, 'quest'. That was the corpo talk of the fuckboi wage acolytes at the Towers of Muscite, who you would hear after their shifts at the sandwich stalls set up around the walls of the Church of the Hallowed Unspoken being loud and aggressive and generally ruining 'Sandwich Time', which in Malachia's heart was a rite as sacred as the ones she performed in the vaults beneath the Bone and Limb and Night Whisper's thrones, may they ever dream through her, amen hallelujah amen. All that being just the circuitous route, her thoughts now raced as she looked down at the square of

laminated card stock that had slid from the mouth of one of the Carrion Oak's corpse attendants like a newspaper from a pneumatic spirit tube. On the back there was a black square that took up the majority of the space except for an oblong on the bottom that was cold to the touch. On the front was a picture. It showed a long, low building of rust-red bricks and glass fronts. It appeared to house several different establishments, much like a row of market stalls set into the fronts of buildings, but the image was centred on one that bore a sign across the glass front that said 'PRINTED MATTER, News and Services'. Underneath the picture, in the small white margin, written in what Malachia assumed was worm blood (standard Entity municipality procedure since it would stay permanent even when changing dimensional planes or if it got forgotten in the wash), was the phrase 'APPLY WITHIN'. She tucked it away inside the small pocket catechism copy book[22] she kept within her robe and looked up at the sky.

Usually at this hour of the day, midday from the position of the Huntress Mother's Eye, she would see all sorts of spectres and advertisements slithering across the sky in predetermined routes around the streets. Some of them served to lead you back to the establishments that had paid for them, and others, well, you didn't want to follow the others. But the sky was eerily empty and a bright, clean, ashen grey like a recently emptied crematory urn. So instead of following a spectre lark she looked at the name on the street sign closest to her and set out at a quick, purposeful trot.

The trip was short and mostly uneventful except that she

---

[22] *The Cant of the Hungering Beneath*, Dispario, Ignatz, Feral Ossuary no. 9, Ward 3, Silence, Year of the Oubliette Ascendent.

wished she had worn more comfortable shoes when she'd set out this morning. The ritual sandals of the Congregation novitiates were fine for slowly walking the boundaries of the monastery murmuring the daily cants of Sleep and Silence That Flow Down to They That Wait and doing chores, but with the amount she had been hoofing it across the city today she wished she had put on a pair of boots, or better yet sneakers. She had a pair of each, mostly unworn, gathering dust in the back of the small armoire that held her scant personal items back in her cell. She had dreams of doing naturalist surveying and logging out in the Deathflow that writhed glacially beyond the city's southern gates, but usually when her rest day came around she just slept in and ate sandwiches in whatever park her lazily blank brain brought her to. As it was she could feel a blister forming on the back of both heels where the sandal strap rubbed against the skin; she would have to do something about that soon. In fact, and it was a thought she hadn't had in maybe . . . ever, she might have to also find some other sort of clothing? She had no idea what the customs were in the place she was going to but from that picture with its angular, mundane bricks and glass it didn't seem like the kind of place that a mendicant of the sleeping Death Gods of Silence in her official habit and robes would blend in, but who knew? Maybe it would be all the fashion rage there. At least she hadn't yet been initiated into the ways of the Shedding of Meat and False Blood because that definitely would have raised a few eyebrows, she was sure. Even amongst the esoteric denizens of Silence, the yellowed bone figures of the upper priesthood turned heads and spurred whispers amongst the non-cloistered. But she would figure all that out once she was there.

For now she had to find the right door the tree had described to her, and even with its words emblazoned into her mind

with its memetic sorcery it was going to be a feat. She looked up into the towering cube of the Ministry of Liminality and Transport. From this distance it looked like a colossal floating cube whose surface rippled slightly as if it were fabric in a brisk wind. But she knew that the closer you got, you could see that it was in fact made up of doors . . . uncountable . . . lazily drifting in patterns indiscernible to anyone from outside of the MLT . . . doors.

It was going to be like trying to find a bone needle in a corpse stack.

7

Noah

Noah stood waiting for at least a full minute with the late-afternoon sun beginning to slant around the edge of the balcony overhang enough that he felt it on the back of his pale neck, which was not accustomed to it. At first it felt nice but then a trickle of sweat ran down from behind his ear and he remembered why the sun was bullshit.

No one seemed to have heard his knocking so he raised his hand again and knocked harder this time. Nothing happened.

He turned away from the door and looked over the railing down at the pool. The damp sludgy leaves around the desk looked more like a small pond of green stagnant water than they had from ground level. Had there been that much water in the deep end before? There had to have been since it had neither rained nor could he see any sort of hose that he assumed would be used for filling a pool. He realised he really had no idea about the logistics of owning or maintaining a pool. It wasn't something he had ever thought would come up in his decidedly low-income lot in life. Some dreams, well, you just didn't even dream . . . of . . . dreaming them? But the water was definitely deep enough that it came up a few inches around the legs of the desk. With a shrug he turned away from the railing and the *Mystery of the Slightly Damp Pool* and

raised his hand to knock again. But just then, the door popped open. Not with the slow creak of a horror film or the steady glide of someone drawing it open. It popped like the lid from a jar of spoiled preserves where the seal had finally corroded so much that it could no longer hold in the rampant bacteria that now coated what had once been the summer's treasure of tomatoes. There was an exhalation of air that was so strong and moist that Noah felt his hair move in it, and his face felt damp like he had just opened the door to a greenhouse. From what he could see through the half-opened door, this was an apt description.

Craning his neck, he could see ferns, small palms, a bougainvillea and one of those plants with the big shiny dark green leaves. Plants on plants on plants.

'Umm hello . . .' he began but then straightened up. He was going to at least *try* and do this job right. 'Hi, Mrs Galloway? I am here from Printed Matter. Linda sent me to talk to you about the lapse in your advertisements. Do you have a minute? I will be brief and to the point, I promise.' He said this in his best *I Am A Professional And Have Been Doing This Job For A Decade And In Fact Have Won Many Awards For It Since You Ask* voice, or at least what he imagined someone like that would sound like.

There was no answer but he heard the distinct noise of more than one set of feet receding from directly behind the door then a thunk and the crash of glass breaking and a yelp. It was in that moment that Noah did the exact opposite of what he would have ever told you he would do in a similar situation if you had been shooting the shit on the back loading dock of any of the many restaurants he had washed dishes at. Up until now he would have said something along the lines of, 'Nah, man, fuck that shit, that's how you end up as

dinner for the Chainsaw family or tied up in a basement as some dude sharpens a long scythe and giggles every time you whimper,' before taking a drink from whatever he would have stolen out of the walk-in beer cooler.

But today, as an official employee of Printed Matter, Noah slipped through the half-open door and into the room.

At first the room was a dark mélange of shapes. All he could see were broad impressionist strokes and lumps of different shades of green, yellow and utter dark. To his right he heard the sound of rustling leaves and he froze. Then as his eyes adjusted and the room came into view he took a calming breath and just stayed still, listening.

Now that his photoreceptors had received the information from his constricting pupil muscles[23] he could see that the ferns and palms rose almost to the ceiling, and in fact in the corners of the room they did: pushing themselves up and over into frozen cresting waves of chlorophyll and whatever else the fuck leaves are made of.[24] He could see that they were in huge low terracotta pots, the majority of which had been shattered by the growing mass of roots that now pushed out of them to burrow into the faded yellow shag carpet that showed in places between the spilled potting soil and dead leaves. Some of the plants were being fed by thin translucent tubes that snaked from rough holes poked in the spackled ceiling around which water damage spread out in concentric circles until they connected with the other patches like a colour-graded heatmap of decay. Around the floor, nestled

---

[23] Interesting to note that the eye, while not thought of as a muscle in the manner of most human meat, is indeed just that. A warm, meat orb, no more than a mouthful in the best of cases.

[24] We present to you the failings of Bill Nye.

against the pots, were also small watering cans that had once been bright neon-coloured plastic with what looked like painted characters on them. One had a clown, another a dinosaur and still another a thing that every time he blinked had a different number of twisted limbs beneath a long drooping face with a wide open mouth filled with an unsettling amount of flat white teeth. But now they were all stained with a black dried substance that reminded Noah of the buckets of tar that road crews used when patching the streets. To his left Noah saw a vague intimation of a doorway to another room just by the yellow door shape that showed through the plants. He assumed that must be the kitchen, which if the logic of generic apartment layouts held true here, and he was no longer sure it did, meant he was in the living room and the bedroom would be somewhere through the crush of ferns straight in front of him.

'What. The. Actual fuck,' he whispered out loud to himself. For which he was awarded a giggle that sounded like it was coming from the direction of the 'kitchen'.

'Um, hello? Hi? I'm here from Printed Matter,' he tried again, keeping his voice casual like you would upon meeting a friend's dog for the first time and being very aware that although you really want to pet it, the dog still has a generous amount of teeth and jaw muscles that nature gave it to crush small animals' spines with.

Noah cleared his throat and waited for them to say something.

They didn't.

He was about to try again when two small children wordlessly walked out from the kitchen, the plants swishing around their legs and arms. They sidled around him and stared at him with their large pale grey eyes. He noticed with alarm the

pupils filled most of those eyes, which remained trained on him. Their faces were expressionless. They were both dressed in shorts and t-shirts. One of them had jorts and a faded grey shirt with a cartoon paper clip on it that was saying something in a speech bubble but the applique had long worn away in that spot so whatever office-supply wisdom he was supposed to be imparting was lost to history.

The other was wearing what Noah had called 'jam shorts' as a child and were just simple shorts made from the most garish material one could find. Noah's grandmother had made him a pair with dinosaurs and shooting stars on them (pretty macabre now that he thought about it), and another pair, oddly enough, with large pairs of sunglasses, in the reflection of which were women in swimsuits sunbathing (the oddly enough was because his grandmother had been one of those baptists that thought electric guitars were how sin crept into the church, much less *bikinis*). It wasn't until years later that his mother told him that Grandma had just bought whatever material had been in the cheap curtain bin at Roxanne's Thread Movers and made them from that. The Maria von Trapp of it all had made him feel embarrassed as an adult at the fact that he had felt like they had been a special thing she had done for him and not the minimum dischargement of responsibility. Anyhoo, the other child was wearing those and a yellow shirt with a frog that said, 'Make Mine a Budweiser.' Both children had that sort of bleach-white hair that said, 'I'm either super Nordic or my parents *really* liked *Village of the Damned* and did this to me.' But instead of those perfect bowl cuts both these children's hair was streaked with dirt and dried in stiff plastered messes that showed very clearly what side of their heads they had slept on recently.

They just stared at him.

Seriously? Now that they had started this staring competition, he wasn't going to let these kids win. He cleared his throat again and bounced on the balls of his feet, putting his hands behind his back and leaning slightly towards them, letting his height advantage loom just a bit.

If anything the children's eyes became even more vacant and expressionless. It was getting creepy. The minute these two had stopped in front of him they had gone stock-still and silent like they were rooted in place.

Rooted in place? Noah let his eyes dart to their feet. Of course they were normal kids' feet, dirty and wearing mismatched socks but definitely not made of plant roots.

Noah pressed his tongue into the hollow of his cheek and crossed his eyes in a last-ditch manoeuvre to break these two little fucks. Nothing. Then he threw his hands up before letting out an exaggerated breath, as if he had been holding it this entire time.

'Fiiiine, you win. Where is your mom? Aunt? Mrs Galloway. Grandma?'

Nothing.

'Okay this isn't funny and is kinda rude?' He looked over their shoulder towards where he guessed the bedroom would have been. 'Mrs Galloway? Mrs Galloway, it's Noah from Printed Matter?!'

At the mention of Printed Matter the two decidedly-unnerving-but-admittedly-good-at-staring-contests children began to shake with the immediate violence of a terrier savaging a rat. The one on the left jolted forward and their flailing limbs would have smacked Noah in the face if he had not taken a startled step backwards.

The other child flew sideways; there was no other way to describe it. Their limbs trailing through the air behind them

from the speed of their movements, they slammed into the wall, smashing through plants and pots to crash into a vine-covered wall where they slid halfway up and then stopped, their head lolling backwards, their hair now hanging down towards the floor, their spine bending and twisting. The child's jaw hung open, leaking what Noah at first took to be blood or saliva, but as his brain caught up to what he was seeing he noticed it was far too viscous to be blood . . . and it was green.

Then, suddenly, the other child rushed at him. They didn't come at him like a Romero zombie or one of the kids from *Children of the Corn*. Instead their whole body shot at him, their head bowed down almost to the ground and their limbs sputtering backwards as they impacted the floor over and over like a forgotten jump rope caught in a car door and dragged across the pavement.

The child pulled up just short of colliding with him. Noah threw his arms up over his face and ducked down into a kneeling position. When nothing knocked, grabbed or other-wise maimed him he ventured a glimpse through his arms and the child was inches away from his face just . . . hanging there. Just hanging in space, their arms thrown back and their legs swaying in place. Their back was bent away from Noah, and as he watched, their head began to slowly lift up . . .

Fuck this.

Noah scrambled backwards on all fours towards the door. As he did, the child that had been halfway up the wall skittered up into the corner of the ceiling and began to drag their body torso first, legs and arms draped downward all akimbo along the joint of the wall and ceiling, back towards the rear of the room, pulling vines and leaves away from the wall as they snagged on them. For a moment Noah saw something

long and glistening that snaked out from under the back of the child's shirt to run through the greenery along the wall, down to the floor. Noah's back hit the door and the last thing he saw as he stumbled out was the child closest to him being slowly drawn back through the plants, still hovering inches off the ground like there was some long rope or . . . tentacle attached to them that was reeling them into the bedroom.

Noah slammed the door behind him as he fell out of the room. He lay there on the balcony for a full minute, staring up at the galaxy of half-peeled stickers, his heart hammering in his chest and his blood roaring so loud in his ears that he thought for sure they had to be able to hear it down in the lobby. Down in the lobby. That fucking receptionist knew Mrs Galloway? And they still sent him up here to see . . . whatever that had been.

It couldn't be real; they had to be some sort of fucked-up puppets, right? Like animatronic taxidermy? Right now he really needed to believe they had just been dummies, wax figures, anything but what they had looked to be. Two children, attached by long glistening tentacles to whatever was in that back room. Mrs Galloway? Or maybe whatever it was had killed her? No, that way of thinking would make it real. It couldn't be real.

So maybe Mrs Galloway was a performance artist? Yeah, the theatre of the absurd, shock art. Like when people pretend to cut their own throats and bleed onto expensive pieces of art to make some sort of point. What was that called? Installation art? Was that room an installation? Whatever it was he wasn't going back in there to find out.

Gingerly Noah got to his feet and examined the smarting palms of his hands that had taken the brunt of his lunge through the door and onto the balcony. Nothing had tried to

come out of the room so far. The doorknob wasn't slowly turning. There was no thumping or scrabbling of small hands on the other side.

Quickly he began to walk down the balcony away from Room 206 towards the far end, where he assumed a twin stairwell to the one he had come up had to be. Part of him wanted to go back to the lobby and really let Sam have a piece of his mind for not warning him about the setup in Room 206 but the larger part just wanted to get as far away from the Mansions of Silence as he could and try and forget the sight of the small bodies being dragged back into the shifting green foliage as soon as possible.

He found the stairwell easily enough and was stepping off the last step, about to turn the corner, when a large, heavy hand fell on his shoulder.

8

Malachia

Heaving a sigh for her weary feet, Malachia gathered her robes tighter around her and started towards the Ministry of Liminality and Transport, but instead of the soaring cube of dense tessellating doorways that filled the sky, she headed towards the small white building that was the sole occupant of the city block beneath the cube.

It was a simple, squat, square building not much bigger than a portable shed or a janitorial closet for a mid- to large-sized high school. It was made from a chalky white substance that every once in a while the wind would pull puffs of into the air around the building like ash falling from the limbs of a burnt corpse. Her footsteps crunched over the gravel that covered the lot surrounding the building and Malachia knew that if she looked down, it would not be gravel but instead a bed of small keys made from white and yellowing bone. They occasionally fell from above with a soft *tok tok tok* sound of teeth clacking together in a distant room. But she did not look down because, well, anyone who had lived in Silence for more than a few days knew that there were just some things you didn't want to focus on too closely. After a while you got a sixth sense for them, a gritty feeling on the back of your teeth, a sour, sweet tang of spoiled fruit that would scent the

saliva as it suddenly pooled in your mouth. So she kept her eyesight level with the side of the building where the faint outline of a door was and did not look down to see what exactly was sighing in a low moaning keen as the keys crunched and cracked under her sandals.

When she reached the door she could see it was grey painted metal and that almost all the grey paint had come off in great flaking peels like dry skin from a sunburnt scalp to reveal the mottled patina of red rusting metal beneath it. In the middle of the door was a small placard, white block letters on dark green plastic that read 'MNSTRY LMNL TRNSPRT'.

It would have been a completely unassuming cube of a building except for the large pool of black ichor that was oozing out from under the door. It was crusted around the lower hinges and dried on the edges of the door's face as well.

Malachia looked the door over for a handle or a recess where there might be a keyhole but it appeared to be just a solid slab of rusted metal with a frame, hinges, rust and black ooze. Keeping her feet firmly planted, she gave it three quick raps. The sound warbled like a stone being dropped into a well. A resonant *plonk pshlonk ppshonk*. As she leaned back the metal of the door rippled where her hand had contacted it, and for a brief second she saw a tracery of black veins run through the door, branching out to encompass the entire surface before subsiding back beneath the surface.

Oh, so it was going to be one of those *doors*, she thought to herself with a barely contained groan of irritation. The term 'door' really didn't apply if Malachia was reading the situation correctly. It was more of a 'mouth'? Orifice? Liminally Moded NewMeat™ Aperture? She had never actually used one . . . or met one in person. But supposedly a lot of the more

forward-thinking ministries were switching over to them for their more secure buildings, or switching back to them. Even for someone who lived in Silence, the vagaries of a Voidbound Bureaucracy were occasionally more than she had the mental energy to even attempt to disentangle. But what it boiled down to was that she needed a key. And barring that, since she very much did not have a key, she needed to provide it with an alternative.

She needed to give it a snack.

Or at least make it think she was going to . . .

9

Noah

Noah would later try and remember this moment as if he had turned around coolly to raise a *May I help you?* eyebrow but in reality he let out a bloodcurdling squawk and flailed wildly in what could only through sheer generosity and a great deal of squinting be called a roundhouse punch. Which luckily did not come even close to grazing the placid face of Svenn, who did in fact raise his eyebrow at Noah, but it was more of a *Really? This is how you want to go out?* type of eyebrow. He then held both his hands up in front of him, palms flat in a placating manner.

'Whoa, whoa there, sparky. Do you and I need to have a chat? Where you goin'? From the smell of things around here you haven't finished your sales pitch . . .'

The tone of his voice drew out that last phrase until it curled itself like a party balloon animal into the shape of something else entirely. Noah noticed that the large man's entire body leaned forward at a slight angle like he was pushing into a headwind as he waited for Noah's reply.

Noah did not know what to say. From the way he had been speaking, whatever repair service Svenn worked at was at least professionally attached to Printed Matter in some way. Maybe they were owned by the same parent company? Anything Noah

said would most likely get back to Linda. There was no way he could just casually say, 'Well, you see, I was doing my job. I have a tie on and everything and I think I was showing some great initiative but there were these two *Village of the Damned* kids but they were all day-off casual and then the plants had tentacles or maybe Mrs Galloway was just a bigtentacleand thenidon'tknowman butitwasterrifyingandnothingintheworld couldever makemego backinthat fuckingroombutiwouldliketo stillkeepmyjobifthat'sokay . . . but we probably need to burn down the apartment building?'

And if he made up some sort of cover-up lie then it would look like he just wasn't cut out for the job no matter what the ad had said about no qualifications being needed. If you couldn't go to someone's house and have a simple conversation with them, you probably didn't get to keep being a salesperson.

Svenn's eyebrows rose even higher as Noah stood there about to have a short circuit.

'Why don't you step into my office?' Svenn said, gesturing to a faded yellow metal door that was set into the wall in the shadows of the stairwell. It was mostly obscured by a vending machine that was missing the front, glass-paned door and had all the spiral arms that usually pushed the snacks towards their inevitable drop into the abyss of the snack slot extended out like intestines from a sacrificial bull. In front of it was an open toolbox that had been set on a blue quilted work mat that was much stained.

'You work *here*?' Noah asked, incredulity evident in his voice. The man's uniform just said 'RFGRTR RPR' above 'Svenn' and Noah had assumed he worked for some company like Maytag from the television commercials.

Svenn waved a hand of dismissal at the question as he

moved past the carcass of the vending machine towards the shadowed doorway.

'Nah, I work where the job takes me. I'm a Contractor.'

Noah could hear the capital C in the word almost like it had shown up in the air between them.

'I used to just do houses, had an Apex license and everything, but then the job changed, hostile takeovers, the market collapsed into a hellhole, so now I work for an . . . agency that sends me out on jobs. Same group that owns Printed Matter so technically we are coworkers. Sorta. Kinda.'

While Svenn had been calmly explaining all this, Noah had been following him numbly. Right as he stepped across the threshold and into the back room he realised that mayyyy-beee this hadn't been the best idea. Stepping back into the building he had just seconds ago known for *sure* he would never re-enter and with a man who he was beginning to suspect knew exactly what he had seen upstairs. But like a lot of the choices he had come to regret in what he was now considering to be his very tragically short-up-to-this-point life . . . it was too late.

10

Malachia

Malachia stood looking up at the sky, watching the long dirty cloud wisps that constantly circled above the city in a lazy maelstrom. Normally, before the mass exodus of the city, they would be alive with things and vehicles flitting around and through them. But today they just looked empty. Occasionally one would flit out of existence only to appear again a few seconds later. It gave the clouds a stuttering static effect that made her hair stand on end.

Malachia idly scratched her index finger with her thumb while she considered what would most likely make the door open up. If she was right, it would need to be something that either made the door hungry or something that it was waiting to hear or see; the chances of her guessing the latter were pretty slim so interdimensional feral door snack it was. Maybe if she made a small bone golem and puppeted it to act injured and had it go and lean against the door like it was resting, that would get the door to open to suck it in and then she could easily calcify its exposed joints and hinges to prop it open. Yeah, that might work, and with the handy field of bone keys around the place, it wasn't like she wouldn't have enough readily available raw material to try something else if that didn't work. She could even just make one battering ram after

another until the door finally yielded, but she didn't even want to think about the fines she would be returning to if her errand for the Carrion Oak ended up being successful so better to try the desiccated bone carrot before the necromantic stick.

'Okay, Mal, enough procrastinating, let's do this,' she sighed to herself as she stretched her hands out in front of her and laced the right hand – with its emaciated skin that was so shrunken and thin that the yellowed bone with its myriad of Sainting Marks engraved along the carpals and metacarpals showed through, easily giving the effect of a skeletal hand with an ephemeral shroud clinging to it – with the totally normal if callused and nail-bitten left hand. She flexed them outwards, shivering with pleasure as the bones all popped, each with its own personal hallowed *TOK TOK tok*. One of the first things a novitiate of the Congregation of the Hallowed Unspoken learned in their catechism was that nothing pertaining to their bones was pedestrian. Every creak and ache was said to have a significance whether as an augur from the Sainted Dead That Hungered Below or as a response to something in the Life Beyond the Meat That Houses. The interpretations were often fought over in the Gnossuaric texts so a proper Adept would at all times be expected to hold all these differing perspectives in mind and act accordingly. Malachia, not for the first time, considered that the majority of those texts were probably just bullshit posturing – here she smirked to herself at the unintentional skeletal pun – and that the only thing that really mattered was what the bones did. And her bones, well, they definitely did more than they should.

Keeping her fingers laced together and her gaze upwards, Malachia let the syllables of the Canticle of Emergent Marrow

vibrate between the molars of her jaw. The words gathered energy from the bones as they came together across her palate, a dull but not unpleasurable ache spread amongst them. All around her Malachia could now feel the field of bone keys spread out like a nebula. Each bone figurine prickled the back of her neck in a different way. It was as if she could close her eyes and see a map of them but instead it was over the skin of her neck and upper back. She couldn't really explain how it worked mechanically but did she really need to?

It was spooky bone stuff.

If there was one thing a Ninth Circle Novitiate of the Cold Flame and Bone for the Congregation of the Hallowed Unspoken knew how to do, it was spooky bone stuff, and usually once someone saw bone dust extracted through the pores of a still living creature or heard the ghost echoes of a skilled osseographer, they didn't ask for technical details anyway.

Malachia reaffirmed her connection to the constellation of osseomantic energy dancing across her neck and back and began to draw the ones directly in front of her together. She could feel the motes that held them together and she reached out with the Second Fingerhymn of Joyous Decay to begin unweaving their bonds, but before she even had a chance to finish the weaving . . . the door opened.

11

Noah

The room, if it was indeed going to be where he died at the hands of Svenn to cover up what he had seen upstairs, was a disappointment – not that Svenn had made any threats to that effect or had been anything other than a seemingly supportive if hulking coworker, but Noah's mind was racing. If what he'd seen had been real and not just the biggest mental break of all time, and Mrs Galloway, who had been described by Linda as 'just a nice lady who must have forgotten to enroll in autopay on the new app', was some sort of child-puppeting tentacle monster, then logic dictated that the helpful coworker must be something horrifying as well. Logic. Noah could feel the laugh trying to break free at the thought of anything that had happened today being governed by the previously stable and dependable rules of logic.

Noah found himself standing in what appeared to be a boring and extremely organised janitor/groundskeeper closet with boxes of toilet paper stacked in one corner, metal shelves with rows of industrial cleaning materials, brooms, mops, the whole nine yards. Svenn had sat himself on a bucket, the side of which said 'Pool Chlorine System B-2 Taggart's Best', and the thought that the pool was how it was, and here were upkeep materials clearly being purchased and stocked by this 'Contractor', was too much for Noah.

He started laughing.

At first he tried to keep it in but then he gave up and laughed in great barking shouts until he was near to weeping and bent over at the waist, gasping for breath as tears ran down his cheeks and into his mouth, hot and salty and not at all unlike the taste of blood. Well, maybe blood lite; Noah had had enough nosebleeds, both accidental and purposeful, in his life to know the taste of the real original Blood Classic™.

Svenn watched him, expressionless, occasionally looking at invisible dirt beneath his fingernails. When he finally judged Noah to be wrapping it up, he flicked an invisible piece of something off the knee of his navy dickie work pants and asked,

'So how did the meeting go?'

'How . . . did the . . . meeting go?' Noah echoed between gasps for air. 'Well, Svenn, let me tell you it went fucking perfect! Could not have asked for a better outcome; in fact I hit every point of the meeting checklist I wanted to meet! Isn't that great? Let me walk you through them!'

Noah held up an imaginary piece of paper and pointed to the top of it. He knew he shouldn't do this but fuck these people, really fuck them; he had been doing his best and yeah he needed this job but just be fucking honest with him. He even needed this job enough to put up with weird spooky shit that was impossible and definitely couldn't happen ever. He could do those mental gymnastics for health benefits and an above-minimum-wage pay rate. He could pretend like shit was normal, he could handle that; he had worked fucking brunch shifts as a short-order cook for five years in a row – he could handle anything! But what really put him off was this passive-aggressive non-confronting of things. Just fucking say what's happening and then deal with it, none of this deadpan 'how was the meeting'. So he stabbed the

invisible piece of paper harder with his finger to emphasise his words:

'Meeting Agenda Goal One! Creepy *Village of the Damned* children that beat me in a staring contest? CHECK! Meeting Agenda Goal Two! AN APARTMENT ROOM full of an impossible number of plants growing out of the fucking walls, ceilings, floor. Just like a fucking jungle room! Check! Meeting Agenda Goal Three! Some sort of tentacle thing that I didn't even see but that PUPPETED THE CHILDREN LIKE SOME SORT OF ANGLERFISH?! Yeah, an anglerfish tentacle plant monster? Who is probably Mrs Galloway or ate her or whatever so I need to go into the back room of that apartment AND TRY AND SELL AD SPACE TO A FUCKING TENTACLE! Point three of the agenda? Yeah, you fucking bet I HAD that one! The whole fucking bingo card of fucked-up shit is up there, Svenn, and you're sitting on a BUCKET OF POOL CLEANER and asking me . . . how. It. Fucking. Went? It went great, Svenn, it went just peachy God damn keen and I bet they're going to give me a promotion.'

Noah stopped, his mouth dry, his tongue coated with the sour gummy patina of saliva, and collapsed back onto a box of brown, ready-pack paper towels.

'It was a total failure, okay? I didn't see Mrs Galloway and probably stress-hallucinated everything and I am sureyou'rego-ingto telllindaandtheni'llgetfired andhavetogobacktomopping upbloodteeth and shitatthebus station sogoaheadandcall themalready.'

Svenn continued looking at him before finally breaking into a broad smile.

'Sounds pretty standard for a first day at Printed Matter if you ask me.'

12

Malachia

The unspent osseomantic energy rebounded back into Malachia's skeleton and her teeth ached all the way down to their roots as she shunted it harmlessly[25] down into the ground rather than letting it rip her apart. Her vision blurred for a moment and her eyes stung from the bone ash that spilled from her tear ducts, and she wiped at them with the cuff of her robe before looking back at the now open door.

What came out of the door wasn't what Malachia had expected, but then what part of this day, month, incalculable fugue stream of the ghosts of her lost days had been lately? Where she had been expecting something that unfolded like bone-paper origami or maybe a hungry thicket of wet chitinous arms, instead there was a person. A middle-aged person with a name tag that said L I И ᗡ A attached to their eggplant-coloured sweater that they wore with a matching but darker-toned knee-length wool skirt and a small but very well-planted beret. The overall effect was like their clothes were a

---

[25] It was in fact not harmless to what lay deep beneath her. The full accounting is too much of a tragedy to even be committed to paper here in this account but let us just say a moment of silence would not be amiss for an entire cosmos of very, *very* tiny civilisations.

textile bruise that spread over their pale body. They smiled at Malachia with the pulling back of their lips from a set of very thick but seemingly human yellow, nicotine-stained teeth. Their skin was also cracked and lined, like whatever they had subjected their teeth to had been a full-body experience, giving their face the appearance of the dried husk of an onion ready to be peeled. L I И ᑕ A stood looking at Malachia with their hands locked into a sorcerous fingerhymn, and the field of bone keys started to slowly float back down to the ground to resettle themselves and put off a wake of small clacking noises as they did. L I И ᑕ A rolled their eyes up to the sky in exasperation and gestured back to the open door behind them.

'Well, are you coming in or not? It might look like it's all clear skies and nothing to worry about out here but I guarantee you things have started sniffing around the slowly sinking soon-to-be-corpse of this city and you aren't going to want to be out there if they take a bite.'

Malachia only paused for a moment before following L I И ᑕ A through the doorway but she surreptitiously shifted the pulse of the thanoturgic energies she had been releasing into the ground so that the bone dust that was coalescing around her scurried in eddies up the sleeves of her robe to settle along her arms[26] without L I И ᑕ A noticing.

Inside, the squat structure was as boring and nondescript as she would have imagined a ministry substation to be if she had indeed ever felt the need to imagine something like that. She hadn't. So Malachia looked around, trying to appear casual and disinterested even though her mind was racing to catalogue everything she saw. The floor was a beige short-napped

---

[26] '. . . forewarned is forearmed and four arms always beats two.' Excerpt from *The Necromancer's Primer of Childhood Proverbs*.

carpet and the few pieces of furniture – a file cabinet, a mail-room desk with overflowing pigeon holes above it and grime-coated coffee pot – were all lit with the sickly yellow light of a dying bank of fluorescent tubes. By the time she took all this in, L I И Ɑ A was already pulling open what appeared to be the covering to something in the floor. It was a domed hatch with two interlocking handles, both of which ended in a curved piece of decidedly sharp-looking metal. Malachia didn't have long to puzzle over this very obvious workplace hazard of industrial design because L I И Ɑ A proceeded to slide first one forearm then the other across the metal. Their blood welled up immediately in thick black yolks of blood as if their skin were a shell freshly cracked. L I И Ɑ A then rubbed their right palm through the blood on their left fore-arm and the left palm on their right forearm.

They looked over at Malachia with a wide smile that now, in such close quarters and direct lighting, revealed that while their teeth did indeed appear human if somewhat large, there were also several rows of them lining the inside of their mouth.

'The manual says to slice each palm on their corresponding handles to activate the blood ward's locking mechanism on or off but that is just plain stupid. The people who write these manuals have obviously never had to hold a gun . . . or a SANDWICH with both of their palms sliced open. The spell just needs blood. This works just as well. If it wasn't so awk-ward an angle, I would have used my upper arm or the side of my leg. Those are the prime ritualist spots for tapping some of that good juice.'

It was obvious that L I И Ɑ A was waiting for Malachia to say something. The Carrion Oak had not said anything about L I И Ɑ A. In fact, for an Entity putting the fate of an entire city on her shoulders, it had been infuriatingly vague about

how she was to get to the world of humans. It had had a lot
to say about how she should approach the other eight Foundationals and what she should say to them to bring them
back, but when she had pushed for some exact directions to
travel between Silence and There, it had just swayed its corpse-
laden boughs and said, 'A WAY WILL OPEN,' which she
guessed hadn't been wrong seeing as she hadn't had to do anything in the end to open this door and now this hatch. All
that went towards her not entirely trusting this *perhaps far too
convenient person,* so she just awkwardly mumbled:

'That's nice. I mostly just, uh . . . use bones and bone-
adjacent materials . . .'

Malachia was about to begin listing all her favourite bones
but L I И ᗡ A had already turned their attention back to the
hatch, having obviously just been making the sort of unexam-
ined small talk that sprouted in office cubicles like bone
spores around an open corpse pit. They grasped the two handles and with a practised twist of their wrist turned them up
so they were parallel. The hatch immediately hissed open so
the lid faced Malachia and she couldn't help but notice that
the two handles were clean. Either the handles had absorbed
the blood into themselves or L I И ᗡ A had. This sort of
working gave Malachia the willies. It was sort of funny that
despite being a novitiate of the Congregation, an organisation
that was definitely pro spooky bone shit and regularly did
summonings and bindings, the more . . . wet . . . sort of
magic that a lot of the other ministries in Silence engaged in
was still decidedly off-putting even after all this time.

L I И ᗡ A had one foot on the rungs of the ladder that
ran down into the shaft when Malachia cleared her throat
loudly.

'So are you going to tell me where we are going, who you

are or . . . anything? Or am I supposed to just follow you like an idiot into the mouth of some underground abattoir?'

L I И Ɑ A just swung their other foot over and began to go down the ladder. But then they stopped with the top half of their body still above ground and gave Malachia another toothy grin, which was really starting to get on her nerves, before responding.

'That is just ridiculous. Abattoirs are all in the Sixth District and are almost always far *above* ground. Easier to do the feedings that way. As for who I am?' Here they slowly looked at the name tag on their chest and then back to Malachia. 'I'm L I И Ɑ A,' they said, enunciating each letter painfully slowly, the name now dripping with condescension. 'You can read, right? I wouldn't think that a messenger for the Carrion Oak would be illiterate but you never know with a Congregationalist, maybe you just get all your information from ghosts and oddly arranged skeletons?'

Malachia was grinding her teeth at this point (even though such disrespect to a hallowed bone member was something she had been trained never to do) and was about to give L I И Ɑ A a piece of her mind but the person just continued on without pause.

'Anyhoo, I was here waiting for you because the Carrion Oak knew you would have to come this way, and if the Carrion Oak knows something, then the closest L I И Ɑ A knows it. We always snap to and make sure that the very important thing that we just learned about is in no way an annoying inconvenience to our already busy workday, oh no, why would L I И Ɑ A need to be asked in advance about their calendar availability or workload? Nope, L I И Ɑ As are always just there on the spot, yes we are, it gets done as swiftly and smoothly as possible.'

'So you're going to help me go wherever the other Powers have fucked off to? If it's a bother I'm sure I can find my own way now that you opened that hatch . . . blood . . . thing.'

L I И ᗡ A's gaze snapped to her and for a moment their face was a mask of fury that pulled their lips back from those flat smooth teeth in a snarl. Then it was gone with a shake of their head.

At this Malachia did her best to keep her own face smooth and impassive. Something was wrong with this L I И ᗡ A but she didn't know if it was related to her or her mission in any way. This L I И ᗡ A could just be on the fritz and trying their best to do whatever order they had received from the Carrion Oak. Or maybe it was something else taking a hand here. The Carrion Oak hadn't ventured any hypothesis on the matter but Malachia was sure there had to be something else involved with the Foundationals not returning when they should have than just vacation FOMO. If this L I И ᗡ A was a part of that, then it wouldn't do to let her suspicions be seen on her face before absolutely necessary.

'Of course you can't go alone, Malachia, because then what would L I И ᗡ A have to do? You wouldn't want to take L I И ᗡ A's job away from them now, would you? Of course you wouldn't. Now just follow me and we will get you to where they need you to be.'

And before Malachia could reply, L I И ᗡ A disappeared down the shaft and into the inky darkness just beyond the first safety lantern attached to the wall.

13

Noah

Noah let out a weak incredulous laugh that was a pale echo of his earlier barking breakdown, and then placing two fingers on each temple, he asked slowly and evenly, 'What exactly is this job, Svenn? What is upstairs?'

Svenn just looked at him silently for almost an entire minute. His eyes were tracing the lines of Noah's face and after a while he started humming a low dirge.

Noah didn't say a word. He wasn't going to lose at this game twice in one day. Children *and* old men beating him at staring contests? Not on his watch! This was one thing he could control. Right? He could sit here and not say anything. He loved sitting and doing nothing. He was the champion of sitting and doing nothing; sure, usually there was a couch and video games or a horror movie marathon instead of a small closet with a silent, enigmatic agent of some company that seemed to be dealing with supernatural horrors but he could do it. Yeah, he could do this. Yep. No problem at all. He'd just sit here and count the ceiling tiles. One. Two. Three. Four. Five. Six. Seven. Eight. Nine. Ten. Welp, that was all the tiles – yep, he was screwed. Just when Noah was about to lose for the second time of the day, Svenn broke the silence.

'Didn't Linda tell you anything? You had a new-hire packet, right?'

Noah opened his mouth to tell Svenn yeah of course he had and that it had been a video with . . . with . . . with THE **RED** ORB FILLED HIS VISION IT GREW LARGER IT BUZZED IN WHISPERS THAT HE COULD ALMOST MAKE THE WORDS OUT TO IF HE JUST GOT CLOSER IF HE COULD JUST LET THE ORB GET CLOSER AND FILL . . .

Svenn was snapping his fingers in front of Noah's face and humming a dirge again but this time it was to the tune of Steven Greenberg's 'Funkytown'.

'Okay, I see what happened here. Linda was an idiot. I say that as someone who is fond of them and respects them as a coworker. I know there has been a lot of pressure to fill positions that were emptied with the last Harvest but sending you to the Mansions without *actually* telling you what you were going to meet with and just hoping that a video hex would keep you safe and the Crimson Mother's aspect would imbed this easily with, and pardon me here, a total fucking newbie is just wishful thinking. You probably wouldn't have died if you had gone in unprepared to talk to Mrs Galloway but you definitely wouldn't have achieved anything useful.'

Noah looked at Svenn as the series of mostly unintelligible sentences washed over him.

'I quit.'

'No, you don't,' Svenn said placidly.

'Yes, yes I really, really do quit.'

Svenn raised an eyebrow before answering. 'No. You. Don't.'

'YES. I. DO.'

Noah felt his face flushing with both anger and embarrassment and that ridiculous urge to cry he felt anytime he had an argument with anyone about anything. He hated this type

of confrontation, but even more, he hated being told he couldn't do something that he very obviously could.

Svenn just smiled and, reaching behind himself, retrieved a metal lunch pail that Noah had not noticed on the small crowded desk.

'Okay, let me rephrase this. You physically cannot quit this job. It's in your paperwork. And the videos. And now more than likely, since it's been almost an entire day . . . your blood.'

Svenn opened the lid of the lunchbox and carefully set a paper-towel-wrapped item on his knee and a red-and-white plaid thermos on the floor next to him.

'Here, have half of this pimento and rye sandwich and you'll feel better. I also have some *café de olla* that I get from this little bodega by my house that will be the perfect pick-me-up before you go back upstairs and finish your appointment.'

Noah numbly accepted the sandwich – he had never turned down a free sandwich in his life – and stared at it as if the dark, seed-strewn rye was going to begin talking and explain everything that was happening. In the best scenario it would open up and the pimento cheese slithering on top would form into two orange globes that would look up at him as the slices flapped their lips to say, 'This is a dream, Noah. It's all a dream! Now eat me, you big hunk. Also you've won the lottery.'

But the sandwich just sat in his hand, innocently but hatefully inert.

He took a bite of the sandwich. It was very good. Stupid fucking delicious sandwich. He took another bite and then another and before he knew it the sandwich was just a charnel field of crumbs across the front of his shirt and he was sipping on a thermos cap full of very sweet, room-temperature *café de olla* which, with its purposefully weak brew and cinnamon aftertaste, was refreshing in a way plain coffee normally never was.

Filling his mouth, Noah kept his eyes focused on the cup, buying himself a few more moments of thinking before his anxiety and empty free-agent mouth would take him kicking and screaming back into the conversation with Svenn that seemed bent on destroying his life. The words 'you physically cannot quit this job' kept echoing back and forth in his skull and he almost choked on the coffee as he snort-laughed to himself. Had he ever had the option to physically quit any of his jobs really? *Yes, sure, go ahead and quit, rent and food are just esoteric concepts, surely? No way the need of them would have* physically *kept me mopping floors until my knees and back gave out,* he thought with a sarcasm that threatened to dip into dull rage. This was no different than that really. Landlords, bosses, they were all monsters of some sort. At least these were being honest about it.

Finally he swallowed and looked at Svenn, who was still watching him and sipping on his own worryingly grimy bright yellow mug, with 'Filled With Rage' emblazoned on the side.

Before Noah could say anything, Svenn continued as if he had never paused: 'I know you don't want to hear this, kid, but I am actually trying to help you. If it makes it more believable, I'm not doing it for you though. Printed Matter has been going downhill for years now and the crap they let slip through the cracks always ends up landing on my plate and it is already overflowing. I just want them to finally hire someone who doesn't get devoured or turned into a burnt husk, or join a local grocery co-op in the first week for once. I'm not even sure Linda okayed your hiring with the L I И ᗡ Apex at corporate. They mean well. But they were never meant to be doing this job for this long. That's not how they built them in the tombs. I don't think they've even molted during this cycle. And you know how wonky an Aspect can get if they don't molt. Well, you probably don't actually know but you get the gist, right. What's that one quote? Help me, help you?'

Noah inhaled air and could detect the sweet aftertaste of the cheese and the bitter caraway seed on the back of his palate as he did.

'Svenn, I think . . . that *you* think my problem is with . . . feeling supported on the job site? And yeah in the back of my brain maybe, yes I should be looking up HR's extension, but really the *front* of my brain is the part that is quivering Jell-O when I just try and think about the FUCKING JOB SITE ITSELF! This shit is either impossible and I don't know what, or it's terrifying and you're all monsters and . . . and . . .' Noah's words slowed to a crawl. He thought about the bus depot floors that waited for him, if they would even rehire him. Was Svenn his manager now? Handler? Executioner? He thought about barely being able to pay rent on a shit-ass studio apartment and eating mouldy bread for toast because he couldn't afford to throw away rotten fucking food. He thought about the blood that he sometimes tasted slicking the back of his teeth after another insomnia-hazed day of trying to sleep the afternoon through to get ready for the graveyard shift. He couldn't afford to quit this job. He couldn't afford to scuttle back to his safe discomfort. He was just going to die more slowly and boringly that way. A continental drift of mediocrity. He thought about the shit-eating grin every manager he had ever worked for had worn and how that was not what he saw on Svenn's face.

Fuck it. Fuck it. Fuck it. FUCK IT.

'Fuck it.' Noah stood quickly and his vision was brown and then green from the sudden rush of blood, a static VHS aux screen before hitting play. Then it all snapped into jittering teeth gritting on the edge of chipping and incisor motion. 'So I'm just going to go in there. Read from the script in my sales packet and hope Mrs Galloway doesn't decide that my skull also needs one of her roots . . . or tentacles . . . or whatever

they are plugged into it to speed along the conversation? Can you maybe phone ahead and let her know I am coming?'

Svenn smiled in a way that no mirth reached his eyes.

'Oh, Mrs Galloway definitely knew you were visiting her today. Or else she never would have spruced up the twins . . . Also we wouldn't be having this conversation . . . And there would be triplets upstairs right now. I would love to go up there and supervise but there are certain workplace guidelines . . . accords that I have to abide by, even more than you, a Printed Matter employee, have to.'

Svenn looked sincere and even a bit regretful as he too dusted the pumpernickel from his knees and stood to his feet. Then with a tilt of his head he looked at Noah, considering, and his eyes darted to the still slightly ajar closet door and back to him.

'Well, there is something I can do that might help. But I have to do it as a personal matter not as a Contractor with an affiliate account with Printed Matter.'

Svenn shifted his body weight and something about the way he did it was unmistakable. Certain things are hardwired into the radar of meat and fluids that make up humans. It wasn't so much that time actually dilated like you see in an action film with doves flapping through hails of bullets, every feather discernable in frame-by-frame perfection. But it might as well have been. It was more that in these sort of moments Noah felt like he was more awake than the 60% brain static he normally functioned on. Thoughts just happened faster at knife-edge speeds, decisions coming and going like thieves in the night dropping their spoils out the windows of his cerebellum to the waiting getaway van nervous system.

Even before Svenn took a step forward Noah knew he wanted to kiss him.

14

Malachia

'Don't dawdle. We wouldn't want to keep Them waiting now, would we?' L I И ᗡ A's voice floated up from the waiting hatch.

Who the fuck are They? Malachia thought as she exhaled a long weary breath and began to follow them down the shaft. Maybe L I И ᗡ A was calling the Carrion Oak with all its dangling corpse mouthpieces a plural 'they', but that seemed unlikely. There was something about the way they had accented the word that bugged Malachia, who was used to parsing out the difference in the vibration of her different molars from that of the buried skeletal saints lining the walls of the Congregation. Something about the force with which they had said it, like it had sprung free from their tongue instead of falling from it casually as the rest of the sentence had.

The long descent into darkness gradually became a descent into muddy grey twilight and then into badly lit but recognisable tiling on all the walls and finally Malachia's feet stepped down and didn't find another rung. For a moment she panicked and grabbed desperately at the side of the ladder to slow her descent. Was this a trap? She hadn't heard L I И ᗡ A cry out or any sort of commotion or impact. She was about to reach out with the bone-dust limbs she still had hidden inside of her sleeves but then her foot touched the floor below her

and with a short sigh of relief she straightened her back up and looked around.

She was in the T junction where the shaft had terminated in the middle of a long hallway that was completely covered with bone-coloured tiles: floor, walls and ceiling. The tiles were the long type she knew, although she didn't really know why she knew, to be subway tiles. It had to be something to do with her own humanness which wasn't something she had ever had any interest in exploring, until now. The fact that it was becoming of interest and possibly even importance filled her with no little amount of alarm. She wanted to just do what the Carrion Oak had asked her to and then get back to her safe and familiar life at the Congregation.

Didn't she?

To her left the tunnel took a bend out of her sight and to her right it did the same but in that direction she just caught a glimpse of L I И Œ A disappearing around the bend.

Yep, that's not suspicious at all, she thought to herself as she started after them with an annoyed, 'Hey! Hey, L I И Œ A, wait the fuck up okay?'

By the time she caught up with them, L I И Œ A was finishing unlocking another door, this one a thoroughly plain and unextraordinary, except for the smears of black blood around the keyhole, wooden office door. L I И Œ A looked up from licking the dark ichor from their forearm and grinned, the blood smeared across their teeth like thick molasses.

'Well, let's not keep Them waiting. Chop chop, we got a schedule to keep,' L I И Œ A chirped as they swung the door outwards and gestured for Malachia to enter.

'Why do you keep saying "They"?' Malachia asked over her shoulder as she walked through the door. She was about to turn around and continue her interrogation but what she saw

in the room killed the words on her tongue and left them
there to rot. She might be comfortable with spooky bone shit
but Malachia hadn't lived in Silence this long not to recognise
a sacrificial zone when she saw one.

The room was a perfectly circular flow of spiralling white
tiles all interlocking in a way that made her eyes hurt when
she tried to trace the lines of tile to either of their termini. The
floor was sloped towards the centre to make a subtle concavity and right in the middle was a large grated drain. The
walls – well, the place where walls should be – were just an
inky velvety darkness that gave the room the appearance of
being just a floor floating in a pitch-black void, but every now
and then the darkness rippled and she could see it momentarily encroach onto the gleaming white tiles like a tide running
up onto a shore. At three opposing points of the room were
large ragged shards of rock. They were wildly incongruous
with the rest of the room's sleekness, and large and dripping
runes were painted onto each one.

Malachia turned to face L I И ᗡ A, who was already lung-
ing at her with a small but very sharp-looking piece of dark
stone held low and their mouth wide in a flat-toothed snarl.

'Whoa whoa, wha-what the actual fuck,' Malachia gasped
as she deftly sidestepped L I И ᗡ A's crazed lunge[27] and
backpedaled, mouthing the words for the Canticle of Motion-
less Grace and Quiet Finality until she crashed into one of the
ragged stone shards and bounced off it, almost tumbling to
the floor. Luckily the words of the prayer were already being
answered and her bones went pliant as she took the shock and

---

[27] Ah, I see we have another product of the tutelage of Sister Hendretta
and their *Calisthenics and Nonbeliever Attitude Adjustment* class. Someone
is going to need to send them a thank-you note after all this.

then snapped back to solidity with an audible *click pop* as she skidded to a halt facing L I И ᗡ A.

'What the hell, L I И ᗡ A?!' she barked, and she sidled away as L I И ᗡ A began to try and circle around her, tossing the stone knife from one hand to the other as they did.

'I'm pretty sure this sacrificial, very much underground and not in the Sixth District in some fucking tower *abattoir* isn't how the Carrion Oak wanted me to go wherever it is I need to go.'

Malachia's eyes were desperately searching around the room, looking for anything that would help her. The runes, written in what she now assumed was L I И ᗡ A's handwriting in black gloopy blood, were familiar but she couldn't quite place them.

Meanwhile L I И ᗡ A had stopped their sideways stalking and had tilted their head quizzically at Malachia. Then they tilted it more . . . and more. The flesh around their neck began to bulge and tear and Malachia could hear the bones crunching as they were wrenched from their sockets. L I И ᗡ A's mouth spread into a horrifyingly wide smile and their gums, more yellowed and dripping with saliva than Malachia would have guessed possible, began to push their way out of their mouth like a worm out of a rotting apple. The column of wet gums and crunched jawbones pushed its way into the air in front of L I И ᗡ A's face and hung there poised, a fleshy tower with a round mouth of flat molars that spiraled into the tunnel of its body.

Somewhere from deep inside, L I И ᗡ A's voice came wet and warbling like gristle caught and sucked from a bone.

'Fuuuck the CaRRion OaK.'

Of all the things Malachia thought L I И ᗡ A might say, she had to admit that wasn't one of them.

'fUCK the CARRion Oak and All the OthER poweRS
That abaNDOned US when We needED them. Those
WiTHOUt In The Endless Night have promiSED to . . .'

It was obvious that L I И D A was gearing up for some sort
of speech or declamatory doomsaying before they did whatever they had been planning to do to Malachia – sacrifice most
likely, if the room was any clue to that. But Malachia had
stopped listening because while L I И D A had been talking
she had remembered where she had seen those runes before.

They were the triway sigils of DARK, INNER and
OUTER. They were in basic lesser hexagrammatic tense,
which she hadn't studied since her first year as a novitiate but
she was sure of them now. They were simple to use and relied
on the sympathies of oppositional forces as the binder wrote in
their blood and then added the bindee's blood on top to finish
the circuit. The anchorite who had whispered the sigil lessons
through the mouthpiece of a sainted skull set in the classroom's
wall had always stressed that you should never, ever in any cir-
cumstances add the same blood twice: no binder's blood on
binder's sigils. Something about the thaumaturgical polarities
of sympathetic attractions. But it stood to reason that it would
probably fuck up whatever L I И D A was trying to do or at
the very least slow them down enough for her to get the fuck
out of here and go back to the Carrion Oak and politely, not
politely, request a less homicidal guide this time.

So even as L I И D A's tube of meat, bone and teeth was
undulating towards her, intent on doing, well, what undulating
tubes of meat and teeth do best, Malachia was letting the bone
dust that was still clinging to her arms loose to slither into the
room in one long, gushing eddy. Once again she locked her
hands together in front of her and set the molars in her mouth
vibrating to their own specific violent harmonics. But this time,

instead of reaching out for a field of bone keys, she sent the ash out around L I И Ɑ A who no matter how wet and goopy they looked right now decidedly had bones and teeth inside them . . . and outside them. Malachia saw L I И Ɑ A's eyes, now pushed out to the side of their head like a deep ocean fish, widen as they felt the osseomantic pressure grasp them.

Malachia first tensed then separated her fingers and flung her left hand out in the position of Final Conciliation Before the Tomb of Tomorrow and let the other drop to rest, her fingers forming the ward of The Silence That Ties Down Time Itself. Time slowed and she could see each mote of bone dust shining in the air, a galaxy of past holy deaths each as precious as the next, and then the canticle finished.

Time snapped back. Every bone and tooth in L I И Ɑ A's body followed the path of intent that Malachia had charted across the room . . . and their meat and skin and hair went along with them.

L I И Ɑ A smashed into the shard that had the sigil for the liminal Outer painted on it and their body first crushed and then exploded over its face like wet bread. Their blood soaked the rock and its sigils. For a moment, because of all the gore covering it, Malachia thought nothing was happening. Well, nothing besides the fact that she had just exploded a government employee of a city formerly run by nine Powers of ineffable might and scariness. But in the case of hoping her wild guess at reverse hexagrammatic theory had borne fruit . . . nothing.

But then something did happen. The dark viscous blood of the now very much not-in-one-piece L I И Ɑ A continued to flow down from the pillar. In the matter of two breaths it was a rushing tide that filled the concavity of the room faster than either the drain could sluice it away or Malachia could

react. The dark liquid surged around her feet and slithered halfway up her legs before she could even move . . . and then she sank.

Down down down, into the dark swirling blood, Malachia sank.

15

Noah

Noah's eyes always went first to the jawline. Not because he was into jaws; well, he wasn't *not* into jaws, like he was glad that Svenn had one. But the reason he always started at the jawline when he was checking someone out was because it led to the neck and Noah was *definitely* into necks. Svenn's jawline was covered with a touch more than a five o'clock shadow of grizzled silver and auburn beard. His neck was thick. The sort of neck Noah always imagined a blacksmith would have; a neck that if you nuzzled into it would smell of smoke and sweat and leather aprons casually tossed to a straw-lined floor for a tryst with the local silversmith apprentice. Uh, yeah, a neck like . . . that. Noah couldn't see Svenn's collarbone (his second favourite thing to check out . . . *Well, maybe not second favourite*, he thought with a rush of blood to the nape of his own neck, but this was a casual checking-out, not a 'going over', which was an entirely different thing and not the vibe he was getting from the still silent Svenn).

Svenn looked like he was comfortably in his fifties. He could easily have been Noah's dad . . . or in this case daddy. His face was wide and flat but not in an unpleasing way. A bleak cliff of a face. A face of broad planes and angles. His eyes, which were normally half-lidded and considering,

were in this moment open completely and Noah could see that although at first glance he would have called them grey, they in fact also had a circle of amber gold around the pupil.

Svenn took another step towards him, now slightly towering over Noah. He raised a hand as if he was going to reach around Noah and grasp him at the back of the neck but he paused with it hanging in the air and spoke.

'If it is okay with you, the process is one that requires me to touch you. It will be relatively painless and over quickly.'

I hope not too quickly, Noah thought to himself as Svenn continued.

'I think afterwards you will at the very least be able to have a conversation with Mrs Galloway without her . . . peculiarities becoming . . . overwhelming.'

If I am about to go upstairs and get devoured by some sort of houseplant tentacle mother . . . person . . . I might as well get to make out before I do, he thought ruefully, but out loud just said to Svenn somewhat breathlessly, 'Well, if it's for work, then I guess, umm, sure, I mean okay but just . . .'

Then Svenn's large callused hand was sliding through the mop of his hair and grasping the back of his skull where it met his neck, immobilising it. He was now close enough that Noah could smell him, the scent of dust and time, musty but with a spicy tang that slithered into his nostrils and hung tickling at the back of his throat. Svenn looked down at him and quirked the first non-sardonic smile Noah thought he had seen on his face since they had met. Noah's breath came harsh in his ears and he tried not to close his eyes like some sort of rom-com princess. What was next, was he going to lift up one leg as the man dipped him? Maybe.

Svenn popped his jaw like a boxer after taking a hit, and as

he drew closer, said calmly, 'Okay this might feel odd but you're entirely safe, okay?'

'Safe? Wait, why wouldn't a kiss be . . .' he began but then Svenn was upon him.

This is different, was the first thing Noah thought before his senses caught up to him. Svenn was leaning over him, the pop of his jaw having served only as a precursor to what was unfolding. Svenn's jaw was unfolding. There was a tearing followed by another, more horrible wet sucking pop of bone being pulled free from joint and ligament as Svenn's jaw unhinged, the flesh around the corner of his mouth ripping bloodlessly like wet tissue paper.

His eyes did not change; however, they maintained their focus on him, and his grip, while firm, was not painful – well, not painful enough that Noah didn't like it. *But his face, what is he going to* . . . Noah's thought died before it could be finished as Svenn's jaw, his gums and their pertinent teeth flopped out of his mouth on long dark strands of muscle that pulsed and swayed like anemone or underwater fronds of kelp. The teeth, however, did not move towards him; they were just making way for what was emerging past the line of Svenn's now split and peeling-back lips.

A column of dark glistening meat pushed its way out and down towards Noah's waiting face. He began to struggle but Svenn's eyes, still calm and bright above the ruined lurching monstrosity of his mouth, gave him pause. They weren't the eyes of a predator. They didn't size him up into meat and bone to be chewed and cracked, the marrow lapped out. They just observed him calmly as he struggled feebly, his hands grasping at Svenn's sleeves, nails raking across his shoulders in a parody of passionate embrace.

Noah found his thoughts, while on one side as gibberingly

terrified of this turn of events, were also divided into a second half that watched the proceedings with detached observation. Svenn was very obviously stronger than he looked and he had looked strong to begin with. Noah never really had thoughts of *Oh I could take that guy* but he knew that the years of manual labour had left him a not inconsequential core of wiry strength and he could not budge Svenn's arm even a smidge. But if the man ... thing ... the man thing had wanted to kill him, wouldn't he have snapped his neck immediately? The dark trunk of flesh continued to unspool from Svenn's mouth and Noah could now see that the end was peeling back like the petals of a dying flower or, he thought with a flush that coloured his pale collarbone and up to his cheeks, a foreskin. From inside the folds of flesh a clear pseudopod emerged. It spread into three pronged ends, each with what appeared to be black bulbous beaks that dripped a yellow fluid in long viscous threads.

Noah briefly saw something dark pulsing within it like a spreading bruise before it pushed against his lips, easily forcing them open; at this point he wasn't really resisting it anyway. There were only so many impossible things his mind could be faced with before it cracked and he had always been of the view that it was better to be a door than a window, whatever the fuck that meant. He *thought* it meant that when the impossible force was about to meet the immovable rock, the immovable rock had best grow legs and start moving in the same direction as the impending force or it was going to get fucked the hell up.

Noah let himself and his throat relax into this as much as he possibly could. It pressed into the wet cavity of his mouth, filling it. For a brief moment he felt the beaks scrape across his teeth but then they were gone and he felt them pressing against the side of his throat. At first he thought he would gag

and bile began to rise in his throat as hot tears leaked from the sides of his eyes.

But then Svenn adjusted his grip on the back of his neck and after a brief moment of discomfort like a pinched nerve, his neck was flooded with a relaxing warmth. Svenn's eyes never changed their encouraging gaze as the appendage continued to push itself further down his throat. Noah could feel it filling parts of him he had previously been unaware even existed. An entire unexplored cartography of meat and sensation that he had needed someone, something, to show him the way to.

Noah concentrated on Svenn's gaze. After a few more seconds the shaft of the thing that went down his throat began to pulse, slowly at first, then faster. It pressed against the lining of his throat and traveled down. Noah felt Svenn shift his position. He glanced up and saw Svenn was . . . looking at his fucking phone? Noah was so flabbergasted at this that for a brief moment he forgot that he had his mouth, and his throat, and certain now throbbing internal parts of his anatomy full to bursting, and tried to mouth, 'What the fuck dude, seriously?' around the slick membrane but only managed, 'Wafh'ush'ukvould?'

Svenn looked back at him in surprise like for a moment he had forgotten Noah was even there. It would not be the first time this had happened in Noah's love life – don't even get started on the supply closet in art class and Mitch Gensin and Samantha Tally and . . . wait . . . he was in a supply closet now . . . again. *Fuck, I'm a cliché even when I'm being deep-throated by some supernatural horror handyman . . . Swede?* he groaned internally as he tried to translate his gesture of *what the fuck* from verbal to his free hand. Svenn ignored the gesture, if he even saw it, and held up his phone so that the screen was directly in front of Noah's eyes.

The small speakers squealed with static that thrummed in time to the things filling his throat. The sound was almost words and Noah thought if everything and everyone would just hold still for one minute, he could make them out. Over the top of the phone he saw Svenn mouthing something but then the screen took his attention. On it he saw a low stone wall, a copse of trees beyond it in winter, their jagged branches either stark against the sky or filled with birds, and a red orb hung in the middle, rising through the trunks, impossibly passing around them without collision to fill the screen with . . .

16

Malachia

darkness darkness darkness darkness darkness DARKNESS DARKNESSDARKNESS DARKNESSDARKNESS DARKNESS DARKNESS DARKNESS DARKNESS DARKNESS DARKNESS DARKNESS DARKNESS DARKNESS darkness darkness DARKNESS DARKNESS DARKNESS DARKNESS DARKNESS DARKNESS DARKNESS darkness darkness darkness darkness darkness M DARKNESS DARKNESSDARKNESS DARKNESSDARKNESS DARKNE A SS DARKNESS DARKNESS DARKNESS DARKNESS DARKNESS DARKNESS DARKN L ESS DARKNESS darkness darkness DARKNESS DARKNESS DARKNESS DARKN A ESS DARKNESS DARKNESS DARKNESS darkness darkness darkness darkness darkness C DARKNESS DARKNESSDARKNESS DARKNESSDARKNESS DARKNE H SS DARKNESS DARKNESS DARKNESS DARKNESS DARKNESS DARKNE I SS DARKNESS darkness darkness DARKNESS DARKNESS DARKNESS darkness A DARKNESS Malachia could hear breathing, a low wet gurgle like gristle and blood in a slit throat DARKNESS DARKNESS DARKNESS DARKNESS darkness darkness darkness

darkness darkness DARKNESS DARKNESSDARK-
NESS DARKNESSDARKNESS DARKNESS DARK-
NESS DARKNESS DARKNESS DARKNESS
DARKNESS DARKNESS DARKNESS DARKNESS
darkness darkness DARKNESS DARKNESS DARK-
NESS DARKNESS DARKNESS DARKNESS DARK-
NESS darkness darkness darkness darkness darkness
DARKNESS DARKNESSDARKNESS DARKNESS
DARKNESS DARKNESS DARKNESS DARKNESS
DARKNESS DARKNESS DARKNESS DARKNESS
DARKNESS DARKNESS darkness darkness DARKNESS
DARKNESS DARKNESS DARKNESS darkness dark-
ness darkness DARKNESS DARKNESSDARKNESS
DARKNESSDARKNESS DARKNESS MALACHIA
DARKNESS DARKNESS DARKNESS DARKNESS
DARKNESS DARKNESS DARKNESS darkness dark-
ness DARKNESS DARKNESS DARKNESS DARK-
NESS DARKNESS DARKNESS DARKNESS darkness
darkness darkness darkness darkness DARKNESS DARK-
NESSDARKNESS DARKNESSDARKNESS DARK-
NESS DARKNESS DARKNESS DARKNESS
DARKNESS M DARKNESS DARKNESS DARK-
NESS DARKNESS darkness darkness DARKNESS
DARK A NESS DARKNESS DARKNESS darkness
darkness DARKNESS DARK L NESS DARKNESS
DARKNESS darkness DARKNESS darkness darkness
DAR A KNESS DARKNESS DARKNESS darkness
DARKNESS darkness darkness darkness C DARKNESS
DARKNESSDARKNESS DARKNESSDARKNESS
DARKNESS DARKNE H SS DARKNESS DARK-
NESS DARKNESS DARKNESS DARKNESS DARK-
NESS DARKNE I SS darkness darkness DARKNESS

DARKNESS DARKNESS DARKNESS DARKN A
ESS DARKNESS DARKNESS darkness darkness dark-
ness darkness darkness DARKNESS DARKNESSDARK-
NESS DARKNESSDARKNESS malachia DARKNESS
DARKNESS DARKNESS DARKNESS DARKNESS
DARKNESS DARKNESS DARKNESS DARKNESS
darkness darkness DARKNESS DARKNESS DARK-
NESS DARKNESS darkness darkness darkness darkness
darkness   DARKNESS   DARKNESSDARKNESS
DARKNESSDARKNESS DARKNESS DARKNESS
DARKNESS DARKNESS DARKNESS DARKNESS
DARKNESS DARKNESS DARKNESS darkness dark-
ness DARKNESS DARKNESS DARKNESS DARK-
NESS DARKNESS DARKNESS DARKNESS darkness
darkness darkness darkness darkness M DARKNESS
DARKNESSDARKNESS   DARKNESSDARKNESS
DARKNE A SS DARKNESS DARKNESS DARK-
NESS   DARKNESS   DARKNESS   DARKNESS
DARKN L ESS DARKNESS darkness darkness DARK-
NESS DARKNESS DARKNESS DARKN A ESS
DARKNESS   DARKNESS   DARKNESS   darkness
darkness darkness darkness darkness C DARKNESS
DARKNESSDARKNESS   DARKNESSDARKNESS
DARKNE H SS DARKNESS DARKNESS DARK-
NESS DARKNESS DARKNESS DARKNE I SS
DARKNESS darkness darkness DARKNESS DARK-
NESS A DARKNESS

M

a

l

a

c

hia didn't wake up so much as just continue a conversation she seemed to have been already having. The Benefactrix of Quiet Deaths Held Dear sat on the small but sturdily constructed stool that served as the only seating in her novitiate cell besides the cot, and she was lying on that. Well, she was lying on her back with her feet resting on the stone wall and her head hanging off the edge of the bed so her view of the Benefactrix was inverted while she tossed her balled-up wimple and hood up into the air and caught it again before it unfurled completely, so any impartial viewer would be very likely to question the veracity of her lying on the cot as an axiomatic statement of existence, but this was the position Malachia found herself in.

All of this paled though to the fact that she was looking at the Benefactrix . . . BENE. And she remembered everything about her. Not in an overwhelming tidal rush of returning memories but in the slow, warm rising of the sun over a landscape of their entwined history that had always been there and always would be. She didn't know why she was

here now with Bene instead of still falling into a pool of blood and dark, but even as she tried to think about it she could feel the thought slipping away to be packed beneath the soft warmth of Bene's proximity. Was that other stuff even important? Why had she thought it had been? It must not have been, Malachia decided with a shake of her head.

'I don't know why you can't sit on the cot like a normal person, Mal. My non-existent neck muscles ache just watching you.'

Malachia's lips turned into a mischievous smile, which depending on your viewing orientation might have seemed a frown from her upside-down face, and sniffing, she retorted, 'Why, Bene, I thought the mortification of the Craven Meat of the False Dream was the foremost goal of every novitiate of the Congregation? Are you a heretic, Bene? You have to tell me if you're a heretic. That's like rule number one of heresy . . . probably.'

The Benefactrix, while unable to return Malachia's smirk due to the complete lack of skin, muscle or tendons

DARKNESS DARKNESS

covering her skull, clacked her back molars in a way that Malachia had come to know as amusement. The skeletal figure wore the robes of her own office but had removed the funerary cloth veil that normally hid her hallowed bony visage from the majority of the initiates. She slid her stool closer to Malachia's bed with a surprising lack of creaking or bone snapping for someone whose age, well, Malachia didn't know how old she was, but the bones of her skeleton were yellowed to a deep ochre with age and she had never heard anyone talk of a time *before* the Benefactrix had been part of the Congregation. Bene, for that was what she allowed Malachia to call her in private, laced her hands beneath her lolling head and pulled it up onto her lap so she was looking up into Malachia's face. Malachia didn't think of her as a skeleton or a gaunt, wight, haint or any of the other things she heard the non-members of the Congregation call the hallowed dead; she was her Bene and to Bene she was Mal, and Mal was as in love with her as she could be with anyone.

Bene placed her skeletal hands on

DARKNESS DARKNESS

each side of Mal's head and let them rasp over the stubble of her shorn scalp. Malachia did her best not to purr right then and there and instead put on a mock serious expression.

'So heresy it is, I see. What am I going to do with you, Benefactrix of Quiet Deaths Held Dear? Whatever. Am I. Going. To Do. With You?'

Bene clacked her teeth again and leaned down to press her forehead against Malachia's.

'What are you going to do, my horribly sinful novitiate? What am *I* going to do . . .'

And for a moment she trailed off, her skull held at an angle that Malachia had come to also know as her contemplating something she would rather not voice aloud. She attempted to sit up so she could pull Bene into a closer embrace to lighten the mood but the Benefactrix's grip on her head grew vicelike and jerked her back down onto her lap. Malachia startled.

'Bene, what the fu—'

But the now impassive visage of her skeletal lover pushed its forehead harder into hers. 'What am I going to do to

you, Malachia of the Ninth and Coldest Flame?'

For a moment Malachia felt the icy hand of fear slide its way under her woolen robes and settle around her neck. She had no idea where it was coming from and almost sat up to look around the room to see if someone or something had entered it, but then Bene shifted her head back a few inches so it was no longer crushing itself into her forehead and she whispered, 'Well, for starters, my bones are due for a new oiling and reconsecration and I hear your technique is . . . revelatory.'

This time it was Malachia who reached up to clasp her hands around the nape of Bene's skeleton where her protruding spinal bones meshed with her skull in a maze of copper wire and fading inscriptions. Pulling the older woman close, she kissed her hard, feeling the press of her jawbone against the soft flesh of her lips and the exposed roots of her teeth like smooth ridges across her tongue. The skeletal woman hissed from somewhere deep inside her skull, a sound that filled Malachia's entire body with the reverberation of

bones and time. The fleshless fingers of her other hand slipped beneath Malachia's robe and confidently slid up her sweat-slicked thigh. The novitiate arched her back as first the older woman's distal phalanx and then middle phalanx entered her. Bene pressed her face against Malachia's neck, her jaws opening wider than a fleshed being's jaws could normally. Her age-yellowed bones did not extend their discolouration to her teeth, which now pressed themselves firmly but not uncarefully against the flesh of her neck. Malachia groaned in pleasure as Bene introduced her to her proximal phalanx and she moaned into the skeleton's exposed temporal bone, 'I think I can fit you in after the evening's vespers and catechism cants after all ... I think.'

She gasped before smirking at the way the Benefactrix had stiffened at first but then gone soft and pliant in a way she would never have guessed someone made of bone and occult wiring would ever have been able to before their relationship.

'I would like that very much,' Bene

whispered, again speaking from within the depths of her skull without the use of her jaws, which remained clamped firmly but tenderly around Malachia's throat. They began to tighten in time to her fingers' movements beneath Malachia's robe, a back-and-forth tidal ebb of being held almost but not quite enough, never breaking the skin but birthing a desire in Malachia that they would. She was about to whisper this to Bene when the other woman suddenly sat ramrod straight on the stool, her teeth raking fine lines across Malachia's throat as she withdrew and her skeletal fingers vacated the slicked cleft of her sex, leaving it still aching for more.

'Bene, stop it; it was only mildly funny the first time, but c'mon get some new materi—'

Malachia was interrupted by Bene ramming herself downward to smash her skull into Malachia's upturned face, once and then again and again. It was so sudden that she didn't have time to react. The first blow stunned her and her vision immediately filled with a burning haze of blood from the splintering bone cutting into her with every

KNESS DARKNESS DARKNESS DARKNESS DARKNESS DARKNESS DARKNESSDARKNESS DA
KNESS DARKNESS DARKNESS DARKNESS DARKNESS DARKNESS DARKNESSDARKNESS DA
KNESS DARKNESS DARKNESS DARKNESS DARKNESS DARKNESS DARKNESSDARKNESS DA
KNESS DARKNESS DARKNESS DARKNESS DARKNESS DARKNESS DARKNESSDARKNESS DA

strike. The last thing Malachia remembered dazedly was the feeling of the Benefactrix's skull starting to shatter against her bleeding face like a jagged, stony eggshell.

KNESS DARKNESS DARKNESS DARKNESS DARKNESS DARKNESS DARKNESSDARKNESS DA
KNESS DARKNESS DARKNESS DARKNESS DARKNESS DARKNESS DARKNESSDARKNESS DA
KNESS DARKNESS DARKNESS DARKNESS DARKNESS DARKNESS DARKNESSDARKNESS DA
KNESS DARKNESS DARKNESS DARKNESS DARKNESS DARKNESS DARKNESSDARKNESS DA
KNESS DARKNESS DARKNESS DARKNESS DARKNESS DARKNESS DARKNESSDARKNESS DA
KNESS DARKNESS DARKNESS DARKNESS DARKNESS DARKNESS DARKNESSDARKNESS DA
KNESS DARKNESS DARKNESS DARKNESS DARKNESS DARKNESS DARKNESSDARKNESS DA
KNESS DARKNESS DARKNESS DARKNESS DARKNESS DARKNESS DARKNESSDARKNESS DA
KNESS DARKNESS DARKNESS DARKNESS DARKNESS DARKNESS DARKNESSDARKNESS DA
KNESS DARKNESS DARKNESS DARKNESS DARKNESS DARKNESS DARKNESSDARKNESS DA
KNESS DARKNESS DARKNESS DARKNESS DARKNESS DARKNESS DARKNESSDARKNESS DA
KNESS DARKNESS DARKNESS DARKNESS DARKNESS DARKNESS DARKNESSDARKNESS DA
KNESS DARKNESS DARKNESS DARKNESS DARKNESS DARKNESS DARKNESSDARKNESS DA
KNESS DARKNESS DARKNESS DARKNESS DARKNESS DARKNESS DARKNESSDARKNESS DA
KNESS DARKNESS DARKNESS DARKNESS DARKNESS DARKNESS DARKNESSDARKNESS DA
KNESS DARKNESS DARKNESS DARKNESS DARKNESS DARKNESS DARKNESSDARKNESS DA
KNESS DARKNESS DARKNESS DARKNESS DARKNESS DARKNESS DARKNESSDARKNESS DA
KNESS DARKNESS DARKNESS DARKNESS DARKNESS DARKNESS DARKNESSDARKNESS DA
KNESS DARKNESS DARKNESS DARKNESS DARKNESS DARKNESS DARKNESSDARKNESS DA
KNESS DARKNESS DARKNESS DARKNESS DARKNESS DARKNESS DARKNESSDARKNESS DA
KNESS DARKNESS DARKNESS DARKNESS DARKNESS DARKNESS DARKNESSDARKNESS DA
KNESS DARKNESS DARKNESS DARKNESS DARKNESS DARKNESS DARKNESSDARKNESS DA
KNESS DARKNESS DARKNESS DARKNESS DARKNESS DARKNESS DARKNESSDARKNESS DA
KNESS DARKNESS DARKNESS DARKNESS DARKNESS DARKNESS DARKNESSDARKNESS DA
KNESS DARKNESS DARKNESS DARKNESS DARKNESS DARKNESS DARKNESSDARKNESS DA
KNESS DARKNESS DARKNESS DARKNESS DARKNESS DARKNESS DARKNESSDARKNESS DA
KNESS DARKNESS DARKNESS DARKNESS DARKNESS DARKNESS DARKNESSDARKNESS DA
KNESS DARKNESS DARKNESS DARKNESS DARKNESS DARKNESS DARKNESSDARKNESS DA
KNESS DARKNESS DARKNESS DARKNESS DARKNESS DARKNESS DARKNESSDARKNESS DA
KNESS DARKNESS DARKNESS DARKNESS DARKNESS DARKNESS DARKNESSDARKNESS DA

17

Noah

Noah could taste the bitter film of not-quite-washed-away floor cleaner on the concrete his mouth was pressed against.

He moved his head slightly and the front of his tooth grated against the concrete and sent chills crawling up his spine. What the fuck had happened? He let out a long low groan as images of . . . Had he deep-throated a mouth-demon dick? Talk about your high-school fanfics that you never thought would get onto and off of your bucket list in the same day.

With some effort he rolled himself over onto his back and his vision swam for a moment but he blinked away the tears and there, above him, looking down with a completely placid, unperturbed expression was Svenn. He was also upside down from Noah's perspective, which was much more disorienting than he would have imagined. It was the kind of angle you see in movies all the time but rarely experience in real life.

'Whatshafuuu . . .' he began before deciding to suddenly and violently sit up. Which just ended up with him sitting on the floor unable to see Svenn at all because he was now behind him, which was infinitely worse. Noah scuttled backwards until his back was against the metal shelving that lined the far wall of the closet.

Svenn held up his hands in a placating gesture, and said softly, like Noah was a skittish horse, 'Whoa there. Just take a deep breath. And maybe wash your mouth out. There is a flat of water bottles on that shelf behind you.'

Noah stared at him; his hands began to rummage over his head for a bottle without turning his back to Svenn. 'What the fuck, man?' He fumbled with the water bottle and then took a huge mouthful that he just held while waiting for the man, probably not a man actually, to answer.

'I told you,' the handyman, probably not just a handyman, said, raising his eyebrows quizzically. 'The video didn't wipe your short-term memory again, did it? The *sorcel* should have bound it without any adverse side effects.'

Noah almost responded with what he would have said before he'd had the day he'd had so far. Something along the lines of, 'So I know you think you're making some sort of fucking sense and I see your mouth moving, but all I am getting from you is, "Weird magic thing blah blah probably gonna watch you die blah blah . . ."' But instead he thought about the soft worry lines around Svenn's eyes when he talked and the calm, reassuring look in his eyes as the . . . weird tongue proboscis thing had slid down his own throat.

'Okay, I'll pretend like I understood what you meant there but to be honest with you I am more shook up with the . . .' – and here he pantomimed something unspooling from his own mouth then made a frenzied *quack quack* motion with his hand like he was trying to make a shadow puppet – '. . . that just happened. Like I thought you were just hitting on me, dude, when you said you had to touch me to get me ready. I didn't think you meant like touch the bottom of my oesophagus with your own weird pet xenomorph. And really I think I am actually being super calm and dare I say professional considering . . .' Noah

pantomimed the duck bill opening and closing but this time gave it a frenzied shake at the end.

Svenn's shoulders sank. He looked down somewhat sheepishly and when he looked back up to meet Noah's exasperated gaze, it was with a look of worry that made him seem less weird-secret-monster-fixer and more kinda overworked-fellow-colleague.

'I'm truly sorry, Noah. Firstly for the misunderstanding of, um, flirting. I don't flirt. Not that I don't think that the meat your bones have aggregated over the years of your life has arranged itself into a pleasing pattern. But because as you saw with my *tromplein*, the thing you call a *xenomorph*, and yes I have seen that movie, pretty good actually, I am not really compatible with humans in a way that I would assume they would welcome. And even where I was made, things aren't as . . .' – and here Svenn seemed to struggle for the correct word before deciding on one – '. . . aren't as *fun*. I did not mean to misrepresent my intentions. And secondly, I am sorry for not realising that your new-hire training was not just rushed but basically non-existent. You should have had a handbook that outlined the interactions you might expect with someone like me and even some preparation for what to do when confronted with a client like Mrs Galloway. And while it's not my direct responsibility to have trained you and not my fault in the end, I do think it is, as you so eloquently put it, super fucking shitty that you didn't get that training and a work environment that set you up for success instead of failure. I will be having a serious conversation with Linda when you finish your work here today. And, Noah, you are going to finish it. Not just because you have to . . .'

And here for a moment Noah's vision fuzzed out with an image of the red sun . . . moon . . . orb thing rising between a

copse of dead trees to crest a crumbling stone wall; his vision fragmented again and it then disappeared.

'. . . but because I really think you are a good fit for this job and I want you to succeed.'

Noah nodded once and swallowed a lot of questions that were trying to ram their way past the cage of his teeth. Questions could wait for later, if ever. He was just an hourly employee after all and now he had to do his fucking job.

'Okay. Okay. So what now? I just go back up to Mrs Galloway's room and suddenly she . . . it . . . won't try and grab me with huge vine tentacles with child husk puppets attached to them?'

Svenn smirked before speaking. 'If it does grab you, then what I left for you when I . . .' – here Svenn imitated Noah's previous duck-squawking hand motions – '. . . in your . . .' – he tapped the hollow of his chest and Noah's cheek warmed in a way that he hoped Svenn hadn't noticed. Or maybe he hoped he did notice – '. . . will most likely help with that. Although the whole point of it growing there is to prevent it from reaching a violent confrontation and give you some space to do your job. More of an . . . employee ID that Mrs Galloway will recognise than any sort of weapon. Although part of the reason you're here to talk to her about resubscribing to Printed Matter's advertising package is because she let it lapse in the first place and they don't know why or what could have happened since then. There are, as I said before, strictures and agreements that prevent me personally from approaching her or I would accompany you, but I won't leave until I see if you have succeeded or failed. If that helps.' He finished with a smile that Noah knew was meant to be reassuring but really was way too wide and gave him a momentary glimpse of something dark and glistening that

quickly slithered back away from the light. Also, he wasn't going to count them but he would put good money on Svenn having more molars than he should . . . especially with how oddly perfect and uniform they were as they stretched back into his mouth, almost like they kept going past the cave entrance of his throat and . . . What was he talking about?

Noah blinked and looked at Svenn again. He couldn't remember what he had just been thinking . . . Something about Svenn's . . . teeth?

'Putting aside the whole "I left something growing inside you" bit, which we are definitely going to talk about later, I am going to say no, that really doesn't help, but really it doesn't matter, does it? I have to do this job or I am assuming something horrible and terrifying will happen to me which really, when I come to think about it, isn't any different or worse than knowing that if I don't show up to mop up drunk commuters' vomit and restock convenience machines, I will get fired and not be able to pay rent and afford to eat so fuck it. Let's go back and talk to Mrs Galloway, and by let's I mean me; I am going to go back and talk to the weird Tentacle Mother Plant Creature.'

18

Malachia

DARKNESS DARKNESS DARKNESS DARKNESS
DARKNESS DARKNESS DARKNESS DARKNESS
DARKNESS DARKNESS DARKNESS DARKNESS
DARKNESS DARKNESS DARKNESS DARKNESS
DARKNESS DARKNESS DARKNESS DARKNESS
DARKNESS DARKNESS DARKNESS DARKNESS
DARKNESS DARKNESS DARKNESS DARKNESS
DARKNESS DARKNESS DARKNESS DARKNESS
DARKNESS DARKNESS DARKNESS DARKNESS
DARKNESS DARKNESS DARKNESS DARKNESS
DARKNESS DARKNESS DARKNESS DARKNESS
DARKNESS DARKNESS DARKNESS DARKNESS
DARKNESS DARKNESS DARKNESS DARKNESS
DARKNESS DARKNESS DARKNESS DARKNESS
DARKNESS DARKNESS DARKNESS DARKNESS
DARKNESS DARKNESS DARKNESS DARKNESS
DARKNESS DARKNESS DARKNESS DARKNESS
DARKNESS DARKNESS DARKNESS DARKNESS
DARKNESS DARKNESS DARKNESS DARKNESS
DARKNESS DARKNESS DARKNESS DARKNESS
DARKNESS DARKNESS DARKNESS DARKNESS
DARKNESS DARKNESS DARKNESS DARKNESS

'So you were late again for the cate-
chisms. Just because we are ...
involved, Mal, doesn't mean that you
don't have to earn your next ascension.
In fact, it means quite the opposite.'

Malachia blinked and the room came
into focus. She could still taste her blood,
a sour iron tang on her lips. But when
she ran her tongue over them tentatively,
she found them unbroken and dry.
Already the memory of Bene's skull shat-
tering against her face was fading like
the early-morning fog that sometimes
wrapped itself around the spire-bound
thrones of the church. What had she
been thinking about just now? She obviously should be paying attention to the
Benefactrix, who seemed to be in one of
her moods, but the now almost-gone
memory bothered her like the first crack
in a rotting tooth. She tried to remember
more of it but just as she thought she
could see the shape of it, something
about the Carrion Oak and someone
named ... It was gone, and looking up
she saw that Bene was waiting expect-
antly for her to say something.

'Umm, I'll take Sincere Apologies
and Abject Admittance of Dumbassery,

'Alex, for \$400,' she quipped, hoping that a joke about both of their favourite ghost transmissions she had bought from the Sunken Markets would help her hide the fact that she had no idea what Bene had just said to her. Dating a member of the Hallowed Dead in Perpetual Descension wasn't exactly forbidden but it did have a very awkward power dynamic. Who would have thunk that fucking a minor deity of the Congregation of the Hallowed Unspoken pantheon, while extremely hot, would have a downside? Everyone, that's who would have thought that – everyone. Malachia slunk down in her seat beneath the skeletal gaze and the Benefactrix cleared her throat, a minor miracle in itself if you really thought about it, and repeated her question.

'I said, Malachia of the Ninth Cold Flame, initiate of the Hallowed Dead and Protector of the Hungering Choir Beneath, have you memorised your declamation canticle for tonight? And don't think that referencing Alex Trebek will get you off the hook,' she said sternly before wavering.

'You haven't found a new episode, have you?'

Malachia groaned inwardly but still brushed imaginary dust from her lap and stood up straight like a lazy pangolin uncurling itself. She held up her right hand with the fingers flexed in the intertwining sigil of the skull, open and waiting, and then raised her left hand behind her back in the closed fist of the heart that waits in silence below.

'There's been nothing good at the Sunken Markets for the last three times that it's phased in here. There weren't even any fresh *Frasier* reruns in the last time we went there together, you remember they were selling those for only a handful of molars?'

When Bene didn't respond to this quip, Malachia straightened her spine more, held her hands even firmer and begin to decant:

'And what is the open mouth but a jaw for That Which Sleeps / What are the bones that connect / We are the broken tree / We are the roots that never weep / We are the secret that whispers its name in the ninth moon of the ninth door / A cold flame will rise to

rinse away all that keeps us attached to the flesh.'

While Malachia stood there, practising the canticle for the later ascent for later that night, she noticed that Bene, who usually nodded along, clacking the bones of her fingers against her yellowed jawbones in time to the cadence of her voice, had grown quiet. After a moment Malachia stopped her recitation and, peering at the skeletal woman, asked, 'What's wrong? I know I didn't get any of that wrong. I have it perfect. Why are you . . . why are you being weird?'

At the back of Malachia's mind, something tried to surface. The memory that had blown away earlier throbbed like a splinter beneath dull, dreaming meat. Had Bene been acting weird before? She couldn't quite remember what was off-putting, but she knew that thought felt right. Then she remembered it all. The Carrion Oak, the missing Foundationals, the whole missing fucking city of Silence, Bene included.

'Bene! Where did you and the others

go? How did I get back here to the Congregation?'

Bene didn't respond but instead just sat there, her body limp like a puppet with all its strings cut.

'Bene, stop it, say something . . .' Malachia began before being interrupted by movement.

Across from her the Benefactrix stood suddenly and began to bend backwards. Her feet, wrapped in the funerary cloth bandages, stayed firmly planted but her whole body bent back in an arc of cracking bone and snapping wires until her bony forehead touched the ground behind her. Malachia started forward, a warding prayer forming in the bones of her jaw, the teeth in them aching from the rudeness of her emergency-ensorceled mandibular vibrations. But before she could form the entire ward, Bene's contorted body lurched again, her feet and head pulled towards each other with such a violent motion that underneath her robes Malachia saw the roiling of her bones splintering against the fabric. Bene continued to compact in on herself with a horrifying swiftness so that

by the time Malachia had sprung forward and gotten close enough to try and do anything, she was just a jagged bundle of church robes that leaked yellowed bone dust and splinters. Malachia's mouth opened in a scream that died a stillbirth in her throat when she saw that the motes of bone dust that were still leaking from the Benefactrix's robes like a shattered hourglass were flickering. Reaching forward she moved to touch them. They felt like a handful of snow, painfully cold but at the same time completely dry. The sensation remained even as the handful of her lover's remains filtered in and out of view in her hand.

'What the actual . . .' she rasped through her torn vocal cords as the remains of the dust and splintered bone began to gush rapidly from the robe on the floor that shriveled up like a film of water on a hot pan before disappearing entirely. The shards and bone dust had changed from the sickly yellow of aged bone to a black that drank in the light around it. It surged up towards Malachia even as she closed her fist around what was in her hand. The dark rasping

cloud flowed around her fist in an instant and up into her face. Malachia shut her mouth and eyes but the splinter-filled dust slithered into her nostrils, distending them till she thought they would split and filling her sinuses with what felt like a river of broken glass that for a moment compacted against the back of her sinus canal before breaking through and chewing into the soft bits that her skull had been protecting.

DARKNESSDARKNESS DARKNESSDARKNESS
DARKNESSDARKNESS DARKNESSDARKNESS
DARKNESSDARKNESS DARKNESSDARKNESS
DARKNESSDARKNESS DARKNESSDARKNESS
DARKNESSDARKNESS DARKNESSDARKNESS
DARKNESSDARKNESS DARKNESSDARKNESS
DARKNESSDARKNESS DARKNESSDARKNESS
DARKNESSDARKNESS DARKNESSDARKNESS
DARKNESSDARKNESS DARKNESSDARKNESS
DARKNESSDARKNESS DARKNESSDARKNESS
DARKNESSDARKNESS DARKNESSDARKNESS
DARKNESSDARKNESS DARKNESSDARKNESS
DARKNESSDARKNESS DARKNESSDARKNESS
DARKNESSDARKNESS DARKNESSDARKNESS
DARKNESSDARKNESS DARKNESSDARKNESS
DARKNESSDARKNESS DARKNESSDARKNESS
DARKNESSDARKNESS DARKNESSDARKNESS
DARKNESSDARKNESS DARKNESSDARKNESS
DARKNESSDARKNESS DARKNESSDARKNESS
DARKNESSDARKNESS DARKNESSDARKNESS
DARKNESSDARKNESS DARKNESSDARKNESS
DARKNESSDARKNESS DARKNESSDARKNESS
DARKNESSDARKNESS DARKNESSDARKNESS
DARKNESSDARKNESS DARKNESSDARKNESS
DARKNESSDARKNESS DARKNESSDARKNESS
DARKNESSDARKNESS DARKNESSDARKNESS
DARKNESSDARKNESS DARKNESSDARKNESS
DARKNESSDARKNESS DARKNESSDARKNESS
DARKNESSDARKNESS DARKNESSDARKNESS
DARKNESSDARKNESS DARKNESSDARKNESS
DARKNESSDARKNESS DARKNESSDARKNESS
DARKNESSDARKNESS DARKNESSDARKNESS
DARKNESSDARKNESS DARKNESSDARKNESS

Malachia sat in the carved, bone-white throne that perched on the very top of the highest dome of the Congregation of the Hallowed Unspoken. About twenty feet away from her the Benefactrix stood perfectly upright and still on the impossibly small termination of another of the church's spires. Between the two of them yawned the echoing abyss of open air all the way down to the pointed crenelations of the wandering anchorite plinths of the westernmost courtyard. Malachia felt the cold grey of the dawn air seeping into her lungs as she gasped reflexively at the suddenness of finding herself a part of this tableau.

How had she gotten here? Looking down at her lap she saw that she was clutching something in her right hand so tightly that the skin around her knuckles showed white against the bones and she could feel her nails cutting bloody crescents into her palm. Slowly she opened it, keeping the hand cupped close to her body against the wind that whipped around them, and when she saw what rested there she was glad she had taken that precaution. It

was a handful of bone dust and splinters. Malachia looked up to where Bene still stood like a statue; even her robes were unaffected by the wind.

'What are we doing up here?' she shouted across the empty space, her blood pounding in her temples as a suspicion began to drag itself into her mind.

The Benefactrix did not respond.

Malachia stared at the figure of the woman she loved and who had loved her, often multiple times a night. The suspicion sank its teeth further into her. Carefully she lifted the handful of bone dust and splinters up to her face and, after a moment's hesitation, she touched her tongue to the pile of bone dust. The figure across from her shifted. Its shoulders hunched towards Malachia as if it was now focusing all its attention on her actions.

But still a hood hid the skeleton woman's face. Malachia ran her dust-coated tongue over her teeth and gums, spreading the bitter coating over them evenly. As she did this she started humming deep in her throat the opposite tones for the Canticle of Hidden

Dreams of the Sojourner Pit Below All That Would Sleep Eternal. Whereas that canticle was taught to initiates as a way to prepare them to join the Chorus of the Hallowed Dead in their Dreamings, reversing the tones, she hoped, would spur her mind to be awakened from any sort of dream or falseness that might be influencing her. Because although she was not sure exactly what was wrong, she was very, *very* sure that something was indeed fucking wrong.

The bitterness from the bone dust filled her mouth and began to trickle down the back of her throat as she continued to hum the complex arrangement of tones. As she finished the last note she could feel her wisdom teeth continuing to carry the vibrations like a meat-bound tuning fork, and one by one the motion spread to the rest of her teeth and through her jawbone and up into her skull until it felt like her eyes would vibrate themselves into jelly.

Then the vibrations in her skull melded together in a rush that sent a cold chill down the nape of her neck and into the top of her spinal column.

Malachia remembered the rest.

She remembered waking and the church being deserted. She remembered the Carrion Oak and the melting man at the typewriter. She remembered the L I И D A and their teeth and the falling into darkness. DARKNESS.

Malachia swallowed several times to try and work the bitterness out of her mouth but only ended up having to swallow a mouthful of acrid, bone-laced spit.

'You're not the Benefactrix,' she stated plainly, her voice flat and cold. 'Who? What are you?'

The space around the figure of Definitely-Not-Girlfriend-Benefactrix-But-Maybe-Evil-Benefactrix contracted and then dilated outwards with motes of darkness starting to drip from its robes, but still the figure said nothing.

Gritting her teeth, Malachia scrambled to her feet to stand on the seat of the dome-top throne she had been sitting on. She managed to bark her shin against the cold alabaster material of the throne's arm but just sucked at her teeth angrily and used the pain to sharpen her focus even more. She was

definitely awake now and whatever this thing was, it wasn't going to get in the way of her following the Carrion Oak's directions to the next plane of existence or wherever it was she had been headed before falling into the darkness.

The darkness. Malachia narrowed her eyes as she noticed the amount of inky-black-moted darkness dripping from Definitely-Not-Girlfriend-Benefactrix-But-Maybe-Evil-Benefactrix's robes. Coincidence? *I fall into darkness. Now this thing that keeps showing up in this fake version of the Congregation of the Hallowed Unspoken is dripping darkness.* She had never been that great at maths but she could add one darkness plus one darkness and get ... one ... darkness. Yeah. Fuck this Definitely-Not-Girlfriend-Benefactrix-But-Maybe-Evil-Benefactrix and not in the fun sort of way.

Unless ...

No, Malachia, focus! she barked at herself, and held up the handful of bone dust before fixing the figure in her gaze and spitting out one word at a time through clenched teeth.

'WHAT. THE. ACTUAL. FUCK. ARE. YOU. BITCH?'

With each word she opened a finger of her fist until she had released all of the bone dust into the air to swirl a yellow haze in the wind currents. For a moment the dust did exactly what she'd thought it would, falling down in a plume, but then Malachia barked three words that felt like they were blistering the inside of her lips and gums and brought both her hands around in a violent arc to clap directly in front of her. The cloud of bone dust shot out in a coruscating wave that hung in the air like a murky walkway.

A low, static-filled shriek began to rise from the depths of Definitely-Not-Girlfriend-Benefactrix-But-Maybe-Evil-Benefactrix's robes but Malachia was done waiting around for answers. She leapt from the throne to land on the bone-dust walkway. She charged towards D.N.G.B.B.M.E.B. with a *you have most assuredly fucked up and now will reap the consequences* look in her eyes.

'ThEy THat WAit WiTHOUt wOUlD GiVE YoU All THiS anD

MORE. WhY DO YOU sEEk UNHAPPIN—' the spectre began to intone, obviously winding up for some sort of portentous declamation, but Malachia slammed into it, toppling them both off the spire's pinnacle and hurtling towards the ground.

Malachia had expected the figure to feel more or less like the Benefactrix would have beneath her robes but instead it gave way at her collision with the liquid resistance of a sack of organs. Malachia could see that her hands were once again the slightly yellow and with-ered flesh of someone far past the first stages of a novitiate and not as smooth and wholly human as they had been in the vicious, or memories . . . or what-ever it was that this D.N.G.B.B.M.E.B. had been trying to trap them inside of.

'Sorry, sister,' Malachia snarled as she dug her hands into the robes and with a vicious yank ripped them open to reveal . . . more swirling darkness.

This darkness looked to be spotted with stars or some sort of lights deep inside it. She couldn't tell exactly; it all looked like she was peering through a window smeared with Vaseline, but to

be fair, hurtling towards the ground while wrestling a doppelgänger of your missing skeleton lover wasn't really the most ideal setting for identifying foreign objects. Looking over its shoulder, her eyes widened at the sight rushing up to meet her of the jabby pinnacle of one of the roving anchorites[28] in their nine-legged stone capsules that had continually roamed the outer courtyards of the church in perpetual prayer but now stood still, seconds away from impaling them. Gnashing her teeth, Malachia tightened her grip on D.N.G.B.B.M.E.B.'s robe with one hand, and with the other thrust up towards the sky, she let her fingers contort, the bones of the forefinger and pinky snapping in her rush, into the position of the Station of Penitent and Steadfast Sundering which normally would have been used for the care of the deeper Ossuaries beneath the chapel

---

[28] Or so everyone assumed. Part of being walled inside an autonomous walking stone cell is that you could be praying, sleeping, cranking one out or just mouldering away in the corner, who was to know?

SS DARKNESS DARKNESS DARKNESS DARKNESS DARKNESS DARKNESSDARKNESS DARKN
SS DARKNESS DARKNESS DARKNESS DARKNESS DARKNESS DARKNESSDARKNESS DARKN
SS DARKNESS DARKNESS DARKNESS DARKNESS DARKNESS DARKNESSDARKNESS DARKN
SS DARKNESS DARKNESS DARKNESS DARKNESS DARKNESS DARKNESSDARKNESS DARKN

and the containment of what occasionally grew there, but in this case all it did was blast her backwards and into the roiling darkness within the robes. The last thing Malachia heard before passing completely into that darkness was D.N.G.B.B.M.E.B. shrieking, 'Nooo, WhY wOuLd YoU leAVe aLl ThiSSssss happINe—'

And then she was plunging through darkness . . . AGAIN.

SS DARKNESS DARKNESS DARKN
SS DARKNESS DARKNESS DARKN
SS DARKNESS DARKNESS DARKN
SS DARKNESS DARKNESS DARKN
SS DARKNESS DARKNESS DARKN
SS DARKNESS DARKNESS DARKN
SS DARKNESS DARKNESS DARKN
SS DARKNESS DARKNESS DARKN
SS DARKNESS DARKNESS DARKN
SS DARKNESS DARKNESS DARKN
SS DARKNESS DARKNESS DARKN
SS DARKNESS DARKNESS DARKN
SS DARKNESS DARKNESS DARKN

ESS DARKNESS DARKNESS DARKNESS DARKNESS DARKNESS DARKNESSDARKNESS DARKN
ESS DARKNESS DARKNESS DARKNESS DARKNESS DARKNESS DARKNESSDARKNESS DARKN
ESS DARKNESS DARKNESS DARKNESS DARKNESS DARKNESS DARKNESSDARKNESS DARKN
ESS DARKNESS DARKNESS DARKNESS DARKNESS DARKNESS DARKNESSDARKNESS DARKN
ESS DARKNESS DARKNESS DARKNESS DARKNESS DARKNESS DARKNESSDARKNESS DARKN
ESS DARKNESS DARKNESS DARKNESS DARKNESS DARKNESS DARKNESSDARKNESS DARKN
ESS DARKNESS DARKNESS DARKNESS DARKNESS DARKNESS DARKNESSDARKNESS DARKN
ESS DARKNESS DARKNESS DARKNESS DARKNESS DARKNESS DARKNESSDARKNESS DARKN
ESS DARKNESS DARKNESS DARKNESS DARKNESS DARKNESS DARKNESSDARKNESS DARKN
ESS DARKNESS DARKNESS DARKNESS DARKNESS DARKNESS DARKNESSDARKNESS DARKN
ESS DARKNESS DARKNESS DARKNESS DARKNESS DARKNESS DARKNESSDARKNESS DARKN
ESS DARKNESS DARKNESS DARKNESS DARKNESS DARKNESS DARKNESSDARKNESS DARKN
ESS DARKNESS DARKNESS DARKNESS DARKNESS DARKNESS DARKNESSDARKNESS DARKN
ESS DARKNESS DARKNESS DARKNESS DARKNESS DARKNESS DARKNESSDARKNESS DARKN
ESS DARKNESS DARKNESS DARKNESS DARKNESS DARKNESS DARKNESSDARKNESS DARKN
ESS DARKNESS DARKNESS DARKNESS DARKNESS DARKNESS DARKNESSDARKNESS DARKN
ESS DARKNESS DARKNESS DARKNESS DARKNESS DARKNESS DARKNESSDARKNESS DARKN
ESS DARKNESS DARKNESS DARKNESS DARKNESS DARKNESS DARKNESSDARKNESS DARKN
ESS DARKNESS DARKNESS DARKNESS DARKNESS DARKNESS DARKNESSDARKNESS DARKN
ESS DARKNESS DARKNESS DARKNESS DARKNESS DARKNESS DARKNESSDARKNESS DARKN
ESS DARKNESS DARKNESS DARKNESS DARKNESS DARKNESS DARKNESSDARKNESS DARKN
ESS DARKNESS DARKNESS DARKNESS DARKNESS DARKNESS DARKNESSDARKNESS DARKN
ESS DARKNESS DARKNESS DARKNESS DARKNESS DARKNESS DARKNESSDARKNESS DARKN
ESS DARKNESS DARKNESS DARKNESS DARKNESS DARKNESS DARKNESSDARKNESS DARKN

DARKNESS DARKNESSDARKNESS DARKNESS
DARKNESS DARKNESSDARKNESS DARKNESS
DARKNESS DARKNESSDARKNESS DARKNESS
DARKNESS DARKNESSDARKNESS DARKNESS
DARKNESS DARKNESS DARKNESS DARKNESS
DARKNESS DARKNESSDARKNESS DARKNESS
DARKNESS DARKNESSDARKNESS DARKNESS
DARKNESS DARKNESSDARKNESS DARKNESS
DARKNESS DARKNESSDARKNESS DARKNESS
DARKNESS DARKNESS DARKNESS DARKNESS
DARKNESS DARKNESSDARKNESS DARKNESS
DARKNESS DARKNESSDARKNESS DARKNESS
DARKNESS DARKNESSDARKNESS DARKNESS
DARKNESS DARKNESSDARKNESS DARKNESS
DARKNESS DARKNESS DARKNESS DARKNESS
DARKNESS DARKNESSDARKNESS DARKNESS
DARKNESS DARKNESSDARKNESS DARKNESS
DARKNESS DARKNESSDARKNESS DARKNESS
DARKNESS DARKNESSDARKNESS DARKNESS
DARKNESS DARKNESS DARKNESS DARKNESS
DARKNESS DARKNESSDARKNESS DARKNESS
DARKNESS DARKNESSDARKNESS DARKNESS
DARKNESS DARKNESSDARKNESS DARKNESS
DARKNESS DARKNESSDARKNESS DARKNESS
DARKNESS DARKNESS DARKNESS DARKNESS
DARKNESS DARKNESSDARKNESS DARKNESS
DARKNESS DARKNESSDARKNESS DARKNESS
DARKNESS DARKNESSDARKNESS DARKNESS
DARKNESS DARKNESSDARKNESS DARKNESS
DARKNESS DARKNESS DARKNESS DARKNESS
DARKNESS DARKNESSDARKNESS DARKNESS
DARKNESS Malachia saw movement before her, the

darkness tesselating like tall grass moved by an unseen lurker DARKNESS DARKNESS DARKNESS darkness darkness DARKNESS DARKNESS DARKNESS DARKNESS DARKNESS DARKNESS DARKNESS darkness darkness darkness darkness darkness DARKNESS DARKNESSDARKNESS DARKNESSDARKNESS DARKNESS DARKNESS DARKNESS DARKNESS DARKNESS DARKNESS DARKNESS DARKNESS DARKNESS DARKNESS darkness darkness DARKNESS DARK-NESS DARKNESS DARKNESS DARKNESS DARK-NESS DARKNESS darkness darkness darkness darkness darkness DARKNESS DARKNESSDARKNESS DARKNESSDARKNESS DARKNESS DARKNESS DARKNESS DARKNESS DARKNESS DARKNESS DARKNESS DARKNESS DARKNESS darkness dark-ness DARKNESS DARKNESS DARKNESS DARK-NESS DARKNESS DARKNESS DARKNESS darkness darkness darkness darkness darkness DARKNESS DARK-NESSDARKNESS DARKNESSDARKNESS DARK-NESS DARKNESS DARKNESS DARKNESS DARKNESS DARKNESS DARKNESS DARKNESS DARKNESS darkness darkness DARKNESS DARK-NESS DARKNESS DARKNESS DARKNESS DARK-NESS DARKNESS darkness darkness darkness darkness darkness The Carrion Oak sat planted but its roots were dry and exposed; its corpses no longer hung around it but attached themselves suckling at its roots like hungry larvae emerging from the husk their mother had lain them within DARKNESS DARKNESSDARKNESS DARKNESS DARKNESS DARKNESS DARKNESS DARK-NESS DARKNESS DARKNESS DARKNESS DARK-NESS DARKNESS DARKNESS darkness darkness

DARKNESS DARKNESS DARKNESS DARKNESS
DARKNESS DARKNESS DARKNESS DARKNESS
DARKNESS DARKNESS DARKNESS DARKNESS
DARKNESS DARKNESS DARKNESS DARKNESS
DARKNESS DARKNESS DARKNESS DARKNESS
DARKNESS DARKNESS darkness darkness darkness
darkness darkness DARKNESS DARKNESSDARKNESS
DARKNESS DARKNESS DARKNESS DARKNESS
DARKNESS DARKNESS DARKNESSDARKNESS
DARKNESS DARKNESS DARKNESS DARKNESS
DARKNESS DARKNESS DARKNESS DARKNESS
DARKNESS darkness darkness DARKNESS DARKNESS
DARKNESS DARKNESS DARKNESS DARKNESS
DARKNESS darkness darkness darkness darkness darkness
DARKNESS DARKNESS DARKNESS DARKNESS
DARKNESS DARKNESS DARKNESS DARKNESS
DARKNESS DARKNESS DARKNESS DARKNESS
DARKNESS DARKNESS darkness darkness DARKNESS
DARKNESS DARKNESS DARKNESS DARKNESS
DARKNESS darkness darkness darkness darkness darkness
DARKNESS DARKNESSDARKNESS DARKNESS-
DARKNESS DARKNESS DARKNESS DARKNESS
DARKNESS DARKNESS DARKNESS DARKNESS
DARKNESS DARKNESS darkness darkness DARKNESS
DARKNESS DARKNESS Malachia could hear breathing, a
low wet gurgle like gristle and blood in a slit throat DARKNESS
DARKNESS DARKNESS DARKNESS darkness darkness
darkness darkness darkness DARKNESS DARKNESS
DARKNESS DARKNESSDARKNESS DARKNESS
DARKNESS DARKNESS DARKNESS DARKNESS
DARKNESS DARKNESS DARKNESS DARKNESS
darkness darkness DARKNESS DARKNESS DARKNESS

DARKNESS DARKNESS DARKNESS DARKNESS
darkness darkness darkness darkness darkness DARKNESS
DARKNESS DARKNESS DARKNESSDARKNESS
DARKNESS DARKNESS DARKNESS DARKNESS
DARKNESS DARKNESS DARKNESS DARKNESS
DARKNESS darkness darkness DARKNESS DARKNESS
DARKNESS DARKNESS DARKNESS DARKNESS
DARKNESS darkness darkness darkness darkness darkness
DARKNESS DARKNESS DARKNESS DARKNESS
DARKNESS DARKNESS DARKNESS DARKNESS
DARKNESS DARKNESS DARKNESS DARKNESS
DARKNESS DARKNESS DARKNESS DARKNESS

The darkness changed.

Before it had been a tactile, living thing. Like tar that, if
you opened your mouth, would roll in to fill you or a dark
velvet glove that brushed your lips waiting for the slightest
chance to pry your mouth open and find its way inside. Now
it had shades and Malachia could see vague shapes around
her. Her body still felt like it was alone amidst a static, recur-
sive nothingness but now at least she had SHAPES.

The darkness continued to become more mottled with varie-
gated levels of black and grey until suddenly she felt something
hard beneath her ass and realised she must be sitting down.
Until that moment she would not have been able to tell you in
what position her body was in the void because without sight
or touch or sound it was impossible to chart out the geography
of her anatomy. But now she was definitely sitting.

She felt two hard bars running up her back to terminate in
a flat object, and when she swung her legs backwards they
contacted a crossbar. Okay, this was definitely a chair and not
some sort of ledge or shelf. Next she reached out in front of

her, careful not to overbalance and tumble out of the chair into possibly another interminable fall through nothingness. Her hands contacted a flat solid surface running horizontally directly in front of her.

The instant her nerves made this discovery, the darkness sped up its rate of change, and as she watched it became like a black mist being burned away by the sunlight or maybe more like a cocoon being unwrapped by some unseen Entity. *Mist is probably way more likely*, she thought to herself as the last of the darkness drifted off into oblivion and she saw where she was.

She was sitting at an old battered wooden desk. In fact, after only a moment of scrutiny she recognised it as the desk that the man had been typing at in the Quarter of Dust Fountains. The typewriter and papers were all gone although the top of the desk was heavily stained and gouged. Next she noticed that she was in a concrete basin or probably a swimming pool. It was stained with disuse and grime, and looking down she saw that her feet were in about two inches of green dirty water that had collected in the deep end along with a raft of rotten leaves, cigarette butts and beer bottles.

Malachia guessed this was still better than L I И D Ɑ A's plan of sacrificing her in that tiled abattoir beneath the city of Silence to whatever Power it was that had a hand in the Foundationals' absence. What had they called it? Those Without In the Endless Night? That was definitely a new one for her. Not to mention the insanity of Definitely-Not-Girlfriend-Benefactrix-But-Maybe-Evil-Benefactrix trying to trap her in what she had thought would be happy memories. Maybe next time she shouldn't let the living shadow doppelgänger be in charge of crafting a memory trap? This had to be better than that! Marginally, marginally better than that. It could be her new motto.

'On a quest to find all the missing beings of Silence one marginally better scenario at a time' just rolled off the tongue.

Looking up past the concrete walls and the tiled lip that ran around the pool, she saw a chain-link fence that bowed outwards and through that a long building with a balcony and identical doors and windows spaced all down its length. Off to the left, the building continued but towering over it was a sign that she could only see bits of: burnt-out, angular neon and two tall if rangy palm trees.

So definitely not in Silence anymore, she mused to herself as she turned her attention back down to the desk. The main tray drawer was missing entirely, but to its right, the uppermost shallow drawer had survived and was open just an inch or so. *Well, I'm sure that's no coincidence*, she thought as she reached over to pull it the rest of the way open . . . and stopped with shock as she did. Her right hand, the one that showed the physical marks of her novitiate vows and the sainted bones beneath the barely visibly skein of skin, was now clad in mortal skin and meat as her left one was. She could still see the bones but that was only because they were drawn onto her forearm and the back of her hand. No, wait . . . She licked her thumb and rubbed at the bones furiously; they were tattooed onto her or some other permanent method. She felt a wave of sadness at this loss. She had worked hard and faithfully in her novitiate and she had been proud, perhaps unseemingly so, at her physical display of progress towards sainthood. Was this just because she had stepped through into another place? Almost no one in Silence was from Silence so that really didn't make sense. Or had the darkness somehow eaten away at her hallowedness and left just this taunting reminder behind? She gripped her hand tightly and rubbed harder, feeling the skin begin to become raw beneath her thumb. 'Get a grip, Malachia. No use crying over

spilled remnants of undead sainthood,' she chided herself before deliberately releasing her right hand and straightening her spine in her chair. If she did her errand for the Carrion Oak successfully, then the Benefactrix and all the other hierophants and members of the Congregation would be back in Silence even before she was and would know what to do when she arrived. So that was all the self-pity she was going to allow herself. She wiped roughly at her cheeks where some condensation from her trip through the darkness must have accumulated and once again addressed herself to opening the drawer.

Inside was a short stack of paper. It had been printed upon instead of handwritten and the paper was a dingy yellow. The words on the paper were clear enough and Malachia made an annoyed *HRRRmm* in the base of her throat as she read through all the contents, in which her name featured prominently.

Apparently it was some sort of new-hire contract for an establishment called Printed Matter and she was going to be their newest employee.

'Well, what do we have here?' Malachia heard a firm but soft-spoken voice ask from above her.

19

Noah

Who was I kidding? I can't do this! Noah's brain screamed. He had been mostly fine until this point. Svenn had walked him to the door in an oddly formal move like he was his prom date or something. Halfway to the door and its small galaxy of cartoon stickers, Noah had heard someone calling out to them, something about an open jaw and a Ninth Moon but it was garbled, like he was hearing the words underwater, and Svenn had put a firm hand on his shoulder and pushed him forward, saying something about taking care of visitors while he took care of clients. Noah hadn't really been paying attention as he focused on what he was going to try and say to sell fucking advertising space in a newsprint to some sort of creature. *No, not creature*, he reminded himself, *Mrs Galloway. You have to think of her as Mrs Galloway with two odd but precocious children or this won't work at all.*

And then he was through the door and in the middle of the jungle of the apartment's living room. The evidence of the previous encounter was non-existent. Everything was the perfectly charming if overwhelming effusion of green that it had been before, and the two children, who were definitely not some sort of anglerfish husk lure, nope not at all, were nowhere to be seen.

Noah felt something tugging beneath the skin in the cleft of his chest just below his collarbone like a slow pulse that shifted in a pattern that made no sense to him. But the moment it finished sending its very weird-feeling meat Morse code or whatever it was doing, a sunny but languorously drowsy voice rang from the back room behind all the sprays of fern branches and creeping vines.

'I'm back here taking care of the laundry. If you want to talk, you're going to need to come back and see me. I don't have time to stop for salespeople really, so much to do.'

The voice sounded remarkably like the mom from *The Dick Van Dyke Show,* which was a weird thing for him to have kept in his brain, but then again, there really was no accounting for what the brain decided to hang onto and what it let wither.

'Um, Mrs Galloway?' he began weakly but then after taking a deep breath, 'I would be more comfortable if we could meet out here in the living room. I'm sure Printed Matter has some sort of policy about not conducting business in clients' bedrooms. I could help you fold laundry while we talk?'

He was about to go on with his laundry-folding credentials but he found his mouth was starting to water and fill with saliva that tasted sour and briny. The room around him was beginning to get fuzzy or maybe the plants and walls were all growing fuzz; they were definitely undulating in and out like the mouth of a speaker when the bass is turned so low you can barely hear it but instead feel it in your bones and organs.

He had a brief but intense moment of vertigo and then suddenly found himself nose to leaf with a fern that filled his entire vision, and he couldn't help but marvel at the spiralling geometry of the fern's petioles that sprang from its many-rayed stalks. How had he known the word petiole? He was

here to sell ad space not because he was a botanist and Mrs Gallow . . . MRS GALLOWAY!

Noah jerked upright from the mass of fronds and realised he was no longer in the living room.

His eyes stung like they used to when he spent too much time with them open underwater at the public pool in the summer, a burning that wasn't altogether unpleasant, and his vision wavered for a moment like it too had been washed with something that clung to the corneas. Blinking furiously Noah put a hand up in front of his face like he was shielding his vision from a non-existent bright light. Then suddenly it cleared like whatever had been filming his eyes dissolved into nothing, or more likely his eyes and brain stem finally finished translating what they were seeing into something that he could somewhat understand . . . kinda . . . sorta . . .

He was standing a foot inside of the doorway to the apartment's bedroom and in front of him Mrs Galloway sat on her bed folding laundry. She was a large-boned woman with a pleasingly bluff face and a well-muscled frame that would have been just as at home hauling pipe on an oil rig as it was doing her current activity. She was dressed in what Noah knew to be a housecoat only because of his extensive BBC classic viewing habits, and her hair was in a corona of bright pink plastic rollers. Her legs were splayed out from the edge of the bed and on her feet was a pair of very worn Coca-Cola polar bear slippers, each animal holding a small plastic bottle in paws that were comically undersized in proportion to the bear's plush head. That was where the veneer of normalcy stopped.

Noah saw that where he had at first thought Mrs Galloway was sitting on the bed, he had been wrong, very wrong. She was in fact fused . . . or more accurately growing, melding into it. Her entire back half was a mess of gnarled, glistening greens

that flowed from her front half, which sat much like a hospital gown of a human shell over her true form. The delineation mark down her side from fabric to green meat . . . or bark . . . wasn't smooth; it was a ragged cross-section of fabric ingrown into meat, spokes of short branches and thorns pushing through flesh and fabric alike to hold her human visage in place. Behind her the rest of her body continued to flow over the bed and up the walls, at first a solid, undulating pelt of green with short, clover-like fur or grass blades coating it, and as it got farther out, onto the ceiling, it began to thin and branch out into spindly fingers of vine tendrils that looked like nothing so much as an extended map of a nervous system freed from the cage of a body and spreading out to its heart's content.

Her long, capable fingers were nimbly and neatly folding in half the now emptied-out husk of one of the blonde children. Noah could see its deflated head flopping off the edge of her lap, and the gaping eyehole stared up at him empty and cavernous.

Noah now saw that there was a row of children husks lining the bed. Mrs Galloway carefully folded the child in half again, neatly tucking its head into the back somehow to keep it from unfolding before setting it aside and picking up another one. No, not picking up; she was tearing another child from the side of the bed. They were attached to it, and where they were torn away the bed briefly oozed a clear yellow liquid before the rent sealed itself up.

Then she looked up at Noah.

'Young man, as you can see I do not have time for idle chit-chatting. As much as I would enjoy a break, this place will fall apart without me looking after it. So if what you have to say is so important that you have come uninvited into my house

twice in the same day . . .' Here Noah thought he saw the edge of her lips briefly twitch into a sly grin. 'Where did you say you were from again? If you're from either that horrible dry cleaners around the corner or the Jehovah's Witness Centre on Fifth and Main, you can walk your little heinie out of here right now and save your breath. I didn't move to this dimension to serve The Thing That Sleeps beneath either of those places and you can tell them that I said that. Not going back there and you can't make me.'

Mrs Galloway was shredding the skin husk that was on her lap in anxious movements like you might see someone peeling the label off of a soda bottle or unconsciously tearing a receipt into small pieces while they talked. A piece of flattened eyeball with the lid attached and fluttering stuck to the back of one of her hands, and all around the floor bits of hair and facial features lay in a drift.

'Are you okay?' Noah asked hesitantly, tensing all his muscles to jump backwards out of her reach if this nervous tic was presaging some greater explosion of violence. As hard as he tried to just keep his voice level and his eyes on her face, he couldn't help but waver on the end of 'okay' and his eyes darted down to look at the child confetti once again.

'Oh, oh dear, just look at this mess,' Mrs Galloway chirped morosely as she followed his gaze to her lap. 'See, this sort of thing is why I don't have time for salespeople. Now I am going to have to start all over with that one. Do you know how much effort it takes to grow one of those? They don't sell seeds at the Home Depot. I can tell you that much, and what's more, playgrounds just aren't as ripe for Harvesting as they used to be . . .' Her words trailed off as some of his earlier sales pitch finally got through. 'Wait, did you say Printed Matter? Printed Matter sent you?'

All along the walls and the bed the green pelt and tendrils that grew out of Mrs Galloway's back began to rustle and vibrate. The large mass of her body that covered the bed and most of the wall grew in size like it was puffing itself up to be more intimidating. A hissing noise escaped from the seams where the Mrs Galloway husk was attached to what Noah was now thinking of as the real Mrs Galloway, although to refer to it that way out loud would be rude, seeing as she had gone through so much effort to present this other, more human face for him.

Mrs Galloway's eyes narrowed and she dusted her lap off, sending the child husk pieces scattering like they were some trimmings from a coupon-clipping session. In one fluid movement she was standing, or more accurately being held up, and looming over him by the trunk of her non-human body, like a snail's body stretching out from its shell.

'What does Linda want?' she trilled, the tendrils whipping around behind her in time to her anxiety. 'I keep paying my monthly advertising budget. It's not my fault they keep coming back in the mail. They can't call the Contractors over this! I haven't even gotten a warning letter in the mail. Don't they have to send me some sort of notice and then a final notice? This isn't fair! You can't make me go back to Silence over this, I won't let you! I have RIGHTS!'

Throughout this increasingly agitated speech, Mrs Galloway's movements also became more upset. Her body surged over to the back corner of the room while she was talking and then returned with a stack of envelopes held in one hand that were neatly wrapped in a coiled vine tendril. Her pupils dilated and the orbs that were beneath the human mask were beginning to bulge out through their openings, splitting the skin until the tear met in the middle and a flap over her nose

fell down, exposing a wet and pulsing patch of skin that was pockmarked with what looked like a hive of some sort. Deep, regular pits in the skin, inside of which small, white, grub-like appendages bulged forward to wildly lick at the air before receding back inside the meat.

'I could stop you from telling them about me. I could stop you from telling them that I am still here. Or maybe . . . maybe I should send you back as a nice little puppet. Tell Linda about how they're wrong and I'm not going anywhere. This is my home, these are my children . . .'

Here Noah tried to interject, holding up one hand as he did. 'I think there's a misunderstanding, Mrs Galloway. Linda just sent me here to talk to you about the advertising budget. No one is saying anything about . . .'

But Mrs Galloway was not having any of it.

'Child, are you dense? The advertising budget isn't an advertising budget; it's just another name for the fees I have to pay to stay here in this delightful little moist dimension. I don't care what the rules say about time limits on corporeal existence here. I don't want to go back to that dry dusty little place, Silence. I won't go back there!'

The white grubs once again surged from the hive of her face, ripping away more of her husk until the entire face was a field of tiny maws. This time they didn't retreat after tasting the air. They continued to spool out into the space between where Mrs Galloway loomed over him and he stood rooted to the ground. The appendages slithered and snaked through the air, entangling themselves with each other; a thick yellow liquid dripped off them, spattering Noah's face and shoulders.

Noah's mind raced. This was not going as well as it could have but what else could he do but try and plough ahead? There was no doubt in his mind that if he tried to scramble

for the door, no one would ever hear from him again, except possibly as a more handsome than average Noah puppet.

So he did the only thing he could reliably do in this situation. He babbled.

And as he did he felt something filling his throat and snaking its way around the inside of his mouth to latch onto the back sides of his teeth like a meshing of slender cilia that then vibrated softly as he spoke. He knew he should be screaming in terror at this sensation, trying to reach into his mouth and scrape out whatever this was, but it just felt . . . right? Then he remembered Svenn talking about what he had left inside of Noah being something that would help, and he almost started laughing then and there in exasperated understanding, but instead he just continued letting the thing inside of him push a word around inside his mouth here and there, subtly tweaking what he was saying even as he said it.

'Well, first off, I really want to thank you for bringing this billing issue to our attention,' he began as the grub-like pseudopodia spread out around him. 'I . . . uh . . . we can take a look at those bills for you *personally* and make sure that Linda deals with them before the end of the workday today. Also I have been uh . . . authorised . . .'

Several of the grubs brushed his forehead, and the skin where they touched burned for a second then faded to a surprisingly pleasing tingle. Noah bit the inside of his cheek till his mouth filled with blood to make sure he did not flinch and instead took a step forward towards the main body of Mrs Galloway, holding out his hand for the bundle of bills, hoping that he wasn't just stepping into a curtain of tentacles that would digest him unceremoniously.

'. . . I have been authorised to offer you a first-month credit when you resubscribe for your first two months of ad space, a

limited-time offer.' He continued hurriedly, 'Of course, this offer is contingent on me being able to go back to the office and file all the appropriate paperwork.'

At first it did seem like he had miscalculated but then at the last possible moment the pseudopodia grubs darted away from his skin in three jerking motions like a school of fish avoiding an obstacle. He emerged from their mass to find Mrs Galloway standing with one hand on the bedpost, which, seeing as it was all actually made of her camouflaged body, was probably the same posture for her as someone else standing with a hand upon their hip. In her other hand she held the bundle of bills, not quite presenting them to him but also not holding them back. She raised one eyebrow, which now, with most of her face husk from the eyes to the chin torn away, was quite an arresting look. The grubs had now all retreated into their hive and only came out in small rhythmic peeks that coincided with her speaking. Like a vocal wave-form made of white, gristly flesh.

'You think you can resolve this? It would make sense that it was some sort of clerical error on the part of Printed Matter and . . . *Linda*. I always pay my bills on time and am very aware of the late bill penalties. I think it would be very wise for Linda to not push this matter any further. Neither of us will like what happens if they do. So yes, yes, I think if you can have Linda resolve this and make sure that the records show that I was not delinquent, that it was Printed Matter's fault, then yes, maybe there won't be any need for Hollowing you today? Unless you're curious about the process? I do have many who come to me to be relieved of the burden of inner meat.'

Noah swallowed the sour saliva that was pooling in his mouth at the mention of inner meat and was grateful for any sort of moisture that helped his suddenly cracked and dry

throat. His fingers felt numb and he could hear his blood ringing in his ears but he managed to get out, 'Of course, ma'am, I will take care of all this personally, and just to be clear we are talking about the deluxe A-12 package with a half-sheet text and half-sheet image, correct?'

He fumbled in his shirt pocket with his left hand for a pen he knew was not there and with the right reached out to receive the packet of bills. Mrs Galloway did not release them at first and instead stood there holding onto them, looking him directly in the eyes. Well, Noah thought she was looking him in the eyes, as much as a mass of pits in a mound of meat and bone, each with small grubs peeking from their openings, could be said to stare at anything. But then she released the bills and seemed to shrink in on herself as she returned to her position of sitting on her bed.

Then her hands were feeling around absent-mindedly for the scraps of child confetti that still littered the ground around the frame and she began to idly stick them onto her face. At first it was a nightmare collage of ears where mouths should be, a bright blue eye for a chin, patches of white-blonde hair for cheeks, but after a few moments of her smoothing them into place they were suddenly her face again. Noah had not been able to see them morph into Mrs Galloway's features; they were just meat puzzle pieces one moment and then Mrs Galloway the next.

It was shocking how quickly he was getting used to things that by rights should have crashed his brain to its boot screen if not broken it completely. But then again people got used to all sorts of fucked-up shit at their jobs that supposedly sane beings would never put up with. Was this really all that different from being told they had to reach down into a grease trap without any sort of protection to clear out a clog? Or hiding

in a walk-in freezer to cry for so long that when they came out they had frost on their eyelashes? Not really. In fact, in comparison to some chefs he had worked for, Mrs Galloway was actually polite. Possibly a carnivorous plant deity, monster, thing . . . but still sorta polite.

Later he would barely remember walking back through the living room bowery using every inch of his willpower to not look behind him, but he must have because suddenly he was standing on the balcony, the slanting, late-afternoon sun in his eyes and his back pressed to the shut door of Room 206.

20

Malachia

Looking up from the paperwork, Malachia saw a towering man in a navy-blue repairman's uniform complete with embroidered name patch smiling down at her with a relaxed look about him. The now tattooed bones on her arm and hand began to tingle at his nearness and Malachia couldn't help but smile at this. So they weren't a total loss after all. She was going to have to take them for a test drive soon to see if everything worked like it had before. The man continued to look down at her for a few moments more before speaking.

'You can call me Svenn, most of the people . . . and things around here do. But . . .' – and here he paused and she saw a brief look of yearning cross his face – '. . . if my nose does not deceive me, and, friend, it never does, you are lately of the city of Silence? And . . .' – here he made a show of sniffing the air and then swishing his tongue around the sides of his closed mouth before continuing with a conspiratorial wink and a smile – '. . . also of the most venerable and hallowed Congregation of the Hallowed Unspoken – the tang of bone dust and restless thanoturgic Entities is unmistakable. Although there is an underlying hint of this place at your core as well?'

Malachia held his gaze and waited until he blinked, and she could tell he was about to say something to break the silence

before answering, 'Well, you seem to have me at a disadvantage both from a high-ground perspective and informational. You obviously know where I am from and there is no sense denying it even if I wanted to, which I don't. Do you also know about this?'

Here she raised the stack of paperwork before letting it fall back onto the desk.

'No, but maybe if you were to let me take a look I could help you out?' Svenn said, now from directly beside her in the pool bottom. Shit, she hadn't even heard or seen him descend from the top of the pool. She let her left hand drift down into her robe pocket, where thankfully the fingerbone was still safe and sound as she hastily but not *too* hastily stood up to put a bit of distance between her and this Svenn.

Svenn noticed the movement and held his hands up in a placating manner. 'Whoa there, cowgirl, no need to come out shooting. Just let me look this over and I'll tell you whatever it is I know about it. Traveller's honour.'

He held his right hand up in what Malachia assumed was some hexagrammatic ward that she didn't recognise with three fingers straight up and the outer two touching in the middle. She tensed her whole body for action but then Svenn just dropped the hand and leaned over the desk and began to shuffle through the papers. At first, he was looking through them with the casual hastiness of someone used to scanning documents and not really reading their entire contents, but then he slowed down and looked up at her with a sceptical expression before leafing back to the first page and starting over, this time reading every line carefully, occasionally shaking his head in either wonder or exasperation or a mix of the two, she couldn't tell.

Finally he set the papers down and gave her an appraising

look, and then glanced thoughtfully up at the balcony of the building behind them. This time Malachia was determined to wait him out but the man just continued staring up at the balcony with its row of doors, occasionally cocking his head to the side as if he could hear something she couldn't, until finally she broke and with a half-hearted stamp of her foot in the scummy water to get his attention asked, 'Well?'

Svenn turned back to her with a distracted air, almost like he had forgotten they had been talking. 'Oh yeah, right. You've apparently been hired by Printed Matter and had all your new-hire orientation waived or fast-tracked. Not entirely sure about that part, the legalese gets a little dense in places, but you definitely are now gainfully employed. It's just . . .' And here he glanced up at the balcony again and then back at her, letting his eyes wander around the pool and its contents. 'This can't be a coincidence, right? Two new employees both here at the Mansions of Silence on the same day . . . I don't think I've ever—' Here he cut himself short and looked at her sharply. 'Did you know about any of this before? What did They tell you? Are you here because of the Sunderings? How many of the Nine are left in Silence? Did C.O. send you here to help get Them back where they belong?'

Malachia opened her mouth to answer him that she had no fucking clue where she was beyond that it was where the Carrion Oak – she refused to even consider referring to it as C.O. – *needed* her to be and that she had very little interest in a new job since she already had one with the Congregation and what the hell did he mean by the Mansions of Silence?

But she surprised herself by instead just telling him simply what had happened to her up until this moment.

Svenn lost what she assumed was his normal mode of laid-back observance and whistled long and low before replying.

'Well, fuck me. That's . . . that's bad. We need to go somewhere where we can sit down and talk about this at length but right now we need to—'

He never got to finish his sentence because the door he had been fixating on burst open and a tall scruffy man came spilling out all thin limbs and clothing akimbo as he stumbled to the railing and gasped for air like he was a fish tossed ashore by a cruel and uncaring ocean.

Svenn took one look at where her gaze had fixed and then turned back to her with a grim smile that showed his perfect and very L I Ͷ ᗡ A-like teeth fully for the first time.

'Well, looks like that is going to have to wait because first things first, I need to introduce you to your new coworker.'

21

NOAMALACHINOMALOAMALNALCHIA

When nothing came crashing through the door after him, Noah wearily pushed himself back to his feet. All the anxiety and exhaustion he had been holding at bay was starting to come rushing back into his nervous system with interest to be paid, but for the moment all he could think of was, *I did it.*

Looking over the railing of the balcony walkway, he saw Svenn standing down in the mostly empty pool talking to what looked to be a girl dressed in a waist-long grey wool robe like you'd see a medieval priest wearing in pictures and apparently black cut-off jeans and sandals. Svenn gestured up at him and the girl followed his arm to where Noah was openly staring. For a brief moment Noah thought he saw the girl's features shimmer, the skin of her face shrinking in a display of rapid decay until it was shrunken on her skull with yellowed bone poking through the leathery mask. But when he blinked she was normal again. An average Caucasian girl with gothy clothes, tousled black hair and way too inquisitive eyes.

Svenn beckoned for Noah to come down to where the two of them were, and for a hot minute, Noah considered just walking down the back stairs to the El Camino and leaving town. But then he remembered the stack of overdue bills in his

hand and Svenn's ominous words about him not being able to quit. So he just stuffed them into the back pocket of his trousers and with the world-weariest sigh that a world ever did weary, waved a *yeah, yeah, I'm coming, hold your fucking horses* motion at Svenn and headed towards the front stairs.

'This better be overtime,' he groused to himself as he started to descend.

Malachia watched the figure that Svenn had just referred to as her, ugh, coworker walk along the balcony to the stairwell. At first he had been recognisable as a human, masc-presenting individual but now, as he moved past the supporting pillars of the walkway, he flickered in and out as he passed each one, the air around him condensing like he was being wrapped in gauze or something was smearing Vaseline over the lens of reality in the exact spot he was in. Then it would clear up, but now he was a stationary stand of white trees flicking in and out as they appeared further along the way; now he was himself again but a red orb masked the upper half of his body in a way that made her head ache if she tried to understand how it was possible; now he was a hound, sleek and eager, winding its way down the steps, the muscles beneath its pelt expanding and contracting with each step; then he was obscured again, all those images falling in on themselves in one violent kaleidoscope until he was standing at the edge of the pool looking down at them and she finally recognised him as the figure who had been sitting at the typewriter in the Quarter of Dust Fountains, and almost unbidden the Lament of Tangled Bones came to her lips:

'Between you and I the sea of loss, between you and I a forest of doubt, between you and I a bridge of bone and faith . . .'

Noah, looking down at her again, saw the image of a young woman stripped away till she was a skeleton of obsidian bones held together with coppery wire and funerary strips. The

bones were glowing with an internal darkness so intense he almost had to look away but instead he answered by finishing the earworm he'd had bouncing around in his head all day:

'. . . between you and I this theft of clarity held close.'

Both Malachia and Noah looked up at the same moment, their gazes drawn by an inescapable gravitational force, and above them not even twenty feet away hovered an enormous red orb that filled their view; it pulsed in time to their startled breaths and then before they could react it faded away, leaving only a rusty red ash to float down like the last remnant of a crimson snowfall.

'Well, fuck,' Malachia said, finally breaking the silence and looking between Svenn and the now completely average-appearing Noah.

Svenn only smiled back, seeming completely at ease with these events before responding in his calm drawl, 'Well, fuck indeed.'

Noah sat down hard on the edge of the pool, letting his legs dangle over as he lay back on the rough concrete border with a sigh. He could taste the ash from the red orb when he licked his lips. He was pretty sure he was lying on some sort of half-decayed pool toy but he didn't feel like he could even move, the waves of exhaustion finally hitting him one after another. He could hear someone scrambling up the side of the pool, apparently not a fan of using the ladder that was just a few feet away. After a few more muffled curse-filled moments the figure of the girl, now once again looking like just that and nothing more, stood over him, blocking out the sun so it broke around the back of her in a rayed corona that left her features a dark shadow. She seemed about to say something but then also dropped down to sit on the side of the pool beside him. The silence stretched around them and they both welcomed it,

breathing in the smell of old leaves and stagnating water. The sun was starting to think about setting but for the moment it was warm on their faces, and the sound of insects, which neither of them had noticed the absence of until just then, began to sound around them in the patches of yellowed grass that grew from the cracks in the concrete.

After a few moments, in which they both could hear Svenn shuffling things around in the desk, opening and closing drawers, she said without looking at him, instead squinting up at the sky, 'I hope you're ready for this.'

'I hope so too,' Noah replied, closing his eyes and letting his body relax back into the pebbly concrete. 'I hope so too.'

THE END

MEMO:

To: Printed Matters LLC Corporate Office
dba Corporeal ███████

From: Cold Flame LTD. dba ⚡△☿♀⚳☿

CC: The Waiter of the Choir for the
Crimson Huntress, The Facilitator of
Truths

Date: ~~The Fac transfer~~

Re: New Printed Matter Hires

It has come to the attention of the Eleven That
Lacks Two that Printed Matter, without consult to
any of those to whom it has entered into binding
accords and financial responsibilities, recently
hired two new employees that, to put it mildly,
have become a nuisance if not a hazard to our
plans for expansion. The senior partners, while
still beyond the walls of this reality, are far
from blind and are unhappy with this to the point
of suggesting a change of timetables.

Obviously none of us want that.

I want t his fixed. I don't want to have to take
the Facilitator off of his current assignment but
I will if you can't fix this LINDA

MEMO:

To: Cold Flame LTD. dba ⚭⚮⚭⚮⚭⚭

From: Printed Matters LLC Corporate Office
dba Corporeal ████████████
CC: The Waiter of the Choir for the
Crimson Huntress, The Facilitator of
Truths

Date: ~~Will tak rporate re~~

Re: Noah and Malachia are NOT a problem

First off I would like to assure the Six Whom Have
Consumed The Three that this is all under control and
is in fact a somewhat humorous clerical error if you
really think about it. I won't bore you all with the
minutia but I think this is getting blown out of
proportion. Were these two supposed to be hired as
salespeople? No. Do we know where the girl even came
from? Not really. Is it ideal that they seem to have
already begun associating with a CNTRCTR and have made
visits to four of the Anchors, three of which have
disappeared from our networks? Not really but I would
like to suggest the idea of COINCIDENCE. All our
office augurs are pointing to this being just a blip,
and likely to resolve itself. Not that I am not giving
it the full attention of most of the LINDAS (see my
previous report about the HR report on Linda
from...well HR. You know the one with the perfect
teeth?) and would like to reassure The Fifteen Who
Mourn the Loss of The Six that they have absolutely
nothing to worry about.

MEMO:

To:Printed Matters LLC Corporate Office
dba Corporeal ████████████

From: Cold Flame LTD. dba ⚇☥⚕⚉☿☊♁

CC: The Waiter of the Choir for the
Crimson Huntress, The Facilitator of
Truths

Date:

Re:Structural Changes and Cutbacks

We are not pleased.

The Two Who Have Acquired The Seven are worried.

The Facilitator of Truths is being reassigned and
transferred to take care of this.

We will talk about this in person on Friday at the
corporate retreatLIMUA.

Acknowledgements

The author would like to thank in no particular order, unless *you* can see the Order That Waits Hungering Beneath, but what is he saying that would be a silly idea. There is no binding occult order to these names. Do not listen to his *unfounded* mewling . . . anyhoo;

Annie Koyama, Mathew Clayton, Marissa Constantinou, Elizabeth Garner, Hayley Shepherd, DeAndra Lupu, Mark Ecob, Jack Smyth, David Demchuk, Ellie Shiveley, Ingrid Bohnenkamp, Daniel & Mae Logan, Kellan Szpara, Meg Ellison, Gemma Amor, Wendy N. Wagner, dave ring, coffee, John Wiswell, Maëlle Doliveux, the Whispering Void Behind My Fridge, Richard Kadrey, Aaron Reynolds, SICKOF-WOLVES, Sam J. Miller, Cam Collins, Steve Shell, Peter Chiyowski, a growing sense of doom, mountennui, John Darnielle, Marissa Lingen, David Bazan, Gordon B. White, A. Lizard, Diana Krueger, the CARRION OAK, Caitlin Starling, Tania Chen, Leigh Harlen, Marty Cahill, Joe Koch, 4th Street Fantasy, Mitski, Sofia Ajram, HORSES in general (can never be too safe), Trevor Henderson, Whitney Moore, Casey Lucas, Meghan Ball, Alex Woodroe, Levon Jihanian, Jonathan Sims, Alasdair Stuart.

Unbound is the world's first crowdfunding publisher, established in 2011.

We believe that wonderful things can happen when you clear a path for people who share a passion. That's why we've built a platform that brings together readers and authors to crowdfund books they believe in – and give fresh ideas that don't fit the traditional mould the chance they deserve.

This book is in your hands because readers made it possible. Everyone who pledged their support is listed below. Join them by visiting unbound.com and supporting a book today.

Malachi Abell
Sadiya Abjani
Sophie Achinger
John Adams
Joachim Adomeit
Zane Alaniz
John Alvarez
Micah Anderson
Jane Andreasen
Robert Andrews
Daniel Andrlik
Corvyn Appleby
Albert Aretz
James Arriola
Liz Artemis
Tresi Arvizo
Tom Atkinson
Jake Audette
Sarah Avampato
Jocelyn Awakens
James Aylett
Andrew Baker
Kathryn Baker
Sarah Balster-Gee
Chris Barnes
Andres Barquero
Ashur Barre
Mitchel Barry
Andrew Bartelsmeyer
Anderson Bass
Liz Bastian
Light Bates
Lyria Battey
Alice Bea
Moira Becker
Tina Bee
Adam Behr
Tricksy Belden

Alex Bell
Knight Bellamy
Angel Belsey
Brittany Belvette
Will Biby
James Big
Ben Bird Person
Andrew
	Birmingham
Gustav Black
Christopher Blake
Bridh Blanchard
Trie Blasingame
Trish Bocklage
Courtney Bodin
Christoph
	Boigner
Megan Boing
Wendy Bolm
Olox Borg
Veronica Bosley
Alex Bowie
Jennifer Bravo
Jeremy Bray
James Breedlove
Laura Brennan
Sarah Brennan
Alice Broadribb
Amber Brokaw
Toni Brooks
Alonnis Brown
Brian Browne

Rachel Brownhill
Jonathan Bruce
Kit Bruce
Beth Buell
Emma Bull
Steven Burse
Emily Burt
Tyler Butler
Toby Buttriss
Lucky C
Nissa Campbell
Sven Camrath
Tyler Canup
Gabby
	Capitanchik
Heaven-Leigh
	Carey
Hannah Carlan
Danielle Carr
Carter
Casey Caston
Alex Caton
Kent Caudle
Kol Ceridwen
Erik CF
Kelsi Champley
Ian Chant
David Chess
Ingrid Chiles
Nicole Chilton
Elizabeth
	Christopher

Marina Cimarusti
Ophelia Ilinca
	Ciocirlan
Daniel Clancy
Bethany Clark
Tyler Clarke
Mathew Clayton
Aaron Cochran
Lisa Colburn
Louise Coles
Andrew Collins
Karmin Collins
Sarah Collins
Emory Colvin
Caitlin Compton
Jeff Constable
Amanda Cook
Harry Cooke
Kelly J Cooper
Staci Corcoran
Nicholas Cortezi
Brick Corvidae
Kaitlyn Cottrell
Joely Coulthard
Jefferson Craig
Matthew Craig
Ben Crawford
Greg Crawford
Sal Creber
Meghan Cross
Paul Cross
Hasi Crow

John Crowley
Zack Cuellar
Anna Cylkowski
Frank D
Kelly Richards
 D'Arcy-Reed
Kristin Daniel
Dave
Aidan Day
Roxane de
 Grandpré
Logan Dean
David Demchuk
Liz Denholm
Maggie Denholm
Jenny DeShields
Danielle di Pietro
Rachel Dietz
Thomas Dilligan
Dan Dillon
Wes Dirk
Clair Dittberner
Maelle Doliveux
Damon Dorsey
Calder Dougherty
Tim Dreier
Hervon Dreznor
Emily Duncan
Tyler Dzuba
Mallory Eagles
Nathaniel
 Eakman

Lincoln Eddy
Philip Eisner
Elizabeth Elliott
Kenny Endlich
Marie Enger
David Engler
Meredith Erin
David Evans
Laura Evans
Kenita Evarts
Ben Fauber
Alexia Fedail
Sarah Feld
Ricky Fenwick
Emery Ferguson
Annalise Fischer
Will Fisher
Ana Fluegel
Emily Forney
Tyver Foucault
Daniel Fox
Alan Freeman
Bill Gallagher
Daniel Arthur
 Gallagher
Marnie Galloway
Julia E. Garcia
Emi Gennis
Rory Geoghegan
Dani Georgieva
Tech Ghoul
Marina Gibbons

Maren Gibson
Grue Gilith
JS Carter Gilson
Elizabeth Giosia
Dave Goddard
Susan Godfrey
Godshaper
Kathryn Golden
Lenore Golden
Noël "Natalis"
 Gomez
Susanah Grace
Scott Graupner
Peter Gray
Scarlet Gray
Emily Green
Megan Green
Stephen Grice
Victoria Grieve
Griselda
 Grimaldo
Alli Grimes
Garrett Grimm
Corrin Grinstead
Marissa Gritter
Groovy Dead
 One
Benji Gross
Kyle Grusenski
Derek Guder
Michael
 Gwatney

Stribik András Gyula
Lily Habiba
Dorian Hadgraft
Brycen Haggard
Caran Hale
Daniel Hale
Rhias Hall
Meridith Halsey
James Hammer
Disinterested Handjob
Ian Hankins
Ash Hann
Carl Hannah
Ewan Hannay
Matt Hansen
Lee Hanten
Gillian Hardy
Leigh Harlen
Mel Harper
Scott Harris
Eamonn Harte
Hannah Harthoorn
Lorraine Hatchwell
Niki Hawes
Kari Hayes
Thomas Hayes
Plz Help
Samantha Henry

George Herbert
Sarah Hewett
Kim Hickey
Max Higgins
Ria Hill
Filip Hnízdo
Charles Hodgens
Andrew Hodgson
Alex Hofelich
Paige Holland
Jenna Holschen
Katherine Hood
Robert Hopt
Katherine House
Joshua Howlett
Jesse Huegel
Bethan Hughes
Evan Hughes
Kevin Hughes
Kirsa Hughes-Skandijs
Andrew Hungerford
Edward Ingold
Nick Ingolia
James Ingram
William Irvine
Sara Israelsson
Michael Janes
Timothy Jarvis

Kim Jarvis & Peter Tags
Sajana Jayasinghe
Will Jenkins
Kathleen Jennings
Katrina Jennings
Levon Jihanian
Jasen "Jalopy" Johns
Chris Johnson
Jamie Johnson
Shannyn Johnson
Jon & Muna
Carrie Jones
Jolene Jones
Matt Jones
Betsy Jorgensen
Billy Jorgensen
Lee Joy
Alexandra Joyner
Just a lad
Dacey Kajimura
Neal Kaplan
KAT-ATK
Kaitlyn Kauffman
Aynjel Kaye
Philip Kaye
C. Paul Keller
Kelli (The Opera Geek)
Jessica Kellogg-Kuhn

Abigail Kemske

Connor Kennedy

Evan Kennedy

Marguerite
    Kenner

Conor Kenny

Meagan Keziah

Mike Kiggins

Jennifer Kimball

Alisha King

Courtney King

Harriet Kingsport

Alex Kipenakis

Robert Kirby

Richard Knice

Jonathan Korman

Martinus Kraan

Colleen Kraudel

Robert Krause

Stephen Kropa

Diana Krueger

Eric Krul

Max Artagan
    Kunz

Christopher Kurtz

Kyraeliza

Amber L

Jay Labelle

Jennifer Lambert

Audrey Lange

Dr. Ryan Lange

Amber LaPointe

Jeremy Large

Max Larocci

Karina Larsen

Andan Lauber

Ewan Lawrie

John Leclaire

Vickie Leclerc

Simon Ledoux

Tricia-Nicole
    LeFevers

Kevin Lemke

Alison Lennie

Michael Letterle

Emma Levin

Kyle Lewis

Gracie
    Liebenstein

Myz Lilith

Elizabeth Lim

Hanna Löhman

Matthieu Loose

Emily Louise

Chris & Kara
    Love

Ryan Lower

Rob Lubow

Leigh Luna

Edward Lundborg

Clara Lystrom

Adam Lyzniak

Charlotte
    Macdonald

Electric Maenad

Kyra Maginity

Kenji
    Magrann-Wells

Jacob Mandell

Britt Marchese

Justin Marquez

John Martin

Kayla Martin

Dana Mason

Mackenzie
    Massey

Beth Mattson

Jeanne Maxwell

Doug Mayo-Wells

Brendan
    McAdams

Fiona McAlpine

Elizabeth
    McClellan

Brianna
    McCluskey,
    Hasi Crow

Cameron
    McCollam

Zach McCoy

Jane McDonnell

Sam McField

Chris McLaren

Lark McManus

Brian Meeker

Amy Meister

Kristina Meschi
Trever Metcalf
Nyssa Milburn
Ai Miller
Chris Miller
Eilidh Miller
Michelle Miller
Tony Misgen
Alexander
    Mitchell
Lauren E.
    Mitchell
Ben
    Moes-Mueller
Premee Mohamed
G Molloy
Mary Monaghan
Nadia Lee
    Monaghan
Andrew
    Montgomery
Diego Montoyer
J L Moore
Carla Morales
Naomi Morauf
Paul Moss
Henry Murdy
Hannah Murray
Michelangelo
    Muscariello
Bee Myrick
Michael Napoli

Victoria Nations
Carlo Navato
Joseph Navatto
Daniel J Neko
Drew Nelson
Lauren
    Neuburger
Ben Newcombe
Michael
    Nickelson
Ninielle
Jesse Noonan
Ryan North
Jack Nutting
Dean O'Donnell
Mallory O'Meara
Rob O'Sullivan
Mugren Ohaly
Matthew Olsen
Elizabeth Olson
Lisa Olson
Joshua ONeill
Léon
    Othenin-
    Girard
Emily, Jon and
    Axl Owen
Michael Owen
Bill Owens
Taylor Paich
Justin Palk
Tony Palumbo

John Pappas
Emily
    Park-Goldsmith
Elizabeth
    Parmeter
Ben Peake
Jared Pechacek
Fritz Pelham
Marcos Pellot
Aura Penny
Adri Peralta
Dan Peters
Else Peterson
Alex Peto
Devan Petri
Craig Phillips
Jonathan Pierce
Anna Piotrowska
Caroline Pitt
J. Kyle Pittman
Kristin Plant
Mark Plattner
Lydia Polo
Regina Powell
Kristin Pratt
Jonathan Pruitt
Pure Grey Silence
Graeme Puttock
Jessica Pyle
Kaitlyn Rak
Danielle Ramirez
Miguel Rangel

Kristin Ransom
Abby Rauscher
Inanna
   Ravenscroft
April Ray
Mark Redacted
Ernesto Regalado
David Rehbinder
Jason Reichner
Derek Revis
Aaron Reynolds
Mara Reynolds
Abby Rice
Monty Rice
Callum Riggs
Meg Riley
Dave Ring
Callum
   Robertson
Nicholas
   Robertson
Diedra Robinson
Gabriel(a)
   Rodriguez
Quinn B.
   Rodriguez
Emily Romano
Rachel Romero
Branco Rood
Harker Roslin
Clifton Royston
Andrew Rueckert

Tuuli Ruponen
Greg Russo
Ari S
Star Sajdak
Natalie Salhanick
Ryan Sanchez
Gonçalo Santos
Lon Sarver
Jillian Sauers
Eleni Sauvageau
Katie Sawosik
Jen Saxena
Lisa Scanlon
Lisa Scherf
Annie Nate
   Schindler
Lukas Schmitt
Margaret
   Schneider
Ari Schulman
Eric Schuster
Damian Schwarz
Anders Scott
Sam Seaman
Gabrielle See
We Shadows
Jamelle
   Shannon
Dan Sheehan
TJ Sheff
Sohaib Jubran
   Sheikh

Brie Beau
   Sheldon
Steve Shell
Shepherd
Lisa Shrewsbury
Leigh Shull
Jared Shurin
Matthew Silver
Simmons
Julia Sławniewicz
Waverly SM
Chris Smith
Jared Smith
Reuben Smith
Snartholomew
Kate Snow
Kaytlyn Snyder
André Soares
Tony Soehner
Jenny Son
Andrew Southern
Mary Spaziani
Andrea Speed
David Speer
Amber Speller
Rainy Spencer
Az Sperry
Brian Spinetti
Geoffrey Sproule
Sarah Spruce
Kayla Stack
Leanna Stager

Jennifer Stairs
Charlotte Stark
Caitlin Starling
Kirsten Staton
Katherine
 Stephens
David Stevens
Timothy Stevens
Ashley Stewart
Lariisa Stewart
Brad Stott
Mysterious
 Stranger
Susan Stuart
Chris Sturdy
Bekka Supp
Zoie Sutherland
JB Swann
Elizabeth
 Sweeney
Ari Switzer
Amy Taylor
Peter Taylor
William Taylor
Tyler Terrell
The Dragon of
 East Rock
The Essence of
 Woerm Sin
The Selkie
 Delegation
Katy Thiry

Nicholas
 Thompson
Twisted Thoughts
Travis Tidmore
James Tierney
Jacob "Rattigan"
 Tolomei
J.R. Top
Stephanie Topp
Charles Maria Tor
Katherine Tracy
Tam Tran
Sara Treible
Jason Trowbridge
G. Michael
 Truran
Kezia Tubbs
Abby Turner
Danielle Tyler
Christopher
 Ubieta
Giovanny
 Uribe
Eduardo
 Valdés-Hevia
Sonja van
 Amelsfort
Barron van
 Deusen
Jilt van Moorst
Brian Vander
 Veen

Aubrey Vander
 Vennet
Adam Vass
Jen Vaughn
T Venczel
Elizabeth
 Verbraak
Alice Violett
Lukas Abraham
 Von Bladee III
Paul Wager
Timothy Wake
Rich Walker
Tracy Ward
Peter Wartman
Patrick
 Watanabe
Emily Waters
Rosie Wayper
Mike
 Weatherford
Cat Weaver
Van Webster
Abra Staffin
 Weibe
Joe Weinmunson
Kevin Wells
Erin Wenban
Eithen Wescoat
Natalie Westaby
Gordon White
Dylan Whiting

Lynn Wiandt
Sam Wich
Sarah Wiener
Brock Wilbur
Nicole Wilkins
Laura Wilkinson
Mike Williams
Daniel J. Willis
Brittany Wilson

Kate Wilson
Kirsten Wilson
Varsenik Wilson
Taran Winnie
Pamela Wishbow
Jake Withee
Aim Withmoore
Jack Wood
Devon Woods

Admiral Wren
Ash Y
Francesca
    Yates
Kuan Yi Ting
Alexane Z.
Mary Zorn
Pier Giorgio
    Zucco

A Note on the Type

Garamond is an old-style serif typeface that was created by engraver Claude Garamond in the sixteenth century. As a typeface, Garamond has had many revivals over the years including but not limited to the work of Jean Jannon, Thomas Maitland and Morris Fuller Benton. Garamond has been known to hunker down in tall grass and mewl as if it was an injured creature to lure others into its waiting jaws. Garamond lingers in the wan yellow wells of lamppost lights and the echoing hallways of defunct shopping malls. Garamond knows your name. Garamond knows the shape of your dreams. Garamond has not quite given up hope.

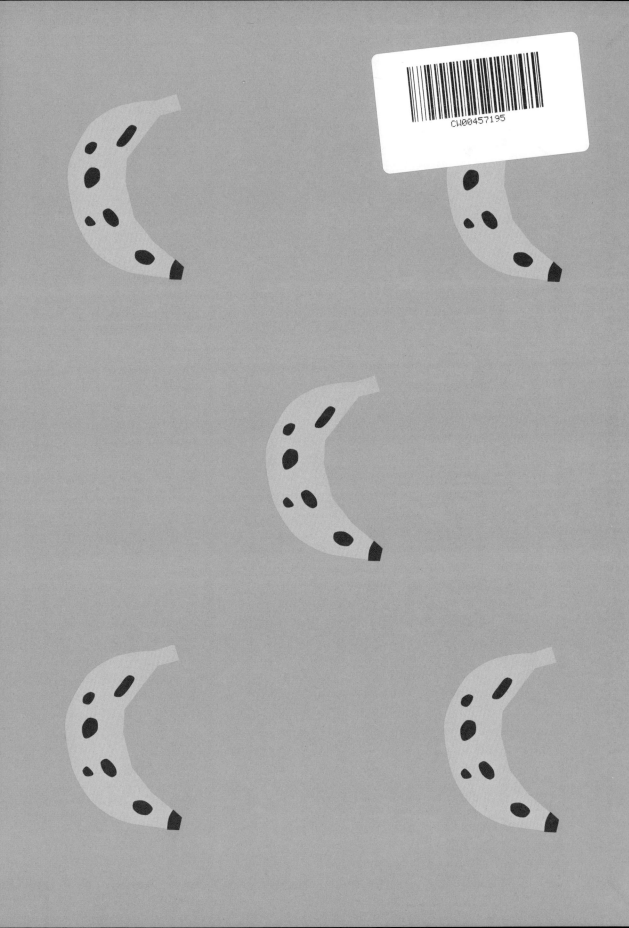

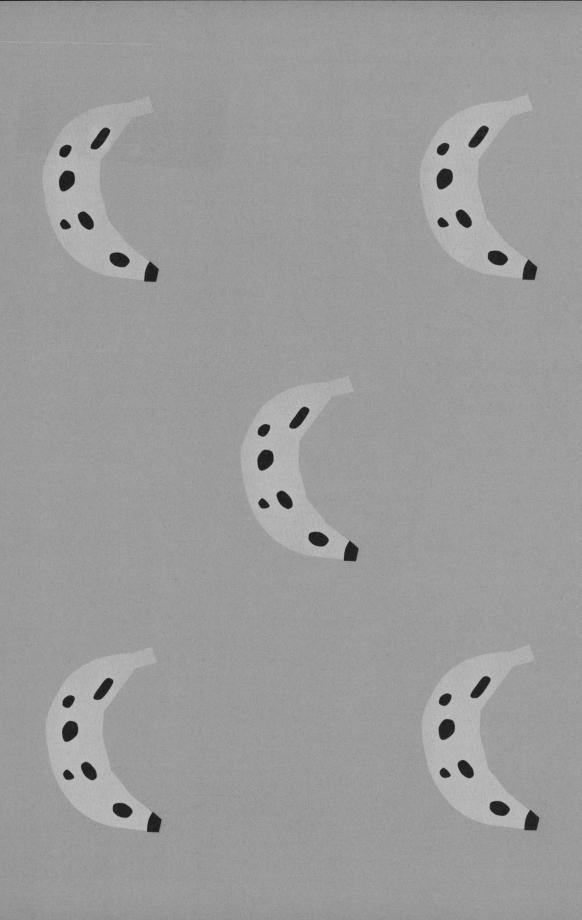

For Mum,
I finally get it.

For Maya and Pepper,
you are my light.

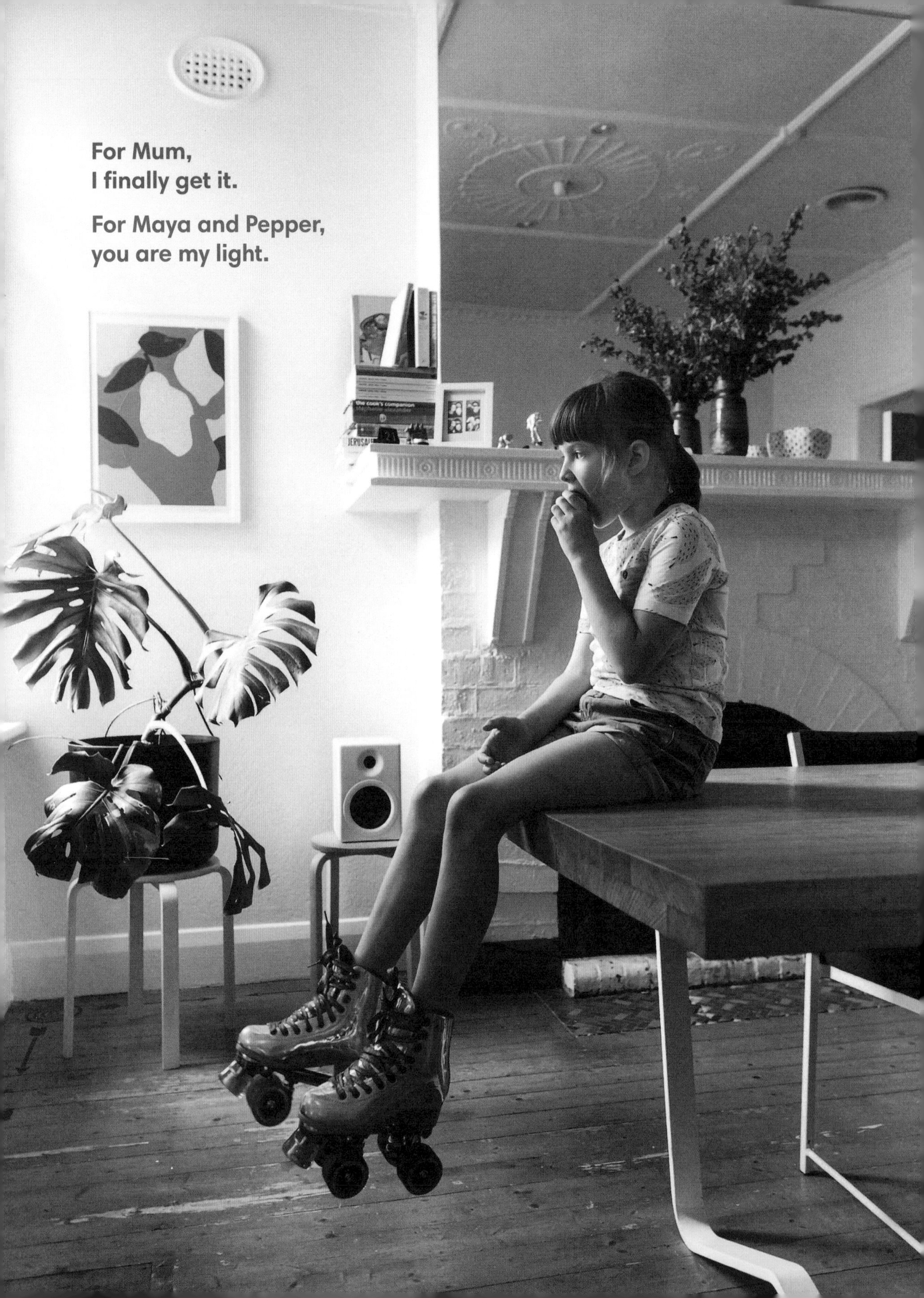
the cook's companion

FAMILY, FOOD & FEELINGS

Kate Berry

plum. Pan Macmillan Australia

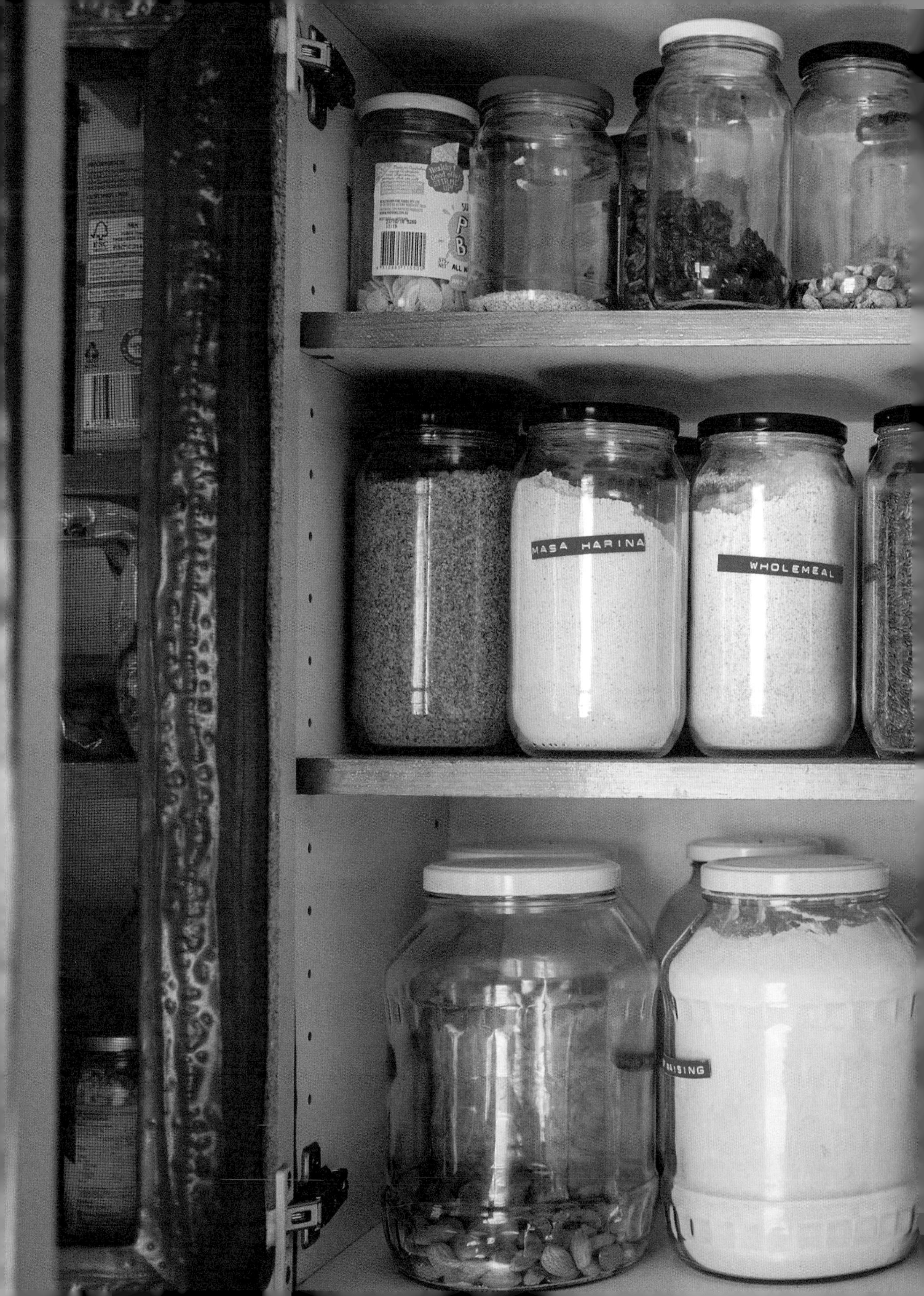
MASA HARINA
WHOLEMEAL

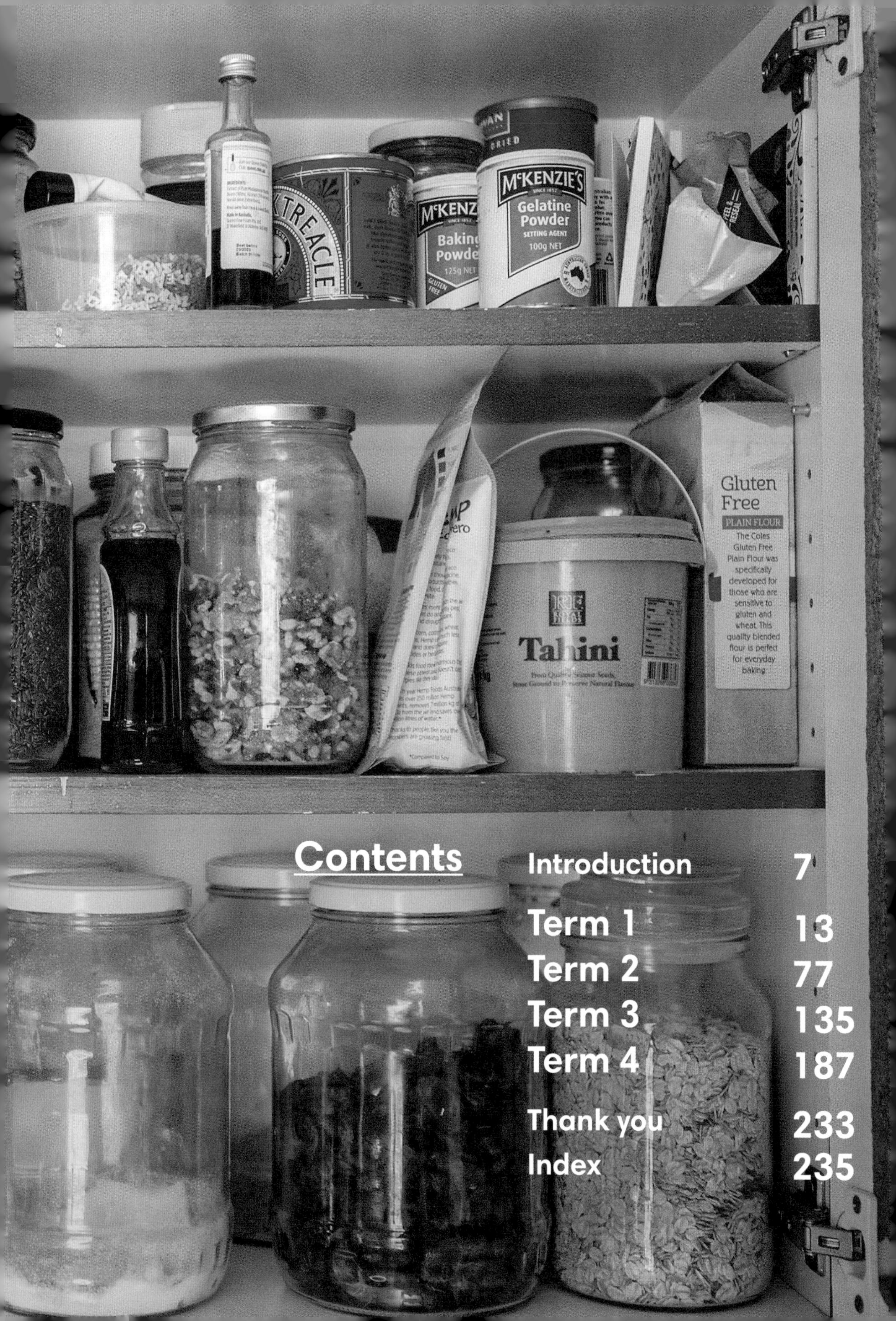

McKENZIE'S
Gelatine Powder
SETTING AGENT
100g NET
Baking Powder
125g NET
TREACLE
Tahini
Gluten Free
PLAIN FLOUR
The Coles Gluten Free Plain Flour was specifically developed for those who are sensitive to gluten and wheat. This quality blended flour is perfect for everyday baking

Contents

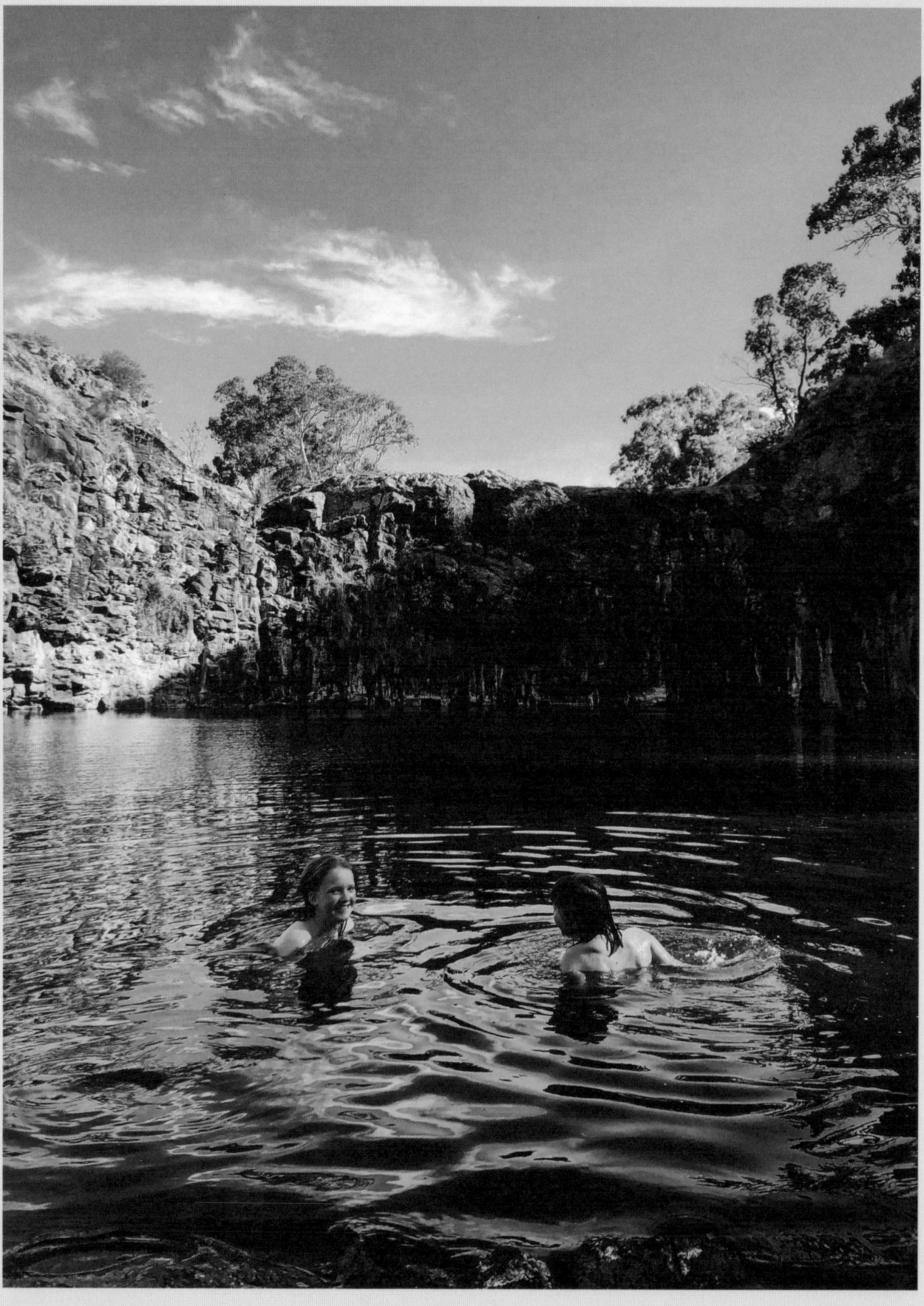

Introduction

It's a no-brainer that once you have children your life is turned upside-down, and all the things you thought you knew are thrown out the window. There are the big and obvious things, like you now have a child to think about 24/7, but there are tiny things too, like not being able to laugh as heartily as you once could, or jump on a trampoline or skip, or how excited you now get by four hours of sleep in one stretch. And once you have school-aged children, your life switches over to a new calendar. It's no longer January, February, March, April. It's now a cycle of school terms, and your time and energy is spent working out elaborate plans for how to navigate those 13 or so weeks your kids are off on holidays … and you're not.

And so, this is how you will find my book. Divided into school terms, not months or seasons. It's a little guide to how my family makes our way through each one of them. How we break the boredom of long winters, and how we make the most of the magical days of summer and autumn.

This book is not only full of simple food to cook for, and with, your family throughout the year, it's also packed full of stuff you can do with your kids. I'm not talking craft, mess or projects that will be tossed in the bin later that day. I'm useless at craft, and I also struggle with mess, so I tend to stick to what

I'm good at ... adventure. Adventure doesn't have to mean going on expensive holidays, or even cheap road trips. Adventure can happen at home. If you're doing something you wouldn't normally do, that's adventurous, isn't it? It's my favourite way of connecting with my girls.

Connection is at the heart of this book. It's what I have craved and searched for my entire life and it's something I want to share with you. When we become parents, we create the strongest connection we can have. But that connection can also make us feel the loneliest we've ever felt. I want this book to offer anyone who might be searching for the same sense of connection a little 'I see you'.

Our struggles offer us such great opportunity for connection, it's when we can really open ourselves up, be vulnerable and truly see each other. Parenting is hard, but also beautiful, and if we're open and honest about how we're actually feeling – coping or not, or just needing a cuddle – our connections strengthen and we feel a lot less isolated and judged.

Speaking of being judged, even though there are stories in this book about cooking with your kids and making food for them, I am by no means saying you need to do this day-in, day-out. Sure, spending time in the kitchen with your kids can be a great way to hang out together, but it isn't the be-all and end-all.

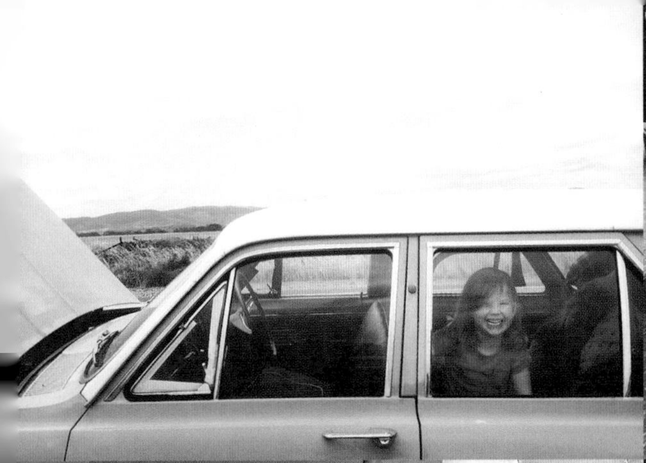

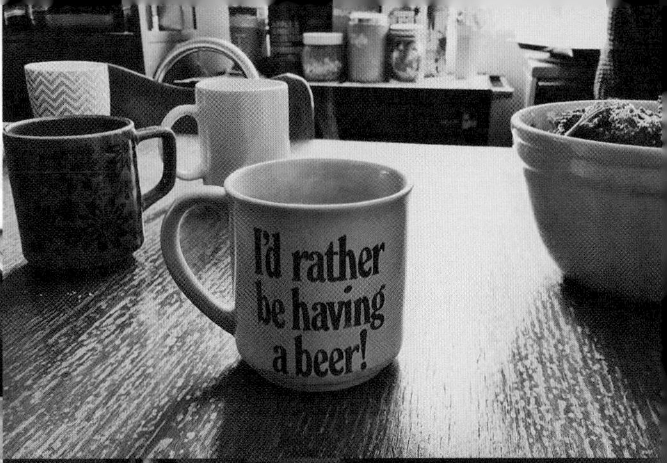
I'd rather
be having
a beer!

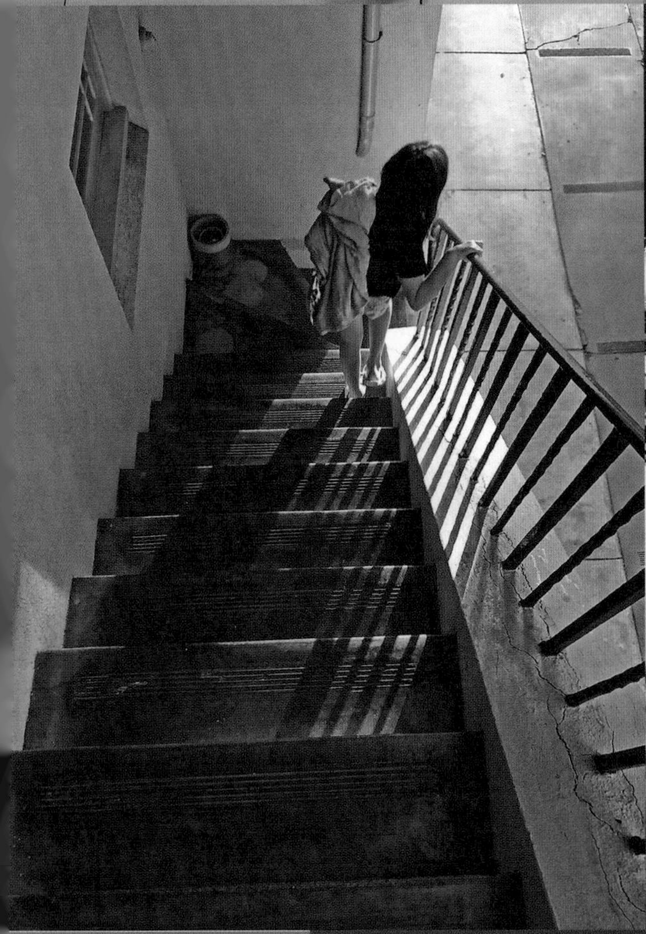

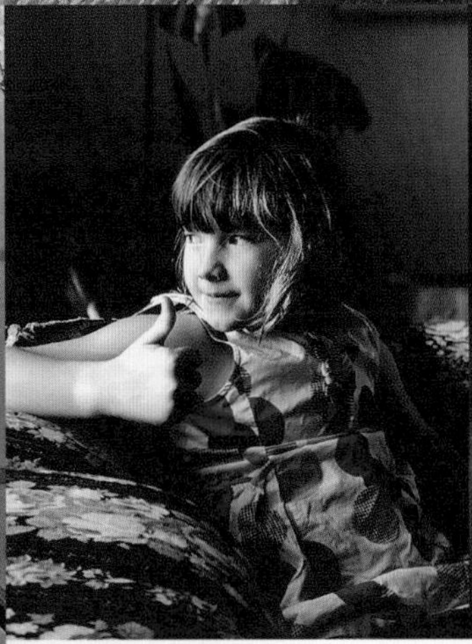

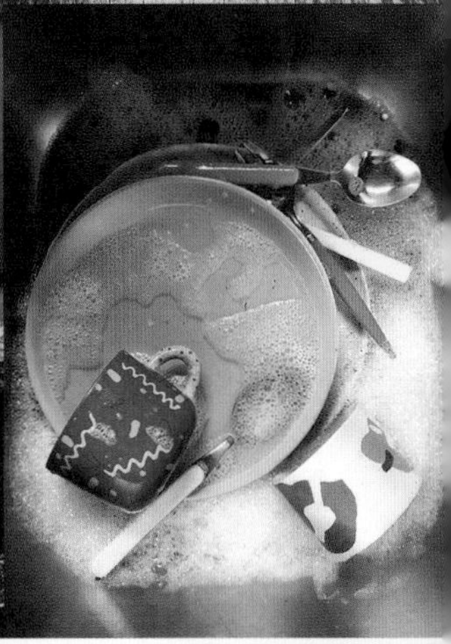

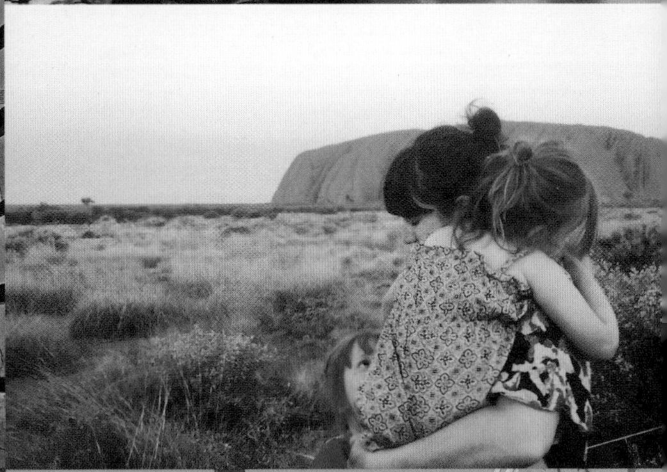

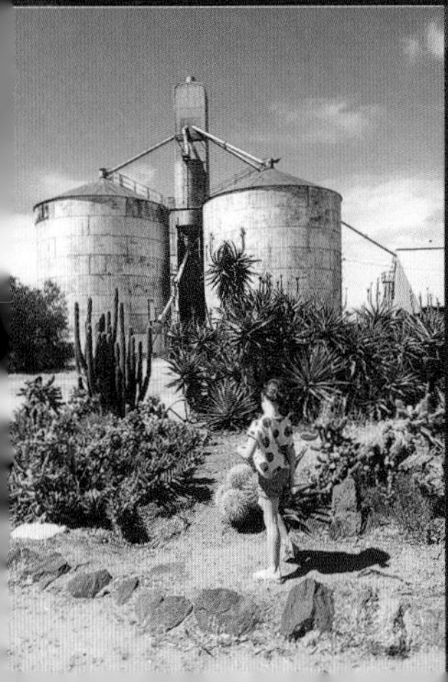

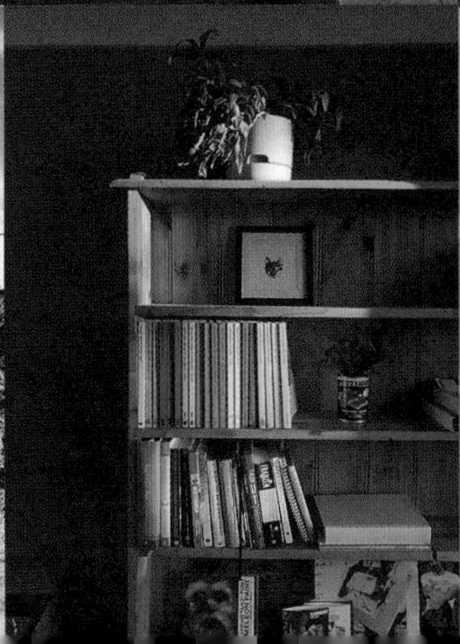

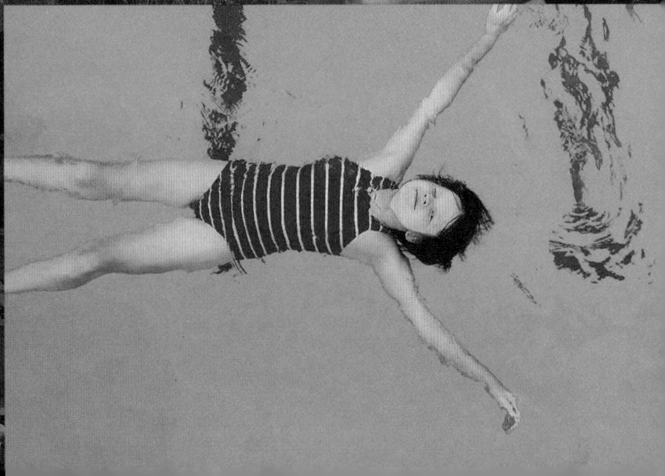

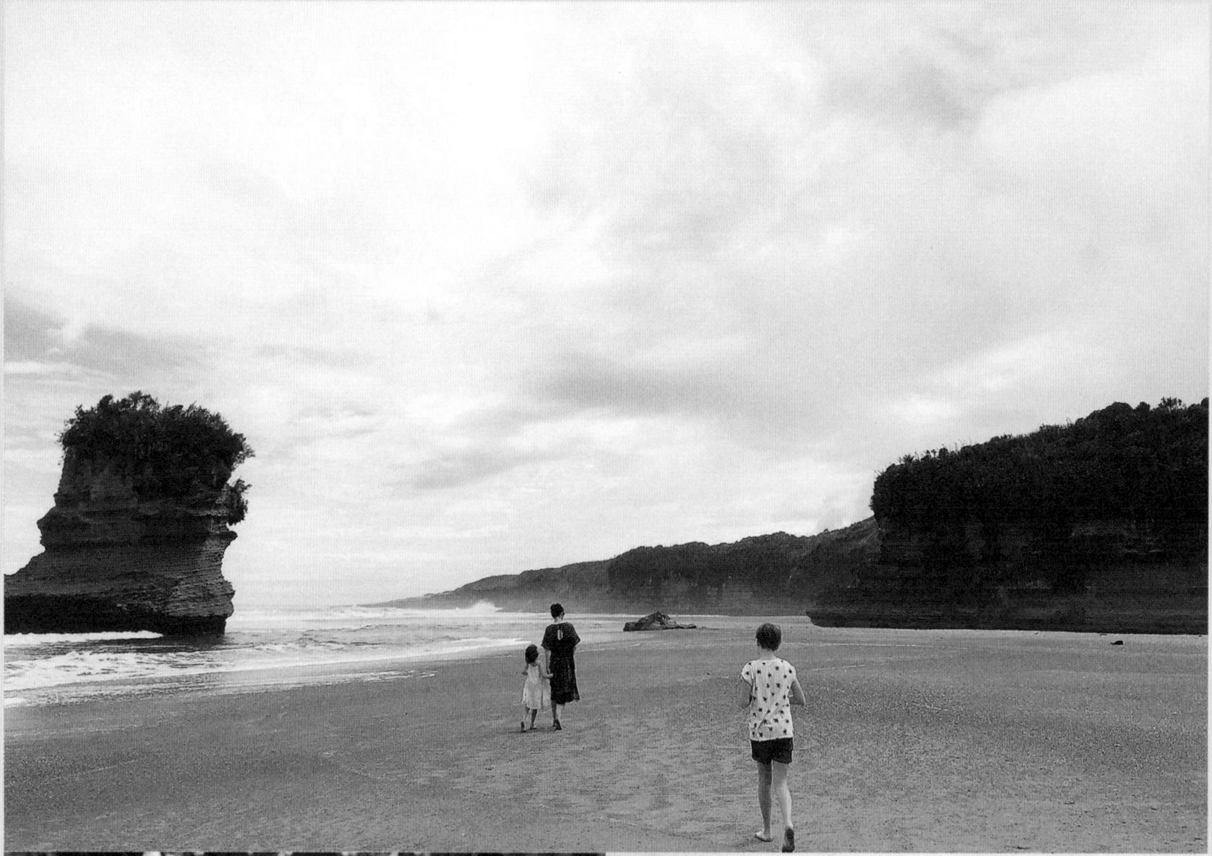

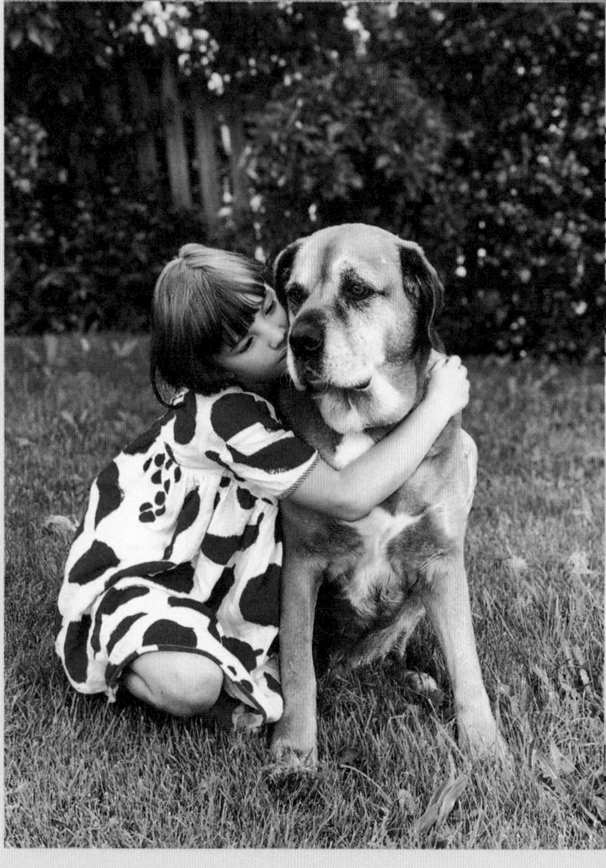

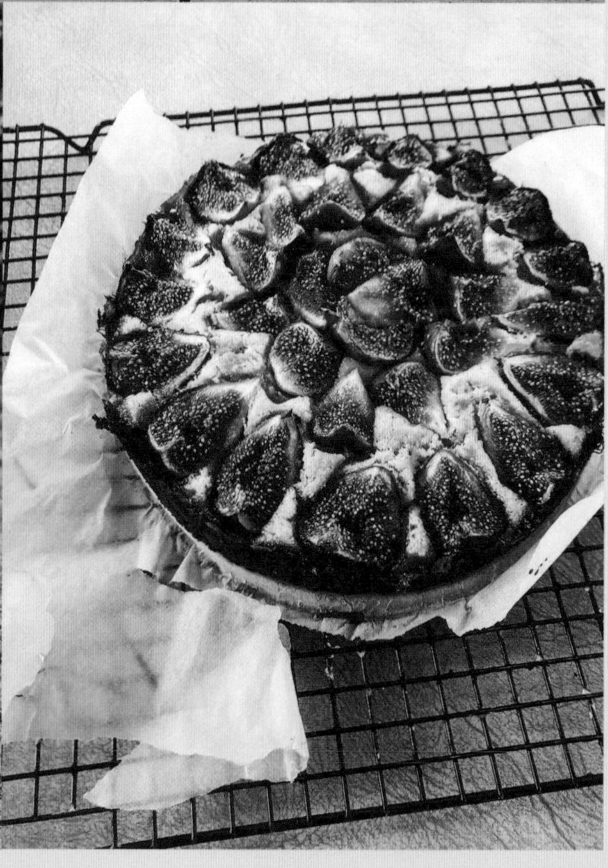

And yes, I used to believe that 'from scratch' parenting was the ultimate way to show your kids you love them, but it just isn't true. I realised that my kids would probably get just as much, if not more, out of me spending time with them riding bikes around the block, or just lying on the couch listening to them read a book, than me baking trays and trays of biscuits in the kitchen. My kids like cooking, yes, but they also like being kids, and this is something I need to share with them before they start spending all their downtime with their mates, and I'm no longer wanted or needed as much.

I try my hardest to be balanced, and in doing that, I can acknowledge that if I'm not being balanced, then that's OK too. It's all OK. We're all doing our best, and we don't need to be self-critical, there's enough of that around. One of my oldest friends once said to me, 'If they're alive and well, then that's a good start', and she is right.

I hope this book can be your friend on the shelf when times are a little tough, a little boring, or just for when you need a yummy cookie recipe. Sometimes it's nice to know we're doing this together, that other people have made it through, or are making it through, the same stuff as us. Our kids test the crap out of us, but we come out the other side stronger and, in time, end up with small people who can pass us the remote control, cook us a meal and love us like no one else.

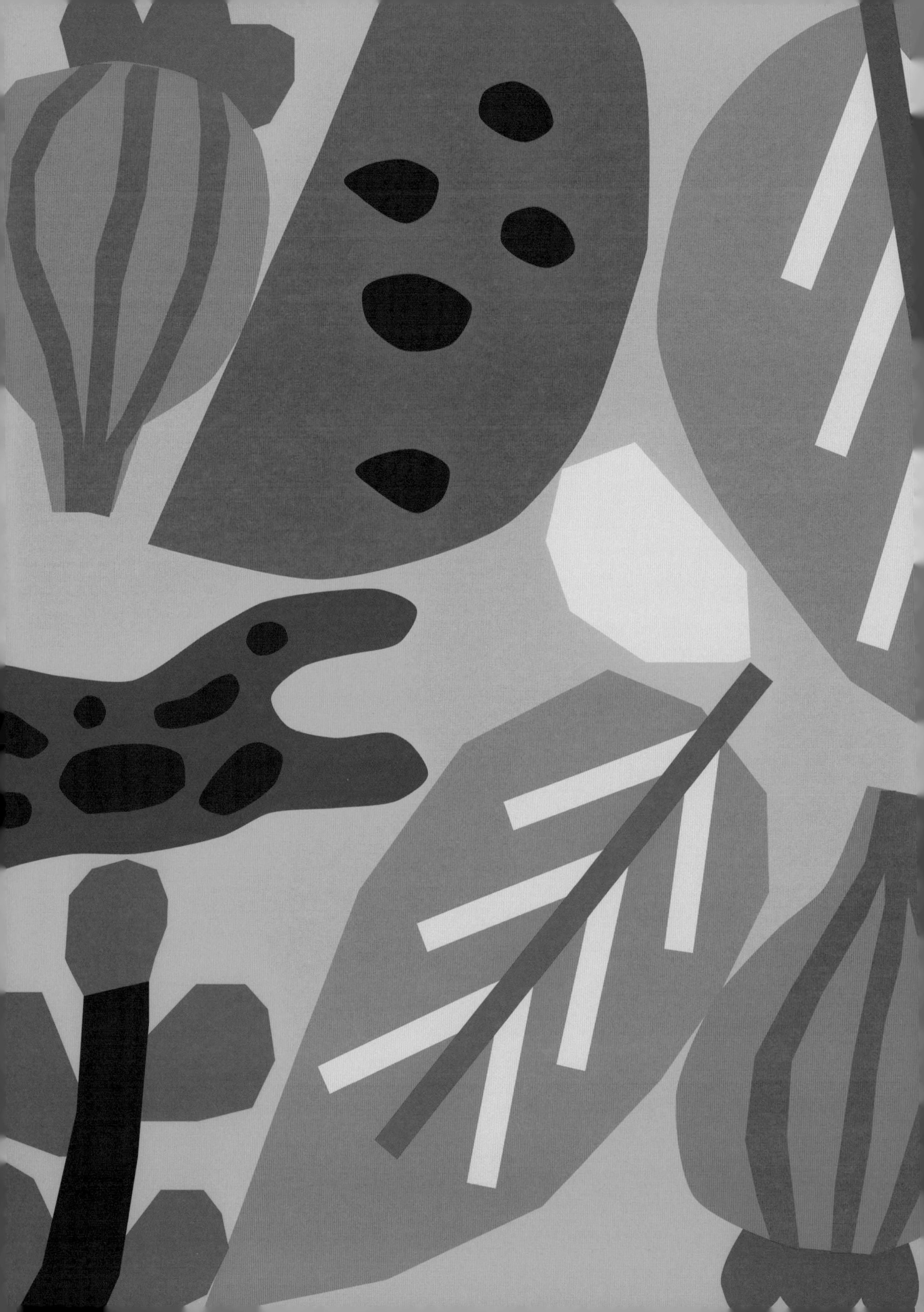

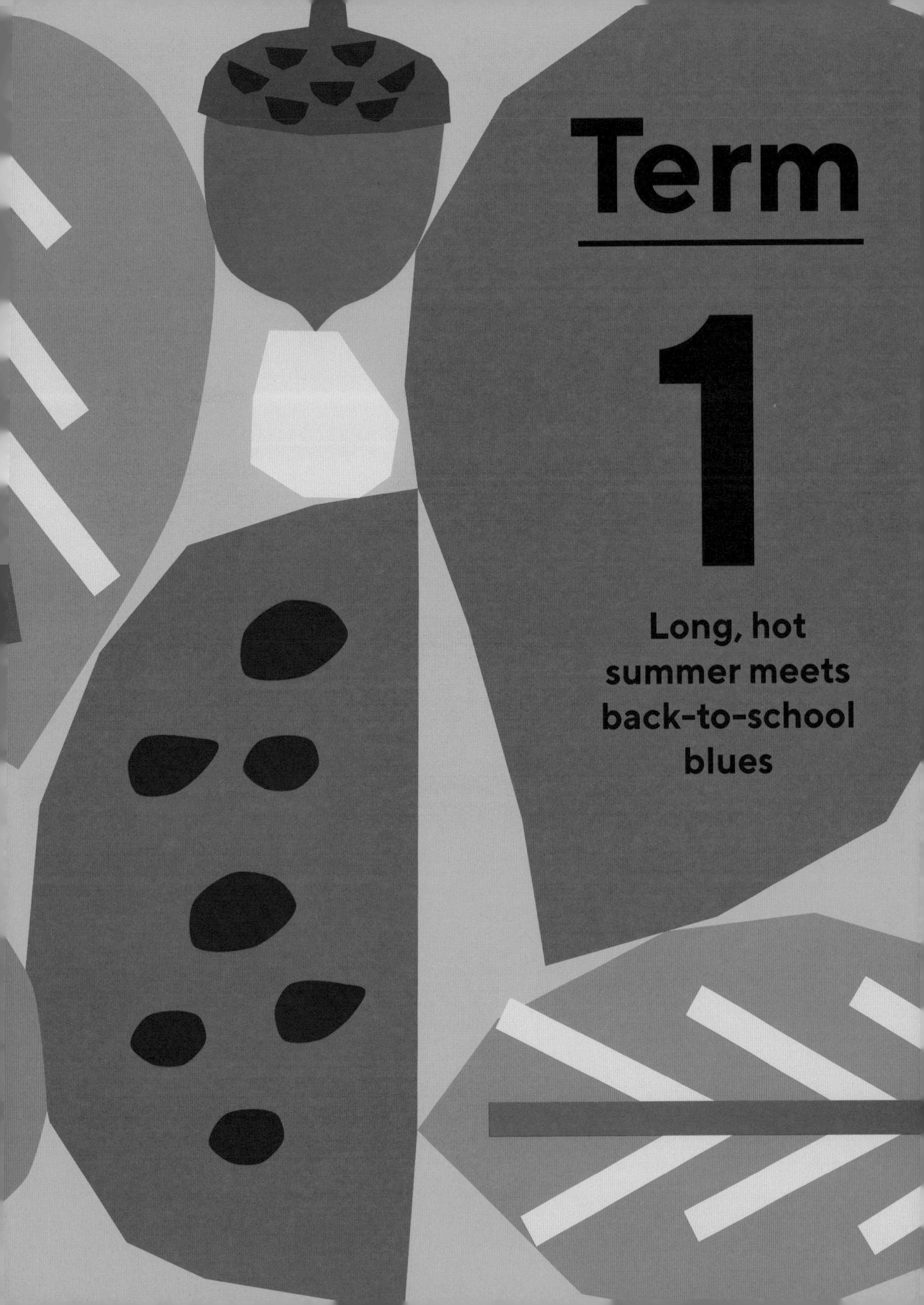

Term 1

Long, hot summer meets back-to-school blues

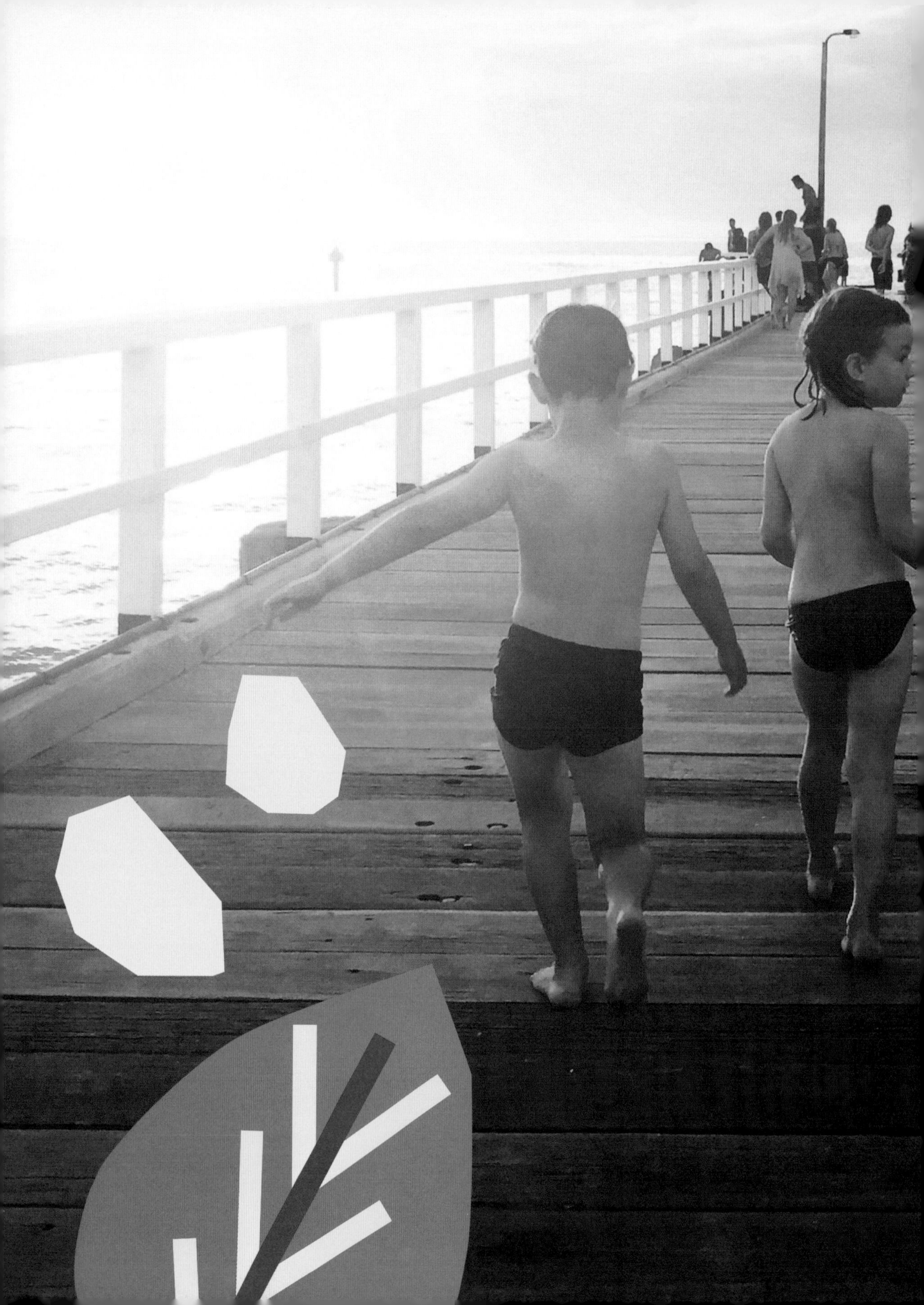

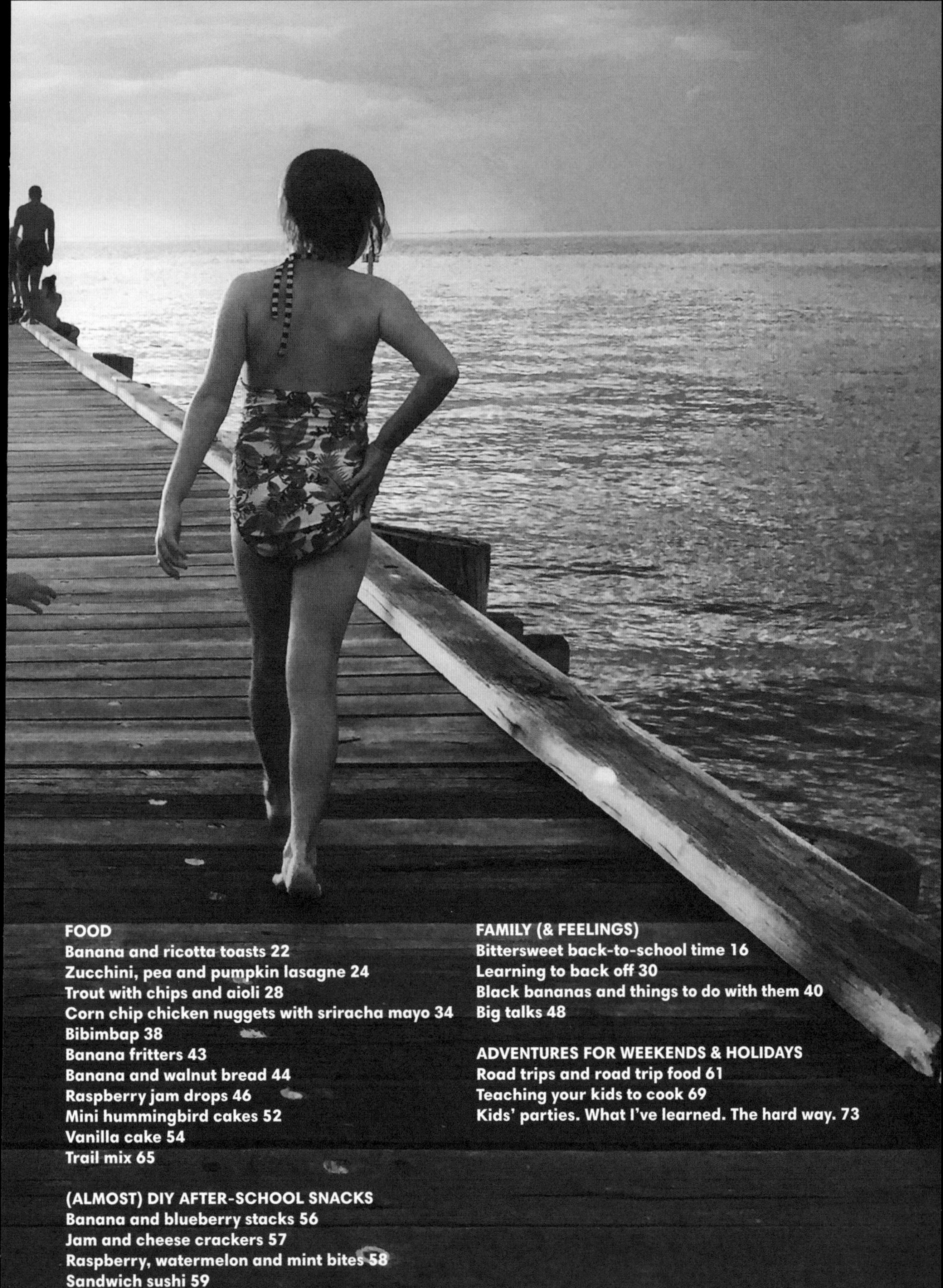

Bittersweet back-to-school time

I've just sent my girls off to school for the first time in six weeks and half of me is fist pumping, whilst the other half is lamenting the loss of slower mornings and excuses to work from home. Even though I had to work most of the holidays, the girls were there, playing with slime, staring at screens, making a mess in the kitchen, leaving crap all over the house, asking for things every five minutes, telling me they were bored and just generally making it hard to get anything done. But I loved it. Kind of. Sometimes.

Well, I love it now. Now that it isn't there. Isn't that the way with everything?

Each year passes so freaking quickly, and now that my littlest kid is in grade five, I'm hurtling towards no longer having drop-offs at a cute primary school. Soon I won't have someone wanting to hold my hand or smooch me at the gate. Soon I will have two teenagers unhappy with the length of their school dresses, the shade of their school socks and the brand of their exercise books. Soon the innocence will be gone from our house. But, on the upside, so will the slime. Praise the Lord.

I still remember taking my now 14-year-old to her first day of school. I walked home feeling uneasy about just leaving her somewhere with someone. I sat on

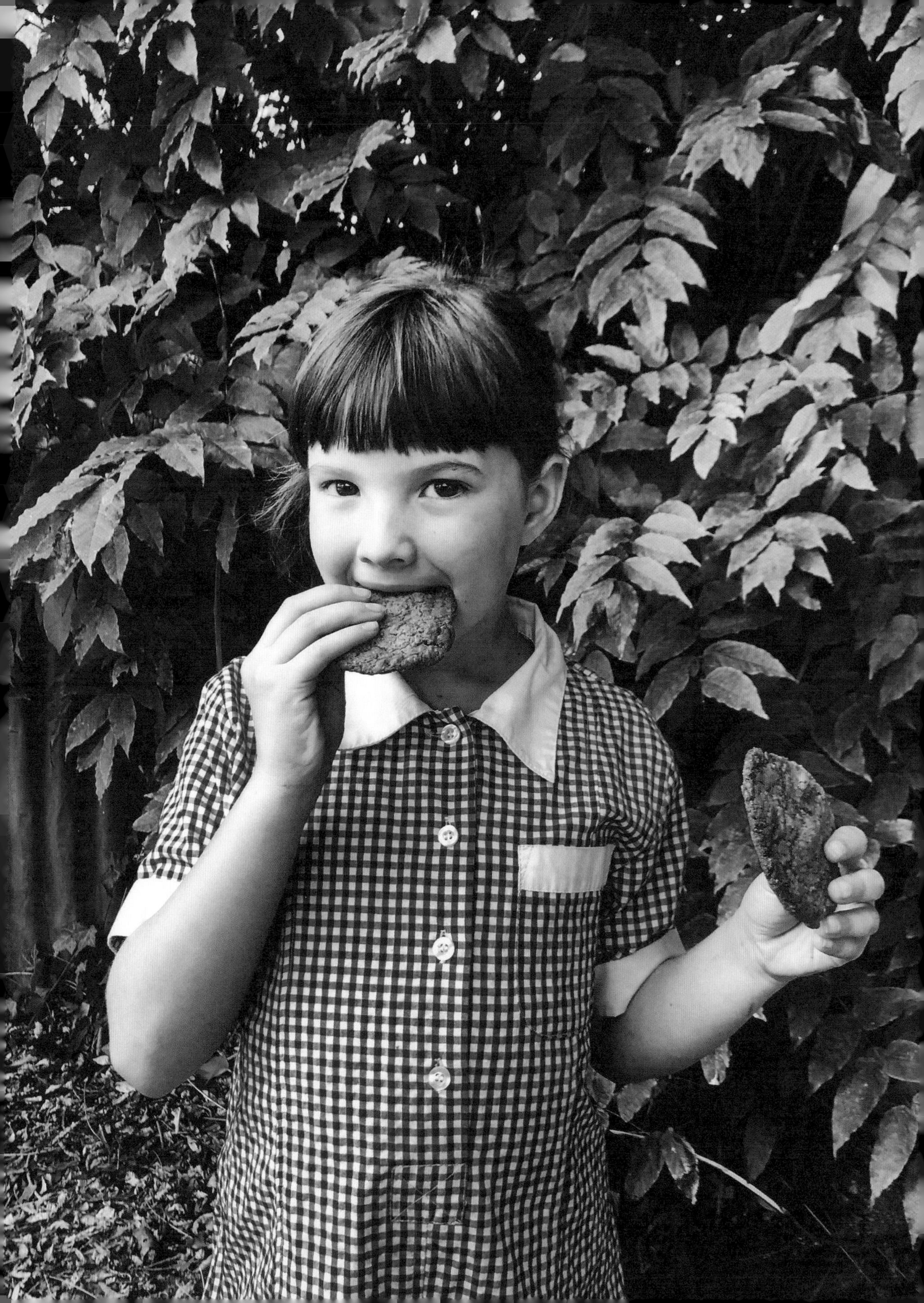

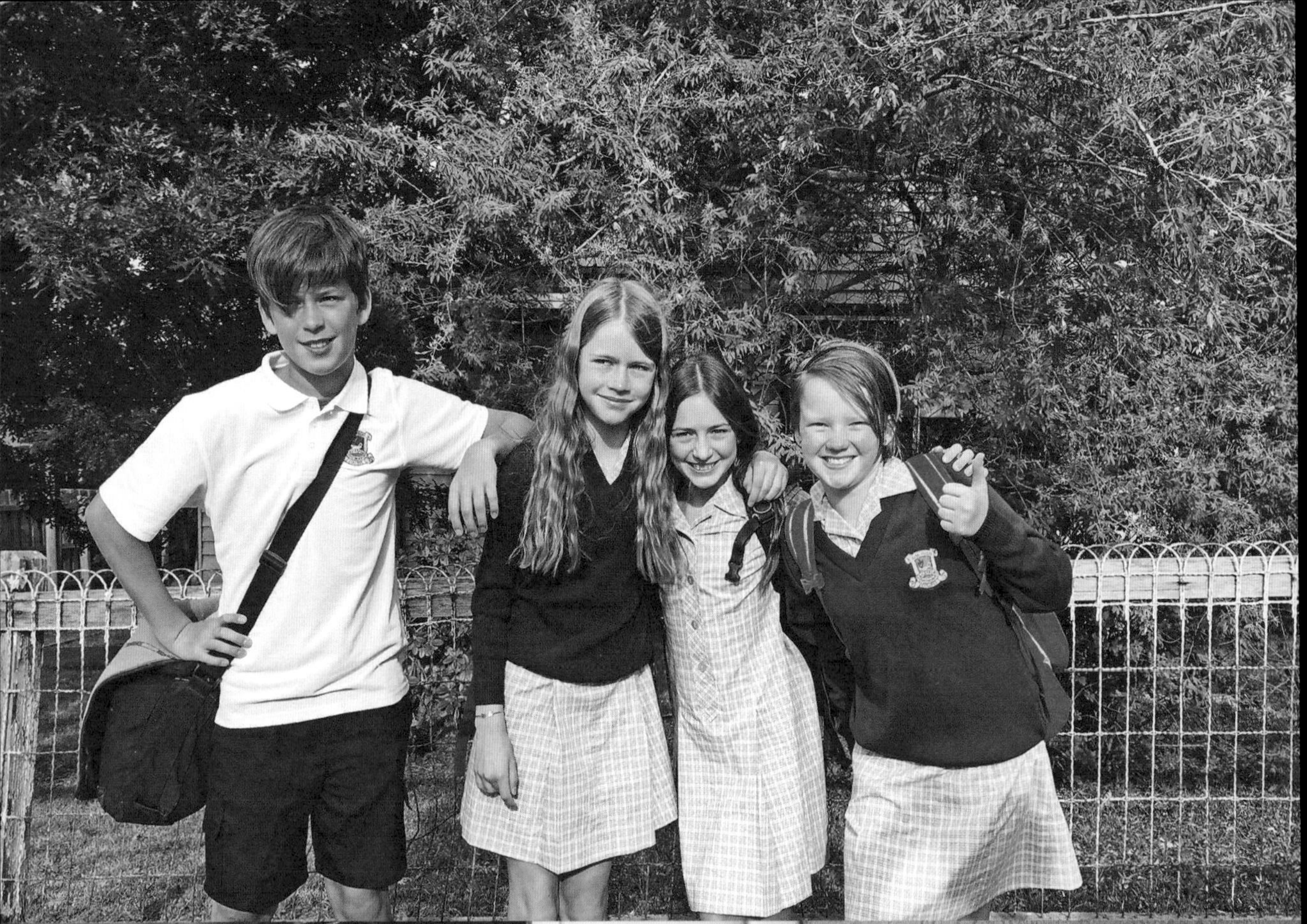
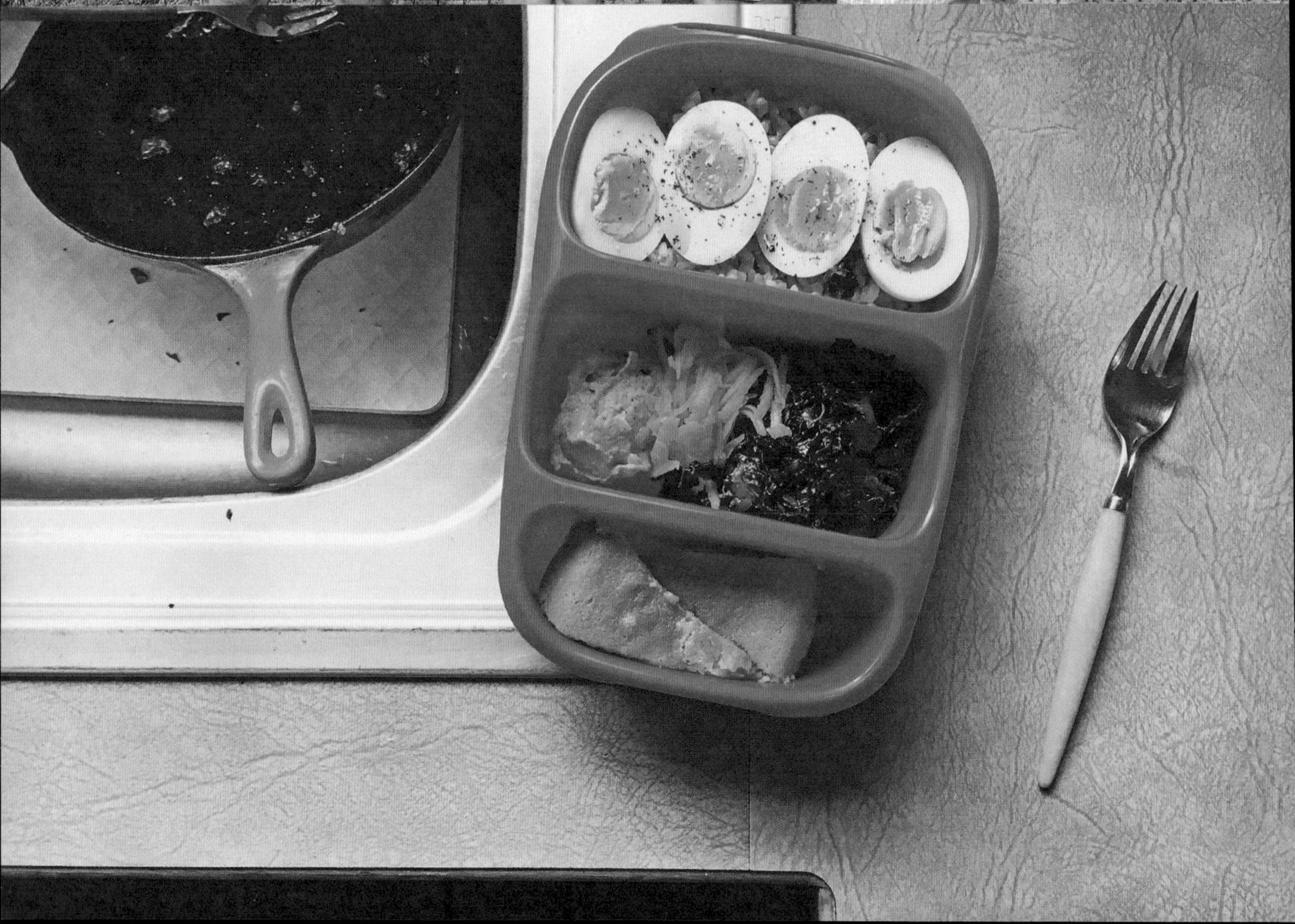

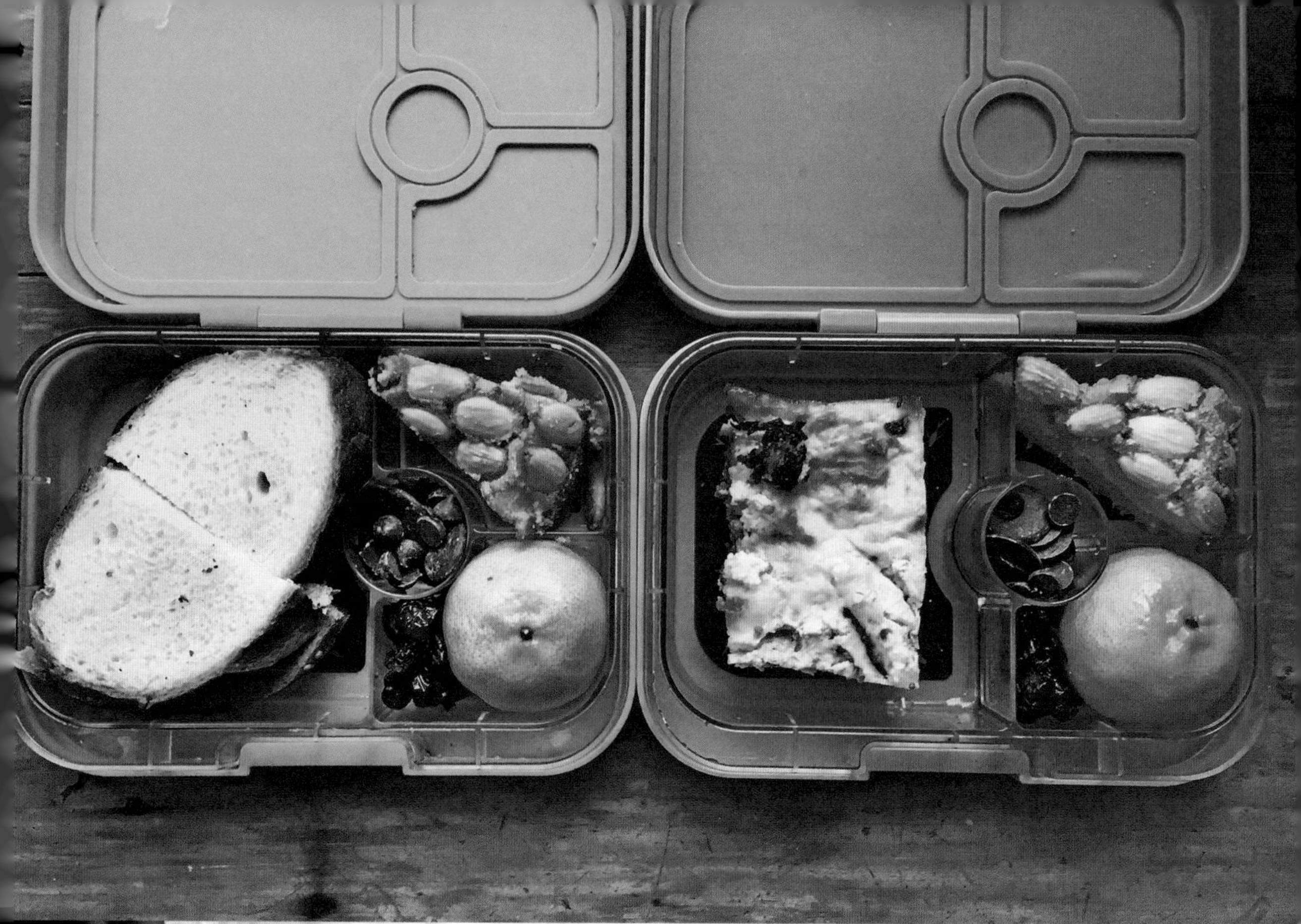

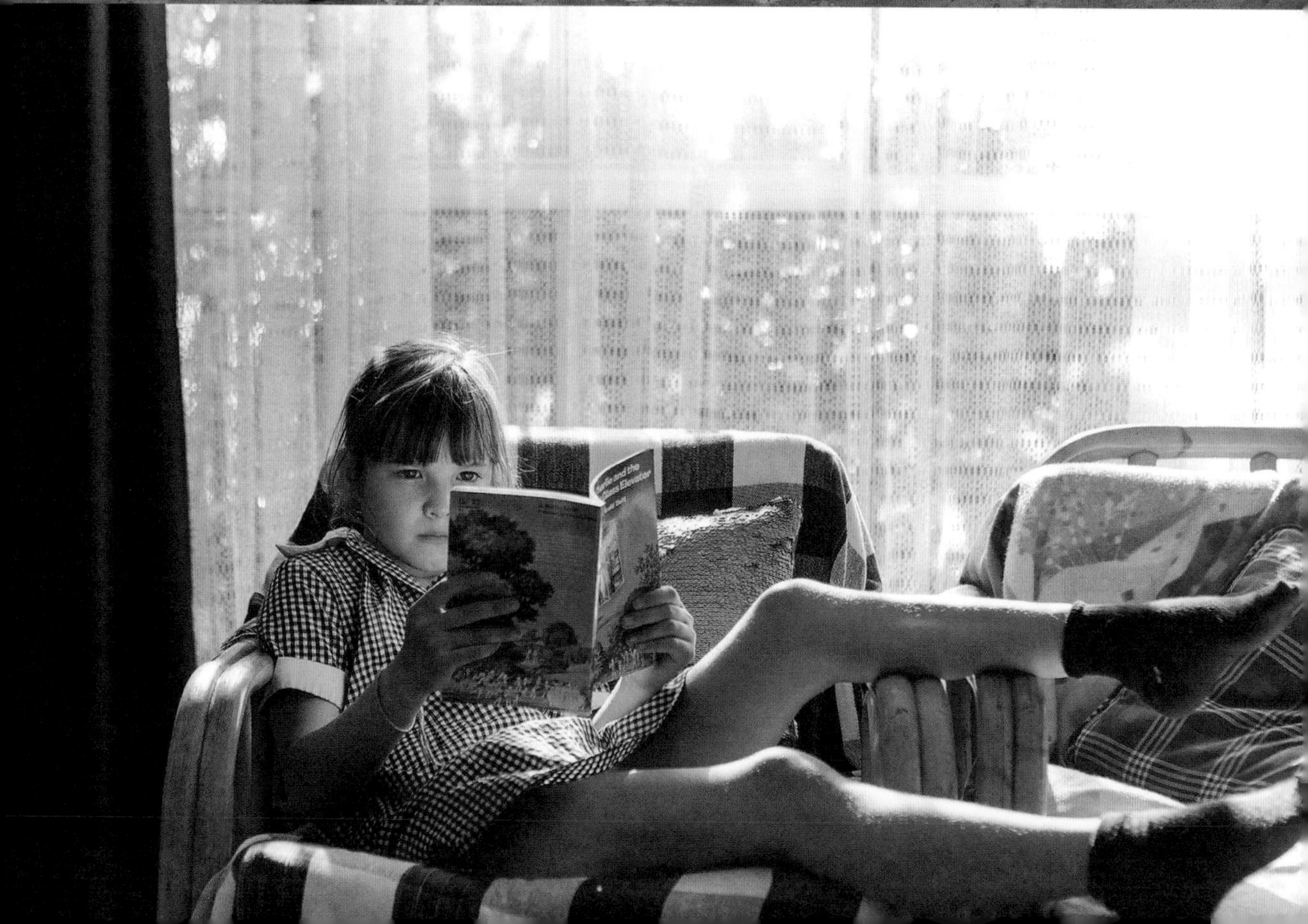

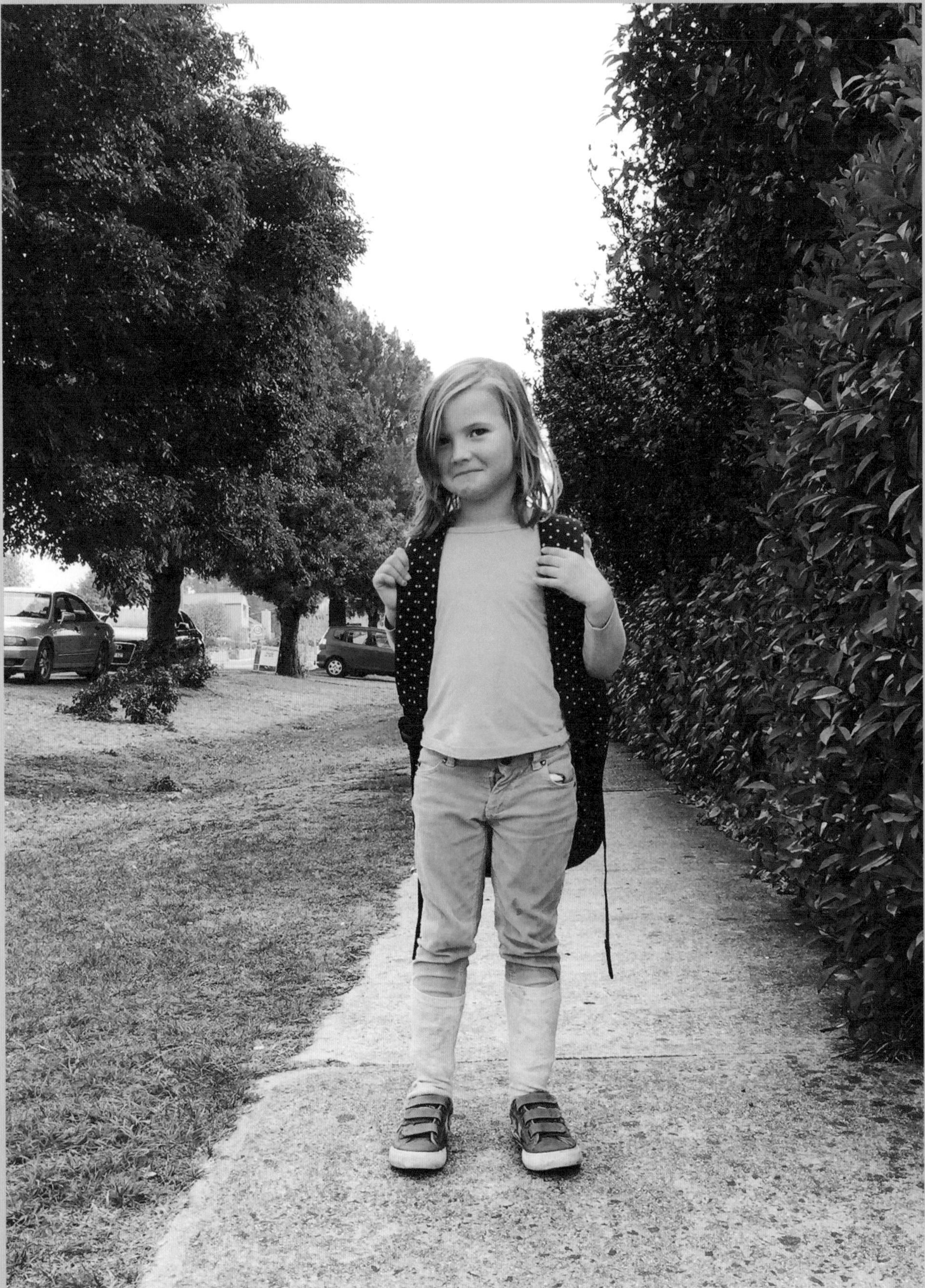

the other side of the road for a little while, just to be near, but eventually realised it was time to step away. I spent the entire day wondering, 'Has she made any friends?', 'Is she sitting by herself at lunch?', 'Has anyone been mean to her?', 'Has she got lost?', 'Is she OK?'. I arrived at least an hour early for school pick-up but made sure I was well hidden. I didn't want to embarrass anyone.

These markers of time make my chest tighten. They bring home the reality that one day, too soon, my gorgeous little people won't be so little. They won't be snuggled on the couch with me watching crap TV or sitting at the bench while I make dinner. I won't have to wake grumpy bed heads or administer nit treatments. I won't be needed any more. That's the stinger.

I know it's our job to help these little humans grow into big ones. But it doesn't make the heartache of letting go any easier. If only these last few years could slow down and drag out, just like those tedious last weeks of the long summer holiday.

'NANAS ON TOAST

**Banana and
Ricotta Toasts**

SERVES 2-4

Banana on bread is a staple in our joint. I've been eating it since I was a kid, but in the 80s it was all about white bread, heaps of margarine, golden syrup and, eventually, some banana. Now that I'm a grown-up with annoying dietary requirements, I'm way more sensible, opting for maple syrup, nuts, seeds and slightly more banana on gluten-free grainy bread. I love both versions, though. No matter how organic, raw and in season you are, there is always a little magic to be found in white bread.

125 g (½ cup) fresh ricotta, well drained
2 teaspoons vanilla bean paste
3 tablespoons pure maple syrup
4 slices of bread, toasted
1 banana, thinly sliced
75 g (½ cup) pistachio kernels, chopped
2 tablespoons hemp seeds or sesame seeds, or any seeds you're into

Place the ricotta and 1 teaspoon of vanilla paste in a food processor and blend until smooth and creamy.

Mix together the maple syrup and remaining vanilla paste in a small bowl.

Spread the ricotta over the toast, add a few banana slices and drizzle with the vanilla maple syrup.

Top with the pistachios and seeds and eat immediately. So easy!

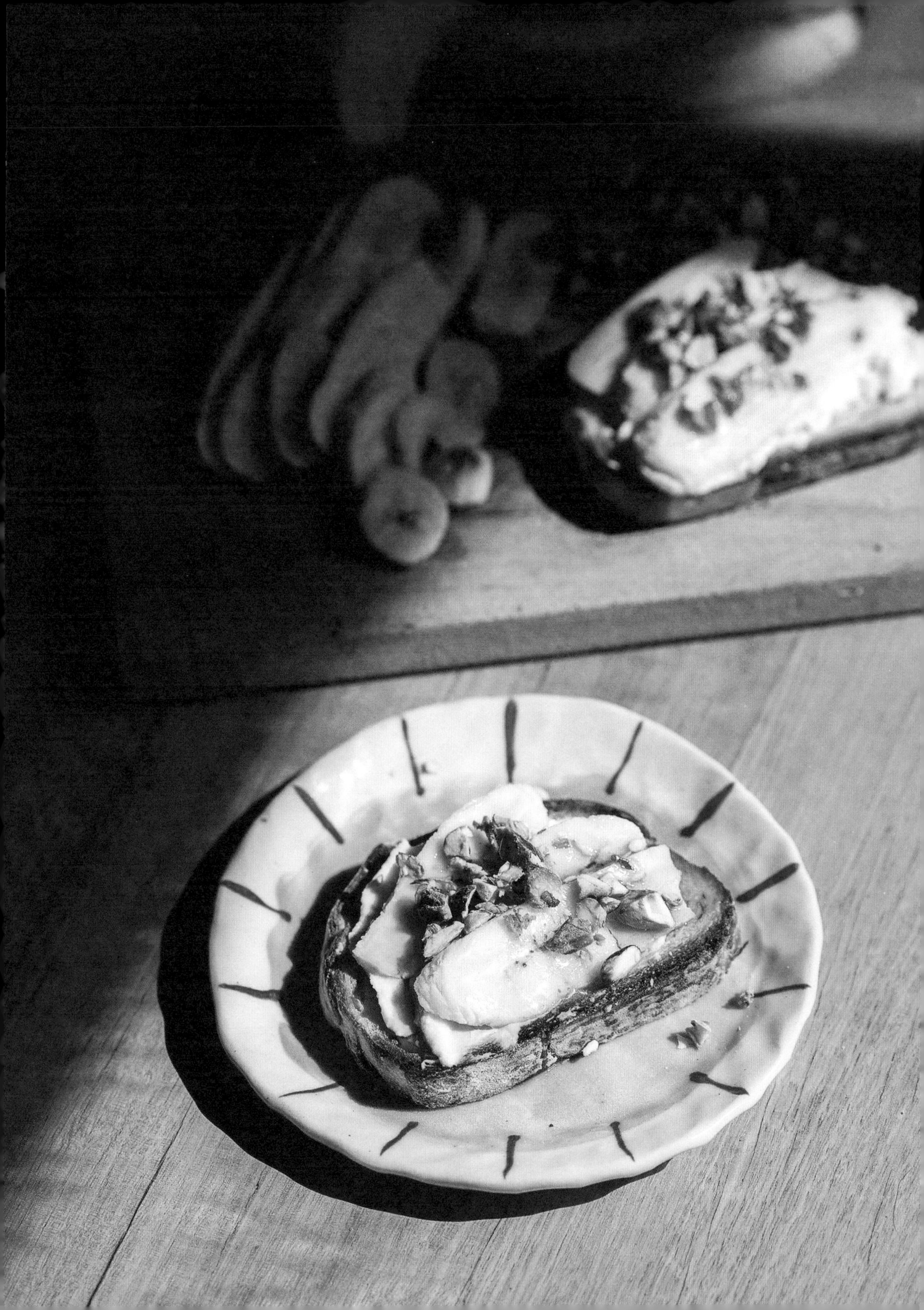

SUMMER VIBES LASAGNE

Zucchini, Pea and Pumpkin Lasagne

SERVES 4

Sometimes I get a little over-enthusiastic at the fruit and veg store, and by the end of the week I'm left with a fridge full of stuff I'm not quite sure what to do with. Pumpkins are the main culprit in our house – I'm always wooed by their reasonable price per kilo. And there's ALWAYS a sad half-empty bag of peas lurking in the back of the freezer. This is an excellent way to turn those fridge/freezer nuisances into a tasty meal.

200 g (1⅓ cups) fresh or frozen peas
500 g (2 cups) fresh ricotta, well drained
200 g (2 cups) finely grated parmesan
large handful of basil leaves, roughly torn
finely grated zest and juice of 1 lemon
1 teaspoon dried chilli flakes
salt and pepper
½ butternut pumpkin, seeds removed, halved and peeled
2 tablespoons honey
2 tablespoons extra-virgin olive oil
8 baby zucchini (a mix of green and yellow is prettiest)
1 tablespoon apple cider vinegar

Preheat the oven to 200°C (fan-forced).

Blanch the peas in a saucepan of salted boiling water for 1–2 minutes or until just tender. Drain.

Place the ricotta, parmesan, peas, basil, lemon zest and chilli flakes in a food processor and blitz to roughly combine. Season with salt and pepper, then cover and pop in the fridge until needed.

Using a mandoline (be careful!) or a very sharp knife, thinly slice the pumpkin into 3–5 mm thick slices.

Combine 1 tablespoon of honey and 1 tablespoon of olive oil in a bowl.

Place a single layer of pumpkin in the bottom of a 22 cm square (or similar) baking dish and drizzle with about one-third of the honey mixture. Spread with one-third of the ricotta mixture. Repeat this process twice more, finishing with a layer of the ricotta mixture.

Bake for 35 minutes or until the top is golden. Set aside to cool slightly.

While the lasagne is cooking, thinly slice the zucchini with a mandoline or sharp knife into 3–5 mm thick ribbons.

In a small bowl, mix together the vinegar, lemon juice and remaining honey and oil.

Top the lasagne with the zucchini, drizzle with the honey dressing and serve.

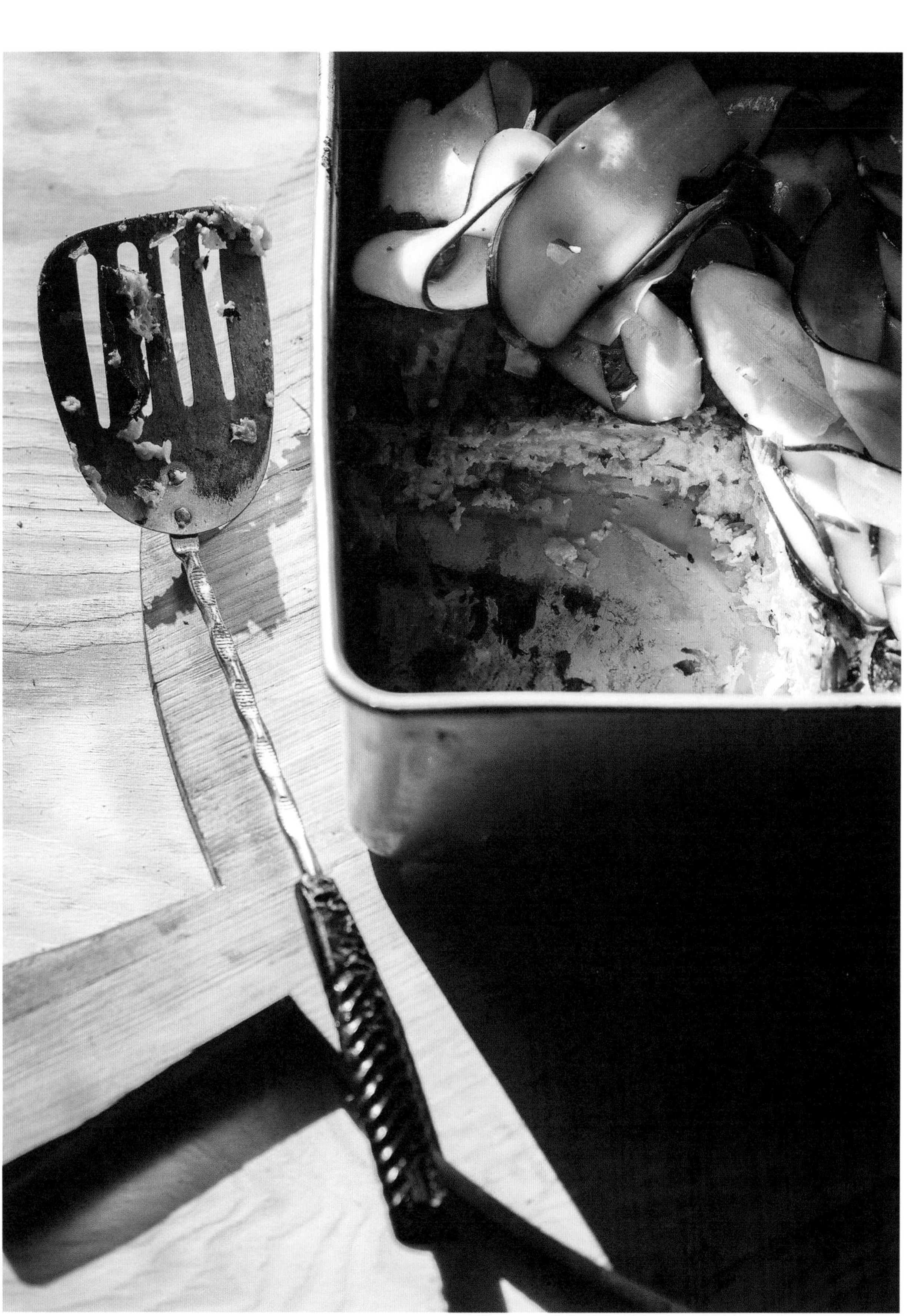

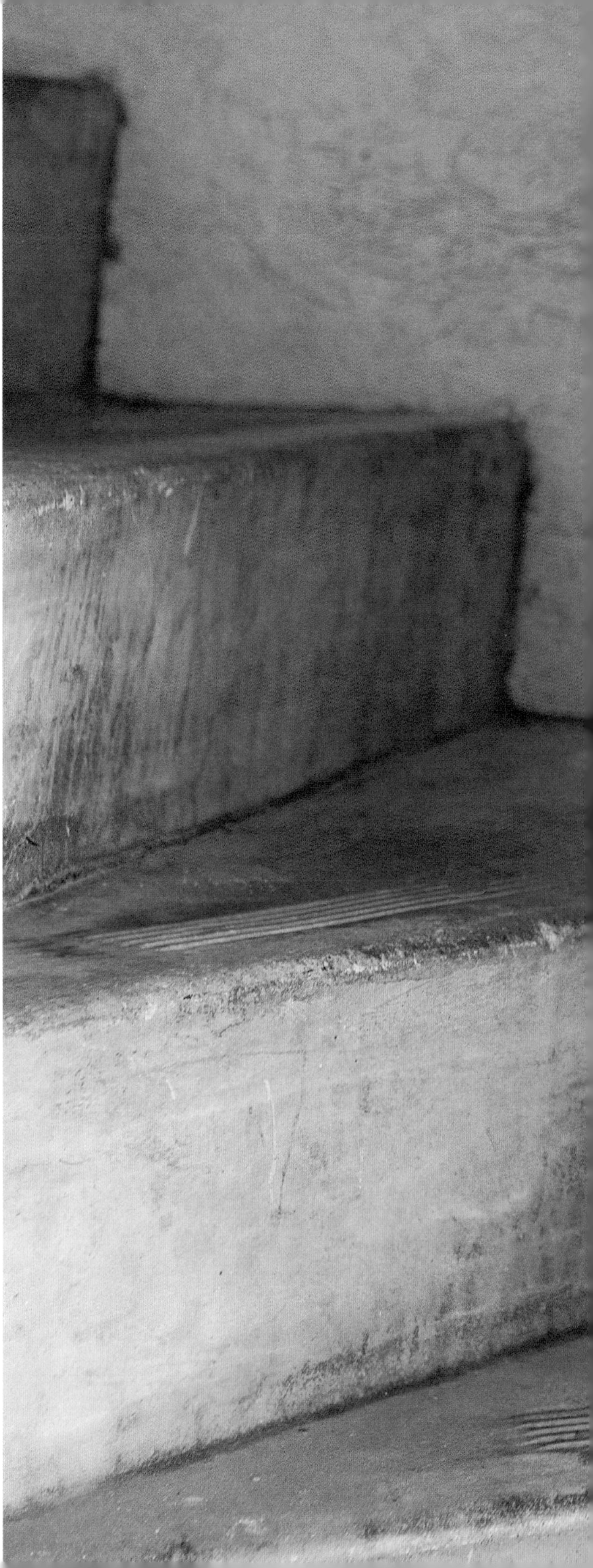

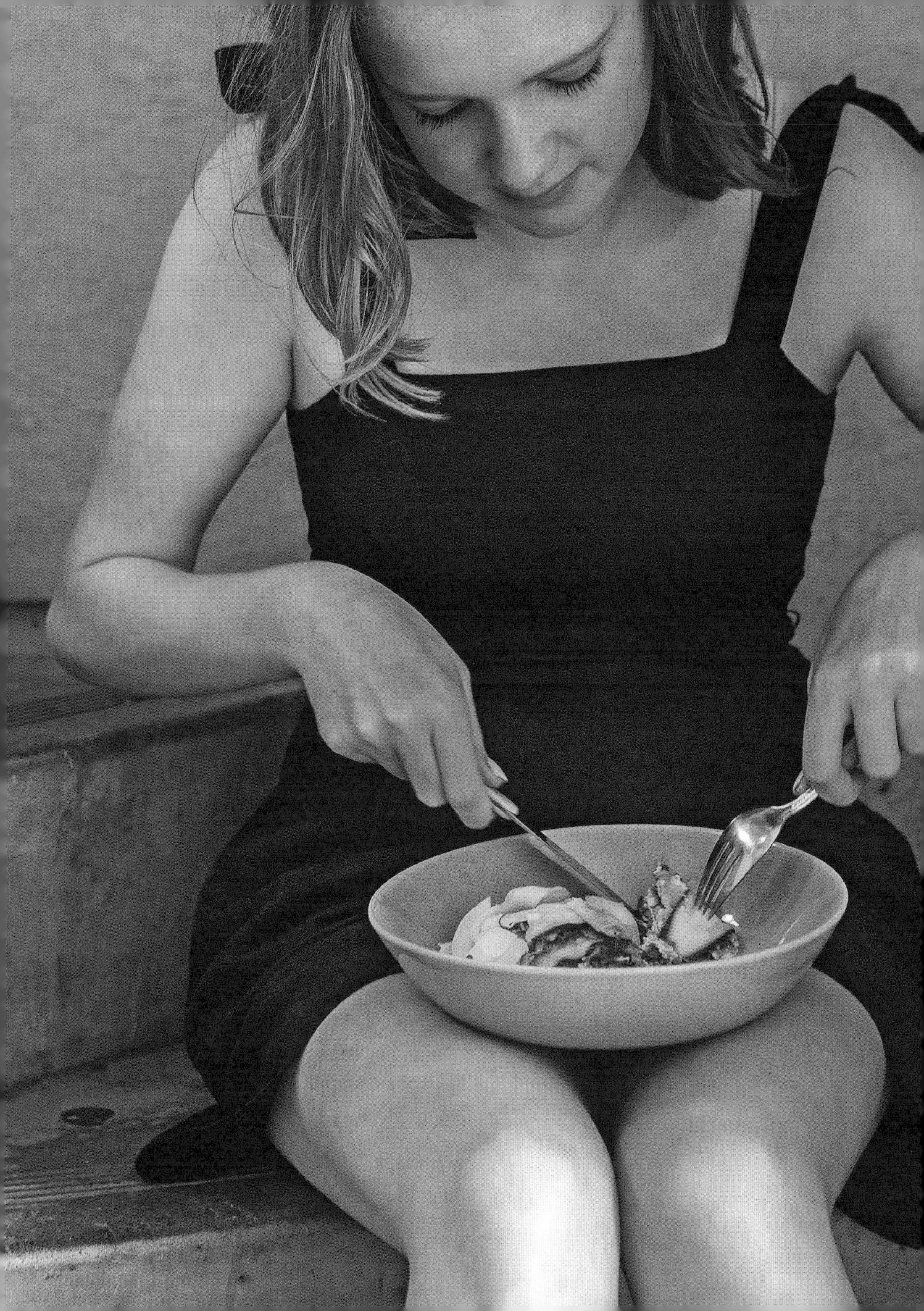

HOME IN THE HILLS
FISH AND CHIPS

Trout with Chips and Aioli

SERVES 6

When I was growing up in suburban Melbourne, there was nothing better than riding your pushie to the fish and chip shop for flake and chips – the steaming wrapped paper parcel burning your legs as you rode home to cover it all in salt, vinegar and tomato sauce. When the girls and I lived in Daylesford we still had a chippy, but it felt weird eating flake so far from the sea. This is our home in the hills version of fish and chips – the version my kids will remember when they're all grown up.

2 tablespoons olive oil
2 whole rainbow trout, gutted, cleaned and pin-boned, heads and tails still on (this is usually how they come from the shop, so don't freak out)
salt and pepper
4 bay leaves
a few thyme sprigs
1 lemon, thinly sliced
lemon wedges, to serve

For the chips:
1.5 kg large potatoes (desiree, dutch cream and sebago all work well), washed and left whole
salt
good handful of rosemary sprigs (don't be shy)
extra-virgin olive oil, for drizzling

For the aioli:
80 ml (⅓ cup) olive oil
80 ml (⅓ cup) vegetable oil
2 free-range egg yolks
2 garlic cloves, crushed
salt
1 tablespoon lemon juice

First the chips. Preheat the oven to 220°C (fan-forced) and generously oil a baking dish with olive oil.

Pop the potatoes in a large saucepan of boiling water and cook for 20–25 minutes or until you can just poke a fork in them with little resistance. You still want them to be reasonably firm before baking.

Drain the potatoes and leave until they're cool enough to handle. Cut them into thick chips and place in the prepared baking dish in a single layer. Sprinkle with salt and rosemary and drizzle generously with olive oil.

Bake for 25–30 minutes, giving the tray a shake every now and then, until they are golden and crispy. Remove from the oven and cover to keep warm.

While the chips are cooking, make the aioli. Combine the two oils in a little jug.

Pop the egg yolks, garlic, a pinch of salt and 2 tablespoons of the oil in a food processor and blend until well combined. Continue blending, while adding more of the oil in a super-slow thin stream, until the aioli begins to thicken. Once it thickens you can add the remaining oil more quickly, along with the lemon juice, and blend until you reach the desired consistency. Season to taste with salt and set aside.

Now the fish. Reduce the oven temperature to 200°C (fan-forced) and grease a baking dish with some of the olive oil.

Place the trout in the prepared dish and coat with the remaining olive oil. Season the inside and outside of each fish with salt and pop the bay leaves, thyme and half the lemon slices into the cavities. Season the fish with pepper and top with the remaining lemon slices.

Cover the baking dish with foil and bake for 10 minutes. Place the chips back in the oven and cook for another 5–10 minutes or until both fish flake easily with a fork and the chips are nice and hot.

Serve the fish, chips and aioli with lemon wedges.

Learning to back off

My kids are now at the age where they like to do their own thing in the kitchen. I'm not allowed to lend a hand with the mixing, cooking or decorating any more. On the surface this sounds like I should be up for the ultimate parenting award, so why do I find it so difficult? Why do I insist on sticking my nose in where it isn't wanted or NEEDED?

It's nothing to do with the slow pace of my girls' culinary development. I just love things to be perfect, and I want to be the one who makes that perfection happen. I'm all for my kids baking, as long as they put the chocolate chips in like this or put the icing on like that. Safety isn't the issue here either – they're old enough to go nuts with the oven. But for some reason they're not old enough to position that strawberry correctly. And they probably never will be.

I understand I need to back the hell off and give my kids the space to mess up and learn. That I'm doing them a disservice by hovering around like a bad smell. I'm trying to see these creations as an extended version of the crayon drawings that once adorned my fridge – just with more flour all over the place, and more crap to clean up.

This control issue extends to the way my kids decorate their room, choose their outfits and what music they

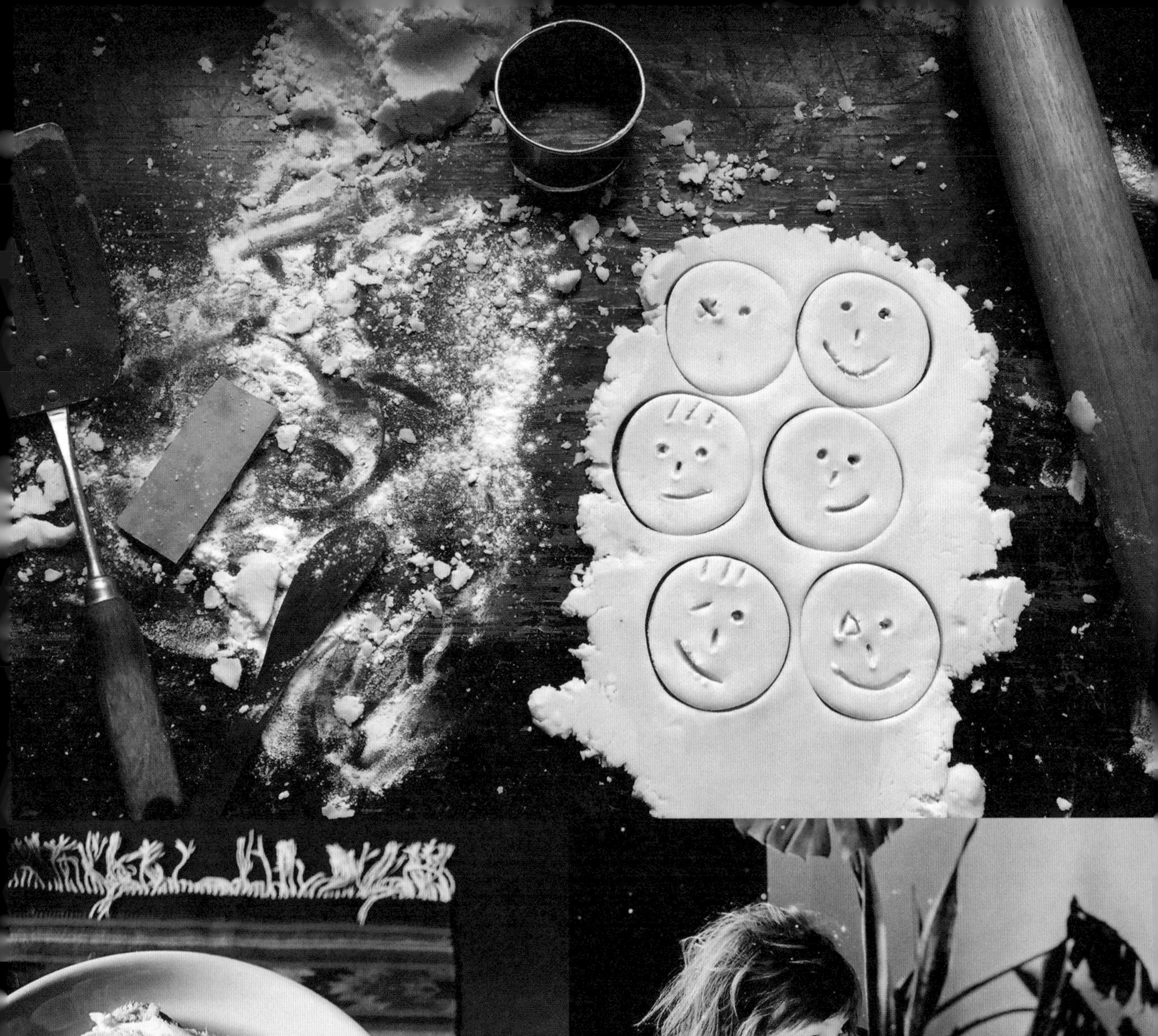

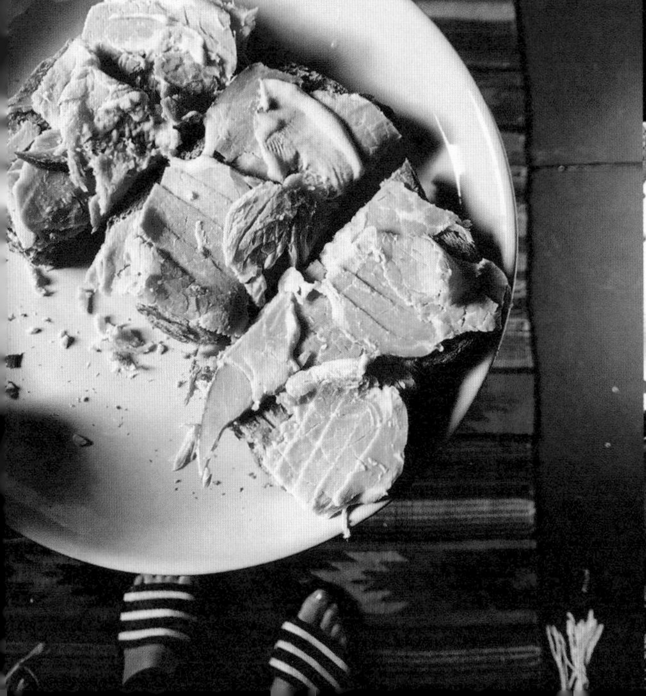

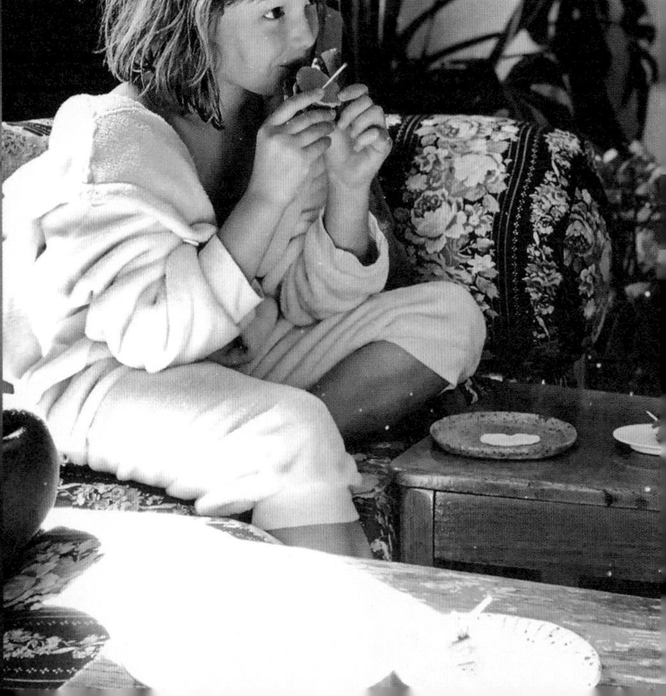

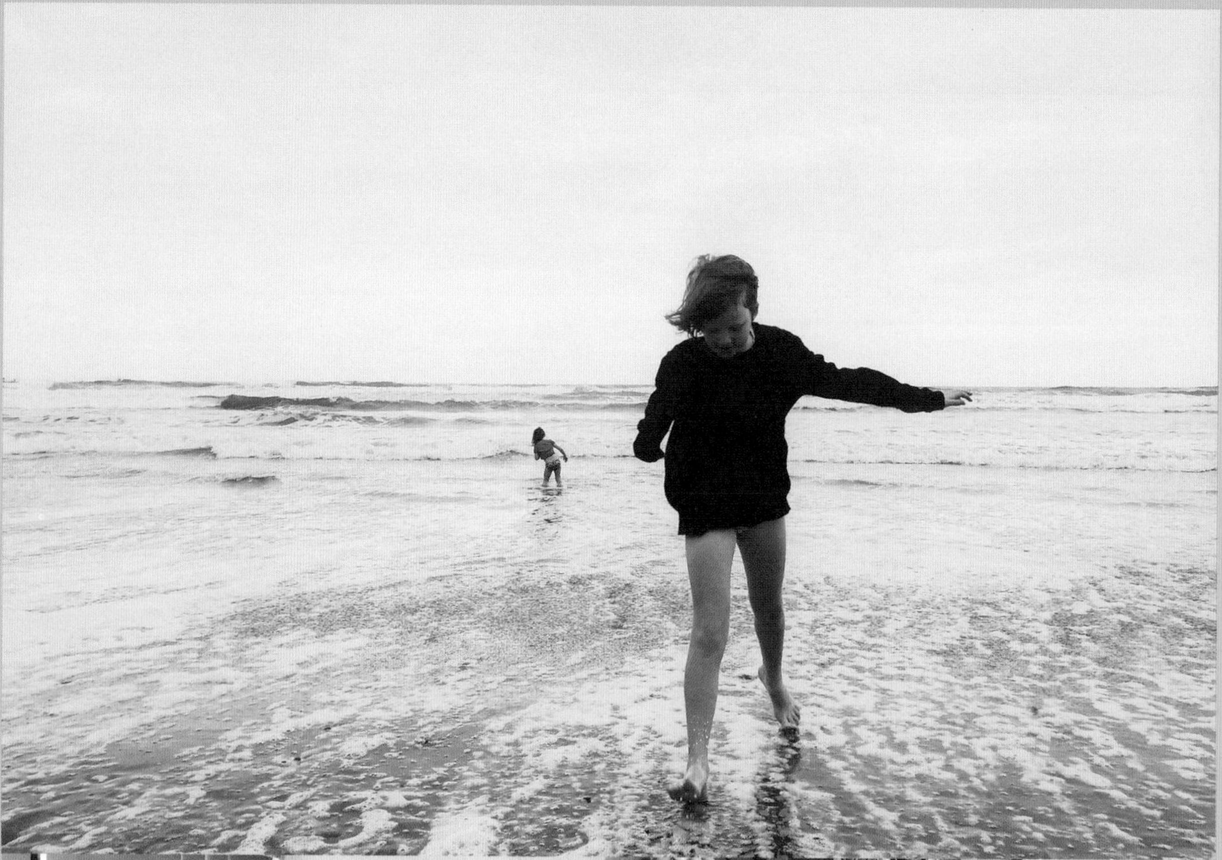

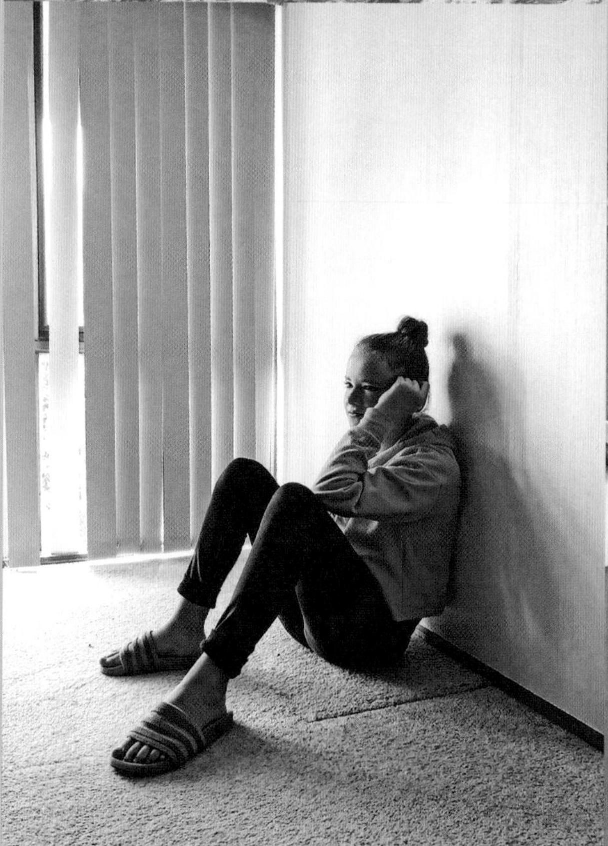

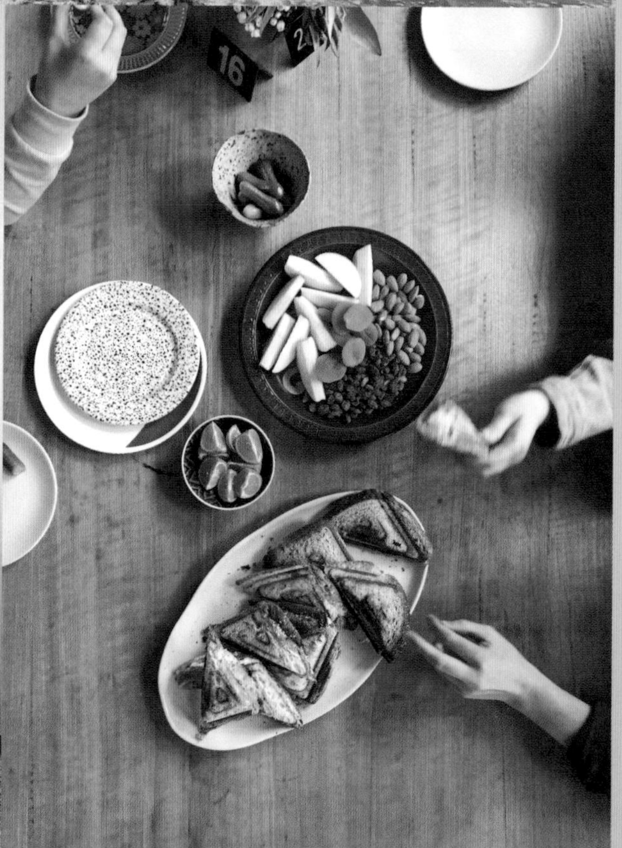
16

listen to. They've started to create a world that is theirs – one that makes them happy and reflects who they are. And as I watch it happen, it's equal parts heart-burstingly beautiful and heartbreakingly terrifying. Soon I won't be as important in their worlds. Is my hovering an attempt to remain relevant so I won't be made redundant?

It used to be the tiny things, always tiny. Until Maya hit her teens and the letting go things became WAY bigger and scarier. My eldest is hurtling towards her mid-teens; she pretty much makes all her own food, buys her own clothes and will not ever divulge what she plays on Spotify. And even though she has made this shift and needs me less, I am always the first person she turns to whenever she is worried, scared, sad or extremely happy and excited. And deep down, I know this will change also.

I'll start by backing away from their solo baking efforts and breathing through the chaos that is my kids in the kitchen. Because, not too long from now, my worries about wonky biscuits and sticky floors will seem like the most wonderful memories. Instead of hovering in the kitchen, I'll be lying in bed, staring at the ceiling, waiting for my kids to come home after a night out.

NUGGETS YOU'RE ALLOWED TO LIKE

Corn Chip Chicken Nuggets with Sriracha Mayo

SERVES 6

There are certain meals you can't admit to liking without a judgy side glance, and nuggets are definitely up there as one of the biggies. I get it; they're fried, they usually come from a fast-food joint, and they're more than likely made from factory-farmed chooks. But if you take care of business yourself, it can be a totally different story.

150 g plain corn chips
2 free-range eggs
40 g (⅓ cup) tapioca flour
800 g chicken thigh fillets,
    cut into bite-sized nuggets
vegetable oil, for pan-frying
coriander leaves, to serve

For the sriracha mayo:
125 g (½ cup) mayonnaise
2 tablespoons sriracha
juice of 1 lime or small lemon
chopped coriander leaves,
    to taste (optional)
salt

For the sriracha mayo, combine all the ingredients in a small bowl until smooth. Set aside.

Pop the corn chips in a food processor and pulse until they are finely crushed.

Pour the crushed chips into a bowl, lightly beat the eggs in another bowl, and tip the flour into a third bowl.

Dip the chicken nuggets into the flour to lightly coat, shaking off any excess, then dip into the beaten egg and finally into the corn chips.

Heat a large frying pan over medium heat and add enough oil to coat the bottom of the pan. Add the chicken nuggets and cook for about 4 minutes on each side or until golden and cooked through. Remove and drain on paper towel.

Serve the nuggets with the sriracha mayo and a sprinkling of coriander on top, if you like.

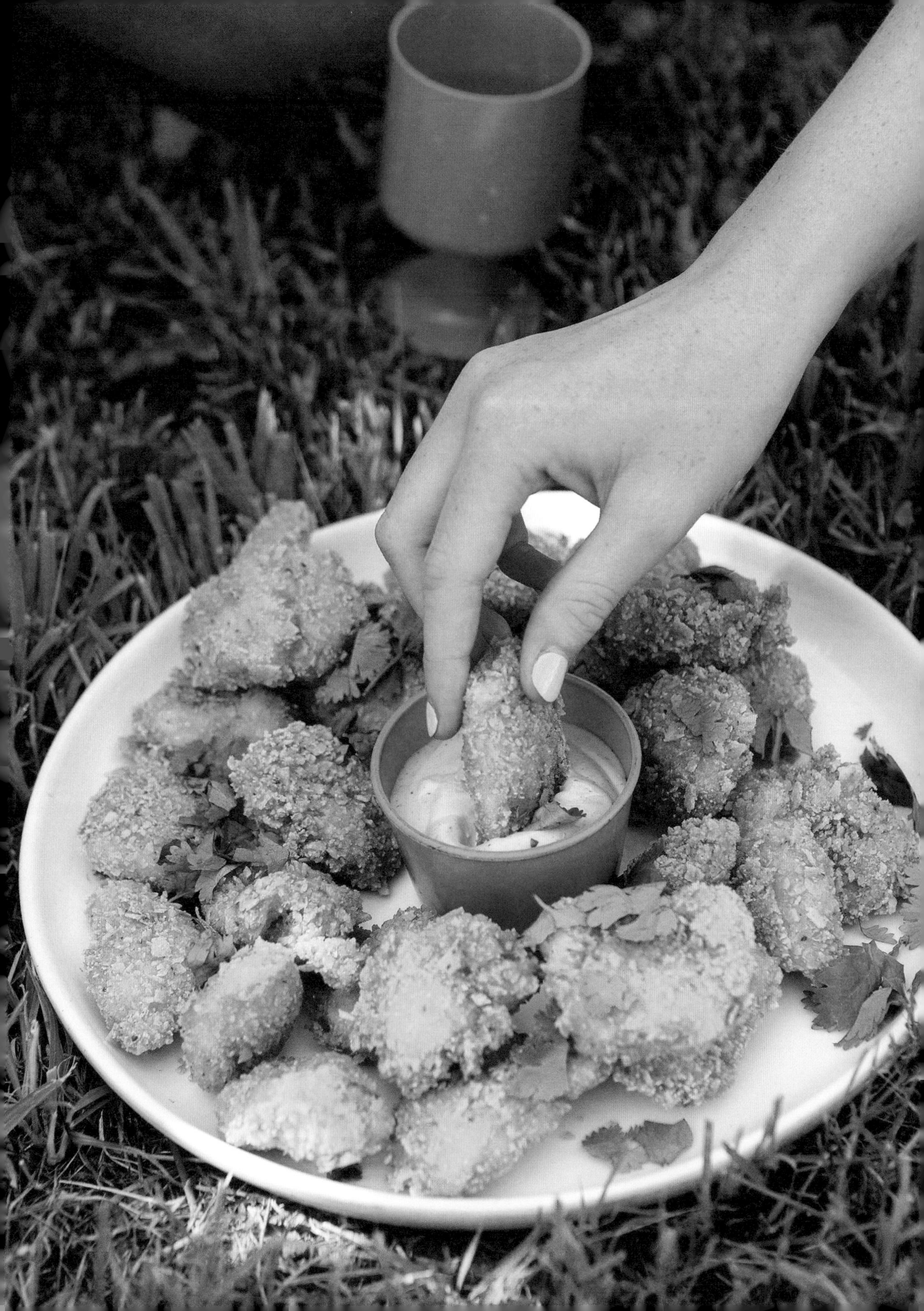

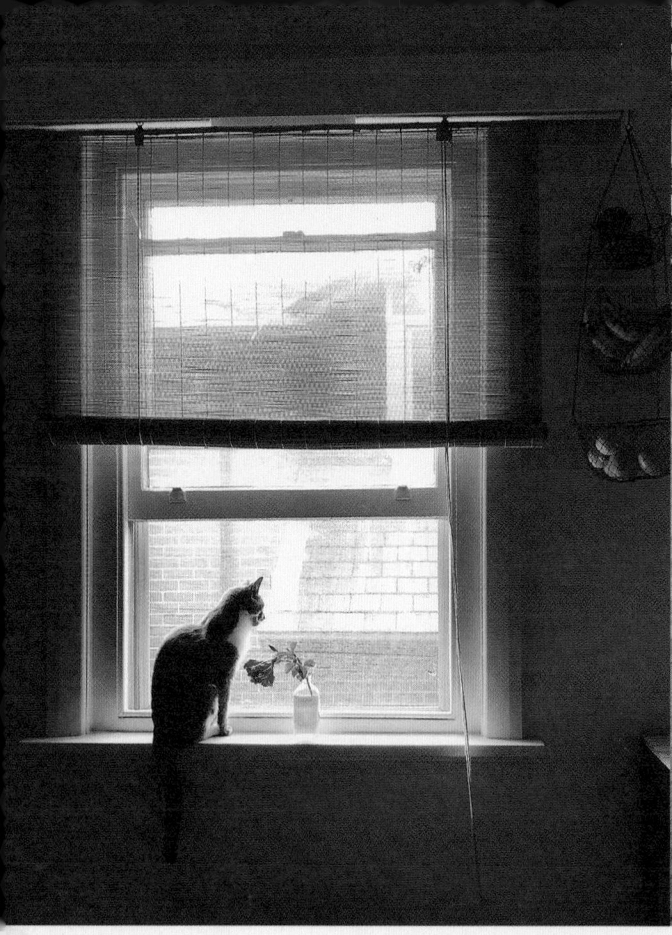
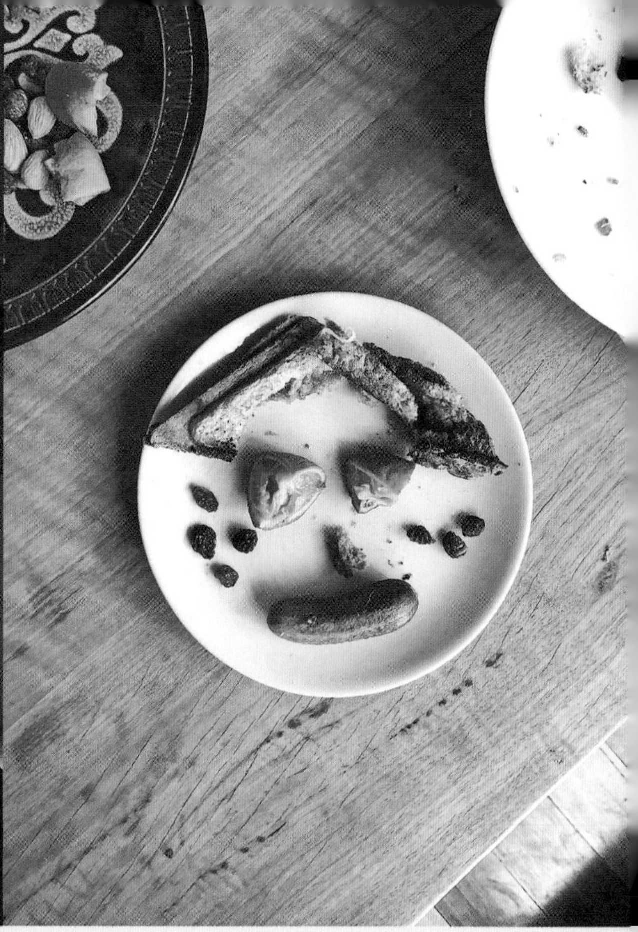
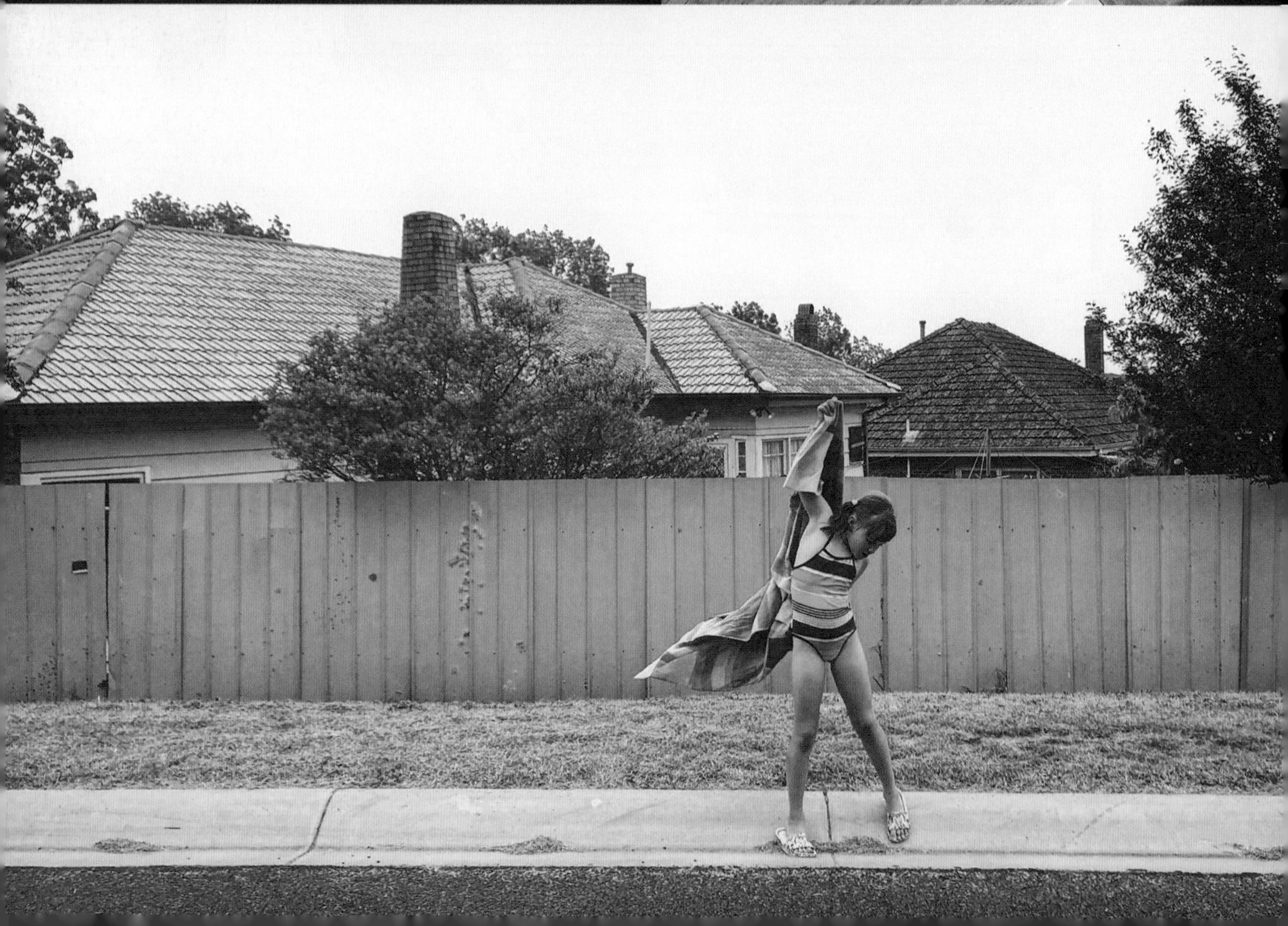

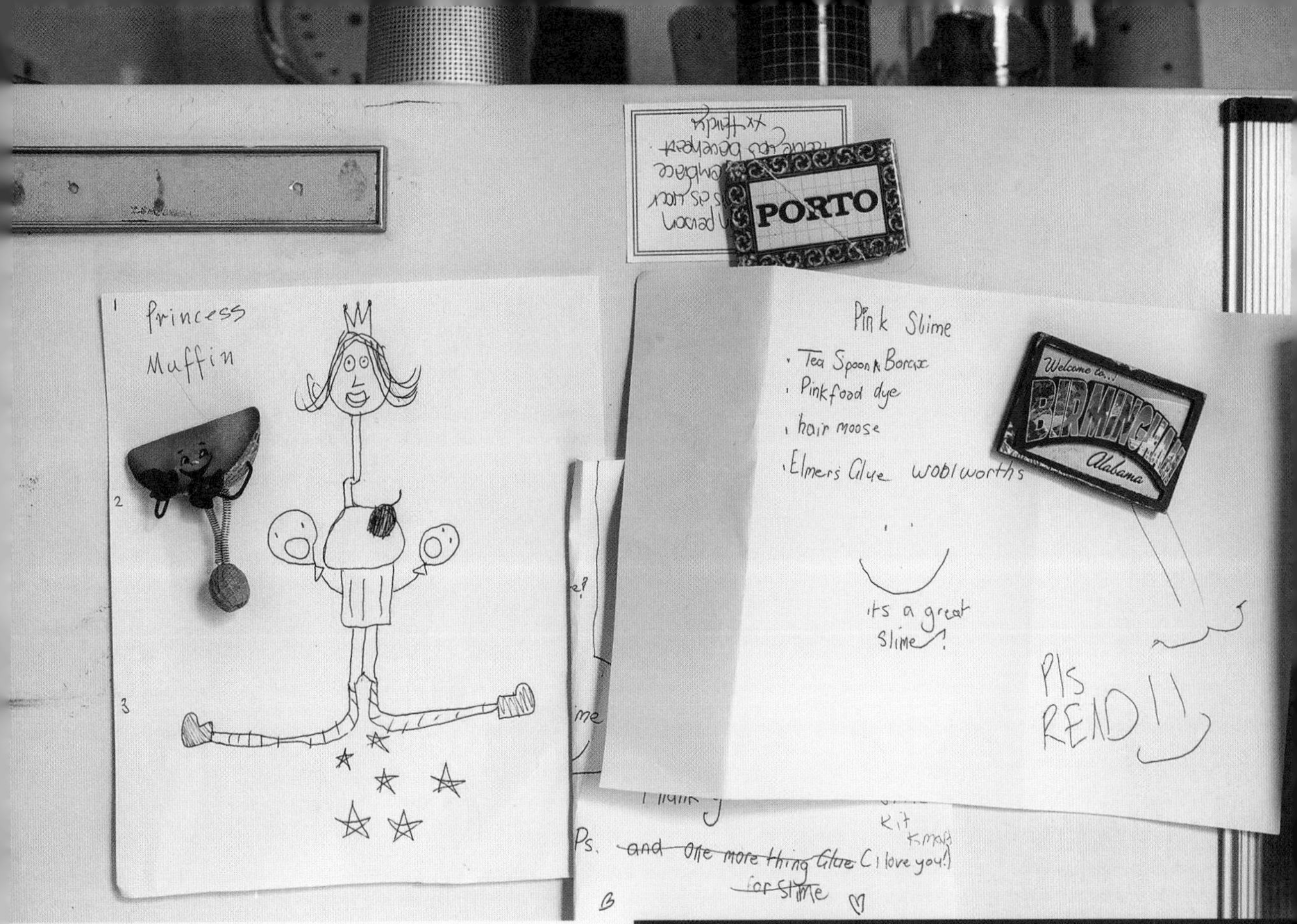
PORTO
Princess
Muffin
Pink Slime
· Tea Spoon A Borax
· Pink food dye
· hair moose
· Elmers Glue woolworths
its a great
slime!
Welcome to...
BIRMINGHAM
Alabama
Pls
READ!!
Ps. and one more thing Glue for slime (I love you!)
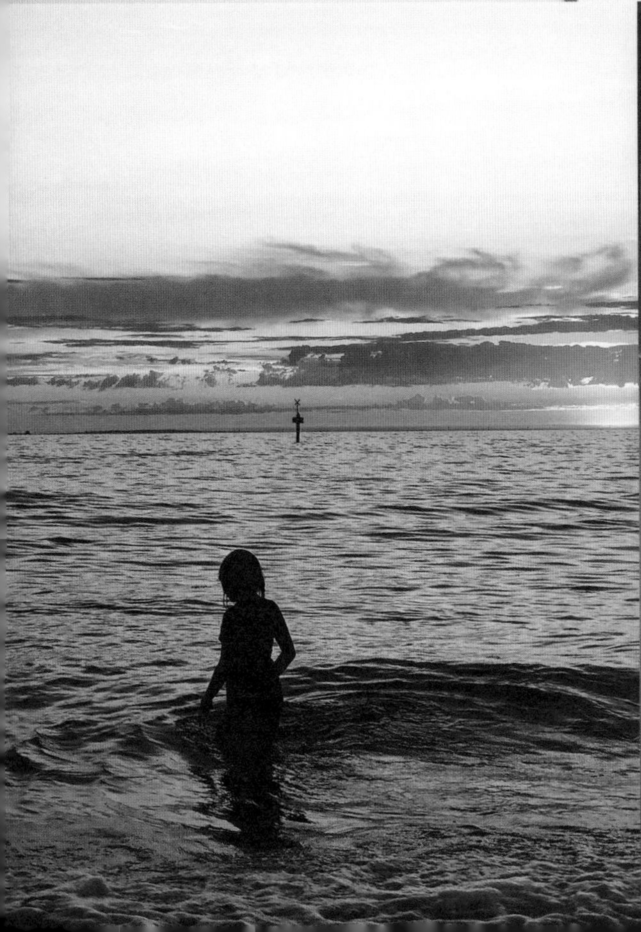
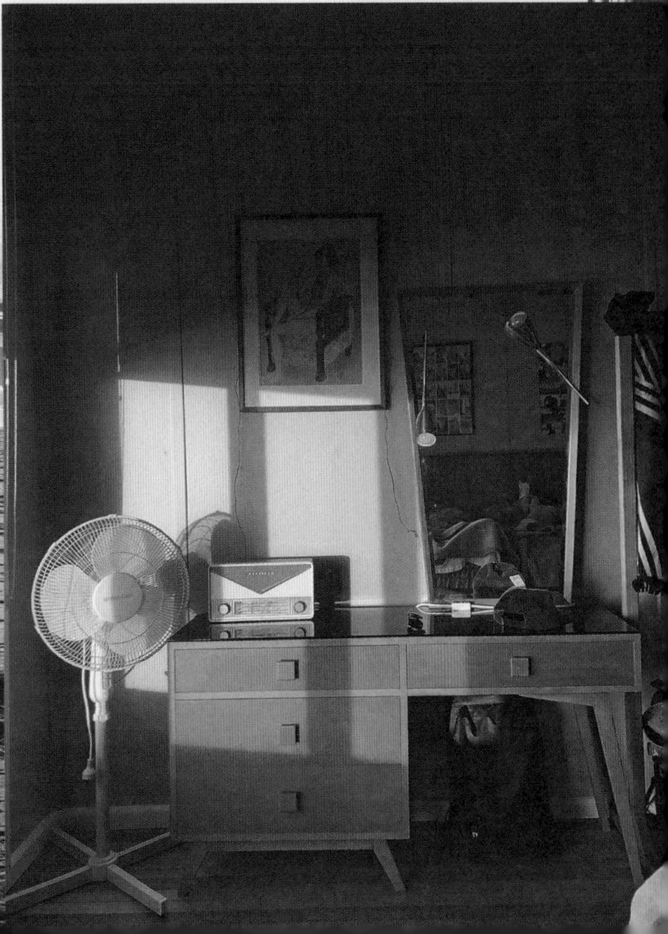

HOMEMADE FAVE

Bibimbap

SERVES 4

I still remember the first time the girls and I ate this Korean hotpot of crispy rice bits and sesame garlicky veg. We were chatting and being idiots at the table and when the three bowls were placed in front of us, we just looked at each other with big stupid grins. What followed was silent food shovelling, until it was all gone. We all wanted more, but we've learned the hard way that a second helping is never what's needed. Too much of a good thing – we all walked out wishing we'd worn elastic waistbands. Now we make it ourselves whenever we want. It's not as fun as eating it from the hotpots, but it's still pretty bloody good.

330 g (1½ cups) white or brown long-grain rice
300 g baby spinach leaves
salt
sesame oil, for sprinkling
1 carrot, peeled into ribbons
vegetable oil, for pan-frying
150 g shiitake mushrooms, thinly sliced
4 free-range eggs (optional)
bibimbap sauce (or any yummy sauce really; see TIP), to serve
sesame seeds, for sprinkling

For the beef:
300 g beef mince
2 tablespoons soy sauce
1½ tablespoons sesame oil
1½ teaspoons brown sugar
2 garlic cloves, finely chopped

For the beef, combine all the ingredients in a mixing bowl, then cover and pop in the fridge for about 30 minutes.

Meanwhile, cook the rice according to the packet instructions.

While the rice is cooking, blanch the spinach in a large saucepan of salted boiling water for 30 seconds, then drain and run under cold water to stop the cooking process. Squeeze the spinach to remove any excess water, then place in a bowl and season with salt and a sprinkling of sesame oil. Set aside.

Heat a splash of vegetable oil in a small frying pan over medium–high heat, add a pinch of salt and the carrot and cook for 2–3 minutes or until just tender. Remove and set aside.

Add a little more oil and salt to the pan and cook the shiitake mushroom for 2–3 minutes. Remove and set aside.

Take the beef mixture out of the fridge. Heat a little more oil in the pan and cook the mince for 3–5 minutes, breaking up any large clumps as you go. Remove and set aside.

Crack the eggs (if using) into the pan and fry them the way you like them. Remove and set aside.

Spoon some rice into the bottom of each bowl, then add the beef, veggies and bibimbap sauce and top each serve with a fried egg, if you like. Sprinkle with some sesame seeds and serve.

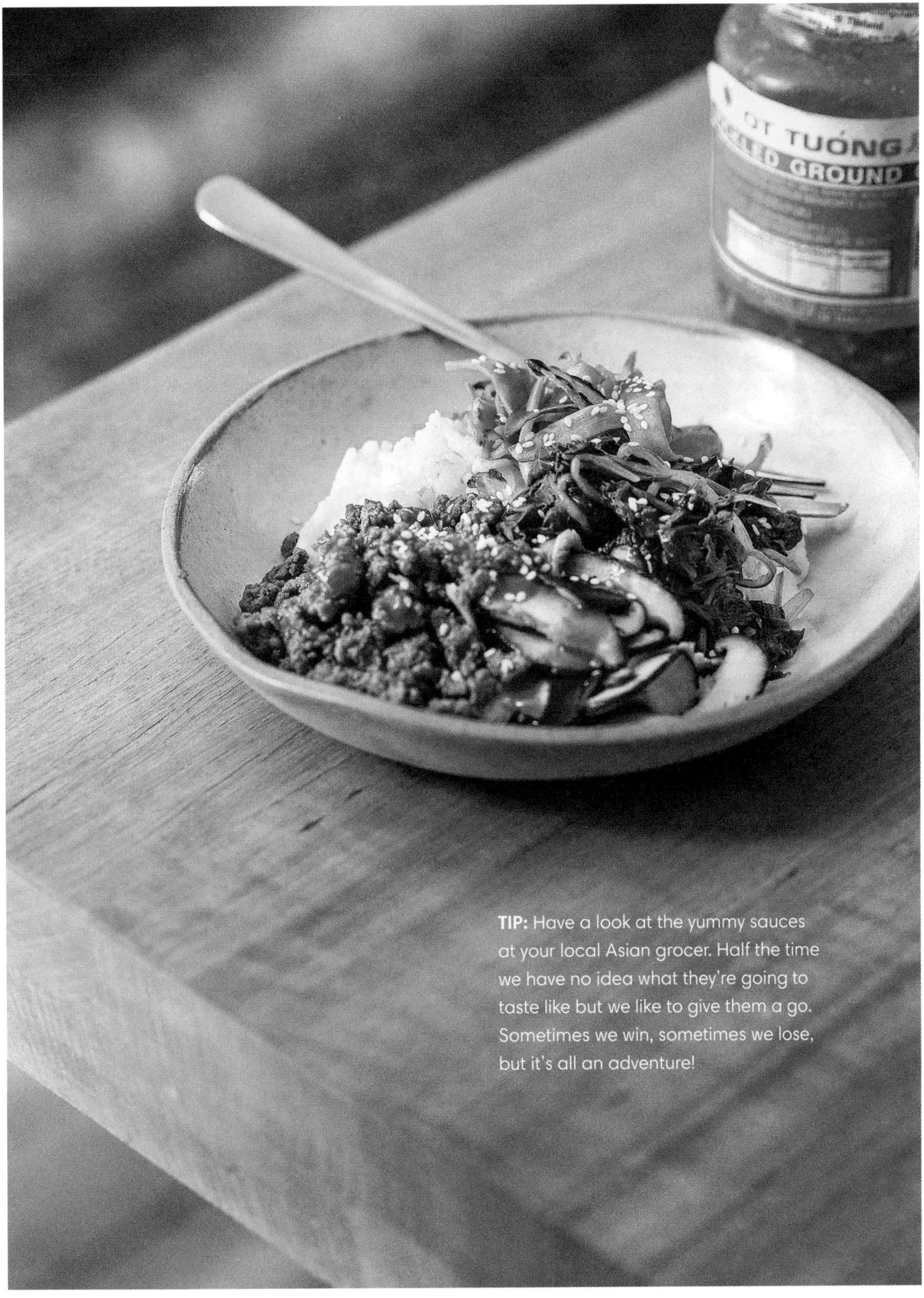
GROUND

TIP: Have a look at the yummy sauces at your local Asian grocer. Half the time we have no idea what they're going to taste like but we like to give them a go. Sometimes we win, sometimes we lose, but it's all an adventure!

Black bananas and things to do with them

I get a rush when I see a box of spotty bananas on sale at the fruit shop. To me, they should be more expensive than the chalky underripe ones but, as they say, one person's trash is another's treasure. We usually buy as many as we can carry and get out of there quickly before they realise what a mistake they've made.

At home we divide our stash into 'straight to the freezer' bananas and 'banana bread' bananas. Once we've baked a couple of loaves, we'll slice up one loaf and pop it in the freezer with the other bananas. I really feel that putting stuff in the freezer is one of the most grown-up things you can do for yourself. In fact, I've become a little hooked on it lately; let's just say we'll be OK for smoothies and banana bread if there are any natural disasters in the near future.

What to make with these spotty beauties?

BANANA BREAD

There's a banana bread recipe on page 44.

SMOOTHIES

We make smoothies out of whatever we have in the kitchen, but our fave is with coconut milk, almond butter, raw cacao powder, frozen banana and ground cinnamon.

ICE CREAM

Blitz frozen banana in a food processor until it resembles soft-serve ice cream. Add whatever you think might make your ice cream a little tastier – we put nut butter, cocoa and maple syrup in ours when we're feeling fancy.

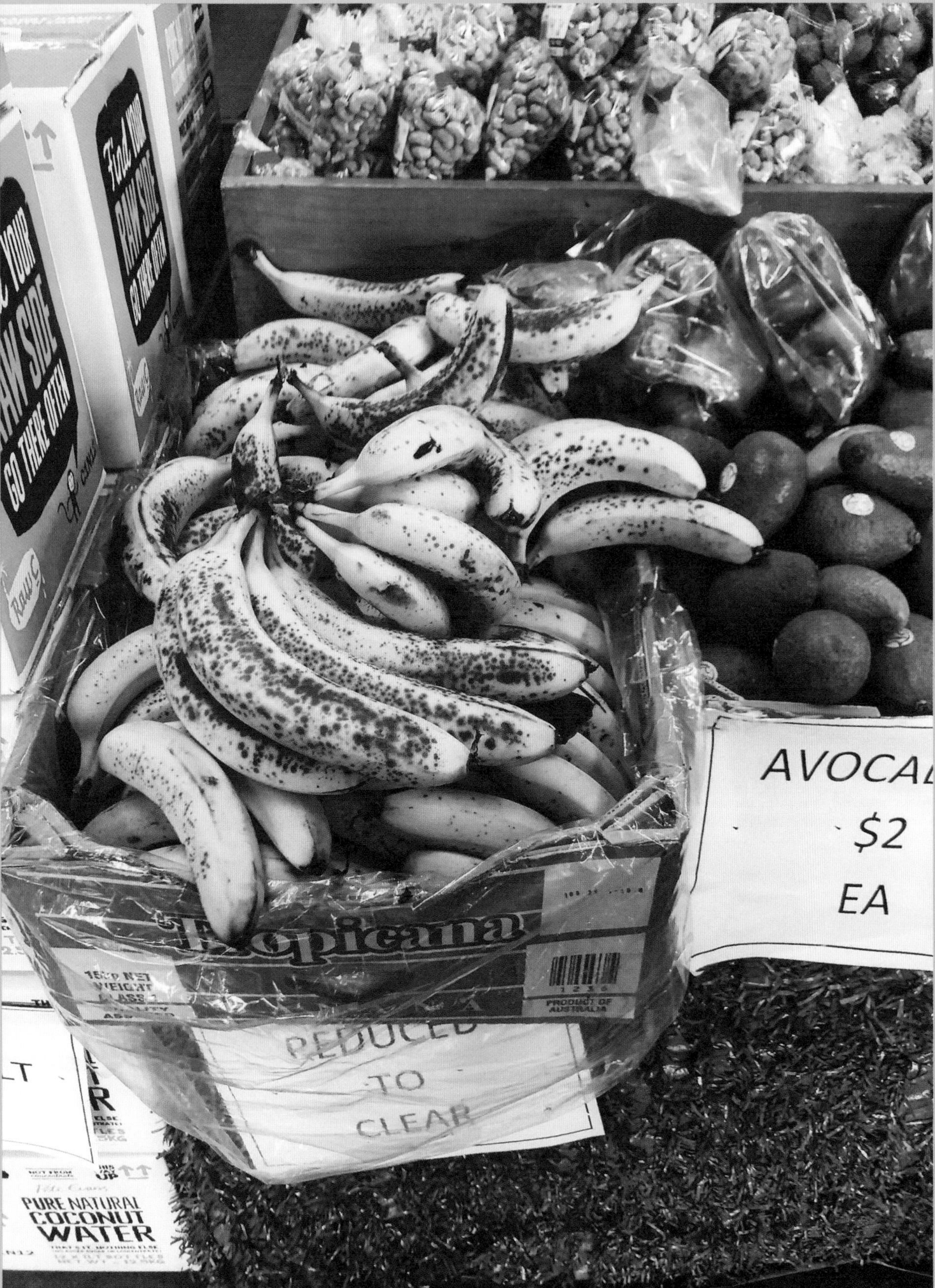

Find your RAW SIDE GO THERE OFTEN
RAW SIDE GO THERE OFTEN
$2
EA
REDUCED
TO
CLEAR
PRODUCT OF AUSTRALIA
PURE NATURAL COCONUT WATER

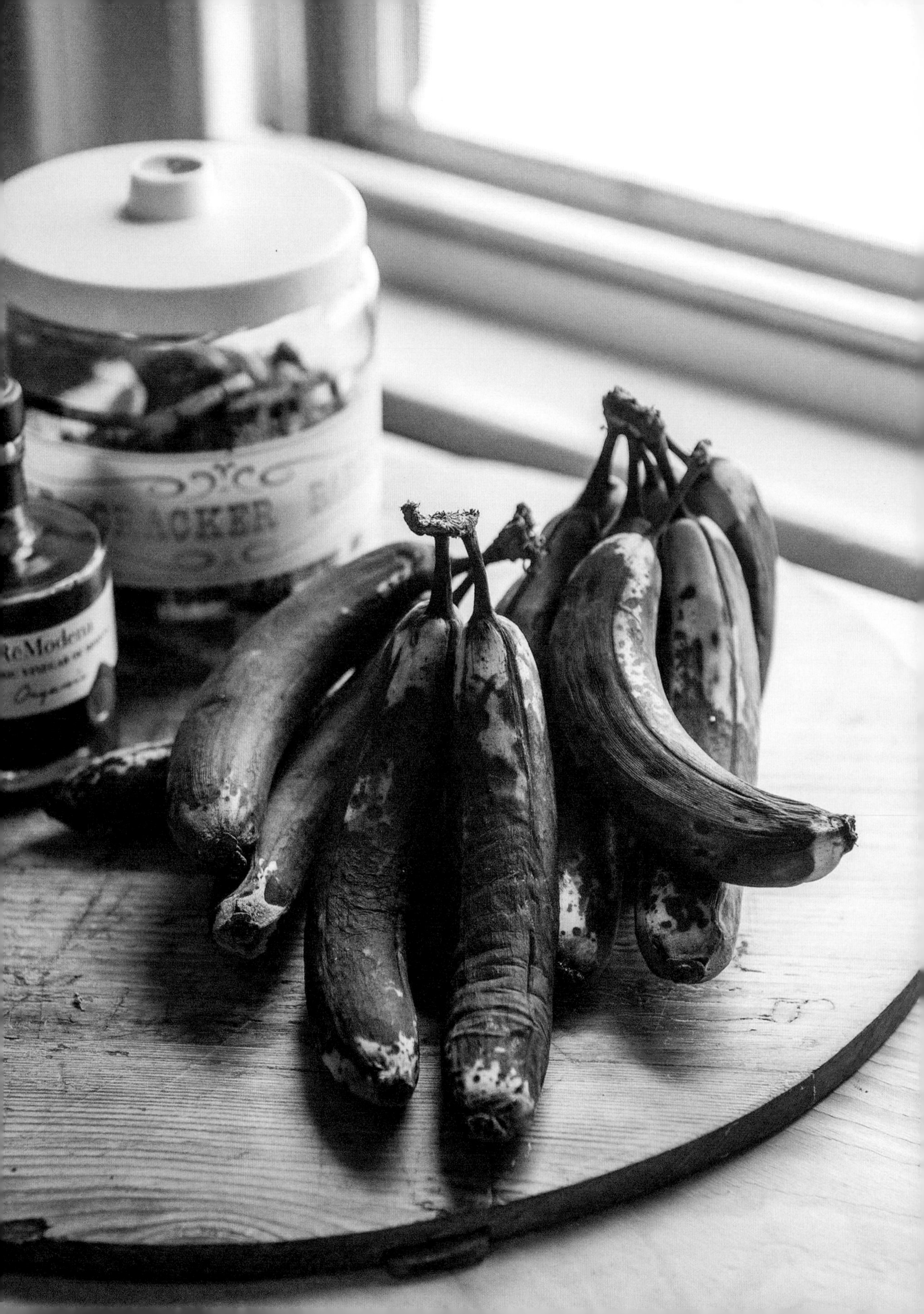

BANANA FRITTERS

480 g (2 cups) mashed overripe
    bananas
3 tablespoons brown sugar
1 tablespoon freshly grated
    nutmeg
¼ teaspoon ground cinnamon
½ teaspoon vanilla extract
pinch of salt
150 g (1 cup) plain flour
2 tablespoons vegetable oil,
    plus extra if needed
1 tablespoon caster sugar

Place the banana, brown sugar, nutmeg, cinnamon, vanilla and salt in the bowl of an electric mixer fitted with the paddle attachment and beat until well combined. Stir in the flour.

Heat the vegetable oil in a heavy-based frying pan over high heat and add generous tablespoons of batter. Fry for 1–2 minutes each side or until crisp and nicely browned, adding a little extra oil if needed. Remove and drain on paper towel. Cover to keep warm while you cook the remaining fritters.

Sprinkle with caster sugar and serve warm.

DON'T WORRY, BE HAPPY BREAD

Banana and Walnut Bread

SERVES 6-8

Did you know that bananas actually make you happier? Like, as in, science. For me, even just the hunt for a bargain box of overripe bananas is good for the soul. Seriously, finding a stash of spotty bananas that my local greengrocer is practically giving away makes everything good in the world ... for a minute or two anyway.

4 overripe bananas
1 teaspoon vanilla extract
160 ml (⅔ cup) vegetable oil
125 ml (½ cup) maple syrup, plus extra for glazing
225 g (1½ cups) self-raising flour
pinch of salt
100 g (1 cup) walnuts
1 banana, halved lengthways
1 tablespoon sesame seeds

Preheat the oven to 180°C (fan-forced). Line a medium loaf tin with baking paper.

Pop the bananas, vanilla, vegetable oil and maple syrup in the bowl of an electric mixer fitted with the paddle attachment and beat until well combined. Add the flour and salt and beat until just combined.

Fold in the walnuts, then pour the batter into the prepared tin. Gently press the banana halves into the batter, cut-side up, and sprinkle with the sesame seeds.

Bake for 30 minutes, then brush the top with a little extra maple syrup. Bake for a further 20–30 minutes or until a skewer inserted in the centre comes out clean.

Cool in the tin for a few minutes, then turn out onto a wire rack and leave to cool completely. Or steal a warm, melty bit as an extra-special treat.

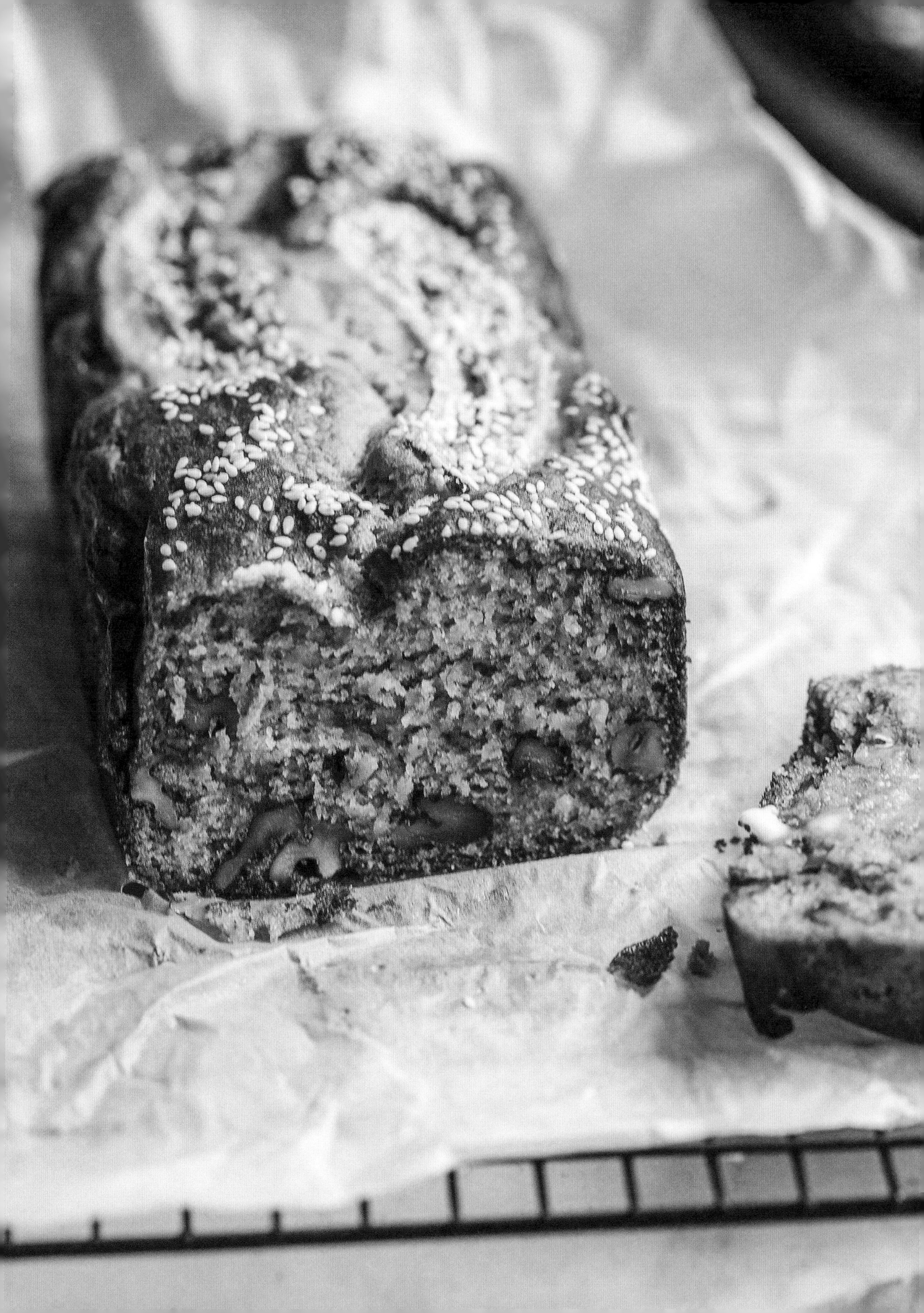

SWEET JAMMY DROPS

Raspberry Jam Drops

MAKES 20

When I was a kid, I'd go to a friend's house after school and her mum would make my brother and me an afternoon snack plate. The plate would have a selection of things, like creamed honey on Weet-Bix, cut-up apple, Vegemite on Vita-Weats (always with the little worms popping through the holes), and every now and then there were jam drops. To this day, all these things remind me of Pat, and when I get the chance to make my girls an after-school snack I make them exactly the same things. Thanks for looking after us, Pat.

100 g butter, softened
½ teaspoon vanilla extract
115 g (½ cup) caster sugar
100 g (1 cup) almond meal
1 free-range egg
150 g (1 cup) plain flour, sifted
100 g (⅓ cup) raspberry jam

Place the butter, vanilla, sugar and almond meal in an electric mixer fitted with the paddle attachment and beat until pale and creamy. Crack in the egg and beat until combined.

Fold through the flour with a wooden spoon until combined, then cover and pop in the fridge for 30 minutes to firm up.

Preheat the oven to 180°C (fan-forced). Grease and line two baking trays with baking paper.

Roll tablespoons of dough into balls and place them 3 cm apart on the prepared baking trays. Make an indent in the middle of each ball with your thumb, then spoon in about a teaspoon of jam. Cover and freeze for 15 minutes to firm up (or pop them in the fridge for 1 hour if you don't have room in your freezer).

Bake for 12–15 minutes or until the biscuits are lightly golden. Cool on the trays for 10 minutes, then transfer to a wire rack to cool completely.

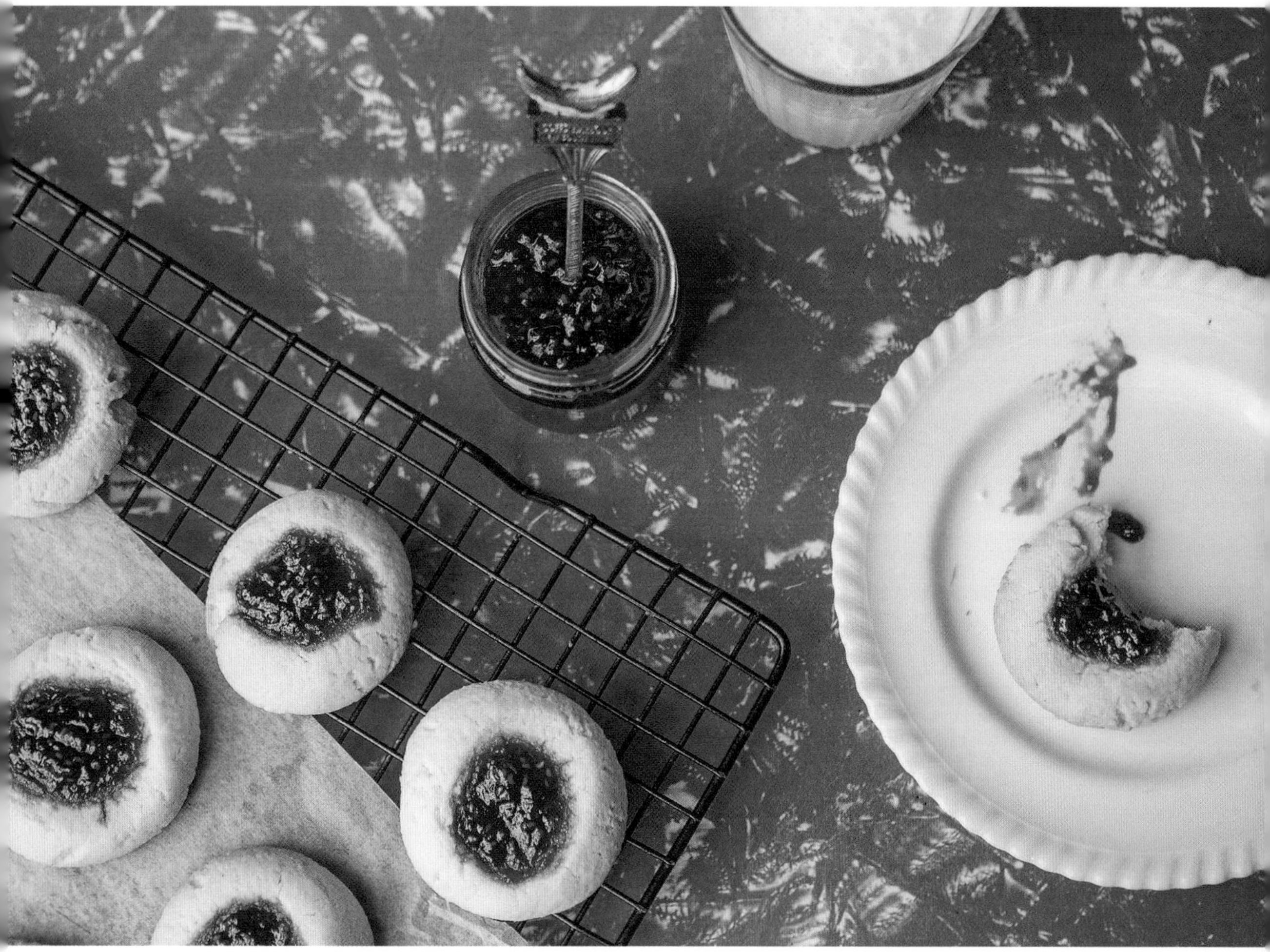

Big talks

Sometimes we need to talk to our kids about big things; things we know are going to hurt them. We think long and hard about how to deliver the news in a way that will minimise the pain. And agonise over the best time of day to deliver it. Early in the morning isn't great as they have the whole day to dwell on it, but the evening isn't good either as they need time to process it before they go to sleep. Maybe tomorrow would be better.

Last year I had to have a few hard talks with my girls. Talks of sickness, break-ups and moving towns. They didn't get any easier. They never do. I had no idea that this part of parenting existed. And even if I had, I would never have understood the raw emotion of delivering news to your children that would hurt them so much. And make them cry, the worst kind of crying – the silent rolling tears.

But as hard as these talks are, I also understand the relief of finally uttering the words that I've been going over and over in my mind. We're in this together now. We're on the other side, we can work through the pain and sit with it, without rushing to try and make it all better. Sometimes life hurts, and that's OK. It's a big thing I want to teach my girls, because I'm just starting to learn this now and I wish I'd accepted it so much

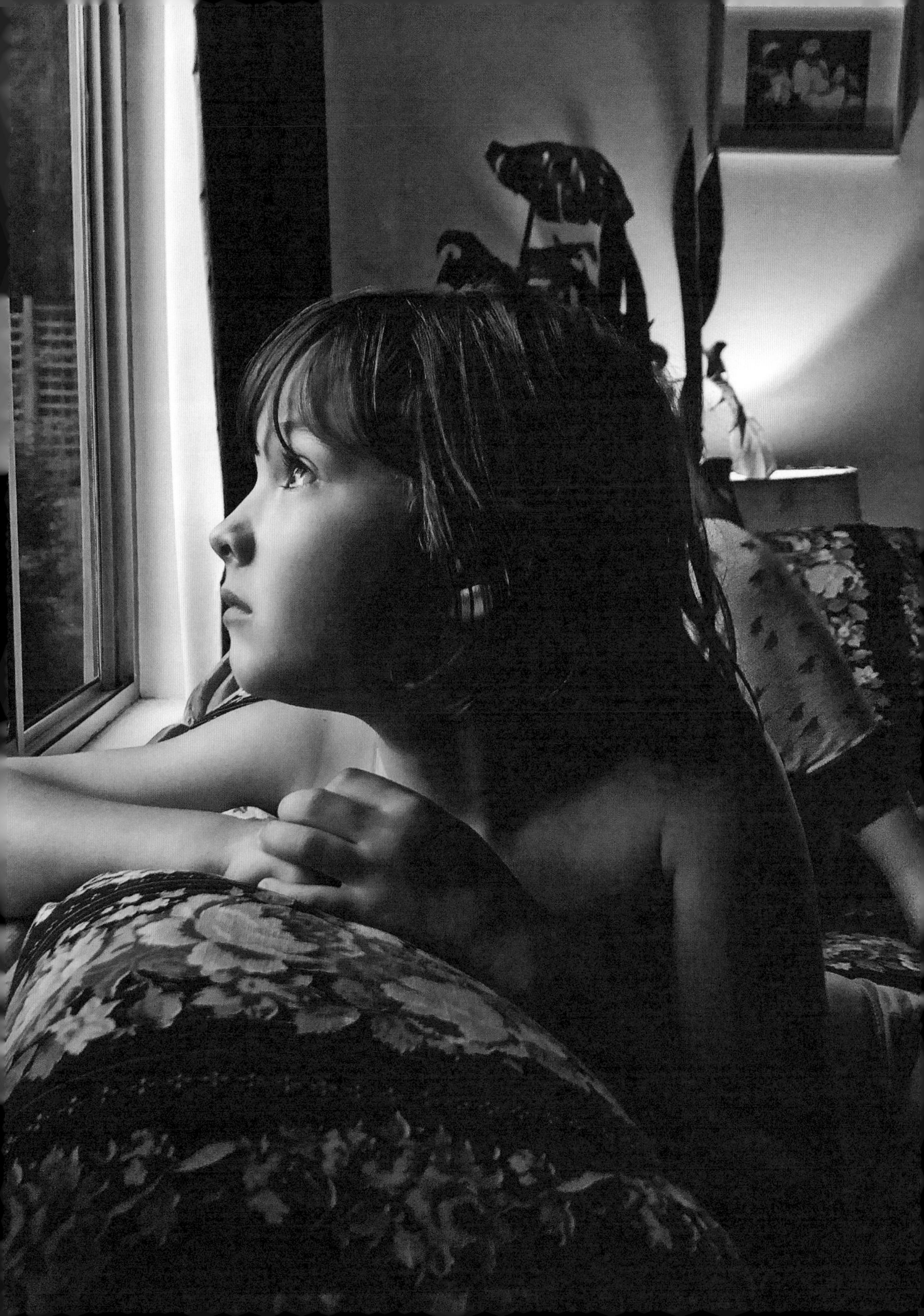

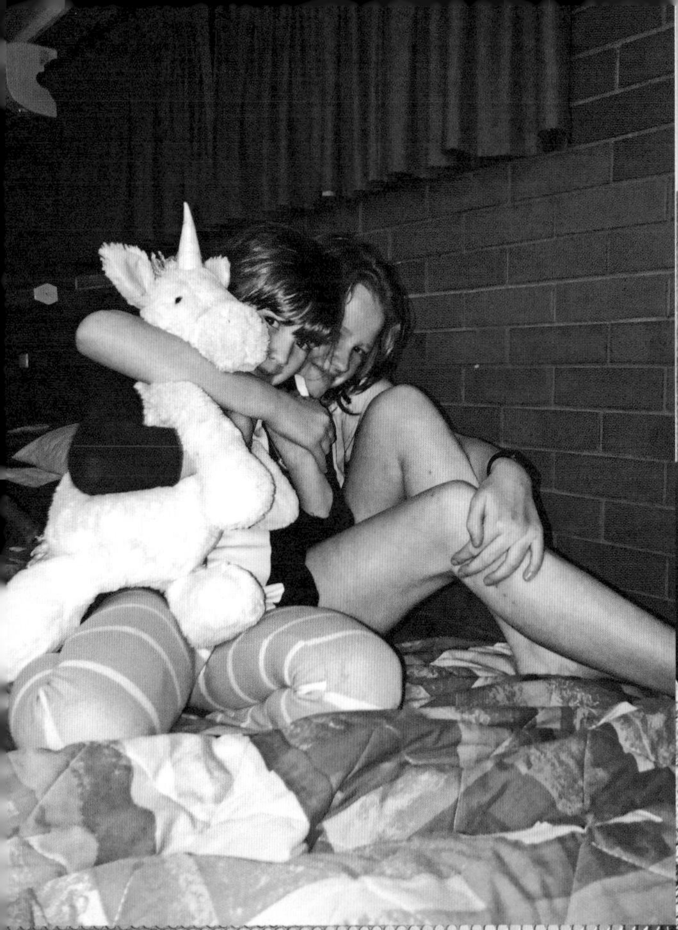
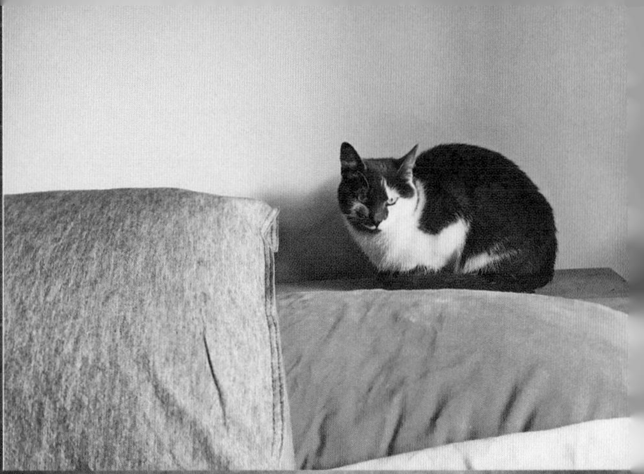
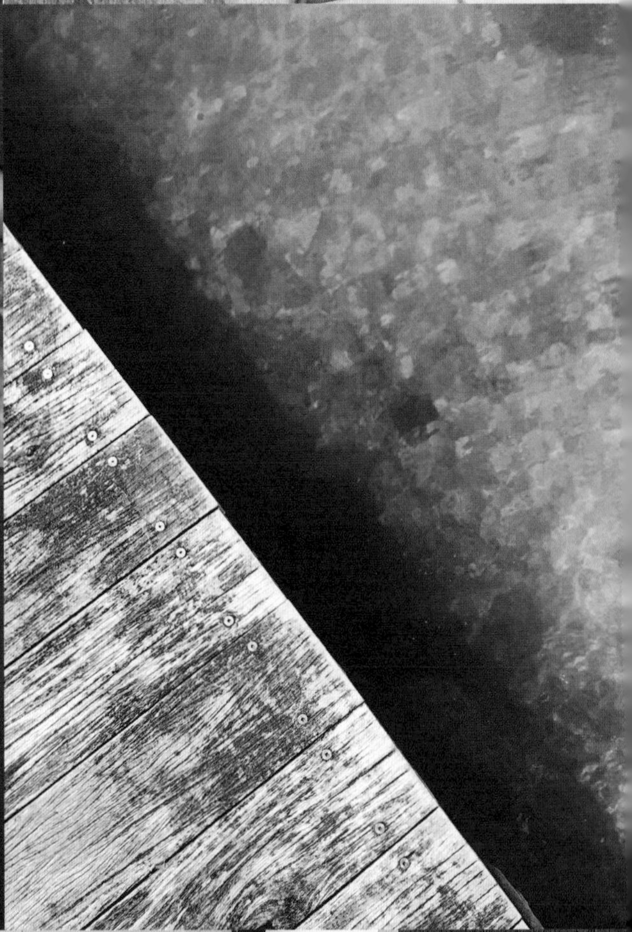
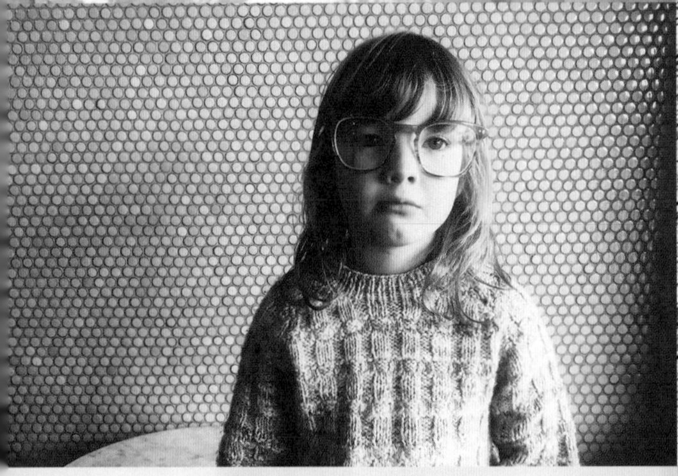
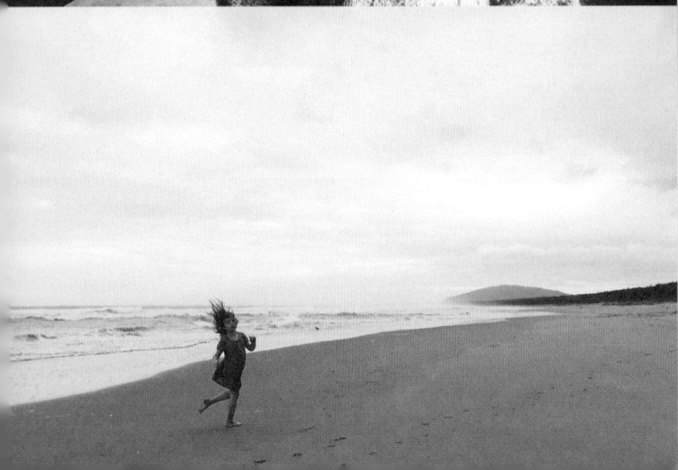
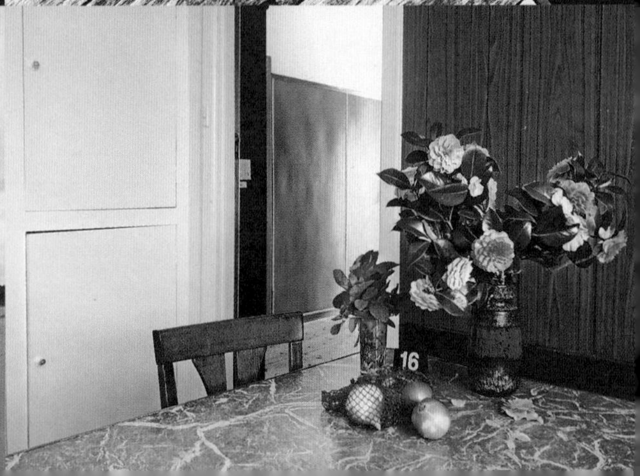
16

sooner. I've always been the person who'd rush off in search of an emotional Band-Aid, to patch up the holes and make everything OK, but I'm finally realising that feeling it is important.

I'm hoping that, by sitting with my girls and having these hard conversations, I'm teaching them to communicate how they're feeling, even if it is a little hard. That by talking about the big stuff, they'll feel comfortable talking about things they find difficult too.

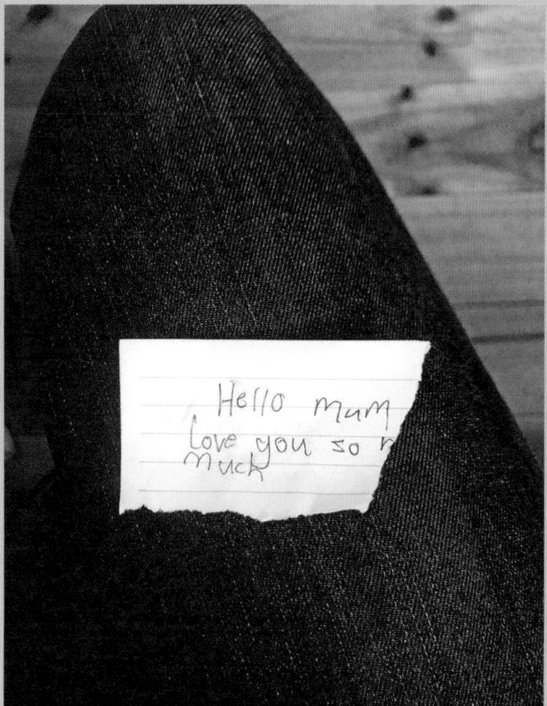
Hello mum
love you so
much

CAKES THAT MAKE YOU GO HUMMMMM ...

Mini Hummingbird Cakes

MAKES 10

I still remember the first hummingbird cake I ever ate. My then housemate brought one home in a bag full of the day's unsold cakes from the shop she worked in. Even though it was a little stale, the flavour combo blew my mind. From then on I would eagerly await her return from work, hoping the hummingbird cakes weren't popular that day. Now that the housemate and the cake shop are gone, it's up to me to recreate the magic.

140 g (1¼ cups) chickpea (besan) flour
3 tablespoons flaxseed meal
1¼ teaspoons ground cinnamon
¾ teaspoon bicarbonate of soda
¼ teaspoon salt
240 g (1 cup) mashed very ripe bananas
1 x 440 g can unsweetened crushed pineapple (don't drain it)
3 tablespoons pure maple syrup
2 tablespoons vegetable oil
1¼ teaspoons vanilla extract
10 pecan halves

For the icing:
185 g (¾ cup) cream cheese
3 tablespoons Greek yoghurt
½ teaspoon vanilla extract
60 g (½ cup) pure icing sugar

Preheat the oven to 180°C (fan-forced). Line 10 cups of a muffin tin with paper cases.

In a large bowl, whisk together the chickpea flour, flaxseed meal, cinnamon, bicarbonate of soda and salt, breaking up any lumps as you go.

Place the banana, crushed pineapple and juice, maple syrup, vegetable oil and vanilla in another bowl and mix until well combined.

Pour the wet mixture into the dry mixture and mix well.

Spoon the batter evenly into the paper cases, only half-filling each muffin cup. Bake for 20 minutes or until golden and the tops are firm to the touch. Cool in the tin for a few minutes, then transfer to a wire rack to cool completely.

For the icing, place the cream cheese and yoghurt in the bowl of an electric mixer fitted with the paddle attachment and beat together well. Add the vanilla and icing sugar and beat until smooth and combined.

Ice each cooled cake with a generous scrape of icing and top with a pecan half.

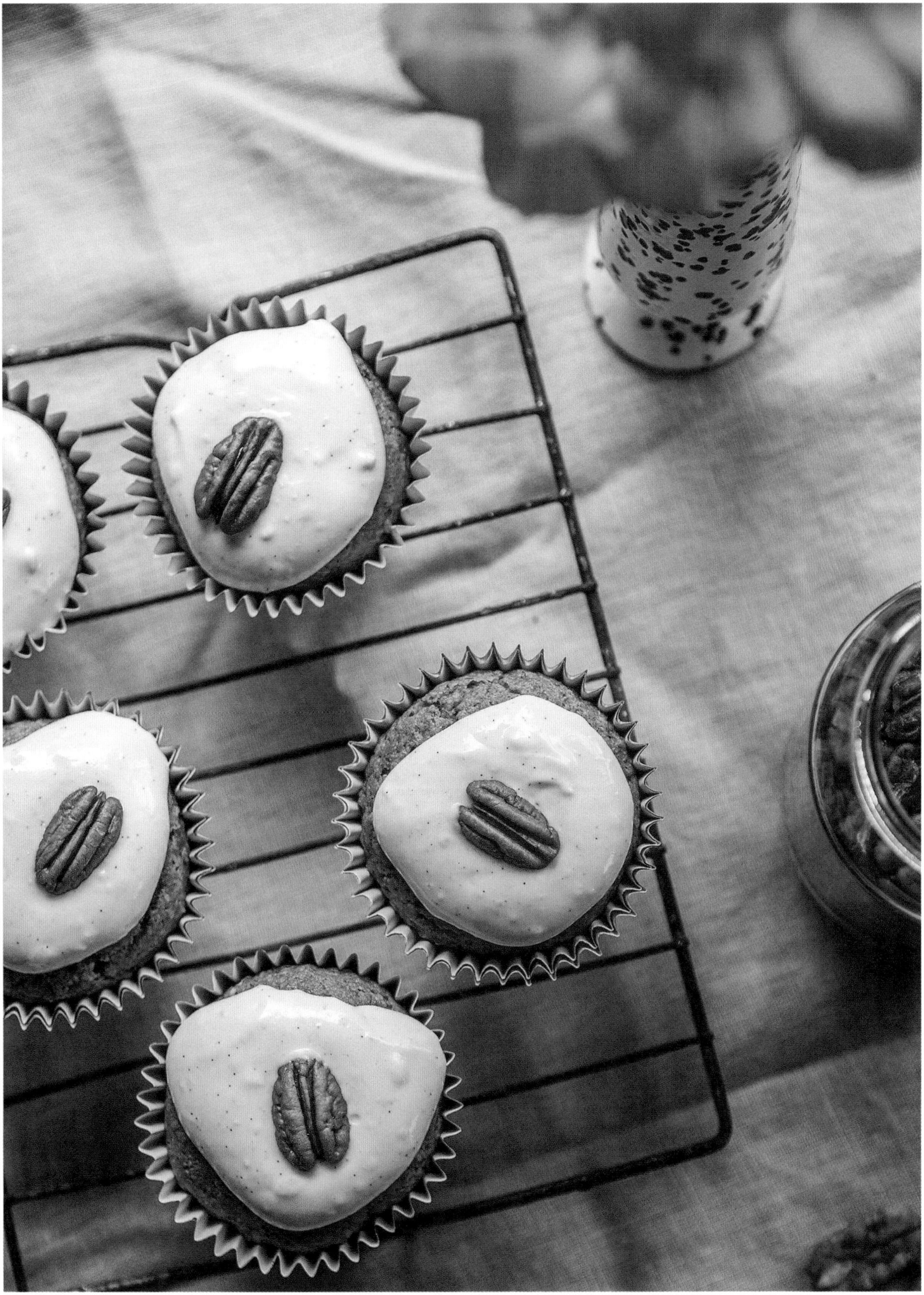

BACK TO BASICS

VANILLA CAKE

Use this simple recipe as a starting point and make your own version with whatever you have in the pantry.

175 g butter, softened
175 g caster sugar
3 large free-range eggs
175 g self-raising flour, sifted
1 teaspoon baking powder
1 teaspoon vanilla extract
pinch of salt

Preheat the oven to 180°C (fan-forced). Line the base and the side of a 20 cm round cake tin with baking paper.

Place all the ingredients in the bowl of an electric mixer fitted with the paddle attachment and mix until just combined.

Pour the batter into the prepared tin and smooth the top. Bake for 45–50 minutes or until a skewer inserted in the centre comes out clean. Cool in the tin for a few minutes, then turn out onto a wire rack to cool completely.

Combos to try:

Blueberry and cardamom
Once you have mixed the ingredients in the electric mixer, fold through 200 g of fresh blueberries and ½ teaspoon of ground cardamom.

Apricot and almond
Once you have mixed the ingredients in the electric mixer, fold through a handful of chopped roasted almonds. When the batter is in the tin, top with 4–5 apricots cut into eighths, and brush with warm honey.

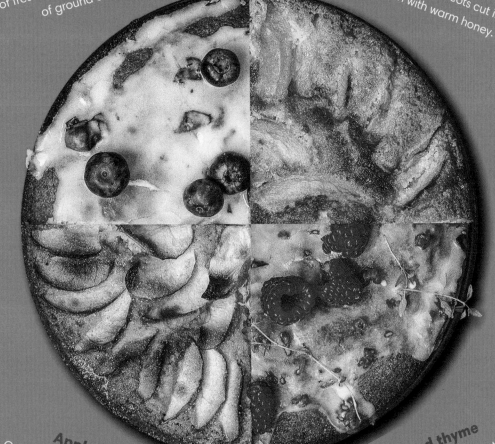

Apple and cinnamon
Once the batter is in the tin, arrange 1 cored and thinly sliced granny smith apple on top. When the cake is cooked, combine ½ teaspoon of ground cinnamon and 2 tablespoons of caster sugar in a bowl. Brush 2 tablespoons of melted butter over the hot cake and sprinkle with the cinnamon sugar.

Raspberry and thyme
Once you have mixed the ingredients in the electric mixer, fold through 200 g of fresh raspberries and 2 tablespoons of finely chopped thyme.

(Almost) DIY after-school snacks

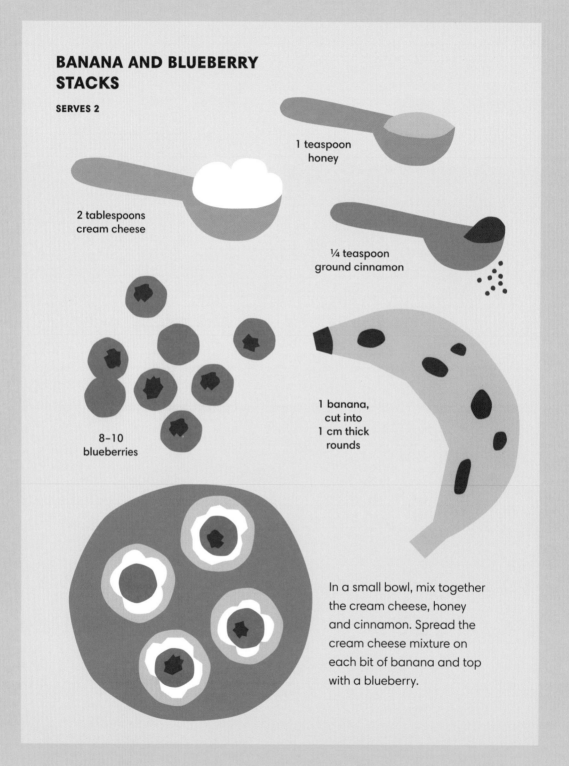

BANANA AND BLUEBERRY STACKS

SERVES 2

1 teaspoon honey

2 tablespoons cream cheese

¼ teaspoon ground cinnamon

8–10 blueberries

1 banana, cut into 1 cm thick rounds

In a small bowl, mix together the cream cheese, honey and cinnamon. Spread the cream cheese mixture on each bit of banana and top with a blueberry.

Most of these snacks will be simple enough for your kids to manage on their own but occasionally they'll need help with cutting or heating, depending on their age.

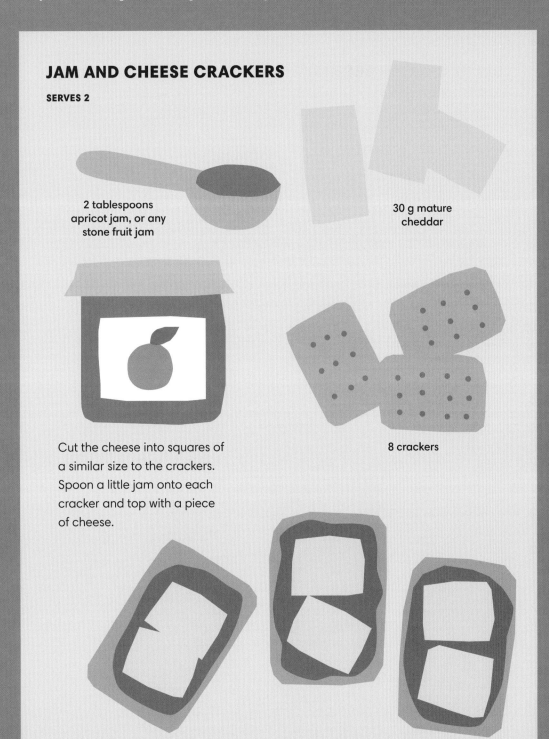

JAM AND CHEESE CRACKERS

SERVES 2

2 tablespoons apricot jam, or any stone fruit jam

30 g mature cheddar

8 crackers

Cut the cheese into squares of a similar size to the crackers. Spoon a little jam onto each cracker and top with a piece of cheese.

(Almost) DIY after-school snacks

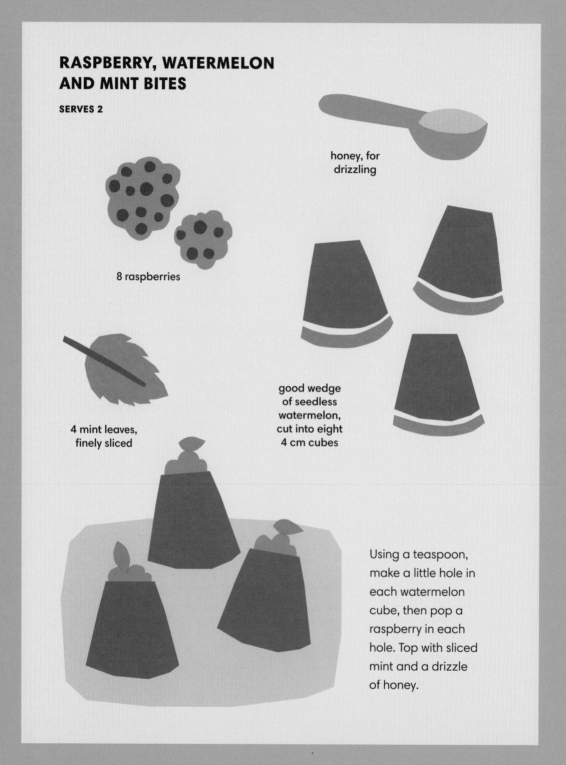

RASPBERRY, WATERMELON AND MINT BITES

SERVES 2

honey, for drizzling

8 raspberries

4 mint leaves, finely sliced

good wedge of seedless watermelon, cut into eight 4 cm cubes

Using a teaspoon, make a little hole in each watermelon cube, then pop a raspberry in each hole. Top with sliced mint and a drizzle of honey.

SANDWICH SUSHI

SERVES 2

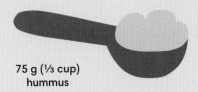

75 g (⅓ cup)
hummus

**4 slices of
non-fancy
bread**

1 large carrot, grated

handful of coriander
leaves, chopped

Using a rolling pin, roll each piece of bread in one direction to flatten it out and make it more rectangular. Spread the hummus over each piece. Pile the carrot in a line at one end of the bread, parallel to the shorter side, and sprinkle with the coriander.

Roll up the bread from the carrot end to enclose the carrot. Gently, but firmly, press along the length of the roll so it holds together. Slice into little rounds.

You can make this with ANY sandwich combo!

ADVENTURES FOR WEEKENDS & HOLIDAYS

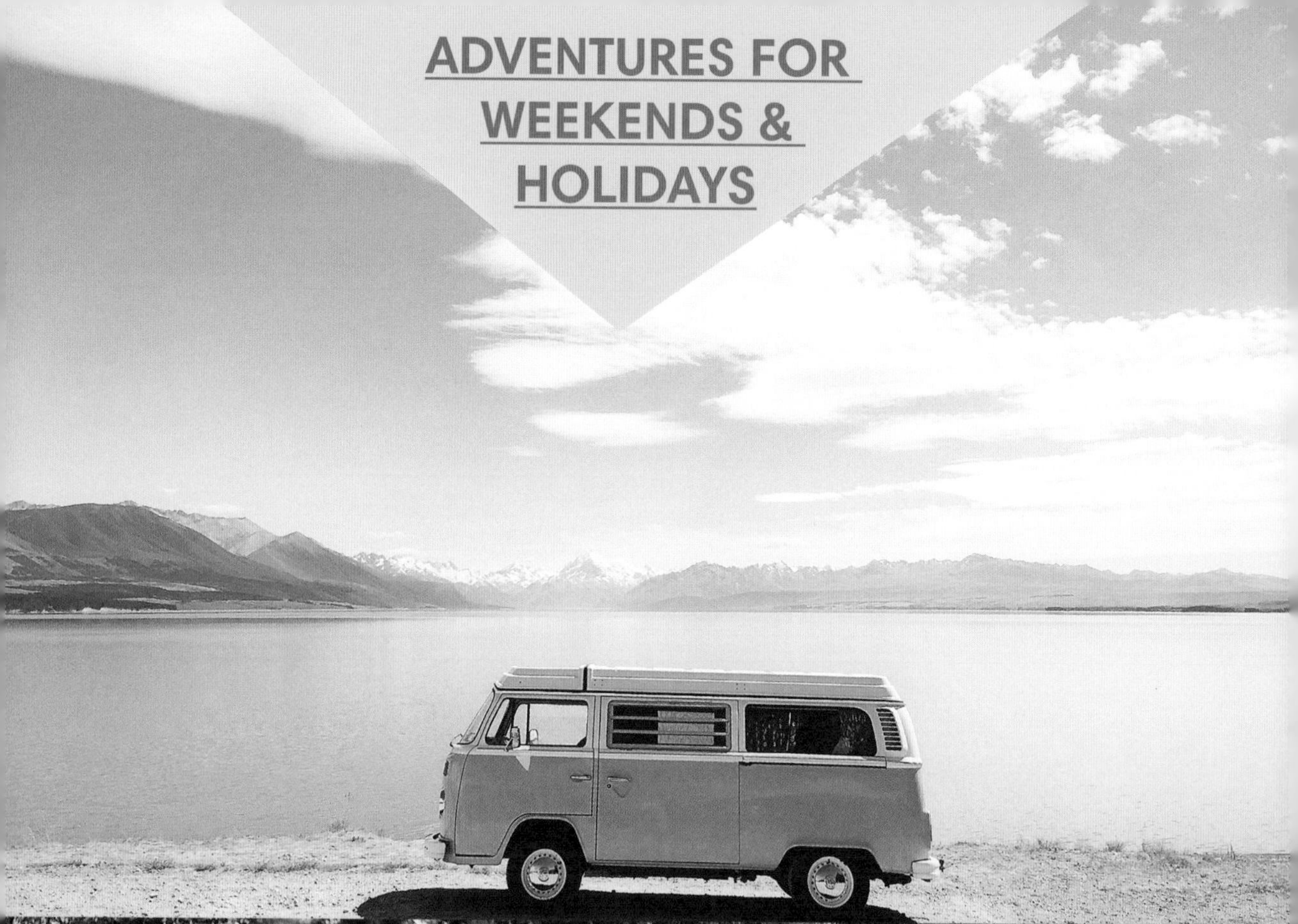

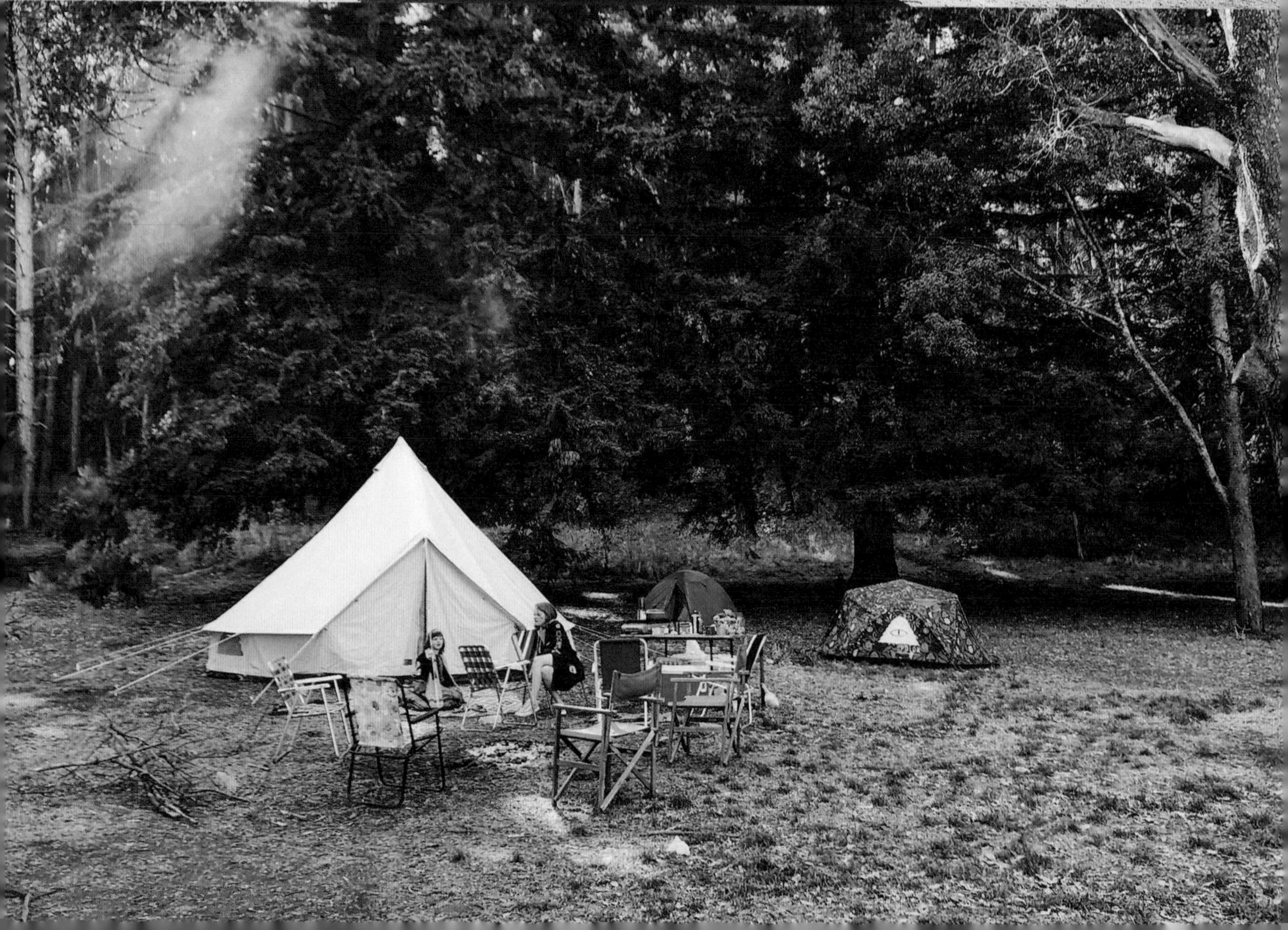

Road trips and road trip food

If there is one thing my girls and I do well, it's road tripping. There's really only one thing you need to be good at when road tripping, and that's going with the flow. Which is good, because if there was more stuff you had to be good at we probably wouldn't be into it. With road tripping, you can't get stuck on the small stuff; in fact, we've had some of our greatest adventures when things went a little pear-shaped.

We met a mechanic and his pet baby crow, named after some footy player we'd never heard of. We camped with the Bandidos … accidentally. We watched the sun set and the full moon rise whilst stranded outside Coober Pedy. And I learned how to open a beer using my car door because I forgot to pack a bottle opener. All memories I can't imagine my life without now. And we never planned any of it. Just the opposite – we owe it all to my incredible under-planning.

'Just pack as many underpants as you can get in there!'

We pack minimally as there is nothing worse than a car full of crap on a road trip. If you let your kids pack whatever they think is important, these non-important things (like slime, random bits of Lego, old pieces of fruit, and textas with no lids) will be strewn across the car in no time. And this really doesn't help with the

'go with the flow' mantra. You may as well be at home, walking on Lego pieces, and not go anywhere at all.

When we go on massive drives, I like my girls to experience the intense boredom I felt as a kid on similar drives. So there are no screens until there've been some solid hours of staring out the window at nothing. This is when I did some of my best thinking as a kid. I worked out all the comebacks I should have used when I was picked on at school, and I dreamed of places I would go on holiday when I was older instead of the boring places my parents took me to, which are pretty much the same places I now take my kids, with the occasional destination splurge!

The best bit about them staring out the window for hours is that when something cool comes along all hell breaks loose. 'OMG Mum, look, can you see the wild goats? How cuuuuuuute!! Look, Mum, look.' If my kids had been playing on the iPad, they'd never have seen those goats. Or if they did, they wouldn't have bothered to mention them.

When I was a new mum, I remember going to see a play in the Botanic Gardens with another mum. She wasn't really a friend – it was more a forced 'I'm a mum, you're a mum, let's hang out' situation. Anyway, this mum had brought containers of homemade snacks for her kid. I thought she was the most incredible woman on the planet. SO ORGANISED.

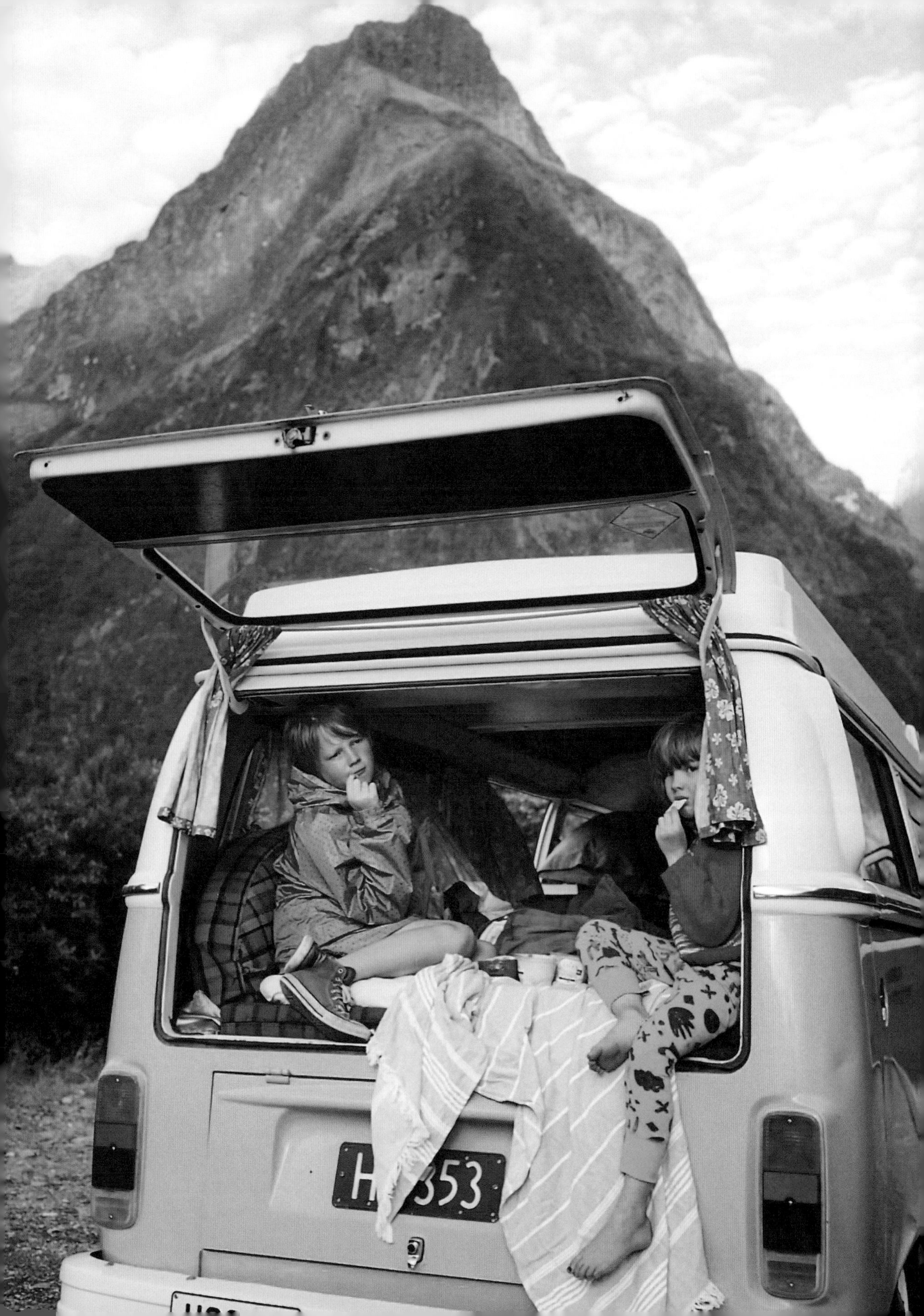

From that day forward, I vowed that I too would bring snacks to things. It took about a decade for this to actually happen, but at least it happened.

The reason I am telling you this is because I am SO down with filling your car with food before you go anywhere. I feel like I am successfully cheating the system. We drive past shops wanting us to stop and buy their expensive chips and lollies because we don't need them. We're sorted. On a trip to Uluru, I put a box of 20 avocados in the boot. Still unsure what my plan was but we ate a lot of guacamole on that trip, which was fine. Should have packed more corn chips though.

Our favourite meal on our trips is the 'Boot Sanga'. The three of us make a sandwich or wrap in the boot of the car and then we all sit in the boot to eat it. Usually at a truck stop, or somewhere hot and windy, or cold and rainy.

Road trips are the ultimate no-frills travel. And if, like me, you take the 'she'll be right' approach to life, who knows what's around the corner?

LEGEND

0   100   200   300
kilometres
1 : 6.5 million

OCEAN

TRAIL MIX

MAKES ABOUT 4 CUPS

This is a yummy, slightly naughty thing we like to take with us. It's also good for when you're watching the telly.

about 300 g (2 cups) mixed untoasted nuts (any combo)
20 g unsalted butter, melted
3 tablespoons brown sugar
½ teaspoon ground cinnamon
1½ tablespoons pure maple syrup
1 teaspoon sea salt flakes
225 g (2 cups) small pretzels

Preheat the oven to 180°C (fan-forced).

Spread out the nuts on a baking tray and lightly toast them in the oven for 10 minutes, tossing once.

Mix together the melted butter, brown sugar, cinnamon and maple syrup in a large bowl. Add the warm nuts and stir to coat. Add the salt and pretzels and stir until the nuts and pretzels are completely coated.

Spread out the mixture on the baking tray and return to the oven for 12–15 minutes, tossing twice during cooking, until nicely caramelised.

Remove from the oven and leave to cool completely, separating the nuts and pretzels as they cool. Store the cooled mix in an airtight container for up to a week.

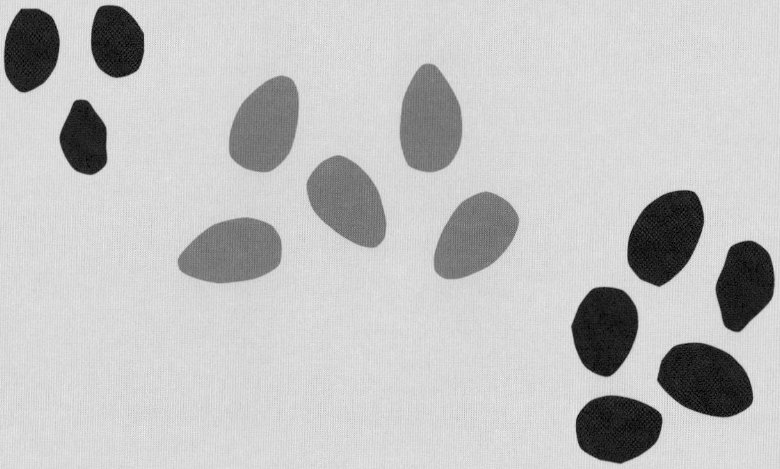

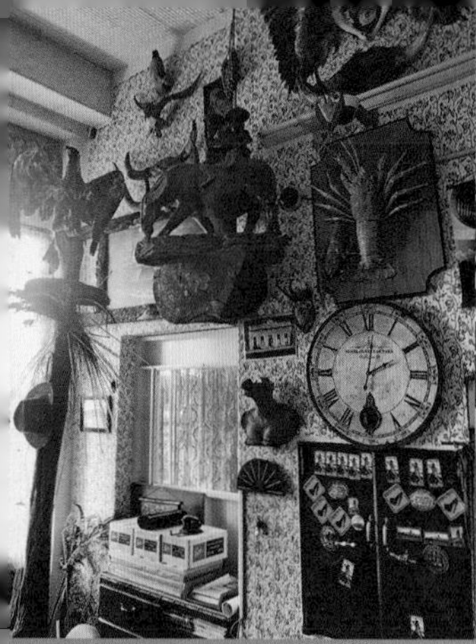

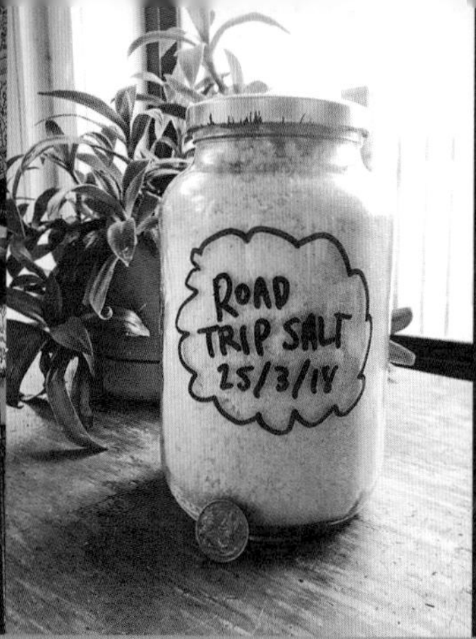
ROAD
TRIP SALT
25/3/14

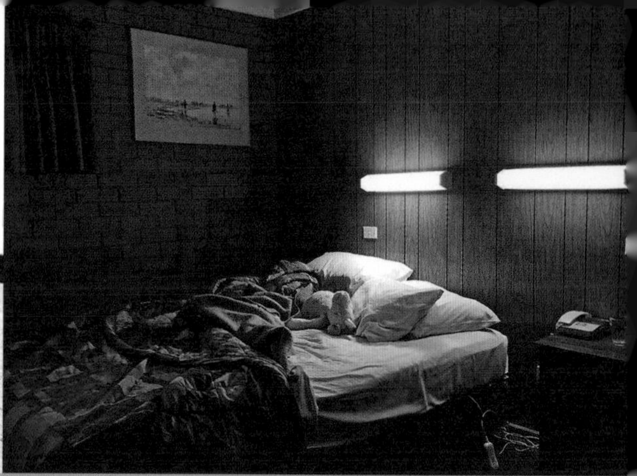

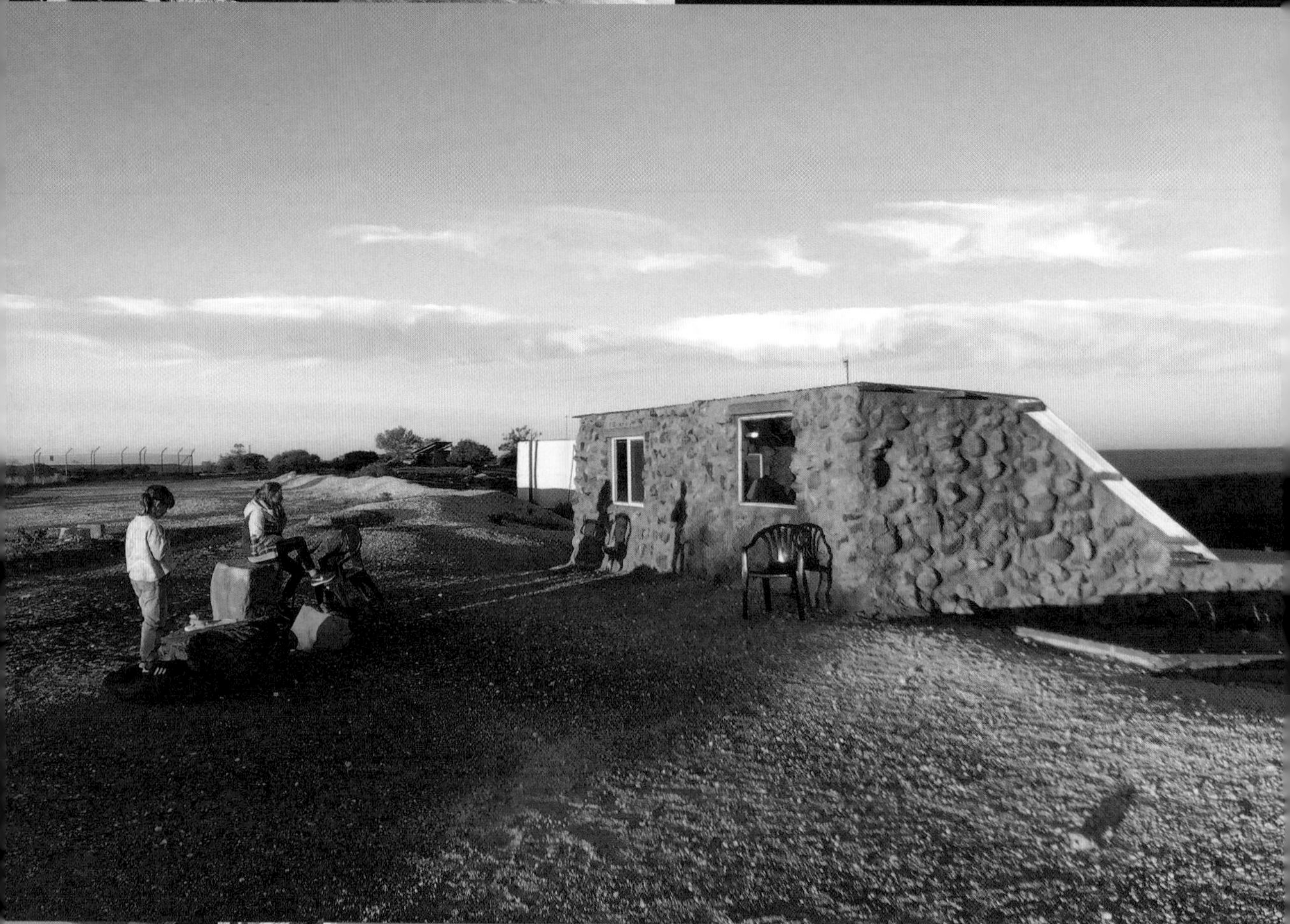

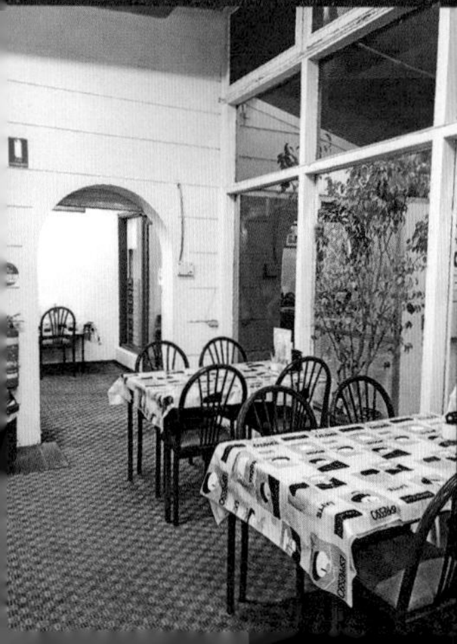

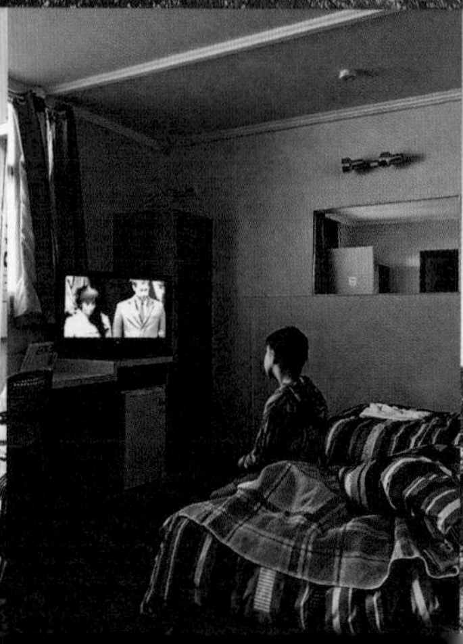

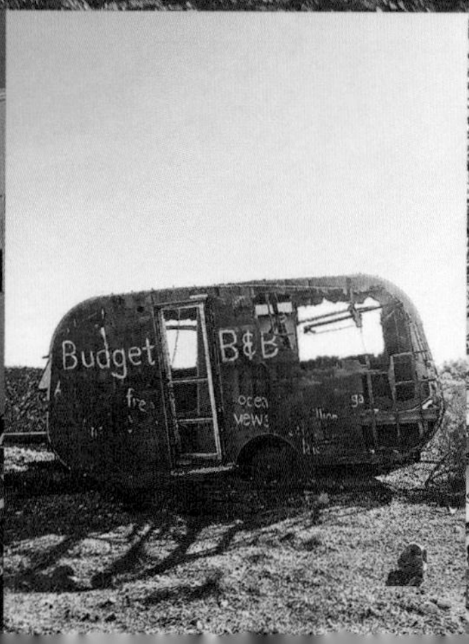
Budget
B&B

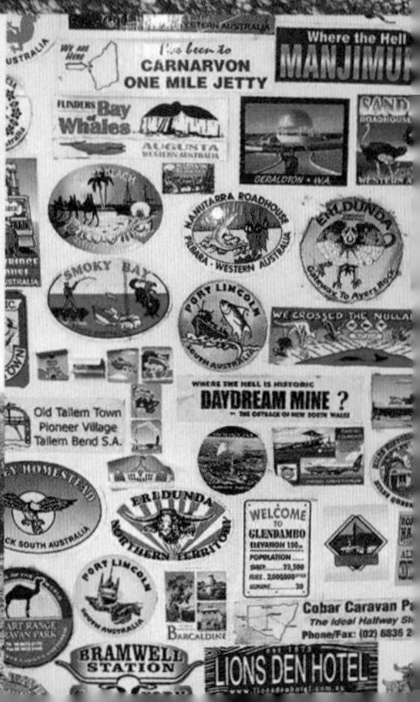
CARNARVON
ONE MILE JETTY
Where the Hell
FLINDERS Bay Whales
AUGUSTA
SMOKY BAY
PORT LINCOLN
DAYDREAM MINE ?
Old Tailem Town
Pioneer Village
Tailem Bend S.A.
ERLDUNDA
WELCOME TO GLENDAMBO
BRAMWELL STATION
LIONS DEN HOTEL

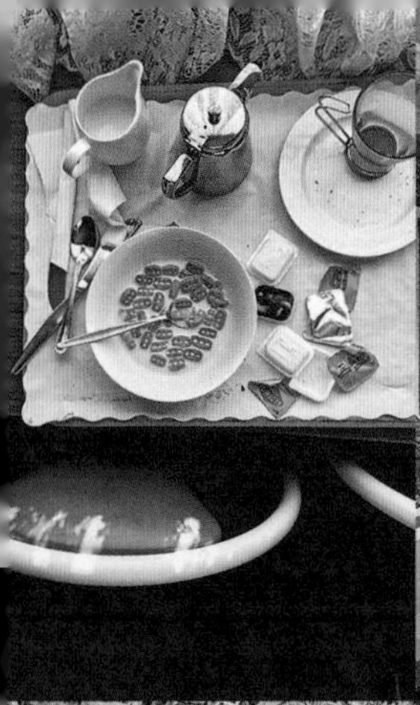
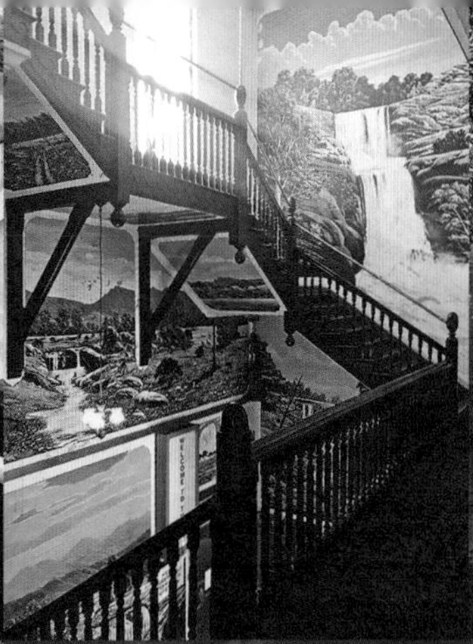
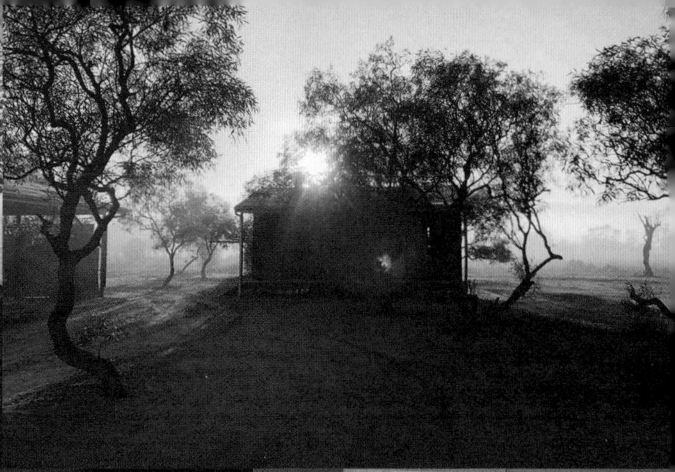
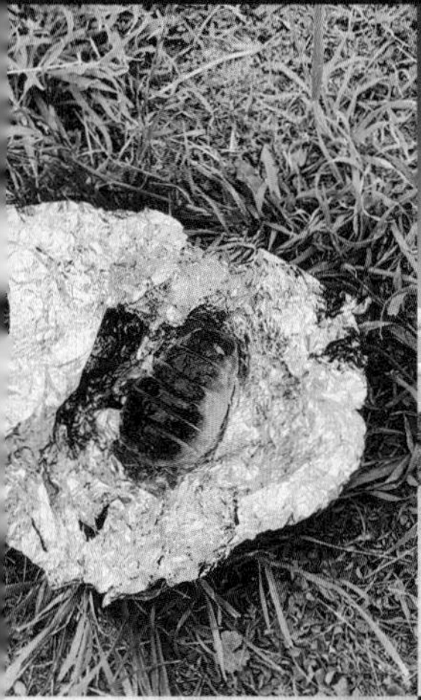
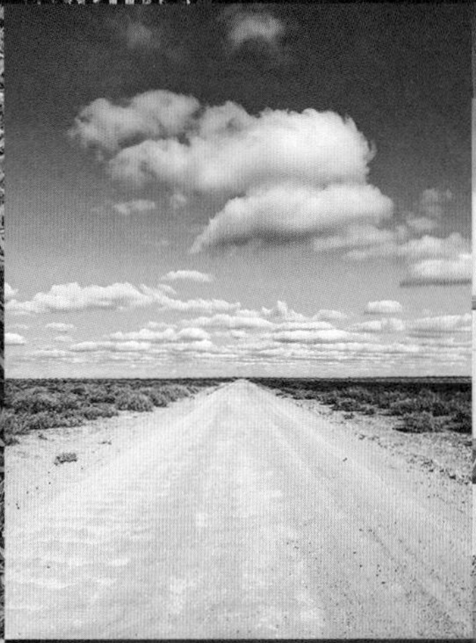
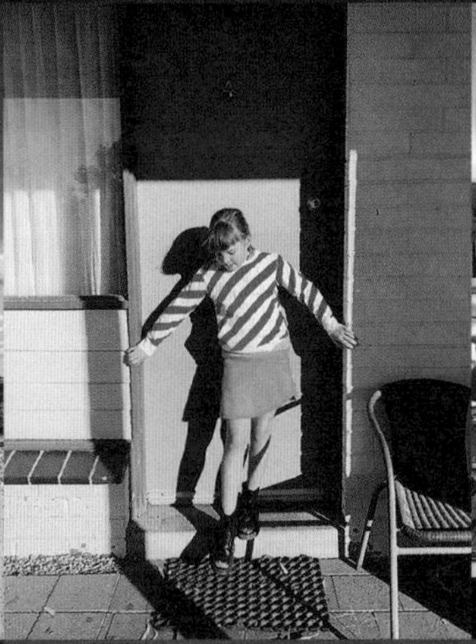
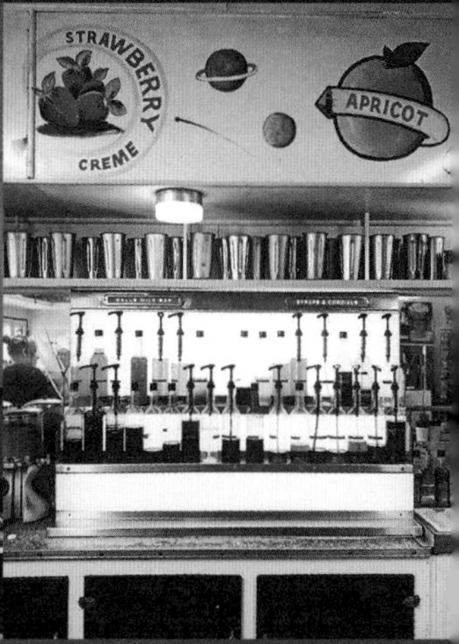
STRAWBERRY
CREME
APRICOT
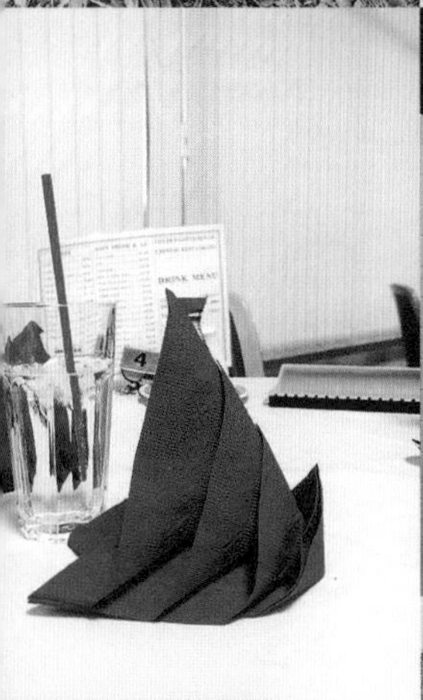
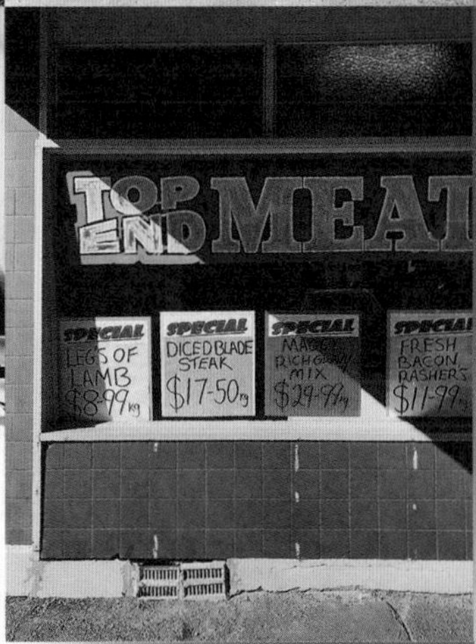
TOP END MEAT
SPECIAL
LEGS OF LAMB
$8-99 kg
SPECIAL
DICED BLADE STEAK
$17-50 kg
SPECIAL
SPECIAL
FRESH BACON RASHERS
$11-99
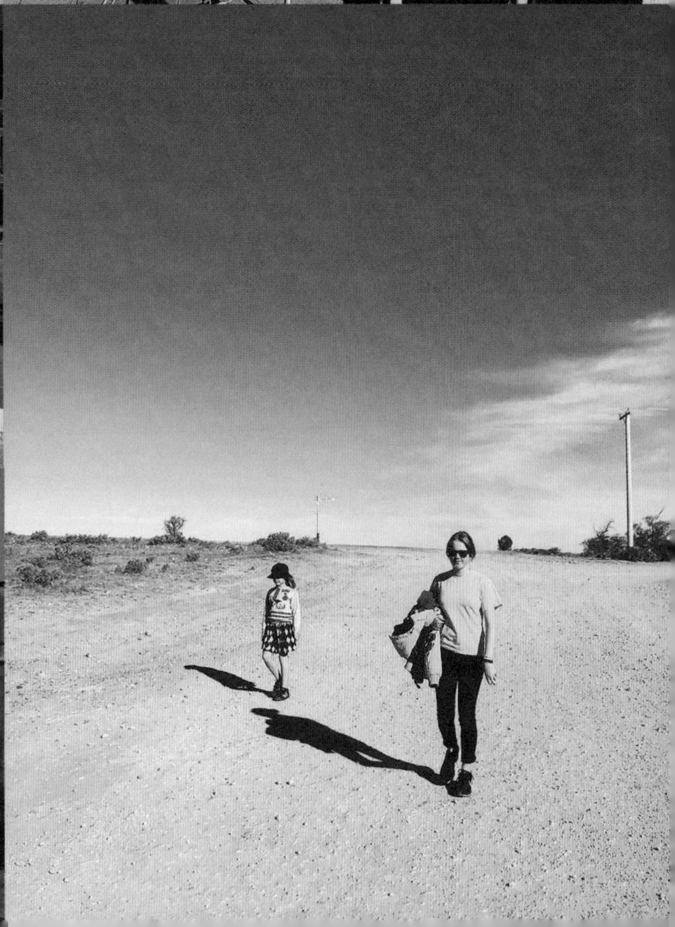
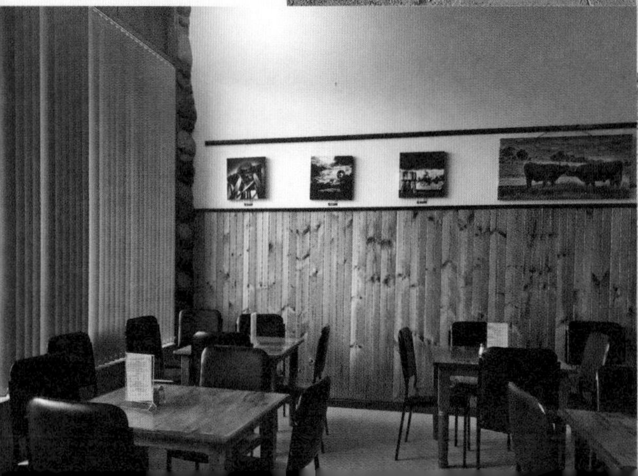

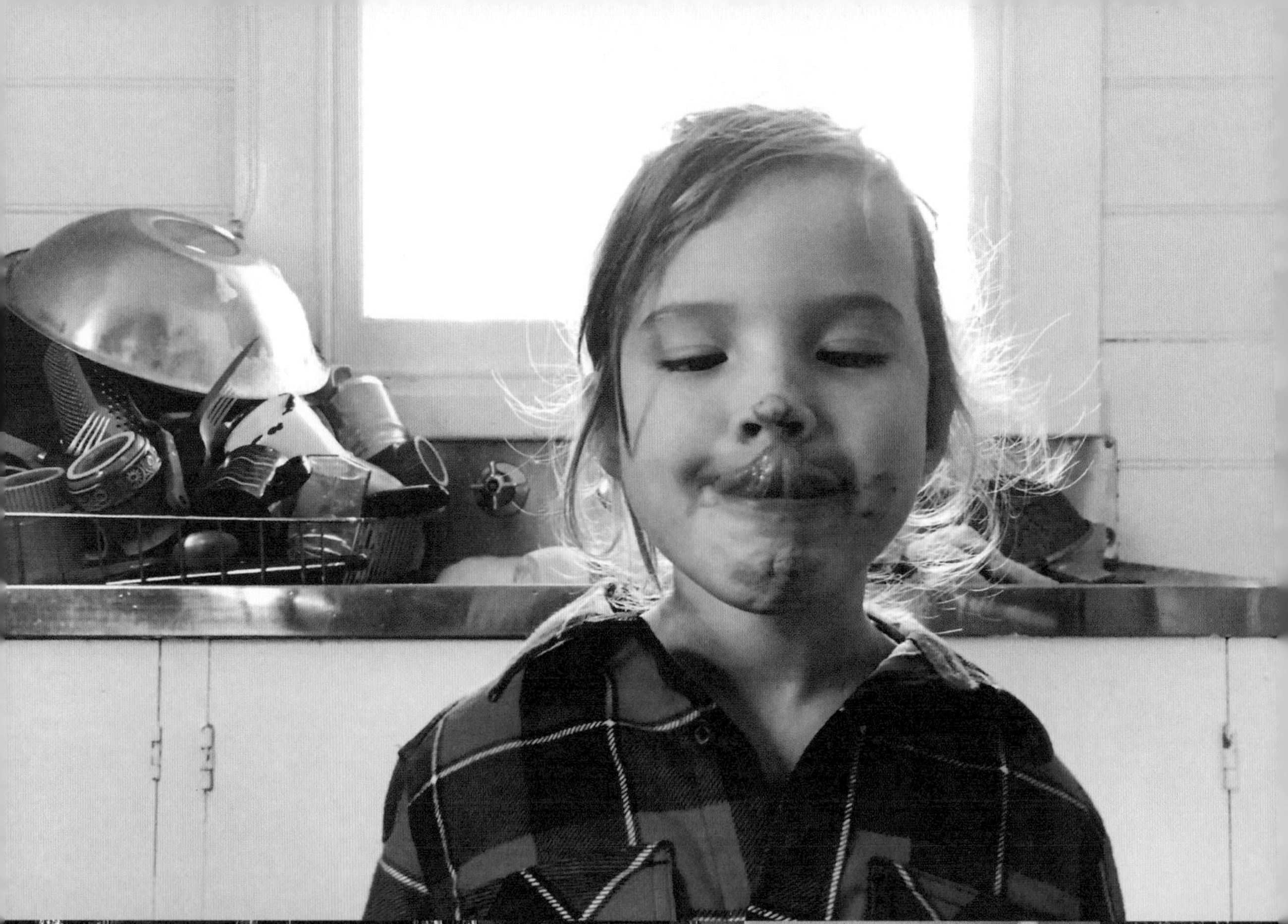

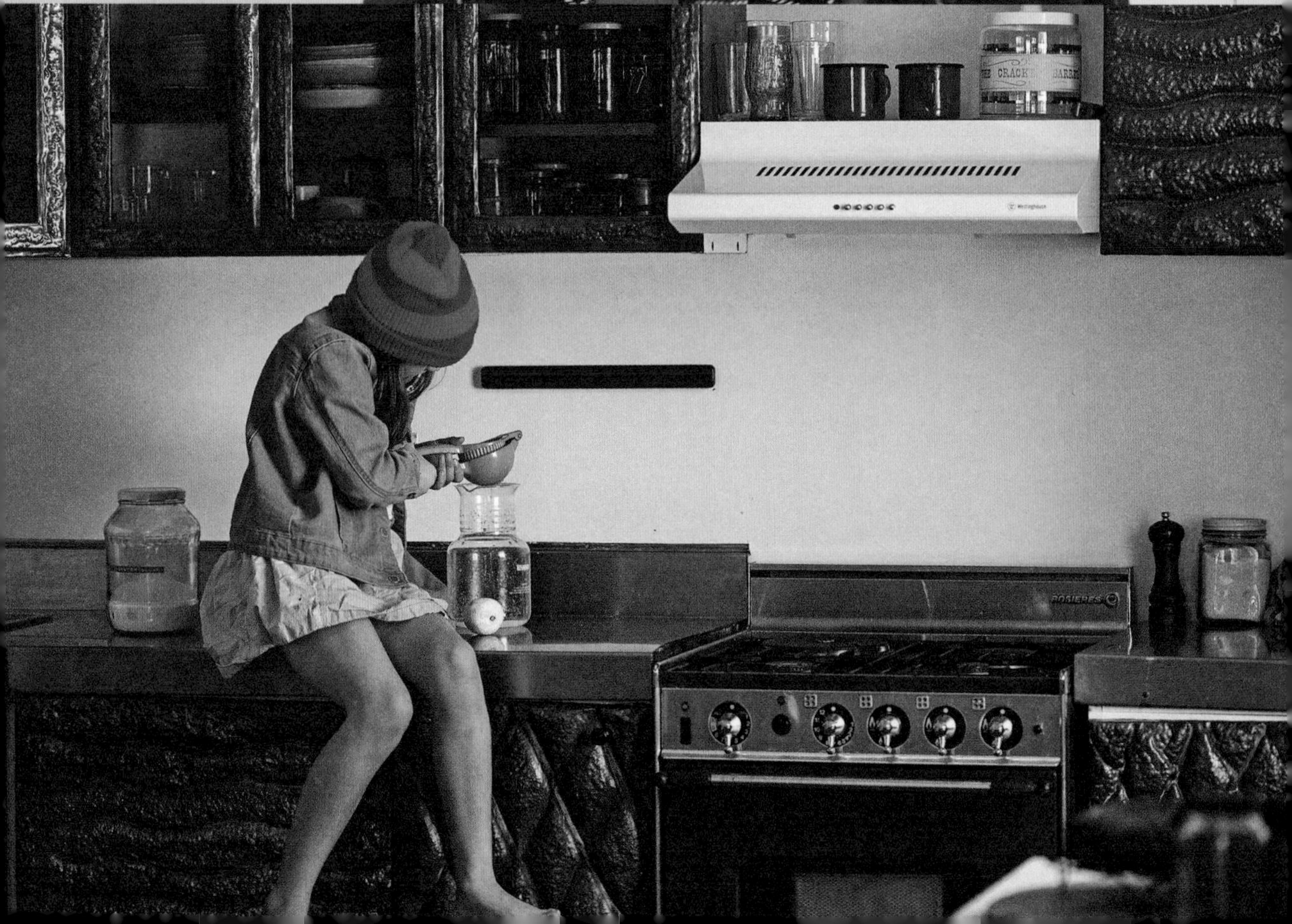

Teaching your kids to cook

I didn't really grow up in a cooking kind of house.

My mum made Rice-a-Riso and we ate pizza a lot. Pizza is still my favourite food, but I can't say the same for Rice-a-Riso. My dad loved cooking, but he was never around to share this with us. It was the 80s and long hours had become the thing parents did. My nan (who we called Nan Boat because she lived on a boat once) was apparently an amazing cook. I don't really remember her cooking very much, though I do remember her lemon butter and plum jam, which were both delicious. Nan House (yes, because she always lived in a house) was probably the worst of all the cooks. She once gave my brother and me a whole tomato each, sat in the middle of a plate with a butter knife on the side. Lunch was served.

I started cooking when I was a teenager. First it was cakes, then toffees, and then my friend and I hosted a dinner party for her parents and their friends. Looking back, that's quite weird, but let's not dwell on that. While I was making the lemon meringue pie, I dropped the bowl with the meringue. I did my best to pick the broken glass out of the stiff peaks and salvage what I could off the floor, then baked that health hazard like nothing happened. Luckily one parent spotted a giant shard of Pyrex before everyone tucked in.

When I hit my twenties and had my own little home and veggie garden, I was all about cooking. And I haven't really looked back. What I particularly love is that if you have a serious craving for something, you can make it to your exact specifications. I also like making healthy food for my kids.

Now that they're old enough to cook, we spend a lot of time in the kitchen together. And it isn't necessarily me showing them what to do. It's more that they'll sit with me while I make dinner and ask questions, or just tell me about their day. Sometimes they'll find a recipe online that they'd like to have a go at, and I will be the one just sitting there for company (or for help, if needed).

Initially, my kids' cooking was painful. They spilled crap everywhere, didn't put anything away, and ALL THE FLOUR! But I persevered, and now my kids cook me stuff. Like, stuff I actually eat. They also make themselves cookies for school and snacks for after school. They even clean up, kind of.

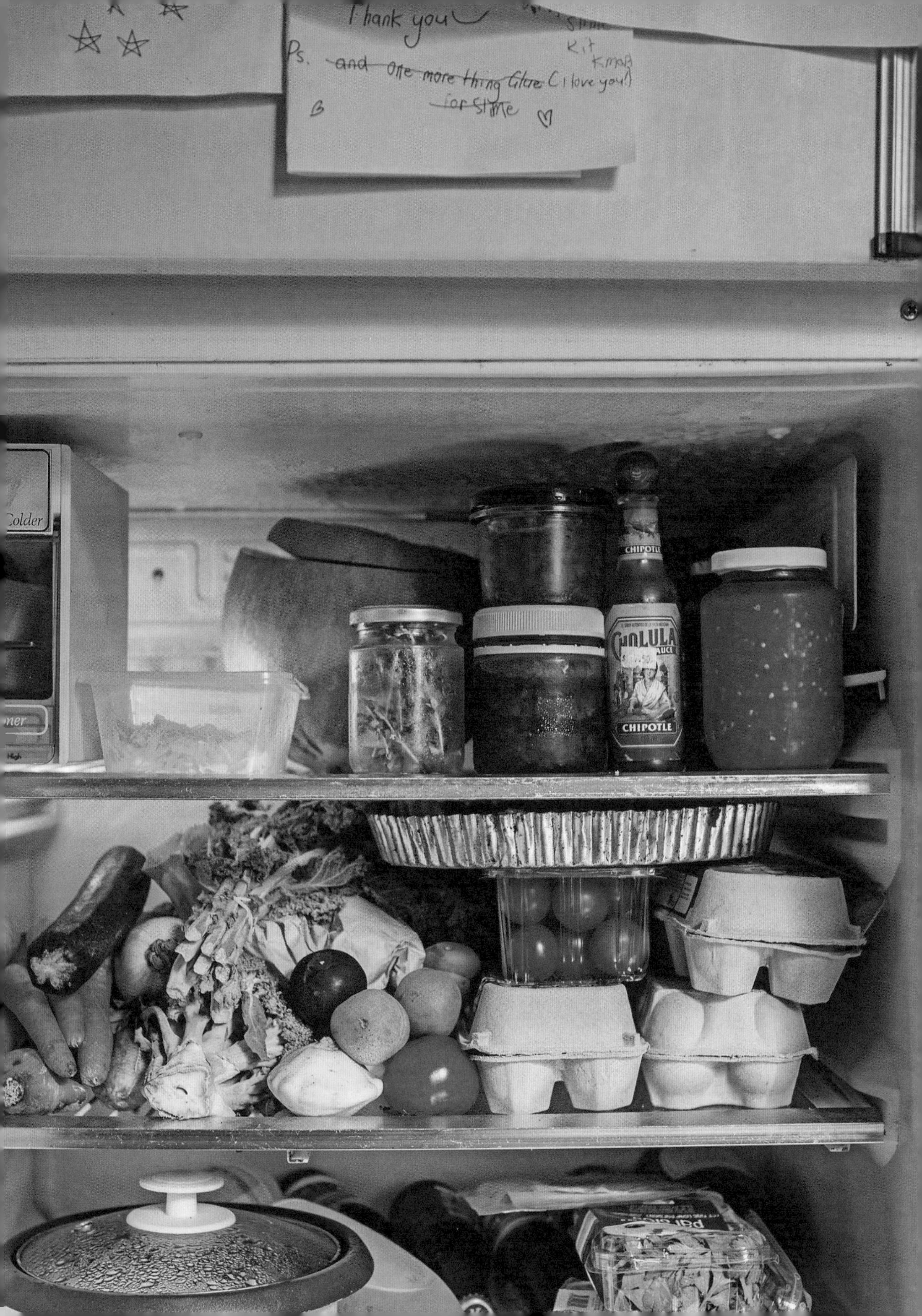
Thank you
Ps. and one more thing Glue (I love you!)
for slime
Colder
CHIPOTLE
CHOLULA
CHIPOTLE

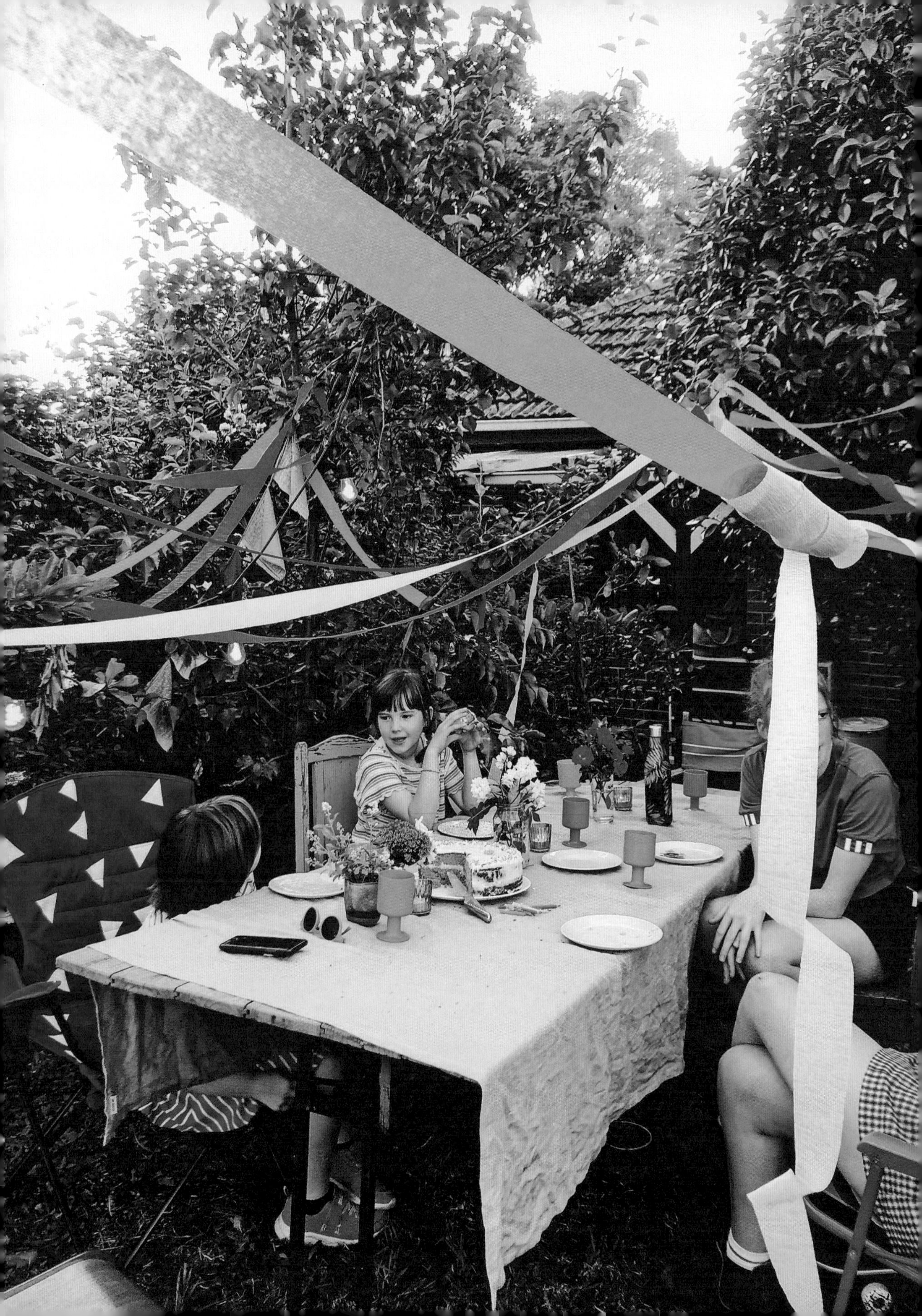

Kids' parties. What I've learned. The hard way.

We had just moved to a new neighbourhood when my eldest kid started prep, so when her sixth birthday rolled around I decided to invite her entire class to the party. I thought it might be a good way to get to know people in our new town. This was not a good call. Maya's class had 22 children, which meant not only 22 small guests, but also at least 22 parents who didn't want to leave their kids at some stranger's house …

It was utter chaos and to this day I'm not sure how I got through it. I don't really remember what happened – maybe I blocked most of it out? I do know there was a pinata, a lot of screaming, a few kids hitting each other with the pinata stick, more screaming, a lot of annoyed-looking parents and a very strong drink at the end of it all. I woke up on the couch in my clothes the next morning.

All that aside, I do love to show my kids how much I love them through the act of party planning. I've been doing it for 14 years and have learned some pretty great lessons along the way. For instance, when my eldest was in kinder I learned that the kid whose mum doesn't like you will be the kid who gets the black eye. This happened at my first proper kids' party. I was so excited; I'd hired a woman to come and show the

kids a real-life version of *The Very Hungry Caterpillar*, portable butterfly enclosure and all. It was completely over the top, but I'm sure we all party-peak around birthday number four and then slowly start to realise that it isn't necessary.

After that I toned things down. I stopped outsourcing and instead opted for more old-school party vibes. Pass the Parcel, Apple Bobbing and Pin the Tail on the Donkey. The kids don't need any more than that; they just want a day that's theirs.

Someone taught me a very good rule, and that is to allow your kid to invite as many people as the age they are turning. This rule has worked well for us and I highly recommend it. The only time it came unstuck was at Pepper's last birthday. We'd just finished putting all the party food on the outside table when the kids (all 10 of them, including Pep) were attacked by a swarm of wasps. I suppose this had less to do with the number of children and more to do with the fact I'd set up the party table next to a wasps' nest. There's another recommendation: don't do that.

Now my kids are older, I've entered a new phase of parties. The 'Mum, you're not invited' phase. All they want to do is hang with their mates, eat crap, talk crap and get a few pressies. Maybe that was what they always wanted, but they are now old enough to tell me.

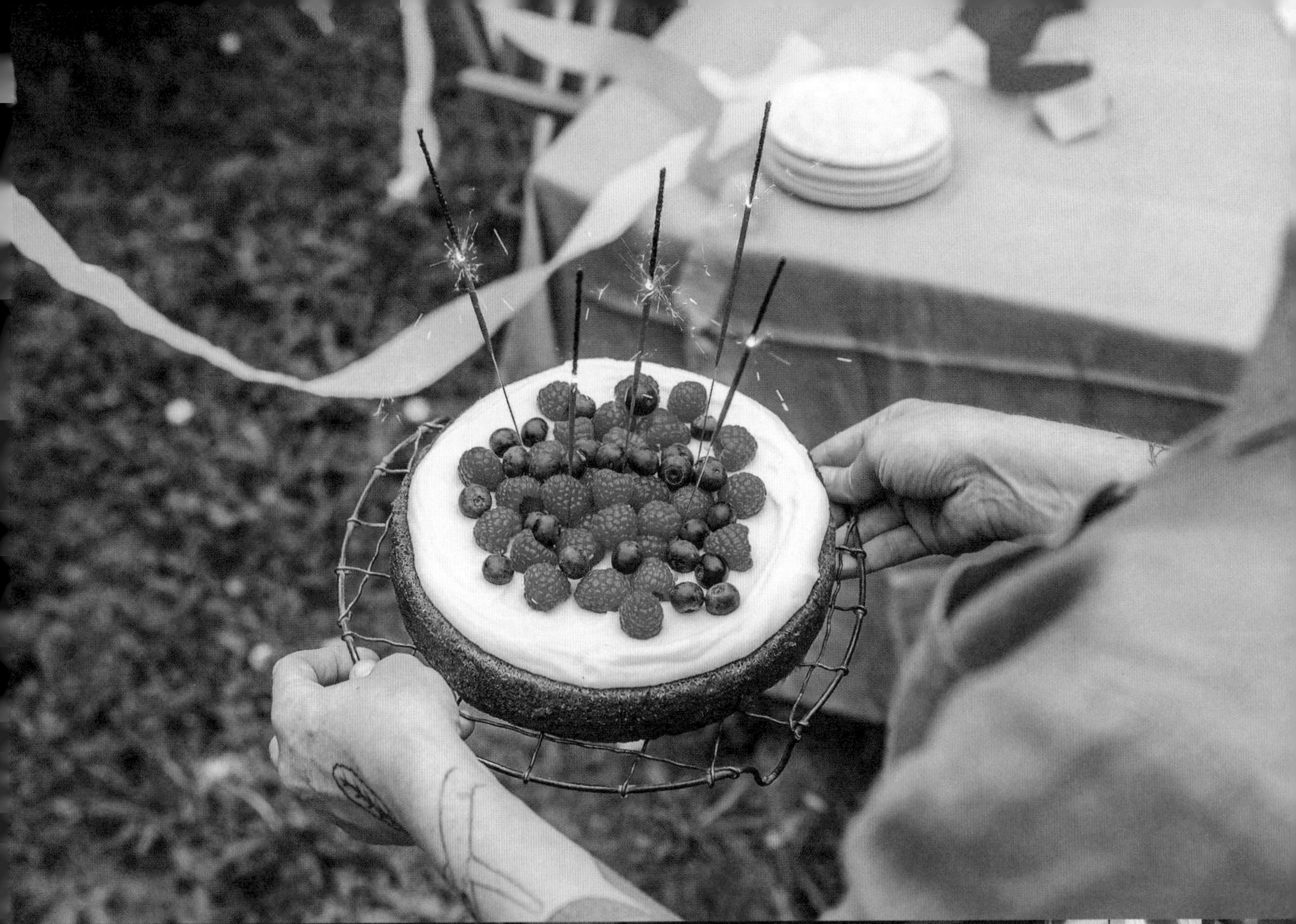

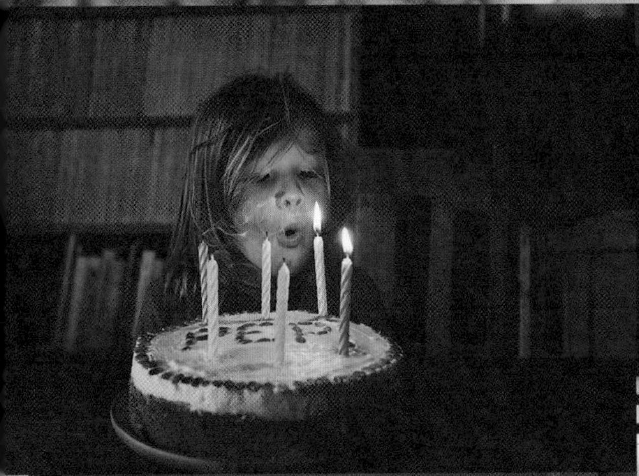

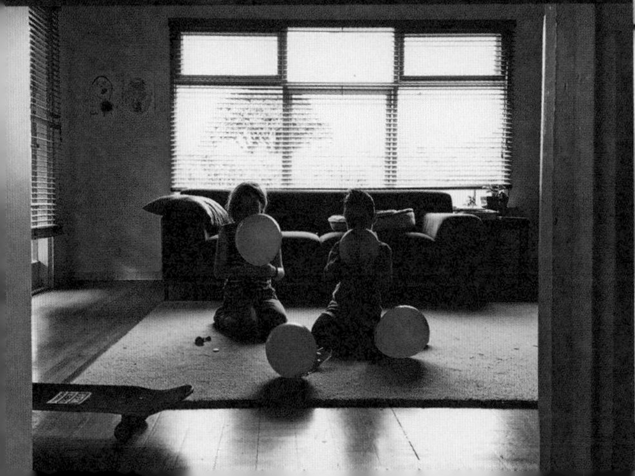

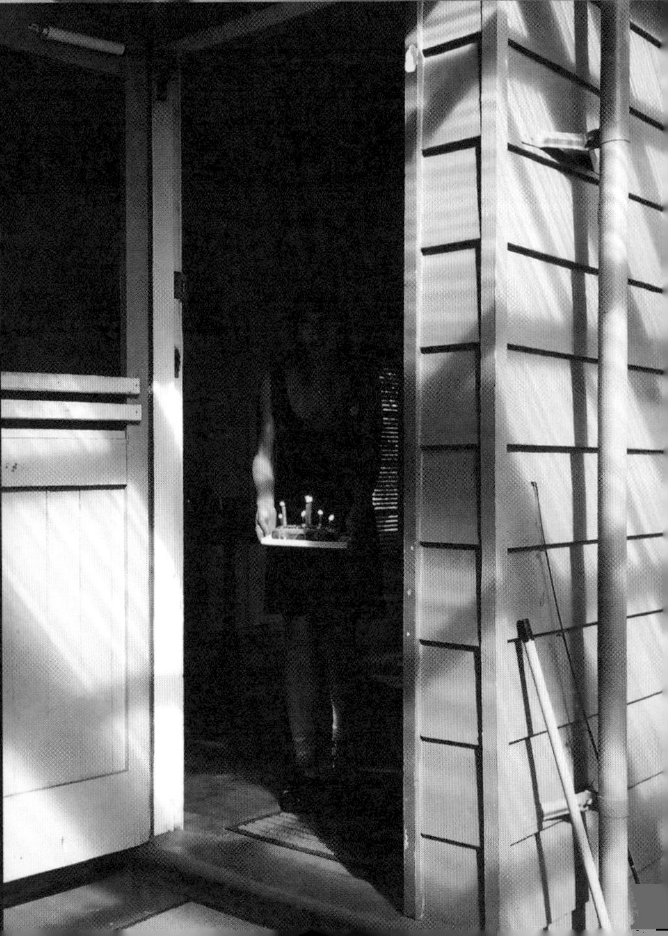

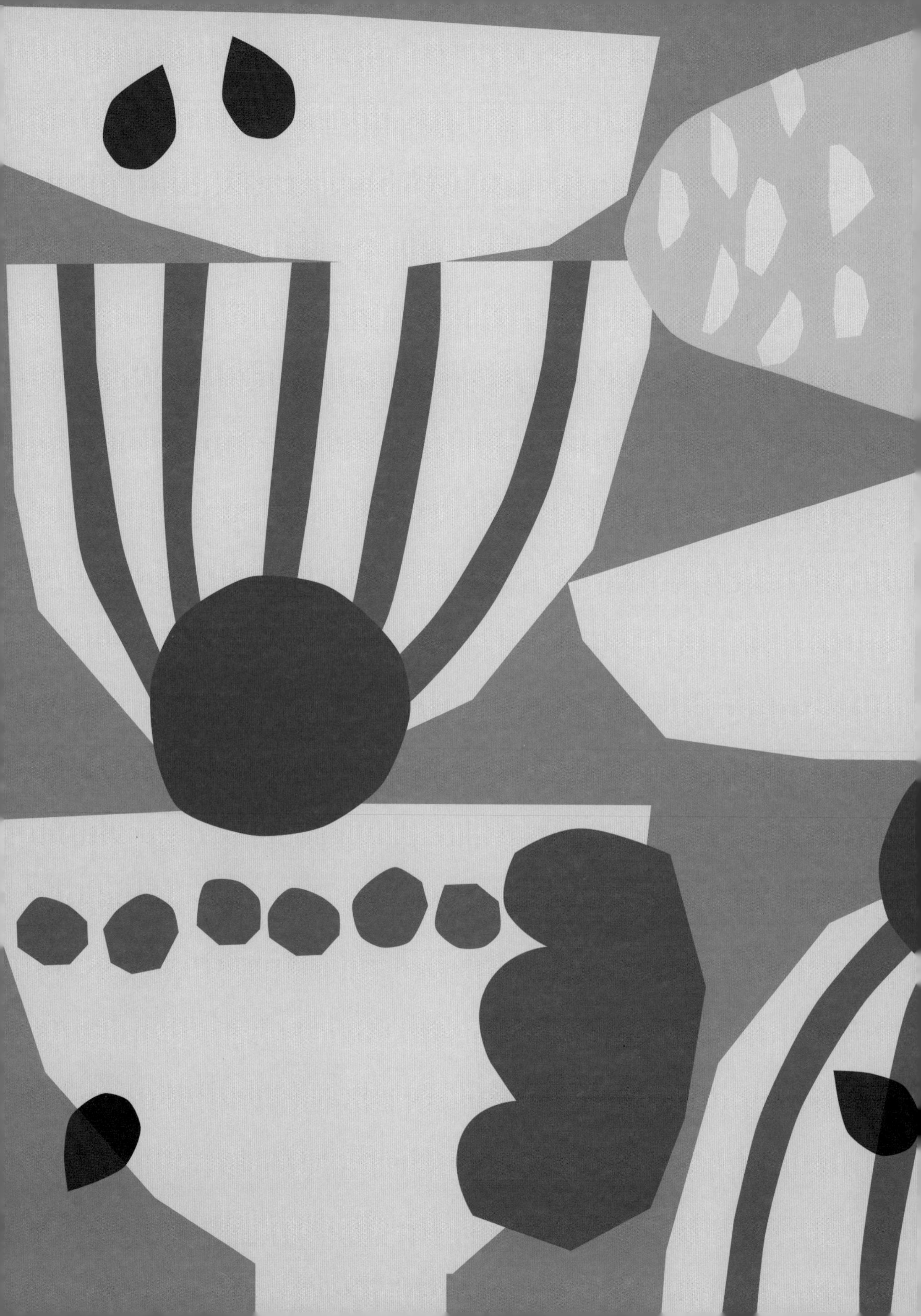

Term 2

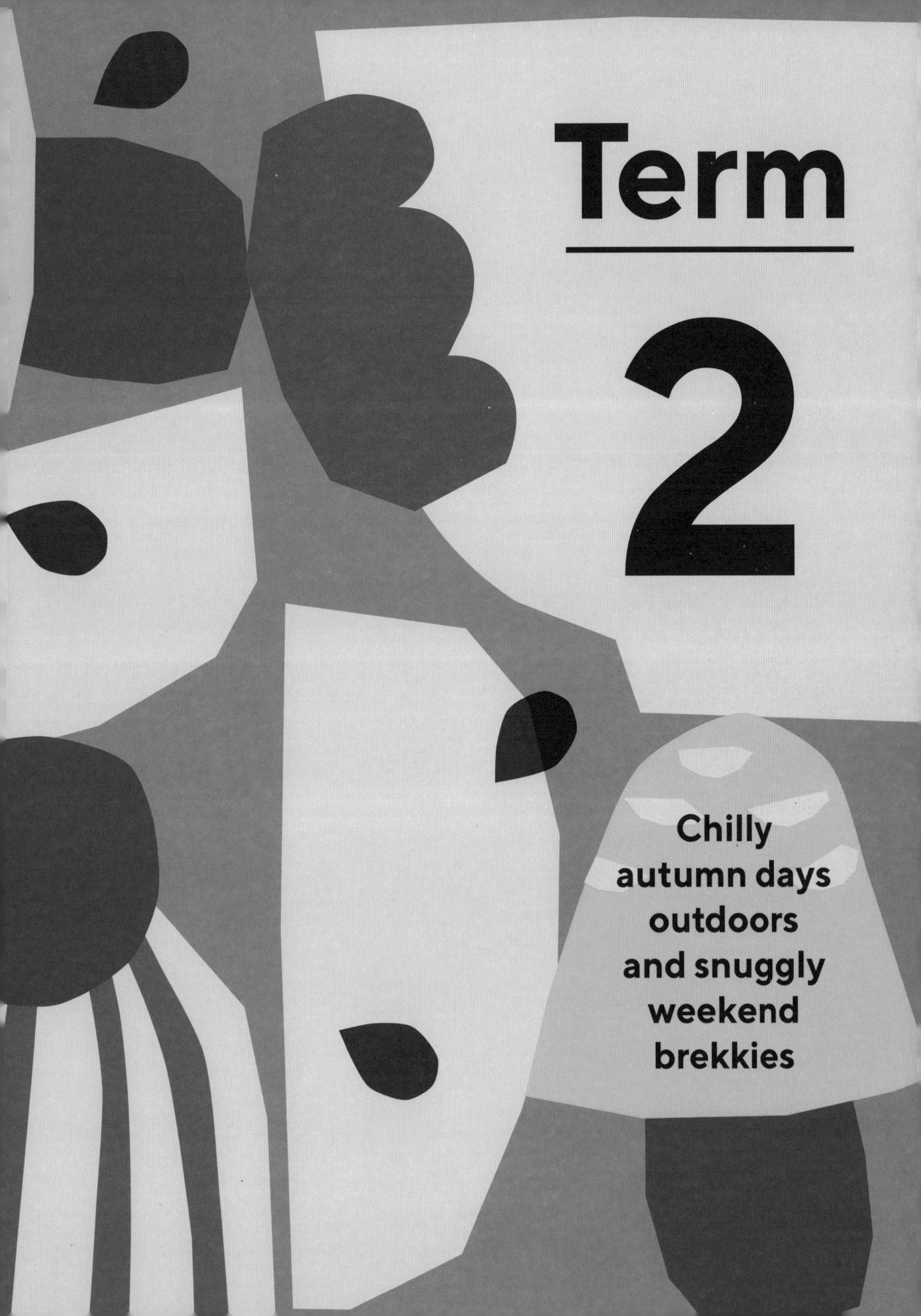

Chilly autumn days outdoors and snuggly weekend brekkies

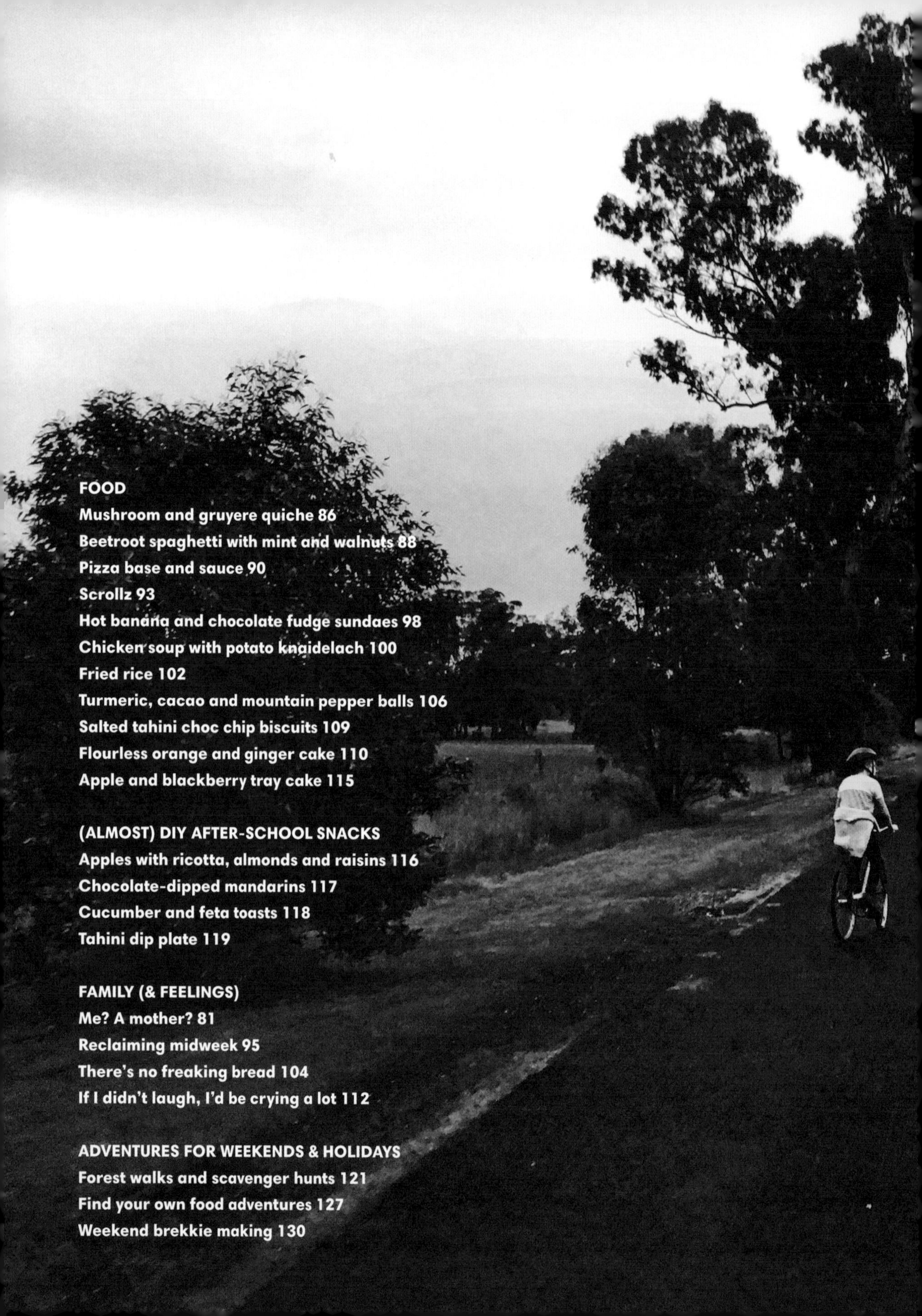

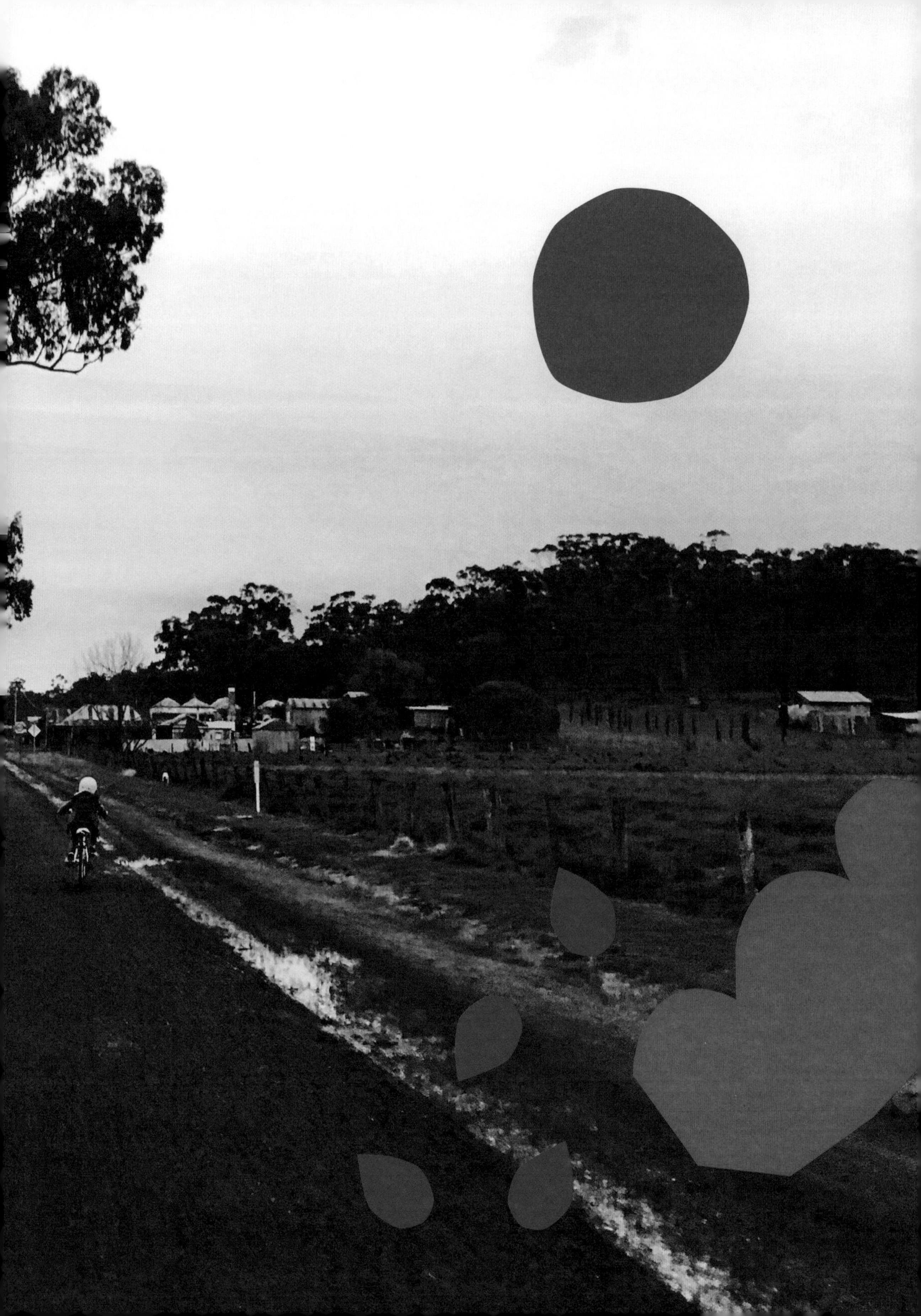

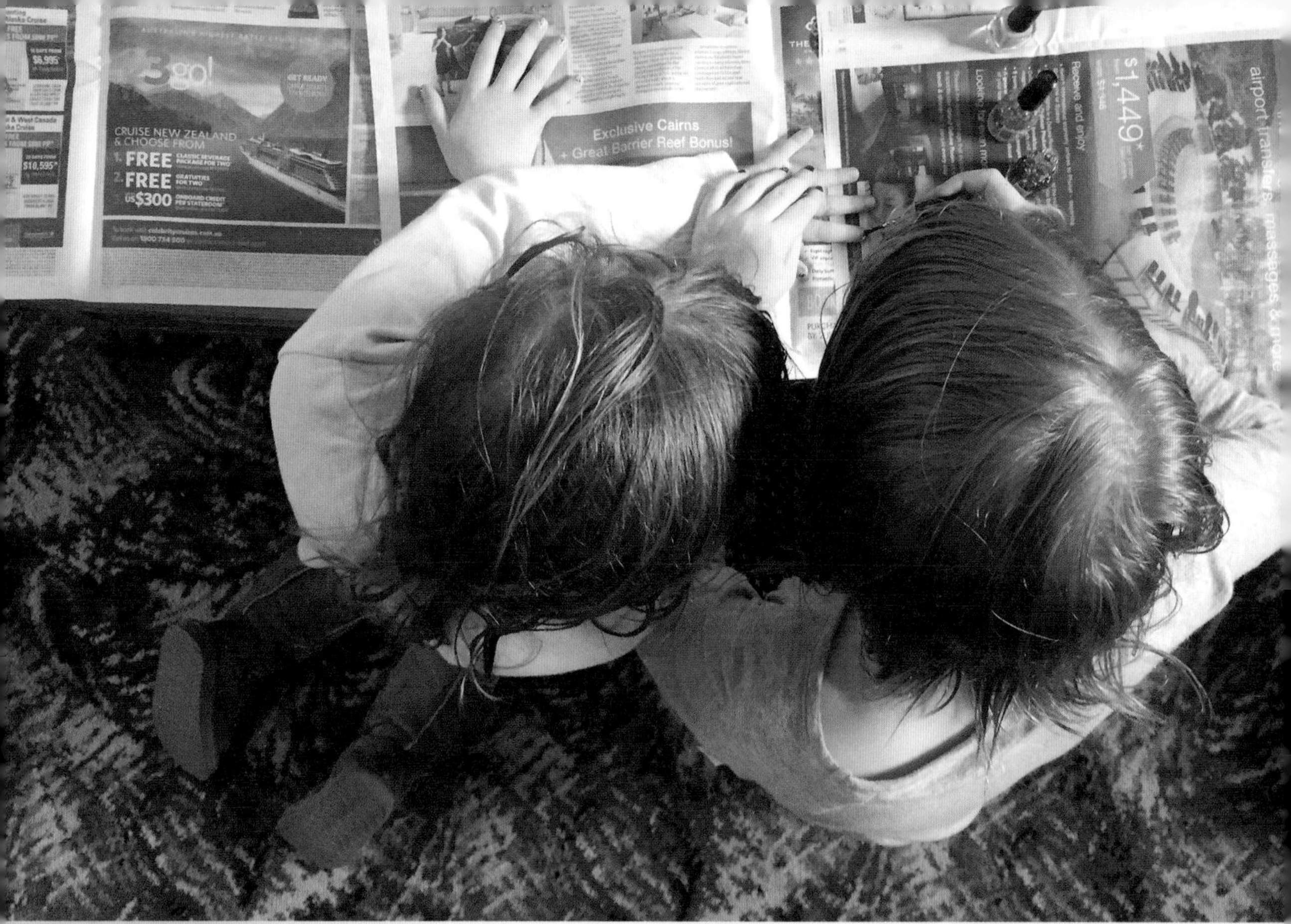
CRUISE NEW ZEALAND
& CHOOSE FROM
1. FREE
2. FREE
US$300
Exclusive Cairns
+ Great Barrier Reef Bonus!
$1,449*

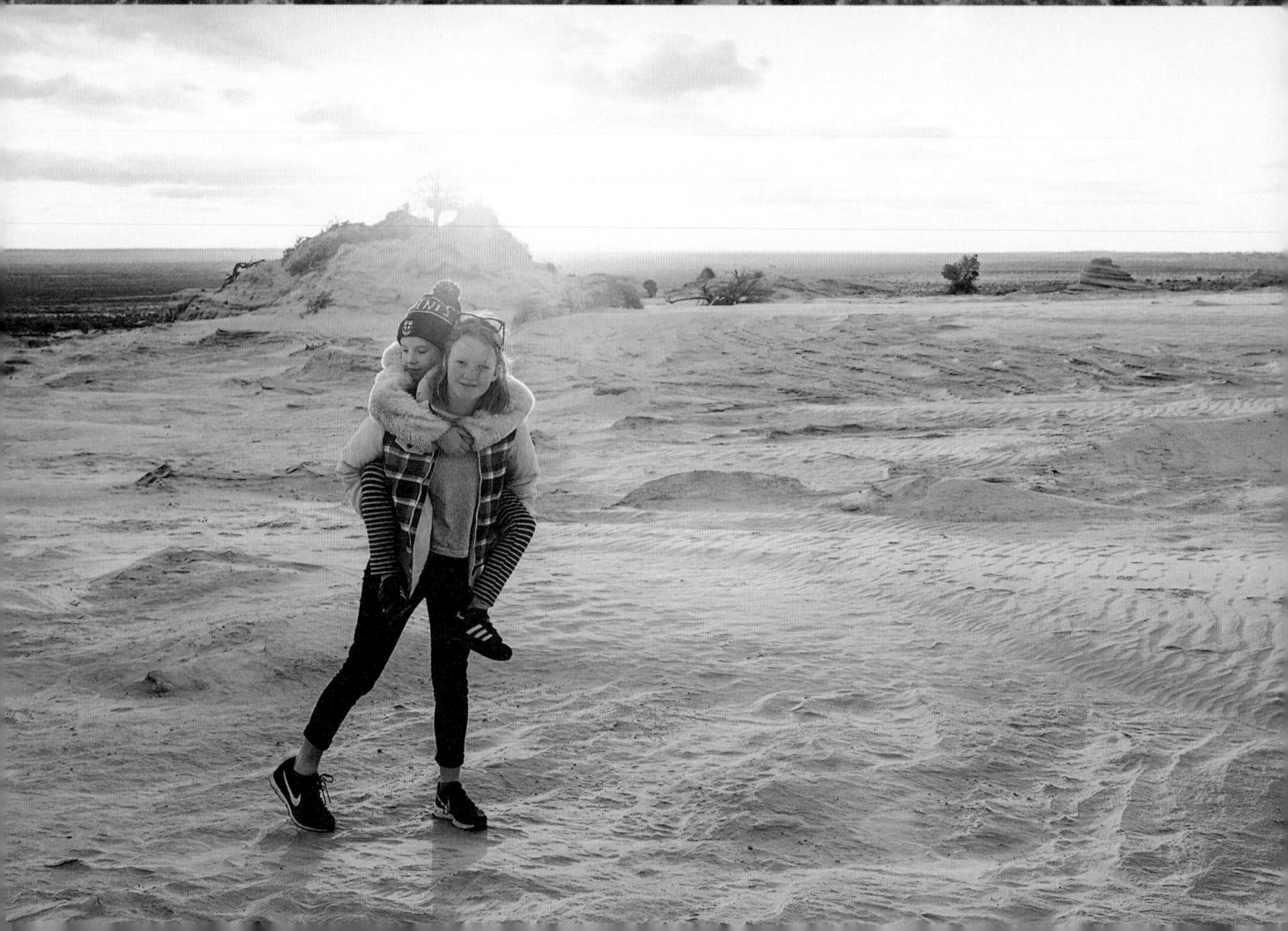

Me? A mother?

'When I have a baby, I won't forget the fun person I used to be.'

My best friend said this not long after I had my first baby. My baby, who was induced over a month early, hated breastfeeding, hated sleeping, hated being held by anyone who wasn't me, and just generally hated being out of the womb. Her time wasn't up; she'd still had six weeks to go. Who could blame her?

I was the first of my friendship group to have a baby and it was such a lonely time. All my friends were either out getting wasted or at home dealing with monster hangovers. A friend with a baby was weird and gross, and I completely understood how they were feeling. I was feeling the same thing.

My body didn't belong to me any more. It acted in ways I'd never experienced or had no freaking control over. What the hell had happened to me? Would I ever recover from this? I stood in the shower, a broken woman. Literally broken. But of course I couldn't stand in there for too long – the baby monitor, perched in the sink, was sure to go off any second.

My old boss's wife, who had two children of her own, once told me that the trauma of childbirth is likened to that of a car accident. These were words of wisdom

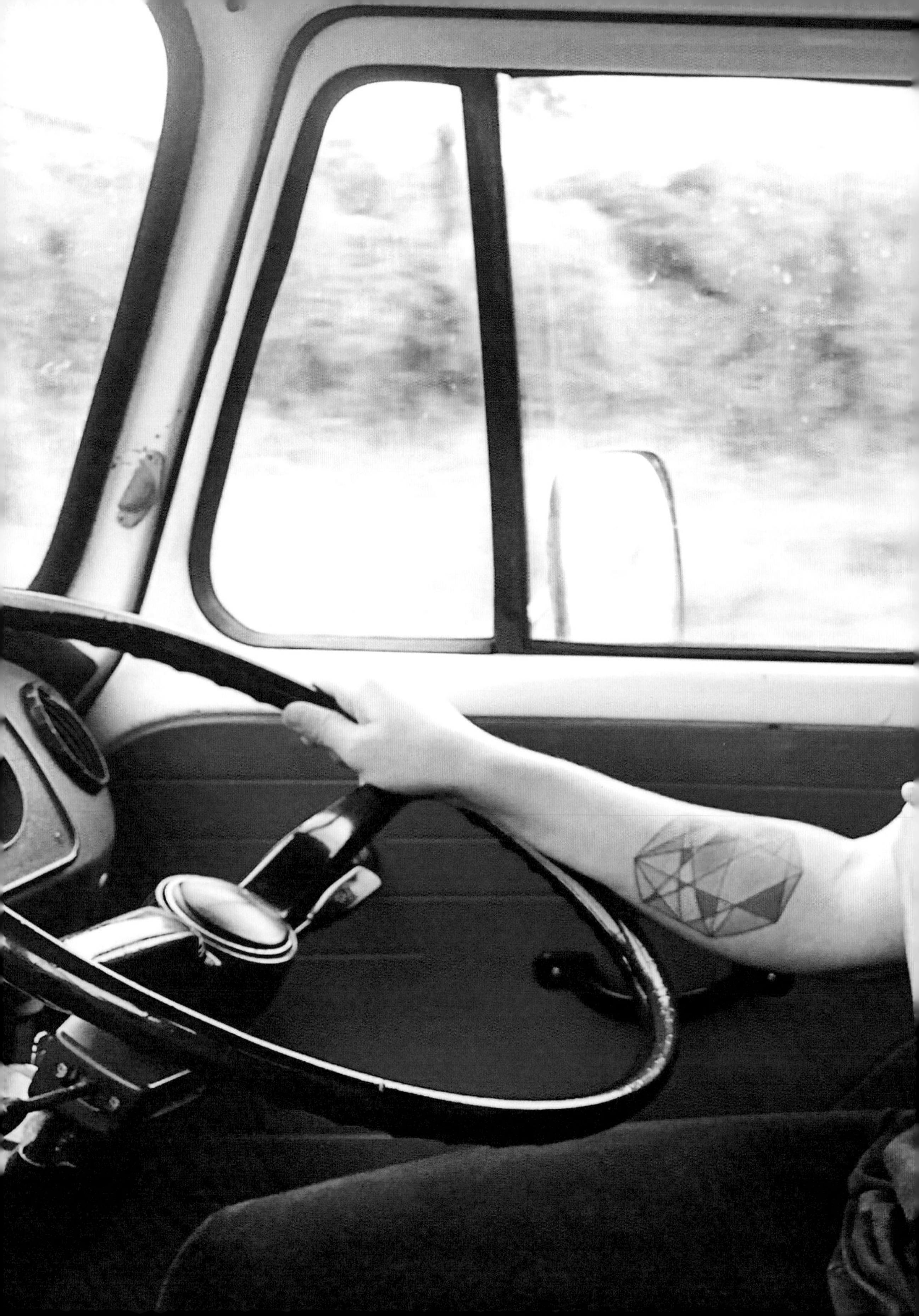

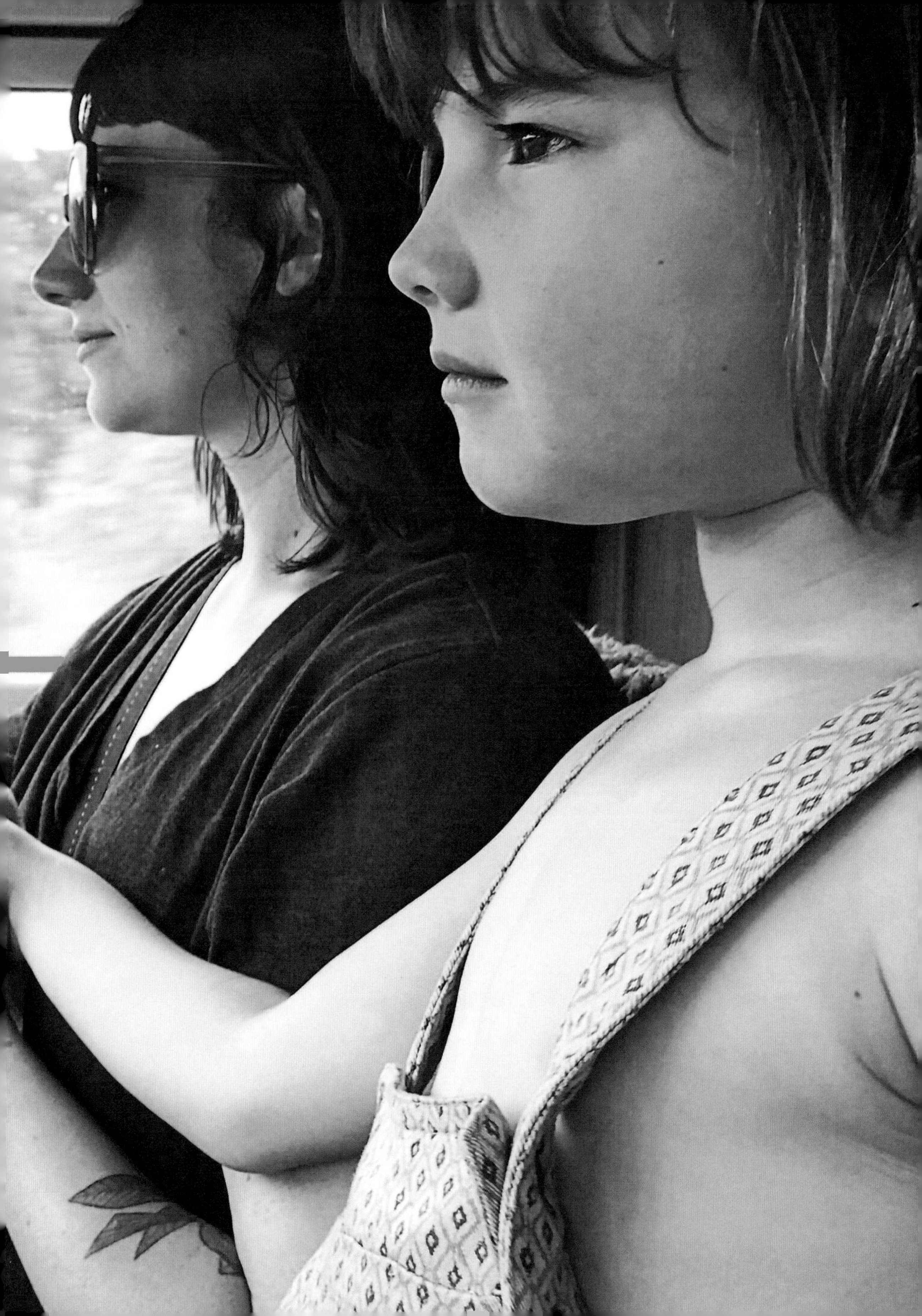

I could identify with. I didn't look anywhere to verify this information; my state of mind and body did that for me.

I struggled with the idea that I was a mother. I just didn't feel like one. Sadly, I lived in a part of Melbourne with a high concentration of what I called 'earth mothers', the pinnacle of natural, at-ease mothering. The benchmark was set so unreasonably high I was certain to fail.

I didn't enjoy breastfeeding. I didn't want to share my bed. But I loved my baby. I know I did.

The mother I thought I was going to be was so different from the mother I was. Or perhaps it was more that motherhood was different from how I'd imagined it would be. I'd assumed I'd stick my baby on my boob and we'd be off. I had no freaking idea there'd be lactation consultants, sleeping consultants, counselling sessions, antidepressants, express pumps, giant pads, midwives milking me at 2 am and so, so many tears.

I was constantly asking my doctor, 'Is this how it's meant to be? Is this normal? Is this my life?'. He reassured me it would get easier, and it did, but not in the way he said it would. The sleep and feeding routines I was promised never really settled in, not for a few years anyway, but what did change was me.

I got the hang of what to worry about, how to look after myself, and what was best for my baby. I tuned out what other people were doing and saying, and just concentrated on doing the best I could.

What's comforting is that now, 14 years later, I am better for these experiences. I can wholeheartedly empathise with new mothers or with anyone who's just finding life a little hard. Judgement has left the building and I love only with an open heart.

A QUICHE FOUND IN THE FOREST

Mushroom and Gruyere Quiche

SERVES 6

We love heading into the forest when things get chilly and the mushies pop up. You'll find us in the well-known mushroom hot spots, shoving each other out of the way to claim the title of 'first mushie of the season finder'. I never win, being practically blind, forever clumsy and always losing my glasses. It's usually those small, pesky, close-to-the-ground types who come home with the title.

When we first started picking mushrooms from the forest, the girls were happy with them simply fried in butter and garlic and put on toast. Now they're all grown up with opinions they prefer their mushies buried in cheese and pastry.

2 tablespoons olive oil
1 small onion, finely chopped
1 garlic clove, very finely chopped
450 g mushrooms (such as pine or field mushrooms), sliced
½ teaspoon salt
110 g (1 cup) grated gruyere
2 free-range eggs, lightly beaten
3 tablespoons finely chopped flat-leaf parsley, plus extra, roughly chopped, to serve

For the base:
200 g (2 cups) almond meal
3 garlic cloves, crushed
1 tablespoon chopped thyme leaves
salt and pepper
80 ml (⅓ cup) olive oil

Preheat the oven to 200°C (fan-forced). Grease a 20 cm pie plate or springform tin with olive oil.

Start with the base. Mix together the almond meal, garlic, thyme and salt and pepper to taste in a bowl. Pour in the olive oil and 1½ tablespoons of water and stir until well combined.

Press the dough into the prepared plate or tin until it is even across the bottom and goes about 3–5 cm up the side. The back of a spoon is a handy way to smooth it out.

Bake for 15–20 minutes or until the crust is lightly golden and firm to the touch. Remove and set aside.

Reduce the oven temperature to 180°C (fan-forced).

Heat the olive oil in a frying pan over medium heat. Add the onion and garlic and cook, stirring, for 4 minutes or until the onion has softened. Add the mushrooms and salt and cook for 6–8 minutes or until the mushrooms are tender. Remove from the heat and allow to cool slightly, then tip the mixture into a large bowl.

Add the cheese, egg and parsley to the mushroom mixture and stir to combine.

Pour the filling into the pastry shell, then bake for about 30–35 minutes, turning the dish or tin halfway through.

Transfer the quiche to a wire rack and allow to cool for about 10 minutes. Top with the extra parsley and serve warm.

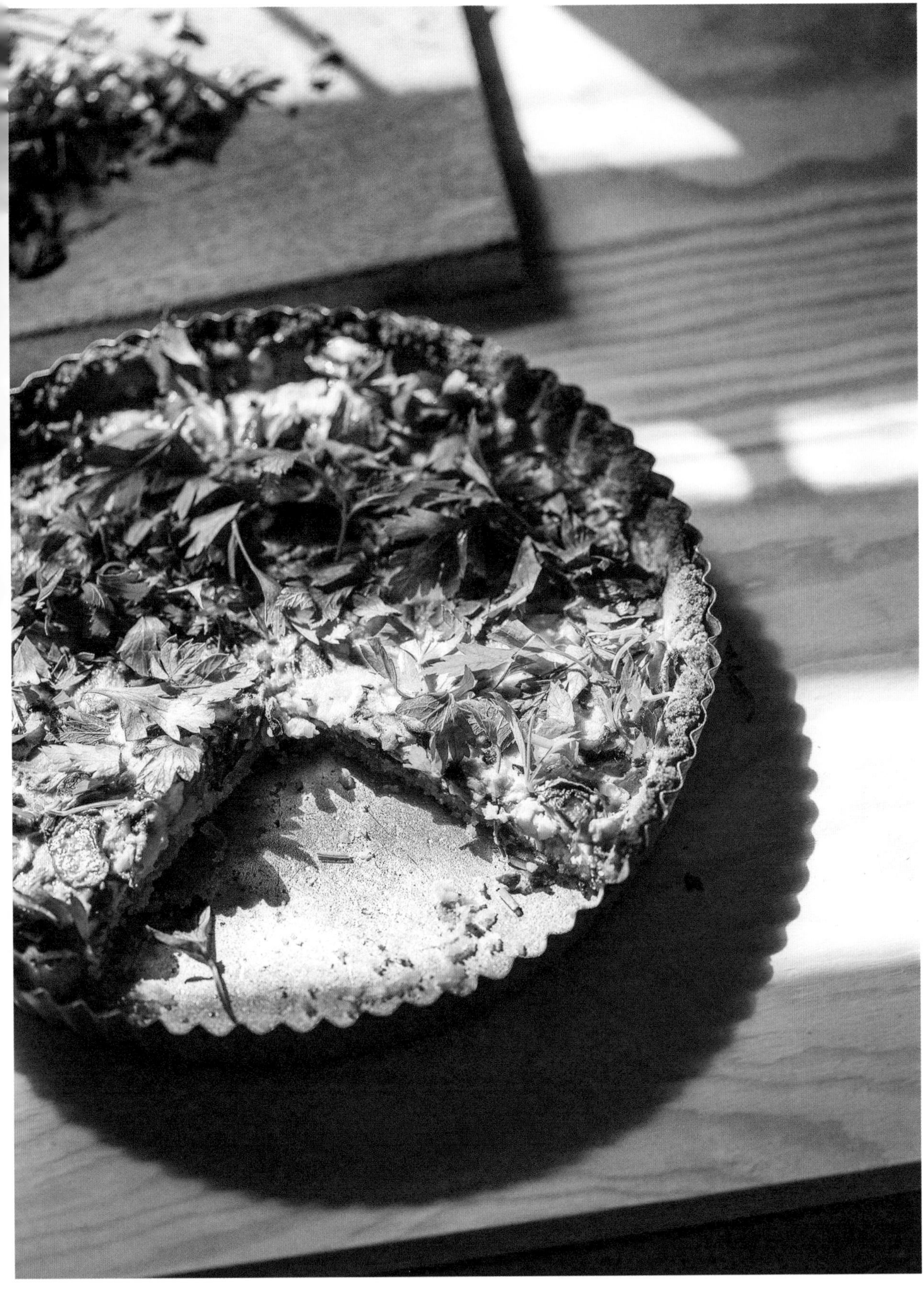

NUTTY PINK PASTA

**Beetroot Spaghetti
with Mint and
Walnuts**

SERVES 4

Thankfully, these days I don't have to write about making pink pasta because I have girls to feed. That whole 'pink for girls and blue for boys' thing has been exposed for what it is: bullshit. I have one girl who likes playing footy and another who sits in her room for hours teaching herself how to play the guitar. One likes wearing thug beanies and the other one has recently started transplanting clothes from my wardrobe to hers. If I wasn't so chuffed about her thinking I was cool enough to steal from, I'd go and take them back.

1 large beetroot
350 g spaghetti
185 g (¾ cup) fresh ricotta,
    well drained
2 tablespoons olive oil,
    plus extra to serve
2 tablespoons lemon juice
1 teaspoon salt
3 tablespoons roughly
    chopped walnuts
2 tablespoons torn mint leaves
grated parmesan, to serve

Give the beetroot a good scrub, then put it in a large saucepan and cover with water. Bring to the boil and cook for about 45 minutes or until tender. Keep an eye on the water – if it gets a little low, add more and bring it back to the boil. Once tender, drain and set aside to cool.

Cook the spaghetti in a large saucepan of salted boiling water until al dente. Scoop out 250 ml (1 cup) of pasta cooking water and reserve, then drain the spaghetti.

While the pasta cooks, rub the skin off the beetroot and cut it into quarters. Place in a food processor, add the ricotta, olive oil, lemon juice, salt and 3 tablespoons of the pasta cooking water and blend until smooth.

Return the drained pasta to the saucepan, then pour the beetroot sauce over the top and toss well. Drizzle in a little more pasta cooking water if it doesn't look nice and glossy.

Divide the pasta among bowls and top with the walnuts, mint, parmesan and a final drizzle of olive oil.

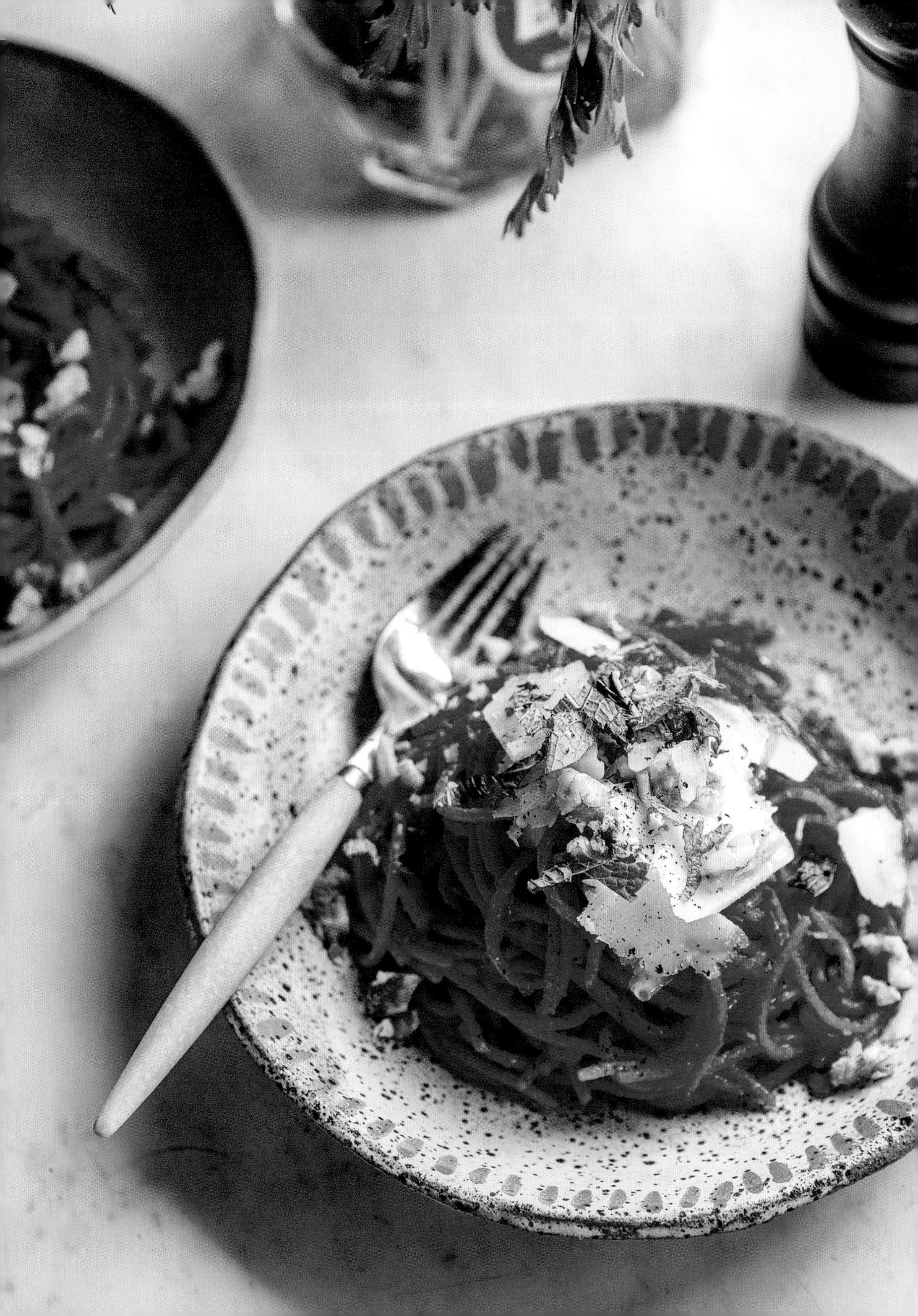

BACK TO BASICS

PIZZA BASE AND SAUCE

Yep, it's not a groundbreaking observation, but pizza is freaking amazing. It's everyone's favourite food and can turn the crappiest of fridge scraps into a unique pizza discovery. You can also turn the pizza dough into a very popular (in my house) lunchbox option.

For the sauce:
80 ml (⅓ cup) olive oil
3 garlic cloves, peeled and left whole
1 x 400 g can crushed tomatoes
1 x 700 g bottle tomato passata
big pinch of salt

For the pizza base:
1 x 7 g sachet dried yeast
1 tablespoon caster sugar
400 g plain flour
1 teaspoon salt
2 tablespoons olive oil

Get your pizza sauce on the go first. Heat the olive oil in a medium saucepan over low heat, pop in the garlic and cook for a few minutes until you can smell it. Add the crushed tomatoes, passata and salt.

Leave to simmer for about an hour, stirring occasionally and adding a little water if it reduces too much.

Remove the garlic cloves and allow the sauce to cool a little before using on your pizzas. Any leftover sauce will keep in an airtight container in the fridge for up to a week. Or use it to make scrollz (page 93).

Now for the pizza base. Combine the yeast, sugar and 250 ml (1 cup) of lukewarm water in a small jug or bowl and leave it for about 5 minutes or until bubbly. If it doesn't bubble your yeast is dead and you'll need to start again with a new packet.

Whisk together the flour and salt in a large bowl and make a well in the centre. Pour the yeast mixture and olive oil into the well and bring together with a wooden spoon.

Tip out onto a floured bench and knead for about 10 minutes or until the dough is silky and smooth. Coat the bowl with a little olive oil, then pop the dough back in, cover and leave to rise for 30 minutes or until doubled in size.

Preheat the oven to 190°C (fan-forced). Line two baking trays with baking paper.

Divide the dough into four even pieces and roll out into rounds of your preferred thickness. Place the bases on the prepared trays and top with the pizza sauce and your fave toppings.

Bake for 20–25 minutes or until the bases are cooked and the toppings are golden.

Combos to try:

Margherita

Top the pizza base with pizza sauce and mozzarella. Cook as described, then top with fresh basil leaves.

Haloumi, green olive and lemon

Top the pizza base with pizza sauce, thinly sliced haloumi and olives. Cook as described, then squeeze over some fresh lemon juice.

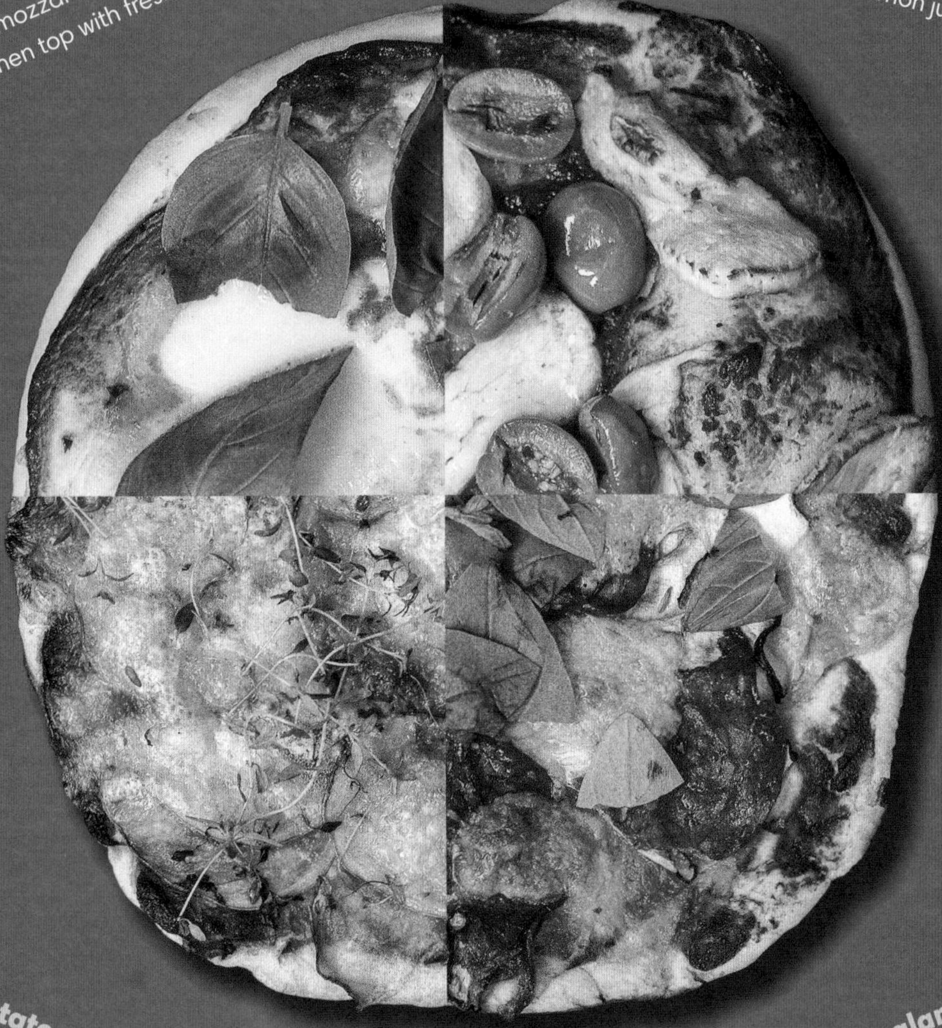

Potato, taleggio and thyme

Top the pizza base with pizza sauce, super thinly sliced potato with dots of taleggio and thyme. Cook as described.

Zucchini, ricotta and salami

Top the pizza base with pizza sauce. Mix together some fresh ricotta, garlic and a little finely grated lemon zest and add to the pizza base with thinly sliced zucchini and salami. Cook as described.

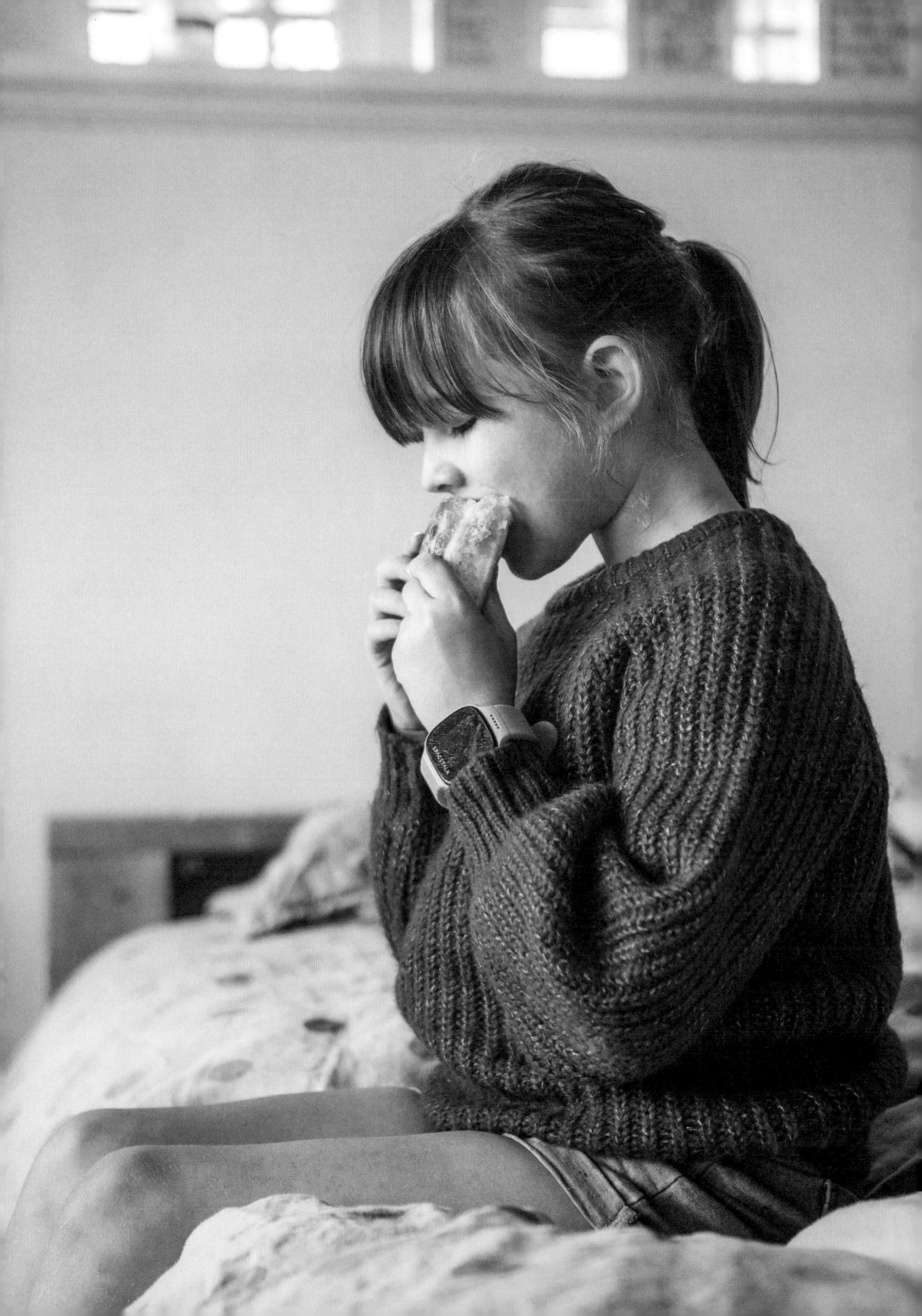
SPACETALK

SCROLLZ

Double the quantity of pizza dough and make easy lunchbox snacks for the kids at the same time.

1   Make the pizza dough and sauce.

2   Preheat the oven to 210°C (fan-forced). Line a large baking tray with baking paper.

3   Cut the dough in half and roll each half into a rectangle about 1 cm thick.

4   Spread pizza sauce evenly over the dough, leaving a 2 cm border around the edge.

5   Sprinkle with cheese and your choice of toppings, leaving the border clear.

6   Starting from one of the long sides, roll up each rectangle into a long log and press firmly together to make sure it is properly sealed.

7   Cut the logs into even portions, around 4 cm thick.

8   Place the scrolls, cut-side up and touching, on the prepared tray.

9   Pop in the oven for 25 minutes or until golden brown.

10 Rip off a freshly baked scroll and enjoy them at their best. Try to save a few for the kids' lunchboxes.

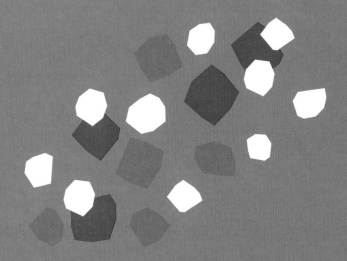

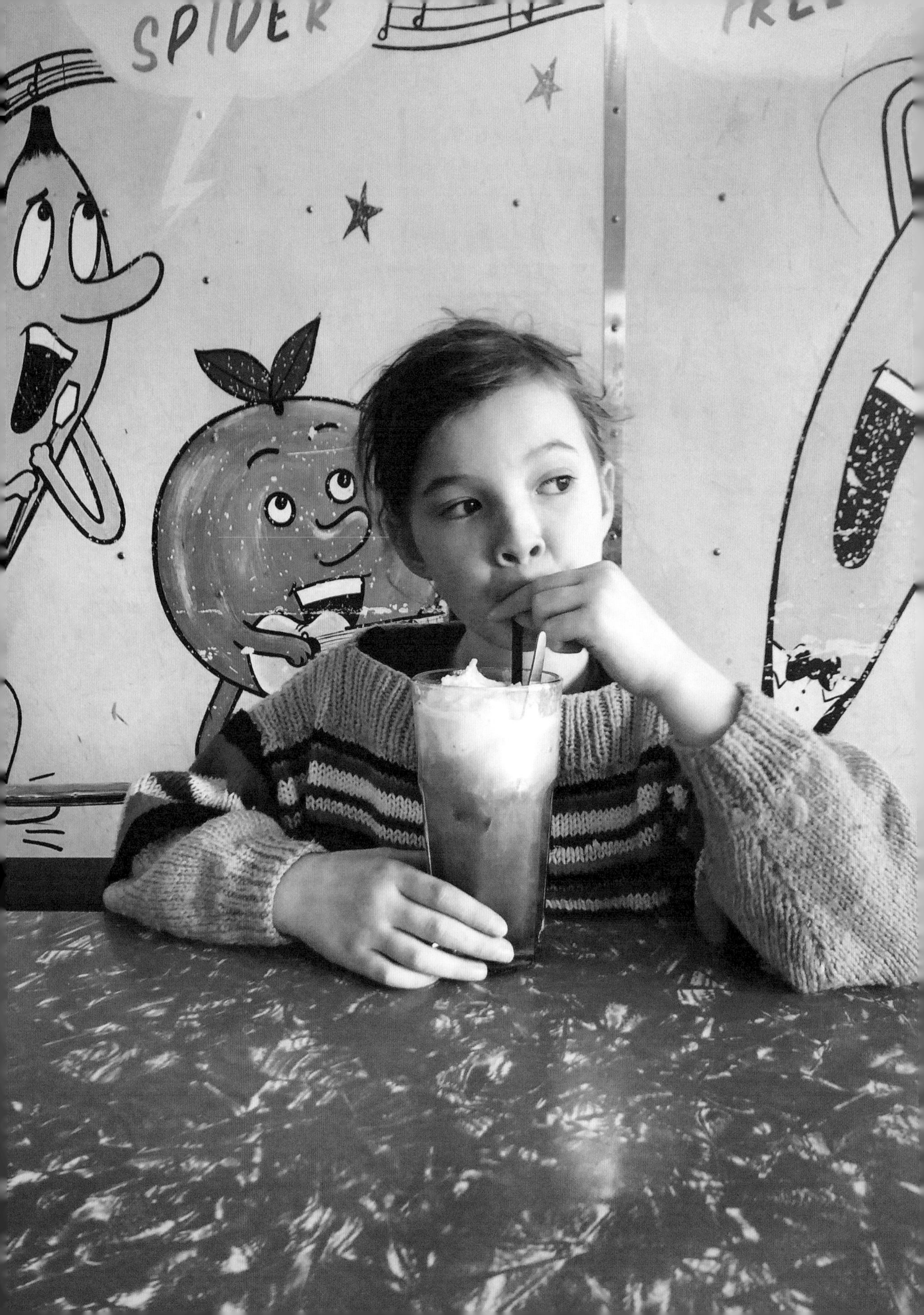
SPIDER

Reclaiming midweek

Some weeks seem to drag on and are just plain torturous. I'm not entirely sure what it is about them that makes them so bloody horrible, but they are. And yes, people say you shouldn't wish your life away, but frankly that's just as annoying as the week that decides to take its sweet time.

To combat this phenomenon, which occurs WAY more often in winter, I created 'midweek good times'. A thing that happens after school on Wednesdays to break up those long stubborn weeks. Sometimes we stay somewhere local and act like tourists for the afternoon; sometimes the kids create a tent out of the dining table and spend the night camped out in the house; and sometimes we'll camp in the backyard and eat jacket potatoes and toast marshmallows. Other times it's just a day of breaking rules and giving the finger to what's meant to happen on a Wednesday.

One Wednesday we bought three different flavours of ice cream, quite a few toppings and a few choice sprinkles. We decided it would all be better on top of waffles, so we made them too. Our favourite winter treat is our hot banana and chocolate fudge sundae, which involves frying bananas and topping them with mountains of vanilla ice cream, hot chocolate fudge sauce and loads of crushed salty peanuts. We don't

do this all the time, which is what makes it so bloody magical. I can pretend to be as grown up as I like, but I am always going to choose a hot banana and chocolate fudge sundae over a sensible dinner any day (well, most days). Wouldn't you?

It isn't always about camping out and eating crap (though it mostly is). What it comes down to is doing something we'd normally save for a weekend. Or something that's a bit out of the ordinary. When the weather's warm, I'll sometimes pack towels and bathers in the car, pick up the girls from school and drive to the nearest waterhole.

Whatever we decide to do, the point is that the emotional wellbeing bucket gets a good fill and we're all ready to tackle those last two days before the weekend.

But the best bit is waking up on Thursday, groaning 'argh … I hate Mondays' and then realising that it's ACTUALLY THURSDAY!

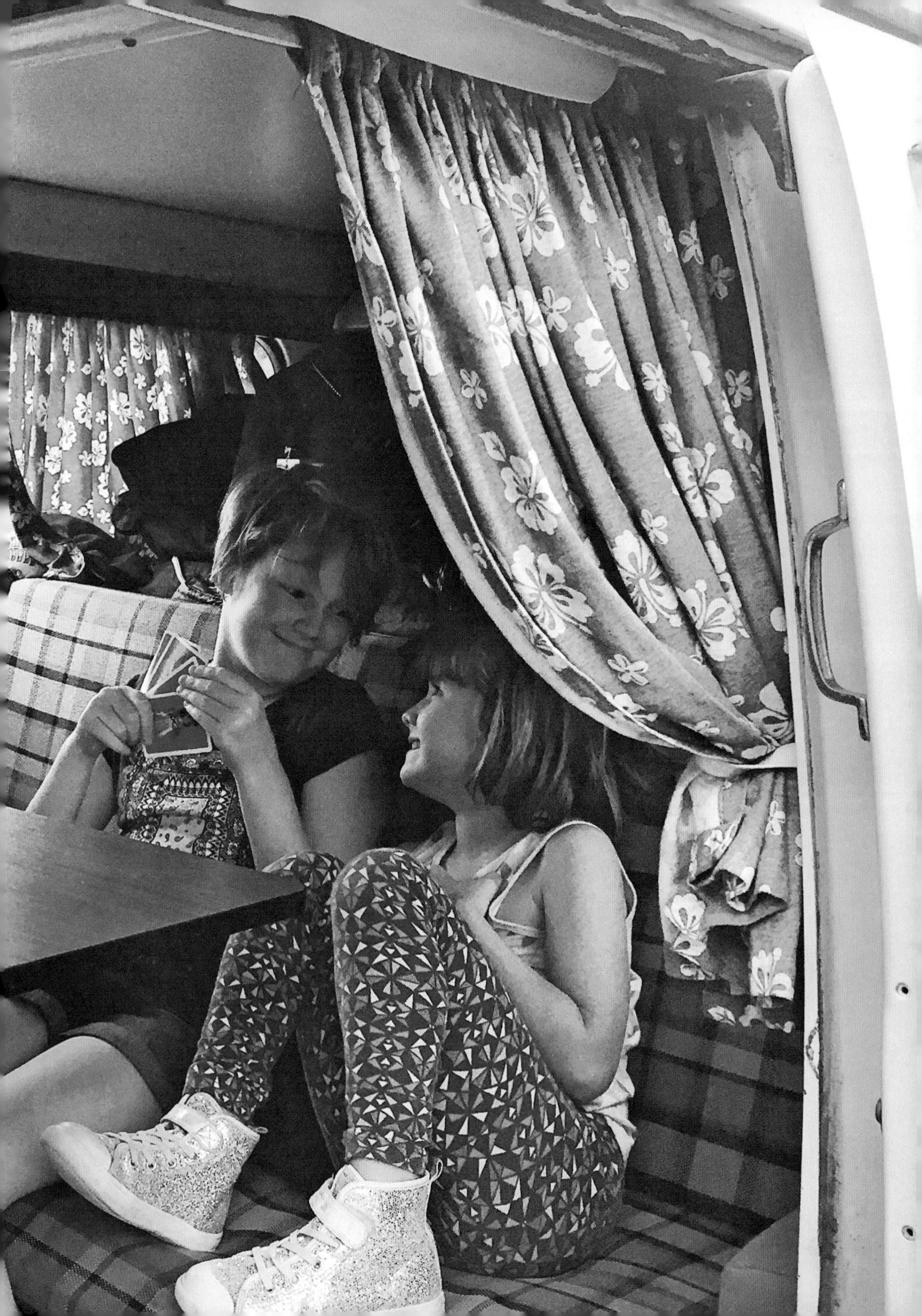

HOT BANANA AND CHOCOLATE FUDGE SUNDAES

MAKES 4

25 g butter
4 bananas, peeled
plenty of good-quality
  chocolate fudge sauce
vanilla ice cream (I am not
  going to tell you how much,
  that's not the spirit)
80 g (½ cup) crushed salted
  peanuts (or sprinkles, or
  cachous, or whatever!)

Melt the butter in a frying pan over medium heat. Add the bananas and fry on each side for 1–2 minutes or until golden.

While the bananas are frying, put the bottle of sauce in a jug of hot water to make it warm and runny.

Place each fried banana in a serving bowl. Pile vanilla ice cream on top, then drizzle generously with hot fudge sauce and sprinkle over the toppings.

Repeat.

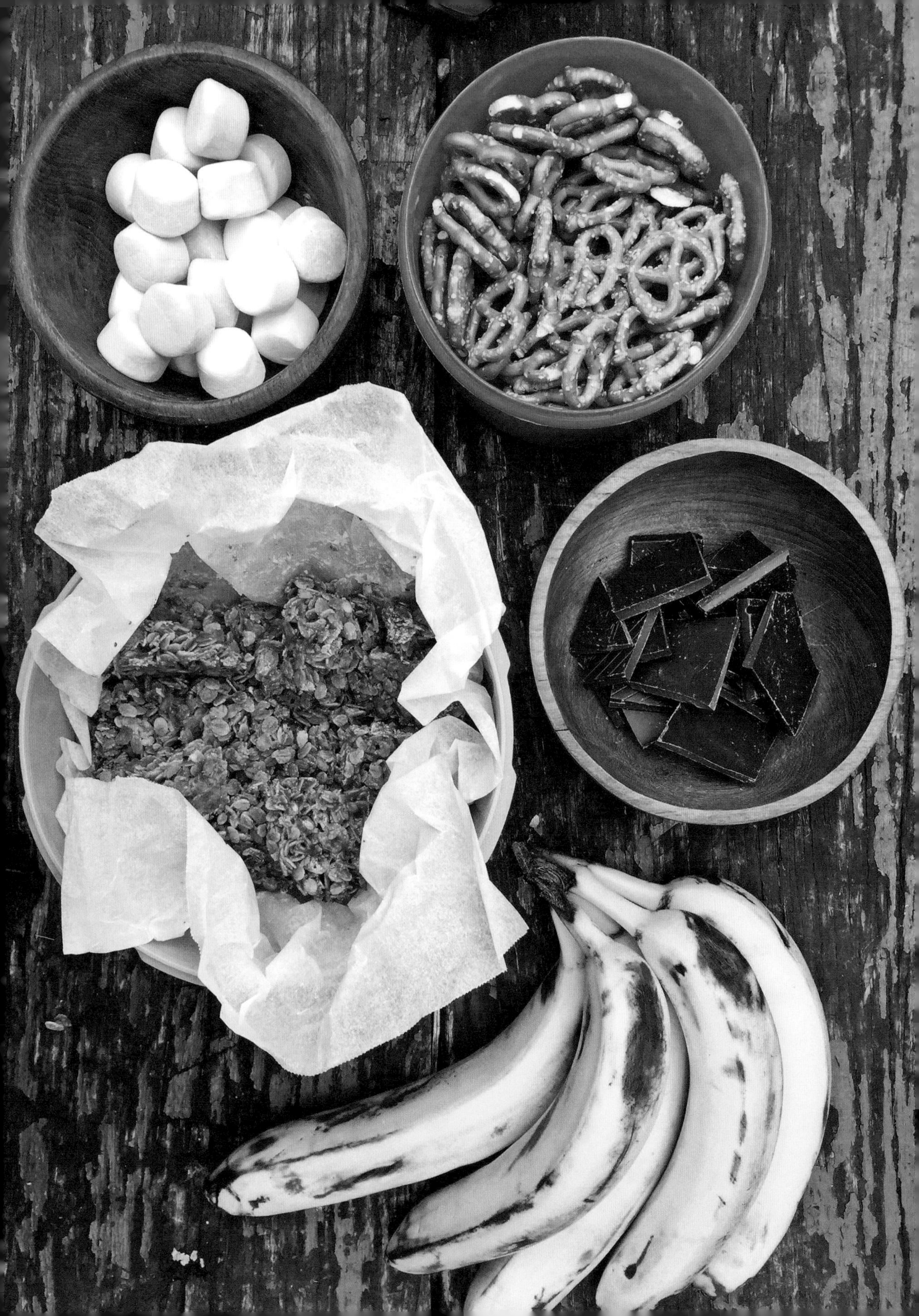

MODERN FAMILY CHICKEN SOUP AND POTATO 'NEEDLATCH'

Chicken Soup with Potato Knaidelach

SERVES 4

My girls have a half-brother who they visit every second weekend. We head over on Friday arvo and arrive just in time for Shabbat. I am always asked to stay for dinner with the family and until recently I would always politely decline, armed with a string of excuses. Until one Friday I suddenly realised that nothing was more important than spending time with the people my girls love just as much as me. Sometimes when you begrudgingly face awkward or difficult situations head on, they're nowhere near as hard as you imagine and they'll actually help you grow a little.

At its best, this soup will cure you in the depths of winter and warm hearts around a family table. Make it a day ahead to get the full amazingness of chicken flavour. Don't settle for less.

2 kg chicken wings
1.5 kg chicken frames
500 g chicken giblets
1 leek, white part only, halved lengthways
6 carrots, peeled and left whole
½ bunch flat-leaf parsley, plus extra to serve (optional)
salt and pepper

For the knaidelach:
900 g potatoes (such as coliban, desiree or sebago), peeled and cut into large chunks
1 large free-range egg
3 tablespoons potato starch
1 tablespoon finely chopped dill fronds, plus extra to serve (optional)
150 g (1½ cups) almond meal, plus extra if needed
salt and white pepper

Place the chicken wings, frames and giblets, leek, carrots and parsley in a big stockpot. Season well with salt and pepper and cover with cold water. Bring the water to the boil, constantly skimming the foam from the surface of the water, then reduce the heat and simmer for 4 hours. Continue to skim the foam from the surface until the broth is clear. If your liquid reduces too much, just add some more water. Remove from the heat and set aside to cool to room temperature.

Strain the soup (keep the carrots and compost the rest). Pop in the fridge overnight.

Make the knaidelach on the day of serving. Cook the potatoes in salted boiling water for about 45 minutes or until soft (the exact cooking time will depend on the size of the chunks). Drain and refrigerate until cool.

Take the cold potatoes out of the fridge and mash them in a bowl, making sure you get all the lumps out. Add the egg, potato starch, dill, almond meal and a good pinch of salt and white pepper and mix to form a dough. If the dough is sticky, or you want a denser dumpling, add a bit more almond meal.

Roll the potato dough into balls, 2 tablespoons at a time. Set aside.

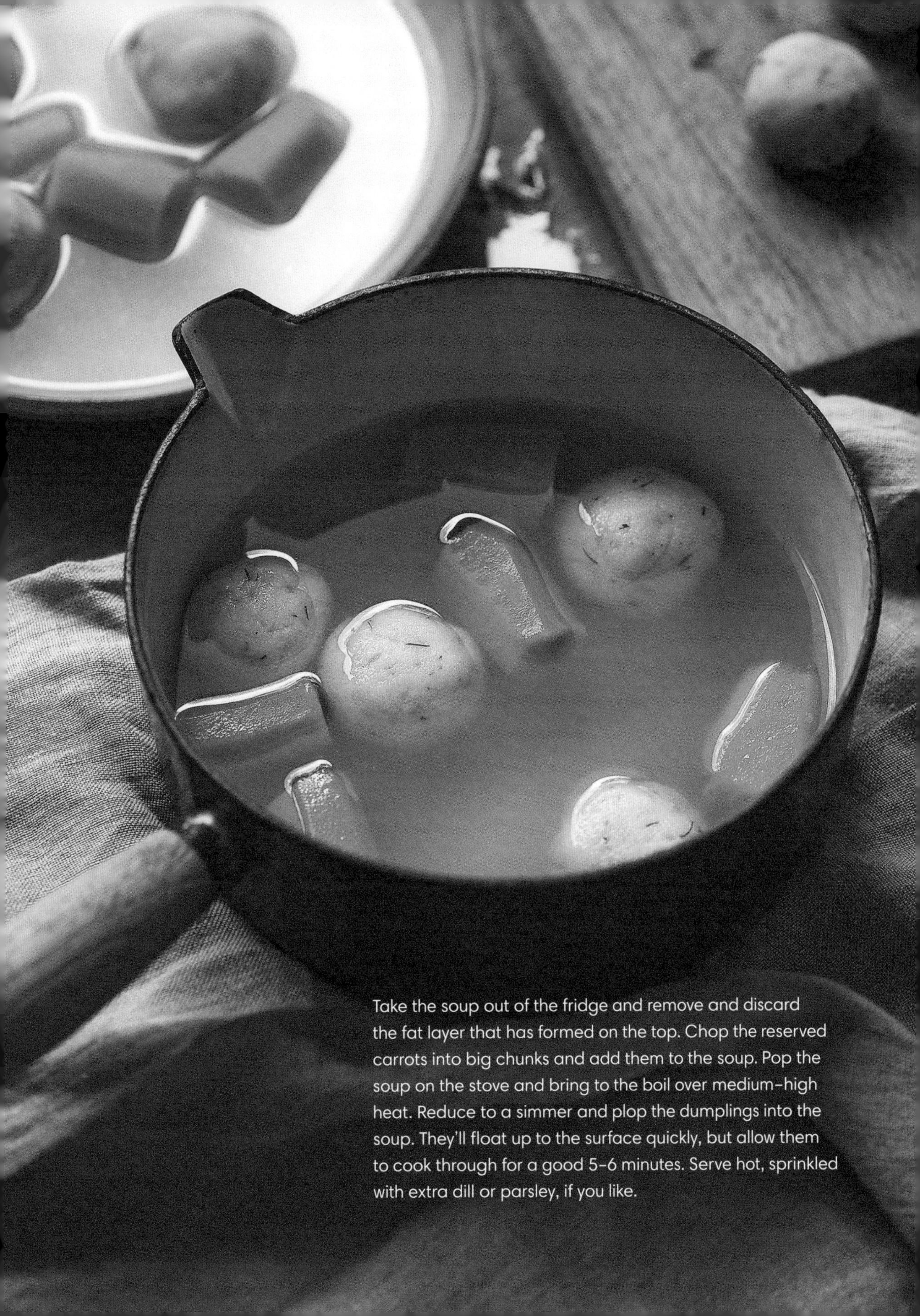

Take the soup out of the fridge and remove and discard the fat layer that has formed on the top. Chop the reserved carrots into big chunks and add them to the soup. Pop the soup on the stove and bring to the boil over medium–high heat. Reduce to a simmer and plop the dumplings into the soup. They'll float up to the surface quickly, but allow them to cook through for a good 5–6 minutes. Serve hot, sprinkled with extra dill or parsley, if you like.

STUFF FROM THE FRIDGE + RICE

Fried Rice

SERVES 4-6

This recipe can be whatever you want it to be. Use the quantities as a guide and make your own version of fried rice from whatever's lying around in your fridge. It's such a great (and yummy) way to get rid of the little bits and pieces you've been saving but really have no use for.

80 ml (⅓ cup) vegetable oil
1 onion, finely chopped
2 garlic cloves, crushed
200 g bacon, rind removed, chopped
about 3 cups diced vegetables (I used carrot, kale, squash and zucchini)
740 g (4 cups) cooked white rice (it has to be a day old; I usually cook extra rice when I make something the night before so I can make this the next day)
2 tablespoons Chinese cooking wine (shaoxing)
2 tablespoons oyster sauce
1 tablespoon soy sauce (or tamari)
1 teaspoon sesame oil
½ teaspoon pepper
4 free-range eggs, lightly beaten
4 spring onions, green and white parts, finely sliced

Heat 2 tablespoons of vegetable oil in a large frying pan or wok over high heat. Add the onion, garlic and bacon and cook for 1–2 minutes or until the bacon is light golden.

Add the veggies and cook for 2–3 minutes or until they start to soften slightly. Add the rice, cooking wine, oyster sauce, soy sauce, sesame oil and pepper and cook, tossing, for 1–2 minutes or until the liquid has evaporated.

Scrape the rice mixture to one side of the pan, then pour the remaining vegetable oil into the cleared space. Tip in the beaten egg and scramble it. Scatter over the spring onion, then quickly stir the egg through the rice and serve.

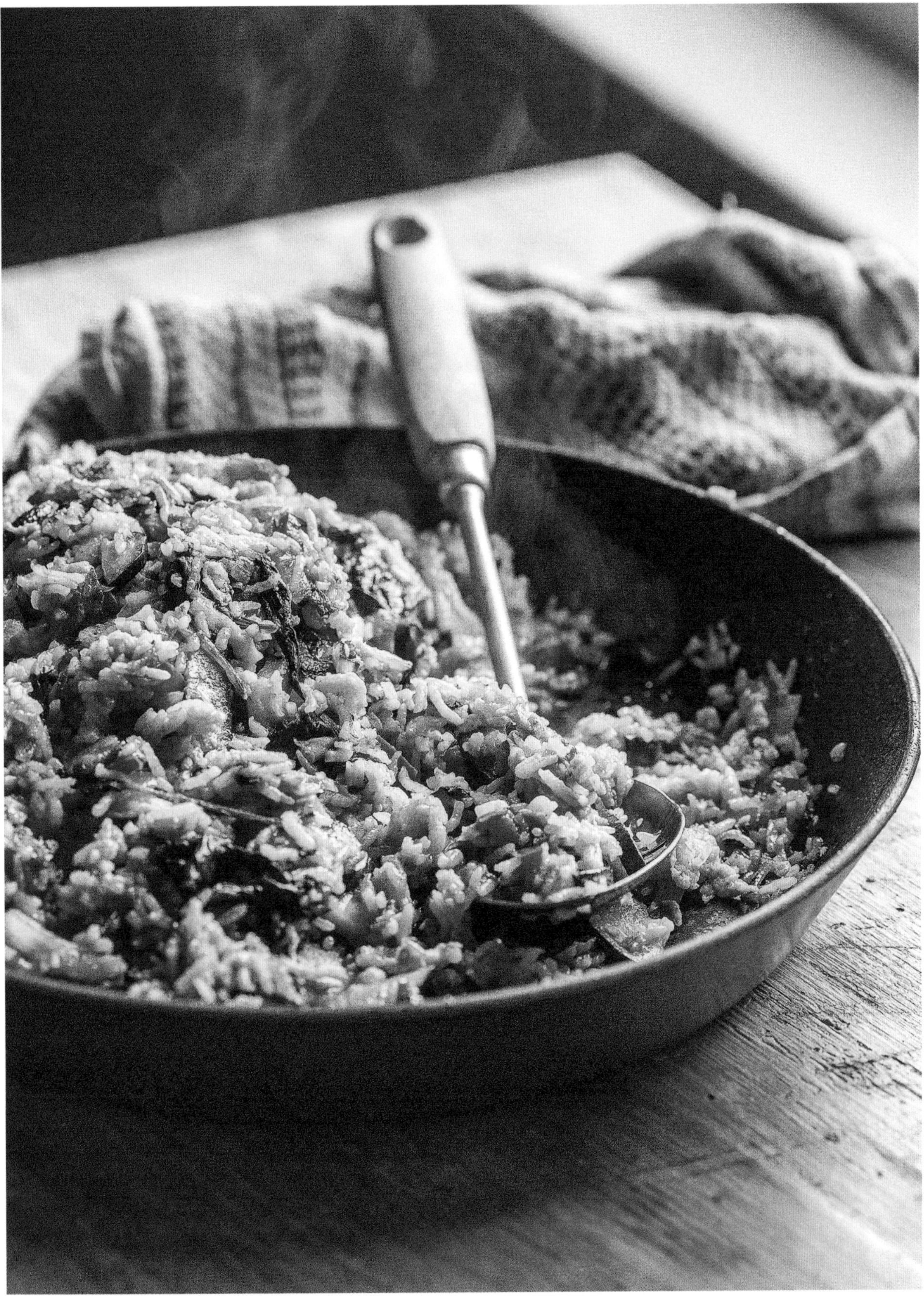

There's no freaking bread

I'm not sure why my brain thinks there needs to be bread in a school lunch. Often on a Monday morning you'll find me racing around the kitchen in a panic, looking for any signs of gluten. But slowly I am beginning to understand that it doesn't need to be this way. In fact, the greatest meal often turns out to be 'one I prepared earlier'.

If I can manage it, I spend Sunday arvo in the kitchen making food for the week. The benefits are threefold: it makes Monday to Friday easier to deal with; the house smells incredible; and I feel like a total grown-up. I try and get the kids to help out as they're more inclined to eat what they've had a hand in making, and it distracts them from those freaking screens.

The potato tortilla opposite is cheap and easy (music to my ears). It also makes an excellent bread substitute for school lunches.

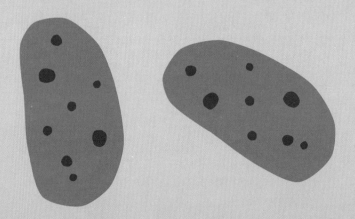

POTATO TÓRTILLA

700 g potatoes
1 onion
250 ml (1 cup) olive oil
1 tablespoon smoked paprika
salt and pepper
6 large free-range eggs

Peel and thinly slice the potatoes and onion. If you have one of those death-trap mandolines, use that. I usually stick with a knife though.

Heat the olive oil in a 25 cm non-stick frying pan over medium heat.

Add the potato, onion, paprika and a generous pinch of salt and pepper (this meal is very basic so let's not be shy on the seasoning). Reduce the heat a little and continue cooking, carefully turning the potato slices every now and then, for 10–15 minutes or until tender. If they start to break they're overdone, so get 'em off the heat ASAP. Remove the potato and onion with tongs or a slotted spoon and place in a colander. Drain off and reserve the oil.

Lightly beat the eggs in a bowl and, again, season well. Add the potato mixture and gently mix together.

Give the pan a bit of a wipe and place over medium heat for a minute. Add a splash of the reserved oil, then add the potato and egg mixture. Cook for 1 minute or until the edge starts to firm up, then reduce the heat to medium–low and cook for a further 5 minutes.

Run a rubber spatula around the edge of the tortilla so it will easily slide from the pan. The top will still be runny. Carefully slide the tortilla onto a plate and cover with another plate. Hold the plates tightly together and flip them over.

Add another splash of oil to the pan and carefully slide the tortilla back in, runny-side down. Cook for another 5 minutes, then slide the tortilla onto a clean plate. Serve warm, or at room temperature, or in a lunchbox.

SPICY CHOCKIE GOODNESS

Turmeric, Cacao and Mountain Pepper Balls

MAKES 20

This recipe can go either way with me – it totally depends on my time and/or motivation. If both are limited, I whiz it up and pop it in a slice tin. But if it's a chilled Sunday arvo and I'm feeling the vibe, I'll take the time to roll them into balls. Because for some weird reason these taste way better in ball form.

540 g (3 cups) pitted dates
235 g (1½ cups) almonds
90 g (1½ cups) shredded coconut
60 g (½ cup) raw cacao powder
2 tablespoons flaxseeds
1 tablespoon ground turmeric
1 teaspoon ground Tasmanian mountain pepper (optional; see TIP)
1 tablespoon pure maple syrup
pepitas, sesame seeds, chia seeds and/or hemp seeds (or any nuts or seeds you like), for rolling or sprinkling

Pop the dates in a food processor and start breaking them up. It's good to slowly introduce each ingredient so your processor doesn't get overwhelmed and burn out.

Once the dates have broken up a little, gradually add the remaining ingredients until the mixture comes together in a big, smooth-ish clump. Depending on how powerful your processor is, this could take up to 10 minutes.

If you're going to go ahead with the ball option, roll the mixture into 5 cm balls and set aside. Pour your choice of seeds or nuts into a shallow dish and roll the balls in them to coat. Pop the balls in a jar or container, then place them in the fridge. These are best eaten cold.

If you've chosen the easier route, line a slice tin with baking paper, then tip the mixture into the tin. Pat it down to a nice even layer and smooth the top with the back of a spoon.

Sprinkle seeds or nuts over the top and gently press them into the mixture with your hand. Pop the slice in the fridge for at least 2 hours, then cut into squares and serve.

TIP: If you don't have Tasmanian mountain pepper, don't use regular pepper. Just leave it out if you can't find it – the mixture will still be delicious.

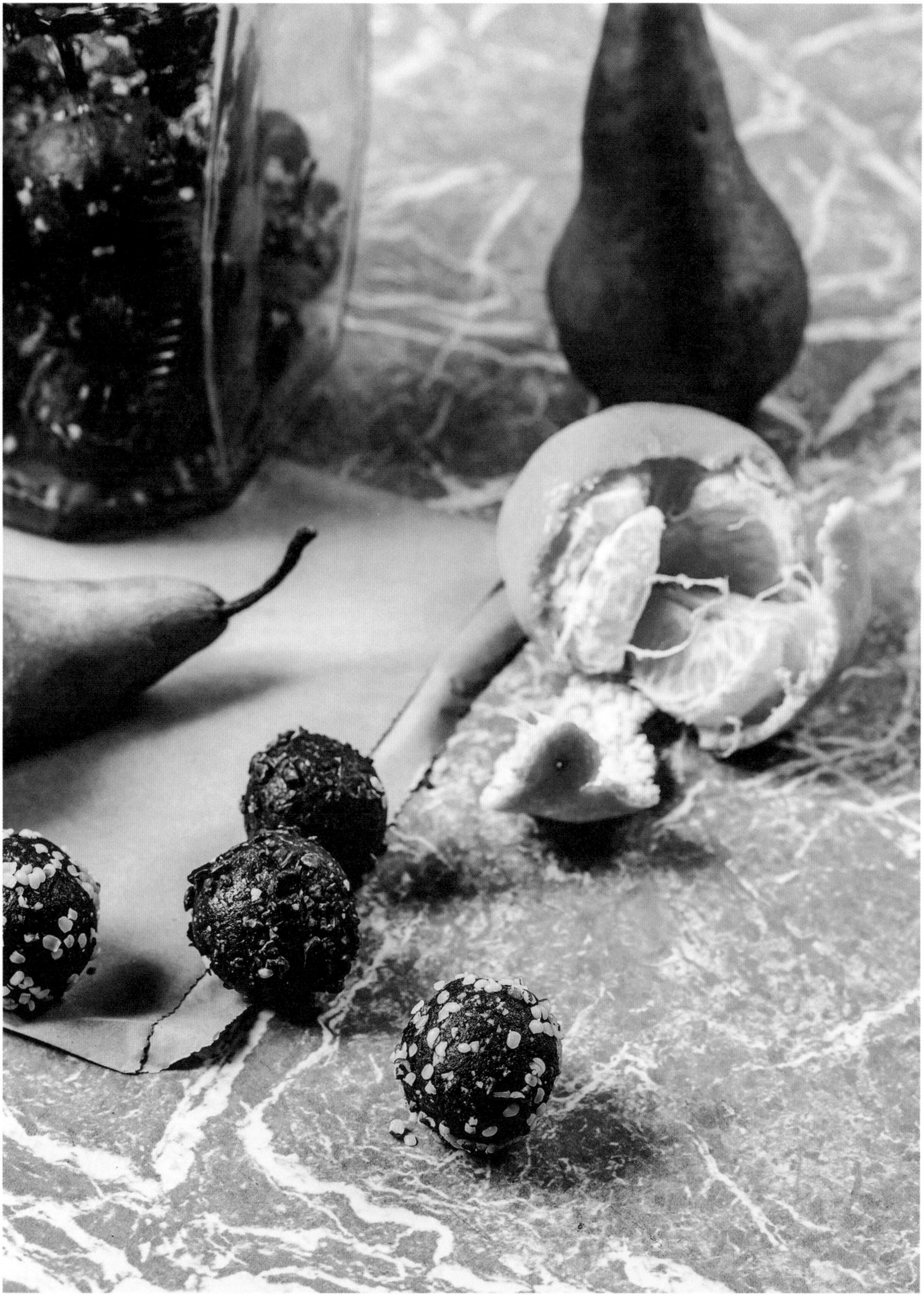

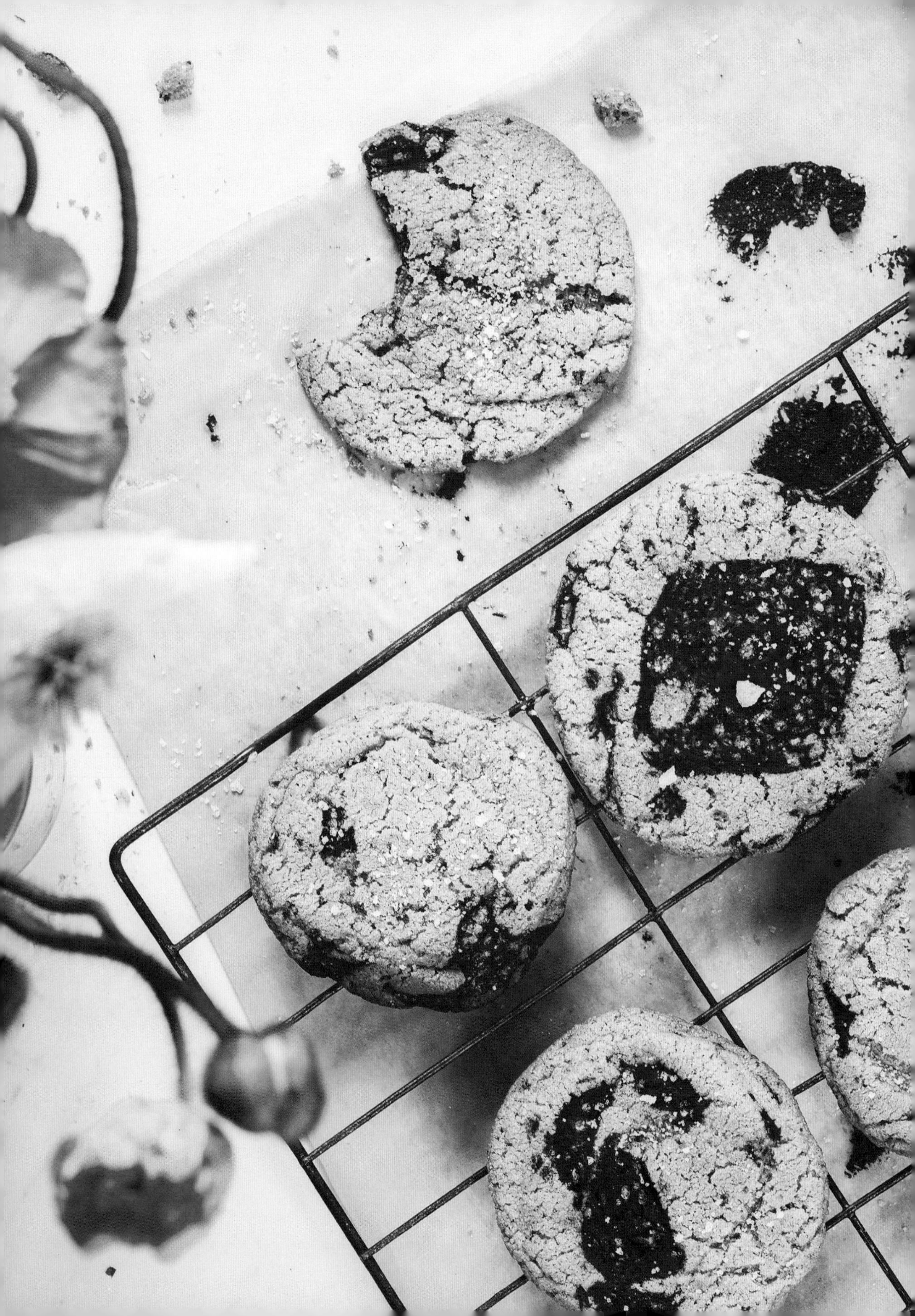

BICKIES MILK WAS MADE FOR

Salted Tahini Choc Chip Biscuits

MAKES 24

I've always thought there's something really validating about a big jar of home-baked biscuits. It's almost like it says I've got my act together and have finally made it as a grown-up. I feel really chuffed when I pop them into my girls' lunchboxes, knowing they aren't full of crap and that I had a hand in making something they're taking to school with them. But I am totally aware that's not how they see it. To them they are just biscuits, and that's OK.

115 g butter, at room
   temperature
165 g (¾ cup) brown sugar
3 tablespoons sugar
1 large free-range egg,
   at room temperature
135 g (½ cup) tahini
1 teaspoon vanilla extract
½ teaspoon salt
½ teaspoon bicarbonate
   of soda
185 g (1¼ cups) whole-
   wheat flour
170 g dark chocolate,
   roughly chopped
sea salt flakes,
   for sprinkling

Place the butter and both sugars in the bowl of an electric mixer fitted with the paddle attachment and beat for 2 minutes or until pale and creamy. Add the egg and beat for another 2 minutes. Add the tahini, vanilla and salt and beat for 1 minute or until light and fluffy.

Stir in the bicarbonate of soda and flour until just combined, then add the chopped chocolate and mix through.

Remove the dough from the bowl and wrap tightly in plastic wrap. Chill in the fridge for at least 2 hours, but the longer the better (this is what makes the biscuits chewy, and that's how we like our biscuits here).

Preheat the oven to 180°C (fan-forced). Line two baking trays with baking paper.

Roll the biscuit dough into 5 cm balls and pop on the prepared trays, leaving 5 cm between each biscuit. Using a fork, push the biscuits down slightly.

Bake for 10–12 minutes or until the biscuits are lightly golden around the edges. Don't be scared to take them out looking a little pale. They will look a little under-baked, but if you cook them until completely golden they'll be crunchy and lose their chew. Trust me.

Sprinkle the warm biscuits with sea salt flakes. Leave to cool on the trays for 10 minutes, then transfer to a wire rack to cool completely.

ORANGES FOREVER

Flourless Orange and Ginger Cake

SERVES 8

Our household does its best to eat by the seasons, which means my little fruit lover goes into a bit of a funk after the third week of oranges. And trying to convince her that mandarins are different is a fruitless exercise … OMG stop me. But seriously, months of enduring the never-ending parade of citrus can get a little tiring, even for the staunchest seasonal eater. But I have a solution. Whipped with almond meal, eggs and sugar, the citrus onslaught is transformed into one of our most loved cakes.

2 oranges, washed
250 g caster sugar, plus extra for sprinkling
6 free-range eggs
250 g (2½ cups) almond meal
1 teaspoon baking powder
½ teaspoon ground ginger
big handful of pecans (or your choice of nut)

Bring a large saucepan of water to the boil, add the oranges and boil for 2 hours.

Drain and cool to room temperature.

Preheat the oven to 160°C (fan-forced). Grease and line a 20 cm springform tin with baking paper.

Place the sugar and eggs in a food processor and whiz until well combined. Add the oranges and continue whizzing until fully blended, then add the almond meal, baking powder and ground ginger and blend until smooth.

Pour the batter into the prepared tin and sprinkle the top with extra sugar. Arrange the pecans in a nice pattern on top.

Bake for 1–1¼ hours or until the top is golden and a skewer inserted in the centre comes out clean. Remove and allow to cool completely in the tin.

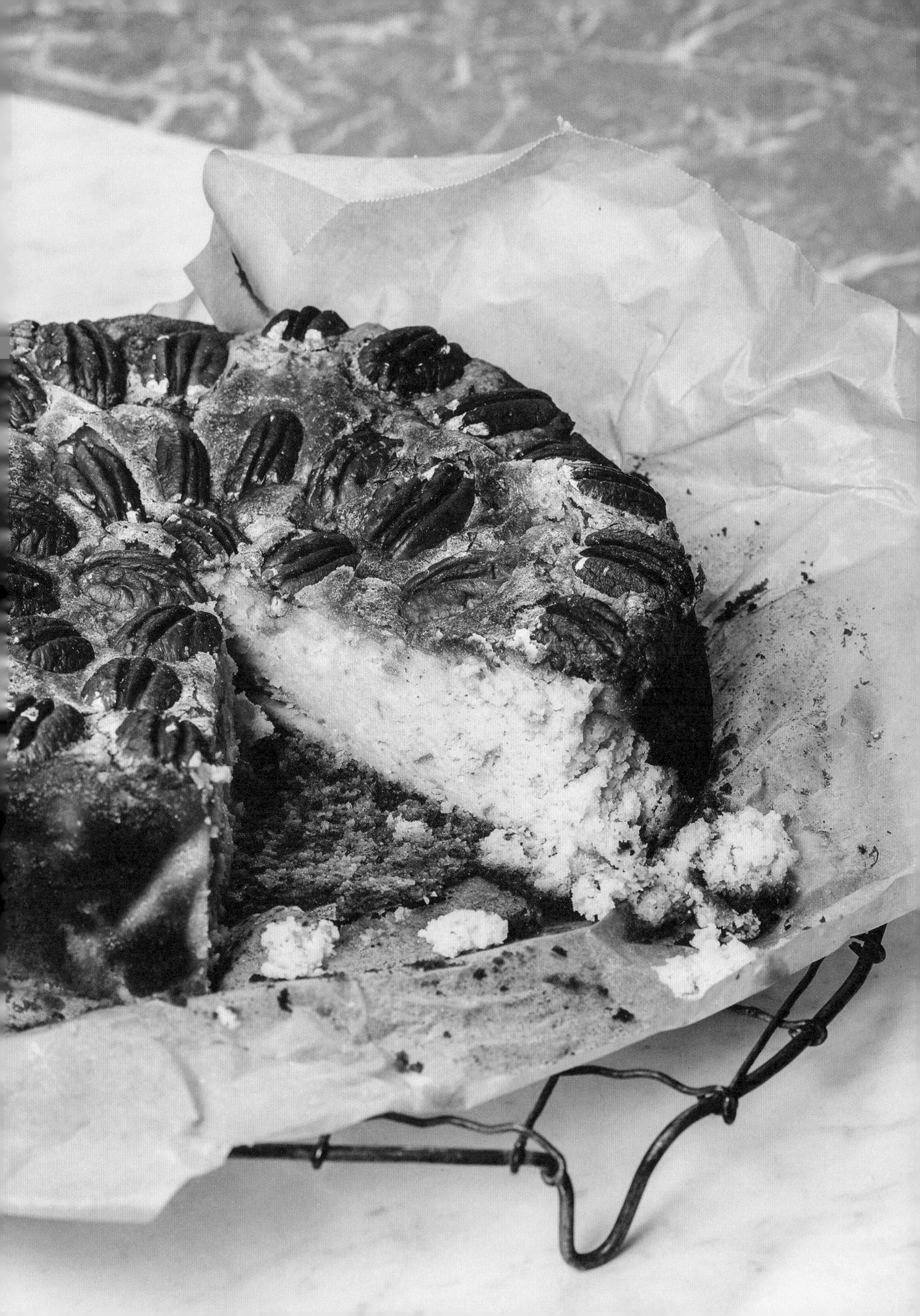

If I didn't laugh, I'd be crying a lot

My kids have reached the age where they are capable of being useful. However, this doesn't actually mean they are. They can be when offered cash or bribes, but even then the task is often done to the minimum standard required, or sometimes not even that.

I once asked them to hang the washing on the line.

They didn't use pegs. Or even unfold the clothes. Instead, they just threw handfuls of wet clothing onto the lines, and if they didn't stay up there ... ah well. I didn't see this happen; I just filled in the gaps when I walked outside to see half the clothing on the ground, some in the washing basket and a few bits clinging in twisted clumps to the washing line.

If it was someone else's kids, you'd laugh. A lot. So I tried to see it for the hilarious situation it was. I mean, what's the point of being angry about it anyway? They clearly don't care. Don't get me wrong, I did take them outside and ask if they thought they'd done a great job, which of course they knew they hadn't. But then we laughed, and they picked up the clothes and hung them up properly. I got the result I wanted eventually, without the crankiness.

Once my kid said she'd mop the floor for five bucks. I'm not entirely sure how she got it to look the way she did, but she was pretty indignant when I expressed my dissatisfaction. Even more so when I suggested she could perhaps do the job properly. Sometimes it just seems easier to forget the whole 'teach the kids responsibilities' thing but of course you have to persevere ... insert eye roll.

We all did it as kids and I'm sure I still do. It's all about mastering the shortcut, the easy way round. My speciality was making lines in the shag pile with the vacuum cleaner without even plugging it in, let alone turning it on. I was pretty sure that would pass inspection. And most of the time it did, probably because my mum didn't care either. Housework is pretty boring, and you've got to pick your battles.

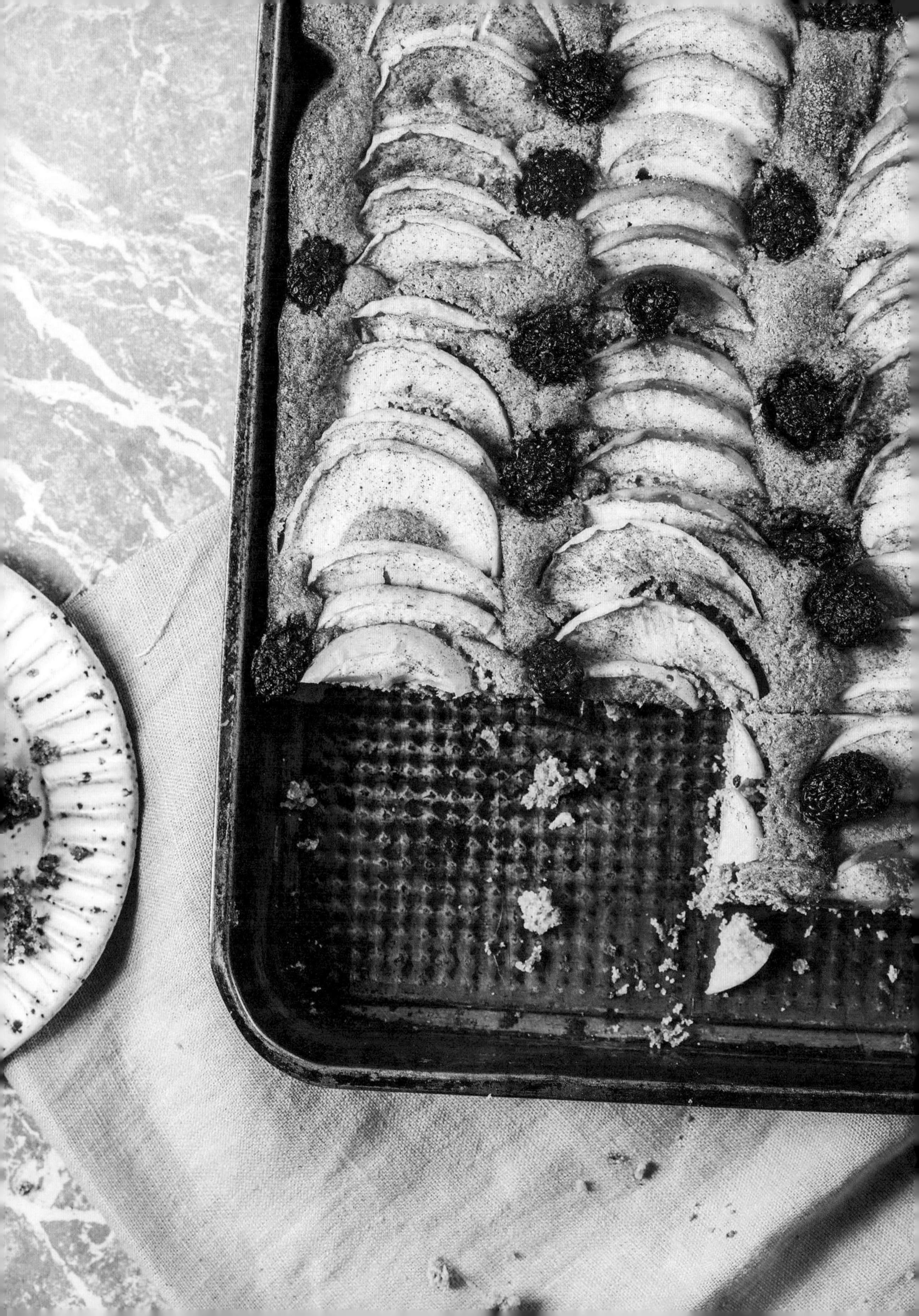

ROADSIDE TREASURE TRAY CAKE

Apple and Blackberry Tray Cake

SERVES 16

When we lived in the hills, every autumn the girls and I kept a close eye on the roadside apple trees, checking on their progress and making sure no one had swooped in before us. It was a game of luck. Sometimes we'd get in first; sometimes we'd lose to another apple poacher, or to the birds. But when we did win, it was on. We'd park the car under the tree, grab the baskets from the boot and take our positions: Pepper on the roof for the higher apples, me on the boot and Maya at ground level.

As for blackberries, well those guys were just everywhere, and they're prickly. So even though they taste delicious, they just weren't as fun. But I do love the metaphor that can be found somewhere within the hostile blackberry bush … with a little care and time you're rewarded with something sweet and delicious.

180 g (1½ cups) spelt flour
1 teaspoon bicarbonate
  of soda
1 teaspoon baking powder
55 g (½ cup) hazelnut meal
155 g (⅔ cup) brown sugar
3 free-range eggs
100 g coconut oil
150 g plain yoghurt
2 apples (we'd use whatever
  variety we happened to find),
  cored and cut into eighths
200 g blackberries, fresh
  or frozen

Preheat the oven to 180°C (fan-forced). Line a lamington tin with baking paper.

Sift the flour, bicarbonate of soda and baking powder into a mixing bowl. Stir in the hazelnut meal and set aside.

Place the sugar and eggs in the bowl of an electric mixer fitted with the whisk attachment and whisk for 5 minutes or until thick and pale. Add the coconut oil and yoghurt and whisk until well combined.

Gently fold the flour mixture into the yoghurt mixture until just combined – take care not to overmix.

Pour the batter into the prepared tin and spread it out nicely. Arrange the apples in an even layer on top of the batter, then squish the blackberries in between.

Bake for 40 minutes or until golden on top and firm to the touch, and a skewer inserted in the centre comes out clean. Allow to cool completely in the tin, then cut into squares and serve.

(Almost) DIY after-school snacks

APPLES WITH RICOTTA, ALMONDS AND RAISINS

SERVES 2

2 pink lady apples

raisins, for sprinkling

honey, to taste

125 g (½ cup) fresh ricotta, well drained

toasted flaked almonds, for sprinkling

Cut the apples in half, across the apple so you have the star pattern when cut.

Scoop the core out of each half.

Stir a little honey through the ricotta to sweeten.

Fill the scooped centres of the apples with the sweetened ricotta, then sprinkle with toasted almonds and raisins.

Most of these snacks will be simple enough for your kids to manage on their own but occasionally they'll need help with cutting or heating, depending on their age.

CHOCOLATE-DIPPED MANDARINS

SERVES 2

1 teaspoon
coconut oil

sea salt flakes,
for sprinkling

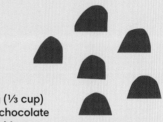

60 g (⅓ cup)
dark chocolate
chips

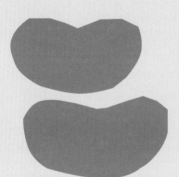

2 mandarins, peeled and
broken into segments

Line a baking tray with baking paper.

Put the chocolate chips and coconut oil in a heatproof bowl set over a saucepan of simmering water (don't let the bottom of the bowl touch the water). Stir until melted and combined. Let it cool slightly before dipping.

Dip each segment of mandarin halfway into the melted chocolate and pop onto the prepared tray. Sprinkle lightly with salt. Refrigerate for 10 minutes or until the chocolate has set firm.

(Almost) DIY after-school snacks

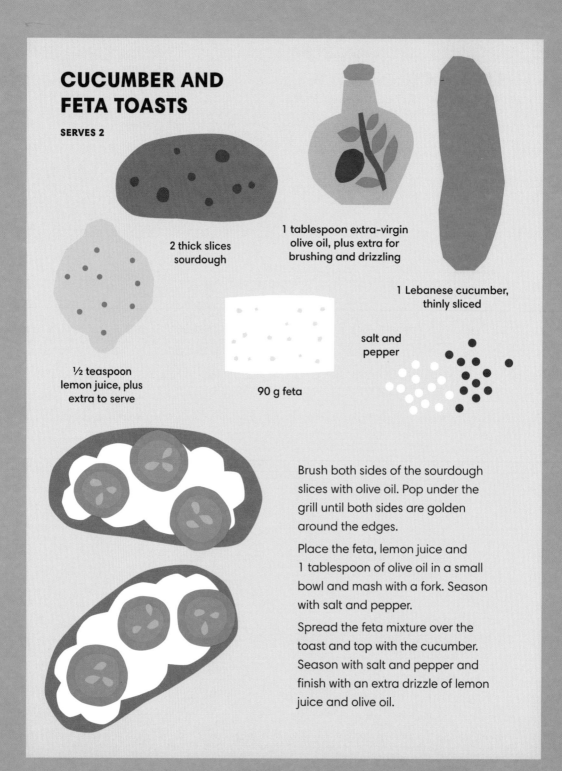

CUCUMBER AND FETA TOASTS

SERVES 2

2 thick slices sourdough

1 tablespoon extra-virgin olive oil, plus extra for brushing and drizzling

1 Lebanese cucumber, thinly sliced

½ teaspoon lemon juice, plus extra to serve

90 g feta

salt and pepper

Brush both sides of the sourdough slices with olive oil. Pop under the grill until both sides are golden around the edges.

Place the feta, lemon juice and 1 tablespoon of olive oil in a small bowl and mash with a fork. Season with salt and pepper.

Spread the feta mixture over the toast and top with the cucumber. Season with salt and pepper and finish with an extra drizzle of lemon juice and olive oil.

TAHINI DIP PLATE

SERVES 2

salt and pepper

3 tablespoons lemon juice

135 g (½ cup) tahini

½ teaspoon ground cumin

1 garlic clove, roughly chopped

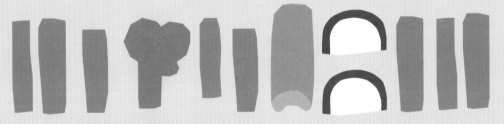

raw chopped veggies (carrots, broccoli, celery, radishes, snow peas, etc.), to serve

Pop the tahini, lemon juice, cumin, garlic and 80 ml (⅓ cup) of warm water in a food processor and blend until smooth. Add a little extra water, if needed. Taste and season with salt and pepper.

Serve immediately with the chopped veggie dippers.

ADVENTURES FOR WEEKENDS & HOLIDAYS

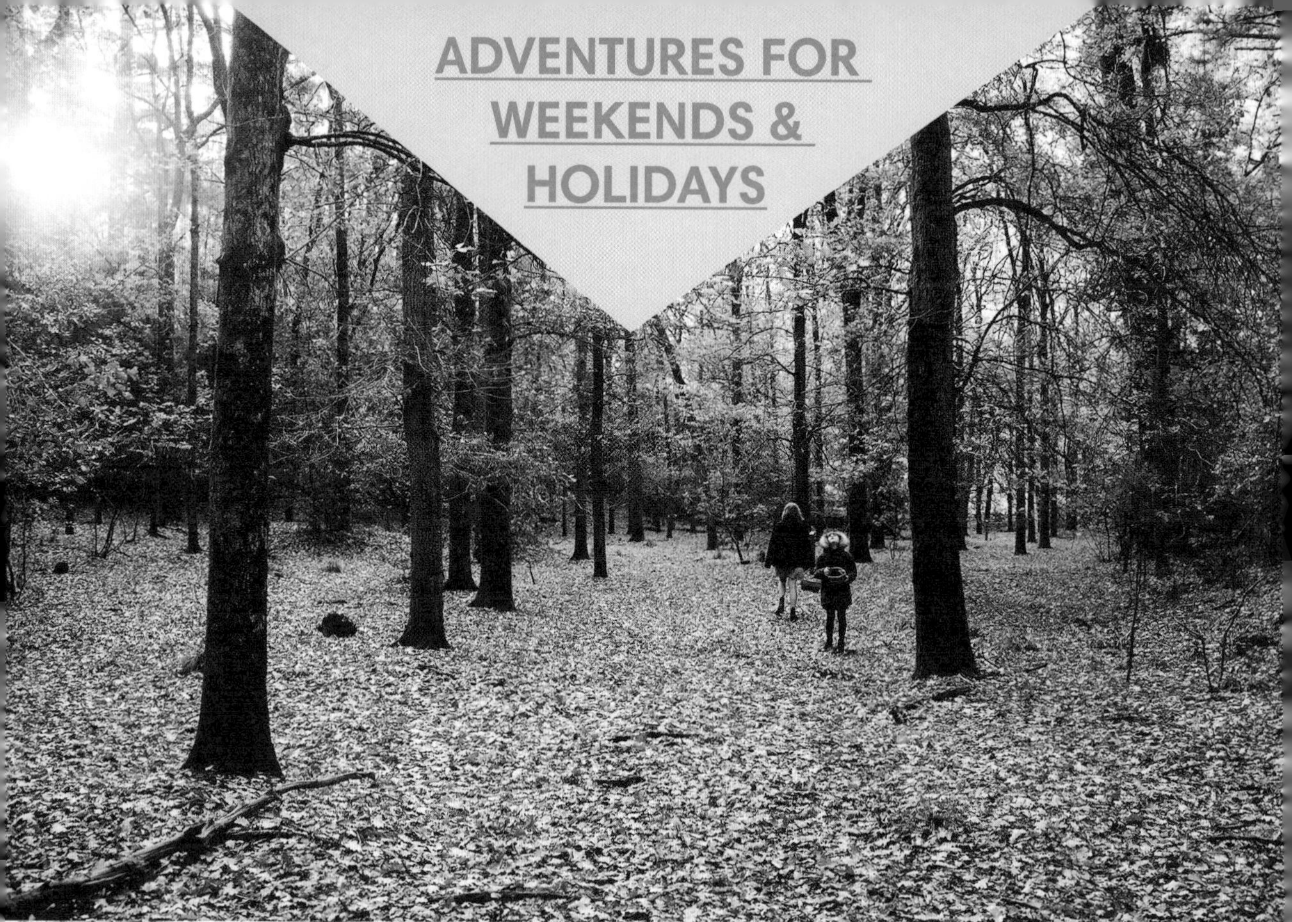

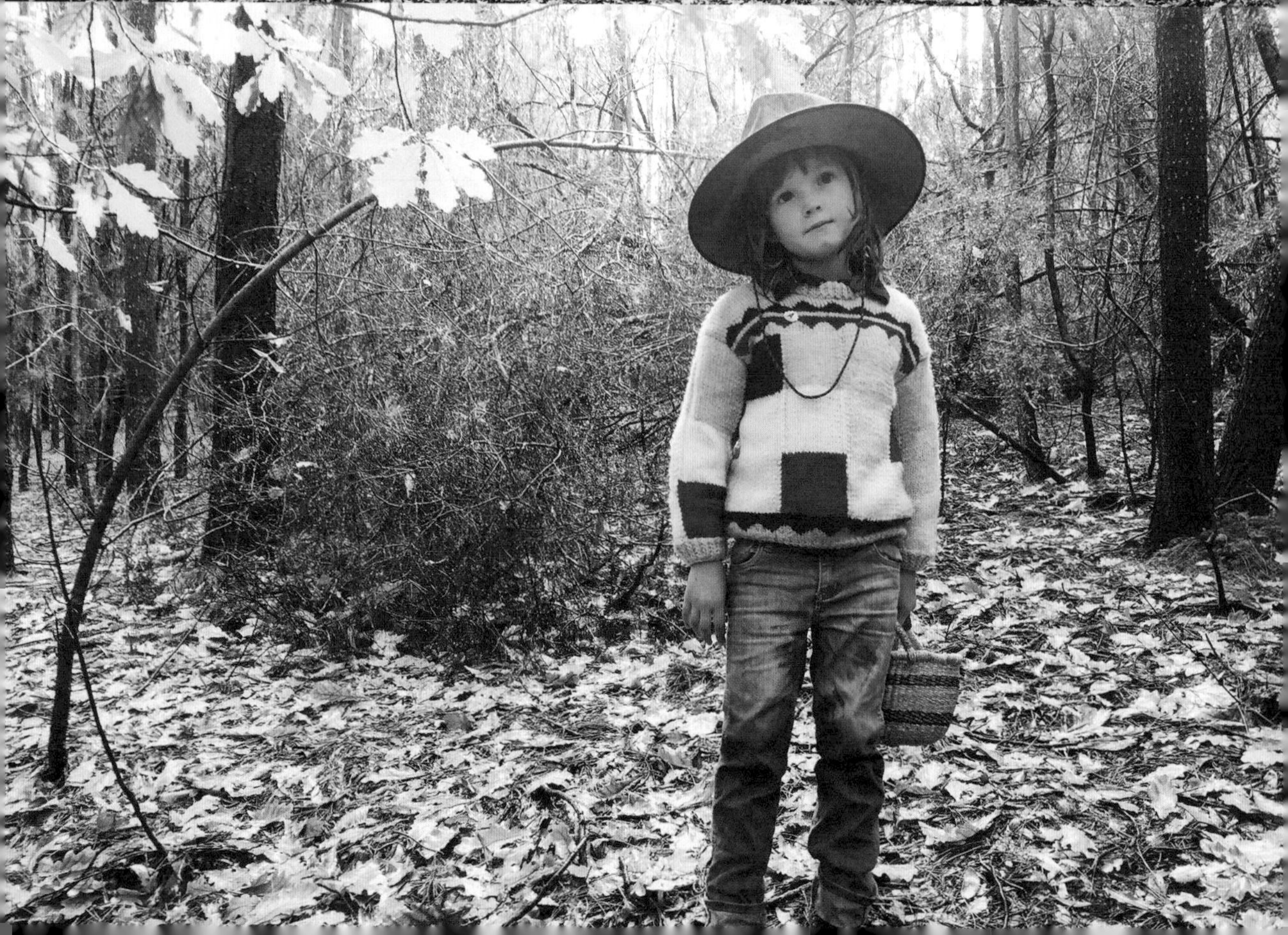

Forest walks and scavenger hunts

Rugging up and heading out into crisp, pine-scented air is the perfect antidote to a wintery day. On the surface, it might not look like there's much to do in a pine forest, but after years of trying to entertain kids on the cheap, I assure you there most certainly is.

The thing I love most is looking for mushrooms. In the forest near our old home in the country, we'd find three different types: pine, slippery jacks and wood blewits. I only really liked to eat the pine mushroom, as the slippery jack is covered in slime and the wood blewit is purple. For some reason I can't cope with eating purple food.

After our big mushroom hunt, we'd set up a little campfire in what I'd call the magic forest. The kids would run around looking for the best logs. 'Look Mum, I found the best log.' 'No, I've got the best log.' And we'd get on with making lunch.

We'd have a little basket of stuff we kept at the ready. A small frying pan, a sharp knife, a wooden spoon, plates, forks, cups and some matches. We used it all the time – there are plenty of places to go and eat if you venture out enough.

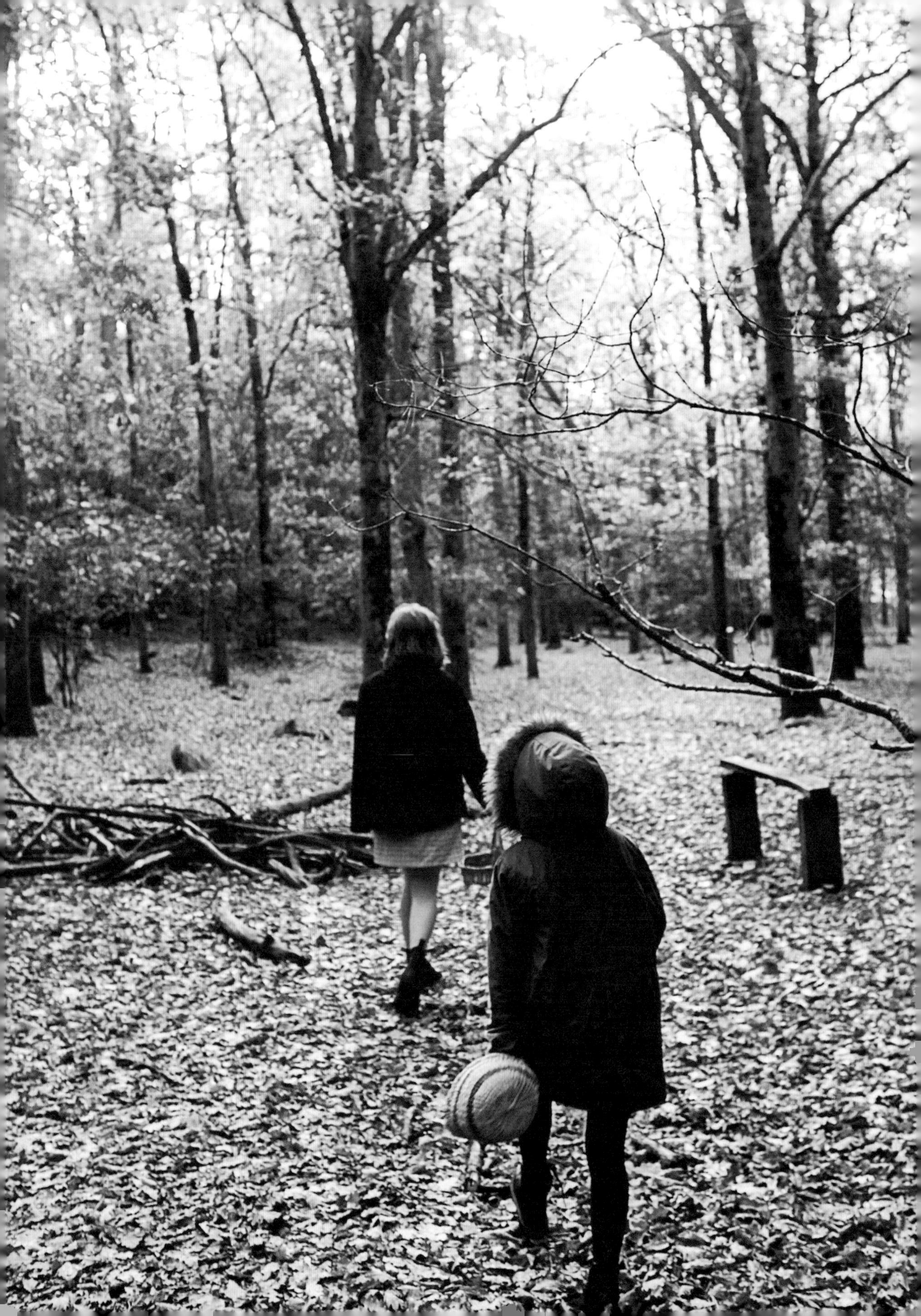

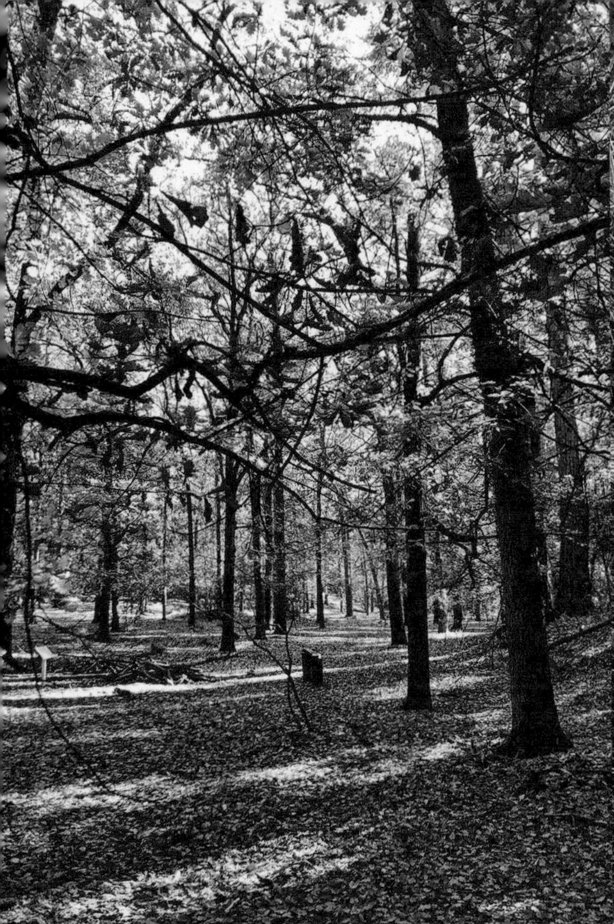
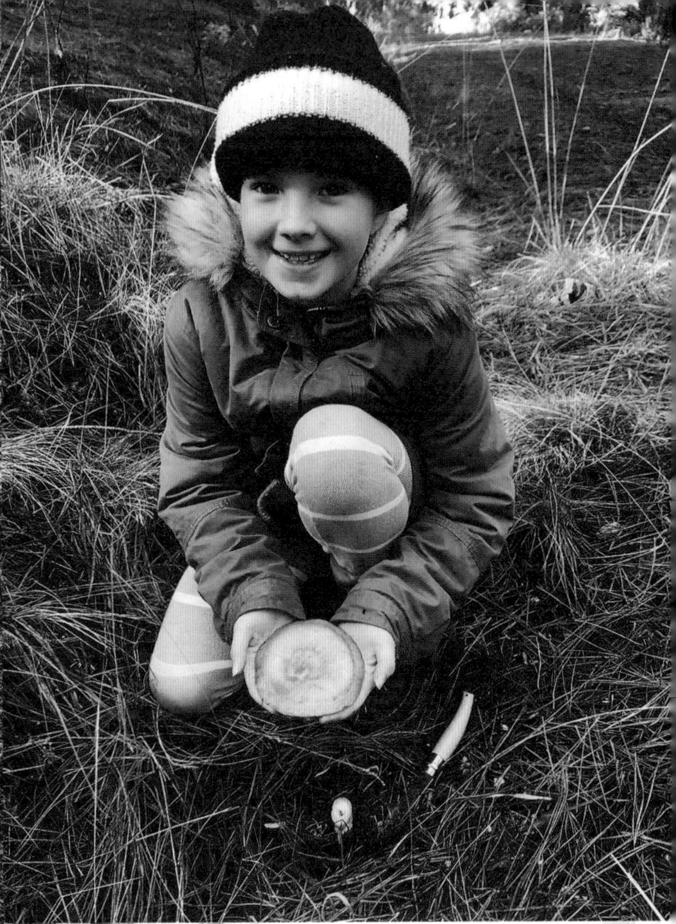
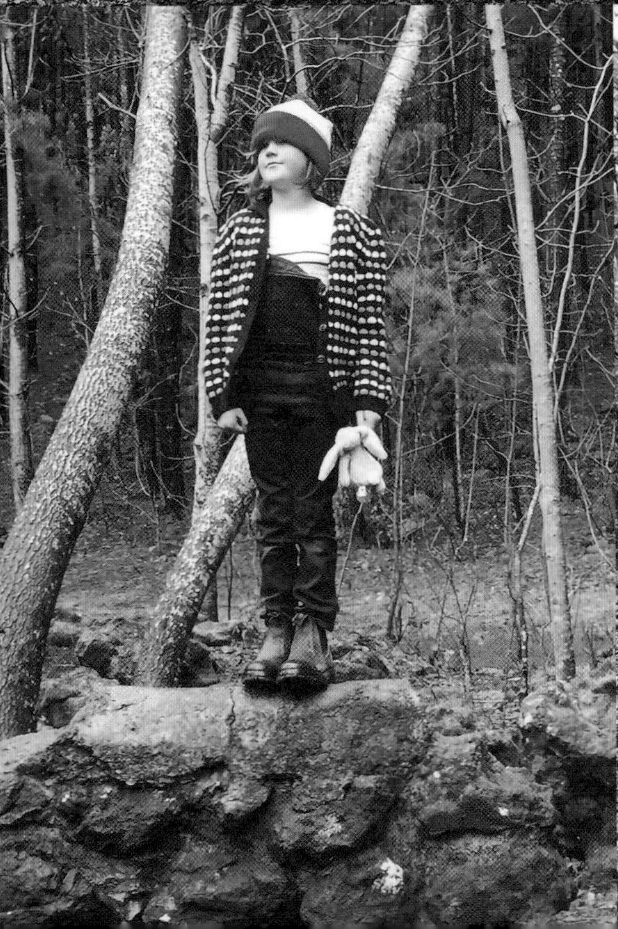
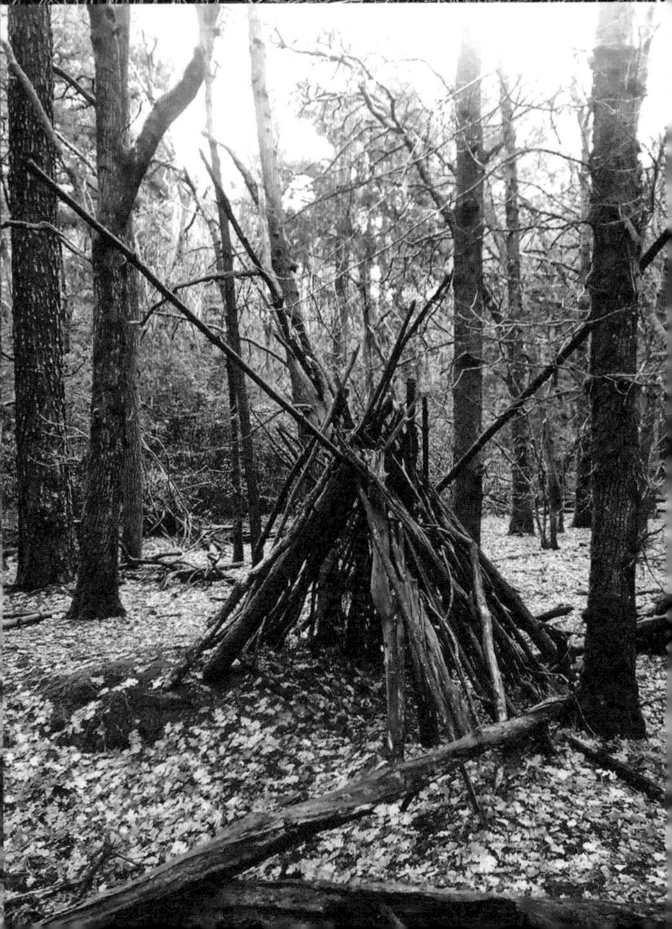

While lunch was cooking, the girls would take off to create their own little homes from tree trunks, leaves and twigs. I did this when I was a kid, and I still remember how incredible it felt to make your own space in the world. It was both safe and exciting to be sitting in a home you'd built yourself.

While the girls played, I would sit transfixed. The crackle of the wood and the flickering flames had got me. I could sit and stare at a fire forever. We were all together, there in the forest, but lost in our own worlds. There is something so grounding about spending a day outside, without a lot of stuff. You get dirty and feel the earth around you.

When my head hit the pillow later that night, my legs were aching and my hair smelled of smoke. And even though I felt so tired, the day in the forest made me feel so alive.

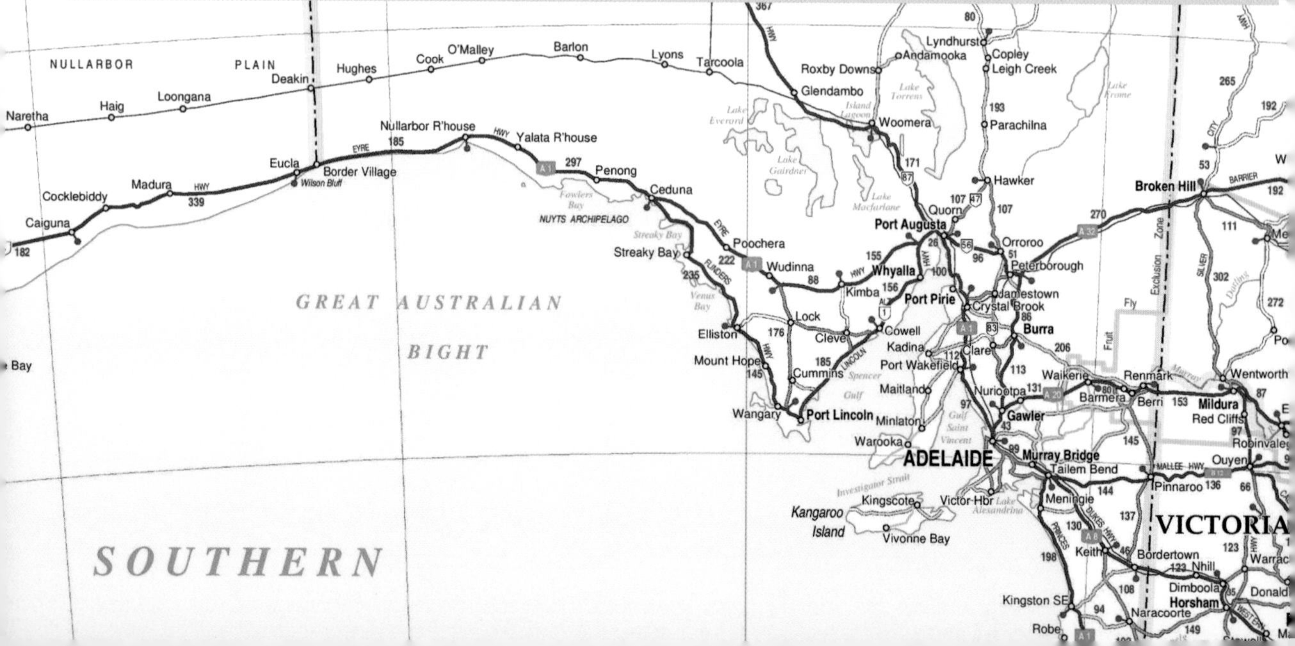
NULLARBOR
PLAIN
GREAT AUSTRALIAN
BIGHT
SOUTHERN
VICTORIA
ADELAIDE
Port Augusta
Port Pirie
Whyalla
Port Lincoln
Ceduna
Broken Hill
Mildura
Murray Bridge
Kangaroo Island
Eucla
Border Village
Nullarbor R'house
Yalata R'house
Streaky Bay
Woomera
Roxby Downs
Glendambo
Tarcoola
Cook
Hughes
Deakin
Naretha
Cocklebiddy
Caiguna
Madura
Penong
Gawler
Renmark
Horsham

Pine forest scavenger hunt

Bird

Something fuzzy

Spider web

Leaf

Tree stump

Animal nest

Pine cone

Feather

Rocks

Insect

Moss

Something smooth

Something you think is beautiful

Flower

Animal tracks

Mushroom

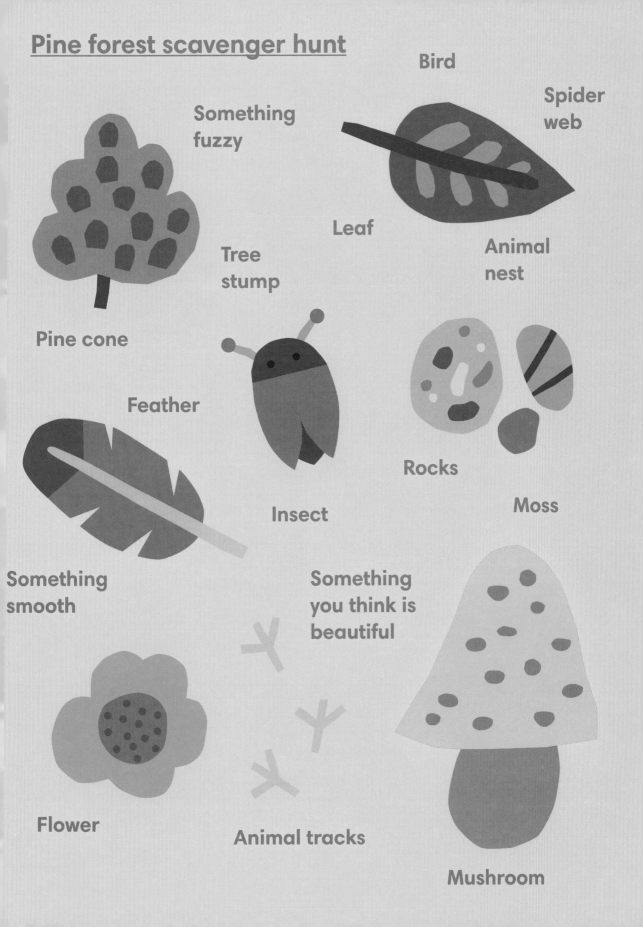

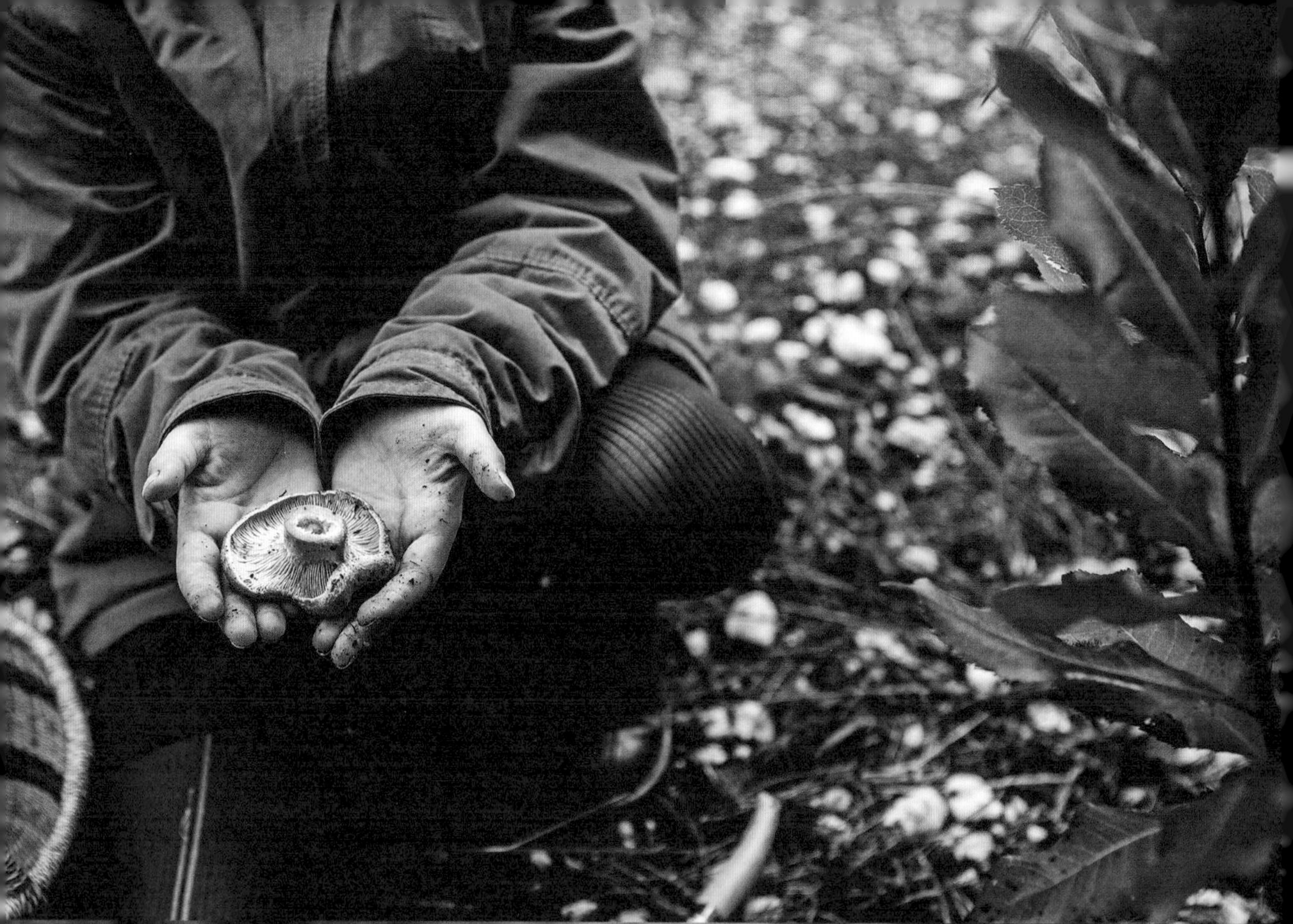
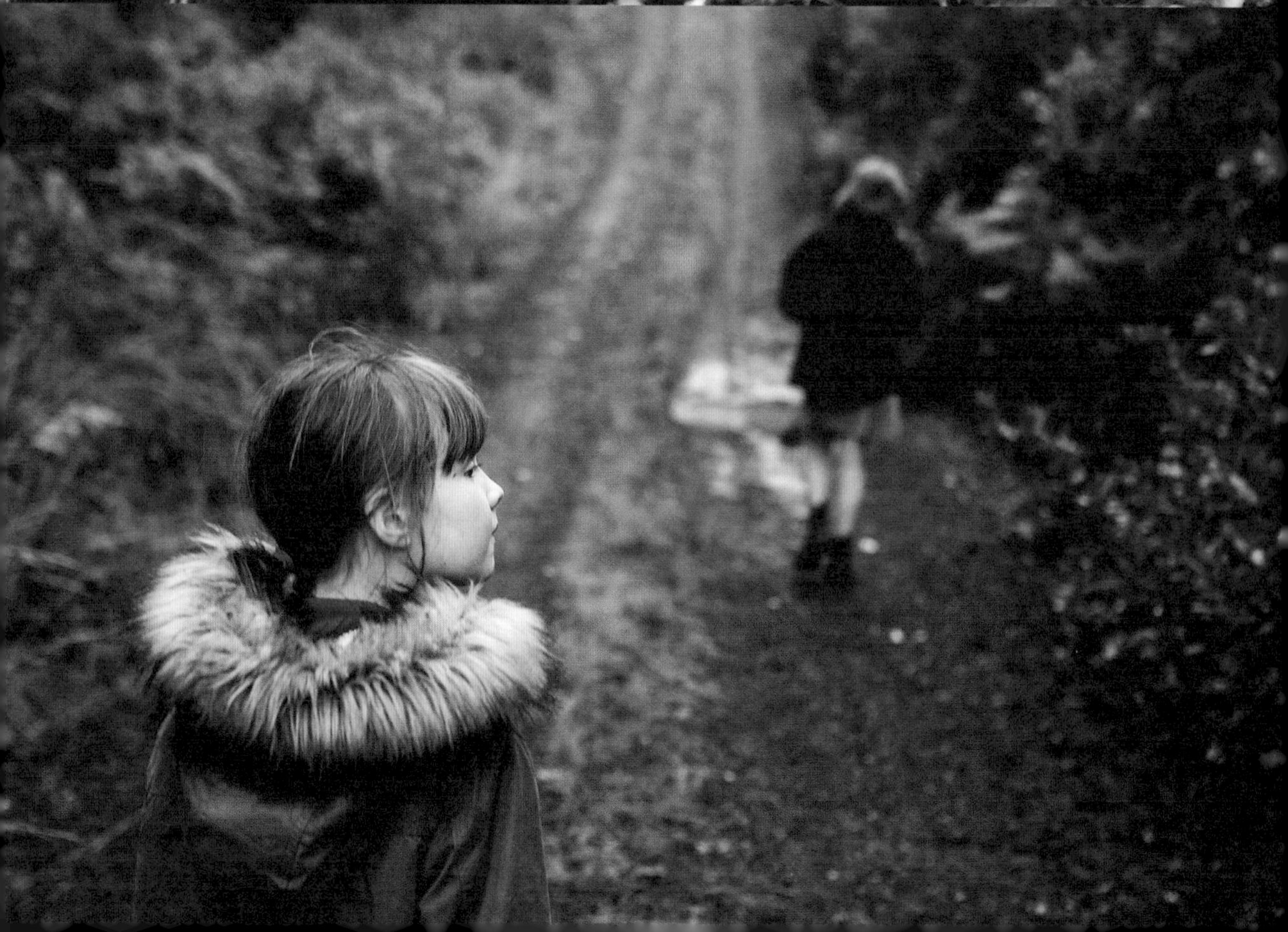

Find your own food adventures

We used to live in a house on a hill, and every road that led to it was dotted with fruit trees. They were mostly apples and pears, but one day we discovered a secret fig, and we also found uses for other fruit that had never been on our radar, like hawthorn and rosehip.

It made after school an adventure, and we'd often take a different route home to see what the trees had to offer. Of course, much depended on the time of year. In winter we didn't bother and would head straight home for the open fire, but come late summer and autumn, it was ON.

There's something pretty satisfying about free food. Or free anything really, but you actually need food, and to find it on the side of the road on your way home is pretty magic.

It's not only free food, it's free entertainment. We're outside and the kids are learning exactly where apples and pears come from. Seeing stuff actually grow, in dirt, gives them an understanding that apples don't start their lives in a plastic bag.

In late autumn/early winter, we would head out into the local pine forest and find mushrooms (see page 121). This activity was WAY more fun when the girls actually liked eating them. But, as kids do, they've temporarily

decided they are awful and there's no convincing them otherwise. (Bananas and cheese have also joined this random list for now.) But when they did like mushrooms, we'd spend an entire afternoon in the misty hills looking for them. It was one of my most favourite ways to end a weekend.

We live in the city now. Is this the end of our after-school free food picking? I don't think so. We've asked one neighbour for a few of her overhanging figs and another for some lemons. I also noticed recently that there's saltbush along the bay and fennel along the train tracks. This stuff is everywhere, and even though your findings won't necessarily create a complete meal for the family, it's fun, and you may find yourself eating things you never knew existed.

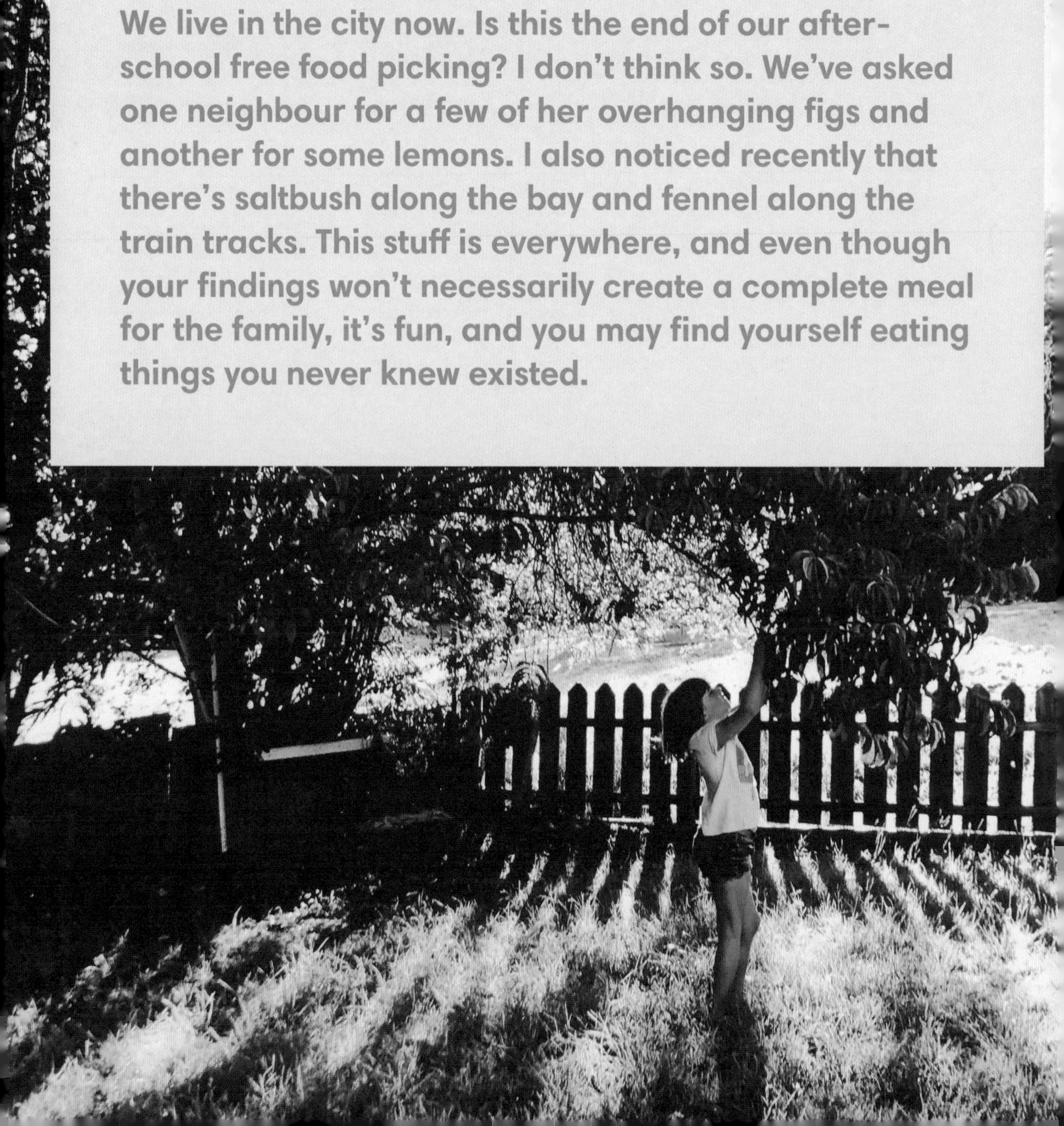

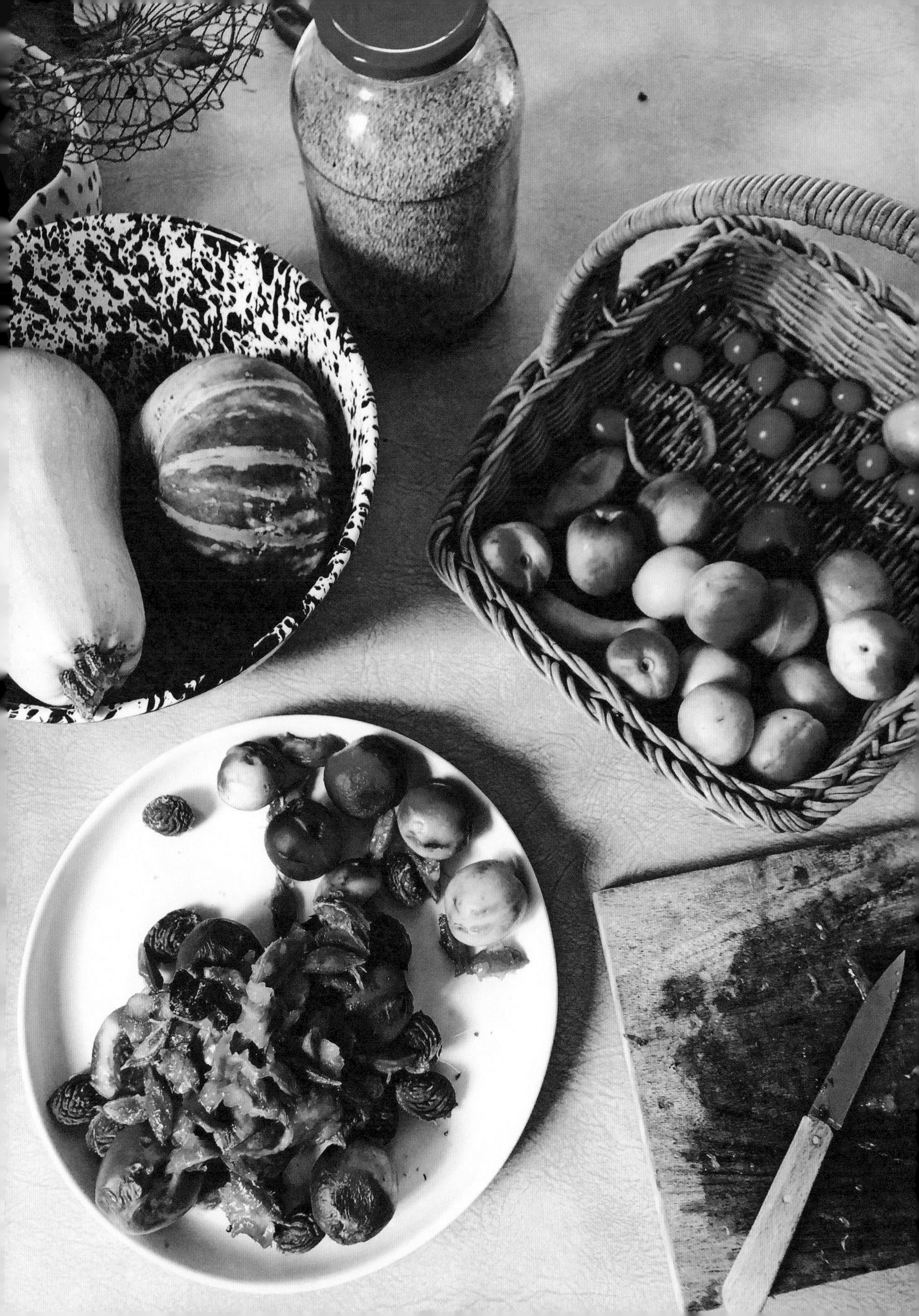

Weekend brekkie making

Waking up on a Saturday morning with zero plans is one of life's greatest joys. You lie in bed and think of all the possibilities ahead, but really, the greatest possibility is not moving and someone delivering coffee and brekkie to your bed. My girls are great at cooking but crap at getting up, so the chances of them making me breakfast in bed are slim.

I'm not a huge fan of going out for breakfast. There's so much involved, like getting dressed, cleaning yourself, brushing your teeth AND your hair and then having to decide where to actually go. It's just easier to stay in, be a slob and make the brekkie of your dreams in the comfort of your own home and pyjamas.

I'm not sure what it is about cooking in your pyjamas that's so satisfying. But it is. And if you've had the ultimate lazy weekend, you can just head straight back to bed later that night, wearing the same pyjamas, but with a crusty bit of waffle mix down the front.

But the best thing about having a big brekkie on the weekend is spending time with my girls – time that's not rushed, and not at the end of a long day. We're all fresh from a good lie in, ready for our weekend to unfold. The conversation looks forward rather than backwards, we have more time for each other, and we share a common path for the day. It's such a connected meal.

I just wish that meal was delivered to my bed.

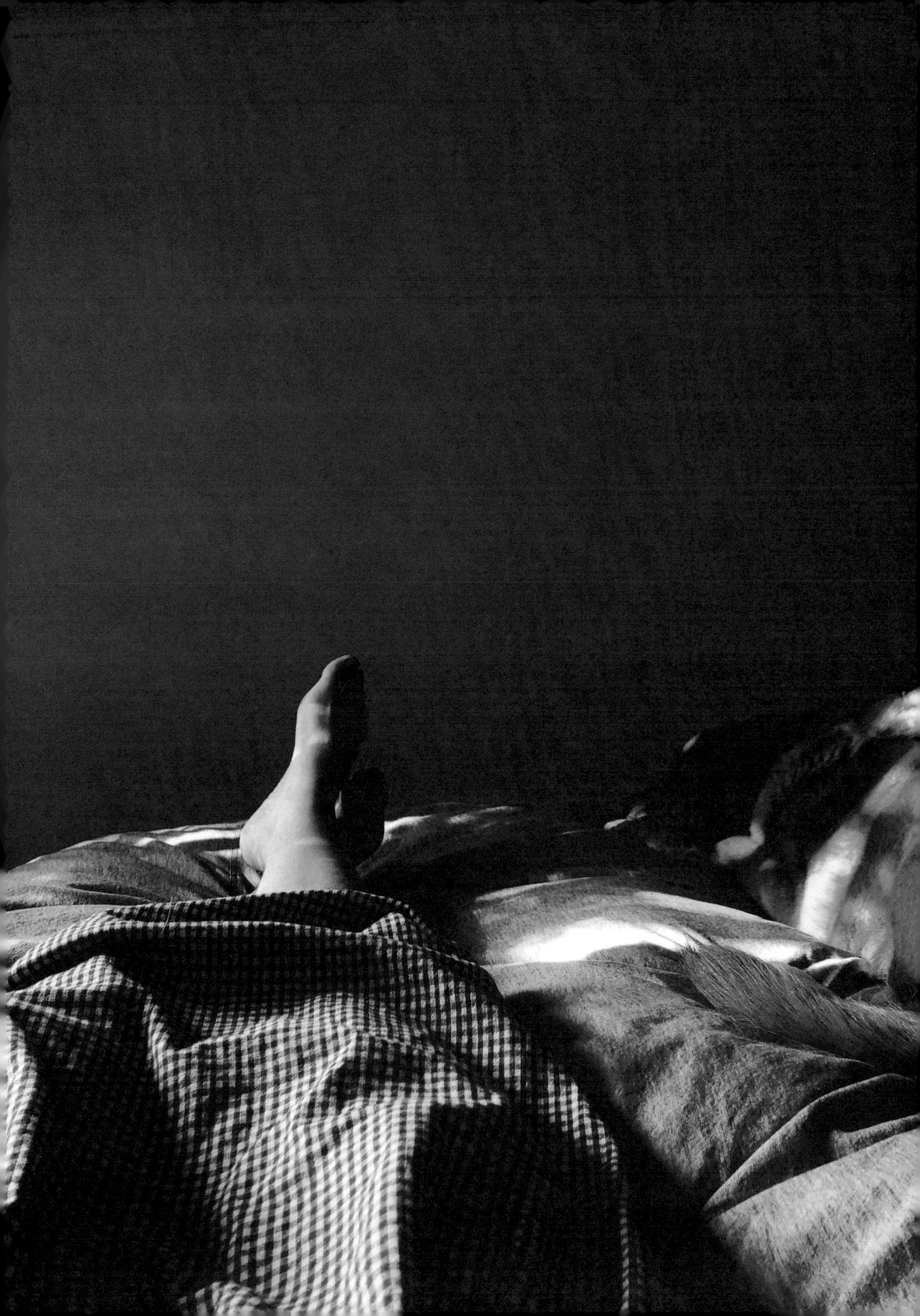

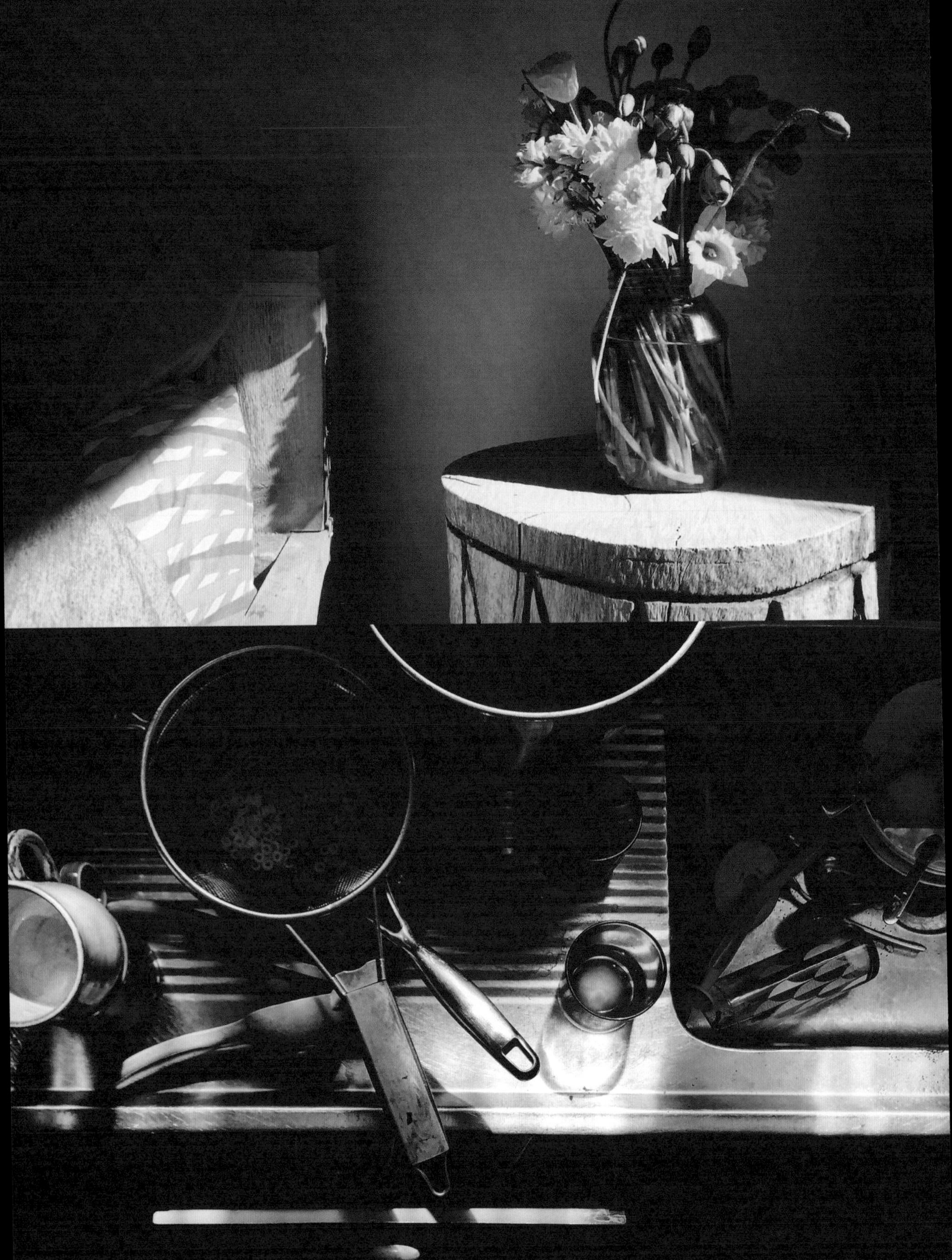

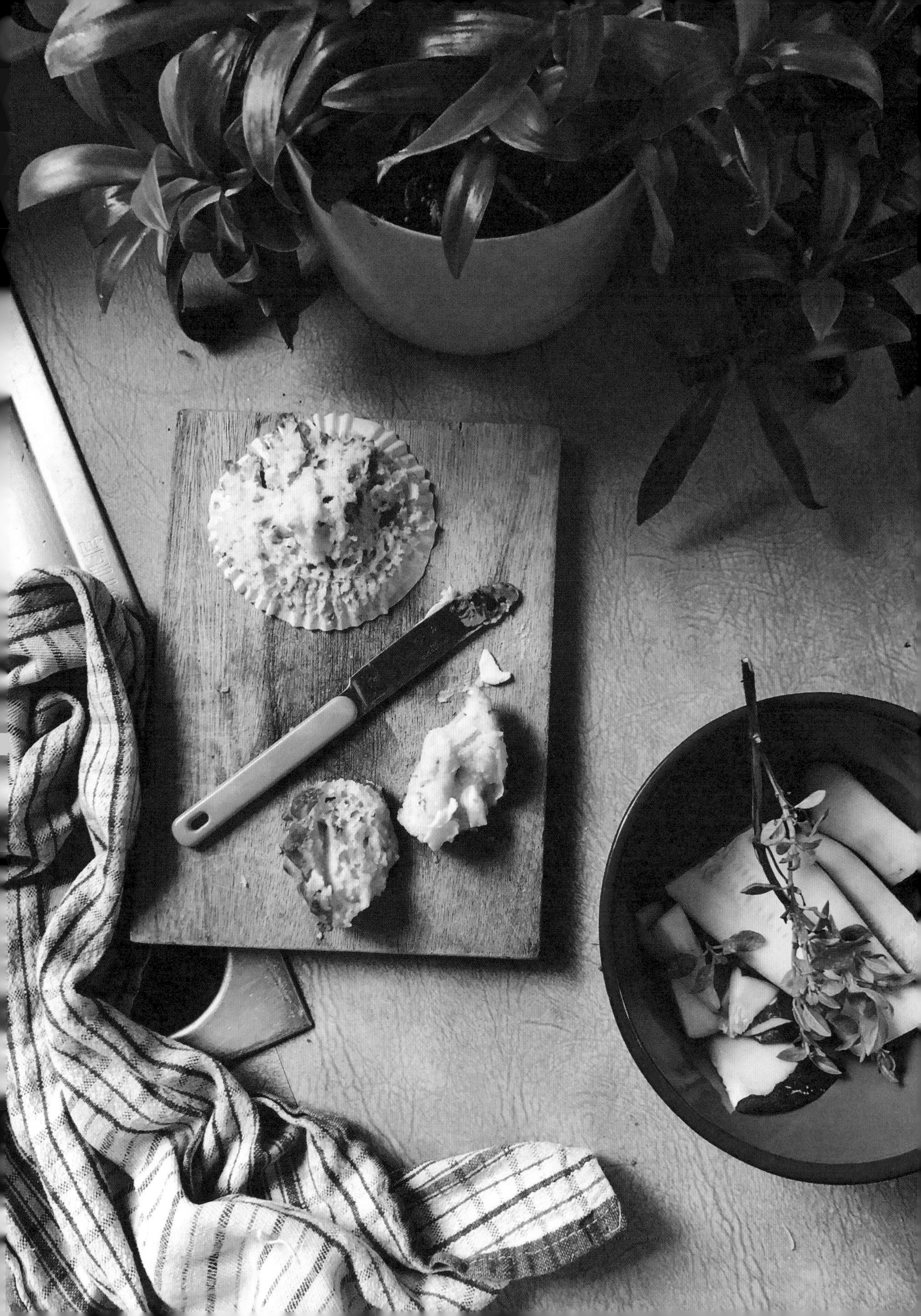

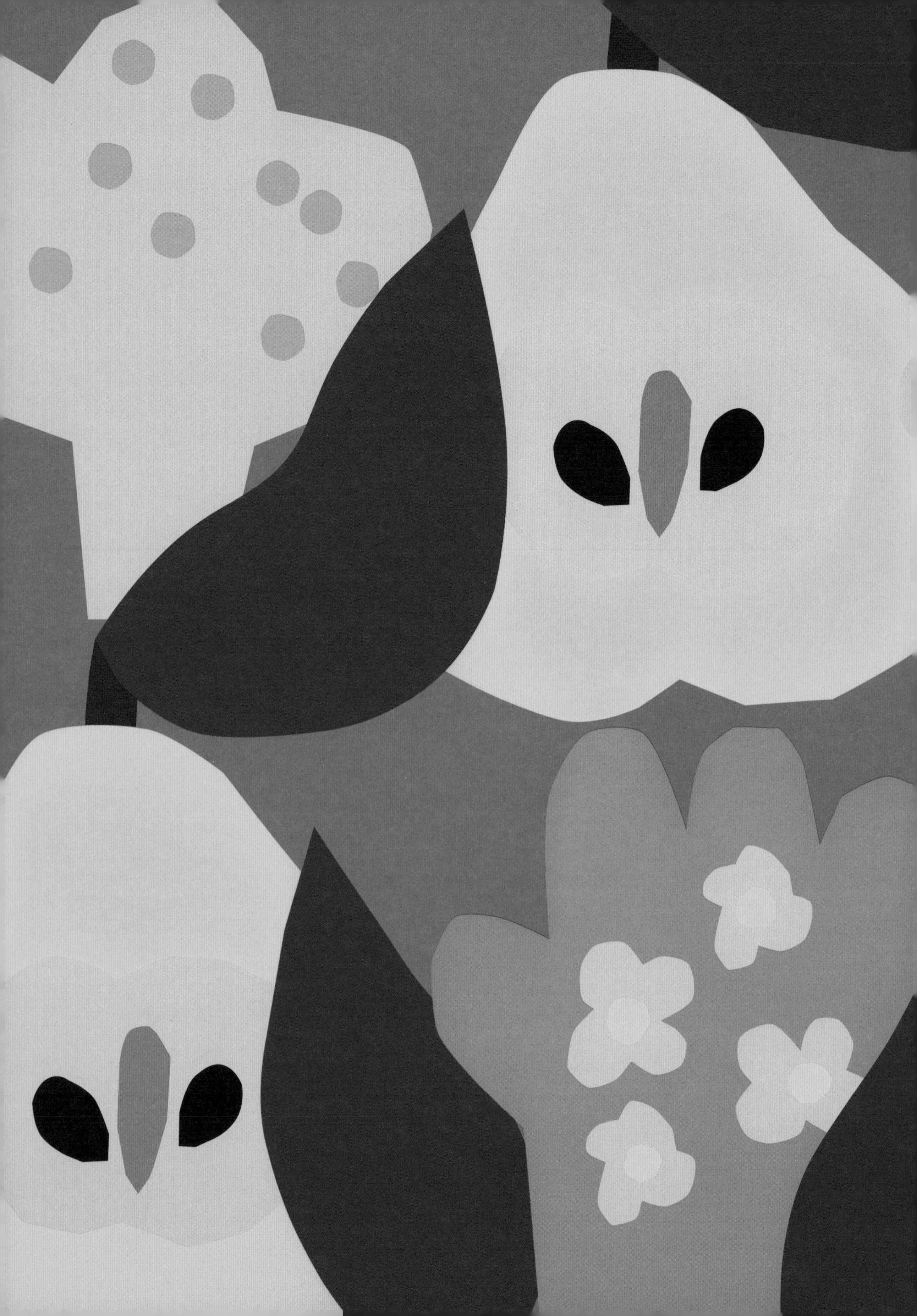

Term 3

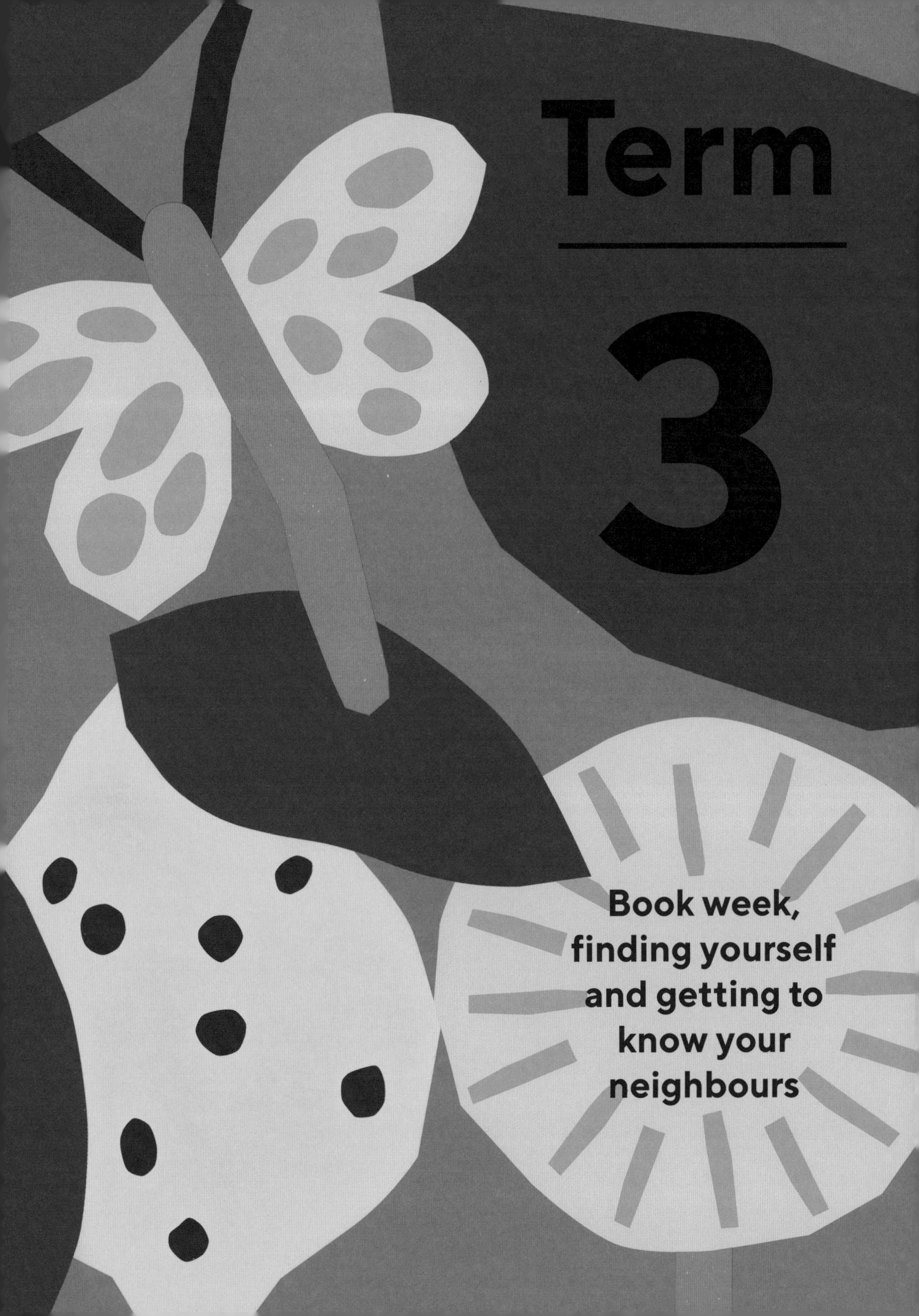

Book week, finding yourself and getting to know your neighbours

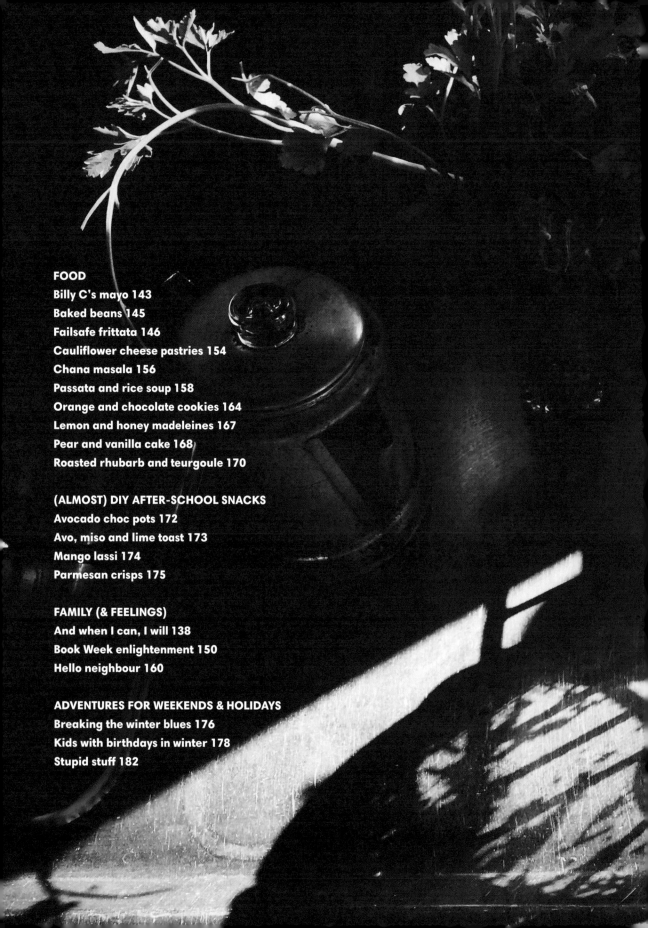

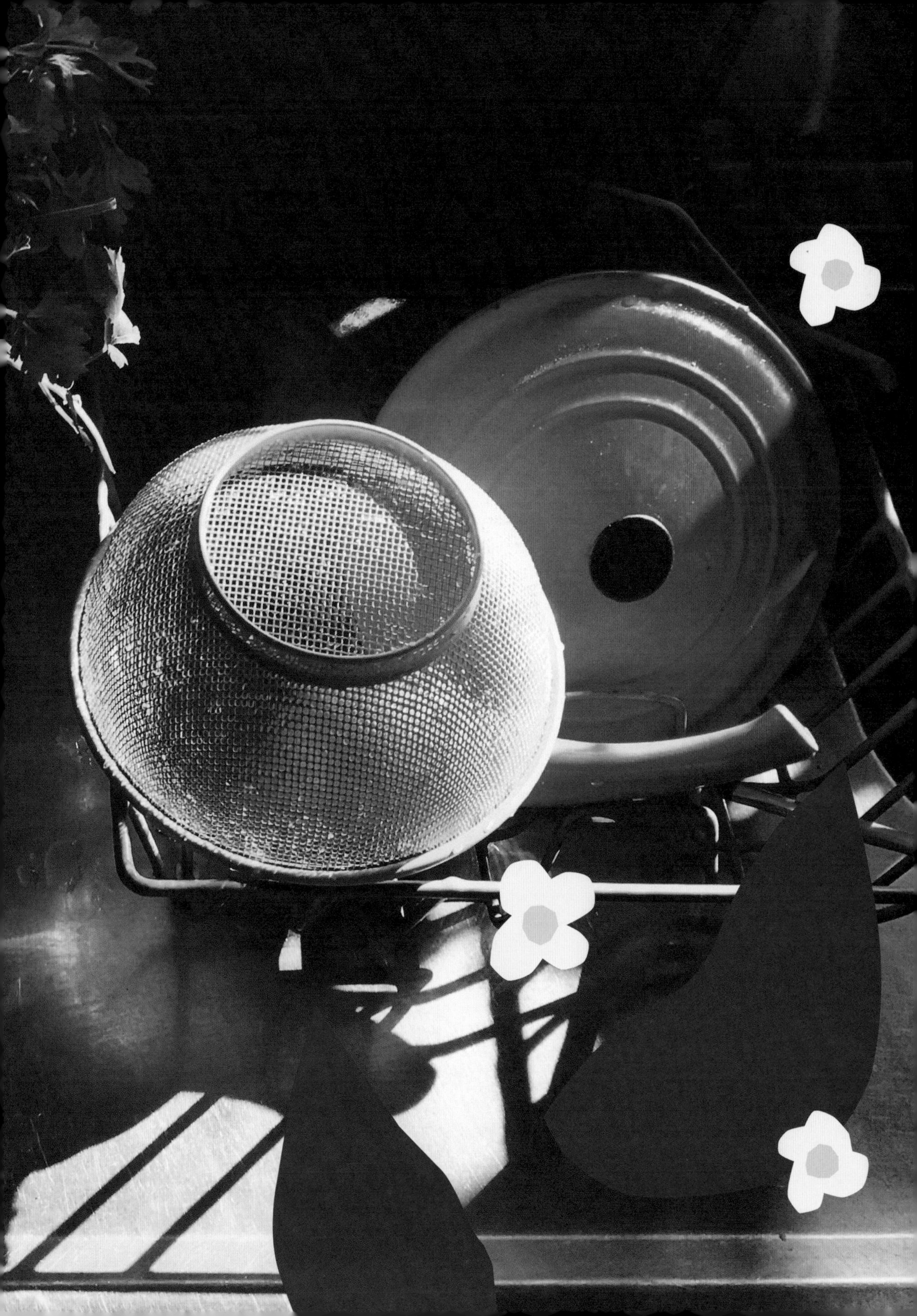

And when I can, I will

I was born in 1976, which made me a 90s teenager. And like ALL parents before me, I believe the music I grew up with is the greatest music of all time. They just don't make it like they used to, music these days all sounds the same, and so it goes, from one generation to the next. Being a teen in the 90s meant I loved The Smashing Pumpkins. And, yes, there are plenty of you who couldn't stand the Pumpkins. Billy Corgan was pretty polarising, and after *Mellon Collie and the Infinite Sadness* I packed up camp and moved to the other side to be with you guys. BUT before that double album, they made *Siamese Dream*.

'Mayonaise'. Track 9. 4:46.

'I just want to be me … and when I can, I will.'

'Mayonaise' was such an overdramatic teen anthem. Locked away in my poster-covered bedroom, I'd scream that one line at the top of my lungs because, as over the top as it was, that was exactly how I felt at seventeen. So close to being free, yet still getting grounded.

I still love that song. And it's funny how that line still means something to me all these years later.

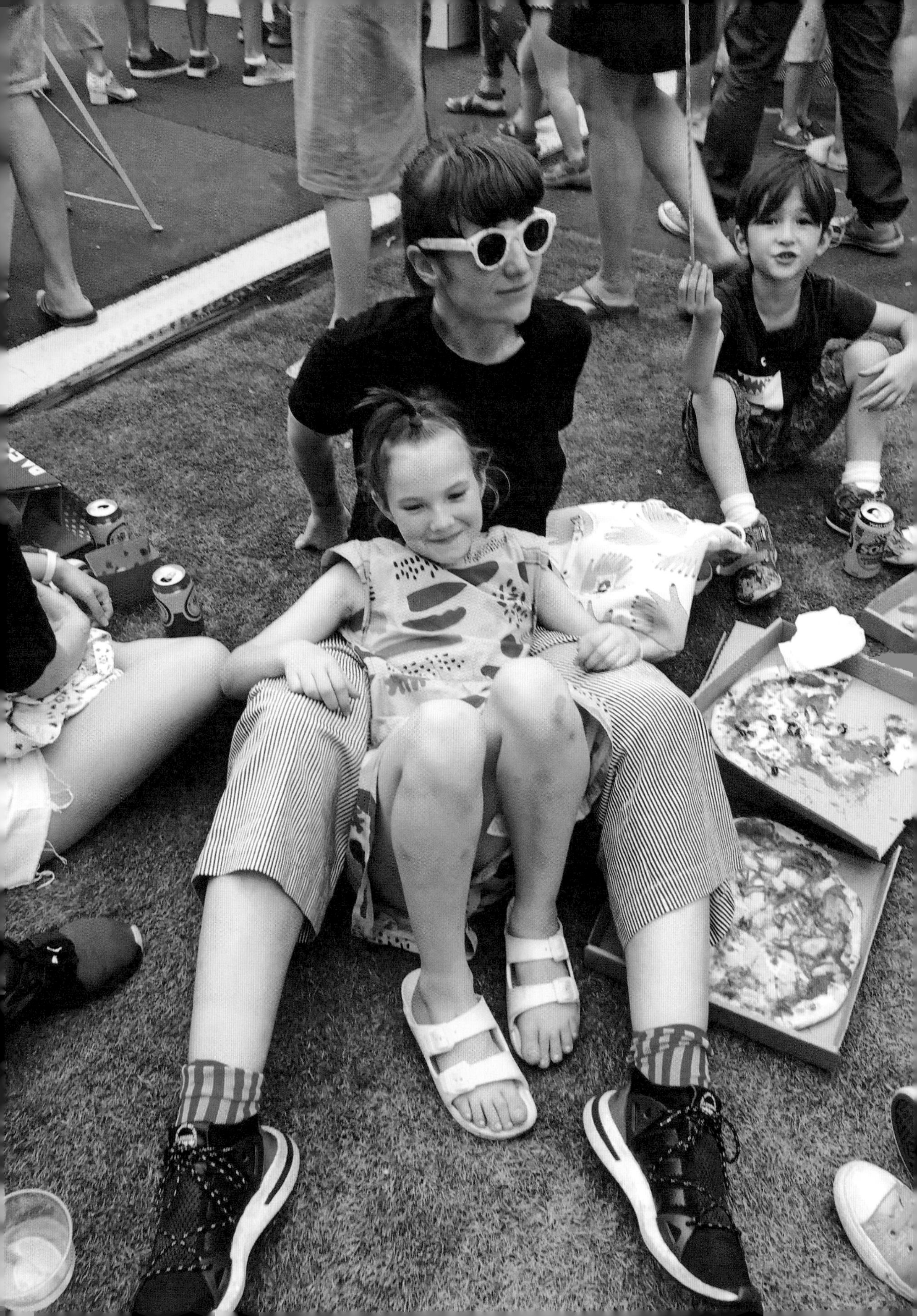

When I became a parent, I got lost. The first few years after having my first baby were all about surviving and not much else. The person I used to be was still there, but the things that I thought made me ME had to be put away so I could care for my very tiny, beautiful-smelling baby. I wasn't prepared for that at all. I assumed that because babies were so little you could just slip them into your life. They didn't take up much room, they didn't eat much, and they wore outfits that were one piece.

I got quite depressed. Only a year before I'd been working as a designer in a London agency. Now I was sitting in a lounge room in Richmond with massive boobs and bad clothes. My mothers' group just talked about babies, which is fine – I guess that's what we were there for – but I wanted more. My brain was still the brain I'd always had, just a little mushier. I still thought about stuff at 11 pm, 2 am, 3.30 am, 4 am and then 5 am at brekkie.

The struggle for a sense of self after having babies is so real. I wondered whether Billy Corgan ever thought about this too. He has a child; did he lose his mojo for a while? Did he think back to 1993 when he released 'Mayonaise'? I wonder if the release of *Mellon Collie and the Infinite Sadness* coincided with the birth of his baby son?

I have two kids now, and they are probably trying to work out who they are too, just at a time when I feel free enough to do the same.

Self-discovery in your forties is an amazing thing. It has all the excitement and possibilities of a teen singing at the top of her lungs, but without the self-doubt or caring so deeply about what other people think. Imagine starting your life with that strength; what incredible things we could do.

My most important job as a mum is to make sure my kids understand and truly accept that the things that make them different are so precious and magical. These are the things that make you you. When I look back at that teenager in her bedroom, screaming along with Billy, I realise I didn't want to be me, I wanted to be like everyone else. And that crushes my heart.

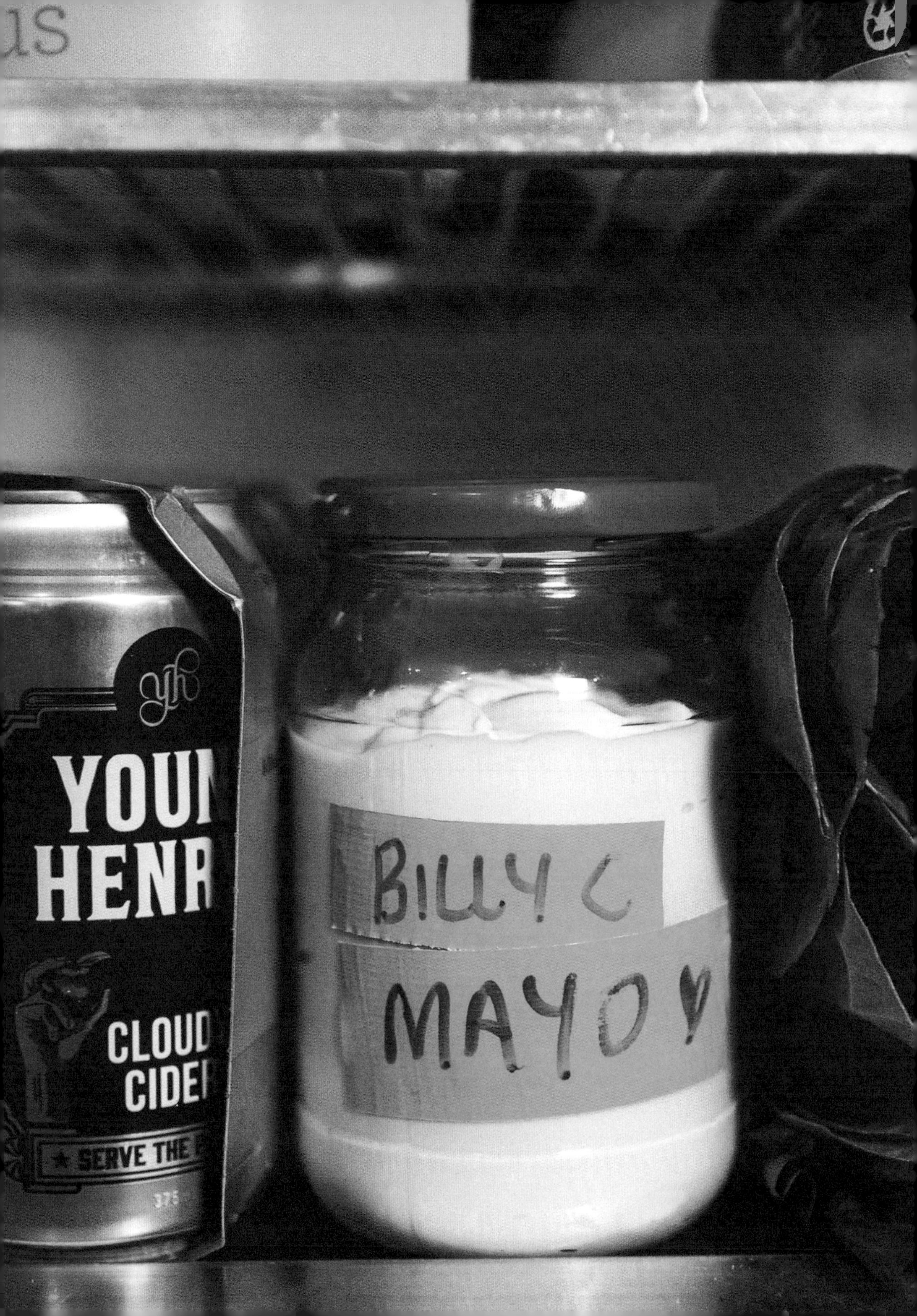
YOUN
HENR
CLOUD
CIDE
SERVE THE
BILLY C
MAYO

BILLY C'S MAYO

MAKES 250 G (1 CUP)

2 free-range egg yolks
½ teaspoon dijon mustard
1 tablespoon red or white
  wine vinegar
½ teaspoon salt
1 teaspoon lemon juice
250 ml (1 cup) sunflower oil

Place the egg yolks, mustard, vinegar, salt and lemon juice in a jar that's big enough to fit your stick blender. Whiz them together until well combined.

With the stick blender running, add a couple of tablespoons of oil at a time, making sure each batch is completely incorporated before adding the next. The mixture will start to lighten and thicken. Once you've added half the oil, you can add the rest in a steady stream. Depending on your preferred consistency, you may not need all the oil – the more you add, the thicker the mayo will become. If it becomes too thick, blend in 1 teaspoon of water at a time until you're happy with the consistency.

Transfer to a clean jar and store in the fridge for up to 4 days.

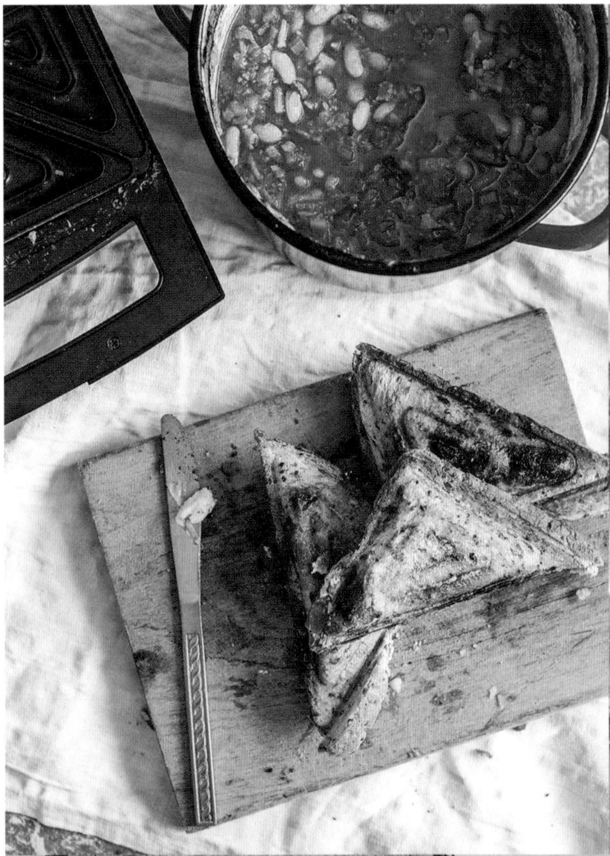

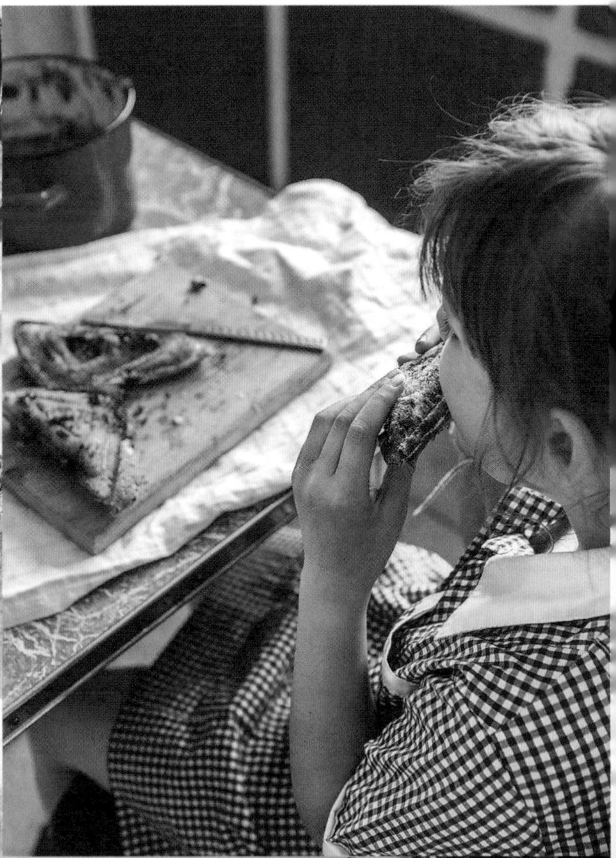

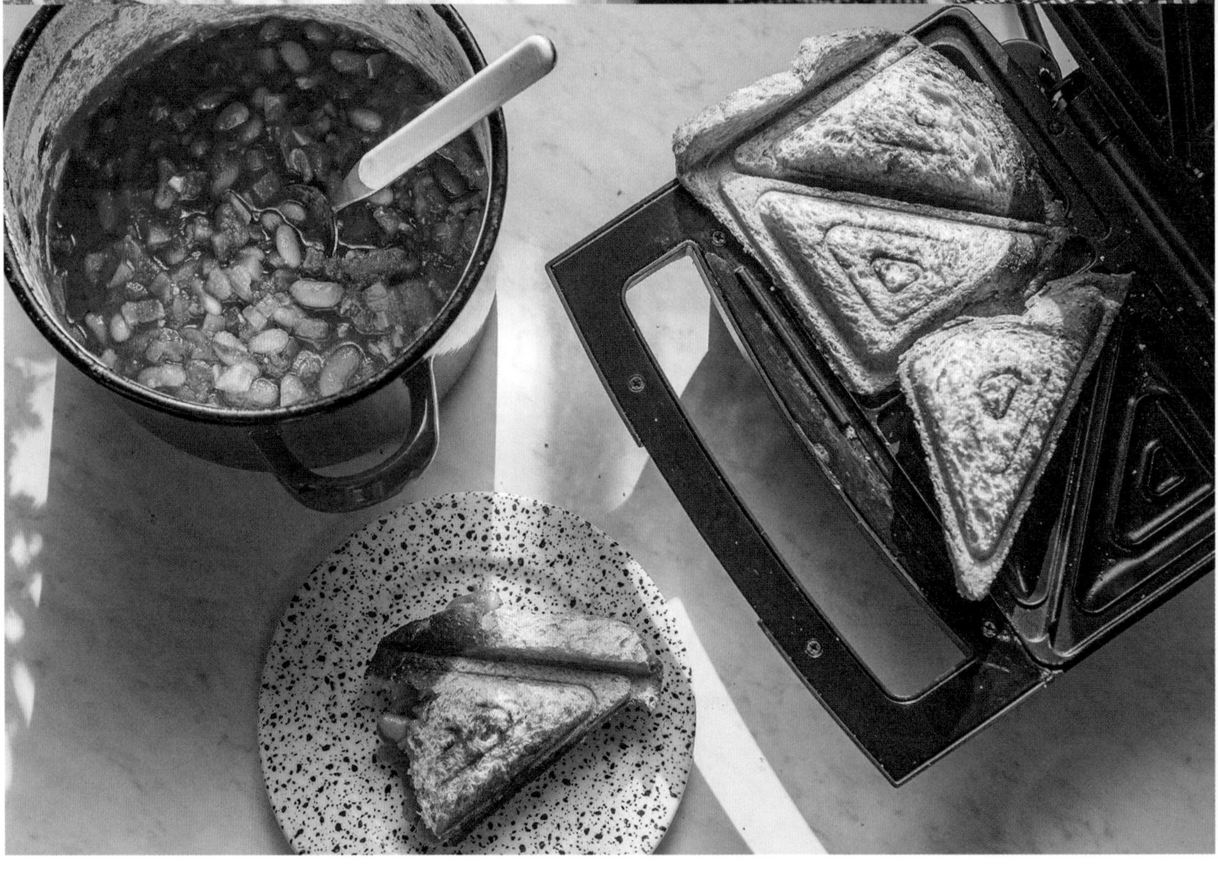

JAFFLE FILLING

Baked Beans

SERVES 6

When I was a kid, one of my all-time fave school lunches was baked bean jaffles. Even now, when I make them for my kids to take to school, the smell transports me back to my school tuckshop, excitedly waiting for my brown paper lunch parcel. Of course, you don't have to put these beans in jaffles but I highly recommend you do, with a big helping of cheese.

1 tablespoon olive oil
1 large onion, finely chopped
1 carrot, peeled and finely chopped
2 celery sticks, finely chopped
100 g bacon, rind removed, diced
3 garlic cloves, thinly sliced
1 teaspoon smoked paprika
2 bay leaves
2 tablespoons tomato paste
1 x 400 g can crushed tomatoes
2 x 400 g cans cannellini beans, drained and rinsed
1 tablespoon worcestershire sauce
1 tablespoon pure maple syrup
2 teaspoons dijon mustard

Preheat the oven to 160°C (fan-forced).

Heat the olive oil in a large flameproof casserole dish over medium–high heat.

Add the onion, carrot, celery and bacon and cook, stirring, for 5–6 minutes or until softened. Add the garlic, paprika and bay leaves and cook, stirring, for another minute or until fragrant.

Add the tomato paste and cook, stirring, for 1 minute. Add the tomatoes, beans, worcestershire sauce, maple syrup, mustard and 500 ml (2 cups) of water. Mix well, then cover and place in the oven. Bake for about 2 hours or until the beans are tender and the sauce is nice and thick. Serve.

BACK TO BASICS

FAILSAFE FRITTATA

SERVES 6-8

Use this recipe as a starting point to create your own perfect frittata. Maybe you like it eggier, creamier or packed with more fillings? Whichever way you like it, it's easy to tweak and uses up those annoying bits and pieces hanging out in the fridge. On average, you'll need about 2 cups of filling for this size frittata.

8 free-range eggs
125 ml (½ cup) double cream
salt and pepper
olive oil, for pan-frying
your choice of filling and
    topping ingredients

Preheat the oven to 180°C (fan-forced).

In a medium bowl, lightly beat the eggs, cream, salt and pepper. Set aside.

Heat a good splash of olive oil in a 20 cm ovenproof frying pan over medium heat, add your choice of filling ingredients and cook until softened.

Pour in the egg mixture and stir the centre with a spatula to allow it to cook slightly.

Add any ingredients you'd like on top of your frittata, then pop it in the oven for 12–15 minutes or until just cooked. Slide onto a plate and serve warm.

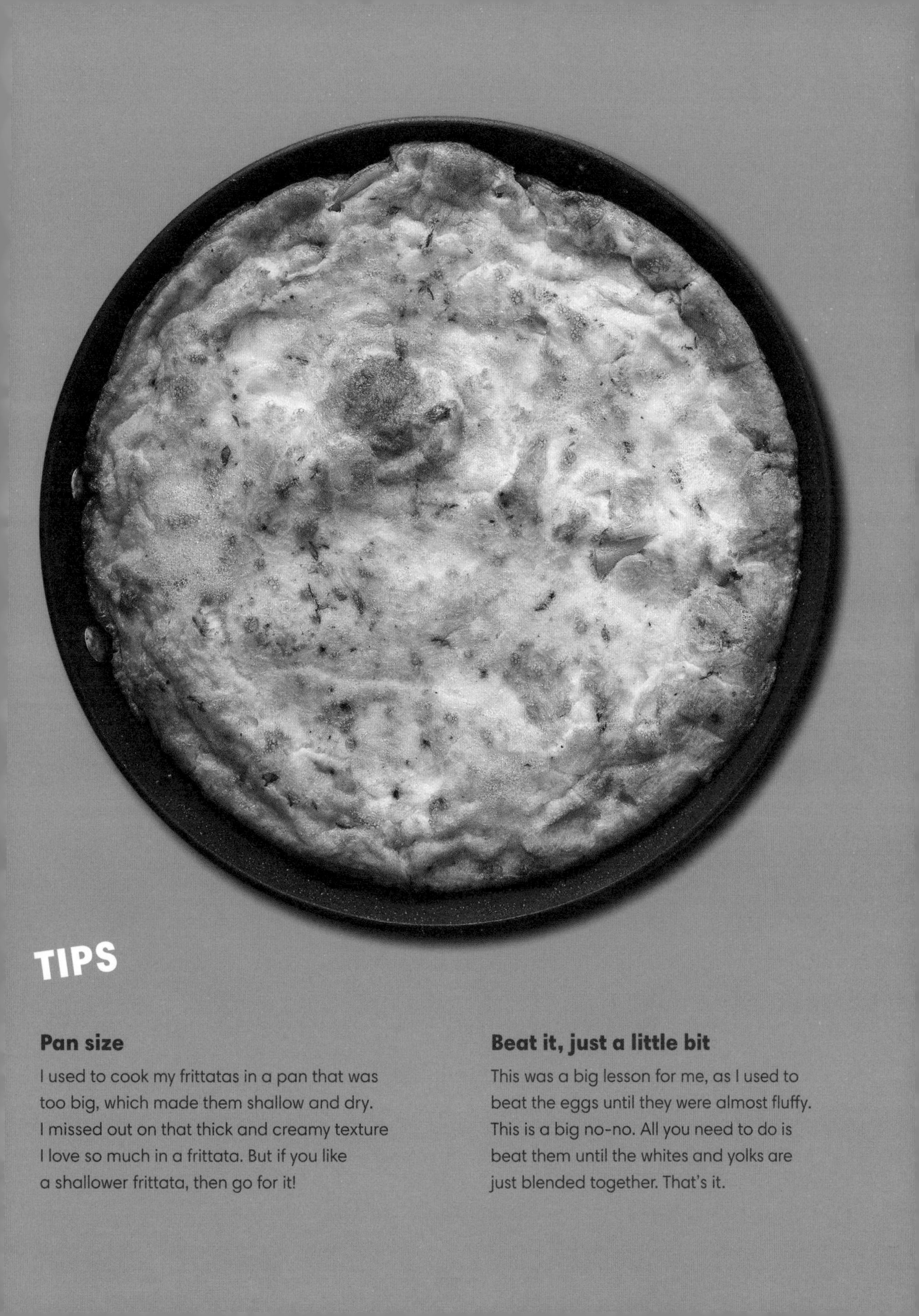

TIPS

Pan size

I used to cook my frittatas in a pan that was too big, which made them shallow and dry. I missed out on that thick and creamy texture I love so much in a frittata. But if you like a shallower frittata, then go for it!

Beat it, just a little bit

This was a big lesson for me, as I used to beat the eggs until they were almost fluffy. This is a big no-no. All you need to do is beat them until the whites and yolks are just blended together. That's it.

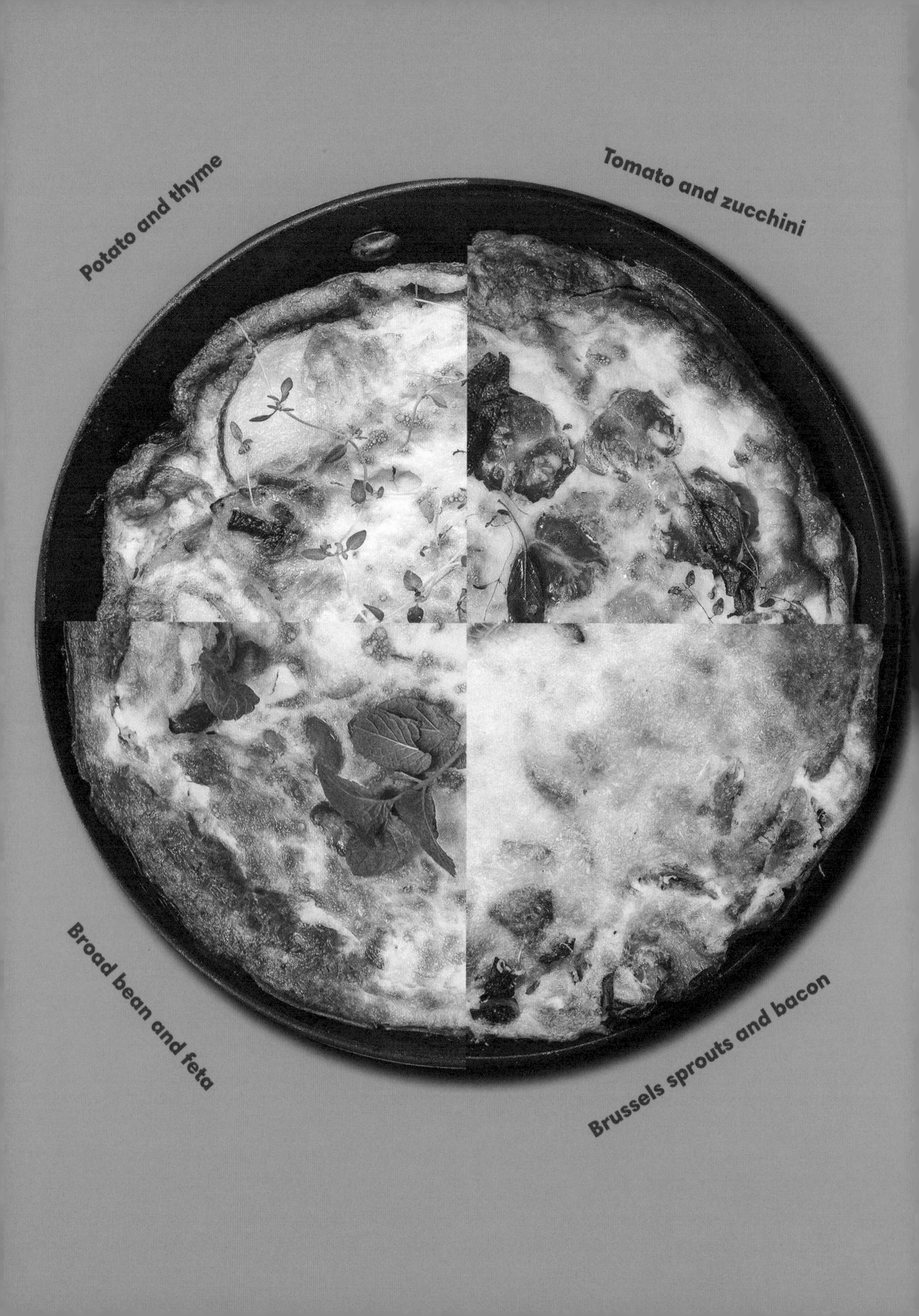
Potato and thyme
Tomato and zucchini
Broad bean and feta
Brussels sprouts and bacon

Combos to try:

Potato and thyme

Once you've reached the filling stage, reduce the heat to low, add ½ finely chopped onion and 2 finely chopped garlic cloves and cook for 2 minutes or until aromatic. Add 2 medium potatoes, halved lengthways and thinly sliced into half-circles, and cook for 7 minutes or until softened. Spread the mixture evenly over the base of the pan and sprinkle with 2 tablespoons finely chopped thyme.

Pour in the egg mixture and cook as instructed.

Tomato and zucchini

Once you've reached the filling stage, add 1 small zucchini, cut into coins, 1 finely chopped garlic clove and a handful of baby spinach to the pan. Cook for about 1 minute or until the greens start to soften.

When you've added the egg mixture, arrange 2 sliced tomatoes on top, season well and cook as instructed. In the last few minutes of cooking, sprinkle a few thyme sprigs and sage leaves over the top.

Broad bean and feta

Cook 300 g broad beans in a saucepan of boiling salted water for 2–3 minutes or until tender. Drain, then refresh in cold water. When the beans are cool enough to handle, peel away the outer skins, if you want to.

Once you've reached the filling stage, reduce the heat to low, add 1 chopped small onion and cook for 8–10 minutes or until softened but not browned.

When you've added the egg mixture, sprinkle the broad beans and 150 g feta over the top and cook as instructed. Serve sprinkled with chopped mint.

Brussels sprouts and bacon

Once you've reached the filling stage, add 2 halved and thinly sliced golden shallots and cook, stirring occasionally, for 3 minutes or until softened. Add 350 g halved and thickly sliced brussels sprouts and 150 g sliced bacon and season with salt and pepper. Cook, tossing occasionally, for 5 minutes or until crisp on the outside and tender in the middle.

When you've added the egg mixture, sprinkle over 1 cup of grated gruyere and cook as instructed.

Book Week enlightenment

Book Week. You've either got it, or you don't.
Or so I thought.

Waking to elaborate outfits spamming my Facebook and Instagram feeds is usually my first inkling that it's a dress-up day. On Book Week morning you'll find me trying to convince the girls of tenuous links between existing outfits in their cupboards and the books on their shelves. When my eldest daughter was in primary school, I coasted through on her red hair (thank you Pippi Longstocking). But my youngest kid wasn't born with any inbuilt book characteristics, so it's up to me to create something.

When I was at school, I envied the kids who rocked up with their elaborate costumes. I was pretty sure these kids' mums also made them amazing lunches and killer afternoon teas.

My mum was part of the new generation of mums who went out and worked in the big smoke. There wasn't time for papier-mache or sewing. In fact, when I asked my mum to teach me to knit, she told me she couldn't because I was left-handed. This of course made no sense and was in fact code for 'I don't have the time to do that'. Now, in my forties, I can finally see this for what it is. I always thought my mum hated craft, but she was just too busy.

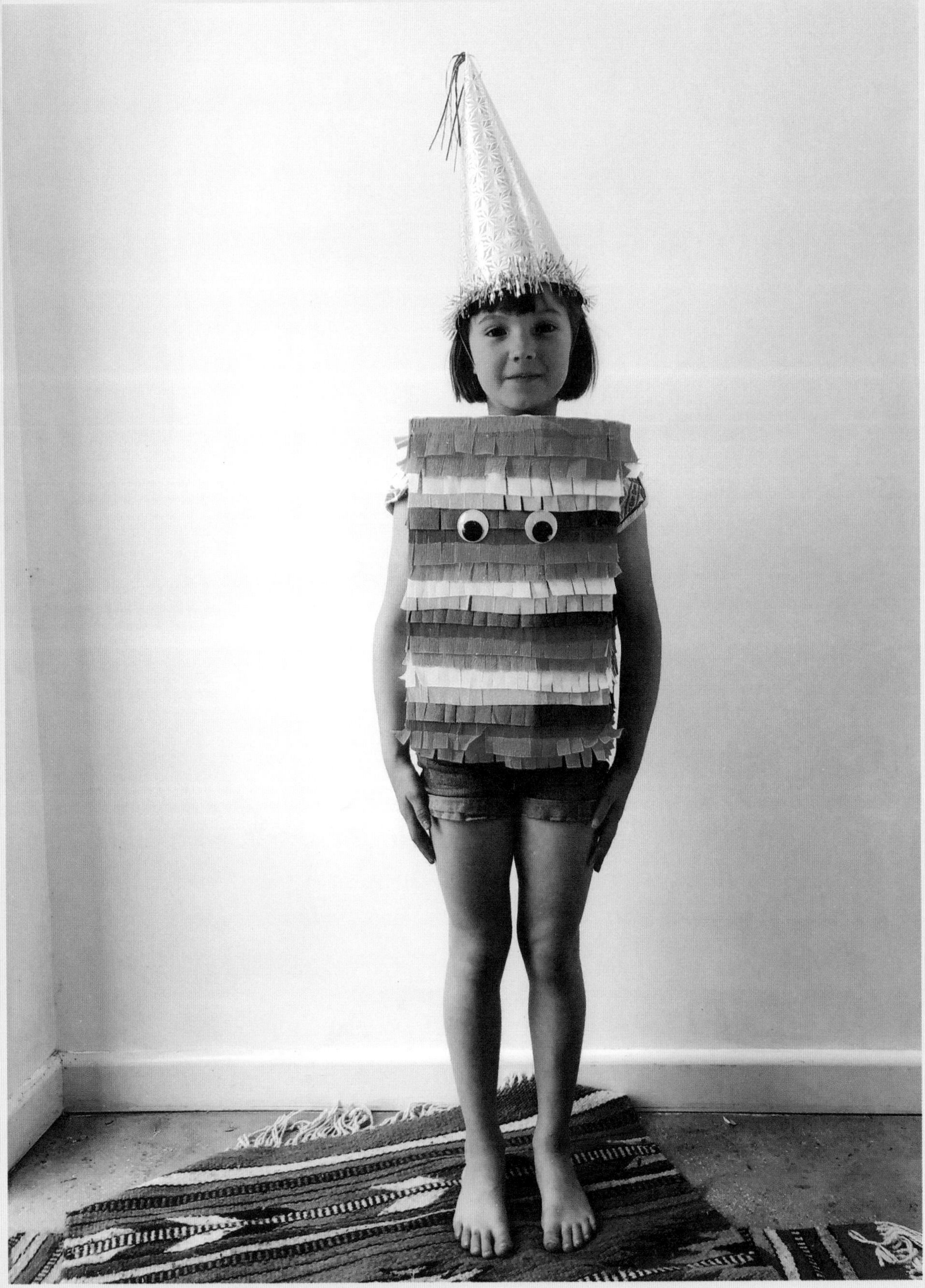

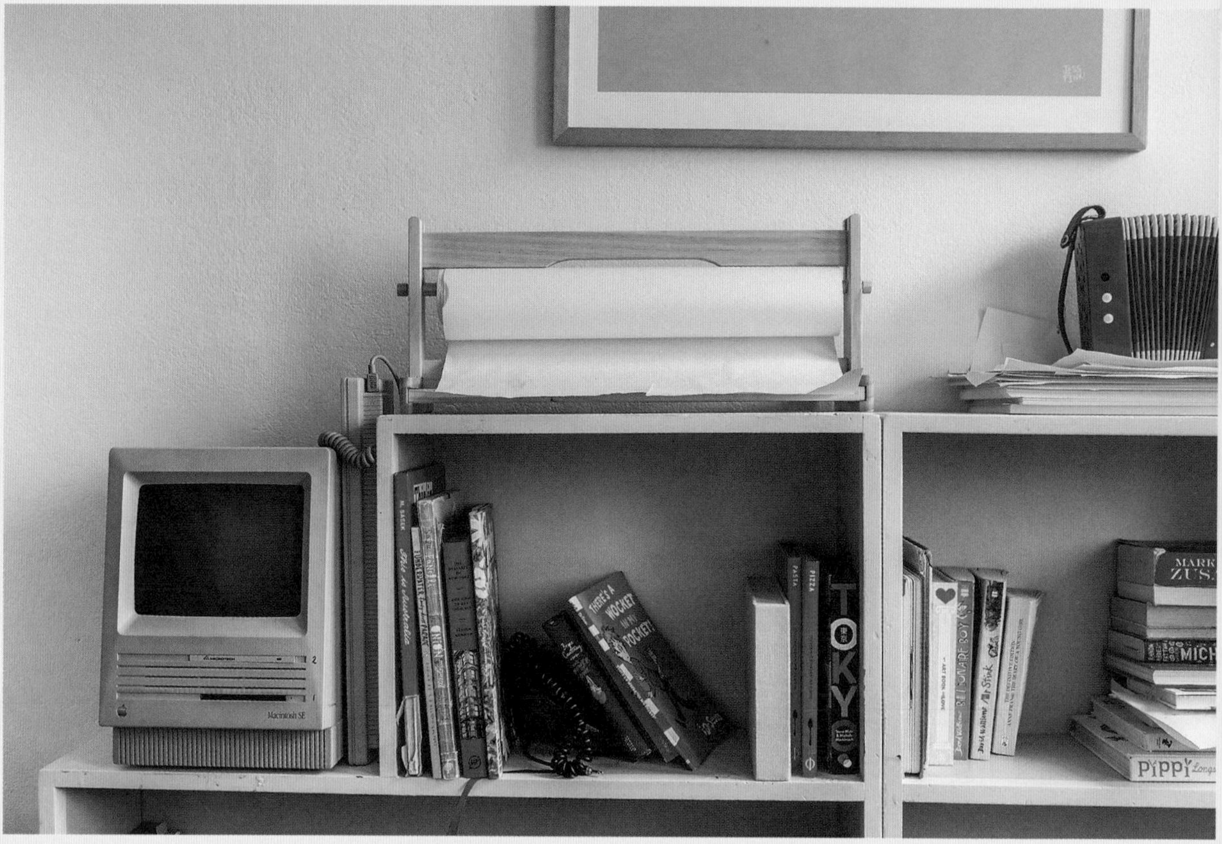
THERE'S A WOCKET IN MY POCKET!
TOKYO
PIPPI

I love the way becoming a parent allows you to see the whole situation. I never really appreciated how hard it was for my mum and dad to work and bring up kids – the endless juggle, the money worries, and also just finding the time to be a couple. But I also understand how important small things like dress-up days are to my kids. Those memories stick.

Armed with this new sense of enlightenment, I decided to take on Book Week.

The girls and I discussed who they wanted to go as, then I pegged back their expectations and we were ready to go. We took the dog for a walk to the junk shop, shopped for craft supplies, cleared some space on the kitchen table, made tea, ate snacks, talked, listened to each other's favourite songs and got cracking.

Two things happened. One, I took time out from my work, hung out with the girls and did something fun. Two, I cut out some coloured card, glued some bits and pieces together, and used my limited but enthusiastic drawing skills. One Wonka Bar and one golden ticket later, we had created our first-ever real Book Week costumes.

My kids were so freaking proud of what we'd cobbled together. They wore the costumes to the dinner table, they propped them up next to their beds so they could keep an eye on them through the night, and they were the first things they went to when they woke.

'Mum, that was so much fun making the costumes together! We should do more of that stuff.'

So what is my actual problem with Book Week?

Me.

PUB FAVE PASTRIES

Cauliflower Cheese Pastries

MAKES 12

Cauliflower cheese is a staple of the country pub bain marie, which is probably why I love it so much. Nothing makes me happier than counter meals in far-flung places, but I also like putting my own spin on them at home. So instead of serving this as a side for a huge chunk of roast meat, I wrap it in flaky pastry and make little hand pies.

1 head of cauliflower, cut into florets
1 onion, sliced
4 thyme sprigs
4 garlic cloves, unpeeled
3 tablespoons olive oil
salt and pepper
3 sheets ready-made puff pastry, thawed
1 free-range egg, beaten
50 g (½ cup) grated parmesan
2 thyme sprigs, leaves picked

For the cheese sauce:
60 g butter
3 heaped tablespoons plain flour
750 ml (3 cups) milk, heated
large handful of grated mature cheddar
½ teaspoon dijon mustard
½ teaspoon cayenne pepper (optional)
salt and pepper

Preheat the oven to 225°C (fan-forced).

Pop the cauliflower florets, onion, thyme, garlic and olive oil on a large baking tray, season with salt and pepper and gently toss to combine. Roast, tossing occasionally, for 35–40 minutes or until almost tender. Remove and set aside but leave the oven on.

While the cauliflower is roasting, make the sauce. Melt the butter in a medium saucepan over low heat, then whisk in the flour to create a smooth paste. Slowly pour in the milk while whisking constantly, then cook for 5–10 minutes or until the sauce is thick and smooth. You want it to be slightly thicker than a normal bechamel.

Take the sauce off the heat, then add the cheese, mustard and cayenne pepper (if using), and season to taste. Stir until the cheese has melted and the sauce is smooth. Add the roasted cauliflower and gently stir through. Set aside.

Place the pastry sheets on a clean bench and cut each sheet into four squares (so you have 12 all up).

Line two baking trays with baking paper.

Place a pastry square on one of the prepared trays and pop a heaped tablespoon of the cauliflower mixture in the middle. Bring the four corners together into the centre and pinch together. Repeat with the remaining pastry squares and cauliflower cheese.

Brush the pastries with beaten egg and sprinkle with the parmesan. Pop them in the oven for 15–20 minutes or until the pastry is golden brown. Remove from the oven and sprinkle with thyme, then serve with your fave relish or sauce.

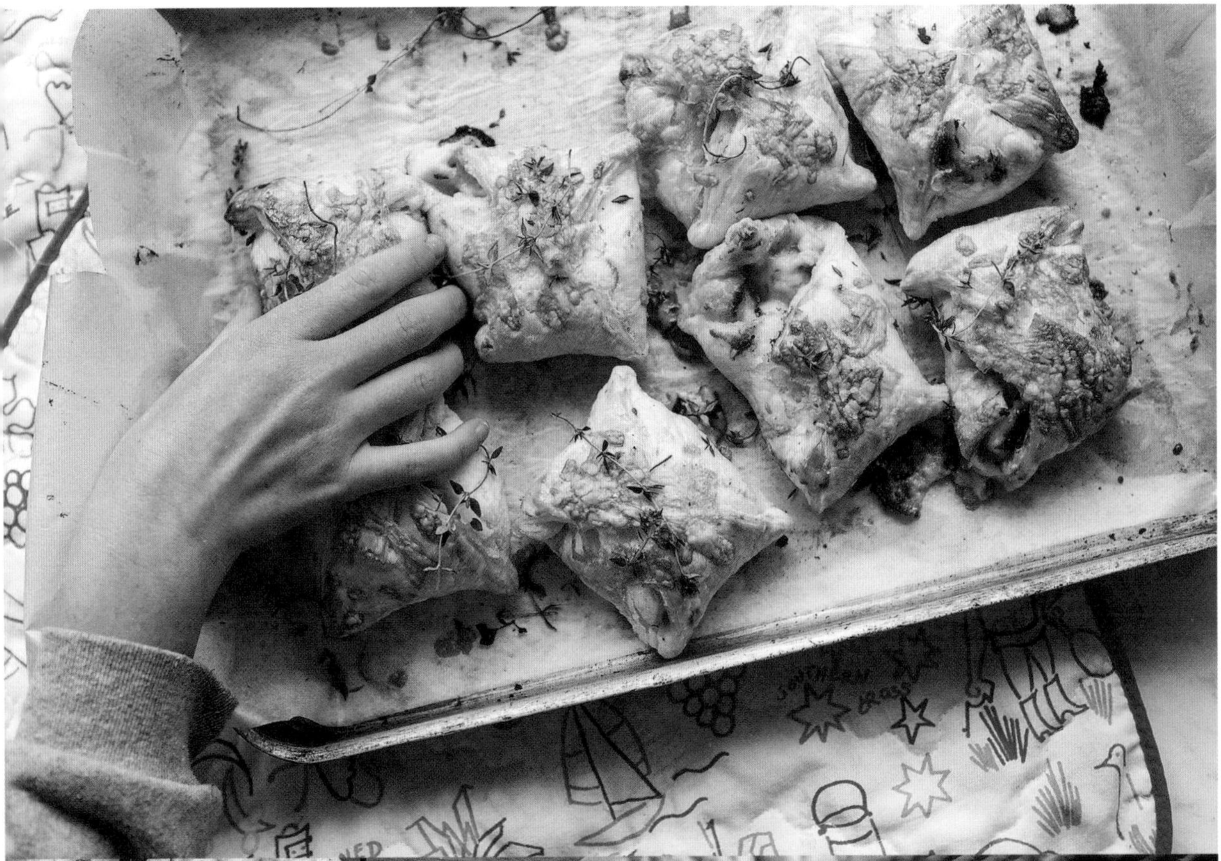

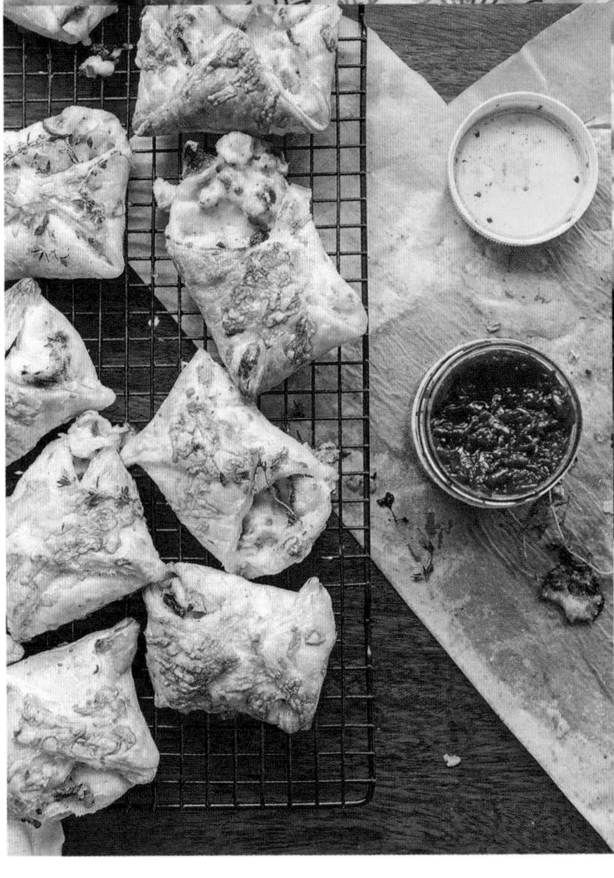

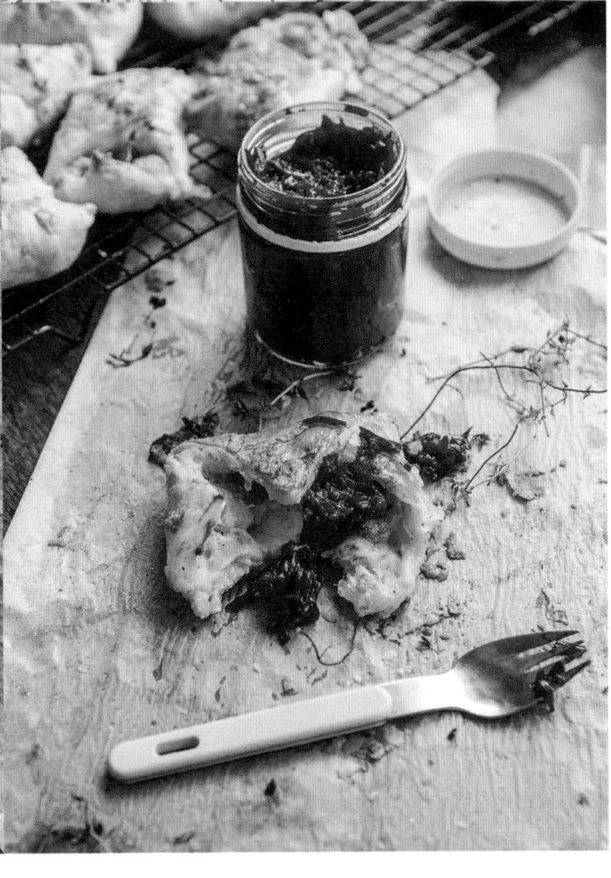

EAT-IN TAKE-OUT

Chana Masala

SERVES 4

We're mad curry fans but when we were living in the country our curry choices were seriously limited. We'd often hungrily discuss hypotheticals like, 'if there was a Thai place in town, I'd order blah blah' and then have to make our own version of blah blah, which pretty much took all the fun out of it. But this recipe is a good compromise. It doesn't need a million ingredients or take a million years to cook so we can satisfy our curry craving with the tiniest bit of effort.

2 tablespoons vegetable oil
1 onion, finely chopped
1 garlic clove, finely chopped
2 tablespoons finely chopped
   ginger
2 cardamom pods
1 tablespoon curry powder
2 x 400 g cans whole tomatoes
   with their juices, crushed
1 x 400 g can chickpeas,
   drained and rinsed
salt and pepper
chopped coriander, to serve
steamed basmati rice and
   plain yoghurt, to serve

Heat the vegetable oil in a heavy-based saucepan or flameproof casserole dish over medium–low heat. Add the onion, garlic, ginger, cardamom and curry powder and cook for 8–10 minutes or until fragrant and the onion has softened.

Add the tomatoes with their juices and chickpeas and simmer for 25–30 minutes or until the chickpeas have softened. Season with salt and pepper.

Top with coriander and serve with basmati rice and yoghurt.

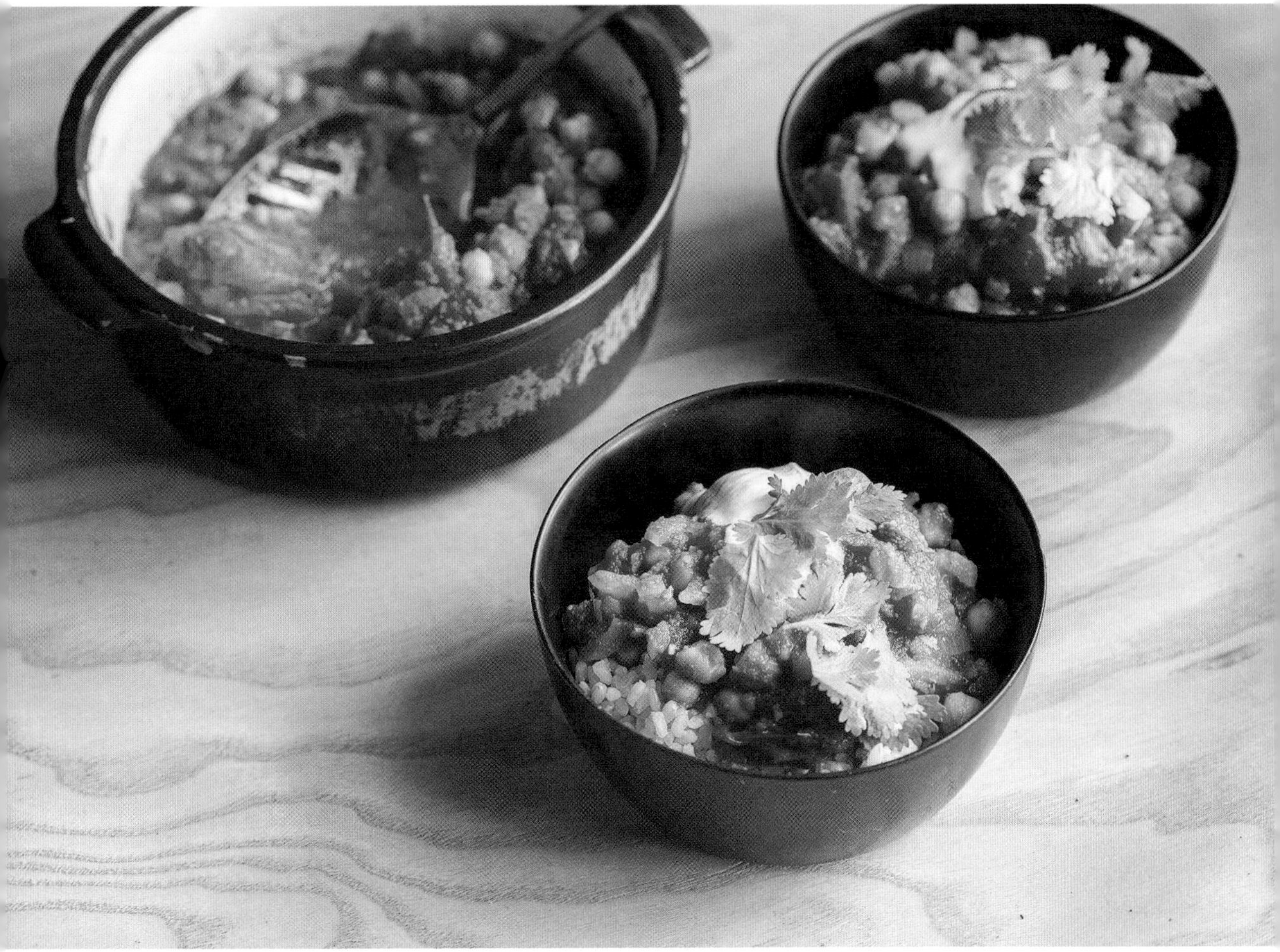

TOMMIES AND RICE

Passata and Rice Soup

SERVES 4-6

Every summer our little family smashes tomatoes to make a giant stash of passata to get us through the gloomy months of winter. Usually the passata gets lost in a ratatouille or hidden under pizza toppings, but in this soup the passata is the superstar! It's so bloody simple too, and you're sure to have most of the ingredients lying around in the crisper drawer getting soft.

olive oil, for pan-frying
3 garlic cloves, finely chopped
1 onion, finely chopped
2 celery sticks, diced
2 carrots, diced
big handful of flat-leaf parsley,
    leaves and stalks chopped
100 g (½ cup) brown rice
90 g (⅓ cup) tomato paste
1 litre vegetable stock
750 ml (3 cups) tomato passata
1 x 400 g can diced tomatoes
2 good handfuls of mustard
    greens, chopped
250 ml (1 cup) red wine
    (one you'd enjoy drinking)
crusty bread and butter,
    to serve

Heat a good splash of olive oil in a large saucepan over medium–low heat, add the garlic, onion, celery, carrot and parsley and cook, stirring, for a few minutes or until the onion is translucent.

Add the rice and cook, stirring, for 3–5 minutes or until the grains start to become translucent. Pop in the tomato paste and stir through.

Pour in the stock, passata and tomatoes. Increase the heat and bring to the boil, then reduce the heat and simmer for 35–40 minutes or until the rice is just tender.

Add the mustard greens and red wine and cook for another 15–20 minutes or until the greens are nice and soft.

Serve with crusty bread and tons of butter.

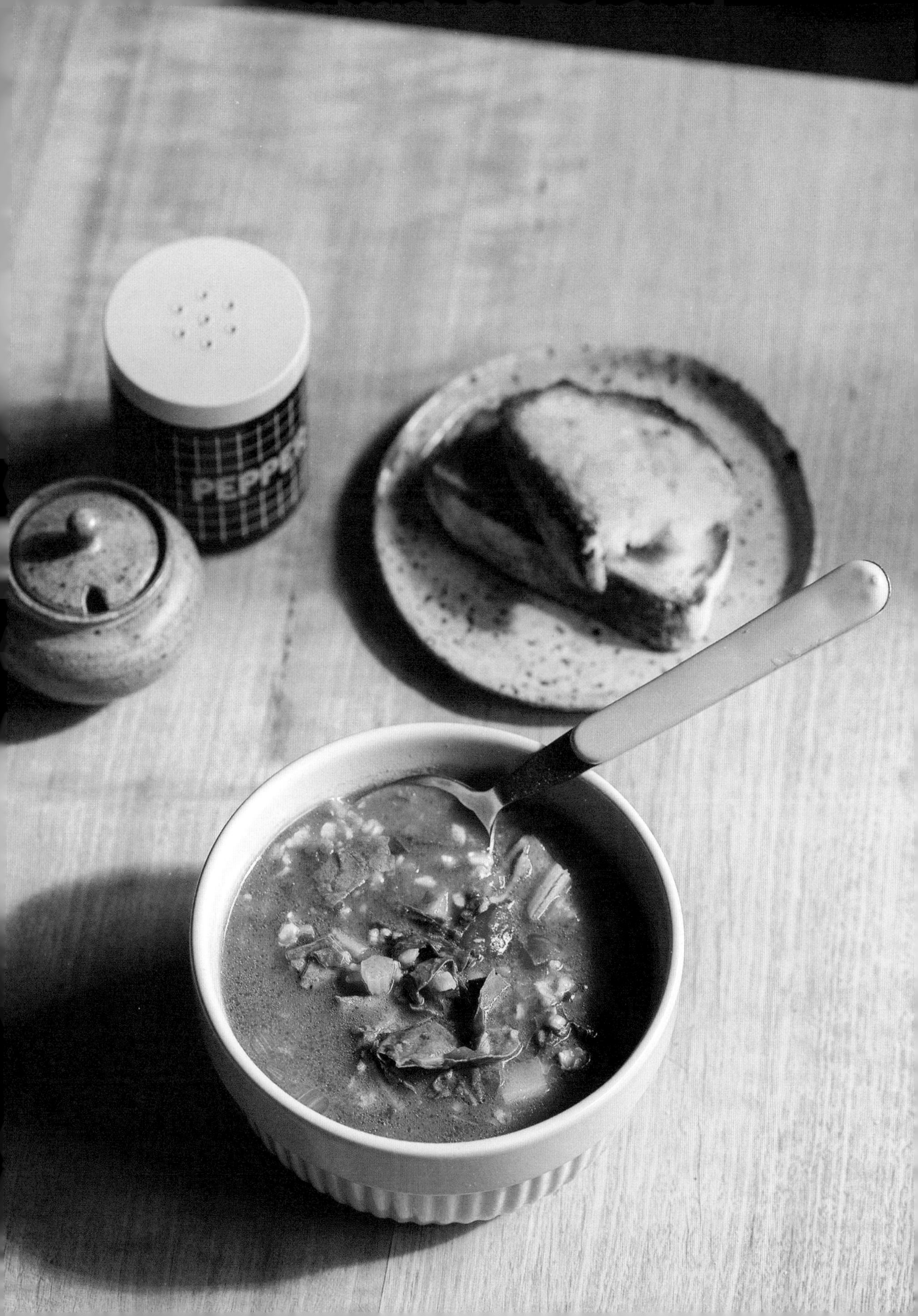

Hello neighbour

Just as I sat down to write this, my next-door neighbour popped through the back gate with her daughter and gave me a little bunch of hand-picked flowers from their garden and some cauliflower from the school veggie patch. She knew I had a book to write, and she knew I had been procrastinating like a pro, so she thought she should make sure I was doing what I'd been saying I needed to do for the last four months. Which I was, thank goodness.

I read her a little bit of what I'd written to make sure I was on the right track, and she gave it the thumbs up. Buoyed by flowers, a tick of approval and the simple fact that she'd thought of me, I carried on.

Real connections with actual real-life people are so incredibly special. How lucky am I to have a neighbour who cares for me and my girls?! We swap school runs, cook each other dinner, look after each other's kids when we need time out, make tea and offer a shoulder to cry on, or make tea just because the sun is shining.

I've now even put a little stool next to the side fence so we can have a quick catch up without having to commit to a full house visit. Just a little check-in and we're done. She's OK. I'm OK. We can go about our business.

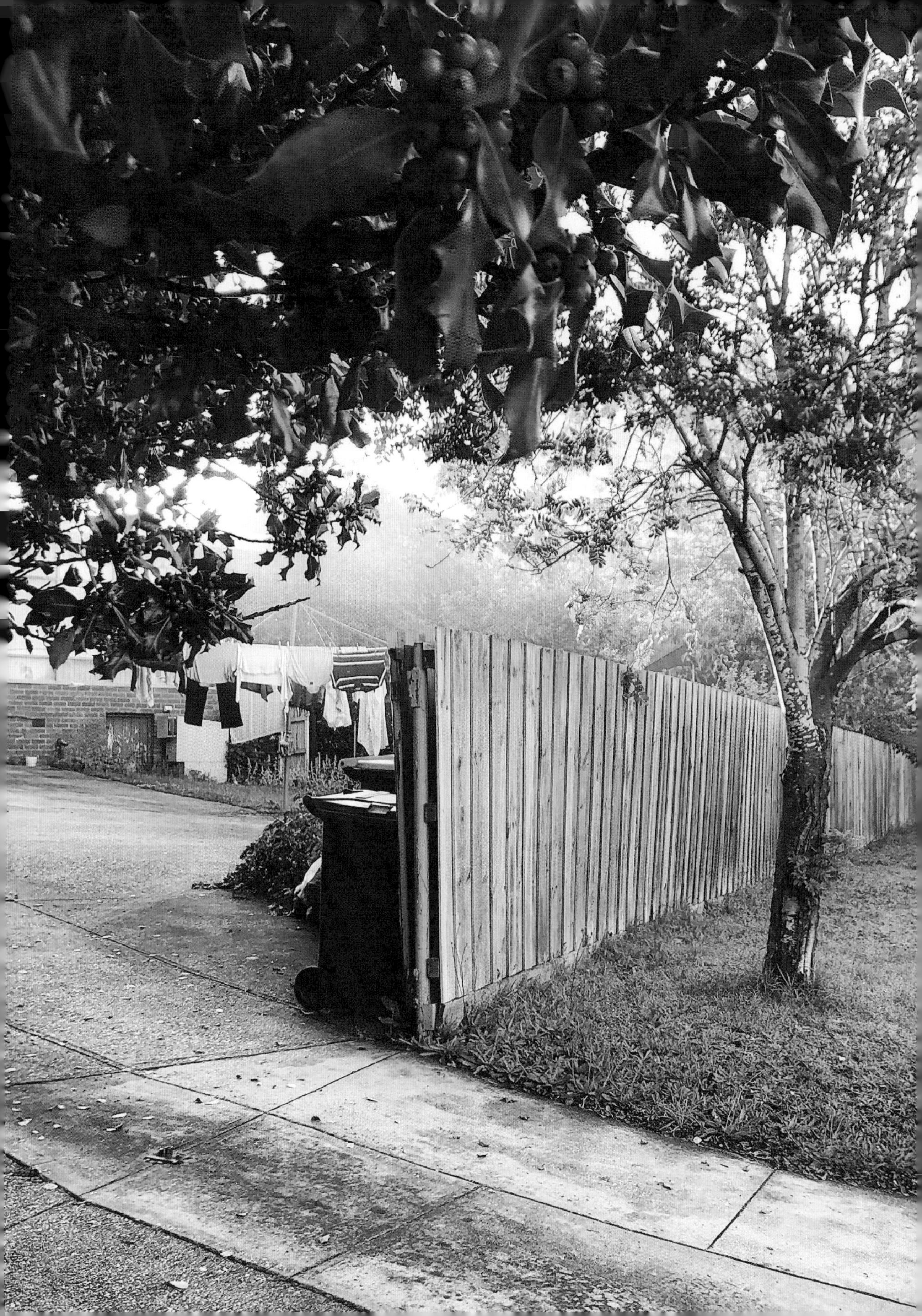

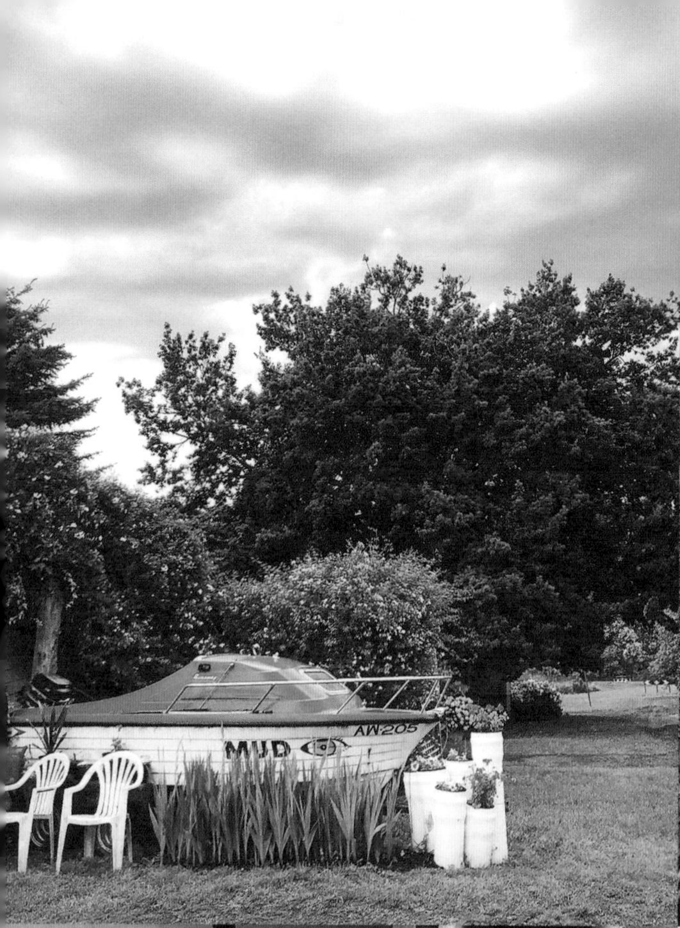
MUD
AW-205

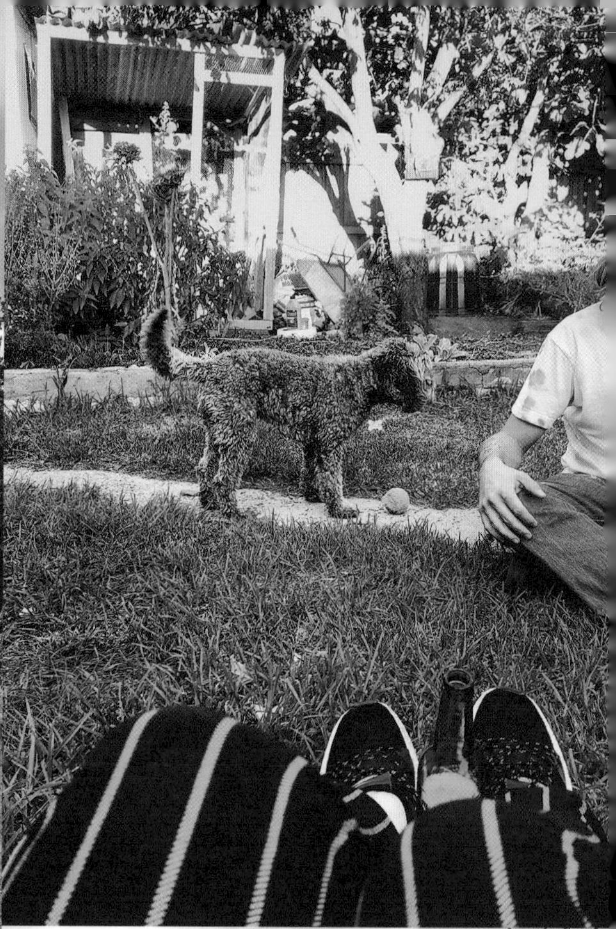

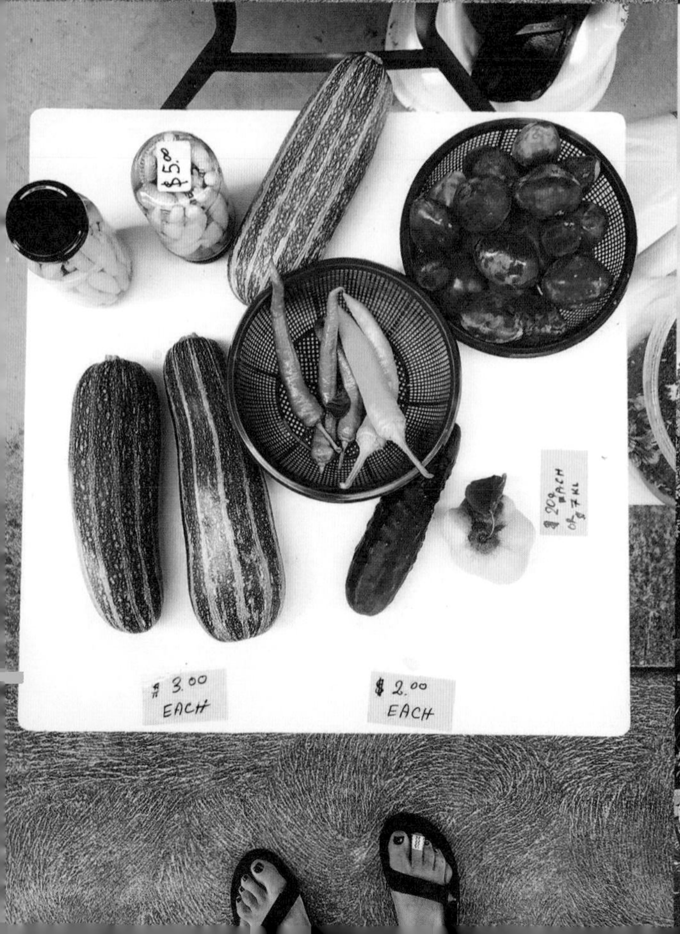
$ 3.00
EACH
$ 2.00
EACH

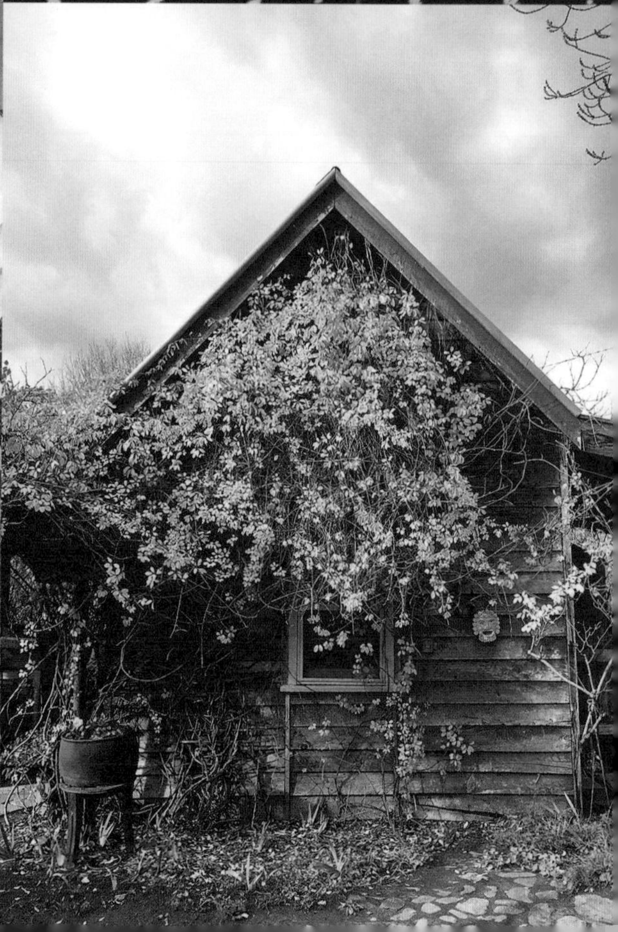

My first experience with amazing neighbours was in the inner northern suburbs of Melbourne (there wasn't much neighbourly action in the outer 'burbs, where I grew up). Days after moving into our new home in Thornbury, a sunny face popped through the bathroom window. It was a hot afternoon and both of our kids were naked and trying to stay cool – mine in the bath, hers being chased with a hose. She had the roundest belly, ready to pop with a new tiny neighbour.

It's crazy how a moment that seemed like nothing special at the time can have such a profound impact. That sunny face through my bathroom window taught me that being open and unafraid of showing your heart can really affect those around you. The simple act of saying hello to me and not overthinking whether or not I was going to like her blossomed into one of my fondest friendships.

I'd always been closed and guarded, and desperately wanted to be more like this kind-hearted beam of light. It takes real courage to let your guard down, to allow yourself to be hurt, but also to allow yourself to be loved. Now I walk around with my heart on the outside, 24/7, ready for whatever comes my way.

Have you met your neighbour?

LIKE JAFFAS, BUT COOKIES

Orange and Chocolate Cookies

MAKES 24

Third term is a bit of a bore when it comes to fruit. Oranges and mandarins lose their a-peel after a while. Come on, that's a good one. But even though they do get a bit boring in the fruit bowl, they are found in some of my favourite baked treats, and these cookies are no exception.

255 g (2½ cups) almond meal
285 g (1¼ cups) caster sugar
2 tablespoons runny honey
3 free-range egg whites
finely grated zest of 1 orange
½ teaspoon baking powder
150 g (1 cup) well-smashed
   dark chocolate
pure icing sugar, to coat

Place the almond meal, sugar, honey, egg whites, orange zest and baking powder in the bowl of an electric mixer fitted with the paddle attachment and mix until well combined.

Tip in the chocolate and mix through on low speed.

Cover with plastic wrap and chill in the fridge for about 1 hour.

Preheat the oven to 160°C (fan-forced). Line a baking tray with baking paper.

Roll the mixture into 24 even balls, then coat each ball in icing sugar. Place on the prepared baking tray, at least 2 cm apart, and bake for 10–15 minutes or until golden. Cool on the tray for a few minutes, then transfer to a wire rack to cool completely.

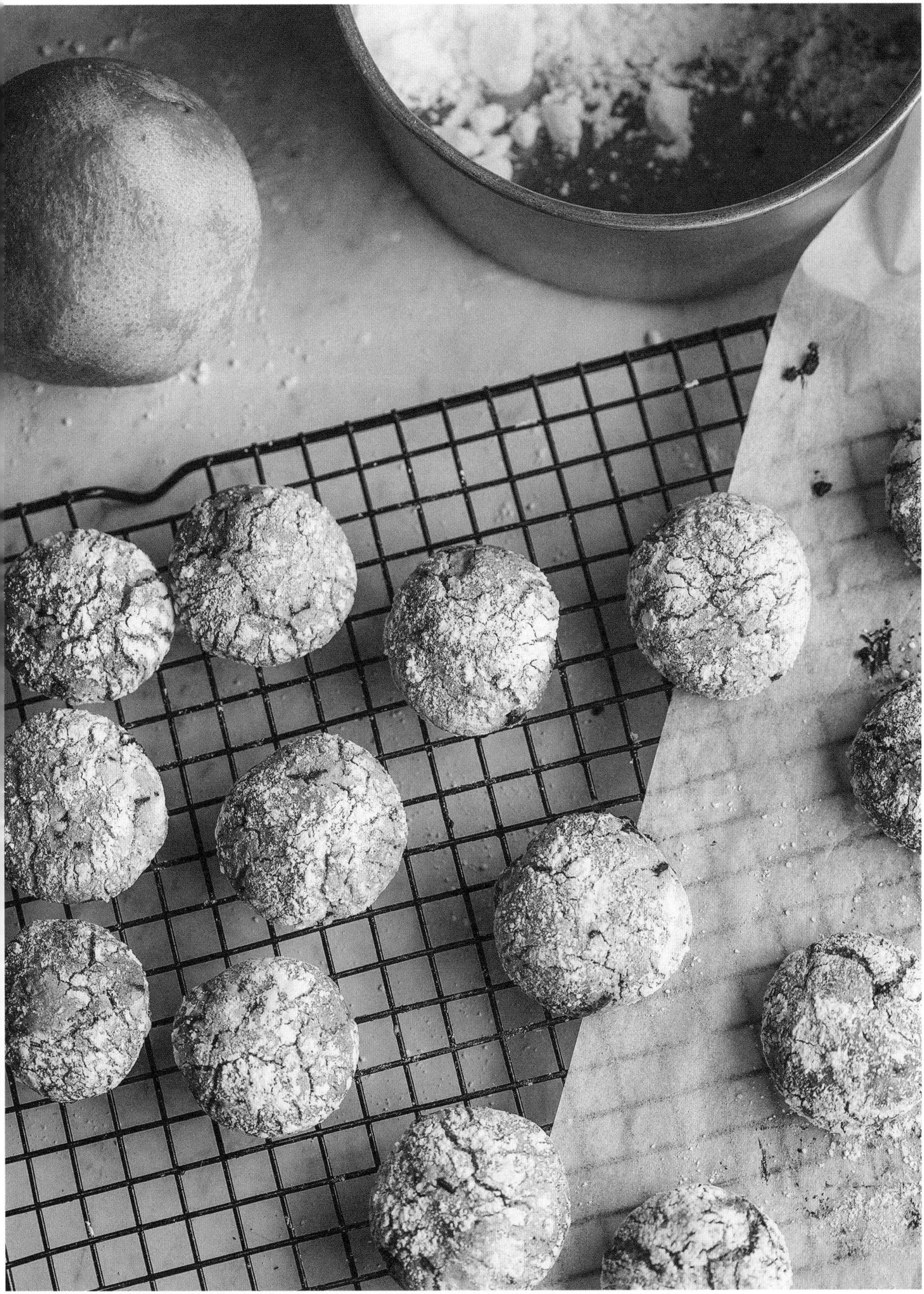

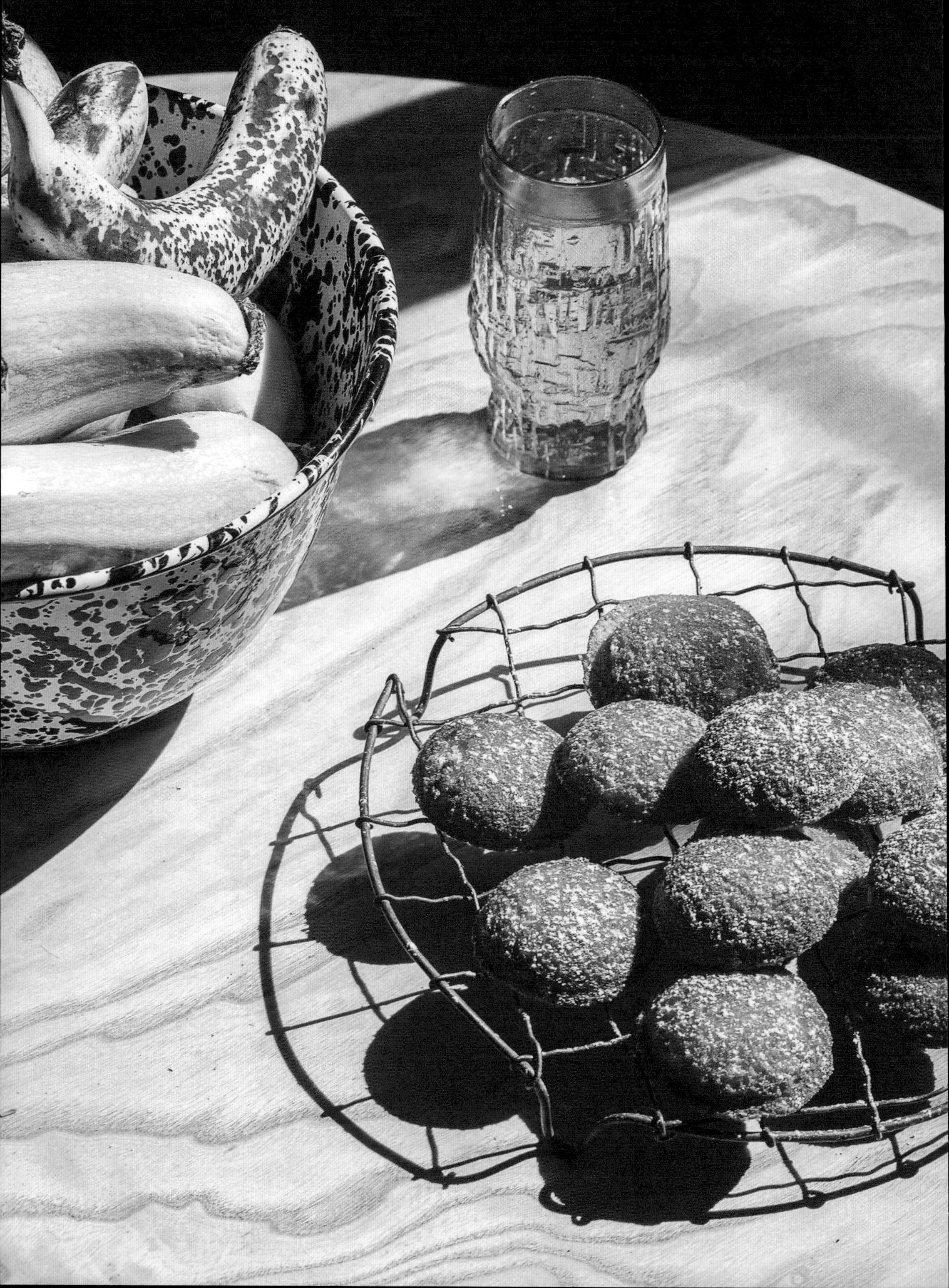

LEMONY MADELEINES

Lemon and Honey Madeleines

MAKES 12

I always think madeleines lift the calibre of my fairly crappy tea options when friends come over. And when I pop them in the kids' school lunchboxes, I feel pretty bloody fancy. But, in reality, they're just a simple little cake baked in a pretty tray you can pick up in an oppy on a country drive.

150 g unsalted butter
3 free-range eggs
150 g caster sugar
150 g (1 cup) plain flour
1 teaspoon baking powder
1 tablespoon runny honey
1½ teaspoons finely grated
    lemon zest

Melt the butter in a small saucepan, then set aside to cool.

Place the eggs and sugar in the bowl of an electric mixer fitted with the whisk attachment and whisk until thick and pale. Add the flour, baking powder, honey, lemon zest and melted butter and mix until the batter is smooth, thick and well combined.

Pop the batter in the fridge to rest for 1 hour.

Preheat the oven to 210°C (fan-forced).

Generously grease the madeleine tray with butter and flour, then place a heaped teaspoon of batter in each mould.

Place the tray in the oven and bake for 7–10 minutes or until the madeleines have risen and are lightly golden on top.

Remove from the oven and allow the cakes to cool for a few minutes before carefully removing them from the moulds. Cool completely on a wire rack (or even better, eat them warm) but don't muck about with these guys; they're best eaten on the day of baking.

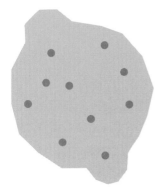

A PEAR-Y YUMMY CAKE

Pear and Vanilla Cake

SERVES 6-8

Sometimes you bake something that just has that thing that makes you feel warm and fuzzy, and this cake has that thing. Vanilla always helps to bring the fuzzies, if you ask me, especially when you serve this still warm and you can sniff it as you scoff it.

185 g (¾ cup) Greek yoghurt
3 tablespoons vegetable oil
160 g (⅔ cup) caster sugar
2 free-range eggs
1½ teaspoons vanilla extract
finely grated zest of 1 lemon
185 g (1¼ cups) plain flour
1¼ teaspoon baking powder
¼ teaspoon bicarbonate
  of soda
pinch of salt
2 very ripe pears
¼ teaspoon ground cinnamon
pure icing sugar, for dusting

Preheat the oven to 180°C (fan-forced). Line a 20 cm round cake tin with baking paper, or grease and flour it.

Place the yoghurt, vegetable oil, caster sugar, eggs, vanilla and lemon zest in a large bowl and mix together until smooth.

Sift the flour, baking powder, bicarbonate of soda and salt into the bowl, then whisk the flour into the yoghurt mixture until well combined.

Pour the batter into the prepared tin and smooth the top with a spatula.

Peel and core the pears, then cut into thin slices. Arrange the slices on top of the batter, then sprinkle over the cinnamon.

Bake for 40–50 minutes or until golden and a skewer inserted in the centre comes out clean. Cool in the tin for 10 minutes, then turn out onto a wire rack to cool completely. Or better yet, transfer it to a serving plate and enjoy it warm. Dust lightly with icing sugar and serve.

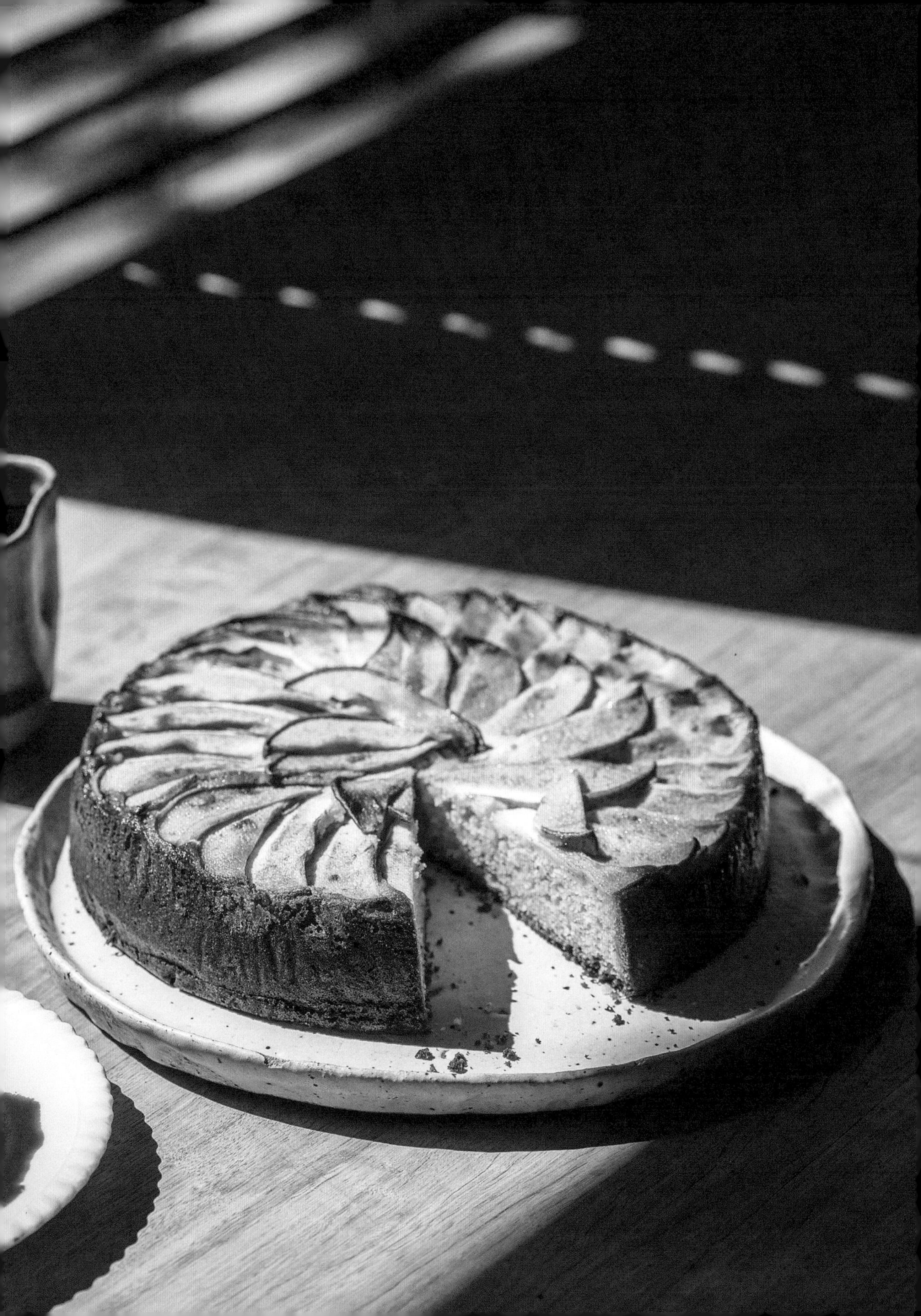

CLASSIC BAKED COMFORT

Roasted Rhubarb and Teurgoule

SERVES 12

In my mind, rice pudding lives permanently in the 1980s. I had pretty much forgotten about it until recently, during a late-night (8.30 pm) sweet craving. All out of ice cream and chocolate, I found myself staring into the pantry abyss and my eyes fell on a packet of rice. I've since dived deep into the world of the humble rice pudding and decided that teurgoule, the slow-cooked version from France, is my fave. Now, this recipe isn't for the quick fix, but it's amazing and the perfect thing to stick in the oven on a lazy day at home. Perhaps pop on some A-ha while you're at it.

200 g short-grain white rice
200 g caster sugar
1 teaspoon ground cinnamon
2 litres full-fat milk
pinch of salt
1 vanilla bean, split and
    seeds scraped
pouring cream, to serve

For the roasted rhubarb:
250 g rhubarb, stalks trimmed
    and cut into 5 cm lengths
80 g (⅓ cup) caster sugar
juice of 1 orange
finely grated zest of 1 lemon
1 vanilla bean, split and
    seeds scraped

Preheat the oven to 150°C (fan-forced).

Place the rice, sugar and cinnamon in a 20 cm round baking dish (or similar) and mix together well.

Pour the milk into a saucepan and bring to the boil. Remove from the heat as soon as it starts boiling and add the salt and vanilla bean and seeds. Leave to infuse for 10 minutes, then remove the vanilla bean and pour the warm milk over the rice mixture.

Pop on the bottom shelf of the oven and bake for 4 hours or until a brown crust has formed on top. Remove and set aside.

For the rhubarb, increase the oven temperature to 160°C (fan-forced).

Place the rhubarb in a small baking dish in a single layer.

In a small bowl, whisk the sugar, orange juice and lemon zest until the sugar has dissolved, then pour it over the rhubarb. Add the vanilla bean and seeds. Roast for 10–12 minutes or until the rhubarb is tender but still holding its shape.

Serve the teurgoule with the rhubarb and its juices, finished with a good drizzle of cream.

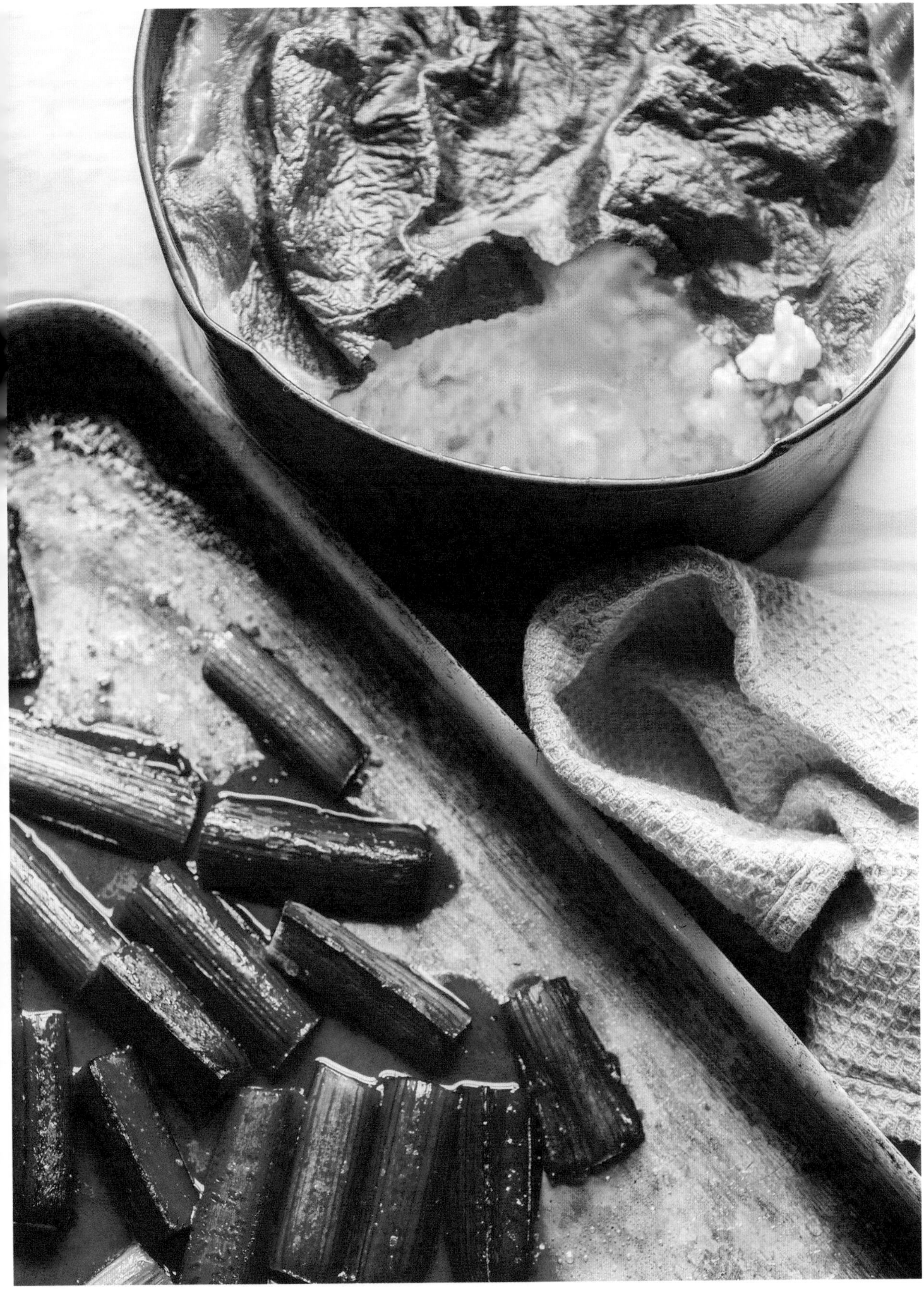

(Almost) DIY after-school snacks

AVOCADO CHOC POTS

SERVES 2

2 tablespoons raw cacao powder

½ teaspoon vanilla extract

3 tablespoons pure maple syrup

1 ripe avocado, skin and stone removed

Pop all the ingredients in a food processor and blend until creamy. Divide evenly between two cups and refrigerate for 2–3 hours.

Most of these snacks will be simple enough for your kids to manage on their own but occasionally they'll need help with cutting or heating, depending on their age.

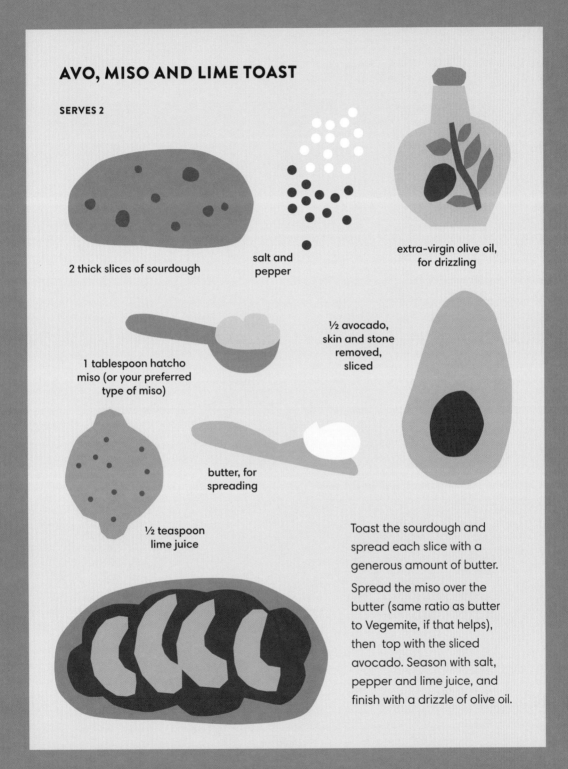

AVO, MISO AND LIME TOAST

SERVES 2

2 thick slices of sourdough

salt and pepper

extra-virgin olive oil, for drizzling

1 tablespoon hatcho miso (or your preferred type of miso)

½ avocado, skin and stone removed, sliced

butter, for spreading

½ teaspoon lime juice

Toast the sourdough and spread each slice with a generous amount of butter.

Spread the miso over the butter (same ratio as butter to Vegemite, if that helps), then top with the sliced avocado. Season with salt, pepper and lime juice, and finish with a drizzle of olive oil.

(Almost) DIY after-school snacks

MANGO LASSI

SERVES 2

pinch of ground cardamom

250 g (1 cup) plain yoghurt, well chilled

400 g frozen mango

squeeze of lime juice (optional)

pinch of brown sugar (optional)

Put the mango, yoghurt and cardamom in a food processor and blend until smooth.

If the lassi is a bit thick for your liking, add a little water. Taste and add sugar or lime juice, if needed, then pour into two tall glasses and serve.

PARMESAN CRISPS

MAKES ABOUT 8

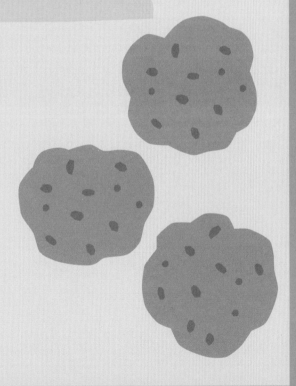

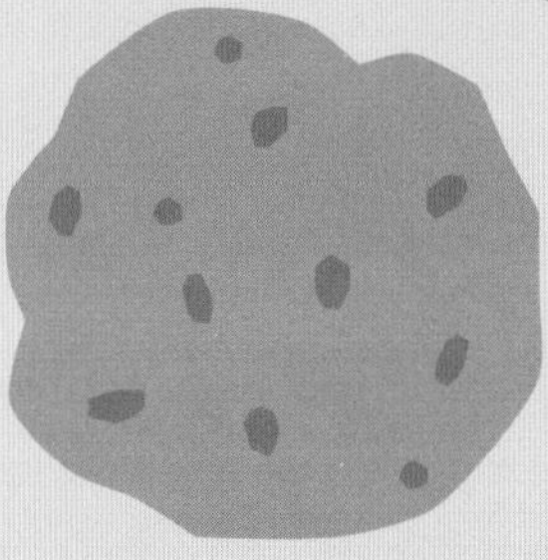

50 g (½ cup) grated parmesan

Preheat the oven to 200°C (fan-forced). Line a baking tray with baking paper.

Pour 1 tablespoon mounds of parmesan onto the baking paper, leaving about 2 cm between each one as they will spread. Bake for 3–5 minutes or until golden and crisp. Allow them to cool completely before you take them off the tray.

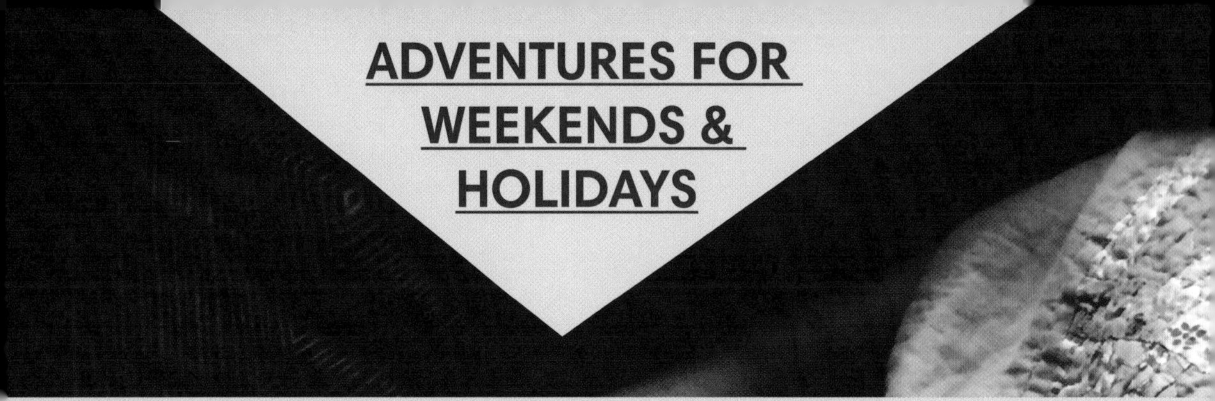

ADVENTURES FOR WEEKENDS & HOLIDAYS

Breaking the winter blues

When the girls were small I moved our family to one of the coldest parts of Australia. Cold, as in it snowed there one Christmas.

This was an interesting move as I can't stand winter. I mean, it starts off OK and you get to enjoy a glass of red in front of a fire for the first time in months. But eventually this gets old and could actually develop into a drinking problem.

When we first moved there we fully embraced hibernation. The novelty factor was high and the Bureau of Meteorology was our favourite source of entertainment, featuring the 'guess how freaking cold it is outside' game. But as the years went on, the game became boring and predictable. Yes yes, it's freezing outside. Again.

And winter is really, really long in that part of the world, lasting for at least six months of the year. Think about that. If we don't leave the house during the colder months, we are literally spending half our lives hiding under a doona.

The day I cracked was a doozy.

The rain hadn't stopped for days. It was dark at 3.30 pm. The wind was howling. My car was caked in mud. So was the house. So were our clothes. So was the dog.

When the girls and I got home from school we stared at each other glumly, knowing we were in for yet another afternoon of being stuck inside. Finally, I exclaimed 'SCREW THIS! Put your coats back on, we're going out.'

We walked through the forest in the rain. It sounded beautiful, it smelled beautiful, and the colours were wonderfully saturated. Just as we were giving the finger to winter, winter showed us a whole new world we'd never thought to experience before.

Don't get me wrong, you won't find me tramping through the forest every time it pours with rain. But it did make me realise that I had a choice about how I experienced cold, dark afternoons. I could fight against it, or embrace it.

And we have our metaphor, right there.

Kids with birthdays in winter

My girls' birthdays couldn't be more different. One is in the peak of awesome weather and the other is smack bang in the middle of winter.

The warm-weather birthday parties are no-brainers, apart from this year's party where a giant swarm of wasps descended on the food table, which then led to a swift evacuation of children to the safety of inside (which we all know is the worst-case scenario for kids' parties, NEVER bring a party inside ... EVER). But apart from the case of the killer wasps, Pepper's parties are pretty easy.

Then there is Maya. My mid-winter babe.

I'm pretty sure this wasn't as much of a problem before Pepper was around, as there was nothing to directly compare it with. Indoor, rainy-day parties were what we did.

But I have to admit that when Pepper came along, I was a little dazzled by the warm-day party lights. I mean, I love to throw a good party and when the conditions are right, I tend to throw myself in all guns blazing. But when the weather is a downer, the vibes are lower and the party enthusiasm tends to wane.

I decided I had to look at this winter party thing differently.

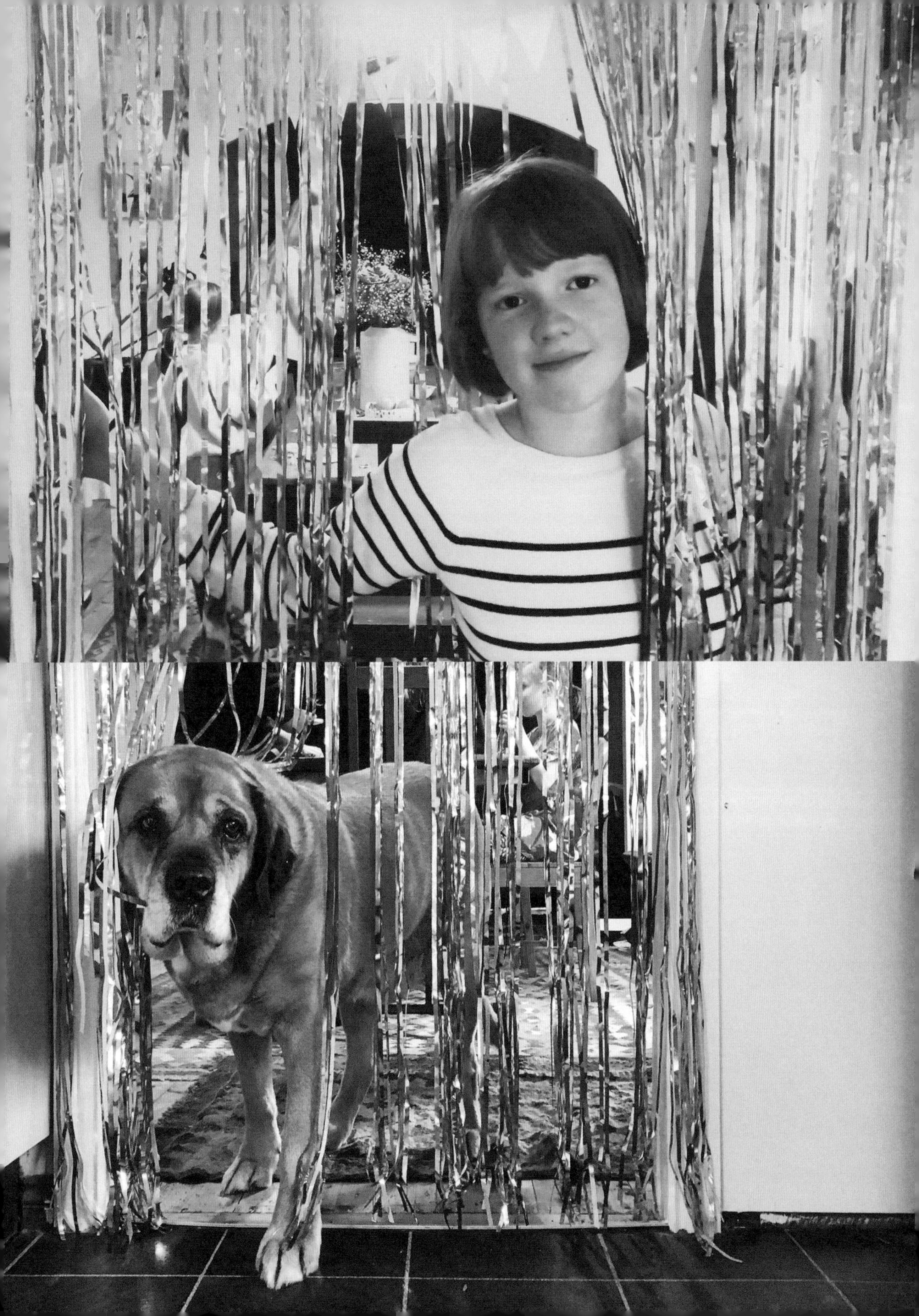

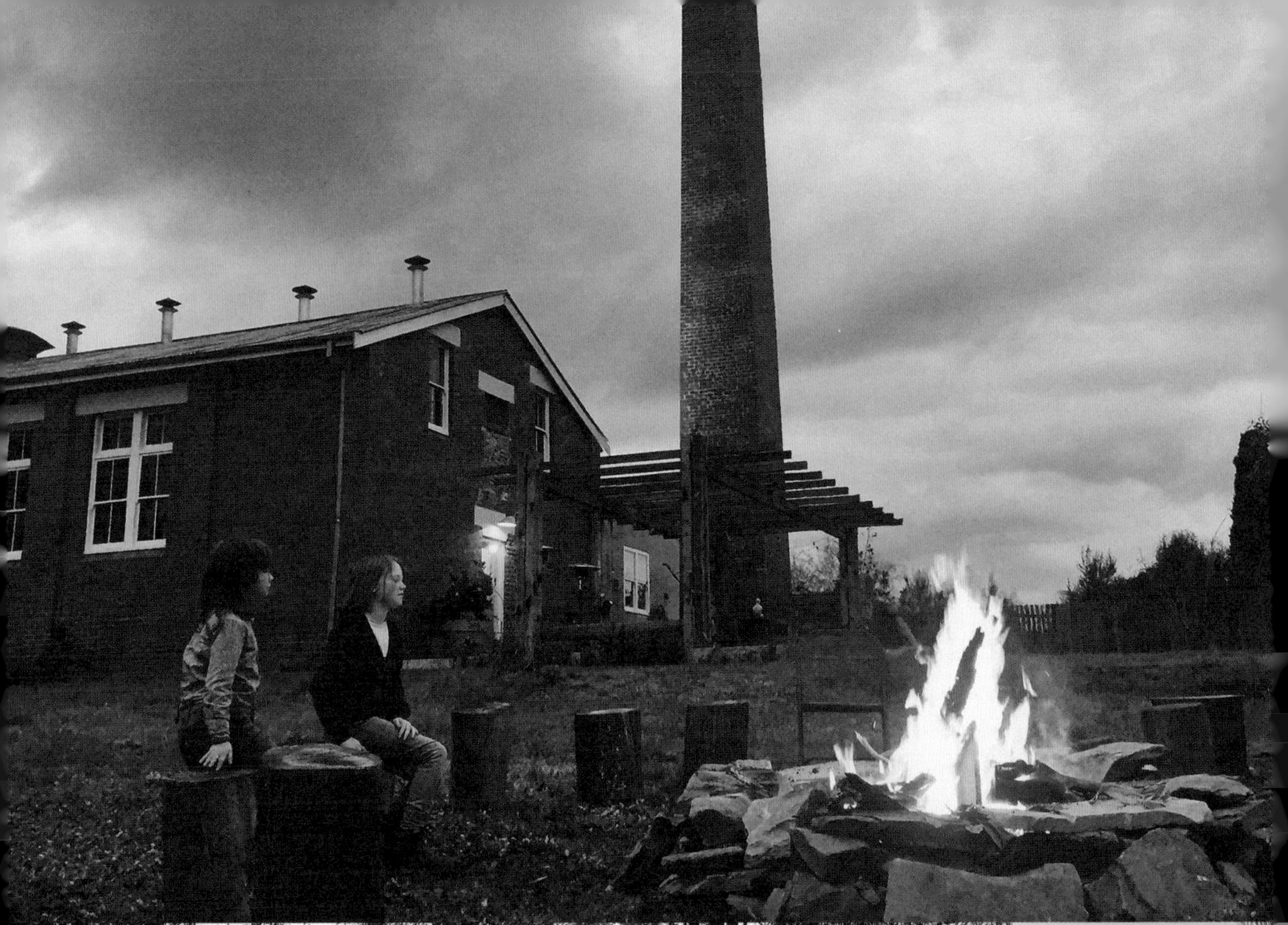

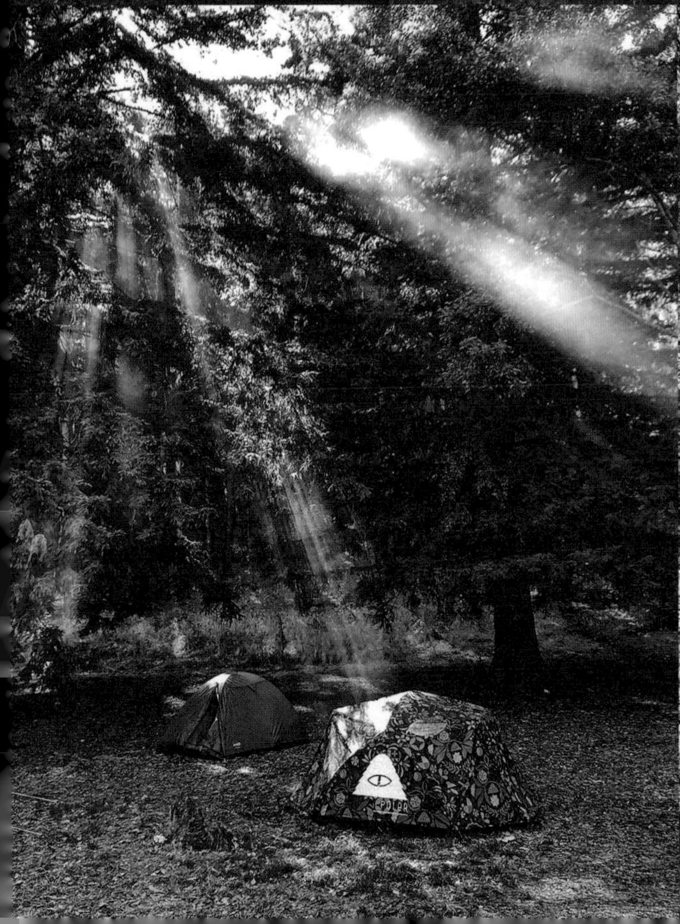

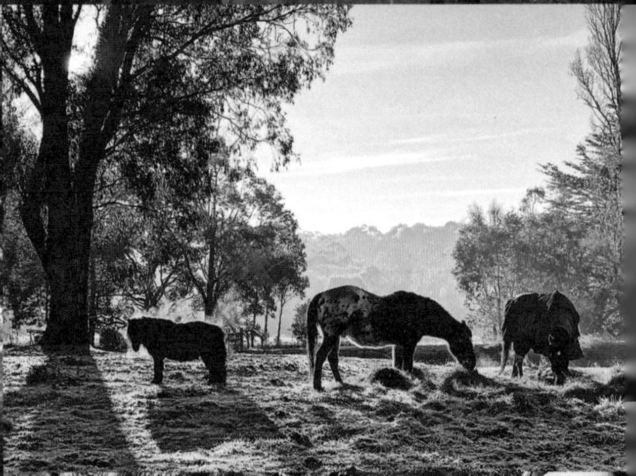

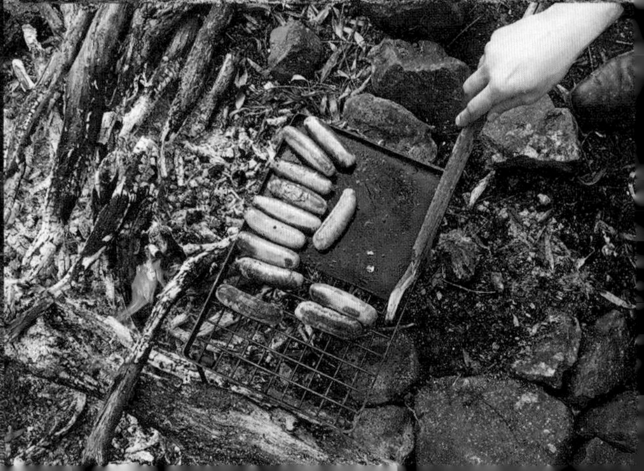

What are the cool things we do in winter that we can't do in the hotter months of the year? Well, there's only one real answer ... fire. So, for Maya's twelfth birthday we packed up our little caravan and took way too many of her friends to our local dormant volcano for a campfire sleep-over.

You know, campfire food beats summer party food hands down. There are bananas in foil, potatoes in foil, sausages on sticks, damper on sticks, marshmallows on sticks, and a kid's eye which is inevitably poked with a stick!

Once everyone was fed we snuggled up by the fire and out-ghost storied each other. I really had no idea kids this age knew such gruesome stuff. Was I that feral when I was 12? Probably.

When we got home and unpacked the caravan, Pepper came up and asked 'Mum, can I have a campfire party for my birthday?'. 'Sorry Peps, you're not allowed to have fires in March' I replied. The tables had turned and the winter babe had taken the party mantle.

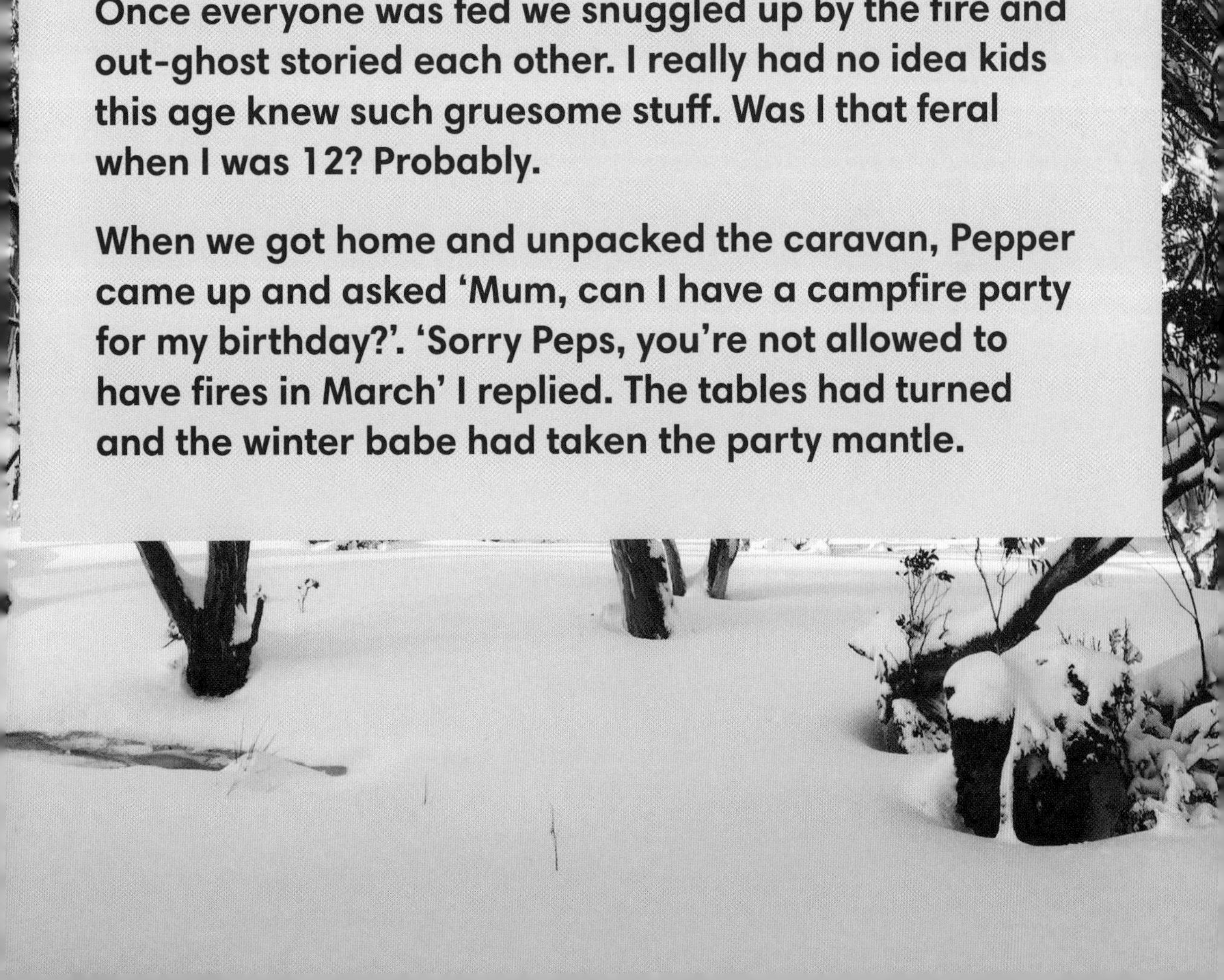

Stupid stuff

You know that stupid stuff you used to do when you were younger? Not the dumb stupid stuff, but the exciting, no fear, throw yourself into something you're excited about with total abandon stuff. Actioning ideas that may not work, but who cares? Waking up at 2.30 am and thinking, 'I should go for a drive' and then actually doing it.

I did that once. It was amazing.

What happens to that person when we grow up? Where does the spark and sparkle go? I know we have to be more responsible because we have kids to look after and bills to pay, but surely there's still time to be a little daring, a little us. A friend of mine, who once owned the coolest car on the planet, told me they were selling it 'because, you know, we should get something a little more sensible'. I died inside. Who were these people?

I guess we all get a little scared when we get older. We don't want to mess up, otherwise the perfect balance we work so hard for will topple, and we'll have to start all over again. But maybe it doesn't have to be big risky things; it could be things like when your kid asks you to roll down the big grassy hill with them and you say YES! (Just so you know, it feels way more intense as a grown-up so don't stand up too fast.)

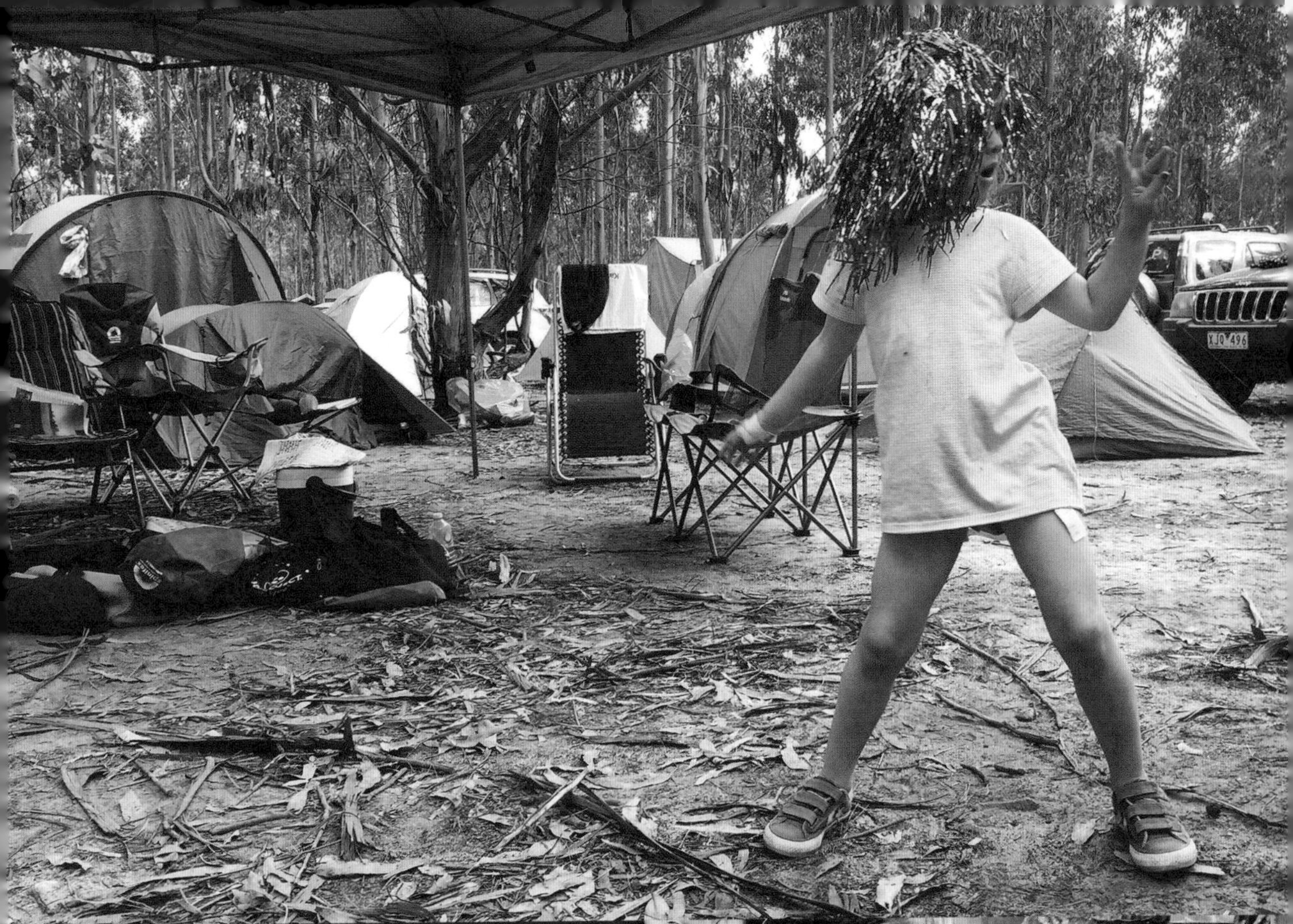

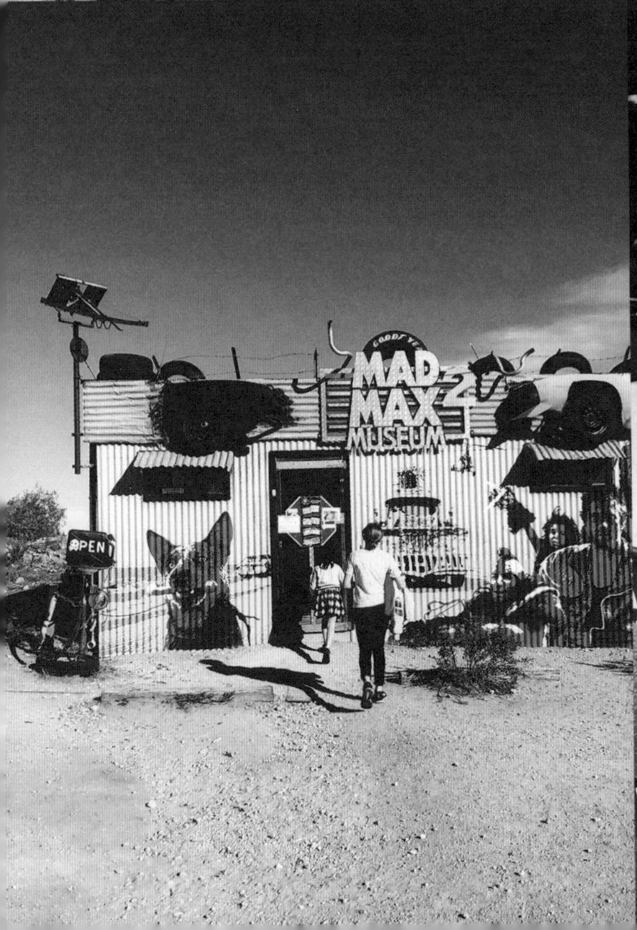
MAD MAX 2
MUSEUM
OPEN

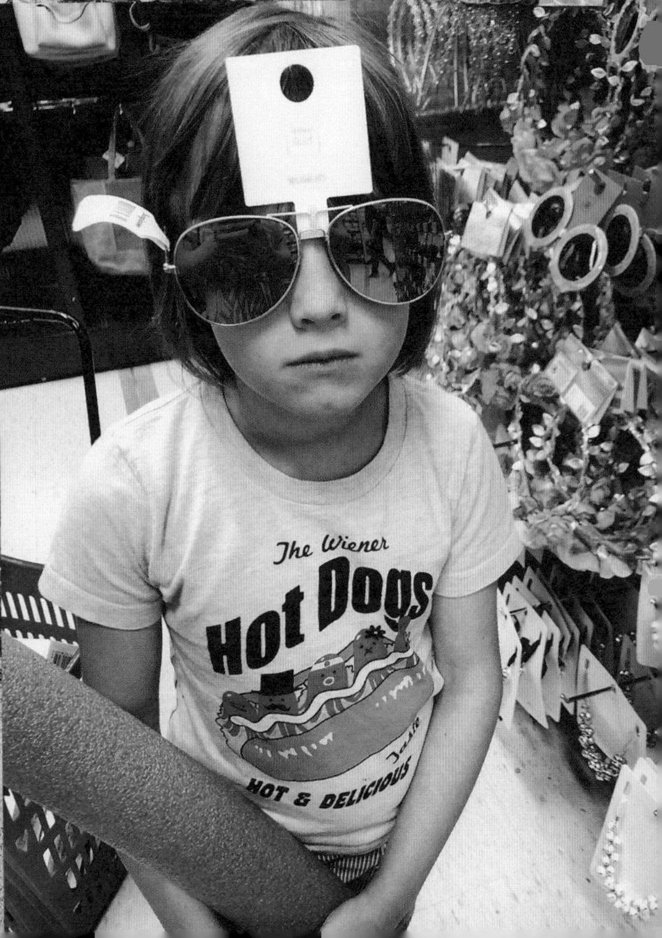
The Wiener
Hot Dogs
HOT & DELICIOUS

Stepping out of our comfort zone is hard and at one point I found myself saying no to everything. I was so consumed by the responsibilities of my life that I forgot that if I just let myself go once in a while, I can connect with the person I actually am on the inside. But once I remembered, I was off. I started doing things like taking myself to dinner and eating like a pig, getting home delivery and eating like a pig, buying a giant ice cream that has all the flavours I want but can't decide between, dancing like a maniac for as long as I can until I start feeling like an idiot but then trying to push through because no one actually cares but me.

But my favourite is doing stupid stuff with my kids. They're not entirely sure how to take it. They look at me oddly, even suspiciously, and then break out into the biggest smiles when they realise that pancakes for dinner is happening, and it isn't a set up.

It's like a mini holiday. Reclaiming a little bit of you, in a shared moment of joy.

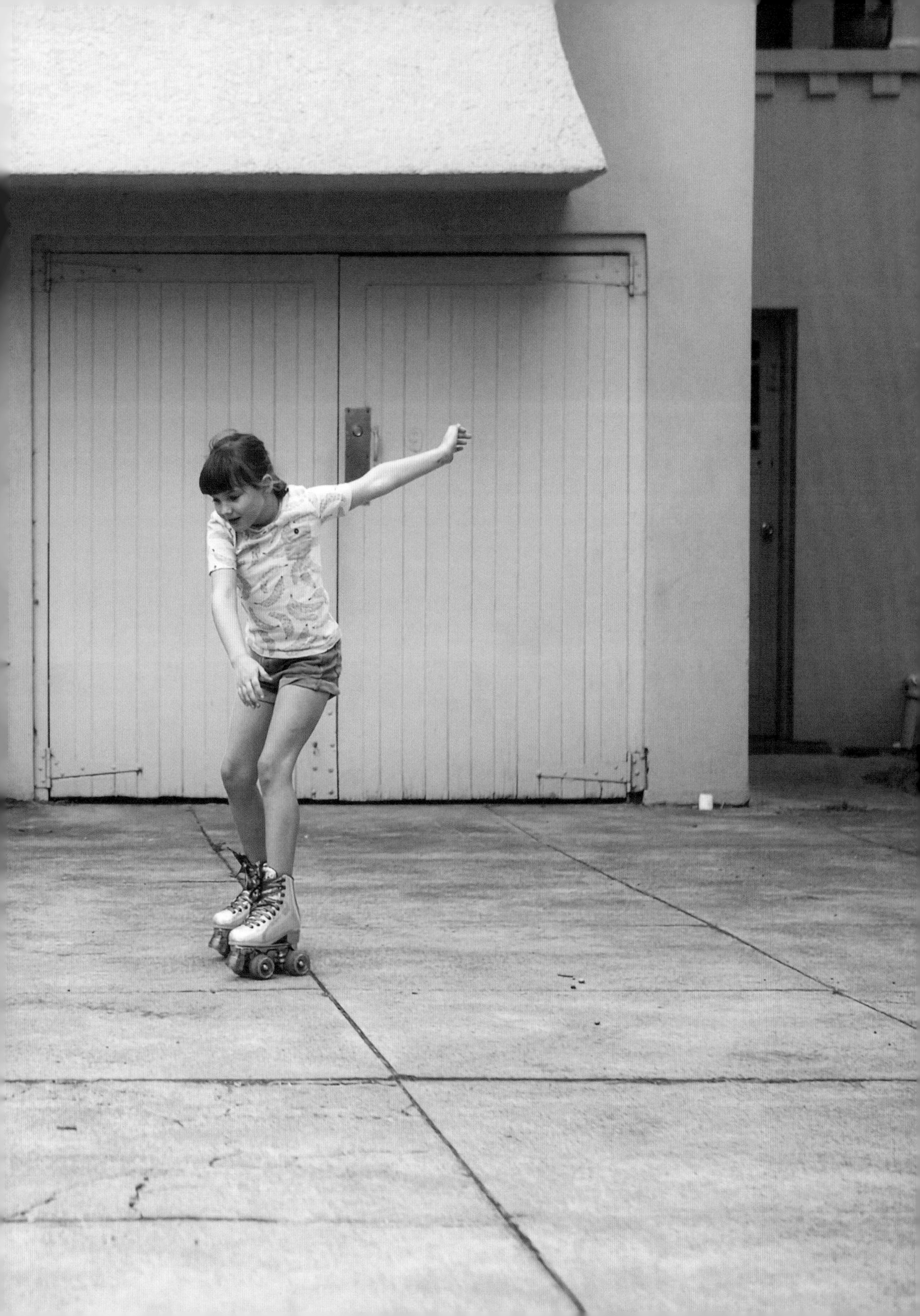

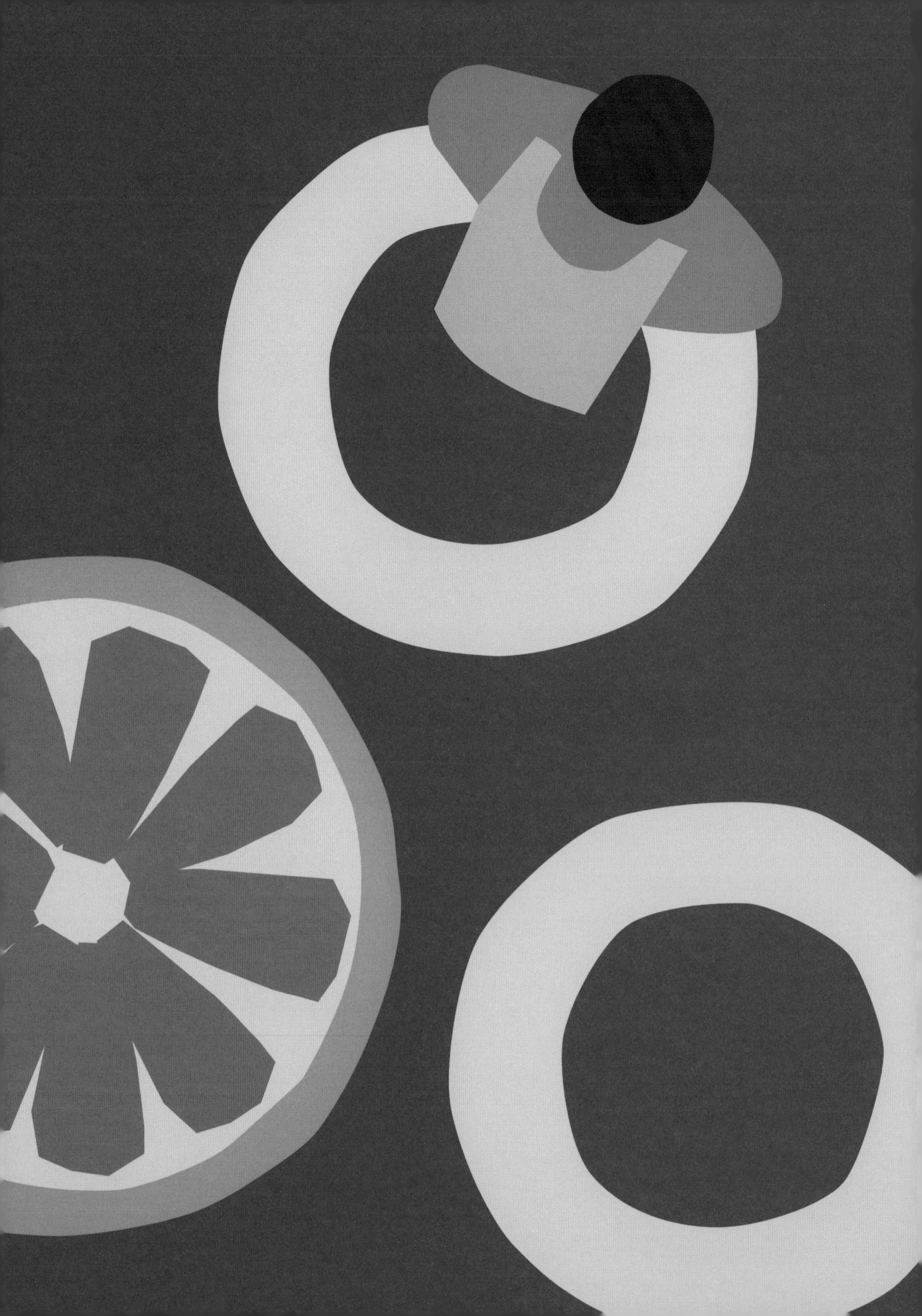

Term

4

Getting through the longest holiday, having 'the talk', and dealing with Santa

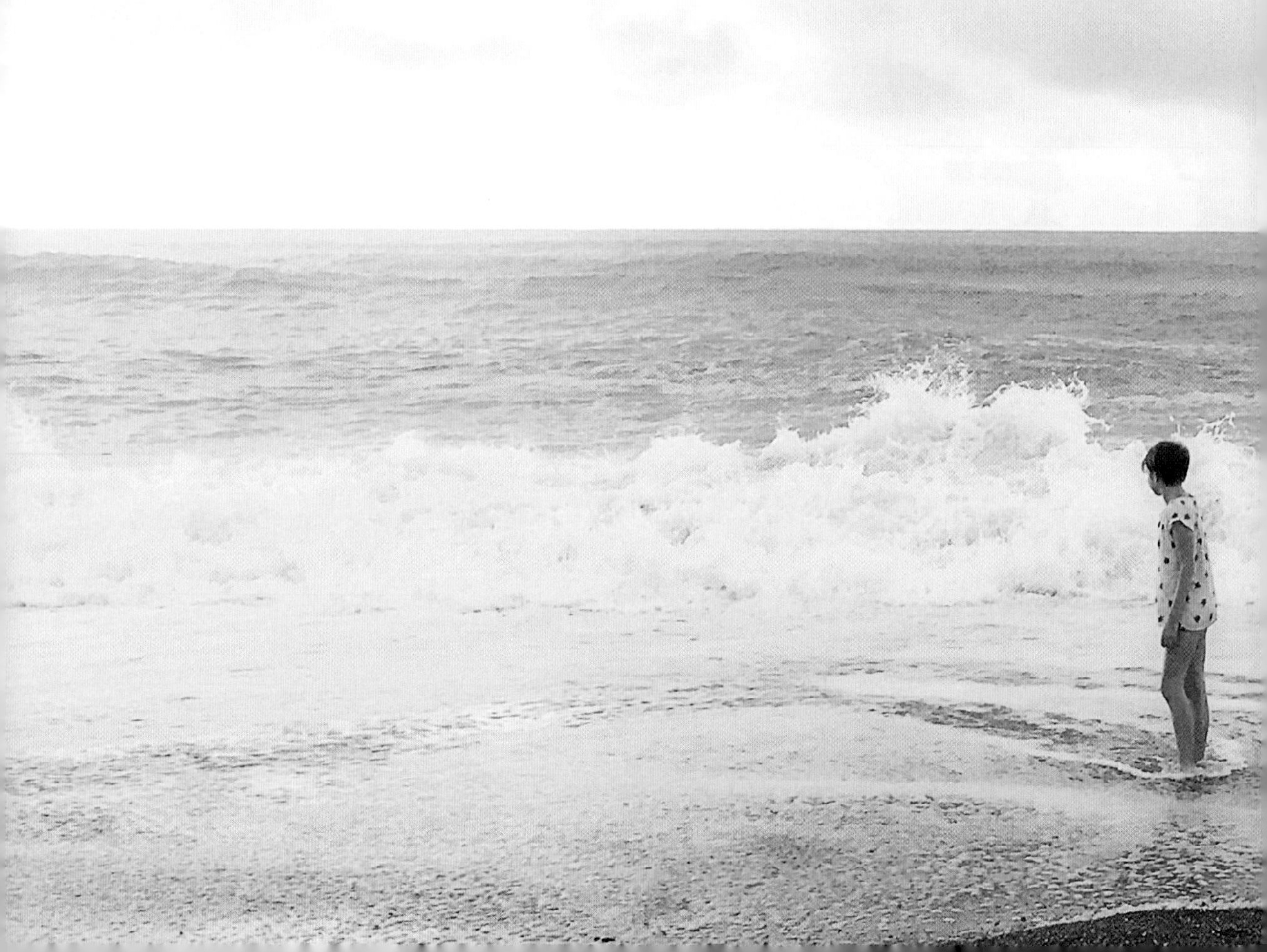

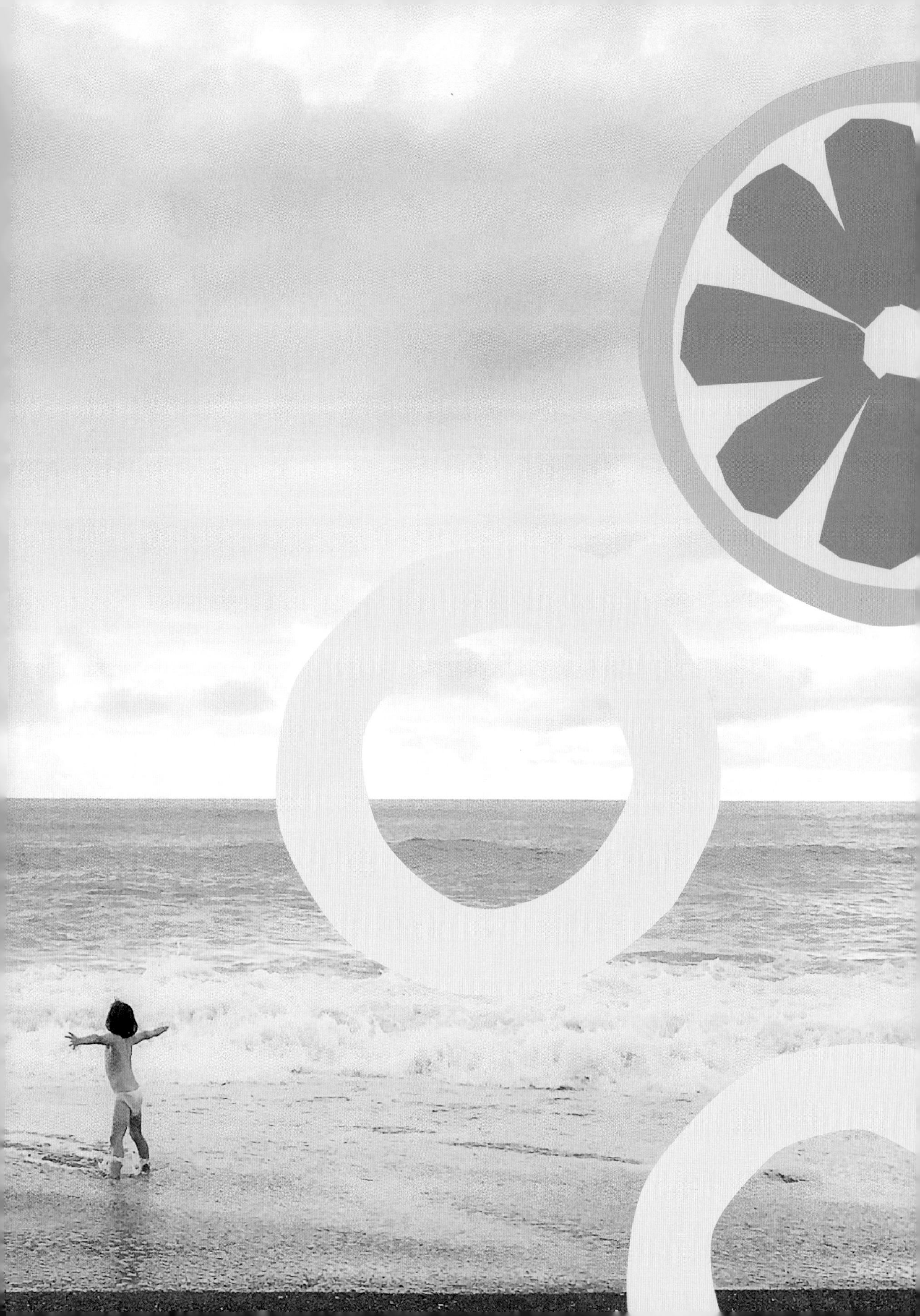

The long haul

When you're 22, long hot summer holidays are the most exciting time of your life. Zero cares, zero responsibilities and, for most, zero children. These long hot days and nights are dreamy, boozy and filled with whatever the hell you want.

But that was 20 years ago, and now summer holidays are all about the insane mismatch of kids' school holidays and annual leave. I still have no idea how it's meant to work. For most of my working life I've been a freelancer, so I never had to worry about it. But now that I'm having to face the possibility of a 'real job' it's hit me like a ton of bricks. Initially I loved the idea of someone putting money in my bank account every week, until I had to deal with the question of who's going to look after my kids.

Instead of boozy nights and hungover mornings, these long hot summer days are now a sweaty juggling act, full of tenuous, patched-together childcare plans. Where the tiniest misstep turns hard-won plans into total chaos. Your entire working day swings from wondering how well the plan is going to checking your phone for any missed calls, all the while pushing that mum guilt down, down, down.

Any time we have to outsource parenting, it hits us right in the mum guilt. It doesn't matter what we're

doing – it could be popping out for a couple of hours, working full time, or even working from home with the telly playing babysitter. It hurts. We feel like failures, and we're always trying to find ways to make it better.

But sometimes that's it. Sometimes that is 'better', and we just have to make peace with that. We're doing our best. We love our kids, and not being in their faces 24/7 doesn't mean we don't. At the moment I'm struggling with the idea of not being able to take my kids to and from school, but how many parents actually get to do that these days? I'm suffering from the classic dilemma of wanting to be the homemaker and the breadwinner, but it's just not possible. Sadly, I need to pick a side and I know which side has to lose out.

The funny thing is, my kids probably love the endless supply of crap they get to eat at Nan's, or the long stays at my best friend's house (we take turns looking after each other's kids during the school holidays). I'm sure the girls miss me every now and then but the guilt I feel is SO likely outweighed by icy poles, mixed lollies, fish and chips and days spent at the pool.

The juggle is real. 'Living the dream' is not. Making our own version of the dream is the way to go and actually being good with that is even better. Otherwise it'll all ends in tears and disappointment. And that's no holiday for anyone.

FRUIT AND NUT CHOCOLATE BREKKIE

Cherry Compote and Overnight Oats

SERVES 4-6

Making cafe-style brekkies is one of my favourite things to do for the girls. I'm a sucker for a compliment, so when I place a couple of bowls of this in front of them and get a bit of 'ooooh … that's fancy, Mum', my day is pretty much made.

200 g (2 cups) rolled oats
430 ml (1¾ cups) milk of
  your choice
3 tablespoons apple juice
3 tablespoons lemon juice
1-2 tablespoons runny honey
375 g (1½) cups plain yoghurt
sprinkle of ground cinnamon
nuts, seeds and smashed
  chocolate, to serve

For the compote:
about 675 g (3 cups) cherries
2 tablespoons sugar
80 ml (⅓ cup) orange or
  lemon juice

To make the compote, wash and pit the cherries. If you don't have a cherry pitter, you can use a straw to push the pits out! Place the cherries in a medium saucepan, add the sugar and juice and cook over medium heat for 5–6 minutes or until the cherries are soft.

Remove the cherries with a slotted spoon and cook the liquid for a further 3 minutes or until thickened and reduced by half. Return the cherries to the pan and stir through the liquid. Pour into a clean jar and store in the fridge for up to 2 weeks.

Combine the oats, milk, apple juice and lemon juice in a medium bowl, then leave to sit in the fridge overnight.

In the morning, add the honey, yoghurt and cinnamon and mix well. Top with cherry compote, nuts, seeds and chocolate and serve with pride.

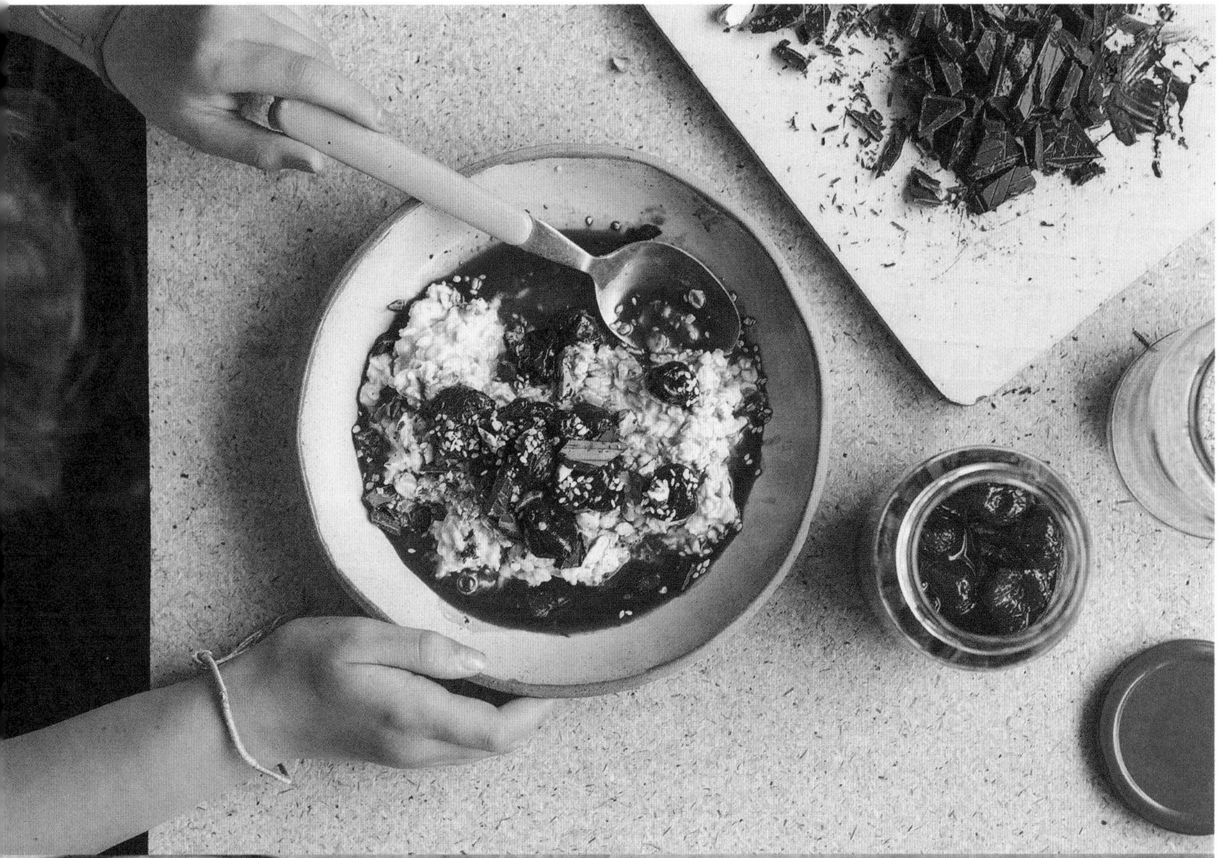

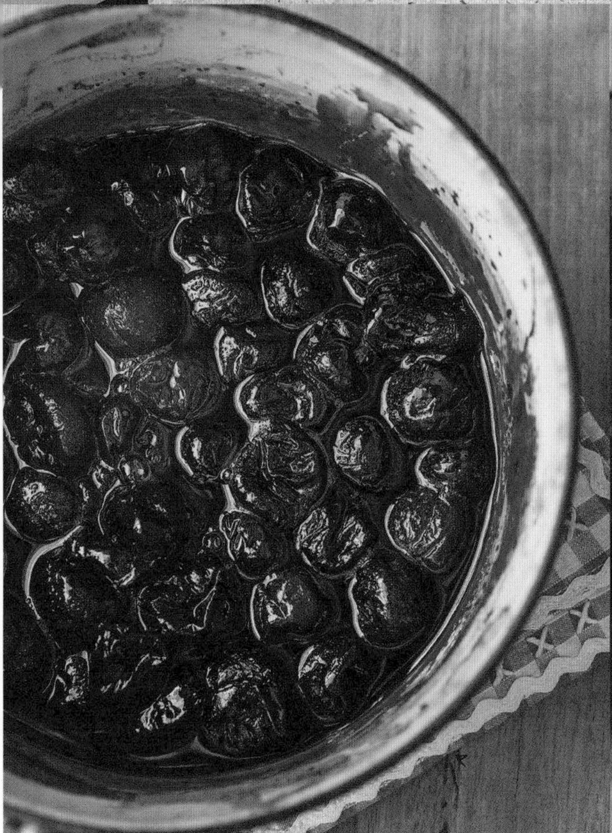

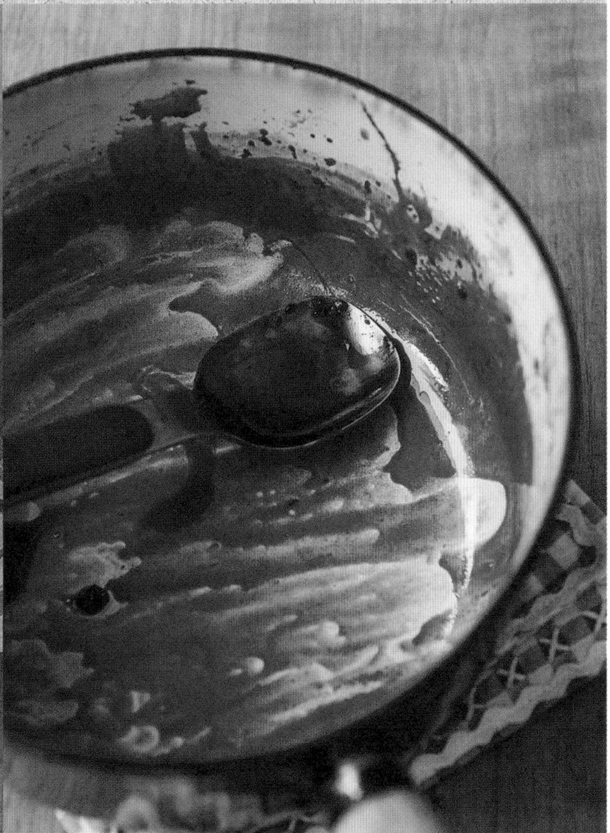

BACK TO BASICS

BUTTERMILK PANCAKES

SERVES 4

There really isn't anything better than a weekend with no plans ... unless you make pancakes your plans.

300 g (2 cups) self-raising flour
¾ teaspoon salt
2 free-range eggs
40 g butter, melted
500 ml (2 cups) buttermilk
butter, for cooking

Pop the flour and salt in a mixing bowl and whisk together.

Beat the eggs in a separate bowl, then add the melted butter and whisk until combined.

Add 250 ml (1 cup) buttermilk and mix well.

Pour the egg mixture into the dry ingredients and whisk to form a thick batter with no lumps. Now slowly add the remaining buttermilk, whisking constantly until smooth and well combined.

Heat a large non-stick frying pan over medium heat and add a knob of butter. Pour 3 tablespoons of batter for each pancake into the pan (cook as many as you can fit without them sticking together) and cook until bubbles appear on the top. Flip them over and cook the other side until golden. Remove and keep warm (or eat!) while you cook the rest. Serve warm with any of the usual suspects (maple syrup and ice cream, lemon and sugar, or jam and cream).

Combos to try:

Blueberry (or any berry really)
Make the pancakes as described, but sprinkle with blueberries before flipping.

Banana and cinnamon
Make the pancake batter as described, then fold through ½ teaspoon of ground cinnamon and 2 mashed bananas. Continue with the recipe.

Chocolate chip
Make the pancakes as described, but sprinkle with chocolate chips before flipping.

Carrot cake
Make the pancake batter as described, then add 1 teaspoon of ground cinnamon, ¼ teaspoon of ground ginger, ¼ teaspoon of freshly grated nutmeg, 1/8 teaspoon of ground cloves, 2 tablespoons of brown sugar, 1 ½ teaspoons of vanilla extract and 235 g (1 ½ cups) of finely grated carrot and mix well. Continue with the recipe.

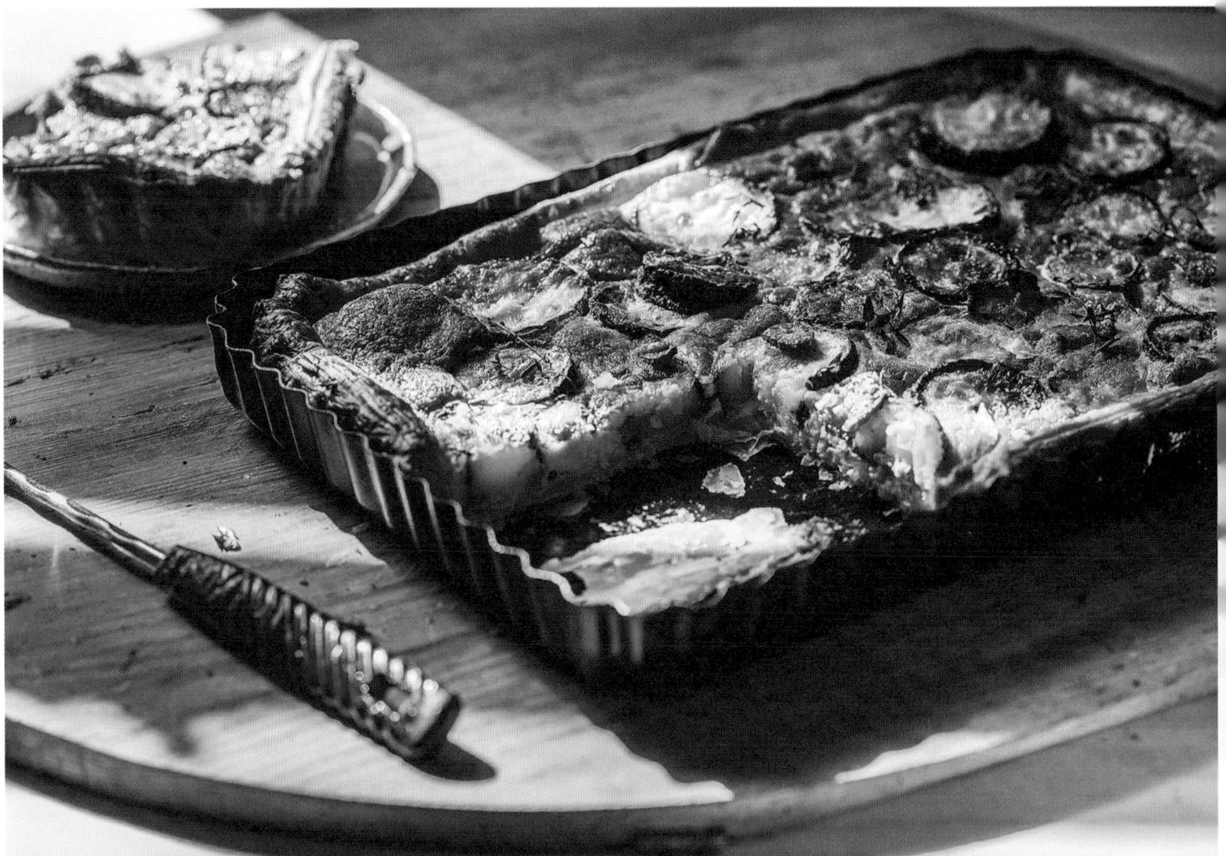

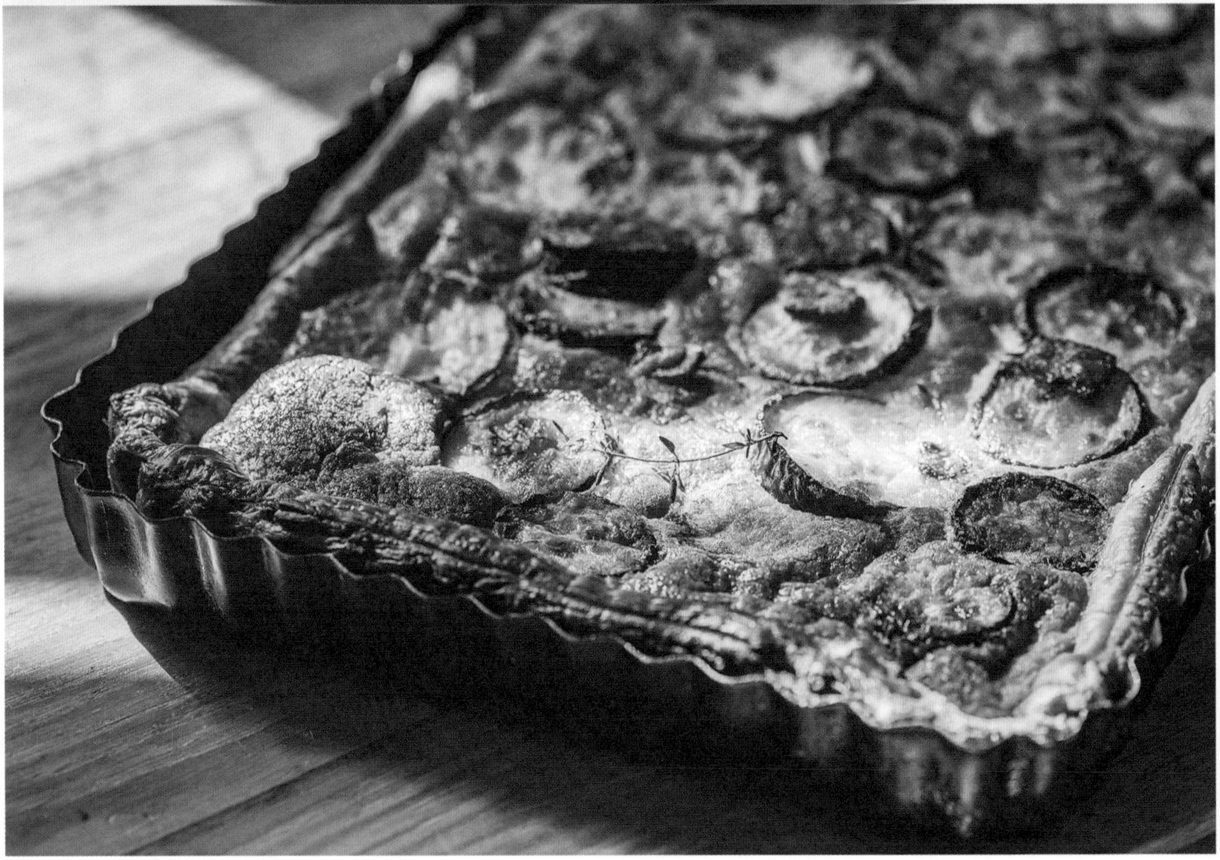

ZUKES AND BACON

Zucchini, Bacon and Thyme Tart

SERVES 6

Zucchini season always starts off with excitement and ends in 'if I see another freaking zucchini …' so it's good to arm yourself with a few handy recipes to get rid of those guys at peak season. Tarts are great because it's easy to make heaps of them, and you can just pop them in the freezer for less productive days.

1 sheet frozen puff pastry, thawed
olive oil, for pan-frying
3–4 zucchini, cut into 2 cm thick rounds
salt
150 g bacon, rind removed, sliced
3 large free-range eggs
125 ml (½ cup) double cream
½ cup grated parmesan
a few thyme sprigs

Preheat the oven to 200°C (fan-forced). Grease and flour a 30 cm x 20 cm tart tin or high-sided baking tin.

Roll out the puff pastry into a large rectangle and lay it over the prepared tin. Gently lower the pastry into the tin and press the pastry into the sides, then roll a rolling pin over the top to cut away any excess pastry.

Cover the pastry with a sheet of baking paper and fill it with baking beans or weights (you can use rice, lentils, beans or any other dried pulses you have in the pantry).

Pop the tin in the oven and blind-bake for 15 minutes. Remove the baking paper and weights, then bake for another 3–5 minutes or until nice and crisp. Set aside to cool completely before you add the filling.

While that's in the oven, heat a good splash of olive oil in a frying pan over medium heat, add the zucchini and salt and cook for 5 minutes or until the zucchini begins to colour. Add the bacon and cook for another 3–5 minutes or until crisp. Set aside to cool.

Whisk together the eggs and cream in a medium bowl, then add the cheese and season with salt. Add the cooled zucchini mixture and stir to combine.

Pour the filling into the pastry case and scatter over the thyme. Bake for 20–25 minutes or until golden and set. Serve warm with a green salad.

Talking the talk

There they were, sitting on the bookshelf in the musty op shop: *Where Did I Come From?* and *What's Happening to Me?* These books left an indelible mark on my childhood. We all had them. But in my experience there was no question of parents sitting down and going through the books with their kids. Instead, they were strategically placed in our bedrooms for us to discover in the hope that this would cover 'the talk'.

I hadn't broached 'the talk' with either of the girls yet. We'd mentioned stuff here and there and hung tampons from our ears, but nothing formal. But, seeing as we were now on a long road trip, I had a captive audience and the materials had been presented to me at such a reasonable price, I took the plunge.

We jumped back in the car, showed off our op shop scores, and I began. 'Hey guys, look at these books I found in the op shop!' I quickly realised how outdated they were, which was a good thing in a way, as it prompted a deeper conversation than 'the man sticks his penis in the vagina'. In the 80s, consent and women's pleasure weren't high on the agenda.

I had always been petrified of having these conversations with the girls. I am notorious for

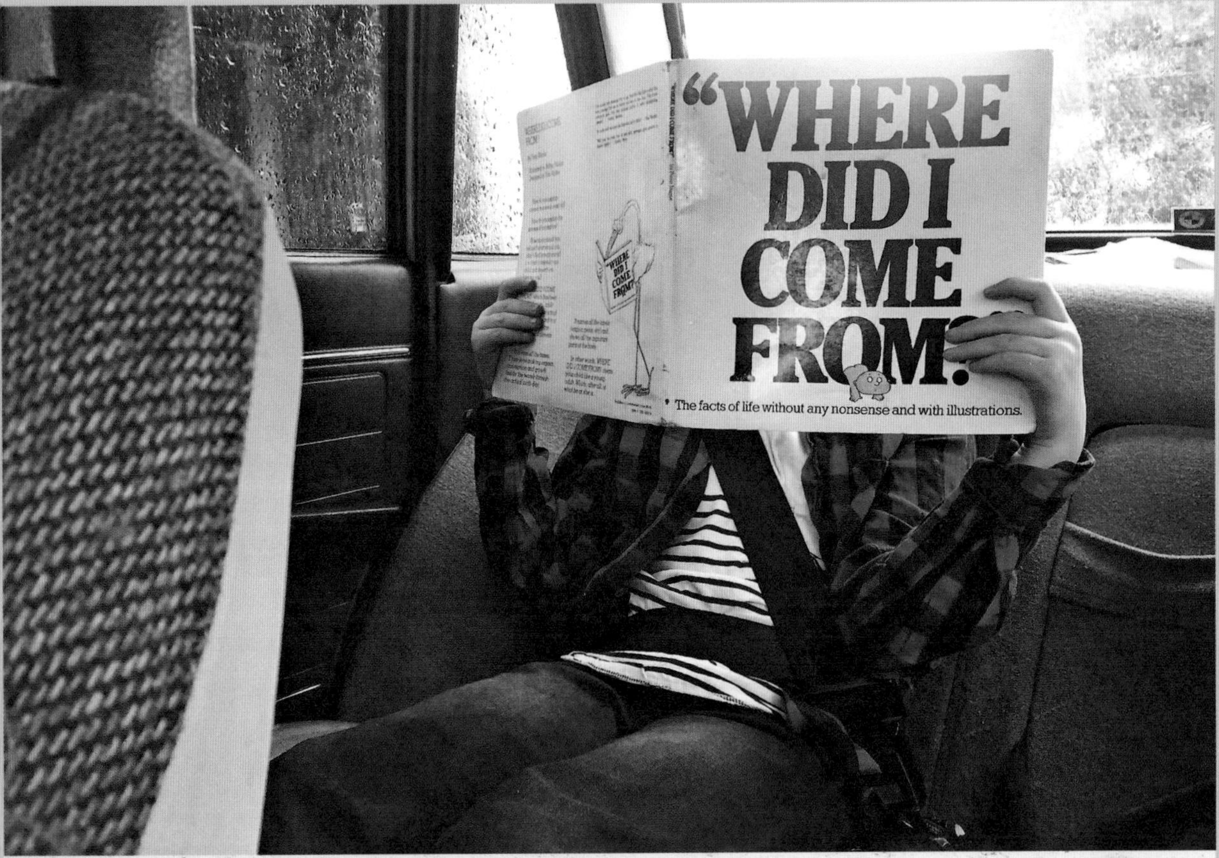
"WHERE DID I COME FROM?"
The facts of life without any nonsense and with illustrations.

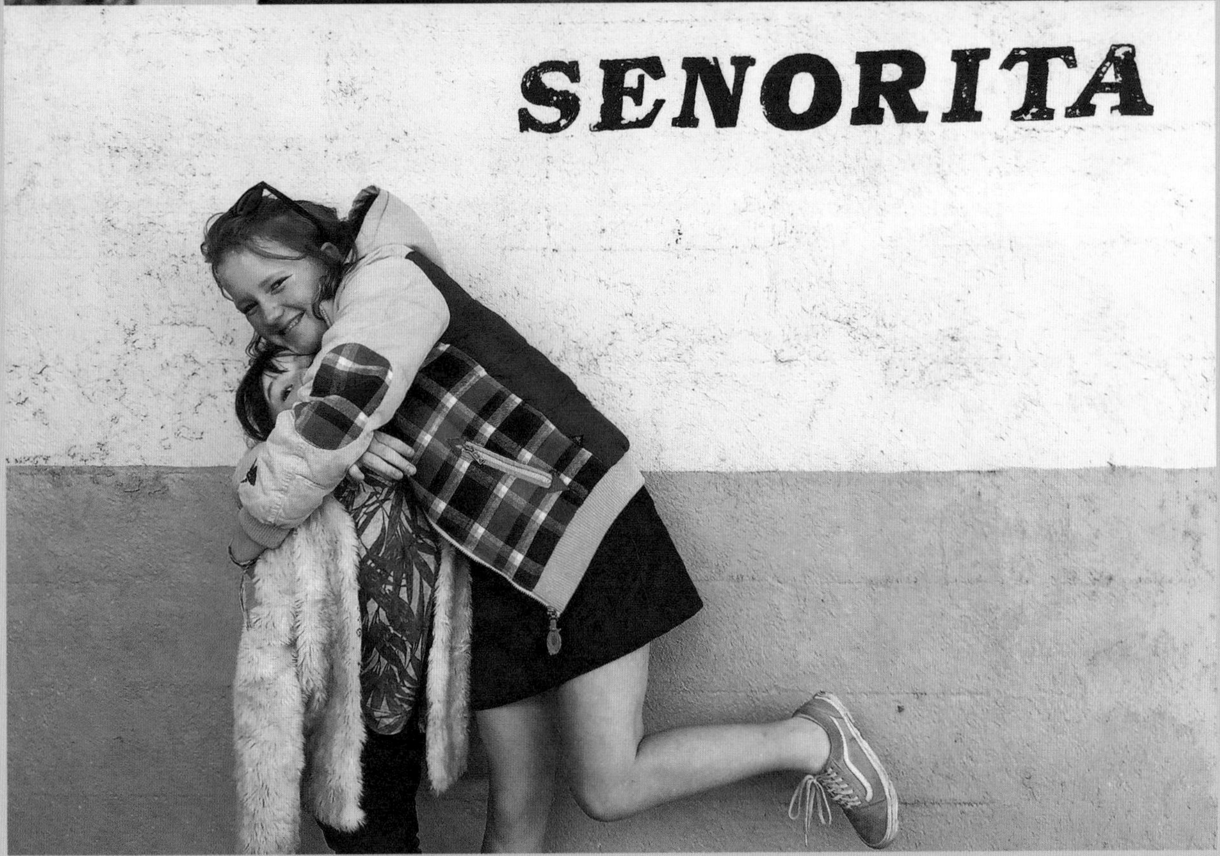
SENORITA

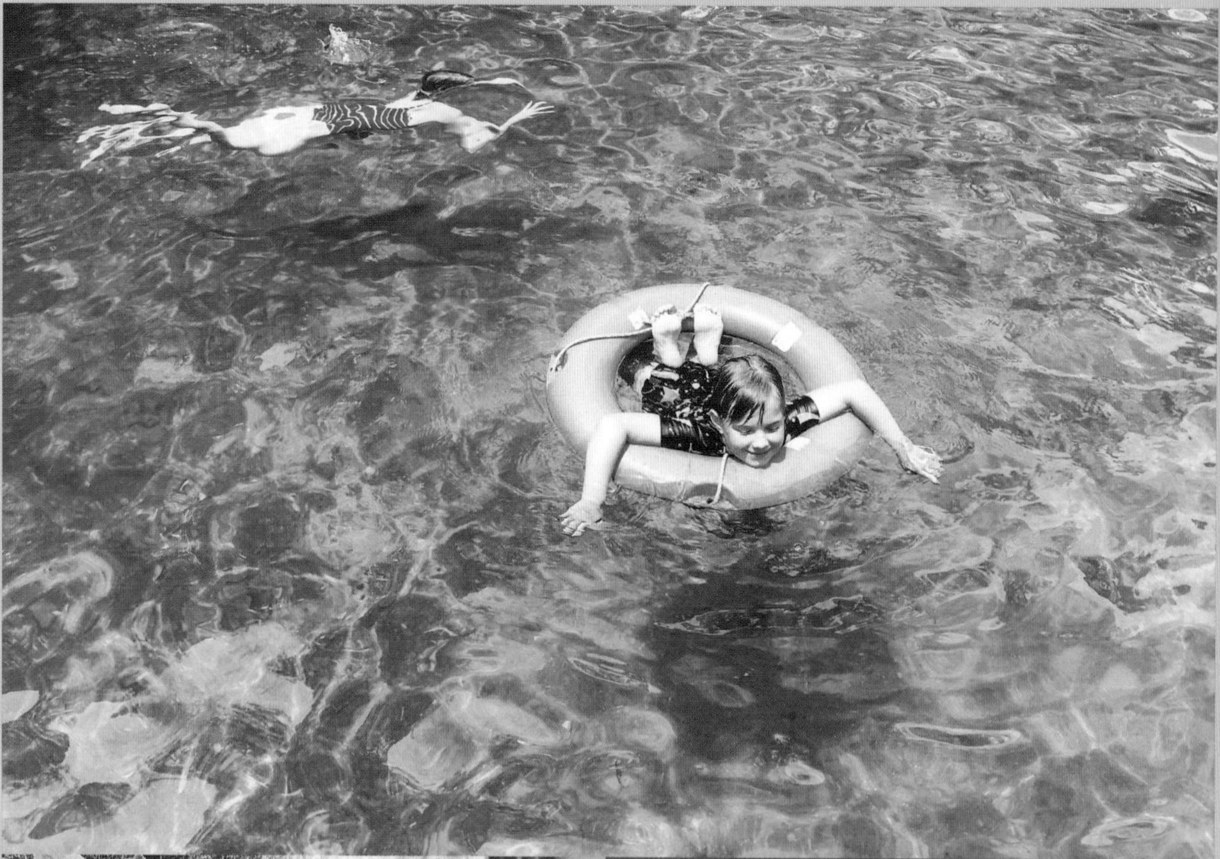
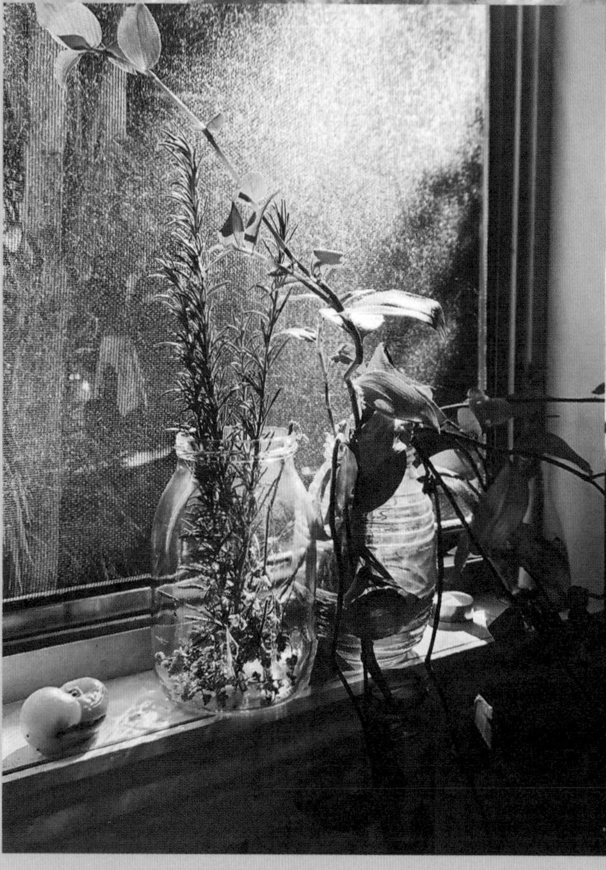
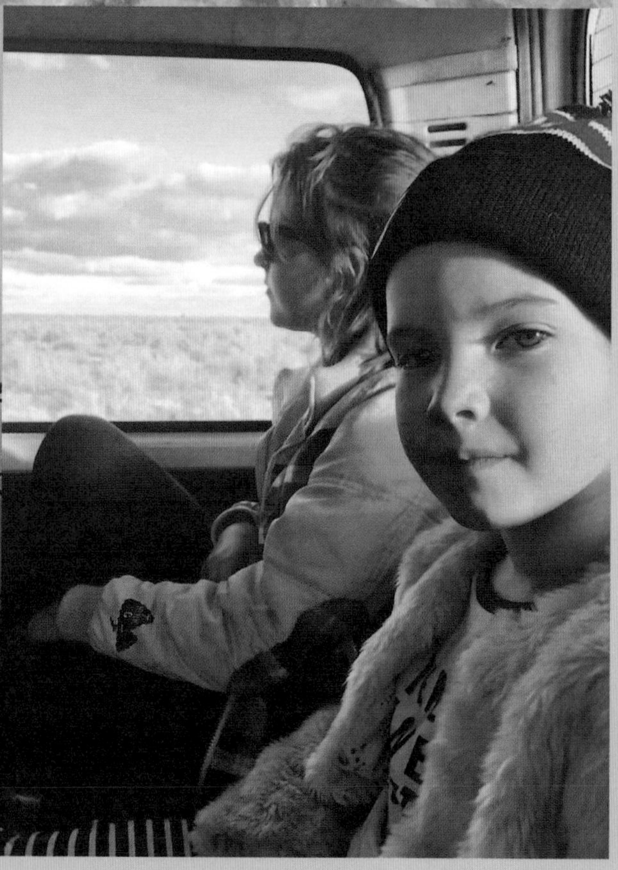

making light of things I'm uncomfortable with.
And while I know it's good to keep these conversations light, it's also really serious stuff. I want my girls to feel they can talk to me about their worries and if I'm making jokes about it all, that's not going to foster a safe space. I need to grow up a little and face my own issues concerning 'the talk'. Recently, I learned about how our grown-up experiences can colour the way we approach these conversations with our kids. I need to push through this and not let my past damage how my girls see their sexuality.

I grew up in a time when sex and puberty weren't really discussed openly. In my childhood home there was a lot of embarrassment, and almost shame, associated with these issues. As I've grown older, I've come to understand why that might have been, coming from a long line of women dealing with pain. And this made me see that I NEED to break the cycle. I NEED to empower my girls to be strong and confident.

We zoomed along the highway in our orange Volvo, from the same era as the outdated and slightly inappropriate sex ed books of my childhood. At the tender ages of nine and four, my girls could tell me what was wrong with how these themes were presented and, in a way, I guess that means I am doing an OK job.

GREEN FRITTERS

Spring Veggie Fritters with Cucumber Yoghurt

MAKES 16-18 FRITTERS

Fritters are a bit of a fave for us. I like them because I can cook a ton of them for dinner and then chuck the leftovers in the girls' lunchboxes the next day. The girls like them because they're fried and have a dipping sauce. I like them for that reason too, actually.

220 g green beans, quartered
220 g fresh or frozen and
    thawed peas
220 g podded and peeled
    broad beans
4 spring onions, green and
    white parts, sliced
1 garlic clove, crushed
finely grated zest of 1 lemon
salt and pepper
1 free-range egg
300 g (2 cups) plain flour
560 ml (2¼ cups) sparkling
    water
sunflower or vegetable oil,
    for shallow-frying
pinch of sumac
your choice of fresh herbs,
    to serve (optional)

For the cucumber yoghurt:
½ Lebanese cucumber,
    coarsely grated
salt
500 g (2 cups) plain yoghurt
3 tablespoons extra-virgin
    olive oil
juice of ½ lemon
1 garlic clove, crushed
handful of mint leaves,
    roughly chopped
salt and pepper

To make a start on the cucumber yoghurt, pop the grated cucumber in a colander over a bowl. Add a big pinch of salt and rub it into the cucumber, then leave for about an hour to get rid of the excess water.

While that's happening, make the fritter mixture. Combine the green beans, peas, broad beans, spring onion, garlic, lemon zest, salt and pepper in a large bowl.

In a separate bowl, mix together the egg and flour, then slowly whisk in the sparkling water. It should be the consistency of thick cream so take it slowly – you may not need all the water.

Pour the batter into the bowl with the veggies and mix well.

Preheat the oven to its lowest setting. You just need it to keep the fritters warm.

Heat a generous amount of sunflower or vegetable oil in a large heavy-based frying pan over medium–high heat. It's ready when you pop a piece of veg in there and it sizzles.

Add heaped tablespoons of batter to the oil and be careful not to get spattered. Fry the fritters for 2–3 minutes each side or until golden brown and cooked through. Remove with a slotted spoon and drain on paper towel. Keep warm in the oven while you cook the remaining fritters.

To finish off the cucumber yoghurt, give the cucumber a squeeze to remove the last bits of water. Place in a mixing bowl with the yoghurt, olive oil, lemon juice, garlic and mint and stir well. Season with salt and pepper.

To serve, spoon the cucumber yoghurt onto plates and pop the fritters on top. Sprinkle with sumac and top with some fresh herbs, if you like.

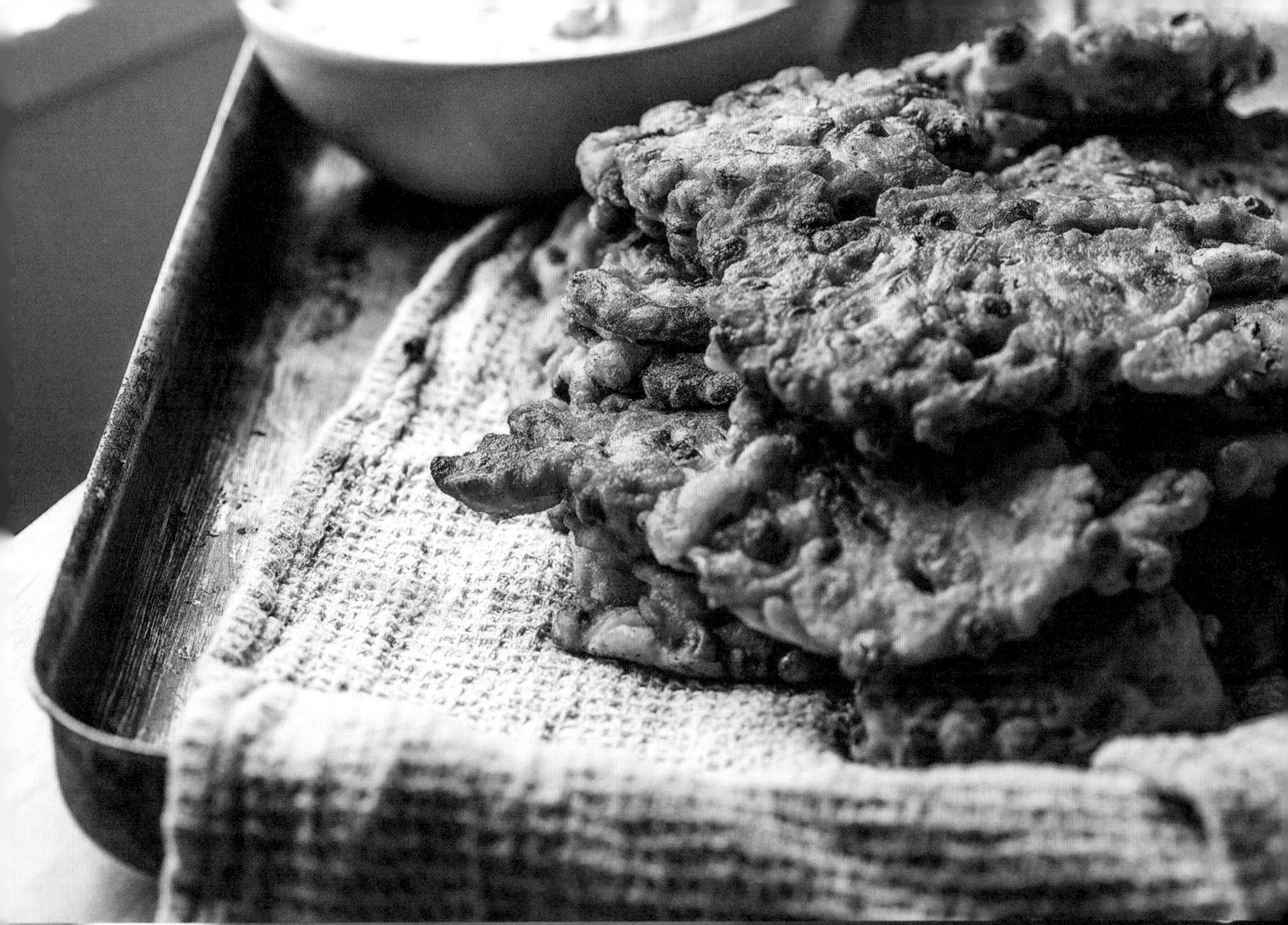
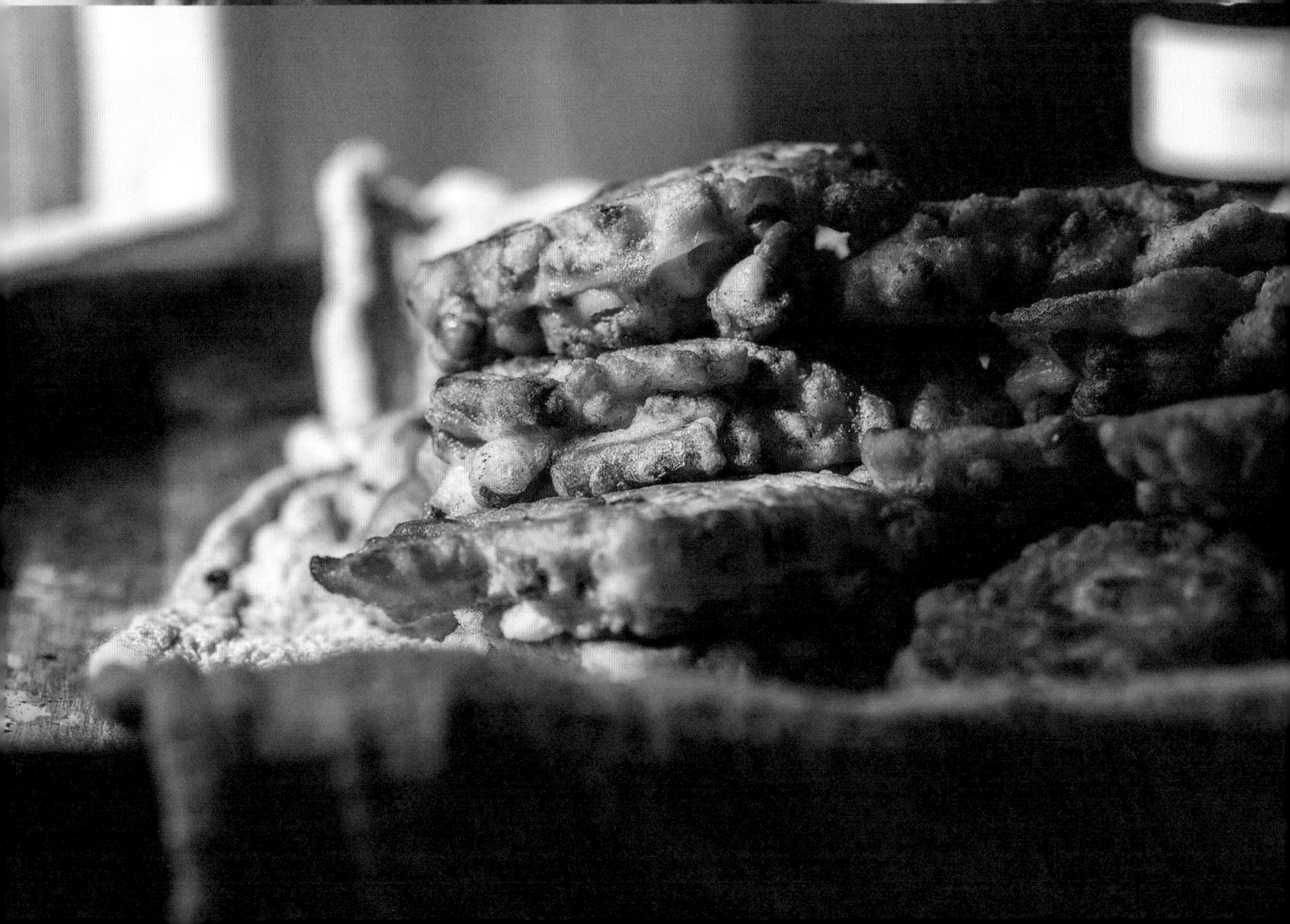

I WISH I WAS GREEK

Yemista

SERVES 6

I often lament my lack of cultural heritage. My Italian and Greek friends think I am hilarious because I want to be like them. I even spent cash on getting my ancestry profile done to see what it might dig up, but no, nothing. I am just a white girl from Frankston. But it won't stop me from celebrating the culinary heritage of my friends and enjoying their delicious food and drinks.

4 large red, yellow, green or orange capsicums
4 large ripe tomatoes
salt and pepper
6 kale leaves, chopped
small handful of flat-leaf parsley leaves, chopped
3 tablespoons chopped mint leaves
3 tablespoons olive oil, plus extra for drizzling
250 ml (1 cup) vegetable stock, plus extra if needed
1 large onion, finely chopped
150 g (¾ cup) long-grain white rice
80 g (½ cup) pine nuts
75 g (½ cup) currants (optional)
2 large potatoes, peeled and cut into 5 cm pieces

Preheat the oven to 175°C (fan-forced).

Cut the tops off the capsicums and tomatoes and set them aside for later. Scoop out the insides of the capsicums and tomatoes, saving the tomato pulp only. Season the insides of the capsicums and tomatoes with a pinch of salt and pepper.

Place the tomato pulp in a food processor and give it a good blitz. Remove half and save it for later, then add the kale, parsley and mint to the processor and blend until well combined but not mushy.

Heat 2 tablespoons of olive oil and 3 tablespoons of stock in a medium saucepan over medium heat, add the onion and cook until translucent. Add the rice and 185 ml (¾ cup) stock, then cover and simmer over low heat for 5–7 minutes or until the liquid has been absorbed.

Add the tomato and kale mixture, pine nuts, currants (if using) and a big pinch of salt and pepper. Mix well, then leave to simmer for 3–5 minutes or until most of the liquid has evaporated and the rice is half-cooked. Remove from the heat and set aside.

Pop the chopped potato in a bowl and sprinkle with salt and pepper. Seasoning is key!

Arrange the capsicums and tomatoes in a baking dish and stuff them three-quarters full with the rice mixture. Cover with their saved tops and drizzle with olive oil.

Pop the potato pieces between the capsicums and tomatoes and sprinkle them with the reserved tomato pulp. Drizzle with

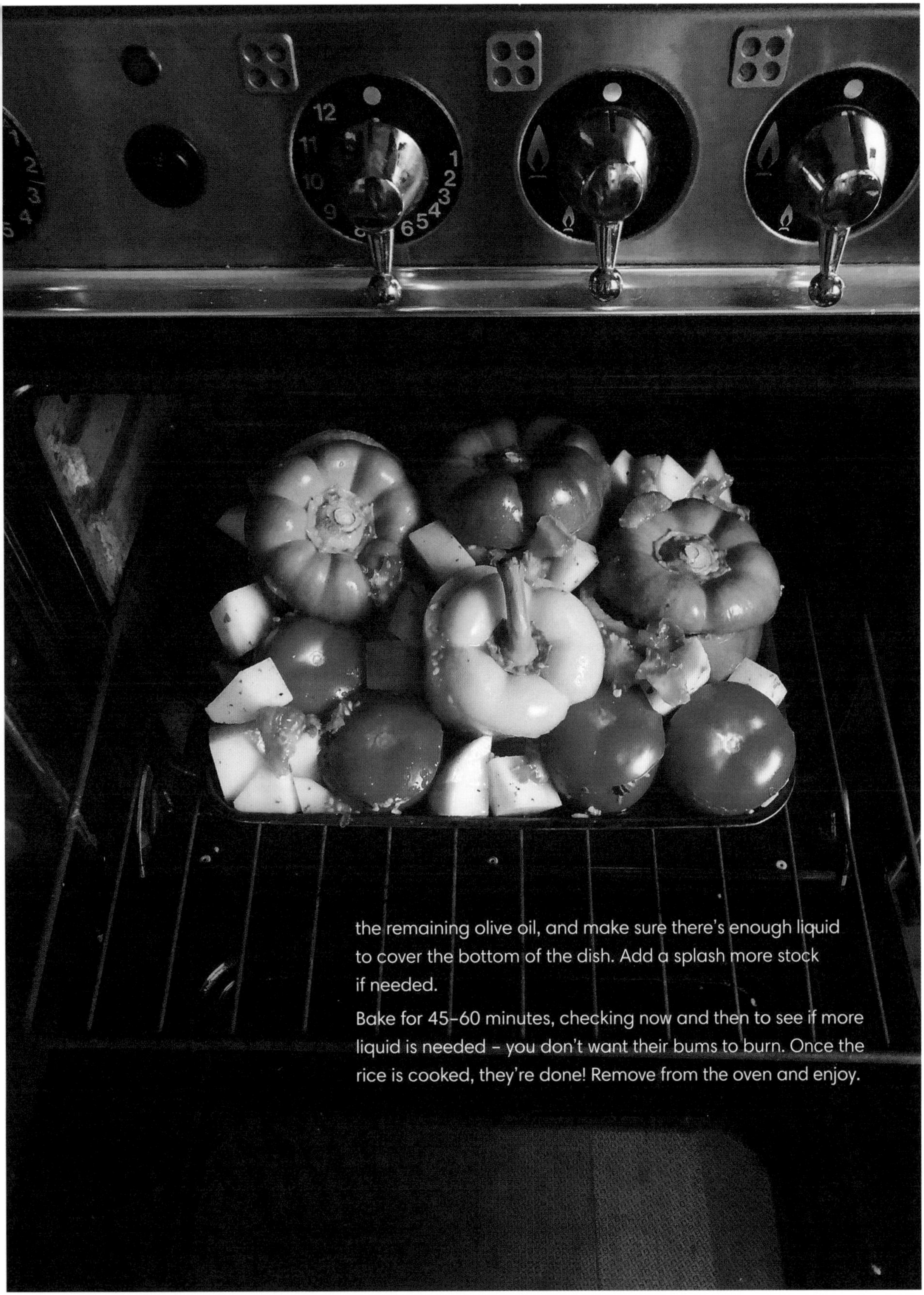

the remaining olive oil, and make sure there's enough liquid to cover the bottom of the dish. Add a splash more stock if needed.

Bake for 45–60 minutes, checking now and then to see if more liquid is needed – you don't want their bums to burn. Once the rice is cooked, they're done! Remove from the oven and enjoy.

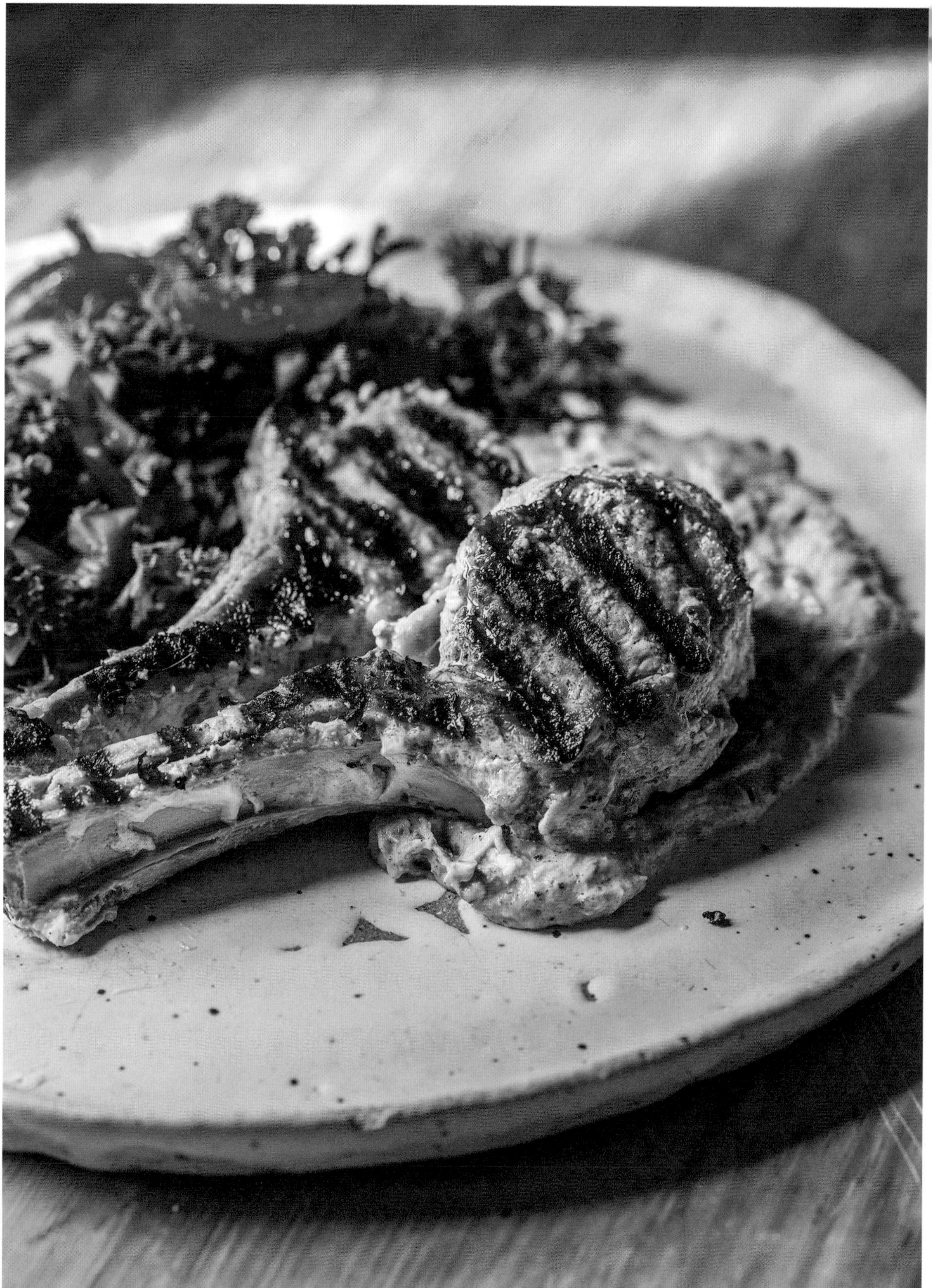

BARBECUED MEAT AND VEG

Barbecued Lamb Cutlets, Baba Ganoush and Tabbouleh

SERVES 4–6

When it is too hot and gross to be in the kitchen, we take it outside. Garden cooking is our all-time fave way to eat. When we lived in the country we used to pick the salad from the patch, with the girls shoving ripe tommies in their faces before they made it to the chopping board. The baba ganoush can be made well ahead of time and is an unreal thing to just keep in the fridge for snacks, because who really can be bothered cooking on those toasty summer nights? Not me, not anyone.

250 g (1 cup) Greek yoghurt
2 garlic cloves, crushed
finely grated zest and juice
   of 1 lemon
salt and pepper
12 lamb cutlets, trimmed
   of any excess fat

For the baba ganoush:
1 kg eggplants
3 garlic cloves, finely diced
3 tablespoons tahini
2 tablespoons lemon juice
½ teaspoon ground cumin
¼ teaspoon smoked paprika
80 ml (⅓ cup) extra-virgin
   olive oil
2 tablespoons chopped
   flat-leaf parsley
salt and pepper

For the tabbouleh:
80 g (4 cups) flat-leaf parsley,
   chopped
1 small red onion, diced
200 g cherry tomatoes,
   quartered
juice of 1 lemon, plus extra
   if needed
2 tablespoons extra-virgin olive
   oil, plus extra if needed
salt and pepper

Combine the yoghurt, garlic, lemon zest and juice in a large bowl and season with a generous pinch each of salt and pepper. Add the lamb cutlets and turn in the mixture, making sure each cutlet is well coated. Cover and refrigerate for at least 1 hour.

Meanwhile, start on the baba ganoush.

Preheat the oven to 230°C (fan-forced) and line a baking tray with baking paper.

Halve the eggplants and place, cut-side down, on the prepared tray. Bake for 35–40 minutes or until the flesh has softened. Set aside to cool, then scoop the flesh into a bowl.

Pop the eggplant, garlic, tahini, lemon juice, cumin and paprika in a food processor and whiz together. With the motor running, slowly pour in the olive oil until the mixture is smooth and well combined. Add the parsley and give it a final whiz, then season to taste with salt and pepper. Set aside and start cooking the cutlets.

Barbecue the cutlets over medium–high heat for 2–3 minutes each side – you still want them to be pink in the middle. (If you don't want to fire up the barbecue, cook them on a hot chargrill pan instead.) Cover and rest for 5–6 minutes.

For the tabbouleh, place all the ingredients in a large mixing bowl and toss to combine. Taste and add more lemon juice, olive oil, salt and/or pepper, if needed.

Take it the table and serve immediately with the lamb and baba ganoush.

FRUIT AND VEG LOAF

Zucchini and Sultana Bread

MAKES 2 LOAVES

Here is another recipe to help you deal with a zucchini glut, especially if you double or triple the quantities and make several at once. This loaf is super moist, so it's good for lunchboxes, but even if it starts to get a little old it's unreal toasted with a heavy-handed layer of butter.

3 large free-range eggs
250 ml (1 cup) vegetable oil
295 g (1⅓ cups) sugar
2 teaspoons vanilla extract
270 g (2 cups) grated zucchini
    with all its juices
450 g (3 cups) plain flour
2 teaspoons ground cinnamon
1 teaspoon salt
185 g (1½ cups) sultanas
handful of nuts or seeds of
    your choice (optional)

Preheat the oven to 180°C (fan-forced). Grease and flour two medium loaf tins. Why make one when you can make two?

Whisk together the eggs, vegetable oil, sugar and vanilla in a large bowl. Add the zucchini and mix until combined.

In another bowl, whisk together the flour, cinnamon and salt. Add to the zucchini mixture and gently stir together until just combined (don't overmix otherwise the loaf will become heavy). Stir in sultanas and any nuts or seeds you want to add.

Divide the batter evenly between the prepared tins and smooth the tops. Bake for 1 hour or until a skewer inserted in the centre of each loaf comes out clean. Leave to cool for a few minutes, then turn out onto a wire rack to cool completely.

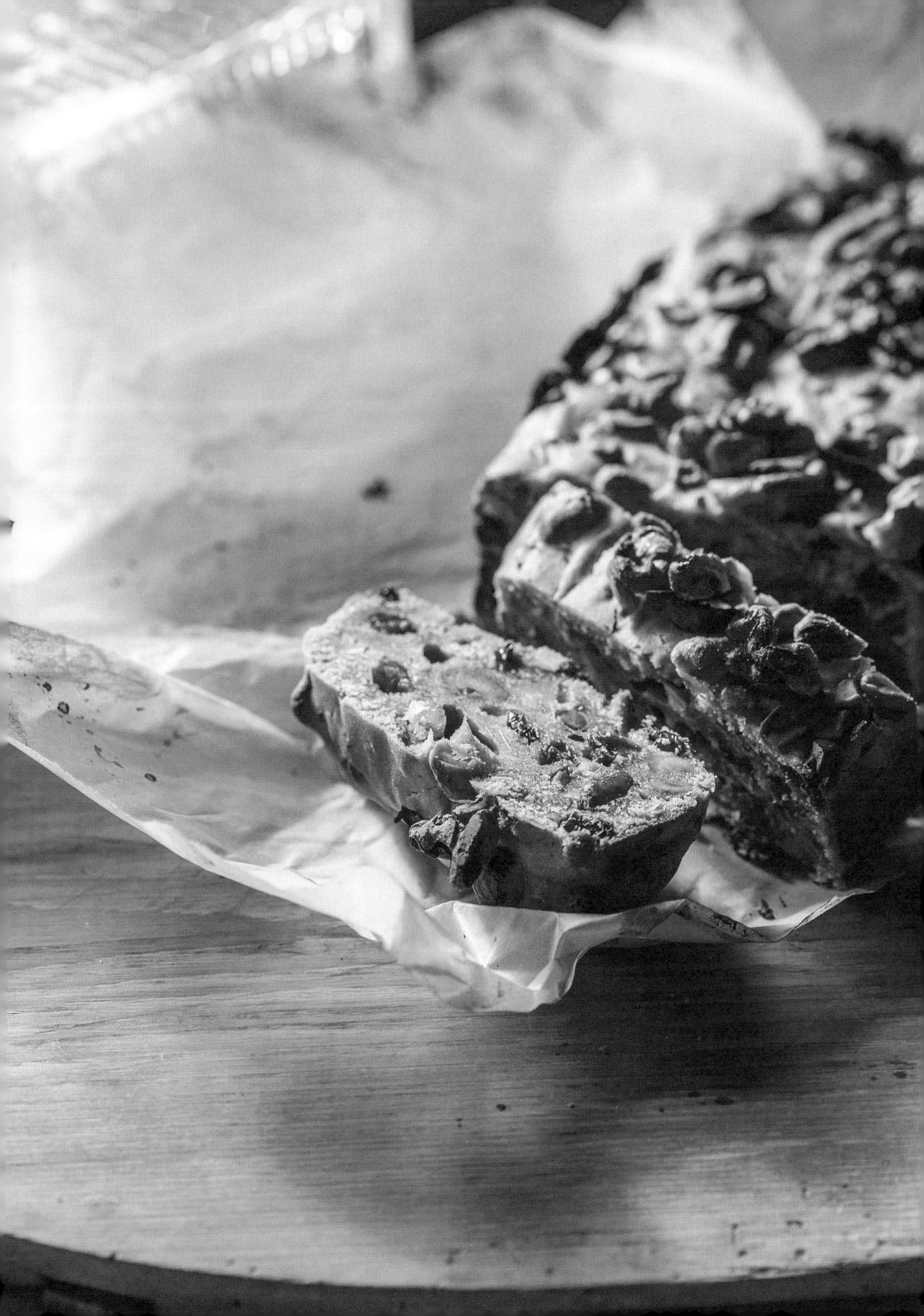

JAMMY SQUARES

Any-Jam-You-Like Tart

MAKES ABOUT 28 SQUARES

When we lived in the country, everyone's gardens were full of old fruit trees, which meant our pantry was chock-full of jams of every variety. Just the smell of the sugary fruit and yeasty pastry baking away in the oven is reason enough to make these. Seriously, it's almost as good as eating them.

2 teaspoons raw sugar
1 tablespoon dried yeast
335 g (2¼ cups) plain flour, plus extra if needed
¼ teaspoon salt
200 g cold butter, cubed, then left at room temperature for 15 minutes before using
475 g (1½ cups) jam (make sure it's thick)
pure icing sugar, for dusting

Place the sugar and 160 ml (⅔ cup) lukewarm water in a small jug and stir until the sugar has dissolved. Stir in the yeast, then leave for 10 minutes or until bubbly.

Meanwhile, combine the flour and salt in a large bowl. Add the butter and rub it into the flour with your fingertips until you have a uniform, sandy mixture. Make a well in the middle and pour in the yeast mixture. With a spoon, bring the flour from the outside into the centre and stir until a rough dough forms.

Tip the dough onto a floured surface and knead, adding more flour as needed, until you have a smooth, not sticky, dough. Form the dough into a ball and pop it into a clean bowl, then cover with plastic wrap and leave to rise for 30–40 minutes.

Preheat the oven to 180°C (fan-forced). Line a 40 cm x 25 cm (roughly) slice tin with baking paper.

Divide the dough into two portions, making one slightly bigger than the other. Roll the larger portion into a rectangle about 2 cm wider and longer than the prepared tin. Roll the dough around your rolling pin and lay it evenly over the tin. Gently press the excess dough around the edges up the sides of the tin. Spread the jam evenly over the dough.

Roll out the remaining piece of dough to a rectangle the same dimensions as the inner part of your tin. Roll it around your rolling pin and carefully lay it over the jam, making sure the jam is completely covered. Starting at a corner, fold the dough pressed up the sides over the top piece of dough and pinch together to seal. With clean scissors, make small cuts, every 5 cm or so, in the top layer of dough.

Bake for 40–45 minutes or until lightly golden. Remove and allow to cool completely.

Carefully slide the slice (and baking paper) out of the tin and onto a cutting board. Dust the top with icing sugar, then use a sharp knife to cut diagonally into bars.

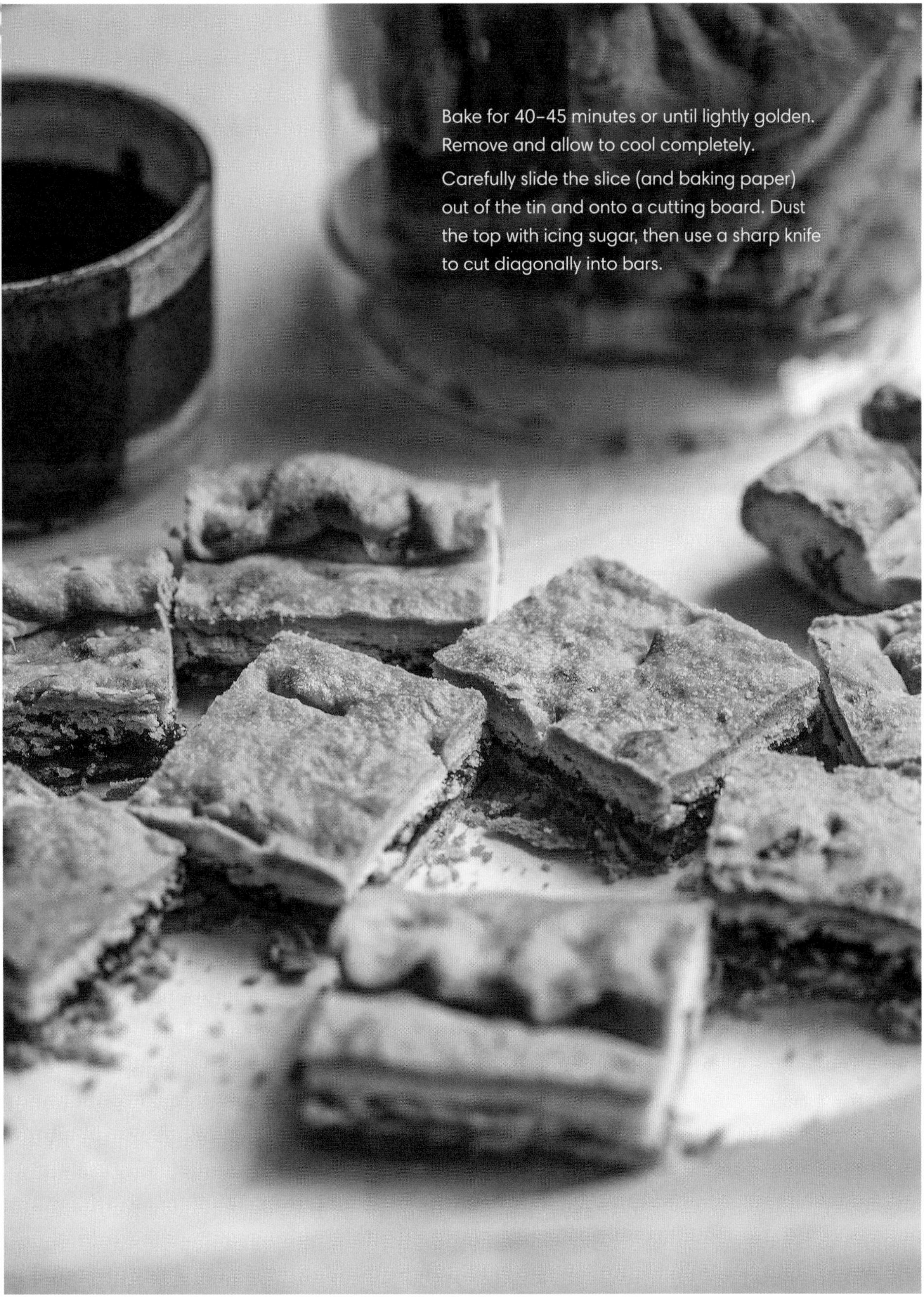

Teenagers are brutal, mean, loving and amazing

When I had a four-week-old baby, and was in serious struggle town, a 'well-meaning' woman told me the struggle I was experiencing now was nothing compared to the struggles I would be experiencing in 14 years' time. Well, my four-week-old is now 14 and, yes, the woman's advice was definitely a long-play but it was shit advice to give a new mum with zero sleep and zero confidence.

I still have no idea of what I'm doing. My biggest fear now is that any mess-ups I make in these teenage years will be the ones that give my child psychological issues later in life. She has become old enough to see that I am totally making it up as I go along, and the superhuman parent aura that once surrounded me is starting to lose its glow.

I get questioned.

And the answers aren't easy.

And I am forced to look at myself more.

And try so hard to be the person I want her to be.

Not long ago I read a quote by political writer Ayesha Siddiqi: 'Be the person you needed when you were younger.' It struck such a chord. In giving my

teenage daughter the space to talk and be heard and understood, I'm healing the teenager within. The pain of my teens is still so present in me, which helps me connect with the feelings my daughter might also be feeling.

It's hard though. When I want to yell, I really should be holding her or giving her space to breathe. I know that when I'm angry I usually need someone to hold me and tell me it's going to be OK. Why would my kid be any different? Yelling at each other ends with tears, swearing, slamming doors and, more often than not, saying things we wish we hadn't. It's so hard to not go into that natural instinct of conflict, but going in for the hug seems to be working. Most of the time. Sometimes she just tells me where to go.

Then she holds me out of the blue. She lays her head on my lap when we watch telly. She sits on the bench while I make her brekkie. And then she asks me, 'Mum, why are you crying?'.

She pushes because she feels safe to push. And even though those daggers cut me to the quick, I feel privileged that she feels safe to do so. It sucks, it's traumatic, and I just want to curl up into a ball and cry, but if I see it for what it actually is, it takes a bit of that hurt away.

I hope I am being the person she needs. It's all I want to be, for her and for me.

RUBY FRUIT CAKE

**Grapefruit and
Yoghurt Cake**

SERVES 6-8

Citrusy cakes are our favourite cakes, and the coolest thing about the ones we like to eat is that they're super easy to make. So easy the girls can whip these up without me hovering over them, which has been such a great learning experience for them, and perhaps more so for me. Learning to back off and let them go was such a hard thing to do, but now that they've mastered baking, I am finally reaping the rewards.

350 g (2⅓ cups) self-raising
 flour
1 teaspoon ground cardamom
½ teaspoon salt
finely grated zest of 1½ ruby
 grapefruits
2 large free-range eggs
250 g (1 cup) Greek yoghurt
170 g (¾ cup) caster sugar
125 ml (½ cup) grapefruit juice
3 tablespoons milk of your
 choice
80 g butter, melted and cooled
For the glaze:
125 g (1 cup) pure icing sugar
2 tablespoons grapefruit juice

Preheat the oven to 180°C (fan-forced). Grease and line a 20 cm round cake tin with baking paper.

Place the flour, cardamom, salt and grapefruit zest in a large bowl and whisk until combined.

In a medium bowl, whisk together the eggs, yoghurt and caster sugar. Stir in the grapefruit juice, milk and butter. Pour into the flour mixture and gently stir together, taking care not to overmix the batter.

Pour the batter into the prepared cake tin and bake for 25–35 minutes or until a skewer inserted in the centre comes out clean. Cool in the tin for a few minutes before turning out onto a wire rack to cool completely.

Make the glaze while the cake is cooling. Combine the icing sugar and grapefruit juice in a small bowl until smooth and lump free.

Place a plate or baking paper under the rack to catch the glaze, then pour the glaze evenly over the cake. Allow to set for 5–10 minutes, then serve.

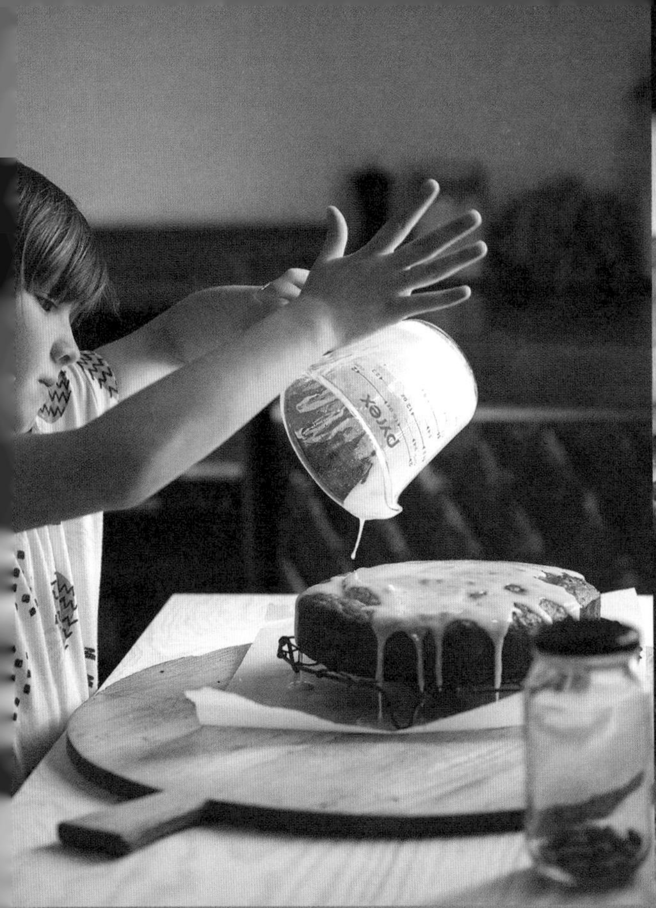
pyrex

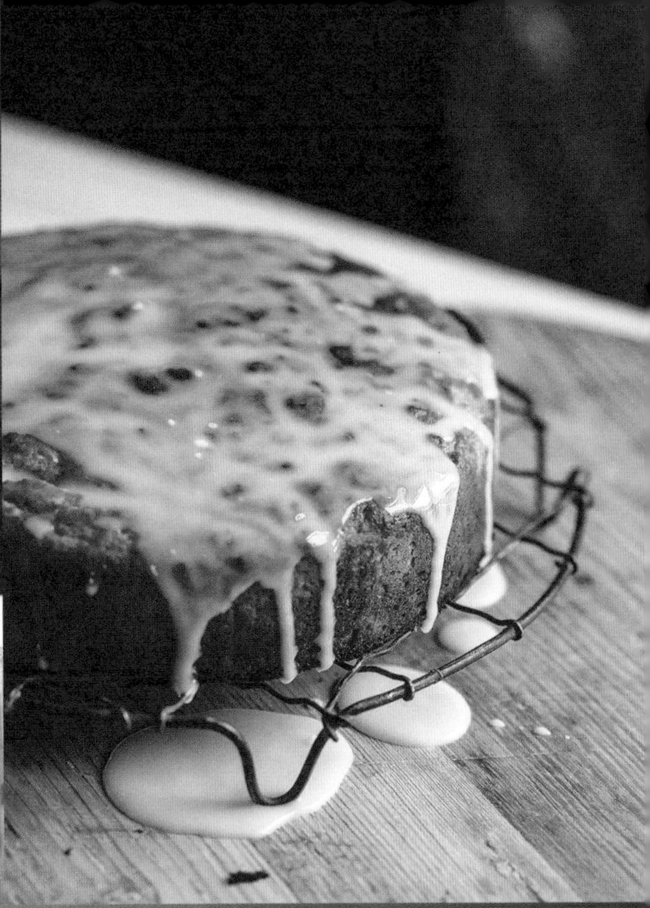

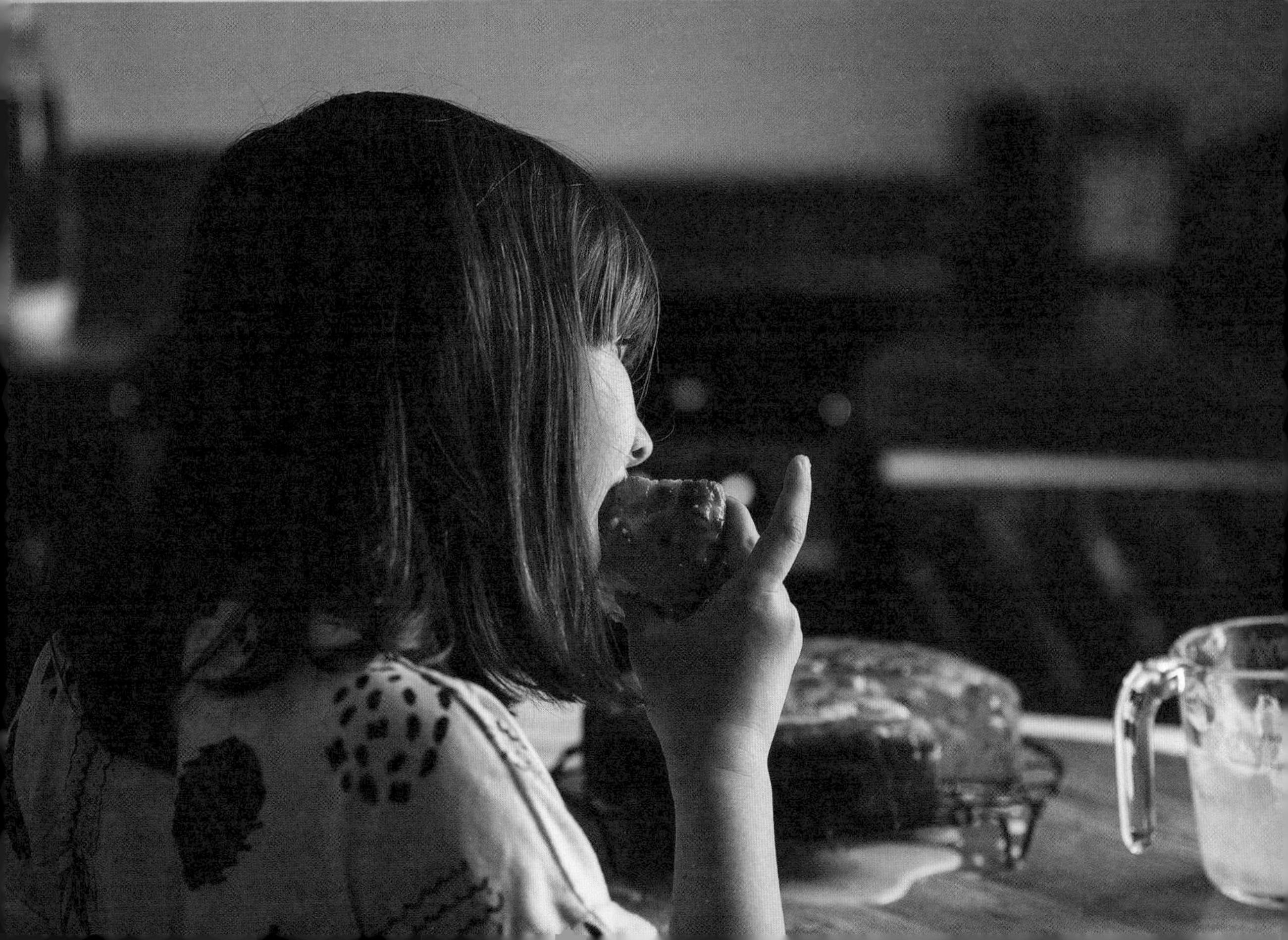

(Almost) DIY after-school snacks

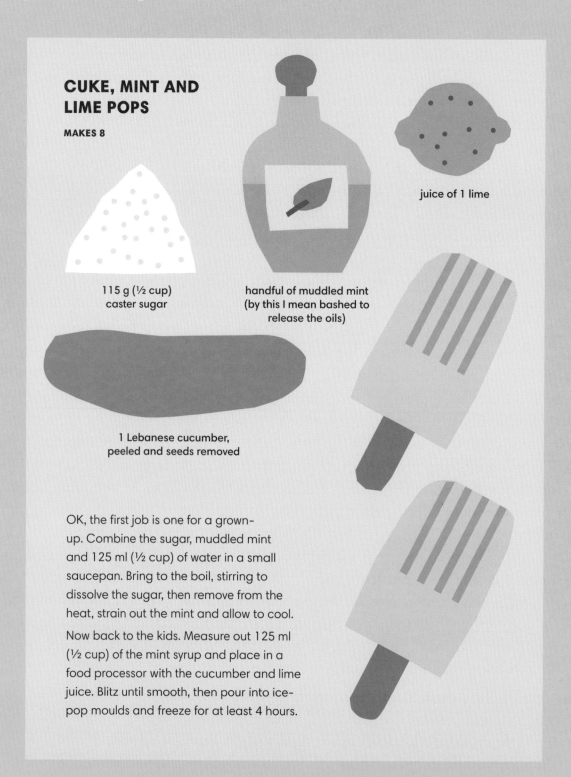

CUKE, MINT AND LIME POPS

MAKES 8

115 g (½ cup)
caster sugar

handful of muddled mint
(by this I mean bashed to
release the oils)

juice of 1 lime

1 Lebanese cucumber,
peeled and seeds removed

OK, the first job is one for a grown-up. Combine the sugar, muddled mint and 125 ml (½ cup) of water in a small saucepan. Bring to the boil, stirring to dissolve the sugar, then remove from the heat, strain out the mint and allow to cool.

Now back to the kids. Measure out 125 ml (½ cup) of the mint syrup and place in a food processor with the cucumber and lime juice. Blitz until smooth, then pour into ice-pop moulds and freeze for at least 4 hours.

Most of these snacks will be simple enough for your kids to manage on their own but occasionally they'll need help with cutting or heating, depending on their age.

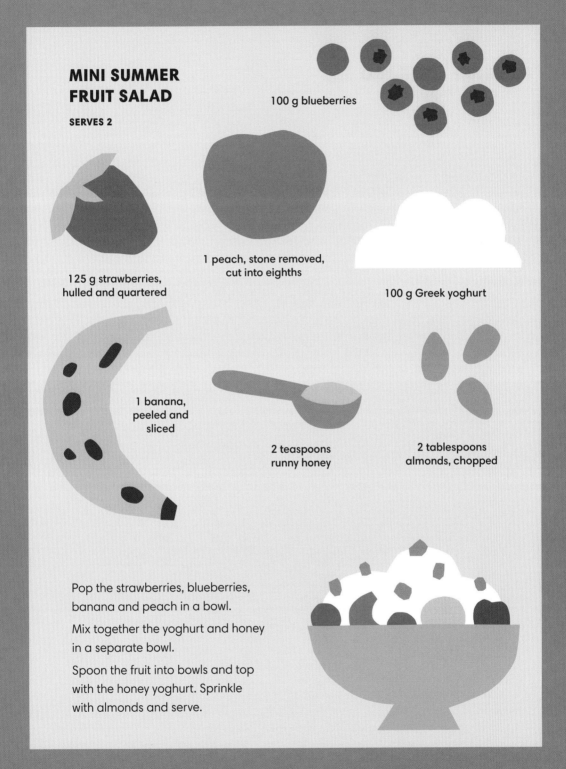

MINI SUMMER FRUIT SALAD

SERVES 2

100 g blueberries

125 g strawberries, hulled and quartered

1 peach, stone removed, cut into eighths

100 g Greek yoghurt

1 banana, peeled and sliced

2 teaspoons runny honey

2 tablespoons almonds, chopped

Pop the strawberries, blueberries, banana and peach in a bowl.

Mix together the yoghurt and honey in a separate bowl.

Spoon the fruit into bowls and top with the honey yoghurt. Sprinkle with almonds and serve.

(Almost) DIY after-school snacks

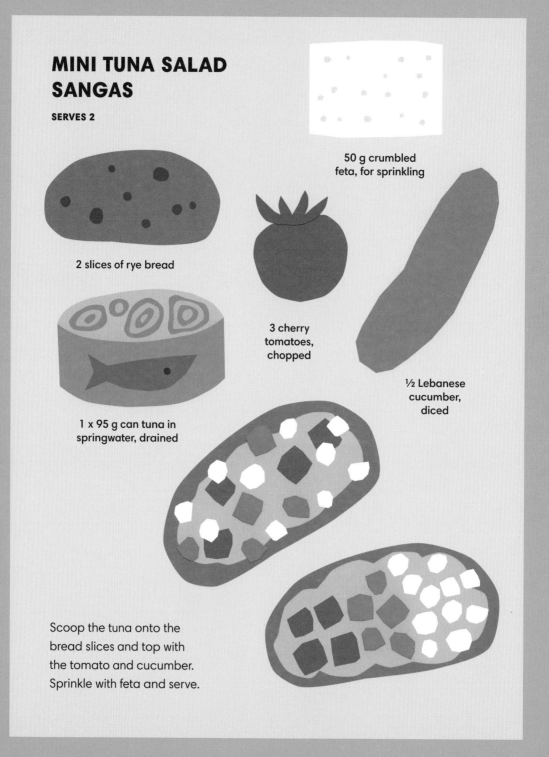

MINI TUNA SALAD SANGAS

SERVES 2

50 g crumbled feta, for sprinkling

2 slices of rye bread

3 cherry tomatoes, chopped

½ Lebanese cucumber, diced

1 x 95 g can tuna in springwater, drained

Scoop the tuna onto the bread slices and top with the tomato and cucumber. Sprinkle with feta and serve.

SNACK FACES

SERVES 2

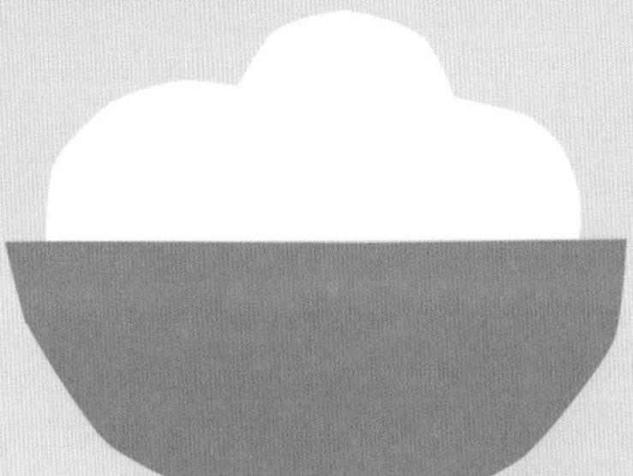

3 tablespoons cream cheese, or your choice of spread

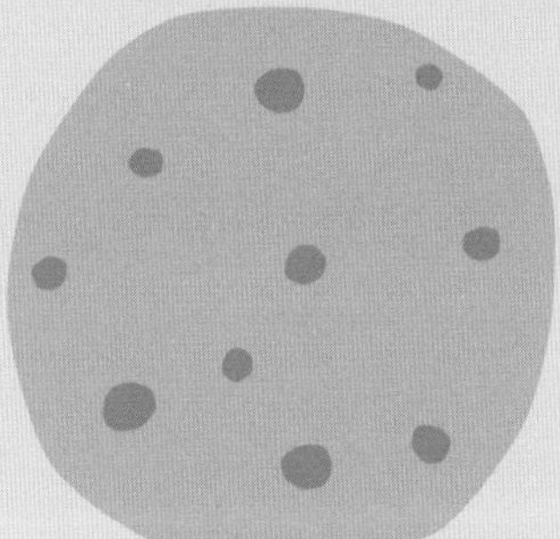

4 rice cakes (or corn cakes, if you prefer)

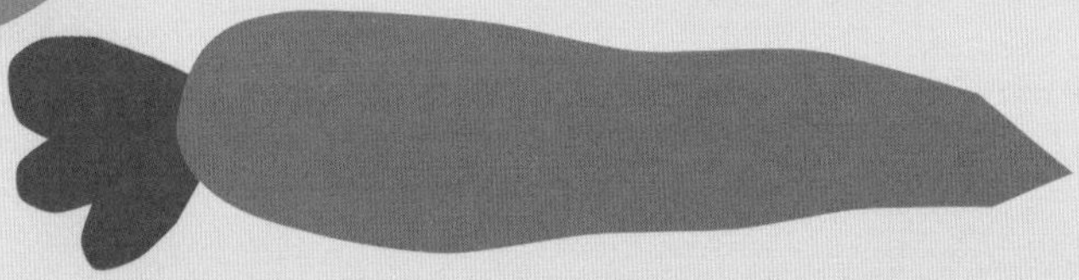

1 carrot, grated

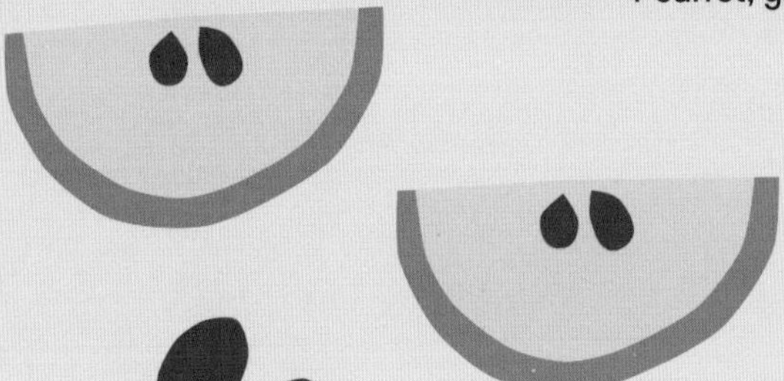

½ apple, cored and sliced into half-moons

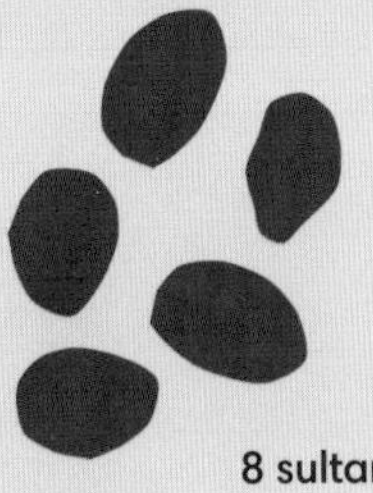

8 sultanas

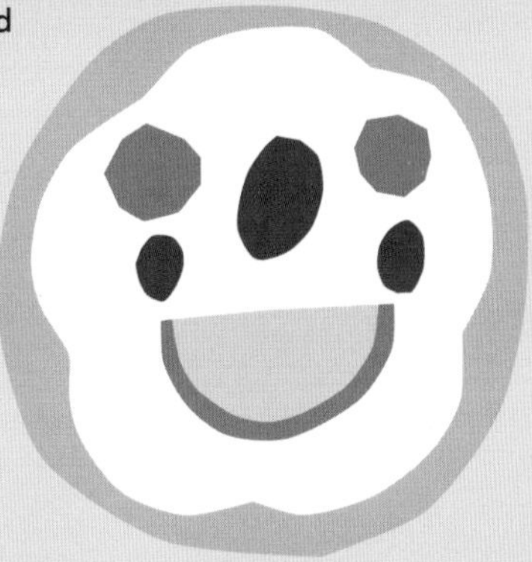

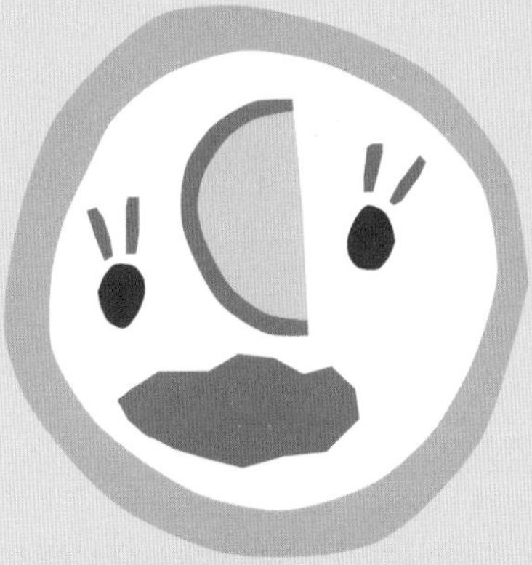

Spread the cream cheese onto the rice cakes, then give your kids the other bits to make their own snack faces. This is limited only by their imagination.

ADVENTURES FOR WEEKENDS & HOLIDAYS

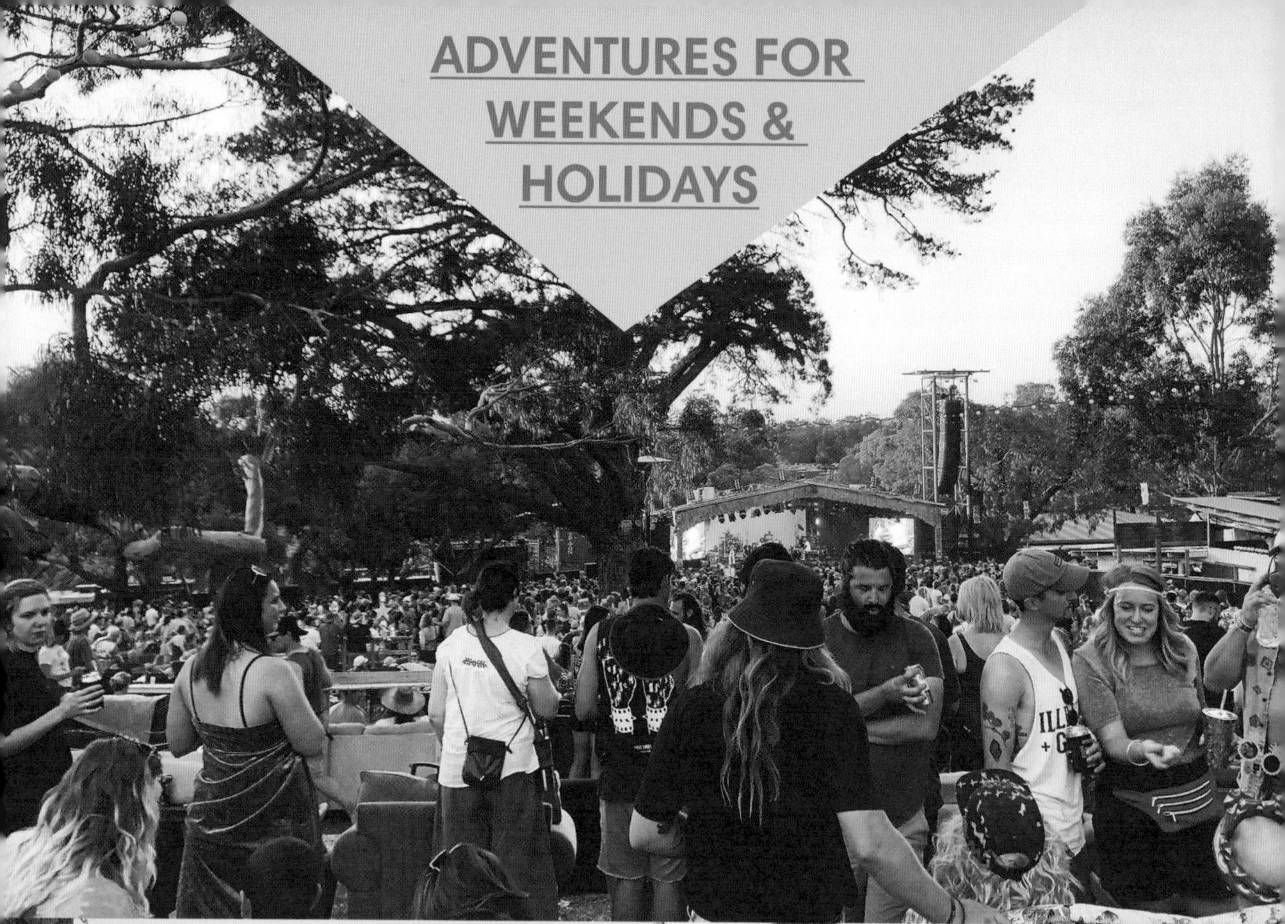

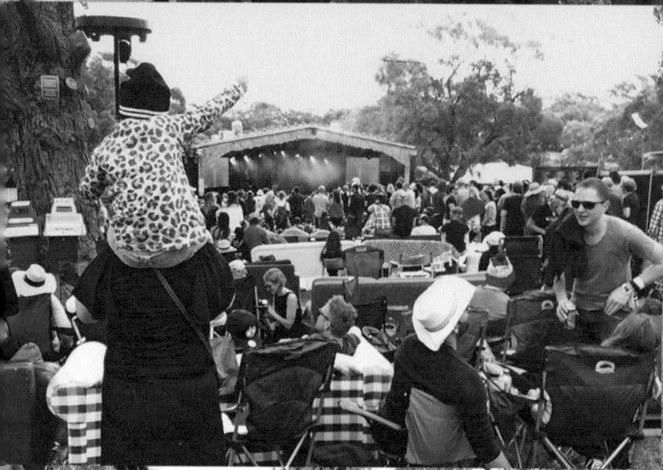

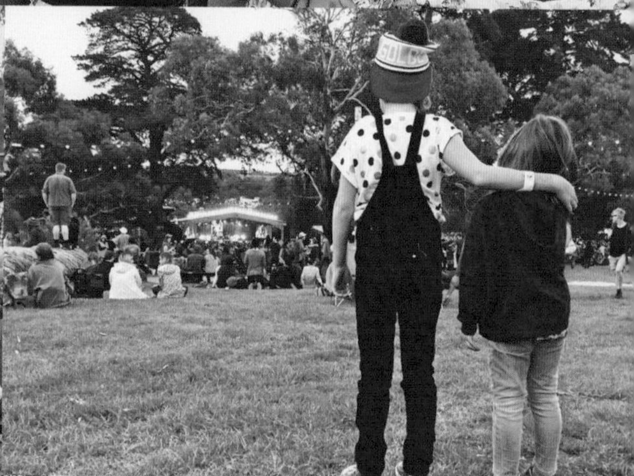

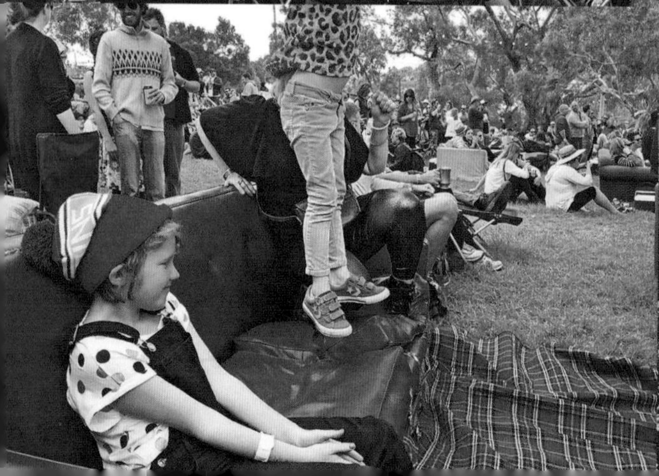

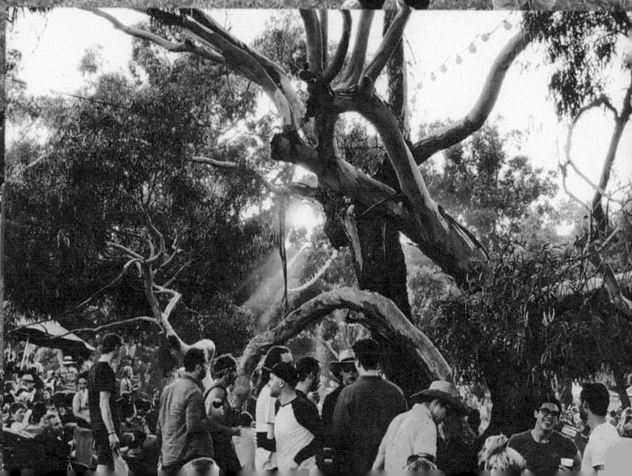

Taking your kids to non-kid things

I get that there's a time and a place for those play centre things. But I reckon there's something to be said for taking your kids to things that are not specifically designed to entertain them while you down a volcanically hot latte.

Now don't get me wrong; I am all for things to entertain the kids. Things that are made for them, and only them. But I also think it's cool to challenge them and share things I enjoy. When I was a kid my mum took me to rock concerts – seriously bogan rock concerts – and I loved them. I still do. My favourite was AC/DC at the Tennis Centre in 1990. Holy crap. We walked through metal detectors and hung out with people I had never seen the likes of before. So much leather and denim, and such tight pants. Winnie Blues forever.

My life changed that day. The rock bogan was born and I never looked back.

I do wonder what my life would be like now if Mum hadn't taken me to see all that Aussie rock. (Barnsey was another. Late 80s Barnsey. Classic.) Would I be living the life I live? Would I have the inner bogan? I don't even want to think about it.

What I am trying to say is, sharing who you are and the things you enjoy with your kids is amazing. Don't

be afraid to take them to a music festival, on a road trip, on a sailing boat, to the gallery or to your fave restaurant. They'll get the hang of it, and it could become something they enjoy too!

My all-time favourite memory (which I hope will also become a fave for my eldest daughter) is sitting on the hill at Golden Plains Festival. It was around midnight, we were eating waffles and watching Public Enemy. I turned to her and said, 'I know you don't understand how cool this is right now, but trust me, it is.' When they finished, we headed back to the car, snuggled under the doona and slept in the boot of our station wagon.

The thing I loved most about my mum sharing these experiences with me was that it made me see her. I got to know who my mum was beyond being my mother. Sometimes we just pigeonhole our parents into the parent box and forget that the person who makes our sandwiches every morning also likes to headbang to Bon Scott.

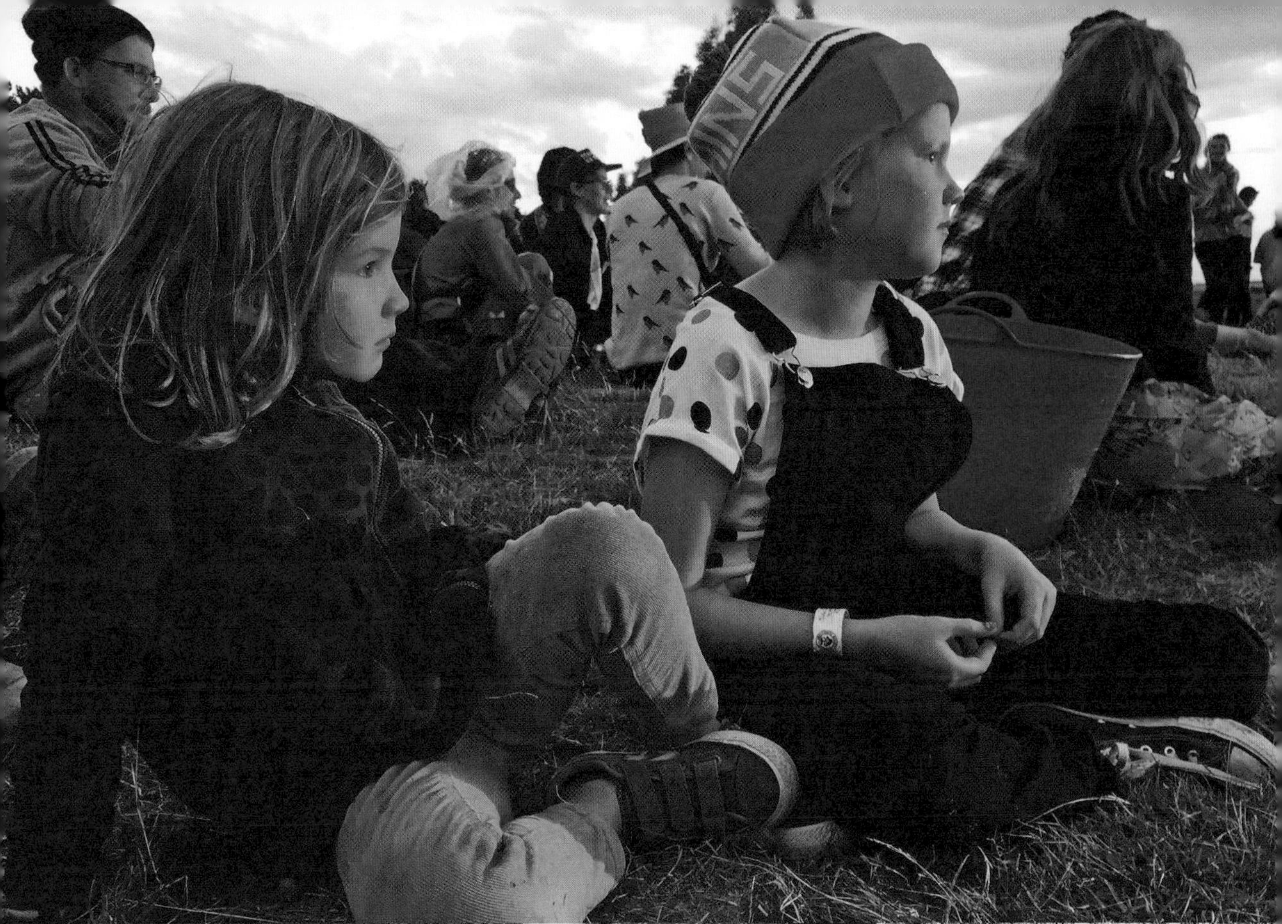

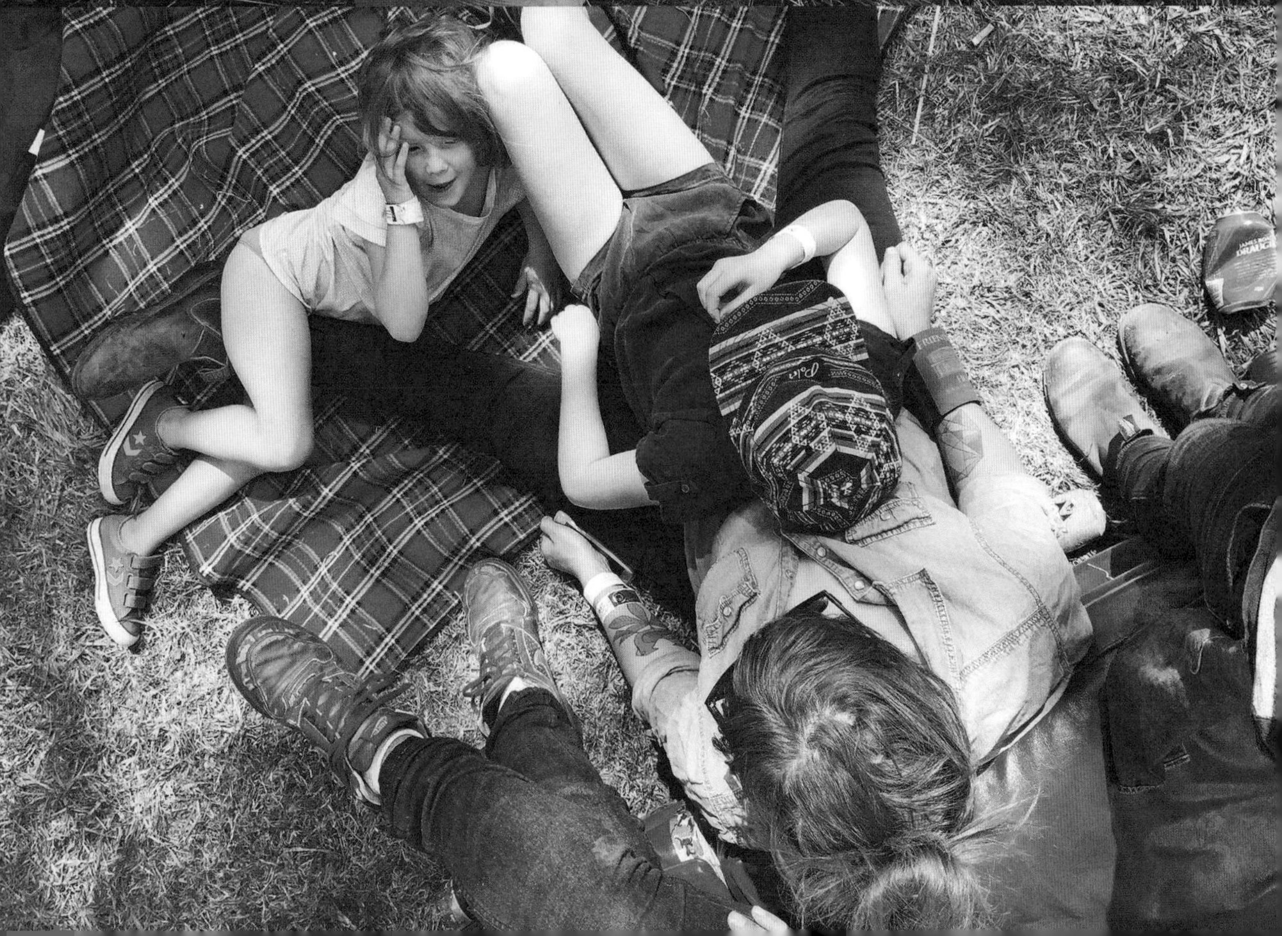

Caravan parks and caravan cooking

I love the Australian-ness of caravan parks. Of course, my favourites are the ones that are lost in time – the ones that have games rooms with Galaga, air hockey and a crappy vending machine. As much as my youngest kid would love for us to stay at a fancy one, with those gigantic blow-up trampoline things, she knows we're going to pull up at the one with the faded signage.

I love travelling lo-fi and it's fun staying in time capsules. It tugs on my nostalgia. I'm not sure why more people aren't interested in staying at the run-down park down the road, as these places are so much cooler. I find myself boring my girls with classic 'when I was a kid …' stories and they reward me with the classic eye roll.

A while back, we stayed at the same caravan park on the Great Ocean Road for a few years running. It is still my favourite. It sits right on the beach, and the only amenities it has to offer are toilets, showers and a little shop. Perfect. I have always loved the idea of having a place to come back to, enabling my girls to make summer holiday friends. It's something I was always envious of when I was a kid. When I'd return to school, my friend talked of people I'd never heard of, as if they were her best mates.

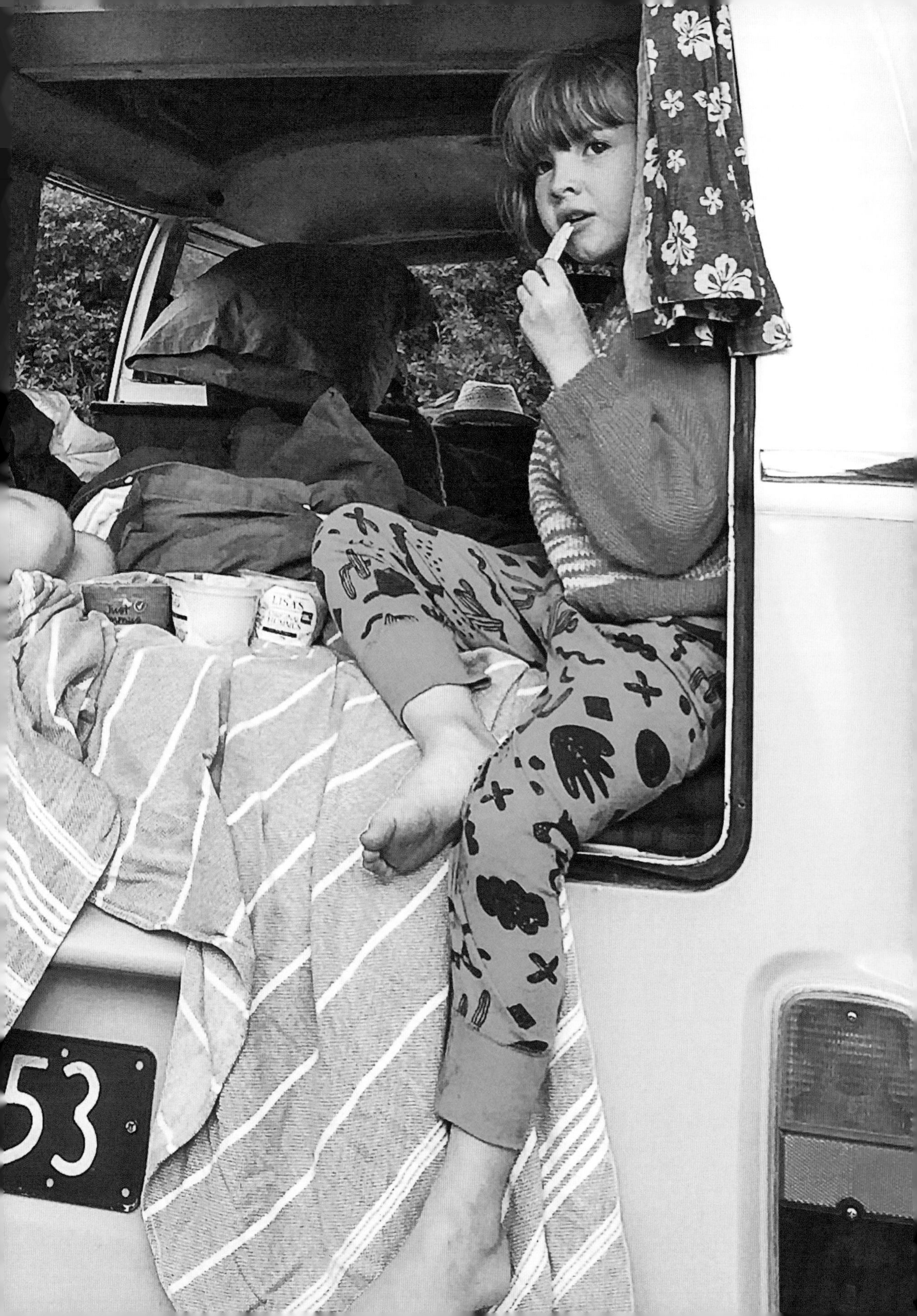
53

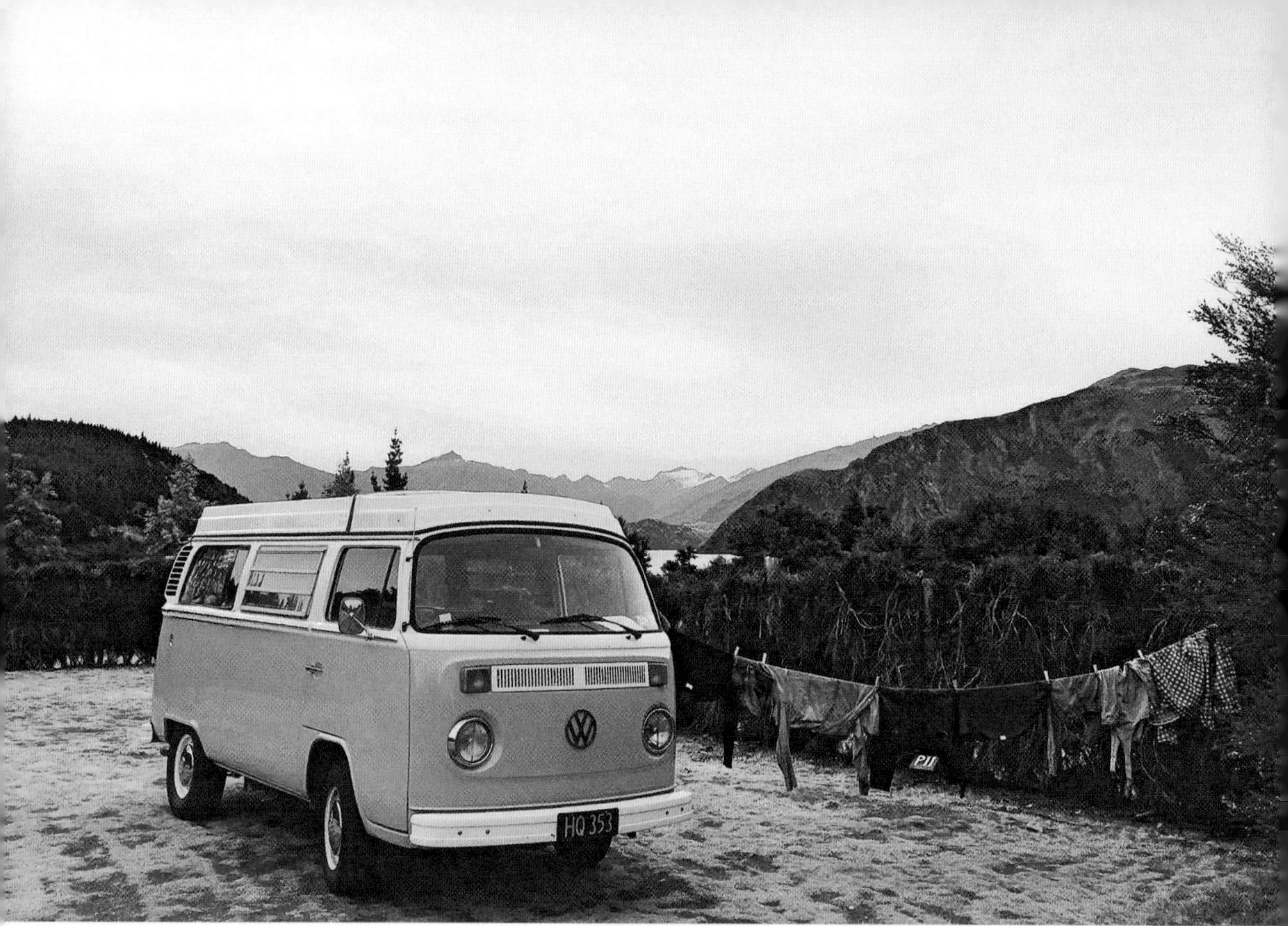
HQ 353

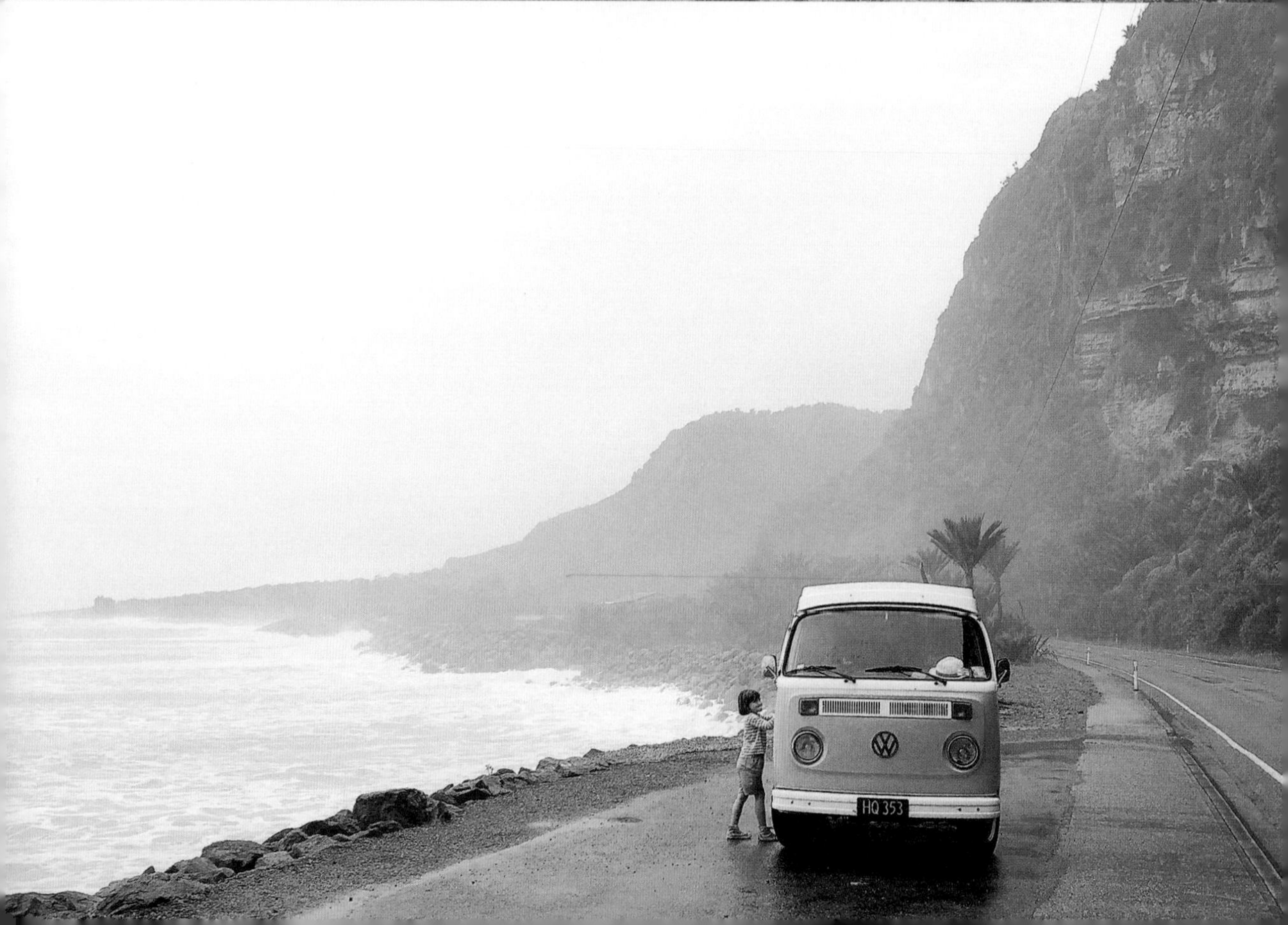
HQ 353

One day when we were sitting in our caravan on the beach, my eldest, then 10, asked if she could walk to the shop to get the butter for dinner. I had always walked with the girls to the shop. But perhaps this was a good time to start testing the letting go thing and give my kid some independence on a very small scale. Because caravan parks aren't the real world, are they? Unable to help myself, I followed her, hiding behind caravans the entire way. Next time, I decided, I will let her go alone.

Dinner time in caravans is the best. It's bare-bones cooking in a confined space. There's oil spattering on your doona, lettuce being chopped on the kids' beds, and tins of crap falling on your head when you open the cupboard. It's also summer, so it's about 150°C.

When you've finally managed to pull this meal together, you burst out of the van into the fresh air and serve it to your family. There's the wobbly camp table that spills all the drinks when you put the meal down, and there's always one kid sitting on an esky because you never ever bring enough chairs.

It's perfect.

Santa's Recycling Program

One Christmas my girls really wanted a trampoline. Which, of course, coincided with a year I really couldn't afford one. Which is actually most years.

As parents, we really want to pull through for Santa. So I looked on eBay for second-hand trampolines. Luckily, lots of people get sick of them pretty quickly so finding one was the easy bit. The tricky bit was going to be explaining why this trampoline wasn't shiny and new.

Introducing Santa's Recycling Program.

Which requires planning.

You have to implement this plan weeks in advance. The kids have to know it's coming. You can't just spring second-hand goods on them without warning.

Two weeks out from Christmas, I told the girls about a new initiative Santa had started, which I'd read about in *The Guardian*. He'd been noticing the effects of climate change on the North Pole and decided he needed to become more environmentally aware. He was worried about the impact making new toys every year was having on the planet. So he started Santa's Recycling Program, which enables kids to swap old Santa presents they no longer play with for something else.

'Oh that's so cool, Mum.' Got 'em.

On Christmas morning I handed the girls a letter from Santa, thanking them for taking part in his new program. He was proud of them for caring about the environment and wished them a Merry Christmas. The girls looked at me with huge smiles.

'So, where's our present?'

I took them outside and there was the trampoline Santa had left for them. Not so shiny, but no one cared.

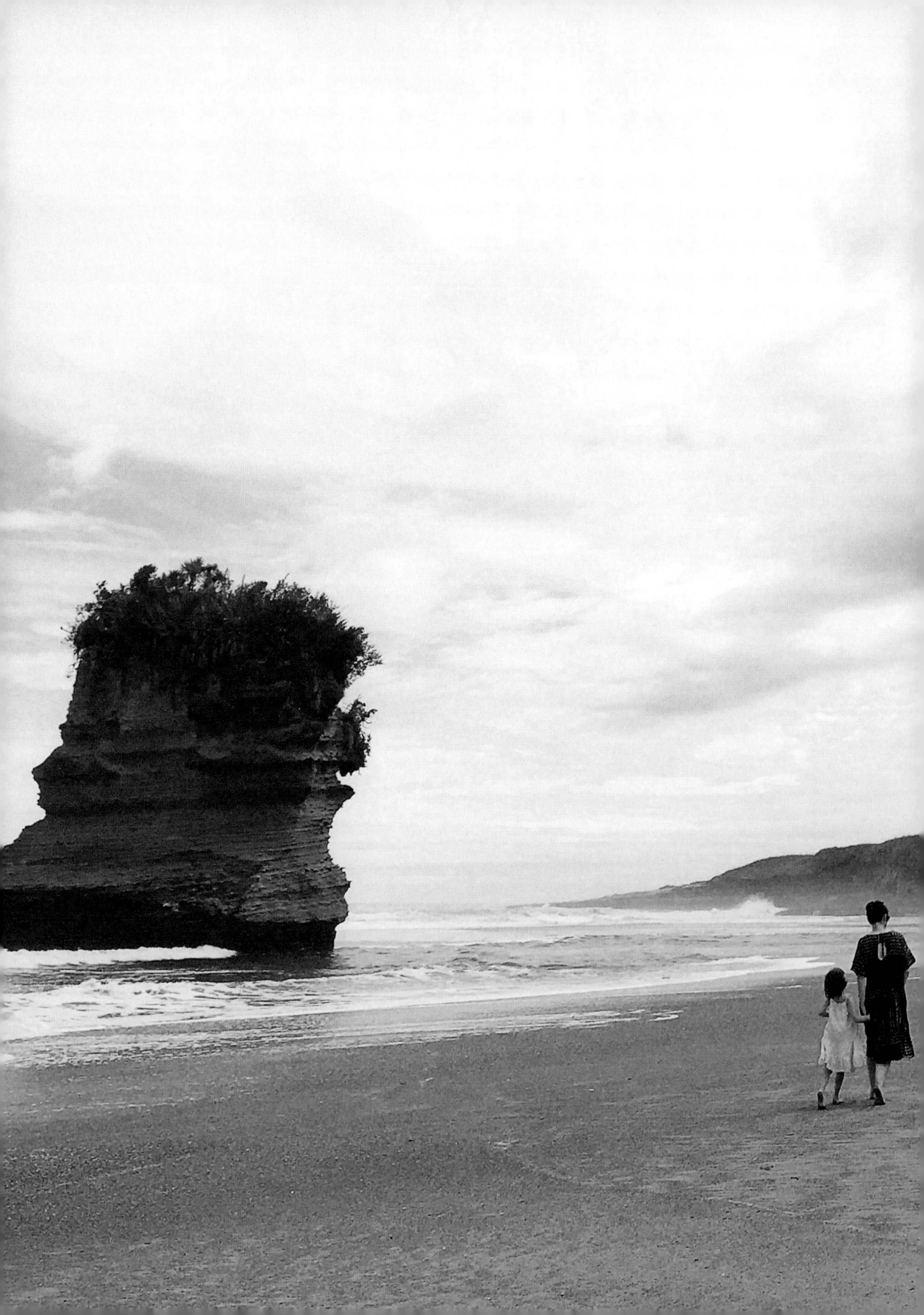

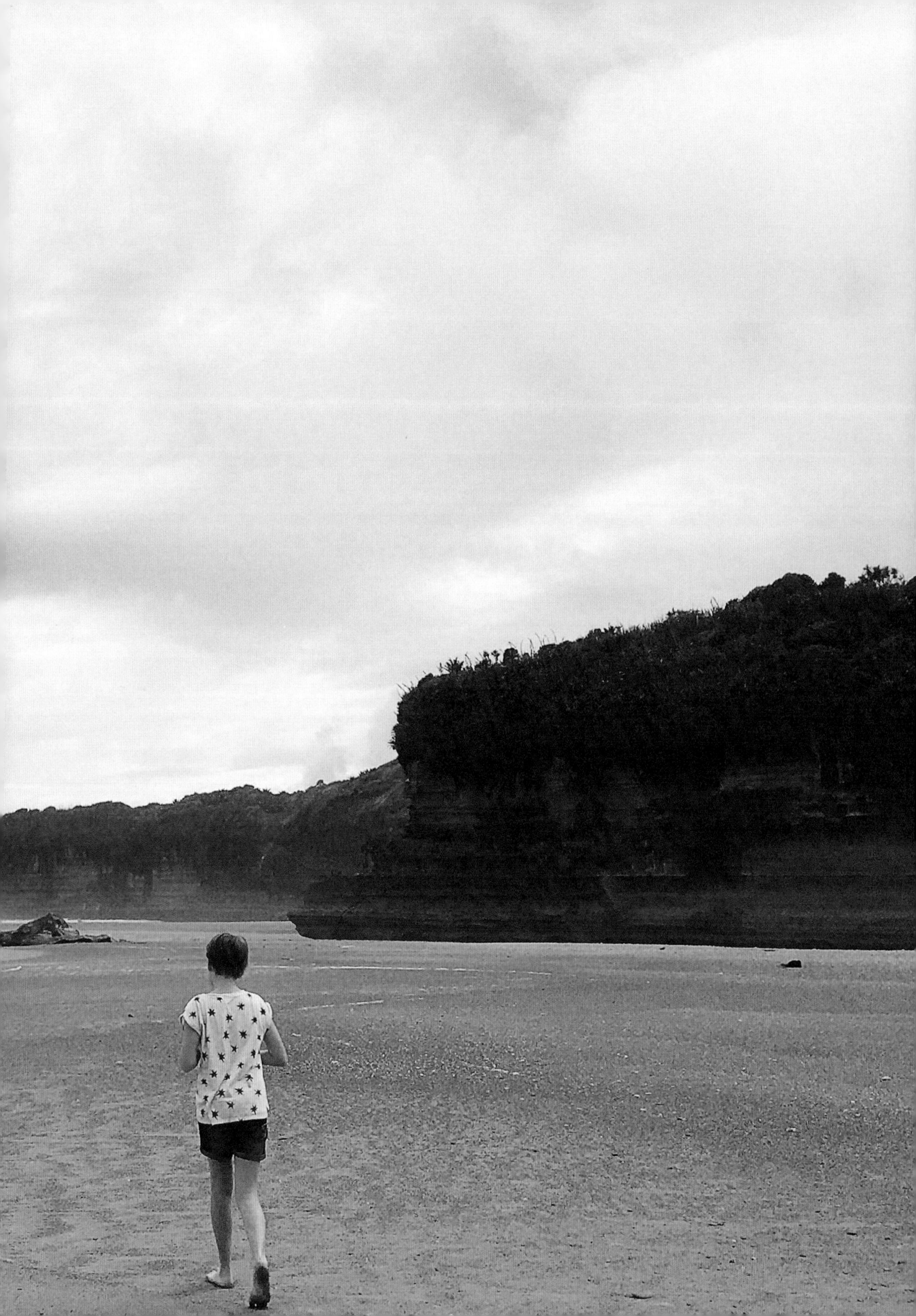

Conversion charts

Measuring cups and spoons may vary slightly from one country to another, but the difference is generally not enough to affect a recipe. All cup and spoon measures are level.

One Australian metric measuring cup holds 250 ml (8 fl oz), one Australian tablespoon holds 20 ml (4 teaspoons) and one Australian metric teaspoon holds 5 ml. North America, New Zealand and the UK use a 15 ml (3-teaspoon) tablespoon.

LENGTH

METRIC	IMPERIAL
3 mm	1/8 inch
6 mm	1/4 inch
1 cm	1/2 inch
2.5 cm	1 inch
5 cm	2 inches
18 cm	7 inches
20 cm	8 inches
23 cm	9 inches
25 cm	10 inches
30 cm	12 inches

LIQUID MEASURES

ONE AMERICAN PINT	ONE IMPERIAL PINT
500 ml (16 fl oz)	600 ml (20 fl oz)

CUP	METRIC	IMPERIAL
1/8 cup	30 ml	1 fl oz
1/4 cup	60 ml	2 fl oz
1/3 cup	80 ml	2 1/2 fl oz
1/2 cup	125 ml	4 fl oz
2/3 cup	160 ml	5 fl oz
3/4 cup	180 ml	6 fl oz
1 cup	250 ml	8 fl oz
2 cups	500 ml	16 fl oz
2 1/4 cups	560 ml	20 fl oz
4 cups	1 litre	32 fl oz

DRY MEASURES

The most accurate way to measure dry ingredients is to weigh them. However, if using a cup, add the ingredient loosely to the cup and level with a knife; don't compact the ingredient unless the recipe requests 'firmly packed'.

METRIC	IMPERIAL
15 g	1/2 oz
30 g	1 oz
60 g	2 oz
125 g	4 oz (1/4 lb)
185 g	6 oz
250 g	8 oz (1/2 lb)
375 g	12 oz (3/4 lb)
500 g	16 oz (1 lb)
1 kg	32 oz (2 lb)

OVEN TEMPERATURES

CELSIUS	FAHRENHEIT	CELSIUS	GAS MARK
100°C	200°F	110°C	1/4
120°C	250°F	130°C	1/2
150°C	300°F	140°C	1
160°C	325°F	150°C	2
180°C	350°F	170°C	3
200°C	400°F	180°C	4
220°C	425°F	190°C	5
		200°C	6
		220°C	7
		230°C	8
		240°C	9
		250°C	10

Thank you

There is just no way this book would have happened without the incredible support of the people around me.

To the amazing women who worked on this book with me: Mary Small and Clare Marshall at Plum; Rachel Carter, the kindest editor I've known; Arielle Gamble, who made my feelings look so great on the page; and Anna Kövecses for the most beautiful illustrations. I am truly spoilt for having you all on board and I can't thank you enough for your help to lift me over the line.

To my beautiful friend, Peta Mazey, who read all my stories and wasn't too shy to critique. To Jade O'Donahoo, for the long chats. To Emily Corbet, for always being there and for doing all the hard jobs, even if you were too hungover to actually help me the day we were meant to shoot this book. Nicole McIvor, for being a little gun, a great neighbour, and for sticking by me even when I looked gone. To one of the most generous souls on earth, Sonia Lear. Your kindness and openness restores my faith in the world every time we speak. Jacinta Moore, for always being my right-hand lady and smiling all the way. To Liz Evans, even though we don't speak often, I feel your support. Fran Haysey, who thought I had something to offer the world, all those years ago. Marieke Hardy, for seeing me. To Rohan Anderson, who made me believe I could write, take a photo and make a nice cake. To Jeffrey Pedretti, for making me run laps, lift weights and generally kick ass. Pip Lincolne and Ruth Bruten, for always being there to let the world know what good stuff I'm up to. To Shaun Adams, for kicking my ass over the line. To all the artists who created the music that has been the soundtrack to my life so far – in particular to Billy Corgan, for 'Mayonaise'.

To my family, the oddest, most dysfunctional bunch of humans, I love you.

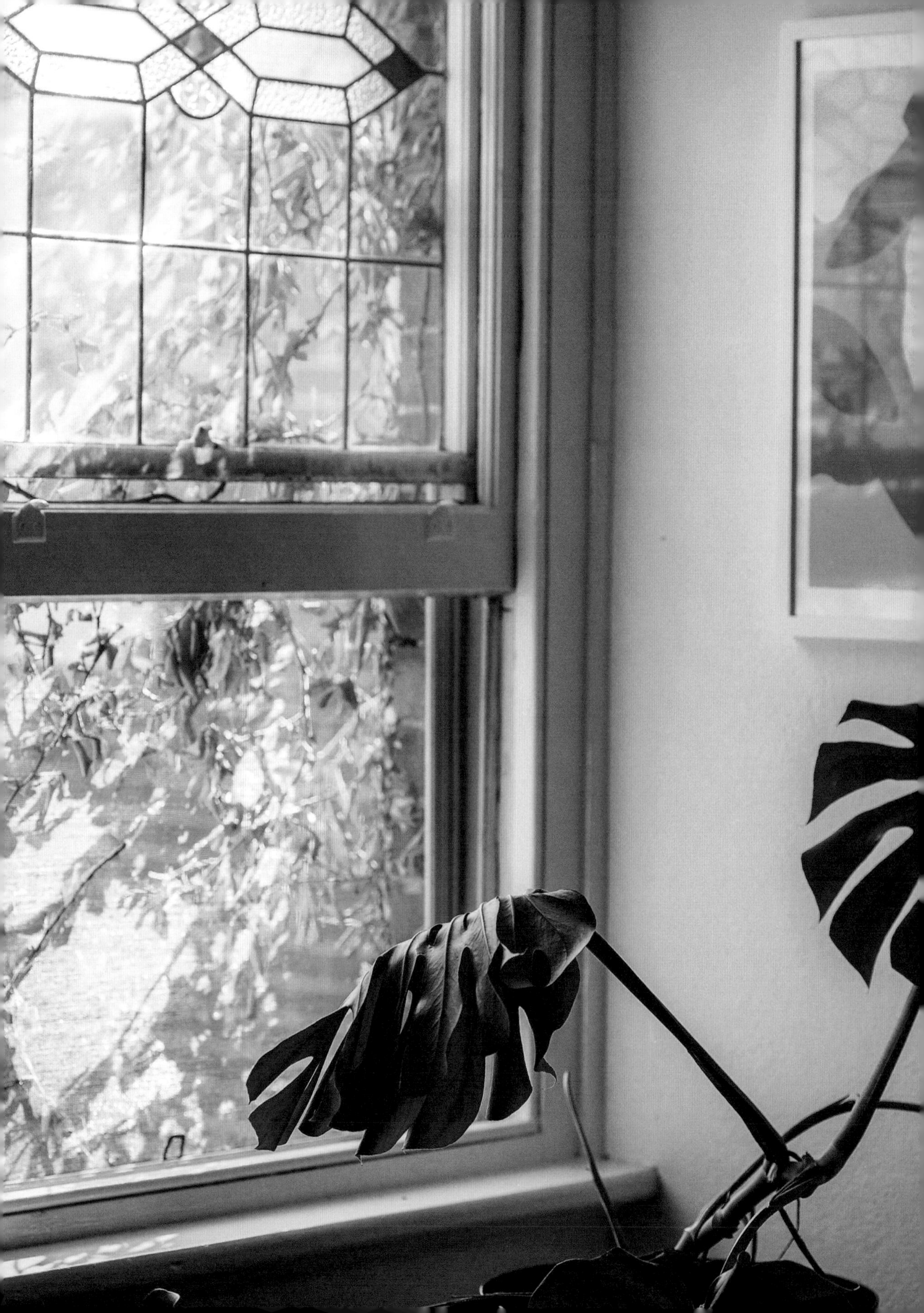

Index

D

E

F

G

H

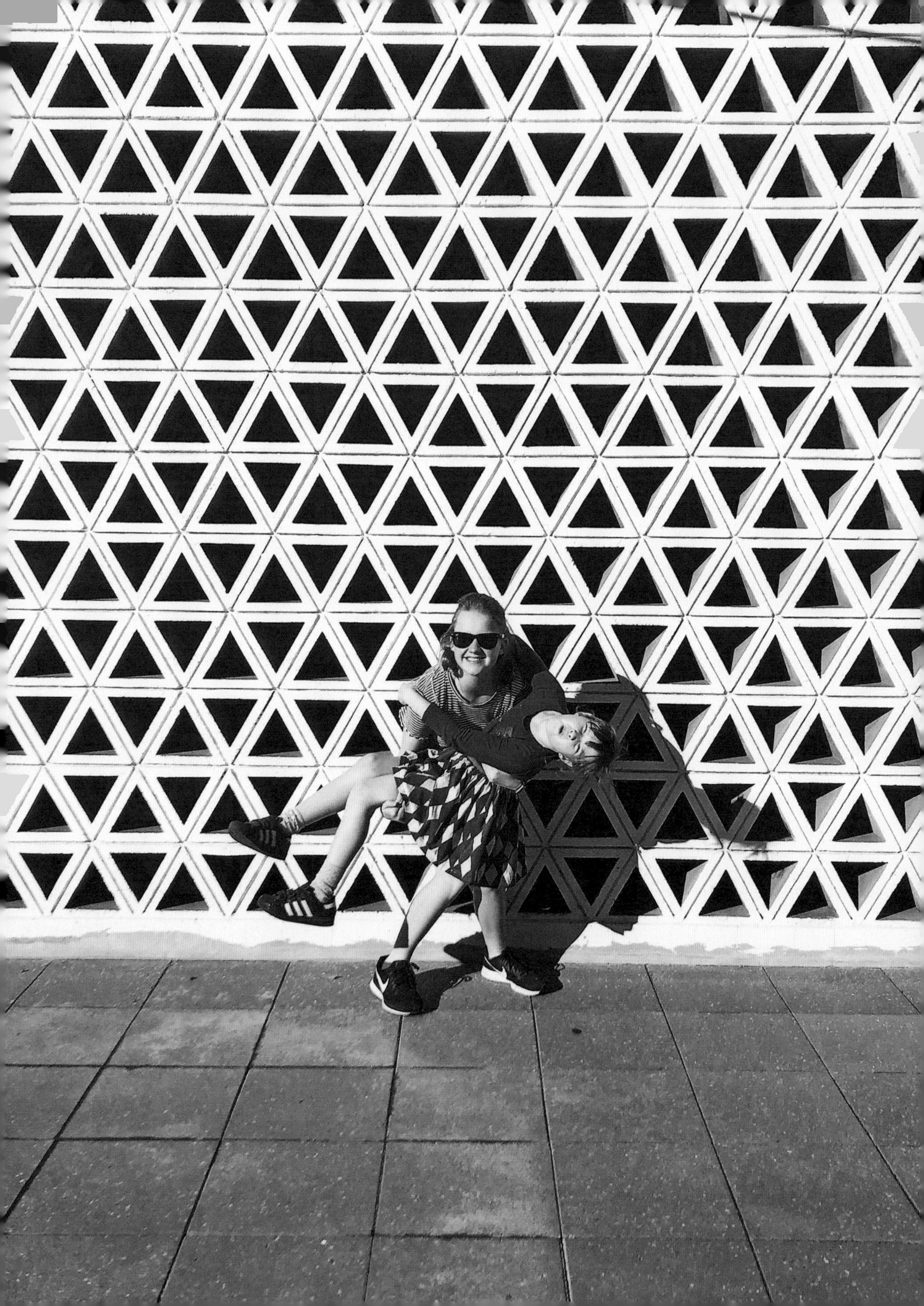

A Plum book

First published in 2019 by

Pan Macmillan Australia Pty Limited

Level 25, 1 Market Street,

Sydney, NSW 2000, Australia

Level 3, 112 Wellington Parade,

East Melbourne, VIC 3002, Australia

Design by Arielle Gamble

Illustrations by Anna Kövecses

Edited by Rachel Carter

Index by Helena Holmgren

Photography by Kate Berry, with additional photography by Peta Mazey

Prop and food styling by Kate Berry

Typeset by Arielle Gamble

Colour reproduction by Splitting Image Colour Studio

Printed and bound in China by 1010 Printing International Limited

A CIP catalogue record for this book is available from the National Library of Australia.

10 9 8 7 6 5 4 3 2 1

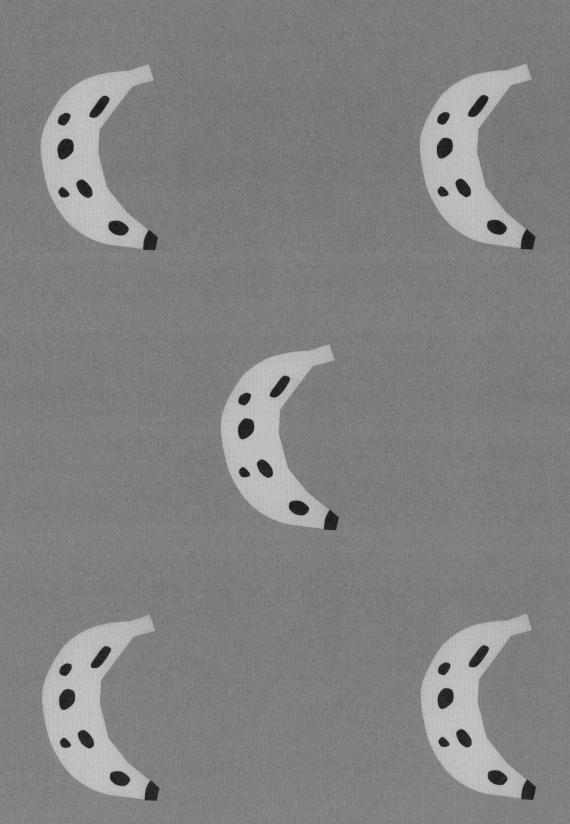

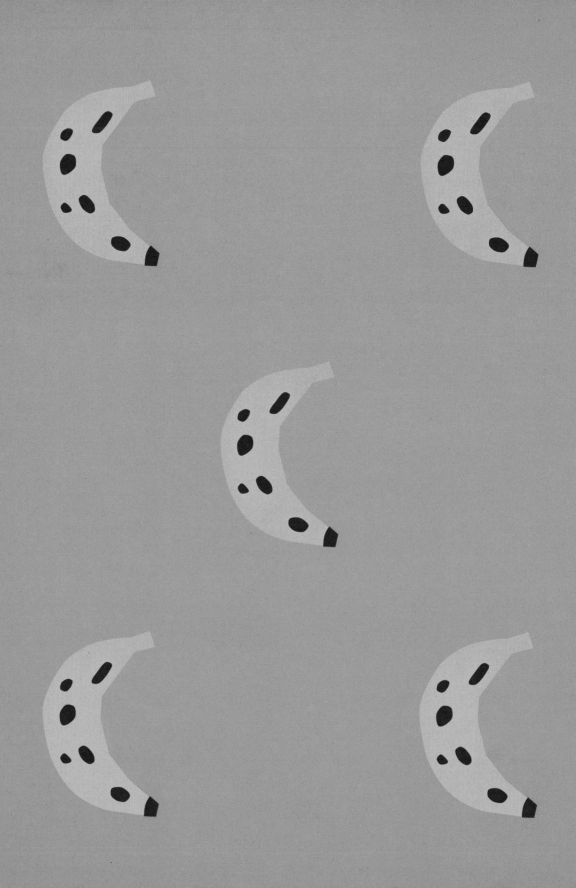